Praise for Michele Mann...

Michele Mannon believes life would be incredibly dull without an endless assortment of books and a good sports match on television—preferably with shirtless men (which is, by the way, her inspiration for writing a debut series featuring hot and oh-so-muscular MMA fighters).

Michele lives in central New Jersey where she divides her time between writing sexy and sassy contemporary sports-themed romances, laughing with her family and caring for not one but three heartless cats. Michele loves hearing from readers, so please visit her on the web at michelemannon.com.

Michele Mannon

KNOCK OUT
&
TAP OUT

⟨H⟩ HARLEQUIN® SPORTS ROMANCE

Recycling programs
for this product may
not exist in your area.

ISBN-13: 978-0-373-60132-5

Knock Out and Tap Out

Copyright © 2015 by Harlequin Books S.A.

The publisher acknowledges the copyright holder of the individual works as follows:

Knock Out
Copyright © 2013 by Michele M. Mahon

Tap Out
Copyright © 2014 by Michele M. Mahon

Printed in U.S.A.

www.Harlequin.com

CONTENTS

KNOCK OUT

To my mother.

For being the grounding force in a family of dreamers; for telling me at a young age to be fearless and that I could be whatever I wanted to be; for being such an amazing person; and for being more than just a parent, for being a true friend. Love you, Mom.

Acknowledgments

I'd like to thank my editor, Kerri Buckley, for her hard work, terrific feedback and encouragement, and for loving my story as much as I do. Thanks to my critique partners and wonderfully talented friends at thevioletfemmes.com, with special thanks to Joanna Shupe and Jenna Blue for their helpful suggestions and for drooling along with me over my hero, Keane. Thanks to the New Jersey Romance Writers for all the support and opportunities to grow as a writer.

Finally, a heartfelt thank-you to our soldiers who risk their lives for our country, and who often arrive home with wounds deeper and less obvious than their physical injuries. According to the Associated Press*, one out of eight soldiers returning from Iraq and/or Afghanistan suffers from PTSD, but only half seek assistance. If you would like more information about how to help veterans suffering from PTSD, please visit homebaseprogram.org/general-information.aspx.

*(nbcnews.com/id/5334479/ns/health-mental_health/t/returning-soldiers-suffers-ptsd/)

Chapter 1

Pittsburgh, Pennsylvania

"Yo, it's the fuckin' ballerina."

The shout rang out from high up in the back row of
the jam-packed arena.

Logan Rettino notched up her chin. No matter how
many times fame reared its ugly head, no matter how
many times a stranger's eyes lit up in recognition, she'd
never get used to her ever-growing notoriety and the
steady chipping away of her private life. Her secrets.

A classic Van Halen song boomed out of the loudspeakers and the crowd went berserk. Sammy Hagar crooned loudly, prodding her onward toward the eight-sided cage they called the Octagon. She tried to shake it off, hoping she'd read the crowd wrong, that they still considered her just a half-naked ring babe with a sign. Step by agonizing step she headed down the ramp and into the main belly of the arena, until disbelief numbed her nerves and gave her pause. Inhaling sharply, she looked around.

Hundreds of widened eyes swung her way and, in one simultaneous swoop, lowered to her chest. Though no one gave voice to the words that followed, they didn't have to—their broad smirks said it all.

The ballerina with the huge knockers.

Great, just great. If tonight's raucous crowd was this thrilled about a notorious ballerina turned ring card girl, you could bet no place was safe.

Logan might have become the fan favorite since her debut as Octagon Girl a month ago, but she was also broke, desolate and weary from the endless media attention, which didn't exactly make this job a cakewalk. Now that her ex Pierre's vicious lies were prime-time news, and these MMA fans knew who she *really* was, all she wanted to do was hightail it back up the ramp and keep on running.

No, she couldn't claim to be New York's most promising ballerina any longer. But hell, the show must go on, right? That's what she was being paid good money to do. Just walk around the edge of a cage and hold up a sign.

Ultimate Fighter fans were gathered at Pittsburgh's Mellon Arena for what was being billed as "The Rumble on the Rivers," a mixed martial arts match-up showcasing the best fighters around, along with a few amateurs striving to make a name for themselves.

Logan was somewhat familiar with boxing and wrestling but Muay Thai and Brazilian Jiu Jitsu sounded more like frou-frou drinks at a suburban chain restaurant than fighting styles. Hey, whatever floats your boat, as long as it pays the bills. Logan knew little else about the world of ultimate fighting, except it paid well for everyone involved. With four bouts under her belt, most of her overdue medical bills had been paid off.

Becoming an Octagon Girl was her ticket toward restoring some semblance of her prior life. Money earned to pay off debt, then save toward the bigger dream of opening her own dance school.

If she could just make it through this bout.

Her knuckles tightened around the Round One ring card as she braced it high overhead. Making her way up the stairs, her pink Nike sneaker caught, and she missed a step. Stumbled, really. Having one's troubles aired in front of an audience had a tendency to do that, make someone falter.

Logan's spine stiffened. As she climbed the final stairs to the cage, the crowd saw a radiant smile, plastered there on her face from years of practice. A dancer's determination to never let them see the pain.

Just you wait, Pierre. Payback is a bitch. If it wasn't for him sweet talking her into that ridiculous reality TV show, she'd be on stage at Lincoln Center right now.

This was not the type of fame she'd aspired to. Public perception of her had belly-flopped into something much uglier. Something of Pierre's making. Infamy eclipsing her hard-won public admiration. All that commitment and self-discipline, blood, sweat and tears. For what?

Considering the crowd's reaction tonight, "make Pierre suffer" shot to the top of her bucket list.

With a defiant toss of her curly blond hair, she leaped up onto the thick mat and positioned herself on the wide rim just outside the fenced-in cage.

The crowd burst out, chanting, "Luscious Logan, dance for us!" For a second, the nickname gave her pause. During her last—and final—ballet season, the audience had dubbed her "Lovely Logan." Evidently, that woman was no more and instead, she had morphed into something more lewd.

Yes, this audience was unlike any she'd ever imagined. But they wanted a show. They wanted her to dance. It was all the encouragement she needed. *Might as well give them something worth talking about.*

At the next corner, she paused. Lengthening her body with arms stretched upward, she came up on her toes. Three perfect pirouettes caused the crowd to come to its feet.

For a moment, she was back on stage…a real one.

Encouraged, a genuine smile replaced her seasoned performer's tight grin. She leaped sideways, toes pointed downward, and landed gracefully. A perfect landing near the ledge and a hair's breadth away from her eager fans a few feet below.

She spiraled and danced across the narrow space to the next corner in perfect rhythm to Sammy's crooning lyrics. Gracefully kicking out her legs, she arched backward. Out of the corner of her eye, she caught the appreciative nod of a well-dressed woman in the front row. Evidently, she wasn't the only one out of place in this crowd.

No, this is my place. The present. A high-paying job I need to keep at any cost.

With masterful precision, her arms circled in a clean rotation as she made for the next corner. The ring card rotated as well, neatly missing the mat as it made its way back overhead.

"Luscious Logan, dance for us!" The loving audience fist pumped the air—another first for her, in a long, long list of them.

She danced toward the eighth and final corner, and cameras flashed. Blinking from the sudden burst of light, she spotted the flurry of activity flanking the steps, blocking the only exit. For a split second, she considered fleeing and turning back the way she'd come and well away from the unwelcoming clutches of a gossipy media.

Win them over, Logan, just like you've always done.

A determination ingrained in her as a young, aspiring ballerina, seasons of performing for sold-out audiences, and the fact that she'd not only fallen short of completing her last televised performance, but she'd actually *fallen*—been dropped, to be more precise— made her relish the moment.

She finished with flourish, her heart pounding deep within her chest. As the music faded, her legs bent into a perfect plié.

With eyes closed against the pumping fists and camera lights, she stole a moment to breathe in the long-awaited, elusive applause. Though instead of sweet roses, it smelled stale and thick with sweaty testosterone.

"Hey, Octagon Girl, is it true you fell on *America Gets Its Groove On*?" Felix Dexter inquired into his mic, his voice resonating loudly from the direction of the broadcaster table running alongside the cage.

Felix thrived on narrating a bout's play by play, most times well before a punch was thrown. How *he* imagined the fight would unfold, like a little boy boasting about a new video game yet to be opened.

Seemed he found something else to be the expert on.

Her eyes snapped open and she glanced his way. The dirty laundry was about to pile up. His question made her clutch the sign to her bosom, protectively. And not a moment too soon.

Felix waved a large notecard in her direction, and prodded, "Is it true Pierre LaFeur couldn't catch you because of your big boobs? He was recently quoted as saying 'It's Logan's fault, for her inability to shift her body so her partner can catch her…without interference.'"

My fiancé. She fought back a scream. *Who cheated on me, dropped me on national television, shattered my ankle, and—as if that isn't bad enough—is now blaming my average-sized breasts for his careless mistake.*

Aside from destroying her career, the jerk had broken her heart and her ankle. Neither had mended without complications.

Sammy Hagar came to the rescue, rasping on and on about finishing what was started. A welcome segue. The crowd's attention swung toward the top of the ramp, a reminder that the crowd wasn't really here to see her, or the two other Octagon Girls. The real performer was entering the arena.

A welterweight, that much she remembered. Her boss Jerry had lit into her for missing the weigh-ins—all four of them. It wasn't like she'd received a job description or a how-to guide when she signed on, but this weigh-in seemed to matter the most. He'd been anxious to feed the new fighter's ego with a grand showing of press, pampering and pretty women. Yet from what Logan had gathered from Jerry's nasty tirade, the weigh-in had not gone well, and she had borne the brunt of his anger.

"One more screwup, and you can forget the huge salary I'm paying you," he'd threatened earlier. This man held her livelihood in the palm of his greasy hand. He could fire whomever he pleased because there was a constant stream of women waiting to be ring card girls, ready to steal her spot. She had to be more careful not to piss him off.

Though Logan had only been working for the slim, squirrel-faced bully a short time, it was clear to her that he'd sell his own mother for a dollar bill. And this particular fighter meant money. The deafening roar of the crowd confirmed it.

Seizing the opportunity, Logan tucked in her chin and descended. Tossing the ring card to the side, she hastened away from the Octagon cage. Rows of Pittsburgh Steelers defensive linemen, or so it seemed, flanked the pathway. She ignored them.

The object of their ear-shattering affection was making his way toward her. Or rather, toward the Octagon. A black sweatshirt framed his body, unzipped and exposing the muscled cords of his upper body, but its hood was pulled up, hiding his face. Camera bulbs flashed, and a chiseled chest, lean, flat stomach, and bulging pecs came into the light.

Unlike other fighters, whose bulk was larger than their frame, this man was proportioned like a fine piece of sculpted marble. A Michelangelo in the flesh, but more brutal, forceful. A beautiful synthesis of strength and physique. With a fondness for art himself, judging by the swirling tribal tattoo that began on the left side of his torso and spiraled down along his abs.

She moved toward the edge of the ramp, making room for him, his entourage and the media to pass.

Except in her preoccupation with the fighter, she'd forgotten the obnoxious fans lining the walkway.

A hand snaked out from the crowd and slid around her waist. Before she could guess his intentions, her back was pressed up against a big, broad chest. In one awkward movement, the rowdy fan lifted her high off the ground.

"Gotcha, Octagon Girl!" the animal snickered. A guy nearby laughed. Someone thumped him on the back as if to say well done for messing with her. No help whatsoever.

With a swift kick backward, the heel of her sneaker connected with his groin.

"Ah, the bitch kicked me!" he bellowed and tossed her away.

Once more, Logan was falling. Falling toward the ground, helpless to stop it. A professional ballerina knew how to fall, unless she didn't see the fall coming.

You'll never dance again. The surgeon's final words still haunted her. The metal rods securing her ankle, the reason. Ballet had no room for a ballerina who couldn't land gracefully. And an Octagon Girl who let herself be tossed around by the crowd would find herself out of yet another job.

She closed her eyes, twisted around, hoping to land with her good foot…and connected with a rock-hard chest. An arm wrapped around her back, securing her, as another reached beneath her bottom. She was yanked upward.

Breathless, she paused for an inhale of sweet air. Only to lose it in a long, rushed exhale as she found herself staring into a set of steel-blue eyes. Exquisite eyes framed by charcoal lashes that went on for miles. Eyes so striking her heart performed a pirouette. Unamused eyes that pierced her to the core. A lifetime seemed to pass before reality sunk in.

The welterweight had caught her. More importantly, he hadn't dropped her—no matter her bra size.

She wrapped her arms around his muscled neck and at the same time, her bare stomach pressed against his. Her skin sizzled with awareness where they touched. An unfamiliar spark of energy that had her leaning in closer and wanting more.

With a soft gasp, she took in his rugged, clenched jaw. High, angular cheekbones led down to full, moist lips pressed together, uninvitingly. But his scowl did nothing to detract from his handsomeness. Beautiful. Much too beautiful to be a fighter.

She lost her breath. Perhaps it was the way he held her against him. Or her very physical response to him— the tightening of her nipples as sure as a snowy Pittsburgh winter.

His somber demeanor didn't deter the giddiness fluttering about in her chest. All was not forsaken this time. The rugged warrior *had* caught her. *Thank God. Thank you.*

Ignoring the jeering crowd, his anxious handlers, the clicking cameras, and even the taut, guarded look of the fighter holding her, Logan angled her head. Awareness registered in his baby blues as she leaned forward. In a year full of firsts, this one was about to take the prize.

She pressed her lips against his with a heartfelt thank-you.

The welterweight's lips parted and, for a split second, moved beneath Logan's own. *He tastes like fresh mint*, she noted before his strong arms gently, yet firmly, pushed her away and settled her back on the floor.

"Jesus, lady, save it for after the bout," one of the handlers said as he tugged her away from the fighter, keeping a firm hold on her.

Over her shoulder, she caught the welterweight's stare before his entourage swept him away.

"Let go," she spat out at the ancient handler and yanked her arm free.

"Tsk, tsk, sweetheart. If you want more of a taste of that cynical devil, better change your tune now. He's got more women lined up than a shoe sale."

The old timer's eyes skimmed over her as they reached the end of the ramp. "An attractive bit like you can do much better than that cold bastard. Unfriendly, somber type, only talks with his fists. Beats the hell out of me why the ladies love him so."

"Listen, you've got it all wrong. I was just…" She stopped short as the handler reached into his pocket, pulled something out, and offered it to her. A card. His card.

"Like I said, *some* men know how to treat a lady." His hands rose up next to his ear in a call-me gesture. Aghast, she could only stare as Grandpa Romeo headed back down the ramp toward the Octagon.

A bell rang, and the crowd began cheering, muffling the stream of curses she'd been holding in. The noise escalated, and so did her disgust at what had transpired tonight, what she'd done. She tore the card, tossed the remnants on the ground, and with the soles of her sneakers, she mashed the tiny pieces.

What on earth had come over her? She'd actually *kissed* him.

"Rettino!" a voice barked out from behind her. "What the hell were you thinking, pulling a stunt like that?"

Great, just twist my bleeding tights.

Logan drew in a breath and turned to face her boss, searching for the words to describe her uncharacteristic behavior. Or behaviors, rather, depending on which "stunt" Jerry was referring to. She bit her lip and prayed that whatever it was, he'd get over it once he'd verbally pinned her ass to the wall.

Gesturing wildly, all five feet of the balding, thinly built man moved in irritation as he closed the distance between them. His hand found her upper arm, and Logan tensed against him.

"Does this look like Rockefeller freakin' Center to you? All you're required to do is hold the damn ring card up over your head, stick out that huge rack, and prance around the cage. Know what? I think all this media attention has gone to that pretty head of yours. I've got news for you, girlie, no one is here to see you dancing around like some spoiled brat who couldn't make it as a fancy ballerina. Now listen to me, one more stunt…"

A horn blared, cutting Jerry off. Logan gazed around as the crowd jumped to their feet.

"Holy shit, did you see that! Andy the Annihilator was just guillotined. He tapped out in seven seconds flat." Felix Decker's animated voice filled the arena as he shouted out a play-by-play over the loudspeaker.

"O'Shea is leaving the cage before the winner is announced." Felix's excitement was obvious by the high pitch of his tone. "He literally crushed Andy the Annihilator but isn't waiting around to be crowned champion. A first, ladies and gentlemen, in MMA history!"

Logan glanced at Jerry. His mouth twisted into a smirk so bold it was comical. She shook herself free of his grip. The more she learned about her boss, the less she liked him.

Though she hadn't bothered to learn all that much about MMA, this was not the case with Jerry. She made a point of asking questions about him, his nature being as horrid as it was. Better keep your enemies close, right? Especially if he was your boss at a job that earned you so much money in so little time.

Not only was Jerry chairman of something called the East Coast Xtreme MMA Federation, he sponsored and promoted high-profile bouts, and was actively recruiting the best fighters out there. It occurred to her that his new welterweight had just handed him a victory—and along with it, some serious money and some bonus publicity. A trifecta. If O'Shea agreed to sign on with Jerry, her boss would be a wealthy man.

In Logan's mind, he'd always be a sleazeball promoter.

Given the abrupt uplift in his mood, Logan seized the chance to reassure him. With a tap to his arm, she drew his attention toward her and hastily began. "Jerry, I'd like to apologize for the shaky start. I need…um, want this job. I'll strut my stuff. Whatever you expect me to do, I'll…"

The mass of bodies on the ramp parted.

Logan fell silent at the sight of the fighter O'Shea. Shirtless and sweaty, the planes of his abdomen flexed as he moved. A sculpted chest, sprinkled with dampened hair, rose and fell with each rapid breath. His biceps tightened as he wiped a gray towel through his jet-black hair. An errant bead of sweat escaped and journeyed across a sharp cheekbone to pool onto lush lips.

Logan froze as awareness of his imminent proximity made her pulse race. Too late, she realized her mistake. She was standing smack in the middle of the ramp. And the fighter stalking toward her seemed preoccupied with drying himself off.

In that moment, she felt so small. Fragile, even. Though not quick enough to get out of the way of the raging bull who'd seconds ago destroyed his opponent and was now bearing down on her. Was this the same man she'd foolishly kissed? Anger reverberated off of him, seeming to fill the rampway.

She blinked as he abruptly halted several feet in front of her.

He looked up through long, wet lashes and narrowed crystal-blue eyes at her. With a final swipe of the towel to his head, he bunched it up in his fist.

The gray ball was sent hurling in the air, spiraled once, and hit her boss square in the face.

Jerry sputtered, and swatted away the offensive material.

How could she forget her boss, rooted in place next to her in the aisle? The indignant expression on his face, that was a keeper.

Perhaps it was the long build-up of tension from this problematic year, or perhaps it was the nervous flutter in her chest at her undeniable attraction to the fighter, whatever it was, Logan did the unthinkable—she laughed.

It wasn't a short, sweet one. This laugh had been brewing for a long time, as if patiently waiting through her painful year of ups and downs—downs far outweighing the ups, that's for sure—for one ridiculous moment to make its escape. It came from deep within the pit of her stomach and erupted out of her so hard her belly ached. Tears wet her eyes as she let go.

Jerry sputtered some more, this time turning a bright shade of red. Raging red. Blood hungry red.

She took a step away from him, inadvertently inching closer to the fighter. An uncomfortable moment lingered with her under the scrutiny of both men. One furious, and the other full of…intent. Watchful. Unreadable.

O'Shea's gaze felt like a caress as it lowered to her chest, then downward to her exposed stomach, pink short-shorts, long expanse of leg, and hesitated on her pink Nikes. Until it shifted to her forearm, and his frown line deepened.

She jumped as two fingers lightly caressed her arm, running across the fingerprint marks Jerry had left. For a split second, something flickered across his pale blue eyes before they narrowed on her boss.

"That's it. I'm done. My final fight. Meet me in the locker room in twenty—you owe me some money." His voice was low and husky, and deadly serious.

The touch of his hands at her waist sent a jolt of excitement through her. Easily, with no effort at all, he lifted her and, pivoting at his waist, swung her around.

Gently, he set her on her feet, off to the side and out of his way.

"What do you mean, you're done?" Jerry squeaked, finding his voice as the fighter brushed past him. "You can't just come in here, win one lousy fight and disappear."

O'Shea grunted and stalked off up the ramp.

Logan couldn't believe it. No one defied Jerry; she'd learned this fact the hard way this morning, when she'd dodged the weigh-in.

Jerry paced about furiously.

What have I done? Logan glanced around, hoping to find a hole to climb into or at least a massive body to tuck behind, before his full attention spun her way.

"Think I'm gonna let a set of tits like you get away with laughing at me? You're fired!" Jerry roared. "Pack your locker and get out."

She placed shaky hands on her hips to steady them. "Jerry, listen to me…" she began but the words dried up. There was no explanation for her carelessness. Her laughter had made him look like an idiot in front of his prize fighter.

Her eyes fell helplessly on O'Shea as he made his way to the top of the ramp.

Maybe *he* was her golden ticket? Someone Jerry coveted. Someone who'd make her boss a very wealthy man. Someone who was clearly capable of getting the job done. Would he agree to kick some ass and, in turn, save her own?

A chill ran up her spine, a kind of body-numbing awareness, reminding her of how mean, how fierce, this fighter was. How unlikely it was she could convince him to help her. She searched her mind for something that she could use in her favor, something that would make him agreeable toward fighting for Jerry.

Who was she kidding?

One kiss. That was their connection. She didn't know him. And, let's face it, what he probably knew about her didn't help.

But that was what she had to do—persuade him to fight. Could she do this?

She had no choice.

"What if I make a deal with you, Jerry? If I get your fighter back, can I keep my job?"

His face pinched together like a rodent assessing a nut as her words registered. For a moment, she thought his temper, clearly visible within his menacing glare, might launch him into another tirade.

She hastily pressed on with her mind-boggling, irrational offer. "I'll get you O'Shea," she stated with a false sense of bravado, "if you keep me on as a ring card girl."

"Ha! You think you can handle him?" he snorted, disbelievingly.

Drawing on the endless tide of humiliation she had endured—and *still* endured—Logan stomped forward and with hands on her hips, glared down at the little weasel.

For once, her troubles were rewarded as his eyes lit up, measuring her, as if noticing her for the first time. His brows pinched together, considering her proposal, then he relaxed. A good sign. He was going to give her a chance.

His eyes fixed on the swaying of her chest, his smirk broadened perversely, and bile rose up in her throat.

"Forget it, Jerry," she burst out, "you misconstrued what I'm saying. I'm not promising to sleep—"

"Tell you what. The qualifiers are in a month. If O'Shea wins all six of his bouts, he'll be headed to the granddaddy of all granddaddies, Tetnus, with a million-dollar purse. You get him to do this for me, you keep your job."

It was hard to contain her excitement. The underlying dread at what she had just committed to, she'd deal with later.

All anyone talked about was Tetnus, the championship fight being held in Vegas in July. A series of qualifying bouts were about to begin around the country—Pittsburgh being one of the main events because of the quality of fighters Jerry had attracted. Only the best fighters within their weight class advanced. O'Shea was the whole package. Jerry knew it. And after tonight's events, Logan knew it. *A big-bodied package all right*, she thought, remembering the feel of his muscled chest pressed up against her.

"You'll get your fighter. I appreciate…"

Jerry held up his hand, Godfather-like. Not a good sign. Judging by the tightening of his mouth, he hadn't forgiven her for laughing. "I have some conditions. For each fight he wins, you stay. Hell, if he wins all six qualifiers and makes it to Vegas, I'll double your salary. But the first time he loses, so do you. Got it?"

Jerry stalked away without waiting for her reply.

Logan inhaled deeply, feeling like she'd bargained with the devil and lost, without an inkling of exactly how she was going to go about getting O'Shea to fight.

Grandpa Romeo. Frantically, she gathered up the remnants of the old timer's card from the aisle, hoping enough pieces remained for her to make out his phone number. He'd help her, right?

By doubling her salary, she'd be on the fast track toward reclaiming her life. Medical bills paid off. A nest egg big enough to launch her dance school. And then, she'd knock Pierre off his toes. Hard. Give him an awful taste of what it was like to be infamous.

This opportunity was her make-or-break moment.

Her gaze narrowed toward the exit at the top of the ramp where the welterweight had disappeared from sight.

"Correction," she said aloud, her determination growing stronger with every word. "You, O'Shea, are going to be my *break-out* moment."

Chapter 2

CORNERMAN: The person a fighter depends upon to guide him/her during a bout

Logan tugged the neck of her black cashmere sweater up higher as a gust of frigid Burgh air chilled her to the bone. The only thing moving quickly this blustery evening was the snowfall—the South Side bus had been late, and her warm skinny latte from The Quiet Storm had slowly chilled just like the rest of her numbed body. Exhaling, she realized that she was going to be late as well, although she didn't know if one could actually be *late* for a surprise ambush of an attractive welterweight.

Late because her best friend Sally had received several encores at tonight's ballet performance, causing it to run longer than expected. Logan frowned in reflection. Backstage, their brief chat should have been about Sally's recent promotion to the Pittsburgh Ballet's principal dancer. Or how wonderfully loving Sally's fiancé was. Kind, too—no way he would ever drop *her* on prime-time television. Granted, he wasn't even a dancer. He worked as a chiropractor who happened to treat ballerinas. But even so, he wouldn't have dropped her. As a matter of fact, he had gotten Logan her job in the Octagon cage, being Jerry's chiropractor and all.

Instead, their discussion had centered on Logan. And the source of all her problems... Pierre.

"I heard your bitter bird of an ex on the radio, of all places. Clearly, he's still pissed off about his precious painting. What did you say to him?"

My painting. No way was Pierre going to keep it, on top of everything else he'd stolen from her. "File an insurance claim, asshole," Logan repeated the words she'd spoken that miserable day a few months back.

The fame pimp had done much worse than drop her on TV's top-rated *America Gets Its Groove On*. He'd kept everything of value purchased for their ultramodern Manhattan duplex, plus the Gramercy co-op itself. The apartment had been a surprise gift to her— one he'd purchased with her hard-earned money.

The sly bastard made sure to itemize everything on the homeowner's insurance policy: the plush, Chippendale living room set, crystal chandelier, wine collection—the list went on and on. And the mortgage, the policy, everything was under his name.

It didn't matter that he'd depleted her bank account to make a huge down payment on *that* place instead of the uptown, pre-war co-op they'd agreed upon, and to purchase most of the furnishings. Without a lawyer, she had no chance of getting her life's savings back.

Sally laughed. "I still can't believe he called the police, like they'd believe you would steal your own stuff! But why haven't you sued that jerk? I told you money isn't a problem if you need it."

Logan shook her head. "Focus on Fiji. Save your money for snorkeling and parasailing and having the perfect honeymoon. Stop worrying. I'll take care of Pierre once my dance school is up and running."

It had been her second trip to the co-op when Pierre had come home, caught her with a Waterford lamp in each hand, and had called the police, resulting in nearly everything being moved back inside. The cops wouldn't let her take anything she couldn't provide proof of ownership for.

But some select pieces, such as an expensive oil painting—a commissioned reproduction of a Renoir piece showing two novice ballerinas en pointe for the first time—had mysteriously disappeared.

Despite Pierre's temper tantrum on the city sidewalk—that painting had been his pride and joy, the object he bragged about most—there wasn't really anything he could do about it. The police had caught on to her money-grubbing ex's number rather quickly. One officer had even arched his eyebrows at Logan, as if saying *"You got off lucky, kiddo, dumping this guy."* Fortunately, Pierre's complaint was added to the precinct's pile of petty cold cases, those they wouldn't waste their time or manpower resolving.

"You constantly amaze me. I wish I had your self-assurance. Your strength."

My stubborn pride.

Sally's comment had made Logan laugh and reminded her of the plaque her mother had hung on the
wall over the kitchen sink so many years ago. It had read
"Pride cometh before the fall." Talk about ironic. One
source of comfort was knowing that pride didn't turn
tail and hide *after* the fall. Along with hurt, humiliation,
defeat…pride was the Band-Aid holding it all together.

She inhaled deeply, the cold air sharpening her
senses. Her conversation with Sally had reinforced her
courage. It was time to rip off the Band-Aid, and peel
away this prideful paralysis holding her back from her
plans for the future.

The qualifying bouts began in three weeks and she
was feeling desperate. She palmed Grandpa Romeo's
pieced-together card in her pocket and quickened her
pace, anxious to reach Finnegan's Pub and get this deal
locked and loaded. Snow blanketed the narrow, winding
street and slowed her progress, until at last, she made
it to the top of the steep hill. She paused to catch her
breath, smoothing a stray lock of hair behind an ear as
she glanced back at the city lights below.

"What took you so long?" Grandpa Romeo, also
known as Sal, demanded, his breath forming a cloud
in the cold air as he came out to greet her. He must
have been waiting at the window. "O'Shea's inside, in
the back. But I've got to warn you, he's in a piss-poor
mood."

Logan straightened. "Great. Do you know why?"
Without waiting for a reply, she headed inside, the old
fox hot on her tail. After all, it really didn't matter why;
all that mattered was the welterweight agreeing to fight.

"Nope. But I'd say it's in his nature. Take me, for example. I'm a friendly guy, wake up with a smile every

morning. That's why I've agreed to help you. I've even ordered you a Ying-*i*-ling." Sal pointed to two tall amber bottles on a small table by the window.

She resisted rolling her eyes, more so from his funny pronunciation of Yuengling than from his assumption that a ballerina would drink a beer. *Ring card girl*, she corrected the mental slip. "Why aren't you sitting with him? You said you guys had plans to 'chew the fat' over a few beers." She slipped off her alpaca knit coat and set it over the back of her chair.

Sal cleared his throat loudly, causing the couple at the next table to look over at him. Did he have something caught in there?

"That's the get-up you're wearing to lure him into bed?"

"What? Who said anything about…I'm not trying to—"

"If this don't beat all," Sal continued, mindless of the reddening of her already flushed cheeks. "A big black turtleneck and leggons. Hate to be the bearer of bad news, sweetheart, but you've got some stiff competition." He ducked, peered under the table at her black riding boots, and shook his head.

"What's wrong with my *leggings*?"

Sal motioned to the naked midriffs and bare legs of the women at nearby tables. Finnegan's inconvenient location didn't deter the local ladies from partaking in a few Friday night beers…and then some, it would seem. Most of the women were dressed more appropriately for a night out at a club in Cabo than a cold Burgh winter. Not that the sight of half-naked women was anything new, given her chosen profession—*professions*, she corrected. Their attire was just…unexpected. Logan peered around the pub, needing to find the welterweight and get this over with. Finnegan's Pub wasn't exactly her kind of scene.

"Should have worn one of them Octagon outfits. A shame to hide a body like yours."

The lustful wink Sal shot her was too much to bear. Tossing his balled-up card on the table, she reached for the Yuengling and took a deep sip. She winced at the bitterness but forced down another long gulp. When in Rome…

"I've got a plan. What do you have on under that tent you're wearing?"

"Listen, Sal, I appreciate your help in tracking down O'Shea. But I'm just going to have a conversation with him—explain my predicament."

"One of them sportsy bras, I hope. You'll fit right in."

Logan frowned but continued, "This isn't a big deal, really. He's a fighter and I need him to fight. If some-one asked me to dance again…"

"You wouldn't happen to be wearing a pair of tight boxer shorts like I've seen in them Victor's Secrets magazine? With them little hearts?"

Logan choked on her Yuengling as Sal stripped her naked with his lecherous eyes. What had possessed her to ask him for help? "Please, watch my stuff." She stood, grabbing her beer, and worked her way to the back of the pub before Grandpa Romeo could stop her.

As she entered the lounge area, her eyes were instantly drawn to the fighter. Her throat went dry at the sight before her.

He was sprawled on a bench in a back booth, one knee bent and legs splayed apart. A hand rested on a powerful thigh and the other held a near-empty bottle.

More than six feet of raw male splendor in repose. Head resting against the wall, he moved a black-labeled bottle to his lips and took a long drink, eyes closed.

And Logan drank him in, every rugged male inch of him. He was too sexy for words. Sexy and, judging by the shot glasses scattered on the table, very, very *drunk*.

She nearly lost her nerve but stepped toward him before she could change her mind.

Like Logan, he was dressed head to toe in black. A simple tight T-shirt, soft, faded jeans, and black leather boots. His fingers clenched and unclenched by his side, a sign he was at least not completely loaded.

Hesitantly, she stood at the foot of the booth. "Can I…" she began.

Frosty blue eyes pinned her to the spot. A glimmer of recognition—or so she thought—flickered, before his lids lowered and shut her out. As if tempting her to finish, he took another swig from the bottle.

Instead of asking permission, she slid onto the other cushioned bench.

"Following me?" His dismissive manner indicated this question was rhetorical, as if women constantly chased him. Hordes of them probably did.

She'd seen the MMA groupies hovering by the arena exits, not unlike her former fans had waited for her after a performance. Except the fighter's fan club was entirely female and these women weren't looking for an autograph, not unless it was emblazed on their naked bodies.

She stiffened, ignoring the flex of his muscles as he shifted, and pressed on, "Um…yes. Sal told me you'd be here. I need your help."

"Sal," he muttered and took another drink before setting the half-empty bottle to wobble next to her beer on the table. "My help? I'm the last person you should be asking for help." Swinging his legs off the bench and under the table, he leaned forward and closed the distance between them.

The act was abrasive and intimidating but his eyes wandered around the room, restless and unfocused. "What I want is to be left alone." Harsh, sharp words coming from pink, plump lips.

Logan sat up straighter in her seat.

"We met a week ago, actually twice, on the ramp at Mellon Arena."

He snorted. Acknowledging they'd met or the quick lip lock they'd exchanged? Both? Or neither? She wasn't sure but given his compromised condition, she'd better reintroduce herself. "My name is Logan Rettino. I'm a baller...a ring girl. Like I said, I need your help." She paused. *Why did this have to be so difficult? Just ask him. He's a fighter, so ask him to fight.*

He pushed his bottle toward her, a look of pure challenge in his blue eyes, but she was uncertain whether it was an offer of friendship or a sign he'd had enough. What harm could one sip in the name of camaraderie do?

Besides, she'd been nursing her Yuengling as if it were the finest Chardonnay. She wasn't about to back down now, germaphobic or not. Alcohol was the great neutralizer, right?

Logan raised the bottle, pressed her lips to the warm glass and took a swig of unfamiliar hard liquor. A blaze of fire ripped across her throat and burned a path into the pit of her stomach. Tears formed in her eyes. "What is this?" she coughed out.

"All you're gonna get...or maybe *not*." The last bit

was said in such a deep, throaty voice, she strained to catch it. It sounded naughty, like he was contemplating tangling his fingers into her hair, pulling her head back, and covering her mouth with his own. *Oh sweet pirouette*. She felt a little bit breathless at the idea. The booze didn't help.

Needing something to do with her hands besides reaching across the table and testing out his "maybe not," she fiddled with the hem of her sweater. Her cheeks warmed, nevertheless.

She came here for a reason, she reminded herself, and taking a roll on a mattress with him wasn't it.

"I'm asking you to agree to fight. Jerry wants you to qualify for Tetnus. From what I understand, it pays really well. And it would help me smooth things out with him. You can't imagine how challenging he is to work for. It's a win-win situation. You'd be paid for a few nights what most fighters make in a month."

Grunting, he avoided eye contact. Instead his gaze rested on her lips. Self-consciously, her tongue darted out and licked off a smidgeon of sticky sweet liquor.

Better sweeten the pot, she thought. "Perhaps there is even something I could do for you in exchange?"

"Maybe."

She gasped as he reached out and ran his thumb along her bottom lip. But when he placed it between her lips so the tip pressed against her tongue, she nearly shot up off the seat.

"Tempting," he murmured.

If her cheeks had warmed before, they were on fire now. *Perhaps I could do something for you?* She'd said the words—a blatant invitation for sex—without thinking.

Perhaps it was her subconscious speaking. *Show me*

the time of my life. Show me how a real man gets down and dirty. Make me forget about my egotistical, limp petunia of a dance partner, who got off more from looking at himself in the mirror than with me.

God knew, she wanted to lick that digit, run her tongue along its expanse and keep going. He was rugged maleness exemplified. *Oh, yeah! Just part your lips a little more and...crinkle my camisole.*

Her indecision cost her.

He withdrew his thumb, shifted back into the position she'd first encountered him in, and rested his head against the cushioned wall of the booth. His eyes closed.

Moments passed. Until it became clear she was being dismissed.

Her thoughts shifted from "oh, yeah" to "oh, no" in ten seconds flat. She wasn't about to let him blow her off her like some overeager MMA groupie. She jumped to her feet, skirted the table and kicked his shin.

His eyes snapped open and struggled to focus on the offending foot. She still hadn't gotten his full attention, it seemed.

Leaning forward, she placed her hands on his shoulders and gave him a sharp push.

With a gasp, she found herself gripped at the elbows, lifted up and yanked forward. Then, he let go. Her legs fell open to straddle his and her breasts firmly connected with his chest. She inhaled in surprise, catching the clean, heady scent of his cologne mixed with the smell of the alcohol on his breath.

He shifted, forcing her closer still, so close she could see her startled reflection flickering within his deep, dark pupils. A face-off—except his crotch rubbed up against her...

For a moment, she forgot everything. Finnegan's Pub, her agreement with Jerry, and even The Fall. Desire stirred, blatant and pure and in shocking abundance. Beneath long, dark lashes, he sat perfectly still, watching her.

She got the impression he was waiting for something. For her to decide what she was going to do with him beneath her. For her to jerk away or lean in, angle her head and grab a taste of him.

Until a loud, piercing whine—the kind someone made when air was constricted within their windpipes as they tried to form coherent words—interrupted them. The source, in all her spandexed glory, stood glaring at Logan.

"Un-freaking-believable. I leave for a few minutes to use the restroom and some whore dressed for a barn-yard tries to steal my guy. Get off him, bitch!"

Logan launched herself off the welterweight in one swift movement, prompted not only by the woman's demand but by the hardened length of male anatomy that had been curved against her ass. He surprised her with a fleeting smirk. *Oh yeah*. At least her response to him hadn't been one-sided.

She turned to face the irate woman, Miss Easywrap in the tight tube dress. "I'm not finished…speaking with him. Give us a second, please."

"Speaking, my ass. I'm gonna count to ten." Rosie—Easywrap's name, according to the enormous necklace perched on her cleavage—pointed to the bar. "If you're not out of here when I come back with a drink, you're gonna be sorry."

Logan put her hands on her hips. She opened her

mouth, then closed it. What was she going to do, fight the woman?

Easywrap gave her a talk-to-the-hand gesture and stalked off.

Logan felt fingers on her arm. "You'll lose. Let's go."

"Thanks for the vote of confidence," she muttered as the welterweight led her into another, more private room, one with a band playing and, hopefully, fewer disturbances. She needed a cold mental shower and to keep her eye on the objective: convince this silent, guarded man to fight.

He gestured to a booth in the back and slid in after her, sandwiching her between the wall and his big body. For several moments, that's how they sat, quietly listening to the band thanking the audience for coming.

"About the qualifiers—"

The waiter approached and cut her off. "Last call. What'll it be?"

"Another Johnny, and a white wine," O'Shea replied, leaning back. His bare arm brushed her cashmere sleeve. A soft, subtle caress.

"Yuengling," she corrected his order. No sense in switching drinks at this point. And more liquid courage was out of the question. Which reminded her how ridiculous this whole scenario was. She should have closed the deal and been long gone by now.

Well, she would have been if the man wasn't so closed off. And if her heart didn't flip-flop at the very feel of him brushing up against her. Close, far too close for comfort.

She sat straighter in her seat as a muscular arm wove its way behind her. Talk about sensory overload—it was too much to bear.

He raised an eyebrow but that was all.

Logan sipped her beer and, beneath her lashes, studied the man next to her as he drank deeply from his glass.

Getting involved with an MMA fighter wasn't like swapping Chardonnay for Yuengling, she reminded herself. It wasn't like he'd ever fit into her world. Besides, tonight was about convincing him to fight so she could keep her job. Nothing more, nothing less.

"Jerry says you're the guy to beat."

He muttered something under his breath. "Bar's closing. Need to find my ride. Tell me, is Jerry...bothering you?"

Drunk or not, the man was perceptive and quick. Should she tell him her job as Octagon Girl was on the line? Quickly, she decided against it. Foolish pride, whatever.

Just do it, Logan.

"Like I said, he wants you to fight in the preliminary bouts coming up next month and qualify for Tetnus. There's a million-dollar purse for the winner."

He moved his arm out from behind her and rested it on the table. His fist flexed.

Logan gasped.

His poor knuckles were bruised and swollen to the size of golf balls. After the break and subsequent surgery on her ankle, she'd never again underestimate the pain someone might be suffering, even from minor injuries. His hands must be killing him.

"Tell Jerry I'm done. No more fights. No matter how many gorgeous women he sends to crawl between my legs."

Logan's temper exploded before she could bite back

her words. "We're having a conversation—that's all. I'm sick to my stomach wondering why everyone thinks I'd *sleep* with you to get you to fight!"

Because you're acting like you would, moron. No denying she wanted this drop-dead gorgeous man and was so freakin' attracted to him her blood sizzled. But this crazy desire for him had overshadowed her objectivity. Sleeping with him to get her way, now that would land her on the disgusting list, right beneath Pierre.

He smirked, appeared unfazed by her outburst. As if to say, "Right, like I couldn't have taken you on the pub bench in the other room."

"I don't get it. It's ridiculous—a fighter who won't fight. If it's one thing I've learned these past few months is that there is always someone waiting in the wings to replace you, even if they suck. I can do that, you know, find a sucky fighter for Jerry and *replace* you."

Desperation was one small step away from irrationality, and as her angry words came spilling out, Logan didn't just walk across that line. She pole vaulted. The chance of Jerry accepting another fighter was as likely as winning the Mega Millions jackpot.

"Thanks for the drink," she snapped.

She dodged his attempt at grabbing her leg as she stood up on the bench's cushion and climbed over him to let herself out.

"Shit," she heard him mutter but she kept on moving, away from the booth, out of the room, and back to the front of the bar. To the table where she'd left Sal to watch her belongings, which was now occupied by a new couple. Her stuff—and Grandpa Romeo, it would seem—had apparently taken a walk.

Bleeding leotards. She caught her stupefied expression in the front window until movement outside broke the image apart.

Her expensive alpaca coat was making its way into a double-parked car, clutched against Miss Easywrap's obnoxious chest. "You…bitch," Logan cried as she sprinted out the door after the blonde. But it was too late. The old Camaro had some pep in it and was halfway down the hill by the time she hit the curb, the only gift from Pierre that hadn't been hauled off to Goodwill along with it. Worse still, her Louis Vuitton wallet and cell phone were secured in the inside pocket.

She tugged the neck of her sweater higher. If she'd learned anything this year, it was how to manage in difficult situations. In this case, she'd simply track down Grandpa Romeo and ask him for his jacket and some money.

Before she could head back inside, people began filing out of the pub—all at the same time. "Sal," she called, searching the crowd for his white head. A cacophony of car engines drowned her out and the snow had picked up, fed by the wind off the rivers far below. With her hands on her hips, she moved undeterred up the sidewalk and back, searching for him.

A white-haired driver passed in a red Chevy pickup, without so much as a glance in her direction. "Sal," her voice rang out weakly, knowing he'd never hear her, but feeling like she had to do something. Run after the pickup? As if that would do any good. She brushed her hands together for warmth. Surely someone down in South Side Flats would help her? If she didn't freeze to death walking down the hill on the way there.

The door of the pub swung open one last time. Six foot two of taut, muscled male sporting a beaten-up, deep green coat—the kind someone in the army might wear—and a woolen bean cap pulled low over dark hair, exited. The welterweight glanced her way, turned and strode a few feet uphill to a black Jeep Wrangler.

Less than a minute later, Finnegan's went dark.

Now what do I do?

She blinked as a horn rang out, invitingly. The Jeep Wrangler flashed its lights, which meant…

Resigned, she walked up the short distance to the Jeep.

"Can you drive?" a deep, husky voice demanded through the rolled-down crack of the passenger-side window.

O'Shea sounded slightly annoyed, but his words defrosted the chill from her body. Everything about the man made her blood run hot—except for his closed-up personality. That was unsettling.

She nodded.

"Get in."

She moved her frozen limbs around the Jeep and climbed into the driver's seat. The vehicle hummed, the keys already in the ignition.

As blessed warmth blew from the vents, she glanced at him beneath half-frozen eyelids. And gasped when once again he flexed swollen, purple knuckles.

"Planning on walking home?"

"No. Your friend Miss Easywrap made off with my coat, cell and wallet—seemed to think they were hers," she shot back, mimicking his sarcastic tone. "How were you planning to make it home? Driving drunk is a stup—"

"You chased off tonight's ride."

An image of the trashy kleptomaniac spread-eagled

across his lap—much like she herself had been earlier—came to mind.

Her body hummed in harmony with the engine, acutely aware of how fully he filled the passenger seat beside her. Logan weighed her options. After all, she knew nothing about him and what she did know wasn't very comforting. Still, the Jeep was warm, she was in the driver's seat, and most importantly, she'd been given another opportunity to persuade him. Life was full of chances. She decided to take another one by leaving with him.

"Look, I'm not going to bite you. Where to?" He seemed exasperated.

"The East End, Friendship. I'll have to break in to my apartment, though, because my keys are in my stolen coat." She pressed her lips shut, realizing how bitter she sounded.

"Hmph," O'Shea grunted. For a second, he sat there, running his gaze over her features. A rush of heat spread up into her cheeks at his appraisal. Opening the glove box, he pulled out a napkin. Reaching across the seat, he gently dabbed it on her damp cheek.

"There," he said, showing her the dark smudge of mascara.

Great, just great. She must look worse than a Pittsburgh coal miner after a long shift.

They remained silent as they drove north. Snowflakes danced across the windshield, growing in numbers and force as they crossed the Monongahela River into the Golden Triangle, where all three rivers—the Allegheny, Ohio and Monongahela—converged. There, the snowfall grew so heavy it dimmed the bright lights from the skyscrapers downtown.

"Looks like we're in for some storm," she commented, not knowing what to say but feeling the need to break the silence.

It didn't work.

She searched for another topic to get a conversation going, hopefully one leaning toward the topic of him fighting. "I don't even know your name. Just O'Shea."

"Let's keep it at that."

The storm brewing outside was minor compared to the one sitting next to her. Why did he have to be so damn difficult? She bit her lip hard, forcing her thoughts on the slight physical pain, and away from the abrupt swell of emotion within. Falling apart right now wouldn't help her in the least.

He pointed left. So typically male, giving directions from the passenger seat, though there was nothing typical about him. "Okay, O'Shea," she commented mockingly, but followed his direction nevertheless.

His low laugh filled the Jeep. She felt his eyes on her, but kept her own on the roadway.

"It's Keane."

Keane O'Shea. Go figure. Short name, short response. Narrowing her eyes, she shot him a look—which he ignored. Instead, he gestured toward an exit sign. Without comment, she carefully slowed the Jeep, exited and headed downtown—away from her neighborhood. A few blocks in, he signaled to turn off onto a side street lined with row houses.

"Number twenty-one."

She stopped the Jeep in front of a rather dilapidated house.

Did I just drive myself to a one-night stand?

Uncertain, she studied the certifiably hot mystery of a man from beneath her lashes.

As if sensing her apprehension, Keane turned and cleared his throat. "Relax. Just a pit stop."

Before she could say another word, he jumped from the Jeep, climbed the cement stoop, and, after someone answered his rap on the door, disappeared from view.

The snow made it hard to see and as the minutes passed, her uneasiness grew. Finally, the door flew open and Keane emerged with a bundle in his arms. A man and woman followed behind him, gesturing wildly.

Twist my tights. What was going on… Did he just rob this couple?

Keane climbed back into the passenger seat, the irate woman right behind him. *Oh my God.* It was Rosie, with the poor fool who'd gone home with her now struggling to stay clear of her flailing limbs. She'd forgotten him already as she tried to claw her way up Keane's body.

Something flew across the center console and landed in a black pile on Logan's lap. A soft, familiar alpaca pile. Searching inside the inner pocket, Logan found her wallet, cell phone and keys. He'd retrieved her coat.

"You son of a bitch! You're taking her home tonight?" Rosie screeched, her tone like nails on a chalkboard. "After all the…"

Logan's mouth fell open, and Easywrap struggled to keep the passenger-side door from closing, despite the accumulating snow and the parting of her dragon-embroidered silk robe.

"Everything they say about him is true. He's a heartless bastard. A great fuck—that's all you'll get out of him. Commitment phobia, that's what he has. The only thing he'll commit to is sticking his big dick in—"

Keane slammed the door shut. Rosie continued her tirade outside the window as they drove away.

Logan was speechless on the drive to her Friendship neighborhood. As was Keane—no surprise there.

Everything about him, from his tight, clenched mouth to his strong build to his dour personality, said run for the slate hills. Yet, perhaps underneath that hard, muscular shell lurked a warm-hearted man? After all, he'd gone out of his way to retrieve her coat and house keys. Dare she approach him once more about fighting?

The Jeep ambled down Friendship Boulevard, fighting snowdrifts all the way. Fortunately, the rooms she rented in the back of an old brick house were close by. Her landlady, Mrs. Debinska, was a widow with an early-to-bed, early-to-rise philosophy. Logan barely saw the reserved, frail Polish woman, though she went out of her way to make sure the old lady had groceries in the house. She hoped Mrs. Debinska was a sound sleeper. Getting busted climbing out of a stranger's Jeep at this hour might upset the conservative elderly woman.

As she turned the Jeep onto her street, the wheels lost traction. In slow motion, the vehicle spiraled in a circle and a half, before coming to rest backward, in a snowdrift, on the side of the road. Logan pressed the gas, but the wheels spun uselessly. Unless he lived nearby, Keane was stuck until morning.

Shaken by this realization as well as by the accident, Logan blurted, "So, I guess this means you're sleeping over."

He shifted his big body around in his seat and looked right at her. Steady, ice-blue eyes captured her own. She felt the heat creep up in her cheeks at the intense scrutiny.

"Wait, that didn't come out…" Her mouth fell shut as he reached over, turned off the ignition and pocketed the keys.

His eyes continued to study her until he nodded. "I guess so."

With that settled, she reached for the handle to her door but stopped when he rested a hand on her arm. Surprised, she turned back his way.

"Everything that happened back there, everything Rosie said…" he began.

Logan jumped in, feeling the sudden need to reassure him. "The woman stole my coat. Do you think for one second I'd believe anything she had to say?"

He shook his head. "Listen…" Pausing, he adjusted his knit cap over his ears, flexed his swollen knuckles and then glared down at the gloves he'd placed on his thigh.

"I have a package of frozen peas in the freezer. Not that you want something cold on you on a blustery night like this—" *Did she really just say that?* "Um, I'll warm some port. It's a habit I picked up during my trips to Paris. So, I'm offering you peas and port."

He didn't so much as crack a smile. Rather, he frowned. She felt like sliding under the seat.

"Logan." Her name rolled off his tongue like sweet butter. "Just so you know, everything Rosie said…is true."

Chapter 3

ANKLE PICK: A wrestling move, where a fighter uses a foot or hand to sweep an opponent off his/her feet and onto the mat

Keane thought it was only fair to warn her. Something about this woman, Logan, appealed to him on many levels. It was best she understand exactly what she was in for because he fully intended to take her up on her invitation. Hell, the high from his fight a week ago had long worn off. Another physical release sounded really good right about now.

Logan brought her finger to her lips in a shushing gesture and motioned him inside. Yeah, fucking her was just the thing he needed, and he'd start with those lips.

Wooden floorboards creaked beneath his weight as

she led him down a long hallway. The keys jingled in her hand as she unlocked the door on the end.

"You can hang your jacket there," she whispered, pointing to the coat rack next to the door. "I'll be right back."

Keane hooked his coat over a knob and glanced around. The small room was dominated by a worn leather couch, with a glass coffee table in front and low end tables at each side. An old, oak hutch holding an enormous outdated television was against the opposite wall, and on the shelf above it sat a neat stack of photo albums. An expensive-looking painting of young ballerinas dancing and two fancy lamps seemed a little out of place, but what did he know about decorating?

He picked up a miniature china figurine, a ballerina with her leg stretched up to the side of her head. With a slight squeeze of his fingers, this little dancer would easily crush. He set her back in place, and settled himself onto the couch. Closing his eyes, he listened to Logan move about.

"Here we go, just as I promised. We need more light. Would you mind turning on the one on the side table for me?"

The small movement of twisting the light's knob reminded him how his knuckles hurt like hell.

Temporary relief came in the form of the tall cup of warmed red wine Logan placed in front of him on the coffee table. Later, he promised himself, he'd forget everything, except the feeling of being buried deep within the attractive female next to him. Resting a hand on his pocket, his fingers wrapped around the bottle of pills inside. After, when he was spent, if it hadn't been enough to quiet his mind, he'd medicate.

"Here you go. Let me see your knuckles." She grabbed his wrist, brought it over to rest on her thigh, and arranged a Ziploc bag of frozen peas over the swelling. "Secret of the trade. An icepack won't wrap around your fingers the same way. I can't tell you how many nights I sat with these homemade packs on my feet. Didn't help the blisters much but nothing beats it for bringing down the swelling."

At the mention of her feet, a memory of her on the ramp in those ridiculous pink Nikes made him frown in confusion. What was a woman like her—dressed in a fancy sweater and classy boots, conservative—doing strutting half-naked in the ring? She brought her legs up Indian-style on the couch and turned slightly to better face him.

Tonight, clothing covered almost every inch of her, from thick, wool socks, to tight, black pants, and on to a large, soft sweater. Effectively hiding the shapely body he'd felt pressed up against him. The memory of her hot little body, her nipples pebbling up hard against him, that tight ass flexing beneath his arm, caused his cock to stir. Those layers did nothing to dim how freakin' sexy this ring card girl was. Fuck, every red-blooded male in Pittsburgh had been talking about this Octagon Girl.

For some unknown reason, the thought annoyed him.

Women threw themselves at him all the time, though he hadn't expected an Octagon Girl to hurl herself into his chest in a full body slam. Or block his exit from the arena. This woman was determined, he'd give her that, tracking him down at Finnegan's and maneuvering Rosie out of bed, so to speak.

"You certainly don't like to mince words," she said sarcastically.

He liked that. She had spunk. He shifted and the movement of the cushion forced her closer. Yeah, she was just what he needed—a temporary distraction from all his problems.

Logan had done something to her hair, pulled it up into a loose bun. Blond wisps escaped and settled around her face. She was prettier than he remembered. Attractive and eager.

Picking up on the heat within his stare, she flushed a pretty pink. He waited for her to act on it. A few seconds passed, and then she spoke. "You knocked Andy the Annihilator out in ten seconds. You're a champion, that's why Jerry wants you on his fight team."

"Seven seconds, in a guillotine." He flexed his fingers. This conversation was going nowhere. The raw insistence in her voice pissed him off. Not at her, at whatever caused it. Shit, he could relate. But him fighting, that wasn't gonna work out for him. Or her. A good fuck—now that would help.

His hand found her thigh and shifted upward. The spark of hunger in her green eyes made his cock thicken. No surprise there, yet he was tempted to smile.

Man alive, she was willing. He leaned further back onto the couch and stretched out his legs. Better if Logan initiated things. Less drama that way, by making her work for it, having her be the aggressor. Someone who'd enjoy exactly what he was offering. Someone who wouldn't break into tears if he didn't talk to her afterward. Or ever again—which he tended to do more often than not.

He relaxed, and waited for her to make good on her earlier invitation.

* * *

Keane's smoldering glances—heated I-want-to-get-into-your-panties kind of looks—were getting more frequent and hotter by the minute. Sprawled on the couch next to her, he didn't say much. Yet he more than made up for the lack of words with the bold caress of his eyes. Not that Logan minded. In fact, she found herself wanting more. But aside from the whisperlike feel of his finger, he hadn't moved to touch her at all. Sharing her albums had been a bad idea.

Twist my tights. Why did she let him open the damned thing in the first place?

An hour had passed while he looked at the photographs, newspaper clips and programs from her most treasured scrapbook, arranged chronologically to showcase the best moments of her life—the story of a dedicated ballerina who had taken Lincoln Center by storm.

"So?" His question made her jump. The port made her mind slow and dumb as she turned over the possibilities of that one word in her mind... *So, what are we waiting for? So, take off your sweater? So, let's take this into the bedroom?*

With a shake of his head, Keane flipped the page of the album balanced between them on his thigh.

Her breath caught. The headline "Ballet's New Royal Couple" was centered on the front page of the *New York Times*. And there they were. A close-up of her beaming like a new mother and Pierre looking at her with loving stars in his eyes. The lying jerk was as smug as could be.

Logan grabbed the offensive scrapbook, snapped it shut and tossed it to the floor. She'd forgotten she'd saved a few photos and articles from the Pierre bonfire.

Leave it to her asshole of an ex-fiancé to put in an un-expected appearance and do the one thing he was great at doing…ruining everything.

Just when Keane seemed relaxed and reasonable. And so damned sexy her mouth felt dry. Just when she'd been building the courage to approach him again about helping her, about fighting, Pierre resurfaced. *Just you wait*, she promised, and braced herself for the forthcoming questions.

"So?" Keane prodded, unaware of how everything she'd ever wanted was lying there, in the album, on the floor. How all the pain from the past year simmered just below the surface, primed and ready to burst. The port and her hopelessly heightened libido didn't help, either.

Stupid. One glance in a mirror would verify it—the ridiculous expression on her face as she stared blankly at Mr. Few Words next to her.

"You're a dancer, a ballerina. So, dance," he stated.

"I broke my ankle," she said, and studied her hands in an attempt to mute the frustration in her voice. "I spent years training, hours every day, since I was a little kid. I'd finally landed a spot in a major dance troupe, a chance at fully living my dream, and now…"

"Let's see," he said, his voice throaty, whiskey-toned.

"Let's see what? You want me to dance right now?"

Without responding, he grabbed her legs and brought her feet over to rest on his calves. With big, sure hands, he rolled down one long wool sock and then the other.

Stunned, she tried to pull away.

"Tsk, tsk," he mouthed, his beautiful lips pursed to-gether.

She'd imagined a fighter's nose would be notched and crooked. Instead, Keane's was straight and perfectly proportioned to his face. With the exception of a square jaw, his features were surprisingly delicate. The sexual tension rolling off of him, however, was pure male. And her reaction was all female, with the way she itched to run her fingers along his high cheekbones.

He tossed her socks to the floor, and arranged her bare feet upon his knees.

Tiny jolts of pleasure rippled through her at his touch. Her feet had never been sensitive—years of dancing had hardened and calloused them. She jumped with surprise when the tender skin on her sole yielded beneath his thumbs. *Not* dancing professionally had one advantage, it seemed.

His thumbs moved up to the indentation between her ankle and heel.

"Hmm, this one," he remarked as a finger ran along the raised scar tissue crisscrossing her ankle. Instinctually, she pulled away. Having him touch her *there*—it felt like he'd skimmed over a vulnerable point deep inside her, the ugly scars hiding the pain within.

He tugged her closer, nudging her bottom upward so that she was balanced on his thigh. Ignoring her gasp, he hoisted her leg straight up in the air, causing her to fall backward onto the couch. Before she could guess what he was about, warm lips pressed against the spot of her injury.

Her hips arched up off his thigh involuntarily.

"No one's ever… What are you doing?" she gasped, as the first flick of his tongue rasped the sensitive flesh of her ankle.

"Relax," he murmured against her tingling skin. Logan's senses had shifted to high gear and she gripped the upholstery beneath her, desperate for something to hold on to.

His tongue swirled over the sensitive skin beneath her ankle bone, over the peaks and valleys of her scar. A light, moist caress, causing a warm tingling sensation to shoot up her leg and burst to life between her thighs. *Sweet heaven.* Keane's wicked tongue laved at her skin. Right on the very spot that had brought her career and her life to a screeching halt, shattering all of it.

Her thoughts spiraled like fireflies on a hot summer night. She wanted to let go. Let her body take over. Forget the agonizing year she'd been through. Give in to just feeling…good.

How could so much pleasure cause so much pain?

His tongue. Him. Her messed-up psyche. She bit back a frustrated cry. It was too much to bear.

She shimmied backward and yanked her leg away.

A low grunt of displeasure was his only response.

Thankfully, her bottom connected with the remote, and the TV clicked on, breaking the awkward silence. Even better, a commercial advertising the qualifying bouts for Tetnus filled the screen, capturing Keane's attention.

She imagined herself a wallflower at the prom, one too embarrassed to dance with the hottest guy in school. The foolish feeling was exactly right, even if she *had* missed her prom for a ballet recital.

The commercial ended and Keane rose from the sofa. Apparently, he was leaving.

"No! You're in no condition to drive, the roads are a mess, and I still haven't talked to you about fighting…"

He glared down at her. "You can forget that. I'm not fighting anymore."

Logan felt like kicking herself. She'd sidetracked, so focused on him, his wicked tongue and her neurosis, she'd hadn't yet convinced him to fight. And now, she'd not only chased him off, but ruined her chances of reasoning with him.

"Look, you seem like a nice person. But I've gotta go. Brave it on foot."

He bent over and retrieved something—a small orange container—from the floor. Then he moved toward the door.

She jumped up. Her head spun from the port.

With a snatch of his jacket, he put his hand on the doorknob. "Thanks for the ride," he muttered, sliding his arm into a sleeve.

"You can have the sofa. I'd really feel better if you stayed."

His glanced at the couch and back at her. His eyes narrowed with displeasure.

"It's comfortable—if you want, you can sleep in my bed and I'll take the sofa. Really, the idea of you leaving during a major snowstorm is ridiculous. There won't be a cab. What else can I possibly say to convince you—?"

"Nothing." He held up a hand in a farewell gesture, and her eyes fell on the small canister in his palm.

"What is that?"

"None of your business. It's been…interesting." He turned to leave but Logan slid in front of him and blocked the door. Close enough she could smell the sweet wine on his breath. Close enough to read the label on the prescription bottle in his hand. Oxycontin. Not only had he been drinking all evening, but he was taking painkillers. She'd taken a few of them during her recuperation and knew how they dimmed the pain. And everything else.

"I'm not letting you leave in your condition."

He grunted. "Little too late to be passing judgment, honey."

"You're on medication. Ever read the small print on the bottle? The print that says don't use with alcohol? The same print that says it'll make you groggy?" She gestured toward the door. "A blizzard is coming down out there. You're likely to end up like the Jeep, ass planted in a snowdrift."

He snorted. "The pills—didn't take any. As far as drinking, I've barely begun…"

"Are you always this unreasonable?"

The glare he shot her said it all.

Still, she tried one more time. Stomping her foot in frustration, she demanded, "What do I have to do to convince you to stay?"

He ran a hand across his forehead and up through his cropped hair. "Nothing. And forget about me fighting. Not going to happen, no matter what you say…or do."

"Forget. Isn't that easier said than done? Look around you, this is all I have—which isn't saying much. My Mazda isn't running because I can't afford a mechanic. I have big plans for this money."

"Hey, you're not the only one with problems."

Logan grabbed his hand and gave a firm squeeze, as if the gesture might stir something inside him, some note of empathy. Hell, at this point, she'd even take sympathy.

"What if the answer to your problem was standing smack in front of you?"

"What if she was?"

"Would you ignore the chance to persuade her to help you? Or would you fight for the chance to climb out from the miserable hole that's swallowed you up? If I can't perform as—"

"Shit," he muttered, interrupting her. He shrugged off his jacket, placed it back onto the coat rack, and moved whisper soft across the carpet.

Turning, she swung the door shut with a resounding thud and snapped the two locks into place. The action gave her a second to process that he was indeed staying, rather than reassurance that he wouldn't leave. Two locks wouldn't stop a man like Keane.

"Common sense prevails." She hoped the satisfied note in her voice wouldn't piss him off.

"Hardly."

The Road to Tetnus commercial came on again, noisily blaring away in the background. Leave it to Jerry to advertise the heck out of these qualifying bouts. Keane's back was to her, yet she could see him balling his fingers into a fist. Guess fighting was a subject best avoided for the time being.

She grabbed him by the elbow and tugged, giddiness mingling with apprehension as he allowed her to lead him into the adjoining room. Her panties were still moist from the job his tongue had done on her skin. She felt herself moisten further at the mere thought of how close they'd come before her freak-out. But recommencing what had been started on the sofa was a bad idea. The emotions caused by his simple, gentle touch on her ankle, on the most broken part of her, were too overwhelming.

Weakness was something she couldn't afford. Multiple times tonight, she'd blown her chance. The scrapbook was a blatant reminder—she wanted all the good parts of her former life back. Pierre would be a bad dream hidden within the pages of her past. Her future was going to be golden, just like she'd always hoped it would be.

But her winning ticket hovered a few feet away, tight-lipped and mean. No, Keane was going to fight. There had to be some way of gaining his cooperation, of convincing him how desperately she needed her job.

Her arm nearly came out of its socket when he didn't move along with her next tug. She released her grip and allowed him to follow her into her bedroom of his own accord.

Her sanctuary. She caught Keane scanning the large room and grinned. Bet he'd never been in a bedroom of this scale and size.

Five enormous floor-to-ceiling mirrors were secured along the length of a wall. She'd salvaged one from the trash and the others she'd purchased on credit from Sally. Eventually, she'd add a barre to match the floorboards and construct a wall to quarter off a sleeping area. For now, the bed was situated mid-room, the headboard pushed up against the wall. Armoires for her clothes and costumes dominated the far wall, leaving a long expanse of floor by the mirrors for dancing.

"Nothing you do will change my mind." His warning was accompanied by a fierce, foreboding scowl, one that questioned her motives and assumed the worst.

Don't be so sure, she thought, but instead replied, "Why don't you take off your boots and sit on the bed?"

Ignoring his sour mood, she slid open an armoire door and carefully selected an outfit best suited to the job ahead. The creaking of the hardwood floors, followed by those of the old bedsprings, spoke volumes. He'd complied, making her feel more confident. More daring.

She glanced in the mirror at the big brute of a man sprawled out on her bed, his back up against the headboard. By giving him a sense of what she was about, maybe he'd be more likely to help her. She thumbed the tulle on her tutu.

"I'm going to make staying over worth your while," she stated calmly, drawing on every ounce of port-induced bravado still within her.

His only response was to raise his eyebrows, daring her. The thumping of her heart was almost enough to send her running from the room, clenching the red-and-gold costume tightly in her hand.

If this doesn't beat all, Keane thought. Classical music tended to grate on his nerves, his preference leaning more toward rock or heavy metal. Though the lovely, rollercoaster wreck of a woman dancing around on her tippy-toes with those long, bare legs kicking in perfect rhythm to the music might just change his mind. Each time she spun around, the frilly white lace on her red mini skirt-thingy vibrated and lifted, revealing her ample tight ass, displayed in something that resembled a Brazilian bikini. Only smaller.

A striptease, of sorts. Keane had had his share of dancers. Male bonding time, his friend Jimmy used to say as he'd dragged Keane into every strip club from Rome to Nagasaki to Ft. Lauderdale. Surprisingly, Afghanistan was a serviceman's paradise; Jimmy'd had more fun there than anywhere else. War did that—

scared the shit out of you, which made the time away from fighting seem unnaturally enjoyable.

So why did Keane's itch to fight—a no-holds-barred, full-blown-brawl kind of itch—persevere like a troublesome hangover?

Keane flexed his fingers. *Fuckin' Jimmy.*

Logan's arms snaked over her head, demanded his full attention. *There's more than one way to scratch an itch.* One faced him now, with an odd, dreamy look on her face. Innocent and seductive as hell.

She bounced, exchanging one bent knee for the other. The little skirt bounced along with her, and his eyes shot to the V between her legs. Nothing visible, yet the idea of what lay hidden beneath that wisp of red material had his cock straining against his jeans.

He shifted on the mattress, adjusting his pants, and not a moment too soon.

Her next move was sexier than any stripper on any pole. Three little spirals and she was beside the bed. Her legs bent, her body lowered, and his breath caught as she pulled one leg straight up alongside her head in a sideways split. Three complete circles followed, her leg held upward all the while. The Brazilian briefs were on full display, much like waving a red flag in front of a bull. A surge of lust grabbed hold of his balls.

And just like that, Logan unknowingly sealed her fate.

The music intensified and her movements followed the tempo as she danced around the oversized bedroom. A half circle and her back arched in a perfect horseshoe. She moved away from him, but not before her lids closed and a satisfied smile spread crossed her face.

A clear challenge there, to ensure that smug, contented look remained while his cock thrust into her or, better still, when he made her scream his name. Keane wasn't the kind of guy who ignored a challenge.

Slowly, he swung his legs off the bed and stood. She didn't notice. Instead, her arms fluttered out to the sides and fingertips wiggled, caressing the air. Slight, quiet movements complimenting the mellowing beat of the music.

With a few long strides, he narrowed the distance between them, coming up behind her. Her chest was flushed a sweet shade of pink, its reflection in the mirror rising and falling with every breath. Heat rose up off her skin. Her hair was a mess, partly still swept up in a knot of sorts but mostly falling onto her shoulders in disarray. One part of her neck was bare, exposed, and to his liking.

The music began to crescendo. In response, she came up onto her toes. As the rhythm built, her bounces changed to small jumps with arms elongated over and upward. The tiny tutu fluttered as he stepped closer.

Hell, he'd been waiting all night for her to make a move, not pull away like she'd been nipped in the ankle by the devil. Her performance was both surprising, and flat-out stimulating.

Also, it was about to end.

On the next jump, his hands found her waist and caught her mid-flight. Her toes pointed downward and her body came to a fluttering halt as she dangled in the air.

"What...?" she gasped and stared at him, wide-eyed, in the mirror.

He let his hands reply, slowly lowering one of her legs to the floor. He hooked the curve of his arm behind her other knee, lifting higher and higher until her leg was back up beside her head. Returning her to this position made his blood run hot all over again.

Gently, he pressed his body against her back, bumping her up against the mirror. Their eyes locked while he waited for an invitation to continue.

She blinked but didn't look away. A myriad of emotions appeared in her somber, green eyes. Uncertainty, nervousness…but, thank God, no fear. Desire flared deep within their depths.

Inch by inch, Keane lowered his head, breaking eye contact. Her back stiffened as his lips found the warm, exposed skin of her neck. He sucked, and her calf muscle twitched against his arm.

"Wouldn't it be…easier on the bed?" she whispered.

He nipped at her neck and worked his tongue in an upward trail to the back of her ear. "Yep," he breathed.

She ground her ass into him. He shifted her foot in his hand. Beginning at her ankle, he ran his fingers downward, over the raised skin of her scar, and still lower, over her bare calf. His other thumb moved in unison, massaging small circles across her inner leg.

Her tight muscles flexed beneath his digits. She liked it all right. A pleasant surprise, those muscular legs of hers. Long, endless legs, with skin so fucking soft, it felt like the fine chalk powder he poured into his fighting gloves.

He returned his tongue to what was becoming his favorite spot on her neck as thumb and fingers journeyed lower still. Flexing his abdomen into her back, he pushed her against the mirror.

His thumb shifted lower and, with fixed intention, rubbed over her panties, right between her legs.

Moving his tongue along the dewy trail to her ear, he whispered, low and deep, "Flex your leg higher." Seeing her dance, that taut, limber body of hers moving, had given him ideas.

She gasped, and for a moment, he fought for control. The urge to unbutton his pants, part the red material between her legs and bury deep inside of her was that strong. Instead, he followed through on what he'd planned on doing since the first time she'd pulled that lovely leg up alongside her head.

He ran his thumb along the elastic band on the scant piece of material covering her center and, with a slight nudge, slid it beneath.

A shiver ran up her back and against his chest as he found her moist cleft.

"Oh my God," she groaned.

He kissed her neck as his thumb pressed deeper, pulled away, and coated her nub with moisture. The movements were repeated, quick and urgent.

She was close. He increased the pressure and felt her shudder. Removing his thumb, he worked two fingers inside her wetness, loving how her inner muscles greedily contracted around him. Tighter and tighter, as he withdrew and, just as quickly, slid his thumb back inside.

It had been a long time since he'd enjoyed bringing a woman to climax with his fingers. Moving his tongue along her neck, he once again licked his way behind her ear. A few nibbles, with his thumb smoothly sliding in and out, had her trembling and ready.

But she had one more move to complete, a prelude to another type of completion. "*Dance for me*," he growled, before swirling his tongue and darting it into her ear. His thumb mimicked the action.

"Now? Later. Oh, please, Keane," she cried out. She felt so fucking hot around him. He promised himself that his rigid cock would find some warmth as well. Sooner rather than later.

"I want you on your toes," he demanded.

For a split second, she hesitated. He slowly withdrew his digit until the pad of his thumb rested on her folds. With a thrust, he buried it back inside.

"Dance. Do it."

"Okay, okay. But please… Oh, my God."

She rose onto her toes of her left foot. The slight shift upward caused his thumb to slide downward, and downward still. Her back arched against him, her leg flexed tighter, and with a throaty moan, she shattered.

Logan's legs turned liquid as Keane lowered her onto her feet and broke contact. She rested her head against the mirror and fought for equilibrium. A drunken headiness washed over her, assisted by the louder-than-Beethoven's-"Ode to Joy" hum running throughout her body, distorting her ability to think.

Keane leaned into the mirror as well, his hands to the sides of her head. Big hands, with long fingers, she noted beneath her eyelashes. Hands she wanted to feel run over every inch of her body. Another rush of warmth spread to the juncture between her legs. God, it had been so long since she wanted someone with such savage intensity.

She'd never imagined dancing could be sexually satisfying. A deliciously titillating kind of foreplay. A naughty overture to what was coming her way. With

Pierre, dancing was always work and only enjoyable in front of an audience. The rare occasions where she'd danced solo for him had been anything but pleasurable—especially when his habit of criticizing her ruined her desire to ever perform for him. The egotistical jerk. Hell, he'd turned her off, never on.

Pierre had assured her other dancers experienced the same hang-ups. Strict diets, strenuous dance rehearsals and the stress of being a prima ballerina were the reasons sex with him was bland, as non-descript as eating a bologna sandwich. What a bunch of bologna.

Come to think of it, since meeting Keane, her libido had shifted from dormant into overdrive.

She couldn't remember the last time she'd felt so incredibly…fulfilled. Unsettlingly so. And to think, this was the appetizer before the main course. All six foot two of muscled fighter.

Opening her eyes, she caught his smirk in the mirror. A quiet invitation. She swallowed hard.

He nodded toward the bed.

"How about…" she began, her voice hoarse with desire. *How about I take a beautiful swan dive onto the mattress, you join me and we go at it?*

He tilted his head and arched an eyebrow, waiting for her to continue.

"…I bring us some water?"

He stared at her for a second. "Okay."

She stepped away from him, instantly missing the warmth of his body but at the same time needing an intermission to find her breath.

"Logan."

Hearing her name roll off his tongue made her want

to sprint to the kitchen, then back. "Yeah?" She stopped and glanced over her shoulder.

"Once we're in it—" he gestured toward the bed "—don't count on leaving anytime soon."

Her body flushed from head to toe. Hell, buckets of water wouldn't quench the thirst she had for him.

"Be right back," was all she could muster before stumbling into the living room.

Late-night host Sophie Morelle's voice filled the silence. The cocky darling of cable television was Logan's favorite after-hours host. Tonight, she was listing reasons why some washed-up actor should star in a new sitcom—something about more strippers in the prime-time line-up.

In the kitchen, she filled two tall glasses, not really paying attention to Sophie. For the first time in months, Logan was eager for what might come next. Starting with the surprise waiting for her in the next room.

It wasn't until she headed back into the living room that she realized who Sophie's guest was. That someone landed an invisible sucker punch and knocked the air out of her.

She dropped the plastic glasses, the water showering her legs and bare feet, the glasses landing hard then rolling in opposite directions across the wooden floor. Not that Logan really noticed, as she grabbed the remote off the couch and turned up the volume. There was no mistaking that smug voice. Pierre.

Logan glared at the TV. The fame hound sat on a chair across from the host, as arrogant as could be, while three buxom women in tight tube tops and tutus were paraded in front of him.

"Pierre LaFeur, a favorite to win *America Gets Its*

Groove On, is with us tonight. Pierre, some people think you're callous for not taking any responsibility for what happened on last season's finale, where you so famously dropped your former partner. Come on, Pierre, her average-sized tits interfered with you catching her?"

"Well…er…for a ballerina—"

"I understand that several other *male* prime-time hosts—not saying any names here—have called you an expert on female anatomy. In the spirit of joining the boys' club and trash-talking women, tonight we're asking you to vote for the biggest set of hooters."

The women pranced across the stage, each stopping to pose in front of Pierre.

When the camera zoomed in on the awkwardly ridiculous expression on his face, Logan attempted a laugh. But her throat constricted tightly.

If the world knew the truth. How Logan had made it through three months on a reality show she'd had no desire to be on. How four weeks before the finale, she'd been basking in the warmth of a standing ovation from her performance before the Queen of England. How one week after Pierre had fumbled his catch and dropped her on the show's finale, she'd caught him in a pretzel position with her understudy, Anya, in her bed.

She felt Keane come up behind her. *Pimp my plié, the humiliation never ends.*

Sophie Morelle continued on relentlessly. "Personally, I find the buzz about your former partner's breasts offensive. But hey, viewers are eating it up—as you well know, Pierre. Clearly, the network is thrilled to have you back this season. But what you might not know is not everyone agrees with you. Her knockers don't seem to be an issue for *this* hunk of sin…"

A picture filled the television screen. Logan let out a dry, inaudible rasp and her eyes darted toward Keane, who was silently towering over her. His eyes shifted from curious to narrowed and pissed-off. The lines around his mouth pulled tighter.

Fearing the worst, her attention swung back to the offensive image on the screen. The paparazzi had really gone all out, bulbs blazing. There, decked out in full, fluorescent pink Octagon Girl regalia was Logan. Shot from the side, they'd captured her pressed up against a sinewy mass of male. Keane, no mistaking him. No mistaking either of them. Or the leering faces in the background.

His hands cupped her bottom and back. Her head was angled toward his. And their mouths were lip-locked in what appeared to be a toe-curling kiss.

"Fuck," Keane growled in her ear.

Sophie continued on, oblivious to the tension building like molten lava in Logan's living room. "A girl after my own heart. Looks like she found a profession that appreciates a shapely woman."

Again, the camera panned to Pierre. A tight fake smile was plastered on his face.

What she'd give to wipe that expression off his lying lips. Before she could muster an explanation for Keane, the photograph disappeared.

Abruptly, one of the women stepped onto the small chair, spread her arms overhead, and leaped forward, aiming for Pierre in a less-than-perfect Logan imitation. Pierre jumped to his feet. His arms circled around her as they connected. He wobbled for a split second but found his footing.

"See," Sophie stated gleefully, "I proved my point.

You *can* catch someone with a rack the size of watermelons."

Having Sophie on her side did not make Logan feel any better.

An oh-so-familiar irritation washed over her. *Just you wait, Pierre.*

Keane moved past her and clicked off the TV. "Your ex? From the newspaper?" He didn't seem the type to appreciate the attention either. Not one bit, judging by the tone in his voice.

What could she say? Even if she could speak—which she couldn't, as a fistful of rage lodged the words within her throat—how could she discuss the depths of despair that sucked the life out of her every time her ex lied about that damned dance?

Oh, she was going to get even with Pierre, that much was certain. Once her life was in balance. Once she was back on her toes again.

"I'm gonna fight, all right."

Her mouth fell open as she stared at him. Perhaps something good had been salvaged from tonight's wreckage.

His thumb caressed her cheek. Something crossed his face. Compassion. Sympathy. Just as quickly, his finger was gone.

"*Not* for the title," he ground out through clenched teeth.

He headed into the bedroom, marched over to the bed and grabbed the folded blanket lying across the foot of it. Moving past her frozen in the doorway, he tossed the blanket onto the sofa. "Better get some rest." His actions were abrupt, but his tone was kind.

Still, it didn't matter. Pierre had ruined the evening.

Her eyes shifted from the pile on the sofa to the Renoir-style painting above it. Revenge was going to taste even sweeter than taking his prized possession.

Just you wait, Pierre.

"Logan." The way Keane stressed the *a* in her name in that deep, gravelly voice of his soothed her irritation. "We'll see how quick your ex-partner is on his feet. Pretty boy LaFool is gonna eat his teeth."

As Keane spoke, his voice changed. Less kind, more menacing. So much so that shivers ran up her spine. His threat said it all.

The market on revenge wasn't exclusively hers.

Chapter 4

FOOTWORK: How a fighter moves his/her feet to best maintain balance, mobility and striking power

*B*am, bam, bam.

The steady thump of someone pounding on the oak door of his Victorian home seeped into Keane's semi-consciousness. He awoke with a jerk, sprang to his feet and immediately reached for his gun. Only his hands came up empty. *Shit*. The Afghanistan/Pakistan border was a world away but at times like this, it felt so real. Realizing his mistake, he rubbed his palms over his face in an effort to wake up. There it was again, loud enough to clear away the last of his drug-and-booze-induced stupor.

The digital alarm read 10:00 a.m. Who the hell was looking for him this early?

His neighborhood, Shadyside, was nice enough, with its Victorian mansions and well-maintained apartments. For the most part, people were polite but kept to themselves. Which suited him fine—he didn't want anyone nosing into his business. Less wise-asses looking for trouble, too. It was the anonymity of this posh neighborhood that made him spend a bit more cash on the place.

Keane made his way downstairs to the foyer and without pausing, threw the door open.

"Dude, did you see yesterday's *Pittsburgh Post*? Your ugly mug is front-page news, though the real reason I picked up a copy was because of that Octagon Girl…Luscious Logan."

Keane glared at Stevie through throbbing, tired eyes. Jesus. Her again.

The memory of Logan's long, firm leg flexed against the mirror plagued him like a frustrating hangover, in spite of how his cock stirred each time he thought about it. He wasn't one to dwell on past hook-ups—hell, getting a ballerina off with his thumb two nights ago hardly rated at all. But something about her stuck with him.

The 6:00 a.m. cocktail hadn't relieved his pounding head, and this unwanted publicity made him want to pound someone else's head.

He moved to close the door in his friend's face. Stevie's reflexes were quicker—it sucked to have sober friends—and he shoved his foot in the doorjamb. "Shit, man. I haven't seen you in a year and this is my welcome?" His friend pushed his way inside.

"Ever hear of a phone?" Keane asked, his tone harsh, but relented by stepping back a few inches. One thing he knew about Stevie: the man was stubborn, with a stiff back that rivaled his own. A trait that had served them both during their third tour together in the Marines.

"Nice place," Stevie commented. He tugged off his jacket and tossed it on a chair, making himself at home as if a year hadn't passed by. The kid was fit, had slimmed down some, and seemed…happy.

"But you, Coach, look like shit." Stevie was joking, but Keane caught the concern in his eyes.

"Don't call me that." Scowling, he changed the subject. "Why the visit?"

"Can't I look up the only friend I have in Pittsburgh? I'm headed to New York City. They want me to train personnel at a new recruitment center. Thought I'd make a stop to see your sorry ass on the way from Ohio."

Clearly, Stevie had overcome his driving issues— the constant searching of the roads for booby traps, the ball-clenching fear you'd experience in everyday situations that flared up when least expected. At least there was hope for one of them.

"So, what's up? You fighting again? Thought you gave that up after…"

"Nice seeing you, Stevie." Keane grabbed him by the arm and muscled him back toward the door. But not without resistance.

They took it to the floor and grappled for positioning, Keane quickly gaining the upper hand. Stevie was an amateur fighter—always had been, always would be. He pinned his friend to the ground and a few seconds later, Stevie raised his hand in surrender. An MMA fighter would have tapped out, proving yet again why Stevie should stay far away from the Octagon ring.

Both men stood, breathing hard. Blood trickled out

of Stevie's mouth and despite having been pissed off by him bringing up the past, Keane felt remorseful. Shit, even though his heart hadn't been in the fight, if you could call it that, he'd hurt his friend.

He nodded toward his leather couch. "Sit. I'll get some ice."

"How about a pot of coffee? Looks like we could both use some." His friend's ability to forgive and forget made Keane feel even worse.

Moments later, Stevie was situated on the couch, an odd expression on his face as he held a package of frozen peas to his lip.

Keane touched his knuckles. The ballerina had been right, the swelling had subsided. For a second, he thought about how she'd carefully wrapped his fist with the Ziploc bag, then pushed the memory away.

At least the peas gave Stevie something to do other than yak at him. Keane welcomed the silence, but not the company, given the present circumstances.

In the privacy of the kitchen, Keane plugged in the coffeemaker, then studied the newspaper he'd retrieved from the floor. They'd gone to the extra expense of publishing a color photograph of that damned kiss. Frowning, he read the headline: *Buxom Ballerina Gets Down and Dirty.*

Scanning the text, the paper crinkled in protest as he clenched his fist and forced himself to read more slowly. If the assholes had dug into his past…flashbacks, nightmares and late-night visits from his dead buddy were reminders enough of his time in the service.

His name was mentioned, but other than that and the freakin' photo, the accompanying paragraph focused entirely on Logan. Shit, judging by the indelicate way they'd dragged out every slanderous detail about her—even daring to praise her dick of an ex, part of this season's favored duo on a lame-ass reality dance show—it wouldn't take long before they focused on him. A sliver of anxiety mixed with anger worked its way up his spine.

He knew that ring girl was trouble the moment they locked lips. A publicity stunt? Doubtful. He shook his head, remembering her reaction to her ex's boob bash on the television. But damn, if he'd known this was what he was in for, he would have dropped her on her ass and there wouldn't have been a photograph.

His life was already fucked without this invasion of privacy.

Tossing the paper into the trash, he ran the kitchen faucet before dunking his head beneath. The cold water, a few cups of coffee and some Advil might do the trick. Preferably before Stevie started asking more questions.

What the hell could he say about returning to fighting, anyway? That a daily dose of booze and pills weren't nearly enough to drive away the demons in his head? That a parade of women and one-night stands wasn't enough of a physical release to satisfy him?

Not that he'd had a woman since his overnight stay with the ballerina. What a debacle of an evening that had been—a restless night on an old couch, an early morning escape through the snow-covered streets of Pittsburgh, and a cock in need of some serious attention.

More thoughts of Logan, this time twirling about in that skimpy outfit, had filled his mind yesterday afternoon. But when his fingers grabbed his hard-on, the fucking evening played over in his head and ruined the pleasure. Not that he didn't get off, fast and furious, but he felt cheated out of having those long legs of hers wrapped around his waist while he pumped into her. Probably for the best, really. Considering her baggage and notoriety, he planned on keeping way the hell away from her.

Stevie wasted no time with his inquisition as Keane returned and handed him a cup of coffee. "Care to tell me what's going on? You look like hell frozen over. And a fight? I thought you said…"

Keane grunted. It seemed his friend hadn't learned his lesson. In a low voice, he warned, "Not now, Stevie. Change the subject."

His buddy gave him a long look but must have read his expression. "Okay, I'll drop it. That's…uh…not the reason I stopped by."

Keane ran his thumb across his temple, picking up on Stevie's nervous tone. Whatever the cause, it wasn't gonna be good.

His friend grew more reluctant with each second passing, until he at last blurted out, "I'm seeing a shrink…a lot of the guys are."

"Good for you." Keane was careful to keep his tone neutral, knowing the angle Stevie was taking here and not wanting to give anything away. This discussion was dead as far as he was concerned.

"No shame in it, you know. It's helped to work out some issues, and stuff." Stevie held out his palm in a let-me-finish gesture. "Something to consider, that's all." He dug a card out of his wallet and tossed it onto the table by the couch without further comment.

Keane drank his coffee and ignored it. He felt his friend's eyes on him, but he ignored those too, until the subject changed.

"Well at least you're getting laid. She's hot, too. Great body. Nice rack."

Oblivious to Keane's anger, Stevie went on and on about the fucking article. And judging by his enthusiastic response, the newspaper's attempt to ridicule Logan had failed. If Stevie was any example, every sex-crazed stud out there, including her wimp-ass ex, wanted a piece of her.

Damn, it was going to be a long morning.

Pulling the hood of his sweatshirt over his head, Keane's legs picked up speed as the ground flattened out. Ten miles was for amateurs, yet he struggled to make it through the windy, hilly streets of Pittsburgh. He was losing what should have been a winnable battle. A string of sleepless nights had made him surly. Mean. And regretting his quest for sobriety.

Last night had been hell.

He'd woken up in a cold sweat, the smell of gunpowder and burning flesh in his nostrils. It had taken several seconds to realize it had been night terrors. That he wasn't in the desert of Afghanistan, on the lookout for roadside bombs and, worse, covered in blood after finding one.

It had taken twenty minutes for his hands to stop shaking.

Something had to change.

How hard could it be? No booze, no pills and no women—a cleaner way of living?

Stevie seemed to have conquered his demons. His visit had Keane rethinking his own bad habits. *Damn.* He wanted the days back when he'd been fit and full of life, both physically and mentally. Days long gone by.

Five miles into the run, he knew it was a lost cause. He needed something more…physical. To jab a punching bag or kick some ass in the cage. Something brutal, where his muscles ached afterward. Where the restlessness within was muted. Running was fine for building endurance. It was the mindfuck jogging around in his head he couldn't endure.

The Pittsburgh Fight Club was within running distance, and in the much flatter neighborhood of Squirrel Hill. Sal might be able to hook him up with a sparring partner. He changed direction and picked up speed.

In under an hour, Keane was dropping punches down on a fairly decent fighter, Frank Tupps. He had to give Tupps credit, the man had a thick skull and even thicker heart. At three minutes and five seconds exactly, Tupps tapped out.

Keane stalked to the corner, stripped off his thin fighting gloves, and ignored the appreciative murmurs of the other fighters. Annoyed that the relentless itch within him still needed scratching, that the fight hadn't done the trick. If the uphill run home wasn't enough to exhaust him, his choice of sleeping aids would be a no-brainer.

Turning to exit the cage, he nearly plowed Sal over.

"Aw, come outta there, Keane. These other fellows aren't too happy with me messing with their sparring time. *Some* fighters are looking to qualify for Tetnus, you know. And they're not going to spar with you—won't risk getting hurt. Not every fighter is a mean bastard like yourself."

Keane ignored the insult—or compliment, depending on how you looked at it. He didn't want the old man prying into his business, so he did what needed to be done. Shut him out.

Unfortunately, the old-school trainer had no sense of self-preservation and followed him across the cage.

When Keane moved to step around him, Sal blocked him with surprising swiftness. "I've set you up for cage time with Jaysin Bouvine in thirty minutes," the trainer offered. "I'm counting on you to give him a run for his money and make him see the light. Show him I mean business."

Keane dodged right, but Sal followed. Why did the old-timer seem so anxious for him to fight this guy?

"How about a hoagie and some protein shakes while we—"

"See you later."

In a full belly slam, Sal hurled himself up against Keane and forced him to stop in his tracks. "Wait…uh… you can't leave. Come on, Keane. I'll order us a roast beef with the works on it. And about Bouvine, Jaysin's been asking for some time with you."

"Look, Sal. Another day. Gotta go."

Glancing over his shoulder at the clock on the wall, Sal looked nervous. He shifted to the right, preparing for another body block.

Keane was ready for him. Faking a right, he side-stepped left and, with a few long strides, got out ahead. He was on the last step when Sal caught up with him.

"I want to talk to you about something."

Keane grunted. It wasn't hard to imagine what the trainer had to say, with Tetnus's preliminary fights just two weeks away.

"Didn't you hear me? I want to talk to you. It's about the girl…Logan."

Keane slowed his pace. Deep down, he was mildly curious about how she was doing—if she'd recovered from her douchebag of an ex's nighttime slander-fest. Having his mug plastered on front-page news still pissed him off, but he wondered how she was dealing with the negative coverage. Annoying or not, no one deserved that kind of treatment.

"What about her?" Keane heard himself say. *Damn, why head down this path? The woman was nothing but trouble.*

"Bouvine's bad news. He's obsessed with Logan, he followed her home last week. She hates the guy but won't rat him out. Thinks Jerry's gonna buy into replacing you with him. Come on, Keane. Why don't you fight?"

Keane ignored the sudden desire to slam his fists into Bouvine's kidneys, repeatedly. But Lord knew, he had his own shit to deal with. "Forget it."

"She's a real *nice* girl. Too good for the likes of—"

"She's a pain in the ass. Later."

"Um, Keane, she's…" Sal's voice was an octave higher than normal. Keane turned slowly.

"The pain in the ass is right behind you, alive and well," Logan said, her hands planted on her hips, glaring at him from a hair's breadth away.

Keane exuded sex—pure, raw sex. He must have just tugged on his black sweatshirt, a section of hem was caught beneath his T-shirt. Black sweats hung low on his hip. One hipbone and the chiseled cut of stomach muscle just above it were exposed. The teasing glimpse of skin made Logan flush.

He'd disappeared from her couch over a week ago,

though thoughts of him remained. A monumental evening she'd relived over and over; the thought of his fingers on her—in her—still sent tiny shivers down her spine. She narrowed her eyes further, fearful her lusty thoughts were written all over her face. Keane shifted and glared back. Scowl or no scowl, the man was sex on legs.

Sal was the first to buckle. "He's all yours," the old fox muttered, and hurried off toward the opposite side of the gym. No help there.

Keane's lips tightened as he realized this meeting was far from coincidental.

With a mixture of awareness and uneasiness, Logan's temporary bravado faltered. Her breath caught as she opened her mouth, ready to speak, but he cut her off.

"N-O, not doing it," he snapped, stalking off to the beverage booth in the corner of the gym. Logan paused. It didn't make sense. Clearly he had just battled it out with someone. If he didn't want to fight at all, then why was he fighting here?

Logan leaned against the counter, blocking his exit. "When Sal texted me that you picked up a bout, I thought you'd had a change of mind. Why else would you be here?"

Keane grunted. The man behind the counter slid over a plastic container filled with a protein shake, and Keane snatched it up.

"Look, I was a little tipsy and emotional the last time we…talked. And I'm sorry about Pierre, the photograph and the newspaper. Little did I know becoming an Octagon Girl would re-spark the media's attention. Pierre's really working the press, he's determined to keep the obsession alive…"

Logan's cheeks warmed at her flimsy words. Keane's gaze ran the length of her body then back up, slowly coming to rest on her chest. Beneath her bulky cable-knit sweater, her nipples perked up in memory.

His features softened, briefly. A hand crossed his temple, then it was gone. "Look, I don't want trouble. When the time's right, that asshole of yours is gonna wish he never fucked with me, you can count on that. But I'm not looking to go beating the shit out of someone I don't even know. All I want is to be left alone."

"Okay, I get it. Truth is we're looking for the same thing. Don't you think I want to be left alone? This isn't the kind of fame I expected, all about my boobs and how I ruined Pierre's chance at winning last season's show. I'm a—*was*—a ballerina, for God's sake." She paused, and swallowed hard. "But I can't run and hide. Look, I didn't know that being an Octagon Girl was going to be like this. And Pierre is making it ten times worse; the fans, the press, the public persona…but it's my job. And it's the only one I've got."

The V between his eyebrows deepened. At long last, maybe he got what she was saying. She pressed on, hoping it was true. "All I'm asking for is a favor—even if you don't make it to Tetnus, I'll have a few more solid paychecks."

"Like I said, we've all got our own shit. Nice chatting with you." Keane tugged the hood of his sweatshirt over his head.

She stood, studying him. Noticed him rubbing a hand over his temple and wincing. Noticed how his knuckles were swollen once more. Noticed him shifting on his feet, the way he wouldn't meet her eyes, anxious to be on his way. Perhaps if she offered him some help with whatever his *shit* was? It was worth a try.

"Maybe we can make some kind of agreement here. An exchange of goodwill. You fight in the qualifiers, and I'll help you sort out your problem. If it's that obnoxious alpaca-stealing thief, I'll gladly help you get rid of her. If it's swollen knuckles, I've more than just frozen peas in my first-aid kit. A rose hip tea blend is a much healthier way of dealing with pain than Oxycontin. When I was injured, after a few pills, I flushed the rest and replaced them with a homemade remedy."

Despite his frown, Logan could see his interest was piqued...or at least he was still listening to her. She pressed on, "I guess you'll have to train, isn't that what fighters do? Whatever you need, I'll help you with it. I spent countless hours dancing every day, for years. I'm extremely disciplined when it comes to practicing. Whatever you need."

Keane shook his head and rubbed his temple once more. "I don't care about you, your wholesome remedies, your training experience, or your guy problems. What I want is to be left in *peace*." He smacked the thick plastic cup against the Formica countertop, and strode through the front door without another word.

That went wonderfully well, Logan thought as she made her way around the Octagon cage in search of Sal. She wasn't about to chase after Keane, though something didn't quite add up with him. He said one thing, but did another. Hadn't she just caught him red-handed—literally—fighting? But instead of the pumped-up energy most fighters had after slamming fists into each other, Keane seemed weary. Tired, even.

Logan sighed. The pirouettes performed by her raging libido every time he was in the room didn't help matters. Time was running out. Jerry wanted a championship fighter. Logan wanted cash, her school, and revenge, in that order, and to get out of this hellish life and move on to a real one. And Sal…well, it was too disturbing thinking about what that old rascal wanted. But he was her only hope right now. The man with a plan, or so he said. A newly hatched Plan B—one Sal promised to be foolproof.

Chapter 5

*STALEMATE: When two fighters are unable to
move forward in a bout*

It was becoming increasingly obvious that Plan B was
a dud. Jaysin Bouvine couldn't fight his way out of a
room full of stuffed animals. Yet he had managed to
piss off enough fighters that they apparently lined up
to kick his obnoxious, loud-mouthed ass. Such was the
case playing out at the Pittsburgh Fight Club between
Bouvine "the Braggart" and Frank Tupps.

Logan winced as, once more, Tupps lifted him up
over his head, raced across the mat, and hurled him into
the metal caging. Bouvine slid down onto his back and
tapped the mat, signaling defeat.

Twist my tutu. She had planned to meet with Jerry

tomorrow, to introduce him to another ultimate fighting hero, the next winner of Tetnus. A man who Jerry'd probably never even heard of and, judging by the outcome of today's series of fights, likely never would.

A week of hoping for the best, that somehow her replacement fighter would stun them all with a surprise Jiu Jitsu move or a lethal front kick, left her with a week to find someone else to foist on an unsuspecting Jerry.

Sal mouthed "I'm sorry" from across the cage and Logan rewarded him with a forced smile. The trainer had a good heart—no gift for training, but a good heart. His kindness, at a time in her life where she'd had very little, mattered.

Every day for a week she'd met Sal at the gym to watch Bouvine strut around in his too-small spandex shorts, mouthing off to anyone who'd listen about his prowess in the cage and elsewhere. He had a scorpion tattoo on his shaved scalp, and he found it funny to swivel his head and arch his eyebrows, as if the scorpion was looking to strike. Or at least that's what Logan thought the silly gesture meant. By the looks of things today, the scorpion had a mouthful of Octagon mat.

When he wasn't fighting, Bouvine was on her like glue. She couldn't shake the guy. If Sal hadn't interfered and warned him away, who knew how she'd get rid of him.

Frustrated, Logan shrugged into her jacket and departed. The only thing she could count on was the bitter winter weather. She tugged up the collar of her alpaca coat as a damp wind kicked up off the rivers below. The weather made her think about getting a mocha latte at The Quiet Storm. Something to cheer her up and pull her spirit out of the dumps.

Despite the blustery afternoon, she chose to walk the mile to the coffee shop instead of catching a bus. Exercise always helped reduce her stress levels, and since her operation, her daily physical routine was improving. Yet at this rate, she'd need to walk around the clock to relieve her anxiety. What would she do if Jerry wouldn't give her another chance?

Her father had remarried and relocated with his wife and two youngsters to San Diego. Prior to that, he'd lived in the home Logan had grown up in, forty-five minutes east of Pittsburgh. But she couldn't bring herself to move west, to show up on her father's doorstep with a shitload of problems. Call it pride, or fairness even, for a father who deserved a second chance at happiness since her mother had passed away. He didn't need her neurosis or the drama Pierre was intent on keeping fresh in the public eye.

Once at the warm coffee shop, she purchased her drink and settled into a table not far from the barista station. But the coffee did little to ease her earlier disappointment with Jaysin. And that led to her thinking about an older, more painful disillusionment.

"A surprise gift for my beloved and talented fiancée," Pierre had boasted when he'd presented her with the co-op. He'd bought it last March, after they'd become the darlings of *America Gets Its Groove On*. Logan had been overwhelmed, scrambling to balance ballet with the show's taping. Her final engagement was in London—though little did she know it'd be the last performance of her career.

Pierre had taken full advantage of her absence. He'd bought the co-op on the sly, then acted as if it was what she'd wanted all along. Just like he'd done with the damned reality television show. After a two-week trip to London, Pierre had picked her up from the airport and, pulling the mother lode of bold-ass moves, had driven her straight to their new home. Logan had blinked back her astonishment—and annoyance, too—as their network of friends came out of the woodwork, clearly in on Pierre's surprise.

What their friends didn't know was that where she and Pierre would live had been an ongoing debate. Logan was adamant about Manhattan's Upper West Side. The hubbub of cultural goings-on, it made sense, with Lincoln Center and other major venues within walking distance.

Also, Logan favored older, more spacious buildings. They offered more room than more modern buildings, and she'd spent months finding the perfect apartment for them to remodel together. She'd imagined one room would be her own private dance studio, complete with wooden floors and mirrored walls.

Their friends also didn't know how Pierre had duped her, how he'd depleted her savings from their new joint bank account for a down payment on the classic prewar co-op of her dreams. Only to surprise her with an ultra-modern, high-rise apartment with windows for walls and chrome accents everywhere, including the kitchen countertop. The only wall in the place separated the living space from the kitchen. With only one lofted bedroom, it had been listed at eight hundred square feet and double the price of what they'd discussed. Gramercy Park was posh, expensive and thirty blocks south of Midtown.

Logan shook her head. Though they'd split the mortgage payments, she'd still been outraged he'd made such an important decision without consulting her.

Turned out, he'd been consulting someone else—her understudy Anya—the entire time. Something their friends *did* know, evidently, but neglected to fill Logan in about.

Logan took a deep sip of coffee, trying to wash away the bitter taste the very thought of Pierre had left in her mouth. But as she set it down on the table, she *heard* him. With a gasp, her eyes fell on the television hanging over the barista's head.

It was Pierre, no mistaking his relentlessly self-satisfied voice. "We hope everyone, and I mean *everyone*, runs out and buys a ticket for our tour. In my opinion, it's a show not to be missed. I've never danced better and it's such a privilege to be selected, along with my partner Anya, for the roles of a lifetime. I've never been happier. And hey, America, don't forget to tune in to watch us on *America Gets Its Groove On*."

Logan felt like snatching her latte off the table and tossing it up at the two pompous faces smiling down on her. The fame whore was using that stupid show to build his career. She knew first-hand how much he sucked as a dancer. He knew it as well. Probably why he was dragging her good name through the dirt—he was bitter about all those years she'd outshone him on stage.

How long was this going to continue?

Since its inception last January, *America Gets Its Groove On* had swiftly become the top-rated reality show on the air. Pierre had often boasted that they were the reason for it. Back then, she'd taken her fame and newfound exposure in stride. Par for the course; dancing was all that mattered, after all.

Now, four weeks into season two, the network was still making a huge production of Pierre's return and Anya's debut. It seemed the fools at the network were counting on Pierre to keep them at the top.

And being the lying, thieving, freeloading mooch that he was, her ex had found a topic for discussion that everyone was interested in. Her. The Fall. Her chest. *His lies*, she added, feeling the burn from the piping-hot coffee trapped in her throat.

Hadn't Sally warned her that he was jealous of her fame? He seemed to be relishing in her popularity now that he'd twisted it into some kind of sick notoriety—where he came out smelling like roses. Where she'd been left to muck about in the dirt. She had to hand it to him, he was right about one thing—a person's dirty laundry was somehow more appealing than their hard-earned success.

The barista approached her, and Logan took a deep breath.

"Thirty-two *C* cup. I'm tall but my small frame makes them seem gargantuan," she said, her tone mocking, which she immediately regretted. It wasn't the barista's fault her ex was a prick.

The girl didn't seem to catch the sarcasm. Instead, she thrust a napkin toward Logan, followed by a shy request. "Can I have your autograph?"

Logan choked on her latte. "What? You want my autograph?"

Star-struck, the barista nodded. But as Logan complied, not knowing what else to do in this appalling situation, the girl leaned forward, smiling broadly, and whispered, "Are you going to attend the performance the end of May?"

Puzzled, Logan frowned. "The finale for *America Gets Its Groove On* is in April." *Though I'd rather be choking on a Quiet Storm panini than tuning in to watch it.* The struggle to forget last April seemed never ending.

"No, silly," the girl said. A wave of dread washed over Logan as she put two and two together. "I'm talking about *La Syphilis*…you know, the Metropolitan Ballet is coming to Pittsburgh in May."

"*La Sylphide*," Logan corrected. "Think I'll pass." With shaky legs and a heart ready to split in two and fall out of her chest, she grabbed her coffee and headed home. The tail end of Pierre's announcement now made sense. Her former company was coming to Pittsburgh, with Pierre in the part of the romantic Scot, James Ruben. And Anya, her former understudy, in Logan's dream role—Sylph, the forest spirit.

But Pittsburgh? Pierre must have rigged it with the director. She didn't have to think too deeply about his motive. A chance run-in with her…man, the fame whore had no shame.

Never had she felt so alone, so defeated. She wanted to crawl into bed and stay there. Since the age of five, she'd wanted to dance. Her mother had sacrificed so much, ensuring Logan had the best dance teachers and access to the top schools, first in Pennsylvania and then in Manhattan. Her mother had been so proud of each and every accomplishment. And the focus on Logan had kept her sane, her daughter's dreams a welcome distraction from side-effects of her chemotherapy treatments. At least she'd seen Logan's successes and not her failures, especially The Fall.

How she missed her mother, her wise ways, gentle

spirit and comforting arms. How she missed the dreams they'd shared together.

A gust of wind whipped around the corner of her block and she buried her face within her coat. As if to add injury to insult on an already horrific day, a news van took the corner at breakneck speed, nearly clipping her. Logan felt like flashing them the bird for airing Pierre's lying mug. She dug deep, and resisted. No way was she sinking to his level. If the press couldn't see through him, if they couldn't treat her with respect, then she refused to engage them. Hell, she was bent on avoiding them.

Polishing off her tepid latte, she quickened her pace up her front walkway, unlocking the door and stepping inside.

She'd survive, just like she'd managed to the past few months. There had to be a solution. A way out from beneath the pile of problems. Maybe Boscov's was hiring and needed a sales clerk?

With a firm push, she closed the door behind her.

It bounced back open. A worn, semi-white Nike appeared, wedged in the doorframe.

She bit back a scream and threw her weight against the solid paneling, ineffectively stopping the person from entering.

And here I'd been thinking my day couldn't get any worse.

He slid quickly inside, quietly pushing the wooden door shut behind him.

Logan pulled her fingers into tight fists, ready to defend herself, as her gaze swept upward. Navy sweatpants, a matching sweatshirt, full but tightened lips, and a pair of piercingly familiar winter-blue eyes. Her breath hitched. Keane had tugged a skull-hugging navy beanie cap low over his forehead, like a movie criminal dodging the police.

She stepped back, both nervous from the fright he'd given her and excited by what his presence meant. Before she could demand an explanation, he moved a finger to his mouth, signaling her to be quiet.

"What a bad freakin' idea," he muttered. "How about we head inside? The reporters are back and looking for parking. Stupid time to go on a coffee run."

You can say that again, she thought. Instead, she whispered her frustration. "So what? I have bigger fish to fry tonight than worrying about what my neighbors are up to." She heard him snort from behind her as she unlocked her apartment door. Too bad, he wasn't coming inside.

"Shit."

She wasn't certain what that one word was all about but didn't have time to wonder as he scooped her up, stepped over the threshold, and kicked the door closed behind them. With agonizing slowness, he lowered her to the floor, letting her body run along his as he did so. A warmth spread through her at the contact.

She took a second to regain her balance, and her wits. "What are you doing here? I thought you'd had enough of me and my problems. Well, they've only gotten worse. You know how you told me you wanted to be left alone? Guess what? *I* want to be alone."

"I was wrong," Keane stated, in a low, calm voice. "I want to take you up on your offer."

For a moment, anger made her doubt she'd heard him correctly. With an open mouth, she peered at him.

"We need some ground rules. None of this bullshit. No press, no publicity, no drama."

Logan snorted. Did he think she enjoyed the attention? Still, hope sprang up within her, but given her recent history of failure, she had to be sure. "What are you saying, Keane?"

The heavy cloud that had made up her day lifted. His lazy grin confirmed it.

"I've decided to fight."

One week was all Keane had to prepare. Logan was undaunted; no way was this opportunity going to pass her by. Nothing would interfere with his fighting in the qualifiers. A profound sense of relief made her feel giddy. For the first time in months, she had something to smile about.

"Pack your things. You'll move in with me." He prowled around her living room like a hungry, caged tiger.

Her smile nearly dropped to the floor. "What are you talking about? I didn't say anything about…"

"I want peace and quiet. No surprises—hate them. No *reporters*."

She pointed toward the small waste can in the corner. "That's where I tossed the remote after you left. Do you think I'm trying to become the next best thing in reality television? This buzz about my…me, it's not my fault. Why—"

"A Channel Nine news truck nearly plowed me over when I got here."

"A news truck? Oh my God, I walked by it—"

"Interviewed the landlady."

"Mrs. Debinska? She doesn't speak a word of—"

"English. Figured that out myself. Suppose they did too."

"How did they know where I live?" Wringing her hands, she paced about the room and tried to absorb this new bit of information.

"Internet. Don't know."

"Pierre was on television exactly an hour ago and a news crew is interviewing my landlady?" *Bleeding leotards, this was worse than she could ever have imagined.* "I've got to get out of here before more show up."

"Way ahead of you, babe." Keane folded his arms across his chest. "Is there a back door? My Jeep's around the corner."

"Through the basement. This is all going down way too fast…"

He grunted. "Do you want to do this or not? If not…"

"Yes, I want to do this," she said hastily, "but I have some ground rules, too. And I plan on holding you to them. We'll even shake on it."

She swore his lips twitched before he responded, "Let's hear 'em."

Logan moved into the bedroom and began tossing clothing into a suitcase, not paying too much attention to her selections. Keane dominated her thoughts just like he did the bedroom. It didn't help that when she dropped a red lace thong, he scooped it off the floor and thumbed the elastic briefly before tossing it into the suitcase. She never expected to be envious of a thong but that thumb of his was magical. Her body flushed in memory.

"Spit it out. Let's hear these conditions."

"You begin early tomorrow morning."

"Agreed. Next."

Logan relaxed. Perhaps this wouldn't be difficult, after all. "No drinking, and no painkillers. I'll bring my medicinal teas. They're much better, healthier."

She glanced up and caught his slight nod.

"I'll help you train however I can. If you are going to fight, I…um…need you to win."

"No sense in fighting otherwise."

The tension in her shoulders relaxed, knowing they were both on the same page. Six winning fights, and the subsequent salary Jerry promised her, would make all the difference in the world.

She pressed on to a more sensitive subject. "If I agree to move in with you, temporarily—not that I've another choice now that the paparazzi have found where I live—you'll have to contact your girlfriends. Note my use of the plural *girlfriends*, as I don't believe for one second that flighty, blonde kleptomaniac is your only one. Tell them they can't come over. It would be awkward, to say the least." All this was said on a long, rushed exhale.

But having her concerns about other women aired was a relief. It would be unbearable if an ongoing stream of women came parading out of his bedroom. And just like that, the thought of another woman in his bed, satisfied and grinning like a cat on cream, made her frown.

"That's it?"

Well, there was one more thing that needed to be said. Logan had had her quota of problems for the year. And as difficult as it was to say, it was best to put it all on the table now instead of later. With a deep breath, she began, "I, um, don't think a repeat performance of our night together is a good idea."

An unidentifiable expression crossed Keane's face, though it wasn't anger. His eyes seemed brighter beneath those long, dark lashes. His tongue darted out and swiped at those plump lips as if moistening them for his reply. Or for something else. Did he do that intentionally to throw her off track?

Her eyes narrowed and her cheeks grew warm. His massive body shifted closer as his lips curled up, causing her inner thermostat of pent-up lust to spike, sizzle and warm her from the top of her head to the tips of her toes. *So much for demands that I've no chance of keeping*, she thought, and was fairly certain Keane had arrived at the same conclusion.

He tilted his head and silently studied her. Like her words were a load of bull, like he could prove it by tossing her to the mattress and finishing what he'd promised the last time he was in her bedroom.

He looked away, breaking contact. "The Jeep's parked outside. How long will this take?"

"Almost done." Logan refocused her attention on the suitcase. Besides packing, she needed to check in with Mrs. Debinska, let her know she'd be gone for a few days, and make sure the old woman's refrigerator was stocked. Maybe call her son, who lived in the suburbs, to make sure he checked in on her.

Her mind raced, so when Keane's fingers touched her arm, she jumped. Gently, he tugged her closer. And closer still. Leaning forward, his husky whisper sent tingles down her spine. "Did we shake on it yet? You know, seal the deal?"

Dumbly, she shook her head no.

"Good. This doesn't count, then."

Before she could guess his intent, he yanked her up against him, angled his head, and pressed his lips over hers. He gave her a toe-curling kiss that made her knees wobble and thoughts swim. A kiss that erased away the day's bitterness and replaced it with something more alive. Something special.

Chapter 6

SWEEP: When a fighter changes positioning, from being on the bottom to being on top

"Oh my God," Logan exclaimed. Keane had barely put the Jeep into Park, and she was out the door and up his sidewalk. "This is *your* house?"

He lifted her bags from the trunk and followed. Having a housemate was going to take some getting used to. Usually it was way too dark for his short-term—*very* short-term—guests to make much of a stink about his home. Plus, he kept them occupied with more important and pleasurable things.

Keane paused on the bottom step and watched Logan follow the wrap-around porch from one end to the other. The night was young. Still time for this houseguest to nose her way right back out the front door. Low-key, quiet and non-meddlesome, that's how he liked to keep things. Logan's antics made him feel uneasy. Once again, doubts about this idiotic plan plagued him.

He unlocked and opened the door, allowing her to enter ahead of him, and almost barreled into her as she stopped short inside the foyer.

"You own *this* house? And here I imagined you living in a fratlike apartment. No offense."

Without responding, he nodded toward the living room.

"Um, can I have a tour?" she asked him, her voice breathless like she'd been dancing or something. "Afterward, you can tell me how I can help you out with training. I want to be useful, plus I'm not one to lounge around, unproductive."

Hmm, he'd like to see her do that, lounging around. Preferably naked. That would be a great help.

He led her through his home and in brief, clipped sentences, answered her prodding questions about his plans for each room. Shame made him hesitant and irritable. Technically, all his renovations could have been completed by now, if his life hadn't gone to hell.

Yet Logan didn't seem to mind the partially sheet-rocked walls or the unvarnished trim in the doorways. Instead, her enthusiasm bubbled as she gushed over the potential in every unfinished project. An enthusiasm reminiscent of Jimmy's. The person who, for the better part of the year, he'd been trying *not* to think about.

The minute she'd started in about the place, he'd had visions of Jimmy doing exactly that. He would have loved the challenge of it. Of renovating the Victorian back to its glory, then flipping it for a profit. Fuck, what was he doing, moving her in here?

An hour later, Keane found the knot in his stomach tightening as he still played reluctant tour guide and revealed small bits about the plans for the house: the re-sanded and re-stained railings on the winding staircase in the foyer, the built-in cherry-wood shelving that matched the window trim in a bedroom, and how the largest room, upstairs and at the back of the house, would make a great—though modern—gym.

His head throbbed like it had been hit by a two-by-four by the time they'd reached the already renovated living room. His stomach rumbled, demanding satisfaction.

"I heard that," she laughed, oblivious of the tension building within him. "Let's talk about tomorrow and then I'll leave you be. I'd like to tag along if you don't mind? A little exercise will do me good. So, what do you think, should we head down to the Pittsburgh Fight Club? There's a boxing bag and plenty of weights for you to use."

"I have weights," he muttered.

"But Sal says alternating various-sized weights give muscles a burst…wakes them up, I guess."

Keane raised his brows. "Sal had you lifting?"

"No, I heard him telling this to another fighter after you…refused me. There's nothing to it, so Sal says."

"Is that right? Seems I've been going about things the wrong way." His tone was sarcastic. Did she think he was a friggin' amateur? He caught her eyes wandering over his chest, assessing the measure of his words. Until she looked away, and a lovely, rosy flush colored her cheeks.

"That's what Sal told me…" she replied in a low voice.

His patience was running thin and his stomach demanded nourishment. He cut her off mid-sentence. "You hungry?"

"Not really. It's kind of late to be eating…"

Keane frowned. When he'd agreed to this insane idea, the thought of someone monitoring his food intake, and even what foods he ate, hadn't crossed his mind. Neither did hours of discussion about his home, his private life, refurbished or not.

Stalking to the foyer and picking up her bags, he barked, "Follow me."

"Yes, sir." He heard the sarcasm loud and clear. At least the woman had a backbone, he'd give her that.

"The bedroom with the wood-burning fireplace is yours for the duration."

"Really! Can I make a fire? Or rather, would you help me with it later?"

He shrugged. If a fire was what it took for him to find some peace, so be it.

Five minutes later, while Keane wolfed down some leftover boiled chicken and brown rice, his mood lightened. Truth be told, his exasperation with Logan was minor compared to the frustration he felt within. Kicking the booze and pills was a lot harder than he'd anticipated, especially after a series of sleepless nights and the nightmares plaguing him.

It was common knowledge that war veterans experienced extreme mindfucks, where the harshest moments of combat replayed in their dreams like a DVD menu screen before you hit Play. But the adage "misery loves company" didn't help much. Which was why Logan's comments about homemade remedies, those herbs, had caught his interest.

Yep, he did it for the herbs, *not* because it pissed him off thinking about that asshole Bouvine following her home. Or how he signed on to kicking Pierre's ass for her. So he tried to convince himself. What did he have to lose? Tossing back a few herbal teas might replace his self-medicating habit. It was worth a shot. Worth a nosy, distracting housemate. And hell, if the herbs didn't work, there was one more way to ease his pain— a method proven on more than one night.

The irony of the situation made Keane's mood lighten further. He liked how she liked his home. Hell, he liked *her*. Looking at her. Touching her. Making her come hard on his fingers. He liked her spirit, the grit it took to pursue him like this. And, fuck, he related to her on a deeper level. Her pain.

Why not keep a smile on those luscious lips of hers?

If her pain was his burden right now, then so was her pleasure.

Hell. Maybe the opposite was true. A heavy dose of pleasure in his life might be just what the doctor ordered.

Logan had had a grand tour of his place, yet there was something he hadn't shown her. Something about the house all his late-night visitors—who were, let's face it, confined to one room in particular—commented on. The old tin ceiling in the master suite. Yep, if those herbs failed, he'd pencil that in on Logan's ways-to-help-him-train schedule. Time on her back viewing his tin ceiling, him between her thighs. Considering her eager response to his kiss earlier, she'd likely be presented with the view, even if the herbs did work out.

* * *

Later that night, it was Keane on his back, studying the ceiling. Alone. Awake with a pounding migraine. Trying to keep the demons at bay. Having Logan take such a liking to his house stirred up memories best forgotten—ones that persisted like a bad toothache.

All his buddy Jimmy had talked about doing after his tour ended was flipping properties in good neighborhoods. A partnership, with the work and the reward split right down the middle. But Jimmy had picked up another tour, and Keane had returned to Pittsburgh alone. The seed had been planted in Keane's head, though. When presented with the listing for the old Victorian home in need of some TLC, he bought it as their first flip.

For a while, the physicality needed for renovating made for a solid night's sleep. The spare bedroom, along with the master bedroom and living room, had been gutted and remodeled his first year back from active duty. All was going okay. Until word that Jimmy's fourth tour had come to an abrupt end—as had his life. The autopsy report was issued. Then everything went to shit.

He rolled out of bed in need of something to quiet his mind. Her door was open and he tapped the wooden frame, skeptical yet willing to try one of those damn teas she'd packed. No answer, not even a murmur. Why would she be awake at this hour?

He turned to leave but the crackle of the red log smoldering in the hearth drew his attention. The room was cold, the fireplace the only source of heat. Swiftly, he strode over to it, grabbed two logs he'd brought in earlier, and banked the fire.

Firelight cast an amber glow on her. She'd showered, he could tell by the damp curls on her pillow. He caught a whiff of sweet vanilla cream; it suited her personality—all proper and feminine. She was a naturally attractive woman, wholesome and clean. He liked that, too. Waking up next to a raccoon-eyed woman, and a trail of lash prints crossing the pillowcases, was a huge turn-off.

The logs took, and he made to leave. Logan shifted, unaware of her visitor. The comforter fell to her waist. His eyes followed but stopped short.

The focus of much debate and discussion rounded snugly against the material of her large collegiate sweatshirt. A perfect set of tits. She always seemed self-conscious about them—he couldn't blame her with all the buzz caused by her moron of an ex's trash talk. Keane would make it his priority to show her, first with his hands, then with his mouth, and then…well, she'd discover soon enough just how pleasurable a well-developed rack could be.

A sigh escaped her, and his cock stirred at the sound. It was obvious Logan was a ball of unreleased sexuality. The way she watched him finger her in the mirror—man, that was hot as hell. One kiss, and he'd have *her* kissing her so-called rules goodbye. No sex? Yeah, right, like that was going to happen. If it hadn't been for the paparazzi stalking her, he'd have taken her right there, standing up against her front door.

For a moment, he contemplated waking her with his hands and his mouth, envisioned her eager response as he ran his tongue from her ear to her neck, and lower. But a good fuck wasn't why he'd invaded her privacy. He'd come for those damned teas.

Once more, she sighed. With narrow eyes, he studied her face for signs of awareness. Her mouth parted slightly but she slept on like the dead. She'd last a day—tops—as a Marine. He was about to reach over and gently shake her awake when he noticed the lift of her mouth. His cock lifted too, and thickened at the sight of her smiling in her sleep.

Shit. Whatever she was dreaming about was doing it for her. As troubled and ornery as he was, he couldn't do it, couldn't wake her. At least Logan's dreams were pleasurable.

Quietly, he made his way back to his bedroom. And resumed his prior activity—examining the tin ceiling.

Hours later, he was up and dressed, but anxious and in desperate need of release. He flicked on the lamp next to Logan's bed and flooded the room with light. "Let's get going."

Logan rolled to her side. Blinking, she struggled upward, suddenly aware of her surroundings.

"What time is it?" she demanded groggily.

"Time for a run."

She rubbed her eyes, then looked at him. "Run? What run? The sun isn't even up. This wasn't what I meant when I said I'd tag along. Why don't you go pump some weights?"

Keane grunted. Power wasn't exactly his weakness, never had been. Endurance was what mattered. The only way to survive fighting two different opponents each night for three nights was by getting the old ticker pumping.

"Meet me in the kitchen in five. Wear layers of sweats."

He ignored her murmur of irritation and went to put on some coffee. Caffeine might help somewhat. A vigorous run, possibly. Still, he regretted not waking her last night, and asking about those natural herbs she spoke so highly of. Regretted not waking her earlier, and seeking relief within her body.

Shit, better keep these thoughts to himself until he was less strung out. Time enough for Logan to find herself flat backed and studying the architectural wonders of his ceiling. That is, after he'd had his fill.

By daybreak, Logan was ready to call it quits. All she wanted was a cold Evian and a comfortable bed to fall into. Exercising to this extreme wasn't normal. Yet, as she turned the corner and spotted Keane on the sidewalk, her thoughts remained just that—thoughts.

No way was she going to piss him off and ruin a chance at reclaiming her life. Even if she'd run miles more than any reasonable ex-ballerina would run in her right mind. She could do this.

Dancing had made her lungs strong and stamina high. And if anyone cared enough to notice the truth, she didn't have two black eyes from her gargantuan breasts knocking her in the face.

At least today's weather was reliable. The sun had melted the blackened snow mounds lining the city's roadways and sidewalks. A few blocks back, she'd even walked past a carrot and a hat on a patch of lawn.

The sidewalk ended and she caught sight of Keane working out in one of their designated meeting spots off in the distance. With a deep inhale, she sprinted off.

Reaching him, she stood panting while he completed an insane amount of pushups. Her eyes fell on his biceps, and how they tightened beneath the snug arms of his sweatshirt with each upward push. If it hadn't been so damned early, rush-hour traffic would be backed up for miles from the heart-skipping sight.

At first, she'd thought this was his everyday drill, run three miles and pump out some squats or sit-ups, run three more and stop for push-ups or boxing thrusts. Until she realized it was his way of waiting for her. Oh, she tagged along, all right, falling far back and jogging along at a comfortable and reasonable pace.

Unable to keep up with his intense running regimen, she tried to make herself helpful in other ways.

"How many was that?" she rasped, still searching for breath.

"Hundred twenty."

The trouble with keeping count of his repetitions was she kept losing count. Too focused on—and oh-so-*aware* of—his every movement: how the muscles in his forearms flexed while jabbing, the way his sweatshirt rose up off his abs during sit-ups, and even the fine, set line of his jaw as he pumped out a few final push-ups. Transfixed, she could only watch, wait and admire him. If it wasn't so dang cold, she'd be drooling like a puppy over a fine, meaty bone.

Keane jumped to his feet, and belatedly, she realized he'd spoken. Wide-eyed, she stared at him, hoping his intense focus prevented him from picking up on the fact she was turned on—so turned on she felt like running her hands beneath his sweatshirt to feel the warmth of his abdomen from all those sit-ups. Or touch the bulging arms, thick with muscle. Or…

"Ready?" he asked while jogging in place.

Am I ever. Logan wanted nothing better than to sprawl out on the sidewalk, preferably with him cuddled up next to her—but Keane was a machine in motion.

For a split second, she thought he was going to hit the ground and pump out a few more. *God, yes, please.*

With a brief, quizzical look, he said, "We'll take it slow. Cool down."

Take it slow. Cool down. The sexy innuendo had her heart doing push-ups. If they weren't standing on a crooked concrete sidewalk on a soon-to-be-busy street...

Keane stood with his head angled to the side and his hands on his hips, studying her.

Fearing he'd guessed her thoughts, she hurried to reply. "Ha, who are you kidding? Your slow is like Manhattan during rush hour. As I said much, much earlier, don't wait for me. I'll either catch up or meet you back at your house."

"No need. We're done for the morning." He nodded toward the roadway and waited for her to jog ahead. Yet, true to his word, this time he ran next to her at a comfortable speed.

"Time to refuel. Are you hungry?"

"Uh-huh." *Yes, but for a taste of you.* How in the heck was she going to make it through the week with him? The man was sexy as sin, and as she spent more and more time with him she discovered that beneath that heart-dropping body lay a humble soul.

She'd come to that conclusion last night during his house tour. He'd painstakingly answered her barrage of questions with short, concise explanations—no surprise there. But something had been playing out within him, an intangible tension she couldn't put her finger on. He seemed almost uncomfortable. Modest about his renovations. Which Logan couldn't quite understand.

His old Victorian house was the home of her dreams.

She itched to pick up some sandpaper and scrub off the chipped windowsill paint in the guest room. Paint an eggshell cream color for the plywood walls and fix a new mantel for the fireplace. And she had told him so.

Painfully embarrassed, that's what his reaction last night seemed like. Clearly, he felt funny about owning such a magnificently dainty house. And this show of fragility made her want to tug him in close.

They jogged through Market Square, side-by-side, passing a woman cleaning a For Sale sign on the window of Rachel's Antiques, and other early risers preparing for the day.

"Here we are," Keane murmured. He had stopped in front of a small luncheonette with warped marine-blue siding and a crooked neon sign in its window. The word *open* flashed brightly.

She shot him an arched eyebrow. "I'm a mess, even for a place like this. When you said breakfast, I thought we would be eating at your house. I haven't showered."

The appraising look he gave her stopped her short. *He likes my just-rolled-out-of-bed-and-sprinted-the-Pittsburgh-marathon look.*

He opened the door and ushered her inside.

The place was packed. The aroma of fresh coffee and sweet buttery pancakes caused her stomach to pull a plié. With all the exercise, she was famished.

A kind, old Irishman greeted them. "Keane, my boy. It's a mighty fine day when you come strolling on in here. It's been too long."

In typical Keane style, he didn't say much but Logan saw him soften beneath the older man's greeting. "Is there a table, Joe?"

"For you, me bucko, there's always a table. Especially when you've such lovely company."

Logan smiled at the elderly man, whose heartfelt greeting was like a warm hug.

Joe led them down the narrow aisle to a back booth. She was surprised how cozy and clean the place was, with its old-fashioned tabletop jukeboxes and red-checkered linen tablecloths.

Settling into the seat across from her, Keane pulled off his cap, lowered his hood and unzipped his sweatshirt. The black shirt layered beneath hugged his pecs but hung more loosely over his abdomen. Logan fiddled with her own layers as she imagined his naked torso beneath.

She had thought her favorite part on a man was his biceps, having grown used to Pierre's strong, firm ones—which in retrospect seemed like ant hills to Keane's Mont Blanc. Yet the breath-catching glimpses of Keane's bare abdomen each time his shirt rose up... nope, she was a certifiable abs-aholic, wanting more and more.

"Need something?" His eyebrow rose, and damn, if his eyes weren't twinkling. Totally aware of her perusal.

She looked down at the checkered napkin and fiddled with the brass ring. Wishing her embarrassment would steal away with her lustful thoughts. If Pierre could only see her now, all hot and bothered. She wanted to laugh, thanks to the handsome man across from her. A virtual stranger responsible for saving her job, her livelihood *and* her sexuality.

Joe returned and distributed the menus, along with a pot of coffee and some cream.

Chancing a glance up, she nearly dropped the menu.

Keane wasn't even looking at it. Instead, he'd put a toothpick in his mouth, sprawled back in his seat, and with something that looked like a predatory grin, was studying her.

Not knowing what to say, she muttered the first thing that came to mind. "Do you know what you want?"

"Yep. Sure do." His reply was immediate, and given in such a low, sensual voice, that this time the menu did slide from her grasp.

"Ah, hum," Joe cleared his throat, breaking the moment. "What will it be this morning? The usual for you, Keane?"

"With a glass of water, too."

"And you, young lady?"

The heat rose in Logan's cheeks. She'd been so busy devouring the man-candy across from her, she hadn't any idea what was on the menu. "Um, how about a grapefruit sprinkled lightly with sugar. And a Greek yogurt. If you don't have Greek, any old regular yogurt will do, I'm not too picky."

Joe chuckled, and kindly remarked, "What does this look like, the Ritz? Me dearie, you're in an around-the-clock meat and potatoes type of place. However, let me see if I can whip up something more refined for a sweet lass like you."

"No, I don't want to be any trouble. Whatever Keane is having will do for me."

A few minutes later, she was regretting her decision. Joe placed not one, but three dishes in front of Keane. One was a steaming plate full of vegetables, mostly broccoli mixed with carrots and a sprout that looked like alfalfa. The second plate had a tower of buckwheat pancakes—Joe had informed her of the special batter he made just for his boys. But the thick sirloin on the third one, rare enough to jump off the plate and bite you back, made her glance around nervously. No way was she eating an enormous slab of meat. Steak was reserved for special, once-in-a-blue-moon splurges.

Frowning, her eyes shot toward Joe, who was watching her reaction with merriment. The same in-on-the-joke look was etched into the raised corners of Keane's mouth. Joe's laugh, when it finally came, was a loud burst of pleasure. Keane's, however, was a low, melodic rumble which caused her heart to thump wildly.

Logan rolled her eyes. "Very funny, you guys. I almost had a heart attack thinking I'd to eat all that."

To her relief, a plate of cottage cheese, mixed fruit and Canadian bacon was set in front of her. Her stomach growled out a hello.

"I'm thinking you've been in me place before," Joe commented, studying her thoughtfully. "You look familiar."

She glanced around nervously and spotted the television on the wall over the counter.

"Food's getting cold." Keane's comment sent Joe on his way.

Logan tried to convey *thank you* with her eyes, but Keane was looking at his plate while stabbing at the vegetables with his fork.

They ate in silence. He wasn't one for long conversations, that was as clear as day. But it wasn't an awkward silence. It was more like a contented lull between two people who'd spent an active morning attaining endorphin buzzes from well-worked bodies. *His* well-worked body.

Logan grinned at the thought.

"That good?"

God, she would have to stop doing that—the object of every fantasy she'd ever had was sitting right in front of her, and wouldn't you know it, she was blatantly eyeballing him with the same consideration that he'd given the steak.

"Really good. The cottage cheese melts in your mouth," she said sarcastically. "Now, how about you fill me in on this week's plan. From what I understand, you're expected to fight two different opponents in two different bouts each night, for three nights straight. That's six consecutive fights." She paused, thinking how crazy it sounded. He must have read her expression.

"It's not like championship boxing. You're in for twelve rounds if you're lucky, and done. In MMA qualifying bouts like these, the fights end quicker. You win and move on until you're the last guy standing. That's how you make it into the big event. That's what getting to Tetnus is all about." His tone had lost its playful quality and she gave herself a mental kick for turning their light-hearted morning into something heavier.

When it came to the topic of fighting, Keane was all business. Instantly serious, more somber, and downright surly at times.

Right now, she was hoping for the least of the three evils—serious.

"Is it enough time for you to get ready?" she asked casually. "You have to win…"

"So, you're suddenly an expert on training fighters?" He chewed a piece of meat and stared at her. A bit of juice coated his full lips and instead of feeling intimidated, she felt…warm.

"Why are you giving me such a hard time about this? You agreed to fight—which I really appreciate—but I don't want to see you lose. Or get hurt. Sal said the key to winning a fight was something about the right balance of technique and strength when grappling on the mat."

Keane snorted, then licked at the pool of juice in the corner of his mouth.

Joe cleared his throat from his spot by their table. "If this doesn't beat all. You're riding me boy about *his* training? Not to butt into your conversation or anything, but you don't know who you're talking to, lass. He wadna have any problem grappling, boxing, or with anything else. This boy's a MCMAP, a Marine Corps martial arts teacher with a fourth-degree black belt. He trains the other blokes how to fight. Jimmy, me nephew, was always brimming with wild tales about Keane, and how…"

"Drop it, Joe," Keane rasped in a hoarse, raw-sounding voice.

Logan straightened in her seat, wondering at the change in him. Seconds earlier, he'd been devouring her with his eyes. But now, in a blink, his gaze had narrowed and his body was tight with tension.

Joe stopped, his mouth wide open. "Your gal, she doesn't know about Jimmy?"

"We're on a need-to-know basis. And she's not my girl."

Logan felt a rush of breath escape her. Keane's words, and the brutal way he said them, cut like a knife. *Not my girl.* It was like he'd grabbed hold of their sweet morning rapport and mercilessly crushed it within his fist.

She wasn't the only one shaken by his abrupt change in demeanor.

Joe folded his arms across his chest. "But you brought her in me place. I haven't seen your mug in months, maybe a handful of times since Jimmy's funeral. What else was I to think?" The Irishman's eyes filled with sorrow. "His death…it wadna something you could control, lad. How were you to know?"

Keane shot to his feet and the plates on the table rattled. "Holy fuck, Joe, shut up."

Logan sat back in her seat, and gaped up at Keane. *He's lost a friend.*

Sympathy welled up inside her, overshadowing her own hurt. She wanted to wrap her arms around him and comfort him. Ease the pain that had unexpectedly surfaced from somewhere deep inside of him. That's what this was, right? Keane's way of dealing with his friend's death? Yet his rough manner made her think twice about consoling him.

Keane wasn't a hug-loving type of guy. Especially now.

His abrupt shift in personality made him downright mean, uncharacteristically so, with the way he was glaring at Joe.

The Irishman looked wretched, wringing his hands and wavering on his feet, and studying Keane intently, as if he was looking at a total stranger, too.

Logan unclasped her numb fingers from the tight knot she'd made on her lap.

And Keane…*oh my God*. He seemed both furious and *devastated*. Like someone who'd just found out about a close friend's death. But hadn't Joe said the funeral had already taken place?

This warrior, this handsome male with a strength and fortitude that was mind-shattering, this private man whom she'd stalked and pestered into fighting in the qualifiers, had some serious issues of his own.

Deeper issues than those she'd already picked up on.

The internal struggle playing out in him spoke volumes—his troubles reached way beyond the booze, the pills, the hard living. Issues that would take more than a few sips of herbal tea to resolve.

Would she be able to help him? Had the teas, exercise, even her companionship, been a source of relief for him?

Or not at all?

Keane stared down Joe, and the Irishman fixed his gaze on Keane, until in the unspoken way of men, they came to some kind of nonverbal accord.

"Let's go. We'll sprint back." His voice was deceptively calm. Normal. She wasn't fooled. Still, relief washed over her. Whatever had played out in Keane's head, he'd gotten a hold on it.

"Another time, Joe," he said abruptly. Keane patted the old Irishman on the arm and softly added, "Sorry."

She followed him out into the bright, Pittsburgh sunlight. With a nod in the direction of home, he took off running. She watched him sprint away, as if the devil had nipped him on the heels. With a sigh, she started after him.

Chapter 7

*FIGHT CAMP: The time leading up to a bout,
when a fighter is rigorously training*

The next few days were more grueling than boot camp.
It was like Jimmy's ghost rode around on his shoulder,
fueling his guilty conscience. *One wrong punch is all
it took, buddy.* The constant reminder was bad enough.
But bearing down on his other shoulder—even more
relentlessly—was Logan. The woman had more willpower than a Marine in basic training. Even in the face
of a mean, sleep-deprived bastard like himself.

She'd gotten too close. Thanks to Joe, she knew too
much about him for his liking. He didn't need her sympathy. She seemed like the type who dreamed of "saving" a guy…little did she know he was beyond help.

Every time Jimmy came up, he found himself striking back, until his message was clear—this topic of conversation wasn't up for grabs. Not that she didn't try. Despite being verbally lambasted, he still caught her looks of concern. Her pity.

Which was why he pushed himself hard, and dragged her along for the ride. Two goals to accomplish: shape up fast and wear her ass out. No, his routine provided little room for discussion or prying, and left them both exhausted by the end of the day.

The streets were quietest at daybreak. A few miles added on to his daily run, broken up with intervals of strength training, ate up the better part of each morning. He made a habit of stopping in the same spots so she could, every so often, catch up to him. He respected her for not idling around somewhere while he hit the pavement. Grudgingly, he liked how she took every hill, obstacle and deterioration in the weather in stride. And for a ballerina, she had a strong set of lungs.

If he wasn't so fucking tired from the nightmares plaguing him, he might have found humor in her following a fighter's diet. She had taken over the task of grilling steaks or sautéing a mixture of chicken and vegetables served over brown rice. No complaints about their bland, lean protein and whole grain diet, eaten for breakfast, lunch and dinner. With the substitution of grapefruit for steak, she followed the regiment wholeheartedly.

Each meal was accompanied by one of her teas. The verdict was still out on if they helped, though his headaches seemed to be less frequent. Her constant brewing and straining seemed to say, "You're not getting rid of me so easily."

Smart woman. She'd caught on to his game.

It was a pain in the ass having someone eyeballing him twenty-four/seven. But he had to admit, she'd given him something to keep his mind on—her.

Two hours of weight-training came after breakfast. The first day, after they had returned from Joe's place, he made it clear her company wasn't needed. The idea of her standing nearby and counting his reps would be a distraction that might get them both killed, which was what he informed her in an abrupt, less-than-gentlemanly manner. She'd stalked out, all stiff-backed, from the bare-bones gym situated between his bedroom and the guest room.

He'd thought about how he'd barked at her earlier and felt a twinge of guilt, remembering the crushed look that had fallen across her features. Which was why he hadn't chased her away when she'd suddenly sauntered in wearing a tight little body-skimming number.

"This is the only room with a mirrored wall. You don't mind if I practice, do you? There's plenty of space."

He had begrudgingly grunted in response. Hell, just because he was a miserable bastard didn't justify hurting her. Letting her stay was an unspoken apology. Or so he had told himself.

Ten seconds into lifting, the real reason had become apparent.

The black tights and low-cut leotard hugged every tight curve of her long, magnificent body. Her muscles flexed as she completed series of squats. Her arms circled up over her head and then back out in front of her. The reflection of her satisfied smile in the mirror had made him add an extra weight onto the bar, prolonging the pleasure of watching her move.

At present, he found himself lifting more repetitions than planned but it wasn't enough. Reality sank in as she pivoted on her toes…nothing but a beautiful distraction was to be had here. Besides, his home gym wasn't equipped to meet his needs. He needed the punching bag, and would force himself to pick up a sparring match or two. "We'll head over to the gym." Like it or not—and who was he kidding? He struggled with this contradicting yin-yang of emotion daily—he was stuck with her.

"Sal is going to be—"

"Just change." His gaze ran over her outfit one last time. "Wear the turtleneck."

They ran in silence to the Pittsburgh Fight Club. Inside, Logan headed off with Sal, leaving him to go about his business without disruption. Or so he thought, until two bouts later when he exited the cage and caught sight of who was bothering Logan.

"Come on, honey. What's he afraid of, the scorpion's strike?" Jaysin Bouvine taunted.

Keane stopped next to a punching bag, gave it a solid jab, and counted the seconds before he had to head over there. The fighter was making weird gestures with his head, swiveling it around and side to side. Probably ate paint chips as a child, with that kind of pick-up strategy. Yet the thought of the guy hitting on Logan pissed Keane off.

He pulled a punch, pausing to glare at Bouvine as Logan turned her back on the asshole and moved over to the Octagon stairs, putting distance between them.

Knowing she didn't return Bouvine's interest didn't make it any better. It took every ounce of discipline he had not to pound the smirk off the jerk's face.

Pulling his arm back, Keane thrust it forward with all his strength. Envisioning *Jaysin's* head. The fact that he'd followed Logan home that time made Keane consider fighting him. Give that bug on his head a solid pounding.

"Call that a jab? The bag is about all you can handle, O'Shea. What's keeping you from a real bout? Come on, man." Bouvine's voice took on a begging quality, like a small boy demanding someone play with him.

But when he swiveled his head and winked at Logan, Keane snapped.

"Let's go."

Bouvine jumped, thinking Keane had just invited him to spar and suddenly looking very nervous. His face fell as Keane walked over to Logan and touched her arm.

"You're leaving? You chicken shit."

Keane caught the look in Logan's widened eyes. She assumed he was stupid enough to jump at Bouvine's bait. Could she see beneath his rigid self-control to the wild, uncontrollable turmoil buried within? The thought made him angrier. He wasn't about to put a beating on this idiot, to have Bouvine's subsequent hospitalization weigh him down even further. Without comment, he nudged her ahead of him.

"We'll be back tomorrow, Sal. Schedule him for a few bouts…with the same fighters as today. Not Jaysin, okay?"

"Anything for you, my love," Sal hollered back with admiration in his voice.

On the run home, Keane sprinted out ahead of her. He heard her shout out, "Wait up!" but ignored it. Bouvine, Sal and every other fighter in the place would have waited. Hell, they'd have given her a piggy-back ride home. Or, more likely, a ride of another kind. What was it about her that made him feel so responsible? So freakin' protective? So close to forgetting about training in favor of beating the living shit out of that worthless ass?

Fuck. Man-oh-man, images of her riding *him* hard were like relentless punches, stirring his blood up past the boiling point. If he was gonna be back in the cage again, he needed to get a grip, and fast. He picked up his pace.

Once home, he headed for the back room, locked the door, and began a series of grueling lifts. Until some semblance of sanity returned.

Keane emerged from the back room so abruptly the bath towel nearly toppled off of her. They were both wet, her from a well-deserved shower and him from a marathon session of lifting. He scowled at her, an all-too-familiar look. She didn't mind, knowing his growl was worse than his bite.

"Sweet Mother of Mary. Put some clothes on," he barked, stepping past her.

For the life of her, she couldn't figure out why his mood had soured sometime between the gym and working out at home. Surely Jaysin and his taunts weren't responsible for the sudden change? Something else was bothering him. Something she wanted to put her finger on so as to better understand him. Keane's muscled chest rose and fell from overexertion, as if he'd tried to physically push away his troubles. A cold draft from the hallway caused her to shudder and for her focus to resharpen on his attire—or lack of it.

"Look who's calling the kettle black. You're showing a heck of a lot more skin than I am." To prove her point, she grabbed the waistline of his sweats and tugged them up a notch. Her thumb connected with the warmth of his abdomen and suddenly, she felt hotter than the shower she'd come from.

He smelled all male, a mixture of Ivory soap and sweat. Beads of perspiration coated his bare chest and dampened his hair. She itched to reach out and run her fingers along the inky, moist path of his tribal tattoo. She shifted, and the movement accidentally caused her to release her grasp on the towel. In one fluffy cascade, it fell to the floor.

She heard his sharp inhale as a flush spread over her body.

Time was suspended, until his hands found her chest. Scooping from underneath, he cupped the weight of her breasts within his palms. His thumbs found her pert nipples. Gently, he pressed, circled and stroked them, then moved lower around her areolas.

The warmth of his fingers sent shivers down her spine. But it was the note of desire in his voice that caused her heart to burst.

"See how you feel in my hands? So soft, so damned beautiful. So perfect in every way."

She melted. The tenderness in his tone and in his touch gave her goose bumps. She leaned in to him, her entire body trembling with want.

Fickle fate interfered as the invasive sound of the

knocker on the front door interrupted the moment between them.

"Finish this later," he stated, his tone rough like whiskey, then broke away.

Logan exhaled a long, disappointed breath. Her breasts still felt warm from his palm.

Quickly she headed for her room, where she pulled on a new set of underwear, a long, loose pink sweatshirt and tight black pants. Running a comb through her hair, she heard Keane's sharp greeting and the murmur of voices echo up from the foyer. Whoever was at the door was uninvited. Yet it sounded as if Keane knew him. She crept to the stairwell and peered down.

"You back? What happened, no one show up for training?"

"Very funny. I told you it was a brief assignment. Decided to check in on you on my way home. When I left here, I was worried. You seemed…well, *hello.*" The handsome man in the foyer grinned up at her. A familiar, semi-fanatical smirk. One filled with recognition. He glanced back at Keane appreciatively. "You have company. Luscious Logan…"

It was all he got out before Keane tossed him on his back in one, smooth move. The man's hand shot out and tapped the wooden floorboards.

"Damn, Keane, let me up. I'll apologize. Stupid thing to say. I get it."

Logan hurried down the stairs, worried for the apologetic man. "Keane, let him up. He didn't mean any harm."

"One more word, Stevie, and you're outta here," Keane warned, and removed his foot from his friend's chest. With a nod toward the sofa, he left them and headed to the kitchen.

Logan frowned as Keane returned with three beers. Drinking wasn't part of their exercise routine. But before she could open her mouth, Keane shot her a look that said "suck it up."

"So, are you two a thing? That kiss was something— a worldwide event. I hear even Prince Harry has commented on it."

Logan just about choked on her Yuengling. Clearly, Stevie had no filter and the incident in the foyer had been dislodged from his very short-term memory bank.

"Stevie—"

Logan cut him off. "I heard Keane mention a recruitment center. Are you in the military?"

Thankfully, Stevie was more than happy to discuss himself. "Yep, I'm home for good. Served three tours as a Marine, one in Iraq and two in Afghanistan. I'm helping a few recruitment centers get up and running. Came from New York and decided to check in with Coach here before I return to Ohio."

Keane drank deeply from his beer.

"Coach? Did Keane train you to fight?"

Stevie laughed and gave his friend a shamefaced smirk. "He tried, but mixed martial arts isn't part of my arsenal. Pretty much sucked at it. Not that this guy wasn't an exceptional coach, he was. Taught some of the best fighters in the Marines some mad skills. I'll never forget the time our friend Jimmy pulled a Kimura in the championship round…"

Stevie trailed off. For a moment, something passed between the two men. Logan searched Keane's face but was met with only an intense scowl. Typical Keane.

Memories had a way of doing that; one person's fond remembrance was another's nightmare.

She inhaled sharply. Jimmy was Keane's nightmare.

Hadn't she witnessed it at the luncheonette? Keane had visibly flinched when Jimmy's name had been brought up. Now Stevie's story was evoking the same dark response from Keane.

Whenever she'd overstepped the boundaries, pushed the issue, Keane had shut her out with his sharp tongue. The threat of him sending her packing if she persisted loomed unspoken between them.

And she couldn't afford it—not with Jerry dangling that money at her. Not with the paparazzi monitoring her every move. These few days were a godsend, despite Keane's mood swings—or rather steadfastly clinging onto *one* mood, that of sourpuss. Case in point was the tension rolling off him now.

"How about I get dinner ready? I'll leave you guys alone for some man time." Logan didn't wait for a reply and headed into the kitchen, fearing Keane might send Stevie packing if she didn't get food on the table soon.

As she seasoned two huge steaks for the stovetop grill and rinsed off lettuce leaves for a salad, her ears were tuned in on the conversation in the next room. A one-sided conversation. No surprise there.

"Did you call that number I gave you?" Stevie whispered in an impossibly loud voice.

Logan pictured Keane shaking his head in the silence.

"I wish you would, Keane. There's no shame in it. A lot of guys experience—"

"Shut up or get out."

Turning the flame up high, she tossed the steaks on. *No shame in what?* she wondered.

She took out a bag of edamame and arranged the green pods to steam over boiling water. Tossed with a dash of sea salt, the high in protein and vitamins soy beans were a better treat than starchy French fries. But Stevie's turn in conversation made her clench a pod so tightly the seed turned to pulp.

"Logan seems real nice, down to earth. Not what I expected at all for a celebrity. Are you two a thing?"

She's not my girl. Keane's comment from Joe's lingered in her mind. Funny, how a few days in his company had changed a simple attraction into something deeper.

There was more than a physical chemistry at play now. An unspoken bond of sorts had formed. Granted, he was as complex as a Manet painting, the sum of many complicated parts. A whirlwind of colorful dots, some small, some large, and for the most part unpredictably placed, but fitting together beautifully as a whole. These glimpses of the real Keane, though few and far between, were the little moments she treasured most.

A shared smile, rare but genuine—which made it all the more special. How his eyes followed her as she practiced her positions. The quiet companionship after a physically grueling day where she'd read on one end of the couch and he'd rest his head back on the cushions and close his eyes, awake but relaxed.

Which was why Keane's response to his friend's probing…mattered.

Still squeezing pieces of edamame between her fingers, Logan braced herself.

Keane grunted. An unhelpful, non-descript sound that could be interpreted as either a yes or no.

Considering her year, Logan should have felt happy his reply was so damned vague. But she wasn't happy. It mattered. *He* mattered.

For the second time this month, Logan felt as if an invisible fist punched her in the stomach. A fight-changing punch, the kind that made record books. The kind discussed, reviewed and analyzed for years to come.

Somehow, in the midst of the dismal debacle that was her life, she'd fallen for this MMA fighter.

Chapter 8

REAR NAKED CHOKE: A common maneuver where a fighter catches hold of his/her opponent by the back

"It all started with a wicked sand storm," Stevie began, leaning forward to place his empty beer next to hers on the coffee table. Keane lounged next to him on the other side of the sofa, deep in thought as he swirled the last of the amber liquid around in his bottle. Stevie had been entertaining her with stories about his and Keane's days as Marines. Entertaining her—*not* Keane, who seemed more distant with each new story and who had been slowly withdrawing from the conversation. The last few anecdotes included a third man, a wickedly sly prankster. Jimmy.

She stretched out her long legs and leaned back in the kitchen chair she'd relocated into the living room, smiling encouragingly at Stevie.

"Another time, our boy Jimmy was out for revenge. Someone messed with his alarm clock. He was late for roll call, but even more annoyed by the sand."

"Why would the sand bother him? Isn't Afghanistan mostly desert?" Logan asked. She took another sip of her second, and last, beer. Tomorrow's training schedule would be hellish with a hangover—not that Keane seemed worried, with his four to her two.

"The Hindu Kush, on the border with Pakistan, is one huge cluster-fuck of mountains. In the 1980s, the Russians found out how desolate and wild they were when they were fighting the Afghans. We didn't figure this out until much later. The hard way…"

Stevie fell somber for a second, and Logan waited, hoping he'd reveal more. Tonight had given her a glimpse into Keane's otherwise guarded past, and she hadn't fit all the pieces together to form a perfect picture of him. Not yet, anyway.

She glanced at Keane. His demeanor was like a storm brewing, anything but approachable; a subtle stiffening of his body like he'd thrown up an invisible wall and dared her to breach it. Something troubled him, and made her want to wrap herself around him and pull him in close. As if sensing her eyes on him, he looked up. His gaze held hers briefly, before he looked away.

"However, we were stationed smack in the middle of the Rigestan, which in Persian means 'country of sand.'" And I'm talking Sahara Desert-like sand, the kind that creeps into your pores and never leaves. Logan, have you ever been in a desert during the night?"

"I spent a few nights on tour in Phoenix two summers ago."

"Well, the Rigestan Desert is a sand trap and if the wind gusts up, sand storms are common. Just so happened, one hit in the middle of the night while Jimmy was catching some shut-eye."

"I thought you slept in barracks or tents."

"Most times, we do…did. Anyway, the sand has a mind of its own. Bent on defeating you, just like the Taliban—though I'd take a mouthful of sand, any day. Isn't that right, Keane?"

Keane simply nodded and took a swig of his beer.

"The entire day, Jimmy picked sand out of his ears, nostrils, you name it. Good-humored sport, he was. Joked about how the sand exfoliated his body so it was nice and smooth for the ladies."

Logan giggled. Back when she had money, a day at the spa exfoliating was common, though most patrons were female.

"It's getting late, Stevie." Keane's tone was low, but firm.

"Okay, let me finish my story and I'll be off."

"I'll hold you to it."

"Jimmy found out that it was Serge, one of the bosses who trained with us and one of Keane's fighters, who messed with his alarm clock, making him late. He rode him all day long about setting up a bout until Serge couldn't take it anymore."

"Was Jimmy a strong fighter?"

"The best, except for Keane here."

Keane drained the last of his beer and the bottle rang out as it wobbled around on the coffee table.

Despite his darkening mood, Logan laughed. The

news of his accomplishments in the cage gave her hope. Everything was going to work out this time. Jerry would get his fighter. Keane clearly knew how to handle himself and win, without getting hurt.

She smiled. A year ago, she wouldn't have been able to imagine herself in this situation. Being an Octagon Girl, never mind one shacked up with a surly fighter with a set of guns bigger than her neck. A man whose world was more foreign than the Hindu Kush.

A big brute of a guy now glaring at his empty beer bottle like it had grown two heads. There was a tightness to his finely sculpted cheekbone and around those firmly pursed lips. Lips most of her ballerina friends would die for. Fascinating lips she wanted to feel pressed on her—every inch of her.

Despite being at odds with her thoughts—not that they noticed, with Keane absorbed in his beer bottle, and his visitor popping edamame beans into his mouth like it was his last supper—she listened as Stevie continued. "Jimmy's last fight—well, really his second to last fight—was one for the record books. I'm sure Marines will be talking about it for years. Unorthodox, to say the least. God, I get a stomachache from laughing just thinking about it."

"Let's have it then. Make me laugh," she prompted, her words lightening her spirits and clearing her head.

"Let's have it so you can be on your way," Keane added, sharply.

Stevie ignored him. "First, Jimmy covered himself in suntan lotion an inch thick, from head to toe. Everything except his fighting briefs. Then, he pulled the ol' tar and feather routine, except instead of feathers, he used…"

"Sand!" she exclaimed, catching on to the joke. "What did Serge do when he saw him?"

"That's the gem in the jewel case. He didn't notice until it was too late. Every time he touched Jimmy, his hands, legs, chest—everything was smothered in soggy sand. He couldn't get a grip on him. The match was over in the first round. I've never seen two more sorrowful figures in my life. Super Sand Men, that's what we called them."

Keane stood, and waved to his friend. "Nice of you to stop by. But it's late…"

Logan jumped up as well, sensing Keane was going to pounce and not understanding why. "I'll walk him to the door, Keane, if you'll take the plates into the kitchen. Leave the left-over edamame on the kitchen table. I'll wrap them up for later."

Clearly, the idea of her walking Stevie out did not settle well with him. He frowned down at her, then turned and gave Stevie a sinister look. Logan wondered, not for the first time, how they were even friends.

"Got it, Coach. No need to worry on my account."

Now it was Logan's turn to scowl. They'd effectively eliminated her from their conversation by using man code. With a loud sigh, she headed off toward the foyer. Stevie's footsteps on the floorboards told her he followed.

"So, you live here now?" he questioned.

"Yes." She ushered him onto the porch, not wanting Keane to catch wind of their discussion. "Stevie, I know he's generally pretty gruff. But there's more than that going on, there's something bothering him. I want to know what it is."

"Listen, Logan, he's changed. Didn't use to be so mean, so quick-tempered. A lot of the guys…" He stopped, and rubbed his jaw. "Keane always did say I have a big mouth."

"Don't let some stupid man code keep you quiet *now*. Come on, Stevie. I want to help him."

"Jesus, why do you women think a man can be fixed like repairing a car, or something? Sometimes, the troubles are so deep, so internalized, no one can help."

"I know you know the answer, Stevie. Is it…Jimmy?"

Stevie looked down at the sidewalk, out into the street, up at the night sky—everywhere but at her. Tight-lipped. No help there.

Logan tried another approach. "We've a few more days of training and then he'll be fighting in the qualifiers. Do you think he'll be okay?"

Stevie snorted. "Does a grizzly eat bunnies for breakfast? Don't worry about him fighting—he's a warrior." He retrieved his wallet and handed her his business card. "Listen, keep in touch, okay? Keane's not so great at it."

"I probably won't be around that long."

Stevie's gaze swept over her from head to toe. Then, his lips curled up, as if he'd discovered a secret he wasn't about to share. With a wave of a hand over his head, he headed down the stairs. But something he'd said earlier had stuck in her mind and begged for clarification.

"You said Jimmy's second to last fight. Who was his last fight with?"

Stevie's shoulders seemed to slump as he turned. Even with the distance between them, Logan spotted the sadness in his eyes. She clenched her fists together, knowing the answer before Stevie even opened his mouth.

"Keane."

* * *

Deep in thought, Logan returned to the kitchen and, scrub brush in hand, went to work on the grill.

Keane had already washed the plates and utensils. He stood quietly by, with his hip angled against the sink and his arms folded across his chest, watching her.

A warm flush heated her cheeks. With a damp hand, she shifted the neckline of her sweatshirt higher on her collarbone and recovered a shoulder. The material had a mind of its own and slid back off. Self-conscious, she scrubbed the grill with renewed vigor.

"What did Stevie have to say at the door?"

"How much he enjoyed your sweet disposition and laughter. I don't know how you are friends, given the way you treat him. The evening started out rough, and despite his attempts to lighten your mood, it ended tense and uncomfortable. I can tell he's a good friend, and a nice guy." She bore down on the grill brush while her point was being made.

Keane snorted. "Nice guy. Just your type, too."

Logan halted the grill brush mid-circle. What was going on in that thick skull of his? He almost sounded…

"Tomorrow, we'll sleep in." His deep, low voice—sexy as hell—caused her to drop the brush. It clanged against the grill irons.

"Sleep in? Saturday's the first two qualifiers." She turned, ran her eyes over him, and wanted to lick her lips. Keane was built better than a model in a physical fitness magazine. But was he prepared for the fights? "Why the change in routine?"

"I'm ready."

"It wouldn't hurt to squeeze in two more days of practice."

"What I need is sleep. A night of solid, dreamless bliss."

"Okay, a nice cup of rose mint tea—"

"Not on the menu."

Logan frowned and stomped her foot. Jeez, three nights until the qualifiers, and he wanted to go on a bender.

"Fine. Drink yourself silly. But remember, you promised me you'd fight and win. I've lived up to my end of the bargain. I've invested a lot of time here and tonight, all you've been is a rollercoaster of nasty and irritable."

Keane shifted off the counter and sauntered toward her.

She continued, undaunted by the powerful man closing the distance between them. Her temper spurred her on. "Mr. Steak-For-Breakfast—remember him? The guy with the wry humor and shit-eating grin? Where did he disappear to? Hell, the times you smile are getting fewer and farther between. I really don't like the way you treated Stevie. Or me."

As he came closer, she sidestepped, moved toward the center of the room, and collided with the kitchen table. With nowhere to go, she folded her arms across her chest. She turned and rested her bottom back against the table.

Tension filled the space. A mixture of her anger, his physical presence, and something else. Arousal?

Still, she pressed on. "You told Joe that I'm on a *need-to-know basis*. Well I have news for you, here's something you need to know…"

Keane moved in closer. With an unreadable expression, he looked down at her. She lost her train of thought, along with her nerve.

One more step forward caused her legs to tangle together, one knotted vine of clumsy.

"Here's what you need to know." His fingers caressed her bare shoulder blade and his eyes narrowed with intent. "Tea isn't what I want, Luscious."

Hearing her new nickname roll off his lips was a game-changer, that's for sure. *Leaping leotard.* The way he said it made her think of all the sexy things her overeager imagination had dreamed of doing with him, in various positions and multiple times, the past few nights. She felt his hands on her hips, lifting her up and setting her on the wooden tabletop.

"This bit of skin has been driving me nuts all night." A thumb retraced the hot path his fingers had left on her shoulder blade.

"Keane, I…"

He slid his body in between her dangling legs, swooped forward and captured her lips, effectively silencing her concerns.

He tasted of Yuengling, not that she minded, as his tongue wound around hers in a sensual twist. So tender, so perfect was his kiss, she felt every muscle in her body fill with music—a heady sensation similar to the rush she always got after a performance. But better. Then he withdrew.

"Open wide," he demanded.

She hesitated, feeling shy and wanton at the same time, though the latter won out. Parting her thighs, she leaned back onto her arms.

The corners of those plump, pink lips turned up. Logan felt breathless, as his ruggedly handsome features transformed by a jaw-dropping, make-me-yours-tonight sensual smile.

"Your lips, Luscious. Open your lips."

God, she'd just spread her legs wide, and he was talking about her mouth!

Her lips parted as she closed her eyes and gasped. Something salty touched her lower lip and her embarrassment was forgotten. Slowly, Keane caressed her mouth with the smooth edamame pod he'd plucked from the bowl on the table, using it as an erotic toy. Her tongue darted out for a taste and he offered up the bean. She devoured it as if it were an oyster, or some other rumored aphrodisiac.

He slowly ran a finger along the moist seam of her lips, making her knees weak. Withdrawing it, his tongue ran along the same path, licking up the salty trail.

Her lips parted invitingly.

This time, his invasion was more aggressive and she found herself breathless from a kiss that made her blood sizzle and skin hot.

He pulled back and caressed her shoulder. "Couldn't take his eyes off this either, ol' Stevie."

Her heart did a perfect cartwheel as she opened her eyes. "I doubt he noticed or even cared about a bit of shoulder."

His mouth moved across her collarbone and over one shoulder, turning her legs into wobbly liquid Jell-O. Then everything seemed to happen at once.

With a gentle tug, he lifted the sweatshirt from her body and over her head. His eyes smoldered, catching sight of her red lace demi-bra. Thank God their earlier encounter had made her toss the tan support bra back into the drawer and dig out this bit of flimsy material— one of several sexy yet unused bras she'd bought after

Pierre had proposed. This particular bra hoisted her boobs up as if offering plums to the gods.

He pulled back. "All night, I wanted another look and taste—no more. You're sexy as hell but too *nice*. Too freakin' good for the likes of me, not my type. Too complicated. And I don't do complicated. Understand?"

Logan tensed. Complicated? He was a poster child for complicated. Sexy and sweet one moment, and snarling deep in his throat and ready to pounce in the next. As for not being his type—just who did this mass of muscle think he was? Mikhail Baryshnikov? He was not even close to being her type…which made her falling for him all the more irrational.

His fingers contradicted his words. They ran upward across her sides, finally angling in for a smooth caress of her breasts.

Her body hummed with need, even if his words still bristled. No strings attached, huh? The liar. *Looks like Keane wasn't going down without a fight. I'll show him nice.* In the recesses of her mind, a familiar horn sounded, like the kind used to announce a mixed martial arts bout. Her opponent stood just inches away, challenging her with his narrowed eyes. She bit her lower lip. Now was not the time for hesitation. Time to strike out and humble her cocky opponent. Reveal the weakness he all but handed to her on a silver platter, one engraved with the words *You're mine.* For once, she was thankful for her tall, thin build and how her average-sized breasts appeared gargantuan—or so she'd heard. *Might as well put these babies to good use.*

Locking eyes with his, she thrust her chest forward and moved a hand to the bra's clasp. His eyes flared as the demi-bra snapped open and she shrugged it off and onto the table. She shifted back onto her elbows.

Her breath caught, and her breasts jiggled. That was all that was needed. The horn had been sounded. Round one was about to commence.

With a low growl, he shifted back, ripped his sweat-shirt over his head, muscles rippling up and down his sculpted torso with the movement, and tossed it on top of hers.

All the breath she'd been holding inside escaped in a sudden rush at the sight of the dark snaking lines of his tattoo. She wanted to run her tongue along its path, along his hills and valleys, and further south. Keane had another plan.

He swooped in, gently grasped her arms and tugged her up, moving her forward to perch on the edge of the table. "Wrap your legs around my waist."

She did as commanded. Her thighs flexed against his warm firm body and she felt herself hoisted higher, their bodies closely connected and his arms secure behind her back. His head lowered, bypassing her lips so his mouth could capture one full nipple. Gently he sucked and rolled his tongue. The wicked man.

Arching forward, she pushed her breast further into his hot, wet mouth.

"Oh, my…"

A few seconds later, his mouth released its prize.

Her nipple pebbled in protest. He pursed his lips and blew. A warm breath of air trickled over her wet areola. Moisture heated her core.

Their eyes met. Hers full of wonder, and his with a sensual, *knowing* gleam.

He adjusted her position, bouncing her against him

as if she were a feather rather than a strong, fit woman. Her erect nipples skimmed along the length of his warm chest, skin pulling on skin—turning them swollen with want.

He maneuvered her onto the table with little effort. This time as she reclined backward, he followed, moving with her and over her. A bowl rattled an instant before his mouth devoured her own.

Time felt suspended. Her emotions ran wild. Nervousness gave way to desire which, in turn, led to disbelief. The tingling of her breasts, the rush of lust through her middle and down between her legs caused her to shudder. Her libido shot into overdrive as he fitted his body over hers. *Oh, yeah.*

She felt the rigid length of him press against her belly. Instinctively, she wrapped her legs around his waist, inviting firmer contact. His growl was absorbed by her mouth.

A quick flicker of self-satisfaction shone deep inside her. All those unsatisfying years with Pierre…what a waste. The heat rolling from deep inside down to the juncture between her thighs wiped away any lasting thoughts of that jerk. Suddenly, it didn't matter whether Keane was her type or vice versa. Nothing mattered more than having this fighter inside her.

Running her hands down his sides, she hitched her thumbs beneath the elastic of his sweatpants and boxer shorts. Before losing her nerve, she tugged them down, over his hips and ass.

His back stiffened along with his cock. Long and thick, and pressing against her mound. Her eyes almost rolled back in her head. She spread her thighs wider.

"A girl could get used to this kind of treatment," she

muttered, her tone ripe with need and *awe*. Hell, she had years to make up for, starting now. All Keane had to do was look at her and moisture coated her panties.

His lips left hers. Her eyes snapped open to see his mouth tightened into a fine line. She had the impression he was going to pull away, a second before he did.

"Where are you going? I thought you wanted this." Her declaration sounded lustful and desperate.

Yanking up his clothing, he moved off the table.

"Fuck." He ran his hands across his temples and back over his hair.

"Keane...?"

"I thought I could do this. But you're gonna end up hurt." He offered her his hand. Her legs swung around and her bottom scooted across to the end of the table as she let him help her down.

Once her shaky legs were planted firmly on the ground, he stalked over to the refrigerator, opened it and took out another beer. With a quick pop of the cap, he brought it to his lips and drank deeply.

"But...you weren't hurting me. You've been nothing but gentle and considerate."

"Fuck. That's not what I'm talking about. You're too fuckin' *nice*," he murmured the last part, then took another swig of beer. "We're done here."

She was in a constant state of confusion with the wild mood swings of his—and this time, her frustration found a voice. "What is your problem? You know, everyone said you were a mean bastard with a heart as hard as steel. But I didn't want to believe it."

The bottle tilted as he swallowed another mouthful. He finally turned to look at her. "Look, Logan, what do you want, for me to nail you on the kitchen table?"

He placed the near-empty beer bottle beside the sink, like he was ready to pick up where they'd left off now that he'd had his say.

His communication skills sucked.

Logan laughed, the hollow sound filling the kitchen. "Is that why you stopped? Mr. Man-Of-Few-Words is now worried about his bedside manner?"

Keane snorted.

"What do you think I wanted, a marriage proposal?" He'd awakened something inside her, a sexual hunger she hadn't known existed. A taste of what she'd been missing. Then he'd abruptly snatched it away, leaving her with that empty feeling she'd felt far too often of late.

An odd expression crossed his features but vanished in a snap. "Nothing's changed. It's just like you've heard, I'm a moody, mean prick. If it's sex you want, no problem. But don't get used to it. Like Rosie said, I don't do relationships."

Rosie. Hearing Easywrap's name was like falling into a bed of thorny roses. Black ones. "You are so infuriating. What do I have to do, mail you an invitation? As if yanking your sweats down wasn't enough of one." She stomped her foot and her bare breasts bounced, reminding her she was topless. Her arms crossed over her chest protectively.

Great, just great. Logan had to hand it to herself, she was a seasoned expert on falling for men who only thought about themselves.

The lines around his eyes softened, but Logan was too furious to care. She grabbed her sweatshirt and tugged it on. *Peep show is over, buddy.*

"Since we're on a needto-know basis, and you've

been so considerate in enlightening me about your own concerns, I have news for you: you're miles from being *my* type." She stalked over to him and poked a finger at his bare chest to prove her point.

He stared down at her intently. "Shit." With another muttered curse, he wiped a hand back and forth over his cropped hair.

"Once our agreement is fulfilled, I'll leave you to the thieving blondes…more your *type*," she added, before marching out of the kitchen and heading upstairs.

Moments later, the front door slammed. Logan had no doubts about where he was headed. She punched a pillow. *Smooth move, Rettino. Way to chase him right into the arms of that spandex-clad airhead. His type of less-complicatedness.*

Chapter 9

DOUBLE UNDERHOOK: When a fighter swings his/her arms beneath an opponent's and knocks them off balance

No more yoyo-mojo, Logan vowed, as she rolled over in bed and turned on the light. If anything, she'd learned over the past year that tomorrow was another day—one she would survive, with or without Keane.

From now on, it's hands-off the merchandise, buddy.

Bad enough her newfound sexuality was like an itch begging to be scratched. But the man she wanted, that infuriating, fickle, unpredictable man, held her at arms' length when all she wanted to do was crawl up within them. And if all that wasn't enough, her newly developing feelings for him weren't reciprocated.

Shifting her sweatshirt back up her shoulder, she tread barefoot downstairs. A cup of chamomile tea might help calm her mind. Hell, she'd drink an entire pot if it'd numb the effects of the emotional rollercoaster she'd been on.

She sighed, and folded her arms across her chest to keep warm against the chill of the living room.

The house was dark and quiet as she followed a path of moonbeams into the kitchen. She poured fresh water into a kettle and set it to boil on the stovetop.

With a sigh, she headed to the living room to wait, and plopped herself down on the sofa. Instead of a soft cushion, her bottom met a solid wall of muscle.

"Holy crap," she cried out, as she lost her balance and tumbled back across the body sprawled out there.

"Persistent, aren't you, Luscious?" Keane's deep voice breathed into her ear.

She squirmed on his lap and tried to sit up, but Keane wrapped an arm around her ribcage, just beneath her breasts, and refused to let go.

"You're back. I didn't see you. What are you doing? Didn't you get what you wanted?"

Keane leaned in, his breath hot against her ear. "What I wanted..." He snorted, tugging her tighter. She felt the heat of his body against her back, all the way from her ankles to the top of her shoulders.

"Keane, you smell like a brew pub. Let me go. We tried this once already, and you weren't interested. Or is that your thing, get hammered and then get it on?" The words came tumbling out, thick with irritation.

"I'm bad news," he said, softly. His hands shifted and cupped her breasts over her sweatshirt. "But I think about you and this," his finger caressed a nipple, as he continued, "all the fucking time."

Despite the rush of lust triggered by her highly sensitive nipples, she halted his exploration. His rejection still stung.

She decided on the truth. "Keane, what I was offering is no longer on the table, so to speak. You made it clear where we stand."

A long exhale of breath said he'd heard her.

"Let's call it a night. Time to sleep it off. Tomorrow, you've got another ungodly day of training. I'm holding you to our agreement, no matter what happens between us."

The arms around her didn't relax. She wasn't going anywhere until he let her. *Why was he here in the dark living room, clearly plastered, and not asleep in bed?*

Perhaps if he talked about whatever was bothering him, he could put his sorrow to rest. And focus on the fight. Focus on…her.

"What's up with you? Maybe I can help. Do you want to talk?"

He stiffened beneath her. "Shit…no."

Logan sighed deeply. Nothing but a headache, trying to help someone who didn't want it.

"Listen, Logan. Everything I said before is true. It's not you—fuck, a few years back when I was a different guy, we might've had a chance."

"You are rather intimidating, but there is a softer side to you that shows up occasionally." Her voice was sharp, and took on a sarcastic quality as she added, "A shame tonight wasn't such a night." *Good*, she'd give him a humble taste of you-can't-have-me pie.

"Hmph, you don't know me. You don't want to know me."

"How much have you had to drink?"

"Not nearly enough."

"Well, that's one too many in my book." She shifted and he held on tight. Quietly, she offered, "I've had my share of problems this year, as you know. Some days, it was hard to get up out of bed, and not just because of the paparazzi. My whole life is broken. Everything I dreamed about is shattered. Yet I get up every day and try to make the best of it."

"You are so naïve," he replied, but his voice sounded hoarse.

Still, his bluntness pissed her off. "Naïve? Maybe, though I'm not about to drown my misery in liquor. Or take my irritation out on other people. If you ask me, that's the cowardly way out."

There was no mistaking the tension in his body beneath her. Yet his actions surprised her. He let her go. She climbed up and out of reach, to the far end of the couch.

But Keane wasn't finished, and what he said next froze her in place. "Cowardly, huh? I'd say it's preservation. Of self and of others."

He sounded downright miserable. Perhaps it was the booze, or a guilty conscience, but Logan sensed he was on the verge of talking—really talking—to her. Whatever it was, it was on the tip of his tongue. She couldn't let him swallow it back.

"Are you having trouble sleeping? Is that why you're here on the sofa?" she asked, a soft invitation for him to confide in her. *Better he be on this sofa than in a bar, or in Rosie's bed*, she reminded herself.

He grunted.

"Why don't I make you some chamomile tea? Relax you so you rest. Even sober you up some."

Keane sat up on the couch, swinging his long legs onto the carpet. Silence followed his movements, and he was once again a large, dark shadow lounging next to her. "I'm going back out for a while."

Logan's heart raced in her chest. Given the time—almost 3:00 a.m.—his business wasn't at a bar. This time, a woman waited for him. It irked her. She'd literally spread her legs for him, and he'd turned her down flat, yet he desired a woman's company. It didn't make sense. Helplessly, she added, "What about training?"

A long exhale sounded beside her. "Look, I'm not backing out of the fight. No need to worry about that—hell, bashing heads in sounds damn appealing."

While his words should have been reassuring, she wanted more from him than the assurance he'd fight. His earlier comment rang out in her head, something about Stevie not being able to keep his eyes off her. Keane had been annoyed. A feeling that showed he was affected by her in some way. *Hmm.* She squared her shoulders. *There was more than one way to tame a fighter.*

Sliding closer to him on the couch, she pressed her legs against his. In the dim light, she saw him hunch over and brace his arms on his legs, as if preparing to stand. Quickly, she held out her carrot. "Your friend Stevie was funny. Nice guy."

"Fuckin' Stevie," he grunted and shifted, ready to stand.

"Is he dating anyone?"

In one swift movement, he was on his feet. Facing

her, he thrust his hands to his sides and flexed his fingers. The moon cast a cool highlight on his furrowed brow, twilight on a desert canyon.

The teapot's whistle sang out, ruining everything.

Logan clambered off the sofa and, without looking at him, moved into the kitchen and turned it off. Listening for the sound of the front door closing behind him. This was what she wanted, right? Her hands-off-Logan approach to dealing with him.

As she sat down in a kitchen chair, she felt his presence in the door.

He hadn't left.

Feeling reckless, and unsure of the outcome but oh-so-sure she was proving a point—especially being they were back in the kitchen—she continued, "Well, is he?"

He shifted, a big, shadowy puma preparing to pounce. At least, that's what she thought he looked like with the tension rolling off of him there in the moonlight.

She lowered her shoulder, hoping there was enough light. The uncooperative sweatshirt cooperated and plunged deeply, revealing a pale, naked shoulder and a good portion of her collarbone. She angled her head and swung her hair, offering an unobstructed view of the side of her neck and a good portion of the top of her arm. Just a taste of what he'd passed up.

The only warning she had of his next move was his sharp inhalation of breath.

In four long strides and one swoop, he scooped her up in his arms. Without a word, he carried her out of the kitchen and living room, up the stairs, down the hall, past the guest room, and then the temporary gym. A well-placed kick and his bedroom door flew open. The vibrating wood echoed the sound of her heart pounding against her chest. Common sense screamed out *caution* but she ignored it.

He stalked inside and over to his bed. With one bounce, she landed in the center of it.

Before she could even mutter the word *yoyo*, he crawled across the mattress and in an instant, his mouth claimed hers.

The kiss made her forget everything. Nothing mattered except his seductive, urgent tongue. She was overwhelmed first by his tenderness, then by a raw, all-consuming sexuality that made her toes curl. It was an endless, drugging kiss.

Until he broke his lips away. "I don't want to hurt you."

He'd made the same comment earlier. He was trying to communicate something important. Something emotional.

Talk about size. For whatever reason, this was a huge issue for him. She certainly didn't want a repeat episode of their kitchen table dance. "Are you really that… big?" Logan questioned, hoping he'd believe the quiver in her tone was from excitement. Well, part of it was.

His massive physique took up most of the center of the mattress as he knelt before her. Of *course* he was big.

He snorted. "That's not what I mean. You'll be prepared to take me, I promise."

Prepared to take me… All the nerve endings in her body tingled at his words. But instead of jumping on him, Logan crossed her legs on the mattress. The air needed clearing, and Keane's troubles needed to be addressed.

"I'm tougher than I look. You don't want a permanent relationship. Fine. Six fights is all you need to win for me to get back on my feet. Then my life will be back to normal. And I'll chalk up our time here together as a necessary transitional stage."

Her declaration sounded hollow. She wasn't the kind of woman who took things lightly—especially mind-blowing sex, which was the only given here. Especially mind-blowing sex with this hunk of a man, someone who, judging by the tightness in her chest, she'd come to care for. *Who am I kidding?*

"You can't help me. No one can."

"Help you with what?"

"Forget it." He stood and quietly undressed.

Her mouth went dry at the sight of him. His erection was beautiful, so strong and masculine, just like every other part of him.

"Take off your clothes, honey."

Whatever he'd been trying to say was lost as his eyes flared, his hands fisted in her hair and, with a gentle backward tug of her head, his lips captured her own.

Logan's eyes seemed greener, bright and shiny. A passion-filled oasis from the turmoil in his life.

A long-overdue reprieve with her fist wrapped around his hardened cock. Fuck, and he'd thought that kiss—the one he'd ended seconds ago when her hand slid into his pants—had been hot. With each long stroke, she broke down any lingering twinges of conscience that reminded him once again how this was a bad idea.

"You're so…um…" she whispered, her tone husky with desire.

He grunted as her palm moved along his length.

"Does this feel nice?" she murmured sweetly.

Nice. That word grated on his nerves, reminding him just how nice he *wasn't*. He felt like rolling her over and fucking her six ways to Sunday, with no regard for how many bruises she'd find tomorrow morning. Instead, he'd settle for smashing his fist into the pillow. Safer for both of them that way. Time to get the fuck out of Dodge before it was too late.

Yanking his leg free, he rolled onto his back. Her grasp on him stayed firm, unbroken. He let out a long, frustrated exhale.

She came up onto her knees. "What is it with you? For the record, I'm not buying it."

"Don't push me. Nice isn't what you'll get with me."

"Bleeding leotards," he heard her mutter. "We've got to do something about this pillow talk. All this yoyomojo because of one silly word."

She cocked her head, narrowed her eyes at him and hesitated for a second before speaking in a low voice, laced with desire. "Then *nice* isn't what you'll get." In less than a heartbeat, she took the length of him in her mouth.

"Jesus." His hips came up off the mattress. The warm, wet pressure felt so fucking good. He'd tried pulling back, both physically and emotionally, but Logan just wasn't getting the message. Better off with someone who knew very little about him, someone who wouldn't be prying into his business, making him talk about things better left unsaid. But for the life of him, he couldn't get her out of his mind. Well, the persistent minx had dug her own grave.

Her head bobbed. He couldn't get enough of her. Weaving his fingers into her hair, he resisted the urge to plunge deeper. Instead, he massaged her scalp with the calloused pads of his fingertips.

Minutes passed and the tension grew as she sucked him hard. Closer, and closer. Finally, the wicked woman withdrew with a loud smacking sound. Keane made a low noise deep in his throat.

"Hmm, Mr. Few Words wants more, does he? Can't remember ever being so turned...oh!"

In one smooth sweep, he flipped her up and over onto her back and pinned her legs open—wide open. His mouth moved between her thighs, his tongue licked and swirled at her core, then plunged deep.

It was her turn to shoot her hips off the mattress. "Oh, my..." she moaned. Seconds later, her thighs began to tremble and he knew she was close.

"Couldn't leave me in peace, could you? I'm going to take you hard and fast. You understand?" He reached for the nightstand drawer where he kept condoms. Tearing the foil with his teeth, he rolled the latex over himself. He moved on top of her and rubbed his cock against her moist juncture.

"Yes, hard and fast." Her legs shifted on the mattress, spreading her wider. "Please."

Tucking his hips back, he flexed and his cock parted her folds. Inch by inch, he glided into her until the thick tip was fully embedded. Despite his warning, he didn't want to hurt her or, truth be told, frighten her with the fierce extent of his lust. She was tight, so fucking tight, and her inner muscles pulsing around him caused him to harden even more.

"God, more. Please... Is this your hard and fast?"

He flexed his ass, driving in another fraction of

an inch, and her hips tilted up to take him in further. "Please…"

"Don't say I didn't warn you, Luscious," he groaned. And with one long thrust, he slid all the way inside her until he was fully seated.

"Oh!" she cried out, shaking. Her legs wrapped around his waist and her hips bucked upward. Butterfly-light convulsions fluttered around his cock, moist and warm. Even in his drunk, lust-fueled haze, he understood her response. A short, sharp orgasm.

Bewildered and *pleased*, he relaxed and waited for the glow to subside before resuming his thrusts.

"You know, the room isn't that dark, Keane. I can see you smiling," she muttered, throaty and deep from her release.

Sexy, satisfied minx. His lips twitched.

"Are you going to grin all night? Or are you going to move…you know, hard and fast?"

His laughter rang out, foreign and carefree. Until she withdrew her hips and gave his cock a long, firm stroke.

He hunched over, his chest pressed on top of hers. His mouth found her neck and with a quick jerk of his ass, he plunged deep, once, then back out. All sense of time and place were lost as he soon found the perfect rhythm.

She sought his mouth and sighed deeply. Her nails ran along his back and her hips thrust up to greet him. Her luscious tits rubbed against his chest in tune with his movements, causing his cock to pulse and swell.

"Oh, my God…"

Her sweet cry brought him to climax along with her.

He must have fallen into a deep sleep, with Luscious as a body pillow pinned beneath him. Either the early morning light filtering into his bedroom had awoken him, or the sinking of the mattress beneath him.

Squinting, he peered at Logan's lovely ass as she bent to retrieve her clothing from the floor.

"Where are you going?" he demanded, without thinking.

She jumped. Holding her clothing to hide herself, she looked over her shoulder at him. "Um…I thought I'd head back to—"

Whether it was alcohol or the fact he wasn't fully awake, whatever it was caused him to spring from the bed and stand before her.

Despite her gasp, her eyes greeted him with a lusty perusal of his body. The effects of her attention jutted out proudly between them.

Reaching, he grasped her waist, stepped back toward the mattress, and sat down, maneuvering her so she stood straddling his legs.

"Put your knees on the mattress."

The look on her face was priceless, a mixture of surprise and excitement.

He quickly rolled a condom onto his rigid length. With one hand, he positioned his cock between her legs and with the other, he tugged her down onto him.

"Your turn to be fast and furious, Luscious."

Her eyes sparkled gently until she took his words to heart. Then, they sparkled brighter than stars in a desert night.

When Keane woke again, her head was nestled on his pillow and her legs were twined with his. Even in sleep, Logan was sexy as hell. Her lips were pink, and plumper than usual—swollen from his kisses. She smelled like sweet vanilla mixed with the scent of their passion. When was the last time he'd studied a woman after sex?

He should feel ornery. Mean. His typical morning reveille. But this wasn't a typical morning. Despite the hangover, he was well-rested and satisfied. The light filling the room said it was midday. Maybe later.

Logan blinked her eyes open, and he glanced back down at her. "You're not getting rid of me now, you know. I could lie here all day."

Warning bells went off in his head. Damn, he wasn't a cuddling, romantic kind of morning guy—even being well-rested.

"If you could see the look on your face. Boy, it's a good thing you established the rules ahead of time or I might be heartbroken right now. What I meant was..." She motioned upward with her thumb.

The beautifully refurbished copper tin ceiling—one of his first renovations. He grunted, careful not to show the swell of pleasure rising up in him. She liked his ceiling.

"The former owner had them covered with drop-ceiling tiles," he heard himself saying. Frowning, he wondered what else she'd be capable of prying out of him if he wasn't careful.

"It's beautiful, Keane. I almost had an amazing ceiling once, in a pre-war apartment I found on the Upper West Side. God, I loved that place. Good bones, you know what I mean?"

Her voice caught, and he studied her face. Sadness lurked behind the green depths of her eyes. "What happened, you sold it?"

She sat up in the bed and self-consciously adjusted the covers around her chest. He followed suit.

"I put up most of my savings toward it but it didn't work out," she responded, her words bitter.

Instinctively, he reached over and slid his arm behind her, cradling her head. "So, what happened?"

"Pierre happened. When we got engaged, we pooled our finances together—which really means he depleted my bank account—to buy an apartment. I'd been away in London, dancing. It was a high point in my career." Her lips lifted but the smile didn't reach her eyes. "When I returned, Pierre'd already purchased a place, and not the pre-war we'd been searching for but a modern co-op. He called it his big surprise, as if that justified his actions. Wasn't the only surprise that jealous, egotistical jerk had for me, either."

Mention of that asshole made him scowl. "You took his ass to court, right? Sued him for robbing you blind?"

She didn't have to reply. Her expression said it all.

"Jesus, why the hell not? Is this why you need me to fight?"

"I don't want to trouble you with more of my problems, Keane. And I want to talk about you fighting—"

"Let me guess. You still own the co-op."

"Half. Well, more than half. But he put the mortgage under his name. He's living there with my understudy. With the doctor bills, and everything, I haven't been able to afford a decent lawyer. Not yet, anyway." She said it so calmly, as if she was resigned to the fact that her ex had stolen money from her, and some other woman was reaping the benefits.

She moved off the bed, gathered her clothes, and gave him a quick, shy grin before leaving the room. "Shower."

Keane watched her naked back as she exited the room. His bed suddenly felt empty.

"I'm going to bash his teeth in," he said to no one in particular.

The first chance he got.

Chapter 10

ROUND: A bout consists of three or five rounds—depending on the MMA organization—lasting five minutes each with one minute in between

Logan told Keane she had a few errands to run. A cowardly fib because she needed time to figure things out. First, recovery time from the toe-curling sex. Even thinking about what they'd done made her cheeks warm.

Second, time to reassess her feelings, and what she wanted from this relationship. Keane had made it abundantly clear he wasn't the kind of guy to make long-term commitments. Was she okay with that? Her body sang out *yes!* oh-so-sweetly, knowing how she'd likely find herself in the horizontal position every night. A frightening, yet appealing thought.

She was falling for him, a fighter, so clearly not of her world, and so not her type. Yet he threatened to be rough and was nothing but… Well, he did hold back when he thought he might hurt her. He'd actually smiled, an earth-shaking, lusty smirk, when she'd found her pleasure. And the big daddy of all surprises—not only did the somber brute of a man have a copper tin ceiling in his bedroom but he was proud of it.

But last night was the first act in a limited engagement. Keane had made that crystal clear. As much as a repeat performance appealed to her, she knew it couldn't happen. A simple fling, nothing more. Harden her battle-weary heart and mute her feelings for him. Besides, her priorities had shifted away from what mattered most.

She needed him to fight and win. Getting too intimate—her skin warmed at the very thought of just *how* intimate they'd gotten—confused things. Blurred the lines between what she needed from him and what she wanted from him.

Logan quickened her pace. Sally was in town, the hometown stop on her Pittsburgh Ballet tour, and after it all ended, she'd be on her honeymoon. Her friend was living the dream and no way would Logan share anything but good news. Sally didn't need a Debbie Downer dimming her spotlight.

She patted her coat pocket and the newspaper folded inside rustled. The rental space sounded like a dance school paradise in the ad. The perfect square footage, a desirable location downtown, and easy access to outside resources, like the Pittsburgh Ballet. Hopefully, there would be good news to share with Sally, if the rental space described in the ad was as good as it said.

* * *

An hour later, Logan was in her seat, in time for the opening of a sold-out performance of *Giselle*. Man, her morning with the Realtor pretty much reflected her year—it sucked. Turned out the potential dance studio *was* exceptional, and exceptionally unaffordable.

She bit back her disappointment and relaxed into her seat. The studio was a dance instructor's dream, with a perfect layout and locale, except for the exorbitant $2,000 a month price tag. Double her budget. Sure, the deal with Jerry was lucrative—tentative, but lucrative—but realistically she was hoping to rent a large place with good flooring and plenty of wall space for under $1,000 a month, so as to save a bit more for start-up costs, renovations, advertising and marketing. She had to be frugal, and smart in her choice of studios in order to make it work long-term.

Watching the ballerinas drift across the stage, the tension in Logan's body lessened. As an audience member, ballet had that effect on her—when she could breathe in the poetry of their movements without the fear of being dropped by a lame-ass partner. Sally was breathtaking, and Logan found the sharp disappointment that had accompanied her into the theatre vanish.

Another rental space existed out there, somewhere.

At the end of act one, she heard her name as the dancers were exiting the stage. Turning her head, she scanned the crowd for a familiar face. A few strangers made eye contact before hastily turning away. The tiny hairs on her arms stood at attention, but Logan ignored the familiar sense of dread as the lights dimmed and act two began.

The tenderness between her legs as she shifted into

the seat made her think of Keane. His touch, and the deep timbre in his throat when he groaned during climax. This morning's smug grin had rivaled the one he'd had over the steak-for-breakfast incident and made her heart dance and her woman's bits warm.

Keep your eye on the ball, she reminded herself. *Six victorious bouts and you'll be home free.* Hadn't Sal told her Keane was the man to beat? A trainer of other fighters—Marines being the toughest in the world and all, right?—yet he didn't find pleasure in it. What had changed for him?

Thankfully, the ballerinas assembled onstage and the familiar routines took over her senses.

Afterward, she headed backstage to chat with Sally, sing her friend's praises, and…oh, hell, who was she kidding? For the first time in months, Logan wanted to confide something in her trusted friend. Something monumental.

The second she entered Sally's dressing room, her mistake became clear. All eyes swung her way. The door leading into the dressing room rattled on its hinges from being forcibly slammed shut. Cameras snapped and lights flashed.

"Logan," Sally called out in surprise. But the swarm of press blocked her path.

"Are you still an Octagon Girl?"

"How do you feel about Pierre LaFeur's performance on this season of *America Gets Its Groove On*?"

"Will you be part of the audience at his May performance of *La Sylphide* here in Pittsburgh?"

"How does that hunk of an MMA fighter like your tatas?" The last was asked by a five-foot slip of a woman, who was clearly a traitor to her gender, and whose breast size was flatter than Interstate I-70. Yet it was her question that brought silence to the chaos.

Logan looked about helplessly, glad her alpaca knit coat masked her curves from the cameras, yet frustrated by the realization that she was trapped.

When it became clear she wouldn't answer, another reporter piped up. "Our sources confirmed your romance with Keane O'Shea is on, and is hot and heavy."

It was too much. They were too much. Notching her chin up, she demanded, "Your sources. Who might they be?"

"Your landlady, for one."

Logan gasped. "Mrs. Debinska? She barely speaks English…"

Two younger paparazzi exchanged raised eyebrows. One reached into his pocket, pulled out a tablet, handed it to her, and then tapped the Play button.

Her mouth fell to the floor. A smiling Mrs. Debinska was on the front stoop of their house. The camera slowly panned in on the object in her hand. The audio kicked in, and a male voice enthusiastically narrated the clip. Stunned, all Logan heard him say was, "America's New Sweetheart Reveals Buxom Ballerina's Bra Size is a—wait for it—38DD." The elderly woman held up her prize for the cameraman. A bra. An industrial-sized, no-nonsense, earth-toned bra. *Her own* bra.

"That's not my—"

A reporter interrupted her. "Is there anything you want to say to your ex? After all, he's been dissing you every chance he gets."

Was there something she'd like to say to her ex? The question was as alluring as a slice of expensive Ahi tuna. But Logan bit her tongue. Throwing gasoline on a fire would only ignite it further. A foolish move. She'd get even with the jerk, in time. Instead, she brought the focus back to someone who deserved it. Sally. "My best friend Sally Jacklyn is on a world tour. I'll gladly pose for a picture with her." She smacked the reporter's tablet against his chest, as if the action would erase that vile video. The way her year was going, it would likely go viral instead.

Moving forward, the reporters stepped out of her way.

"Oh my God, Logan. I'm so sorry. They've been at this all day. The dressing rooms are bursting with bodies. My director is thrilled with the media attention and is permitting it. I tried to warn you but your voice mail is full. Didn't you get my text?"

Logan threw her arm around Sally and smiled for the cameras. "Is there somewhere private we can talk?" she whispered in Sally's ear, quickly turning for another photo. Hard to remember a time when she didn't mind having her picture taken.

"Follow me." Grabbing her hand, Sally tugged her into the small lounge connected to her dressing room. "No one enters. Got it, Stanley?" she told the huge bodyguard who'd body blocked them a pathway out of there. The door closed.

Logan flopped down on a long, pillowed chaise, and Sally did the same next to her.

"Are you okay? I've been sick with worry about you. With my schedule, I haven't had time to track you down and demand to know why you aren't returning my texts. The Octagon Girl gig sounded so promising, a chance for a new start. How was I to know that Pierre would stoop so low? You must be mortified. Devastated by his betrayal."

"Mortified, yes. Devastated…no, not anymore. Everything he's done—ruining my life, my career, my future—has been to save his own reputation. All those practices where we'd worked on the positioning of his feet were a waste. You know he tends to keep them too close together. I really tried to help him correct that. Nothing helped. Bet the talk shows don't know that juicy tidbit. All it would take is a slow-motion replay of The Fall and someone who knows what they're talking about to run commentary on Pierre's stance just before he drops me…"

"I can't believe you've kept quiet about this." Sally sounded appalled. "It wasn't like you came at him bare-chested and lathered in butter cream, or something equally slippery. Women have a way of restraining these." She gestured to her chest. "It's called a bra. Are your boobs bigger than your standard ballerina's? Probably. Are they so incredibly massive they'd blacken your partner's eyes at ten feet away? Not a chance."

"I should have stuck it out as a solo artist."

Sally shook her head in silent agreement. Then she added aloud, "What a jerk! You need to make a public statement. Immediately. How long are you going to let him get away with his lies?"

"I'll get even with him when the right time comes. Going to the press, though, you can forget about it. I'm not giving him the satisfaction of acknowledging him, or an opportunity to publicly humiliate me again. Being famous is one thing, but *notorious*—that's a whole different animal."

"But Sophie Morelle loves that kind of thing. She's

been sticking up for you and your breasts the entire time."

"Sally, that's what Pierre wants—craves. He's a media pimp. Dancing isn't enough of a high for him anymore. He wants to be famous, at any cost. I don't know why I didn't see it sooner. What classically trained ballet dancer puts his career on hold for a reality TV show?"

"One who can't dance," Sally exclaimed.

"You know the expression 'what goes around, comes around'? All this bullshit he's dishing is going to swing his way. And I'm not going to be there anymore to prop him back up. That's Anya's territory now."

"Jeez, I've been so busy. Is there anything else I missed?" Sally demanded.

Oh, yes. Her breath hitched thinking about it. About him. But how to begin?

"Guess what else? I'm not frigid. Not by a long shot."

Sally's pinched, pity-infused look dissipated. "Frigid? Who said you were frigid? I've known you since high school, know all about your first kiss, etcetera." The question was rhetorical though; Sally knew as well as she did that the same jerk who was dragging her name through the mud had given her a complex. "Oh, my God! Tell me you got naked with the fighter."

Logan couldn't suppress a smile. "You know the feeling you get in your cells, your body and soul, when you lift up on your toes? How every muscle fills with music? That's what Keane is like…maybe even better."

"Holy shit! You're a couple? That kiss did look pretty hot. And he's gorgeous. Who would have thought someone who gets his face bashed in for a living could be so pretty? A real feast for the eyes…an *eyegasm*."

"Mr. Eyegasm has proven himself the expert source of some mind-shattering multigasms."

"Holy hell. Really?"

Logan nodded, reaching out to smack Sally's hand in a high-five.

"Now we're talking. Is it serious?" Her friend studied her face, reading her expression in the silent way that only best friends can communicate.

Logan spoke, needing to clarify things before her friend got the wrong idea. "It's casual...a temporary deal." In an attempt to keep the discussion positive, she added, "To think I might have spent my life with a man who doesn't know how to make my body dance."

"Wow, I don't know what to say. I know that look. When you said his name, you were glowing with happiness. Good for you, Logan. It's about time."

Logan frowned. It had been such a long time since she felt happy about anything, the emotion was nearly unrecognizable. Which made her say, "Hopefully, you'll be back in Pittsburgh before fall."

The word *fall* startled them both. Yet somehow it didn't seem to sting as much as it once would have.

"Logan, I have to ask you something...personal."

She sighed. If hordes of reporters had the right to demand answers, why shouldn't she allow her best friend a shot? "Whatever you want to know, Sally. You are my best and dearest friend. I trust you completely."

Mimicking the way one of the paparazzi had rolled his eyes over her, Sally asked in a stern, serious tone, "A 38DD? Did your seventy-something, Polish-speaking landlady—America's New Sweetheart, Mrs. Debinska—just bamboozle the paparazzi with the mother of all lies and pawn off one of her granny bras as yours?"

The situation was so ridiculous—the whole scope of it was absurd—but Sally's expression was priceless. Laughter welled up and out until the two of them crouched over with their hands on their stomachs. Just like old times.

Full of good cheer, Logan headed home after a lovely meal of fresh salmon and basmati rice with Sally at their old hang-out, McCormick and Schmick's. In her haste to leave earlier, she'd forgotten her cell phone at Keane's. Not that calling him was something she planned on doing—reporting in was such an I'm-your-girl type of action. But she felt guilty that he might be wondering where she'd disappeared to.

Until she caught sight of the woman struggling with Keane's front door. An obnoxious blonde Logan had hoped never to set eyes on again. She had a death grip on the door handle with one hand while the other clasped the sides of her leopard-print blouse together.

Logan halted dead in her tracks. Breathless from the invisible grip tightening around her windpipe and squeezing all the air out of her. With nowhere to hide, she tucked in her chin and prayed the woman wouldn't spot her, frozen there on the sidewalk in front of the neighboring house.

A myriad of emotions washed over her—primarily anger. She had resigned herself to having a temporary fling with Keane. Temporary meaning a few weeks, even a week, not less than twelve hours. Despite his no-strings-attached warning, it hurt. And two women in one day? Too gross for words.

The alpaca thief didn't see her, now too busy trying to keep the front door open with both hands and her right hip. Her chest heaved with her efforts. There was no missing it, with her blouse flying open every time her hip hit the door.

What the bleeding leotards was going on here?

"Come on, hon-eeey. I waited for you at Finnegan's last night, but you were a no-show." Rosie's whiney voice was so loud the current patrons at Finnegan's could probably hear her from all the way across town. "Let m-eee back in."

Logan wished she hadn't heard. Or at the very least, had been at Finnegan's and too drunk to let one woman's long-winded wail crush the delicious daydreams she'd reveled in all day. A fool, that's what she was. Hell, he'd warned her, but she'd gone ahead and wondered about an exclusive, if not long-term, relationship with him anyway. Now she had to worry how many other women would be showing up on his porch.

At last, Rosie gave up and was headed down the sidewalk, buttoning her blouse. The front door opened, and a goose-down jacket came sailing out and over the blonde's head. She scooped it up, struggled into it, and gave the front door a stiff middle finger before stomping off down the street.

Mercifully unobserved, Logan stole up the sidewalk. With her hand on the doorknob, she moved to enter and proceeded to fall into the house as the door flew open.

"Jesus, go home." Keane's voice rumbled in anger.

The sight of his bare feet made her head snap up. Her mouth went dry. Keane stood before her with a white cotton towel slung low on his hips. Water matted the fine black hairs on his chest and head. She inhaled sharply and caught the clean soapy scent of him.

Recognition mixed with irritation filled those baby

blue eyes of his. "Where the hell have you been?" he demanded. Nothing compared to the anger building within her.

"Why do you care? It looks like you found a way to amuse yourself today. Last night was nice and everything, but I'll know better than to hook up with Mr. Can't-Keep-It-In-His-Pants again."

"You didn't answer my question. Why did you disappear like that?"

"I don't know what pisses me off more, the fact that you could entertain another woman less than twelve hours after our…whatever, or the fact that you did the deed with that disease-infested thief."

"Shit, it's not what you think."

"Proof you'll fuck anything—serves me right for sleeping with someone like you. A fighter! Six months ago, you wouldn't have even registered on my radar. What was I thinking?"

"She just showed up."

Logan had been down this road before. When she'd discovered Pierre and Anya in bed, she'd kept quiet. Dealt with the hurt silently, privately. Now, she felt like yelling, with so much pent-up anger the tin tiles would fall off his ceiling.

"She stopped by to see if I needed…anything."

"Humph, like someone to wash your back in the shower? Guess you did need something, huh? Clearly, you're okay now." Despite the bite in her words, her eyes betrayed her with a full body scan, checking him out from head to toe. The damned towel angled lower on his hip, revealing a good portion of hipbone and the small indentation below it. She inhaled sharply.

"Look, if you'd been here seconds ago, you'd have seen me toss her out on her troublesome ass."

Point taken. Logan felt her anger lessen but pressed on. "So that was why she was buttoning up her blouse on the way out?"

He shot her a piercing look. "She's persistent. Hell if I know how she got in here. Picked the lock—"

"I know you said this was temporary, that you didn't want a relationship. I've accepted that. But don't you think it's insulting—and gross—to roll from one bed into another? Or is it okay when you shower together afterward?"

"That's not what happened. She threw herself at me. I wasn't biting," he said, clearly exasperated. "I'm not used to justifying myself, Logan. But nothing happened." His body seemed to vibrate and the damned towel loosened as he moved.

Her gaze lingered on the unstable knot at his hip. If he swung himself ever so slightly, that sexy dimple below his hipbone wouldn't be the only part of him on display. She clenched her fist, refraining from tugging the bit of cotton lower. *Who am I kidding? He's my type, all right. An upward trade, from Snickers to Neuchatel truffle—if you knew enough to lick your way through the hard, gritty surface.*

Logan flushed. She'd known enough to do much more than lick.

"Hell, after last night—" He didn't finish his thought. "I warned you. We keep things simple and uncomplicated. But I've been straight with you from the get-go and I'm being straight with you now. Nothing happened. Take it or leave it."

Aside from the towel, he had nothing to lose. Maybe

she was a fool twice over. She shook her head, struggling to believe him, and struggling to ignore the spark of desire flaring up inside. "I've been played before," she confessed softly. "It's difficult to trust again."

"Trust is about all I've got to offer." Keane shifted on his feet and the towel another fraction of an inch. She didn't dare more than a quick glance or she'd be lost. He pressed on, seemingly unaware.

"Your ex Twinkletoes is an asshole. But guess his type is more your speed..." His words sounded soft, wounded. Until his voice took on a sharper tone. "Last night was fun and all. But no more hookups. No commitments, except for the fight. I want space and privacy. And no questions. We're strictly business. Agreed?"

"Agreed," she murmured, wondering if her instincts were right, that her comments had gotten under his thick skin. That somehow, she'd hurt him.

"Agreed," she restated, a bit more firmly. Keane was a means to an end, after all. Last night—*and this morning too*—had been a mistake. She should thank him for refocusing her, reminding her of her priorities. A fun, unemotional, short-term fling with him worked in theory. But today's afterglow and the way her heart churned at the sight of Miss Easywrap on the stoop should have sent warning signals to her brain. She'd been as unemotional as a surfer riding a tidal wave. Still was.

The dimple just below his hipbone made her heart turn a cartwheel. As if she'd ever give up running her fingers along that brazen display of flesh. He'd awakened something within her, and she was reluctant for it to be extinguished. Besides, she could see his body reacting to her inspection, his penis rising at attention just for her. Clearly he still wanted her.

What would he do if I reached over and tugged the bit of cloth from his hips? Instead, she inhaled sharply and made to turn away.

"Look at me."

Her gaze lifted, and she wondered if he'd guessed her thoughts, conflicting as they were.

"Jesus, have you heard a word I've said?"

He shook his head as if he wasn't sure what to do about her blatant assessment, or his body's undeniable response to it. Let him deny the attraction that always sizzled between them, no matter their mood or topic of conversation. The elephant in the room she was struggling to ignore.

"We'll focus on the qualifying bouts, and getting a good night's sleep." He moved past her toward his room. "That's all," he muttered.

Logan headed to her room, irritation fueling each step. Keane would fight, and she should have been overjoyed. He was doing her a favor. Her livelihood depended on it. But their exchange left a bitter taste in her mouth. Was it because he'd given voice to what she'd been struggling to say—that theirs was a business agreement? Probably. As if she was just another notch on his belt, forgotten and dismissed. She flopped onto the mattress and willed herself to be just as unaffected by him as he seemed to be by her.

Why did she feel like she'd danced her last dance?

Chapter 11

*CUTTING WEIGHT: What a fighter does before a
weigh-in to quickly drop pounds in order to meet
the weight requirement*

As if Jimmy's nighttime visits weren't enough of a
pain in the ass, Keane was now haunted by a shapely
form in a skimpy pink tutu. One moment he'd been
dreaming of fireman-carrying his injured friend out of
an ambush, the scent of blood and gunpowder strong
and potent. Then quicker than a car bomb, the picture
changed.

There was Logan, smelling like sweet vanilla cake
and spiraling around on the tips of her toes. Her tiny
skirt lifted with every turn, exposing flaming-red
panties. Worse still, she was topless, her full, luscious

breasts bouncing freely. Keane ran his fingers along a
brow bone. Nothing like waking up with a pounding
head and a throbbing boner.

*Take care of business and maybe the headache will
stop*, he hazily thought, kicking off the bedspread and
readjusting his body.

A muffled noise came from his bedroom doorway.

Immediately wide awake, his eyes shifted toward
his dream-lurker, now standing in the doorframe. The
early morning light cast an innocent glow about her, especially with that deer-in-the-headlights expression on
her face. His morning wood blatantly filled his white
boxer briefs, as her eyes fixed on him, and, just as blatantly, looked her fill. For Christ's sake, she was acting
as if she'd never seen a semi-naked man before—never
seen *him* naked before.

He flipped the covers off a leg, shifted on the bed,
and looked away. But the damage was done. Her sweet
yet naughty demeanor—a total turn-on—was now im-
printed on his brain. Damn, she was hot as hell. He liked
that she wasn't afraid to hide her desire for him. For a
second, he contemplated getting her all fired up about
something so her cheeks flushed pink and firecrackers
sparkled in those green eyes of hers, and then tossing
her onto the bed and sinking deep inside of her.

But yesterday, there'd been hurt in her eyes, which
reminded him of their agreement. No sex. Strictly business. A relationship was the last thing he wanted. Blissful aloneness, that's all he wanted, along with a good
face-pounding. No prying questions or sympathetic
shoulder to cry on. He'd avoided plenty of the nice ones
in the past, since they tended to cling tighter and cause
more drama. Logan fit into this category perfectly.

A shame. Besides his physical response to her, he liked her. There was very little *not* to like about her. Despite worming her way into his dreams and poking her nose into his business, he respected her for sticking up for herself, and demanding answers about Rosie—even if yesterday's argument had triggered warning bells in his head. His sense of self-preservation said keep her at an arm's length.

"I wanted to tell you I'm not running this morning. I need to head down to the gym early and soothe Jerry, if that's even possible. Though, the fact that he now has his fighter should do the trick."

Keane grunted and climbed out of bed. Ignoring the way her eyes widened, he opened a dresser drawer and pulled out clean sweats.

"We ended on a bad note yesterday. I just want you to know that I am really thankful you agreed to fight. A few wins and I'll have enough money for my dance school. Then I'll be out of your hair."

She fell silent as he pulled on his sweats and a clean, white T-shirt. He frowned, mulling over this new bit of information—a dance school? So the Octagon Girl job was temporary? He frowned. For some reason, the news did not sit well with him. In their short time together, he'd gotten used to her just like those bitter herbal teas of hers.

"That is, unless you want me to move back home to Mrs. Debinska's sooner rather than later?"

Shit, why did she have to be so damned persistent? She was his until the preliminary bouts were over. "No," he said harshly.

She exhaled. "About last night—"

He shot her a look as he tugged on some socks. "A business agreement. Your herbs for my fists."

"But you said the herbs didn't help. That you needed…um…more." *More.* His cock stirred at everything that one simple word contained, but he ignored it. Oh yeah, he needed more. More uncomplicated. Less likely to twirl around in his dreams in a skimpy costume. Less likely to fill his mind with images of her voluptuous body.

He grabbed his sneakers, slid them on and quickly tied the laces. Anxious for this conversation to end and for his solitary run to begin before he changed his mind.

Black- and pink-striped sneakers came into his line of vision. One stomped in front of him. He looked up. Her hands rested on her hips. "You are the most exasperating, closed-mouthed man I've ever met. A business relationship is exactly what I'm agreeing to. I know you don't want sex, or anything. Bad idea going forward. But this is awkward for me. Say something."

Fuck. It wasn't a good idea—not at all. But sex was exactly what he wanted from her at that moment, with her breasts swaying and her luscious lips slick from her tongue. Her blond hair bounced, and her green eyes glimmered as daggers shot out of them. Her lips parted slightly in a breathless sort of way. She was stunningly beautiful in her rage. Even as she stomped her foot again, madder than a drill sergeant.

He had to get out of there and fast.

Abruptly he stood and made toward the door. Peace and quiet was what he'd settle for. Time to calm his tired mind and ease his throbbing temples. "Later."

"Jerry's expecting you at the gym by noon for the

weigh-in. I'll see you there, right?" he heard her shout from halfway down the hallway.

Cameras flashed and Logan blinked. She forced her lips to remain frozen, twisted in an upward pose, as if scores of lenses and eager-eyed reporters weren't fixed on her. At least Jerry had penned them in like sheep, corralled in the press booth at the foot of the stage.

"Looks like your boyfriend is a no-show. If he's not here in five more minutes, you're done. Not only will you never work as an Octagon Girl again, that skinny, pantyhose-wearing ballerina boy's interviews are going to sound mild compared to the bullshit I'll say about you." Jerry smirked and gestured to the mass of media. Countless cameras clicked, snapping away at this prime photo op.

Logan inhaled a calming breath. No point in arguing with the man. Instead, she tried reasoning with him. "You changed venues, Jerry. Who knew you switched the weigh-in to the arena? Keane probably headed over to the gym. Be patient, he'll be here." She resisted rolling her eyes. Jerry's last-minute change in venues was a real problem tonight, with fighters wandering in late and with two other Octagon Girls being no-shows. The new girl, Chloe, was hiding in the locker room, immobilized with a severe case of stage fright. Logan had been forced to handle the crowd single-handedly.

Another silent prayer was issued. When Keane realized the weigh-in was bound to be more frenzied than a Justin Bieber concert, he might not show. Logan couldn't blame him. She'd been stuck on this stage, a high-definition screen blaring highlights from previous fights overhead as a steady parade of fighters stepped

on and off the scale and Jerry paced around like a mindless, squirrel-faced chicken.

All fighters from every weight class weighed in tonight, in advance of the eighteen bouts to be fought over
the next three nights. The winners of each bout would
proceed on to the next fight, and so on, and so on, until
the best fighters within their class battled it out to qualify for Tetnus. So far, twenty guys had stripped down to
their boxers, stepped on the scale, and had made weight.
Well, most of them had.

Four fighters had been disqualified for being too
heavy. There had been a big hubbub over something
about Jerry fiddling with the weight requirements. Outrageous. How could he get away with such a thing? Yet
Logan wouldn't put it past ol' Squirrel Face to manipulate things in his favor. She needed to speak to Keane
beforehand, give him a heads-up. Plus, she needed reassurance that Keane could now make weight.

Where was he?

Everyone except the featherweight fighters and the
two men pumped up to be tomorrow night's showcase
fight—Keane and his first welterweight opponent,
Young Gun—had weighed in.

"Come on, man. We don't have all day!" someone
shouted from below. Logan kept her smile in place, even
as Jerry shot her a scowl before heading for the mic.

"Keep your fuckin' panties on. Young Gun Willie
is already backstage. We're waiting for the Guillotine
Grappler, Mr. Tap Out Central, and the fighter to beat,
our own…um…"

She felt like rolling her eyes. Some emcee he was,
one too cheap to hire a professional broadcaster.

"Boom-Yay O'Shea," a voice squeaked from somewhere up in the rows of bleachers. An area assigned to hard-core MMA fans who ventured out into the cold Burgh winter to bear witness to several men taking turns on a scale.

"Boom-Yay O'Shea," repeated the crowd, easily pleased with the silly nickname.

Twist my tutu. No way was Keane going to like this name, nor the entire spectacle playing itself out here. Nervously, she glanced up the ramp toward the entrance, hoping he hadn't arrived and overheard.

Jerry held his hands up, his palms facing the crowd, as if that might stop their chanting. Then he spoke. "Let me remind you that tomorrow night Sunrise Sessions presents 'MMA Monster Mayhem,' an evening of tremendous, world-class MMA action. Doors open at seven and the first fight is at eight."

He sucked in a deep breath, and continued, "The fights are winner-takes-all format, meaning if a fighter wins, he'll fight again that same night. If he wins the second bout, he'll move on to the next night's fights, until a victor in each weight class is announced the third night, after bout six."

She jumped as Jerry stalked up, his face lurching inches away. "Three more minutes," he threatened. "Now get out there and entertain them."

"You want me to what? Dance?"

"Dance? What the fuck…no! What I want is for you to parade your luscious body around the stage and keep these guys excited. Show off another one of the new outfits I bought you. Didn't you see them in your locker? There's one for each series of bouts unless I fire your ass. See, you're an *ass*-set too." He leered the last words, his humorless attempt at a pun. The creep.

The outfit in question wasn't that flimsy. A bright aqua V-neck halter top was tied around her neck at the top and fell to mid-waist, covering her more effectively than some of the leotards she'd worn to ballet practice. Matching boy shorts hit the crease of her legs, but only in the front. The back was cut diagonally, so the bottom half of her cheeks peeked out. Clearly, the focus was on her *ass*-ets. Zippity-doo-dah.

Wanting to distance herself from the squirrel-faced creep, Logan squared her shoulders, put her blue Nikes in motion, and did what Jerry demanded. She marched across the stage, halted, and struck a pose. The clicking of cameras told her she had their attention.

Pivoting on her toes, she moved back across the stage and posed for the photographers on that end of the corral. Click. Click.

As long as the cameras did the talking, Logan was fine with this…*performance*. Years of being onstage had prepared her. As she added more sway to her second sashay across stage, the realization struck that she was *more* than fine with this. With the media focused on the present rather than her mangled reputation, Logan discovered that for the first time as an Octagon Girl, she was the boss. She was in charge of her own notoriety. The audience was *hers* to win over their attention and respect, *hers* to perform for like she'd itched to do, *hers* to enjoy.

Overhead, the television commentaries switched over to music videos. Bon Jovi's "Livin' on a Prayer" had the audience singing, and Logan smiling. If she had to pick an anthem for herself, this would be it. Sure, she'd been down on her luck. But life was on the upswing.

She hit the edge of the stage and pivoted smoothly on her toes, keeping her arms neatly at her sides, resisting the urge to stretch them overhead as she spun. Giving the press any reminder of her ballerina days would be a bad idea.

Halfway across stage, she glanced toward the entryway. Where was Keane? He'd given her a promise, albeit a reluctant one, and her trust was in his big, burly hands. *Trust is about all I've got to offer*, he'd said.

He'd be here, all right. Hopefully before ol' Squirrel Face pitched a hissy fit.

A guitar solo rang out. She catwalked across the stage in perfect rhythm, her back straight, arms swinging slightly, feet crisscrossing, feeling like the Gisele Bundchen of the MMA world. Training alongside Keane had sculpted her muscles in a curvy, more obvious way than the firm, tight lines she'd acquired from dancing. The new lift in her backside being the most notable—and most obvious in this get-up.

She stopped mid-stage, rose up on her toes, and twirled, landing to jauntily face the audience. They loved it—she could tell by the flashing bulbs and, smack behind them, from the grinning male faces in the first row. One bizarre guy in a Santa hat even blew her a kiss.

Why, I'm grinning too! Incredible.

With a toss of her head, she made a forty-five-degree turn, stretched one long leg forward, and continued along her imaginary runway. And mentally stumbled as she caught sight of the tall figure partially obscured by the temporary curtain hanging at the side of the stage. Fascinated, she watched a set of familiar yet furious blue eyes give her the once-over. *Keane.* Jerry's welterweight had finally arrived, as hardened and mean-looking as ever.

The smile fell from her face. His earlier dismissal still stung. How dare he stand there, one massive muscle of irritation, and burst her small, fleeting bubble of happiness. Yesterday's confrontation danced around in her mind, too. Strictly business, he'd said. Well, she'd introduce him to *her* business, that of being an Octagon Girl. Whether he liked it or not. Give him a taste of her…assets, and show him what he'd be missing with her new you-can-look-but-don't-touch policy.

The thought of his hands on her made her face warm, but pride spurred her on.

She shortened her steps. Channeling her inner supermodel, she swayed her hips from side to side and thrust her breasts forward, hoping to catch his attention. Her mind played over every naughty moment they'd shared that last, mind-blowing evening, fueling her movements. She hoped it was all there, reflected on her face for him to see.

Plastering a sultry smile on her lips, she turned first to the snapping cameras and then to the welterweight hidden offstage. *Remember, this is just a business arrangement, dear Keane*, she mentally scoffed, strutting closer and closer to him.

He shifted, and she wanted to believe that slight movement was her touchdown, a sign of her effect on him. But she wasn't sure.

She *so* wanted to be certain.

Prancing closer, she noticed the way his arms folded across his black zip-up sweatshirt and his legs angled down in an inverted V. A casual stance, except for the tight curl of his fisted fingers. She didn't dare make eye contact.

Over her shoulder, she flashed the crowd another Cheshire Cat grin. Slowly, she stopped, pivoted on her toes, and twirled so she faced the audience. Just feet away from the sexy welterweight off in the shadows. Making sure her back was to him, she rose up on her toes and struck her best model pose yet. Boy, she'd give anything to see Keane's reaction right now. *Would he even notice the cut of her boy shorts?*

The music ended and so did her impromptu time-to-torment-Keane performance. *Now what?*

Logan hesitated. She could exit toward Keane or walk back across the stage toward Jerry, who'd finished befriending the brunette and was back to shooting her dirty looks.

Thankfully, she didn't have to make that decision. Jerry spotted Keane—she could tell because he threw his hands into the air in a my-prize-fighter-has-finally-fuckin'-arrived gesture, and was now hastily approaching the mic.

"Uh, hum…*ladies*—" Jerry's neck pivoted toward the brunette "—and gentlemen. I'm Jerold Batelli, Chairman of the East Coast MMA Federation."

"You said the same thing an hour ago, man! Where's the welterweights?"

But not everyone was displeased. The brunette reporter had her camera fixed on Jerry, as if to capture every nuance of his handling—or mishandling—of the weigh-in. *Enjoy the fleeting sunshine, Jerry.* Logan knew full well how the press was a fickle friend. One moment showering you with praise, and the next leaving you floundering on your ass. And if there was someone in need of a thorough lambasting, it was that weasel.

Jerry noticed the attention as well, and his chest swelled out like a baboon's as he continued, "Welcome once again to Mellon Arena and to the event you've all been waiting for. This afternoon, we've been weighing in—get it, weighing *in*?—on our featherweight, welterweight, and heavyweight contenders."

Two-months-too-late Santa rolled his eyes in disbelief. As if he had room to talk in that get-up. Though stand-up comedy wasn't exactly Jerry's forté.

Oblivious, he continued, "Let me remind you that in order to compete, featherweights must not exceed the weight of 145 pounds, welterweights 168 pounds, and heavyweights 265 pounds."

Keane had told her that making weight was always a pain in the ass. That fighters frequently had to cut thirty to forty pounds to do so. And how, in days leading up to a bout, fighters did crazy things to slim down. Fasting, electrolytes, hours in a sauna—whatever it took. Logan frowned, trying to remember what he'd said about the maximum for welterweights. Wasn't it one hundred and seventy pounds?

Unfortunately, she was certain that was it. Her mouth had dropped open when he'd told her his training weight and she'd wondered how such a wall of splendidly muscled man could be that light.

"Shit," she heard Keane mutter behind her. Logan stiffened. How could one curse word carry so much meaning? Although she didn't turn around, she could feel Keane's movements through the vibration of the stage, as he jogged or jump roped or whatever he was doing to make the floor sway under his sudden exertions. The rest of the air sizzled out of her bubble. Oh, hell. He was worried about making weight…which meant big trouble.

She swallowed hard.

"Let me first introduce the pretty ladies of the MMA, our Octagon ring girls."

Splitting leotards! Surely Jerry wasn't planning on announcing her, being that she'd just spent minutes parading across stage.

"New to the cage tonight is the charming Chloe Morris." A stunning, drop-dead-gorgeous girl in an Octagon outfit matching Logan's own walked out on stage. Logan blinked, wondering if this was the same person who'd been curled over a bench and moaning uncontrollably back in the locker room. Chloe made her way to Jerry, her face brighter than a cherry on an ice cream sundae. Yep, still nervous—you could tell by the way she wrung her hands together—and shy. Poor thing. Logan felt her embarrassment. Yet the crowd didn't care one iota and fist pumped the air in greeting. *It pays to be beautiful.*

"Another newbie to MMA…Miss Rachelle Getz."

No one appeared on stage. Logan had an ample view of the other side, behind the curtain. It was empty. *Another one bites the dust*, Logan thought.

"Rachelle Geeeeeetz," Jerry trilled, craning his neck back toward the curtain. Chloe's pink cheeks were nothing compared to the deep, crimson flush that spread across Jerry's face in a blotchy webbed pattern. *Yep, another one bites the dust.* His Octagon Girl was a no-show. Logan could almost feel sorry for him, until she remembered how he'd treated her when she herself had missed weigh-ins. Rachelle was in big trouble.

Jerry must have remembered as well, judging by the look he shot her. So much for mending matters with the ketchup-colored Squirrel Face.

"I want everyone to stand up and put your hands in the air for the one, the only only…Luscious Logan!"

"Asshole," Keane snapped but, except for Logan, it fell on deaf ears. The audience had begun to chant "Luscious, Luscious, Luscious!"

Logan was not about to join the red-faced party by the mic. Instead, she remembered Keane whispering her new nickname, how much she liked hearing it roll off his tongue in that sexy, low voice of his. The thought calmed her.

How you treat this audience and the press affects the impression they form of you, she reminded herself. Hadn't she seen that moments ago during her quasi-modeling strut? Clearly, she was the most popular Octagon Girl. Granted, Jerry had fired nearly everyone else, so in a way, it was popularity by elimination. But nevertheless…she was in control here.

As she crossed the stage, another idea danced around in her mind. Keane needed to shed weight quickly. Maybe she could buy him a little time.

Her arm shot up. In a gesture similar to the Queen's wave, but with her fingers rolled in tight, she motioned into the air.

The crowd loved it and fist-pumped back.

Raising both hands overhead, she began to clap until the entire auditorium mimicked her actions. Then she strutted her stuff, making sure to move as far away from Keane as possible. Away from Jerry and Chloe too; the first was definitely not pleased by further delays in his schedule, and the second looked so shocked, her mouth gaped open.

"Luscious, Luscious, Luscious," her fans chanted.

In a year full of firsts, this one was a keeper.

Chapter 12

HIP THROW: When a hip is used to first knock an opponent off balance and then to flip them onto their back

"**W**hoo, hoo! Loving them shorts, honey!" Sal hollered, coming to stand next to him. From his position behind the black curtain, Keane had a clear view of the events unfolding on stage.

He sent an uppercut flying toward the curtain, trying miserably to ignore both the old-timer and the sway of Logan's sweet ass on display for the entire arena.

"Look at her go. That's my girl, working the crowd and all."

Keane kept up a steady jog. Even from this angle on

the side of the stage, he could tell his eyes weren't the only ones fixed on her ass. He sent another fist flying.

"Glad I didn't miss this."

"Shut up, Sal," Keane shouted. *What the hell is she doing?* There was no explanation for the scene playing out on stage right now. Jerry spoke into his mic several times but the crowd's chanting—*Luscious, Luscious*—drowned him out. The chanting from this crew pissed Keane off, so much so that he wanted to grab the guy with the brightest smirk from the front row and grind his nose into the stage. Right next to Jerry's, after he got his hands on him.

Jerry had intentionally riled these animals up. He was going to pay for it, too. Although, Logan seemed to be…what the holy hell *was* she doing?

"What I wouldn't give to be you for a night," Sal muttered.

Keane tossed another jab at the curtain and picked up speed. He wished the locker room had a sauna or even a hot tub, someplace to sweat out two pounds of excess water weight.

"Jerry might have an eye for girly wear but there's not much else good I can say about the guy."

"Is this even legal?" Keane demanded. Furious. So much so he wished the old timer would leave him alone before he did something he'd regret. Of course that asshole's messing with the weight requirement was illegal, and stupid beyond belief.

Nothing Keane hated more than going into a fight riddled with surprises. He'd made a habit of being careful, of evaluating ahead of time the skill level of his opponent, of weighing the odds of what the potential outcome might be. How the fight was being managed. Shit, was an honest, well-run fight too much to expect?

Why cut the weight requirement by two pounds? It didn't add up.

"God knows, it should be. Those hips in those shorts are definitely illegal. Makes a man forget all about fighting and turn the old heart a-thumping."

What the fuck? Keane stopped mid-stride, barely holding off on turning the old-timer's head a-thumping, and glared at the irritating man. Sal shifted nervously on his feet as awareness of his mistake dawned on him.

"Eh…um…we're discussing Jerry. Right. Did you know about his change in venues? Waited around for a while until the kid at the smoothie bar told me about the arena."

"That fool lowered the weight requirement to 168 pounds," Keane said, as he began a series of jumping jacks. Two pounds less than the standard UFC requirement didn't seem like much. That is, it wouldn't have been if Keane hadn't hydrated with excessive amounts of Logan's herbal teas to shake off a wicked headache. Dumb move. If he had known Jerry would be messing with the weight restrictions, he'd have waited until afterward.

"God knows why, but Jerry's probably using DREAM or another MMA organization's weight classes instead of the UFC's," Sal replied, surprised.

Keane jabbed in between jacks. Up-downs might do the trick but it was a risky move working out his muscles while trying to cut weight.

Sal moved off to the side, came back with Keane's jacket, and tossed it to him. "Put this on, it will help you break a sweat. I've some experience outmaneuvering the scale. If all else fails, you can file a protest about Jerry's screwball switch with the UFC execs. I'm itching to do so, no matter what happens."

Jogging in place, Keane slid into his jacket. For once, the old-timer's training experience came in handy.

Feedback from a microphone pierced through the chanting and the crowd hushed. "You're walking a thin line here, Logan," Jerry threatened in a low voice, which the mic picked up and carried. "Stand over by Chloe at the back of the stage...now!"

"Aw, leave Luscious alone. She's the only thing keeping me here while you get your fighters organized." This came from a fan in the second row, an idiot wearing a Santa hat.

Keane exchanged punches with the air, a right hook promised for Jerry, and a left upper-cut for the smug Santa Claus and his lame attempt at scoring points with Logan.

Logan walked to the back of the stage, providing every guy looking to score with a full visual of her ass cheeks. She must have sensed his irritation because her eyes searched him out.

For a moment, they stared at each other. Then her lips moved, mouthing, "Are you okay?"

Damn how her concern bothered him. He turned away. Yeah, once Jerry's nose bled from the face-plant he'd put on him after this whole debacle was over, then he'd be okay. Damn, why had that asshole changed the weight requirement?

No logical answer came to mind. Jerry announced the featherweights and two smaller fighters took to the stage. Another break in MMA protocol. A lucky one. Clearly the asshole was riling the crowd up for his fight

with Young Gun by saving their weigh-in to the end.
It'd be a major fuck-up on his part if Keane couldn't
shed the two pounds.

One at a time, each man stripped down to his boxers
and bare feet and stepped onto the scale.

Keane picked up his pace. It was a matter of minutes before he'd be called on stage. Luckily, a handful
of reporters had been allowed out of their pen and were
snapping close-ups as the featherweights struck a few
muscle poses.

Jerry's shrill tone filled the arena. Time was up.

"Now for the men to watch, the pairing you've all
been waiting for. Two amazing fighters. Welterweights
with equal ability but very different styles."

Keane neatly alternated between a few quick jabs
and a series of kicks. Every second counted.

"First up, introducing Willie 'Young Gun' Reyn-
olds."

He used the last few crucial seconds to beat out some
high leg lifts. The weigh-in was going to be a crap
shoot, a slight chance in hell he'd make it.

"The official weight for Willie is 156 pounds."

"Where did he recruit this—" Sal muttered, but was
cut off by Jerry. Not breaking pace, Keane shrugged off
the heavy jacket and threw it at the trainer.

"And now I want to bring onstage his opponent and
the fighter to beat. Introducing the King of the Guillotine, Mr. Tap Out Central, our very own Keane 'Boom-
Yay' O'Shea."

A fuckin' circus freak show, that's what this was. All
he wanted was a good, clean and challenging bout. The
kind of fight he missed. Keane gritted his teeth. For a
second, he contemplated cutting out, until he caught

sight of Logan on her tippy-toes, anxiously looking toward him. A less than subtle reminder of his promise.

Without breaking stride, he jogged out and over toward the group surrounding the scale at center stage.

A fist waved at him threateningly. A small, unfighter-like fist connected to skinny arms with barely any muscle tone. Those arms lead to a lean, tight chest shaped like a wannabe Marine recruit's—one who Uncle Sam would send home packing within a day. And damn it all, wouldn't you know the face topping it all off was…young. The kid wasn't twenty, if that.

This was Young Gun Willie? His opponent in the showcase match-up?

He scowled at Jerry. The jerk simply shrugged his shoulders.

Right then and there, Keane knew the truth—the change in weights hadn't been a mistake or a result of Jerry adhering to an alternate set of guidelines. Jerry had done it so this unsuspecting amateur could go up a class and fight as a welterweight. Lose as a welterweight, too.

Keane stopped jogging, knowing it was too late to dodge the inevitable. He wasn't about to back out now, not in front of everyone. Not in front of Logan. He wanted to jab someone's face in, anyone except the baby-faced sacrificial lamb Jerry'd recruited.

Resigned, Keane stalked up to the scale, ignoring Logan's anxious expression.

Damn, the kid didn't stand a chance. *If* Keane made weight.

Twist my tutu, what's with him? Offstage, Logan had been trying to get Keane's attention for the past few minutes. He'd briefly caught her look, then snatched his gaze away and blatantly ignored her.

At least he was taking the weigh-in seriously. Judging by his earlier actions, she was under the impression he was worried about it. Why else would he suddenly burst into exercising? Yet, now he appeared…calm. As if the weigh-in didn't matter—which perhaps to him, it didn't.

Logan and Chloe stood near the back curtain about ten feet behind Keane. The kid, Willie, stood off to their right, preoccupied with making odd, I-am-trying-to-look-mean-but-only-seem-ridiculous faces. Jerry had positioned himself off to one side of the scale, just out of Keane's reach. Smart move. Keane looked ready to throttle ol' Squirrel Face.

A raucous AC/DC song, "Back in Black," boomed overhead. An appropriate song, as Keane's track suit covered his back in black oh-so-well.

He kicked off his beat-up sneakers and tugged his sweatshirt over his head, mussing his hair into a just-rolled-out-of-bed look.

Her breath caught when the tight dark T-shirt followed. This was a sight she'd never grow tired of; deliciously taut pecs and abs that made you want to run your tongue along their grooves. She blushed, thinking of how she'd done just that, remembering how his muscular chest pressed her down into the mattress, how strong he was—all over.

"He's hot," Chloe whispered. No arguing with her there.

Mr. Eyegasm slid his thumbs into the waist of his sweatpants and, with one fluid tug, yanked them down his legs. Stepping out of them, he presented her and

Chloe with two perfectly shaped butt cheeks outlined by soft white briefs.

Despite having watched the other fighters strip down, Logan exhaled deeply, and an honest-to-God grunt came from the woman next to her. Keane was just…the total package, like caramel cream inside a bonbon. He tasted just as fine, too.

"Boom-Yay O'Shea!" the crowd began to chant. Keane's rear end tightened along with the rest of the mass of muscles so amply displayed in front of them.

He shook his head, as if the slight gesture would stop the excited crowd. Raising one foot, he went to step up on the scale, hesitated and stepped back. Placing his hands on his hips and turning slightly, his head swung around so he could look directly at…Willie. She shifted on her feet, wanting—*needing*—a sign of reassurance. Instead, he ignored her completely.

What the blazes was he doing? Why wasn't he stepping up on the scale? Damn. His actions spoke volumes. He wasn't going to make it.

He turned a fraction of an inch more, presenting them with a perfect profile as he assessed Willie thoughtfully. Raw restrained power reverberated off his chiseled form. Six foot two of sweaty, rugged male caused a surge of adrenaline to fire through her and her heart to thump wildly. The intricate tribal tattoo rolled across his body like a dark inky wave as his muscles flexed even with the slightest of movements.

Chloe shifted next to her but Logan didn't care how her companion responded to Keane. How could any woman not react to such male perfection? His face was downright beautiful, with strong cheekbones, a well-proportioned nose—no knots or bumps from fighting there. Logan licked her lips, remembering the taste of his own full ones.

The fine sheen of moisture coating his chest drew her gaze lower. Still lower, she sought out that mouth-watering indentation above his hipbone, fully displayed just above the elastic of his low-hanging briefs. But even her favorite spot didn't hold her attention long as her eyes continued downward, to the large bulge nestled within the thin cotton material. She felt drunk, lightheaded, giddy, knowing the full extent of what was barely concealed there. How so perfectly masculine he really was.

"Hold on there, Jerry. One more thing," Sal called as he jogged across stage with a towel in his hand.

The spotlight overhead seemed brighter, the heat more intense. She needed a towel, a moistened one. Something to cool down her raging libido.

Sal snapped the material and tossed one end to Jerry. They stretched it out in front of the scale and formed a sort of barrier between the crew onstage and the crowd. Low enough that the audience and cameras could still see their faces.

Against her will, her eyes shifted, then quickly lifted. No one held a candle to Keane in briefs…not even Marky Mark in those Calvin Klein ads. Close but not close enough. Interesting how the only piece of clothing Keane wore that wasn't black were snug, white briefs.

"Come on, Keane," Sal urged, breaking the sensual spell.

She snuck another peek. But as she glanced up, her eyes collided with Keane's bright baby blues. Something changed within them. The fine creases, so prominent when he was angry, softened. A hint of an oh-so-naughty smile tugged at his lips. He *knew* what she was thinking.

Then, without breaking eye contact, he stripped off his underwear.

The crowd picked up their chant of "Boom-Yay O'Shea!" Chloe let out a nervous giggle. And Logan, blushing furiously, tried her very best not to look. Not with the way Keane stood, studying her—almost daring her with his beautiful body.

A second later, his expression changed. He shook his head, turned and stepped up onto the scale.

"Whoa. For a second there, I thought he might wrestle ya down onto the stage," Chloe leaned in and whispered in her ear. With that, the girl fell silent again, probably checking out the eyeful of ass standing there on the scale.

His upper legs were muscular, thick and corded. His hips narrowed, setting off a small, tight ass, white as baby powder compared to his darker skin elsewhere. Powerful buns.

"One hundred sixty...eight pounds," Jerry shouted, pleased and excited. "We have a fight, everyone."

Babyface stepped toward the photographers and struck a pose with fists up and legs bent.

Keane stepped off the scale, uncaring that his jewels swung about with his abrupt movements. Bending at the waist, he grabbed his clothes off the floor, stepped into his briefs and sweats, and swiftly tugged the T-shirt back over his head.

Jerry reached out to touch his arm but snatched it back, thinking better of it. Instead, he gestured toward Young Gun, muttering, "Picture time."

Chloe gasped as Keane sauntered toward them.

Barefoot, his sneakers dangled from his fingers and his sweatshirt and coat were swung over an arm. "Let's go." With his free hand, he lightly grabbed Logan's elbow and nudged her to move.

"Piiictuuuure time, Keane," Jerry repeated loudly, sounding more anxious and irritated.

Keane led her across stage toward the curtain as if he hadn't heard Jerry's order.

Logan forgot about Jerry, the audience and the reporters snapping shots from the corral. Her awareness shifted to the man at her side. The lingering warmth from the fingers that had just been on her elbow.

The surprising feel of his big hand, as it touched the bare skin of her backside and propelled her forward.

He led her along a small corridor in the underbelly of the arena. Once at her locker room, he stopped, his palm leaving her ass to hit the door open. He followed her inside.

"What's wrong? You made the weigh-in. You were worried about it, right? I could tell by the way you were exercising. What else—"

"He's a kid." Keane hunkered down on a bench in front of the lockers. Dropping his gear, he braced his forearms against his legs. One palm ran across his face and his fingers skimmed over his brow bone.

"So, you'll win the first bout easily."

"You are so fuckin' naïve. How many fights have you watched?"

Logan looked down at him. His hand cupped a cheek as he studied the floor. Something was drastically wrong. He wasn't exactly angry...more pained. Upset.

"Huh?" Though rage simmered below the surface, judging by his prodding. He wasn't going to like her answer. "Um…I've worked five bouts, including yours. They all ended quickly. There was no need to stand around, watching and waiting. Jerry's so busy, he doesn't care whether I stick around while the other girls work. Up until now, I never wanted to watch someone get his face kicked in or getting slammed into a mat. It's not exactly my type of performance. So I usually keep to myself inside the locker room. But don't forget, I worked with Sal at the gym and observed many sparring matches, mostly with Jaysin Bouvine. I suppose for an Octagon Girl this sounds odd—"

"Now what?" This word was muttered in a voice so low, Logan almost missed it. She'd rather have him angry…she didn't know how to deal with this unidentifiable emotion. This wasn't anger, but something more frightening. Something deeper, more tragic.

She reached out, wanting to comfort him, and touched his arm. He pulled it back as if burned, but his head swung up and his blue eyes shimmered with raw emotion.

"Can't do it."

His words felt like a jab to the solar plexus and left her breathless.

"What can't you do, Keane?" she whispered, fearing the worst.

He wasn't going to fight.

All the time spent cajoling, worrying, training and hoping. Just as she was growing into her Octagon Girl role. Just when her future seemed brighter…

She waited for him to finish, for him to say that one word that would crush her dreams… *fight*. But when a few heartbeats passed without further comment, she marched away. Her hand was still warm from where she'd touched him, yet her throat had tightened from his rejection.

"Fuckin' Jimmy."

Fuckin' was right. And why bring Jimmy up now? It wasn't like he was here, telling Keane not to fight.

Her locker was around the other side. The shadows from the broken fluorescent overhead fit her mood perfectly. She entered the combo and glared at the stack of Octagon Girl outfits in cellophane, neatly piled on the top shelf and labeled with the number of each bout. Outfits that now wouldn't get used. Jerry was going to be pissed off at the unnecessary expense once he recovered from his coronary after learning Keane wasn't going to fight.

She swallowed hard and listened for Keane, hoping he was still there. But what did she expect, his emotions on a platter? Not his style.

Hastily kicking off her other sneaker and tennis sock, she headed toward the end of the row of lockers and turned the corner. His big body stopped her dead in her tracks.

"Keane," she breathed.

Time halted for a fraction of a second. Not a second after that, Keane was on her. She was grabbed, spun around, and pushed up against the hard locker by one hundred and sixty-eight pounds of tight-lipped male. His head angled and ducked in for the kill. He kissed her with such force her world tilted. Her body cried out for more. *More.* Forgotten were her pride, worries and any lingering sense of preservation. All she wanted was him.

His knee wedged between her legs. One arm slid around her waist. His free hand tugged at her top's knot and yanked it free. A low growl vibrated up lips. He stepped away and tore off his black T-shirt.

"Grab the bench."

She shot him a look. His jaw was tight, mean. But the heat in his baby blues spoke volumes. There was need there, a desperation she felt to the bottom of her toes. She said a quick prayer that Chloe wouldn't wander in, and then, as fast as her shaky legs could carry her, she did as she was told and found the bench.

He placed a warm palm on her back, bending her forward. She clutched the sides for support. Before she knew it, her boy shorts were sliding down her legs. She stepped one foot out of them, leaving her completely bare. A rustling of clothing behind her made her skin prickle with anticipation.

An arm wound around her waist, adjusting her. A hand ran along the length of her back. A knee pressed between her legs and widened her stance. His palm caressed her buttocks, one at a time. A slight slap caught her off-guard. She gasped.

"That's for what you did earlier. On stage."

His fingers fondled her moist folds. A shiver ran up her spine and continued, even though he broke contact.

He bent farther over her and reached around to grasp her breasts in his hands.

Feminine intuition took over. Her hips thrust back and connected with the hardened length of him. She wiggled.

Keane grunted.

His tip found her warmth. One smooth thrust and he filled her completely. A hand shifted from her breast to between her legs, his fingers expertly stimulating her nub. He slowly withdrew, plunged and massaged her until she was panting. He was everywhere at once: his wicked hands caressing her, his massive body surrounding her, his warm lips pressing against her skin, his careful handling making her entire body shake.

She wasn't alone in her need. His mouth paused from suckling her neck as he made a sound low in his throat. His chest heaved against her back as he pressed her forward.

Nothing had ever felt so wonderful. So beautiful. So naughty.

On the next earth-shaking plunge, he grunted, "Condom."

"Uh…"

"Shit, don't move, hear me?"

She heard his sneakers on the thin carpet as he left the locker room. Her skin flushed pink. *Splitting leotards*, here she was, bent over a bench with her bottom in the air, more than ready for what was coming next, in the women's locker room!

The door vibrated, and Keane returned.

"Lock it, okay?" She heard the metal lock snap into place.

"Told you to stay put," he said from behind her. Every fiber of her being was on high alert. She heard his clothes rustle as he stripped off his pants, a box hit the carpet, and the condom lightly snap before he rolled it on himself. "Now you're gonna get it."

He tugged her upright, rotated them around, and sat on the bench, yanking her firmly down on his lap with her back to him. Her legs automatically spread as she took him in one smooth thrust. Her groan filled the locker room.

His legs spread wider as he lifted her upward and tugged her back down, his pace quickening.

Her body shook as pleasure rolled over her.

A slight shift of her hips caused him to hiss. His pace became frantic. Small kisses found an ear, cheek, until her head turned and her lips captured his.

Incredibly, her body welcomed every rough inch of him. Squeezing her thighs into his legs, she arched at his withdrawal and dropped down on his thrust. The fingers at her waist tightened as their rhythm intensified. Like the swirling path of his tribal tattoo, her release coiled up within her, beginning deep within her womb and snaking its way up into her chest.

He must have sensed it. Slowing his pace, he ground up into her and urged her on. She rose and crested in a huge tidal wave of warm, slick moisture.

"Logan," he said, the low gravel in his voice resonating deep inside her. His arms wrapped around her body and he pulled her in tight. She felt his heart beating wildly as his chest pressed up against her back. He thrust up into her hard as his own wave followed her over and, together, they shattered.

Afterward, she felt his forehead pressed against her shoulder. His long, warm breaths caressed her skin. He wasn't the only one breathless. Mindless. Speechless. No words could describe what had just happened. She had never felt more connected to someone, so in tune to their every movement, every breath. A euphoric feeling filled her senses. It was even better than a standing ovation. She'd never felt so desired, so thoroughly *pleased*.

He sat back, but the warmth of his body remained.

She wanted him to hold her. What she didn't want was for him to let go.

One hand left her hip. *He's going to pull away.*

A good thing his back was to her. She feared her rush of emotions for this beautiful, troubled man were plastered on her face like a neon billboard. *This is a business arrangement with benefits to him. Don't get all adoration-eyed and...emotional.*

Another rush of pleasure ripped through her as she stood and slid off of his semi-erect penis. How was that even possible?

His other hand fell from her hip. Yep, aside from the hard evidence to the contrary, he was done. His purpose—and passion—had been served. Better for her to be the first to move away. Distance herself before he did. Without looking at him, she crossed the small space and bent over to retrieve her shorts.

"Leave 'em, baby."

He moved behind her, snatched the shorts away, and hurled them across the locker room. His arm snaked around her waist. He hoisted her up against his chest, and sauntered off toward the glass-enclosed showers, grabbing a towel from her locker en route.

Logan had always believed that of all athletes, ballerinas possessed the greatest stamina. She was happy to be gloriously, deliciously, and oh-so-thoroughly proven wrong.

Chapter 13

BUTTERFLY GUARD: When a fighter hooks both ankles inside an opponent's thighs to prevent him/ her from moving. Often used to get out of a Sub-mission Hold and often followed by a Sweep

Three times. Three locations. Three positions. That's what it took for his troublesome mindfuck to go away. Or so Keane wanted to believe. Except he was pretty sure the first time, with Logan bent over the bench, had done the trick. The other two times…well, he'd rather not dwell too deeply on the itch he couldn't seem to stop scratching.

Logan winced as she brought the dinner plates over to the kitchen sink. He tensed, almost spouted an apology, until he spotted the satisfied smirk of her lips. He relaxed, only mildly disappointed that the source of his itch was too tender for a fourth round. Hopefully, that meant she was also too tired to probe further into his fucked-up psyche.

He'd put her off the first time she tried questioning him about the comments he'd made in the locker room. Silenced Miss Inquisitive right smack in the middle of his foyer, too. Jesus, the couch or a bed would have been more comfortable. Yet Logan hadn't seemed to mind.

Shit, how was he supposed to explain his mind-fuck—the memories and *guilt* plaguing him—to her?

Since he'd gotten the news of Jimmy's death, Keane had taken care when selecting sparring partners and opponents. Tough, brawny meatheads out for blood were preferable. Well-trained professionals. Hard-heads who could take a punch and recover from a knock-out.

"One day, I'm gonna kick your ass," his reckless friend had joked.

Little did he know how his promise had played out in Keane's guilt-riddled conscience. Every night since his friend had died, Keane had had his ass kicked all the way from Pittsburgh to New York City, and back.

Except, fighting was all Keane knew. Up until Jimmy died, it had been one of the things he most enjoyed. Now, it was a necessary release. Nothing more, nothing less. With carefully selected opponents, ones he couldn't hurt too badly.

Jimmy wasn't the only reckless one. Why had he promised Logan he'd fight with freakin' *Jerry* picking his match-ups?

"Dessert?"

Logan had changed into that sweatshirt that drove him nuts, the one that fell off a shoulder. Her shoulder was bare, creamy and smooth except for the mark his lips had left on it. She waved the can of whipped cream in front of his face.

"Will this be too much sugar with the blueberries?"

He studied her and contemplated what he wanted to eat with that whipped cream. It wasn't fucking blueberries. Something must have shown on his face, and her cheeks flushed pink.

Damn, she was an unexpected surprise. His renewed rush of lust was a surprise as well. And Keane didn't dig surprises—hated them, as a matter of fact.

"I didn't know if consuming processed sugars before a bout was good for tomorrow's performance."

Here we go. Her unspoken question was tactfully hidden there. Are you up to fighting? Shit, what was he going to tell her when he didn't know the answer himself?

She pulled out the chair next to him and sat. He had to give her credit for the way she silently waited for his answer. The blueberries were carefully spooned out into two bowls, the canister shaken vigorously, and whipped cream painstakingly spiraled on top of each dish.

Still, he couldn't keep his hand off her. Redirecting his attention away from that shoulder, he reached out for a piece of loose blond hair and curled the soft strand around his finger before tucking it behind her ear.

The air sparked brighter with unspoken passion. She looked at him, green eyes alight with desire, her lips parted and ready.

It would be so easy to clear the table with one swipe of his arm. Press her onto her back and use her nipple as the topping for his whipped cream pie. Luscious and sweet. And too sore from his rough attention.

He hesitated. Her eyes widened in confusion. Then he pulled the stupidest, most asinine move of all time. He kissed her. But not his typical foreplay kind. Not the kind designed to get into a woman's panties or onto her knees. No, this kiss was light. Gentle.

She withdrew, stood, and then situated herself on his lap. Leaning into him, she gently kissed his forehead, cheek and lips. Her eyes were filled with emotion, a mirror image of his own. Full of… *Holy shit!*

His head snapped back. Moving her off his lap, he jumped to his feet. *What the fuck is wrong with me?* Maybe it was his cock doing the thinking here? That was the most likely explanation, though he didn't want to dwell on it.

"Gotta get up early before the fights. Get some sleep," he heard himself say. Avoiding her eyes, he stalked out of the kitchen. Tomorrow, he'd fight and win. Find a way to make the kid tap out. Without fuckin' killing anyone.

Every MMA fan within a hundred-mile radius of Pittsburgh was crowded into Mellon Arena for the first round of qualifiers. The crowd was a mixed bunch, from executives and blue-collar workers to college kids and middle-aged fathers. All passionate about this emerging sport, and easily excited when their favorite fighter pulled a surprise Kimura, Muay Thai or any other technical move that showed off their spectacular fighting style. Or so Logan had heard; she wouldn't know a Kimura from a kimono unless it showed up as part of a dance costume, not that she'd been dressed in any recently—except the red number.

Her cheeks flushed at the memory.

Hopefully, she'd find someone to serve as her translator for all these funny-named fighting terms. Tonight, after her Octagon Girl performances, she planned on sticking around for Keane's bout. Curiosity played a part in her decision, but she was worried too.

Her housemate was quite the enigma. One-two-three, he'd pinned her on the foyer floor and pushed inside her. Then four-five-six, she was crying out his name in a toe-curling climax. The beautiful man's stamina was mind-boggling—not that she was complaining. But that wasn't what worried her.

Since the weigh-in, he was either all over her or... withdrawn. After the final foyer tryst, he'd gone from blazing hot to Arctic cold in one second flat.

Logan closed her locker and tugged at the hem of her shorts. Maybe she was overthinking this? After all, Keane was up at dawn training and bulking up for tonight's fight. She'd barely gotten a passing grunt out of him in the few times he'd taken a breather. But he was here at the arena, and more importantly, he was ready.

"Is it safe for little ol' me to come in?" Chloe strutted around the lockers with a big ol' grin on her face. Confident and carefree, a far cry from yesterday's battle with the jitters. Logan was happy for her, impressed at how she'd overcome her shyness. This Octagon Girl might be here to stay.

"The janitors are all a-buzz about the mysterious flood in the locker room. Water drippin' off locker doors, lockers not anywhere near the showers. Large wet footprints...good thing I headed straight home. Lordy, who knows what I might have walked in on." Dangling Logan's blue boy shorts by the label, she waved them conspiratorially.

Logan laughed. Wow, Chloe had a sense of humor, all right. Grabbing the shorts, she tossed them into a nearby hamper.

"Rumor has it that drop-dead gorgeous fighter is ya boyfriend. He's hotter than the devil's anvil, for sure. Way dang envious!"

"A mutual business arrangement, that's all."

"Yeah, right! Friends with benefits, and so on... sugar, I near about fainted at the weigh-in. That hunk is hot for ya. The way he's fixin' on ya, pretty much sums it up. M-I-N-E."

"It's complicated." Logan sighed. Now she sounded like a Facebook status. Once more, she yanked down the hem of her shorts. Today's version were even smaller and more annoying, with the bits of red material gathering between her cheeks.

Chloe, clad in an identical outfit, giggled.

"Just you wait until you're up in the Octagon ring, strutting around with the wedgie of all wedgies." Logan tested the knot at her neck, making sure it was secure. Two miniscule strings were all this red and white tie-dyed tube top had to hold her in place. If her chest had been any smaller, it would have given her a uni-boob. "Guess Rachelle bailed. Jerry's going to flipping freak."

"Jerry shmerry," Chloe mumbled in a rich Southern accent. Every so often, it became more pronounced.

Texas, Logan decided.

"My daddy will have him fired if Jerry gets all buggy-eyed and puffy-faced on me again. Ya know, when he's mad, he looks like an ol' toad."

Yep, a Texas belle with a rich daddy, one who'd miraculously recovered from her nervousness back at the

weigh-in. What Logan wouldn't give to see Chloe serve
Jerry a slice of humble pie.

"Not a toad but a squirrel face. His eyes pinch in
and his cheeks bloat out like he's storing winter nuts."

Chloe burst into laughter. "I like that. Squirrel Face."

"Are you ready to check in with him and work out
which bouts we're announcing? I'm doing the welterweights."

"Ya certainly are."

Logan rolled her eyes. "You seem more comfortable today, Chloe. Aren't you nervous about working
with this crowd?"

They made their way around the lockers and over
to the door. Perhaps she should have asked herself that
same question, because her stomach tightened and her
pulse sped up. She took a deep dancer's breath, hoping
to calm her nerves.

"Nope. Not nervous," her partner announced. "Not
much of a drinker, but those five shots of Stolichnaya
in my latte done did me good. Soon, I'll be smilin' like
a half-mad bobcat."

Leaping leotards. Just add watch-out-for-pissed-
drunk-Octagon-Girl to today's list of worries.

The announcer's microphone pierced their eardrums
with a blast of feedback, hushing the crowd. Logan
clutched her ring card tighter. It was time for the welterweight bout to begin. She hadn't seen Keane all night.
Hopefully, he'd been warming up in his locker room
while she'd been busy strutting her stuff for two prior
bouts.

If she hadn't been so concerned about Keane, she
might have enjoyed herself. The fans and press had

grinned and wildly fist pumped the air, enthusiastic about her appearances. It reminded her of those last precious performances at Lincoln Center when her future had been full of such promise. At the time, Pierre had turned green with envy. Oh, if she'd only known then.

Logan yanked at her polyester wedgie. Aside from the wedgie, Squirrel Face and the tabloid press eagerly waiting for her to mess up so they could feed the drama hounds, the performer in her was beginning to like her temporary job as Octagon Girl. Hey, might as well enjoy the spotlight. And tonight she'd be heading home with a new, crisp paycheck.

"Ladies and gentlemen, all eyes on your favorite busty ballerina and Octagon Girl, Luscious Logan Rettino."

Later, she was going to have a talk with this guy about straightening out his boring, repetitive rhetoric. *Get over it already*, *buddy*.

She hoisted a number one ring card overhead. Knowing what to expect, she calmly moved down the ramp. Hundreds of eyes swung her way. A few steps up and she positioned herself on the rim of the cage. Cameras rose for a picture. With a hip thrust out, she took turns giving each of them a jaunty smile.

"How about an interview, Logan?" one young reporter yelled up at her.

A popular Aerosmith song filled the arena and saved her from responding. She pranced off in tune with the beat.

Chloe waved up to her from a seat below, smiling and cheerful with several bouts under her wing. Fortunately, she'd made it through her bouts without trouble. The shots in her latte apparently had waited to kick in.

The fan-boy babysitter in Logan's seat next to her had better not get too comfortable.

Before she knew it, her performance had ended. Glancing out toward the entryway, she searched for Keane. No luck. She propped the ring card up against the side of the stairs as she claimed her seat.

Chloe leaned in. "This is my first fight."

"Mine, too," Logan shouted back. Tonight, she'd announced the first few bouts but hadn't stuck around to watch them. She never did. Instead, she'd headed into the arena's underbelly, hoping for a moment with Keane. He was nowhere to be found. After that, Chloe had consumed most of her time, and at present, the little Texan lush was swaying in the seat next to her. Soon, Chloe'd be doing the Texas two-step, if she didn't face-plant first. *Better keep her next to me and within sight.*

The music took on an ominous beat. "Weighing in at one hundred and fifty-six pounds, with a black belt in Seibukan Jujutsu and with fists that pack a lethal punch, introducing welterweight Young Gun Willie."

Chloe burst into giggles beside her. "A black belt in Chewbacca juju-juice."

Logan grimaced.

Young Gun Willie moved down the ramp. Confident. Determined. A close-up of his face filled the wide-screen TVs. He pulled a reverse *Mona Lisa*, pressing his lips tight and mean while his eyes sparkled with delight. Logan wasn't sure what exactly being an expert in "Chewbacca juju-juice" entailed. Or if it was enough to keep Keane at bay. She knew Keane was worried about fighting such a young kid—the fact he was doing so at all was a little surprising after his reaction yesterday.

She hoped Willie would be okay in there, for Keane's sake as well as his own.

Willie made a grand showing of stripping off his clothing as he jogged around the inside of the Octagon cage.

"Now introducing the King of Tap Out, the Guillotine Grappler, the man who forced Andy the Annihilator into submission in seven seconds flat. The one, the only, Boom-Yay O'Shea!"

Logan jumped to her feet. Along with hundreds of other eager eyes, she searched the entryway at the top of the ramp. No music accompanied Keane's introduction. Only the murmur of the anxious crowd was heard.

Seconds seemed like hours. The buzz of the fans escalated. Logan bit her lip as her gaze fixed on that one spot, waiting. Hoping.

A swarm of trainers—Jerry's people—filled the entryway and began moving down the ramp. Keane was there, sequestered somewhere in the middle where Logan couldn't see him. The image on the Jumbotron screen shook as the cameramen jockeyed for a clear shot of him as well. Finally, it steadied. And Logan grinned.

In a typical fuck-you gesture, Keane had pulled the hood of his black sweatshirt over his head and now kept his chin down as he approached the cage. She didn't have to see his face to know what she'd find there. Clearly, this grand spectacle didn't fit his low-key style.

Keane entered the cage. Ignoring Willie, the crowd and Logan—did he even know she was sitting there?— Keane jogged in place and jabbed the air.

Sal did see her, waving to her as he positioned himself in Keane's corner.

"How about both welterweights make their way to the center," the announcer in the cage directed.

Instead, Keane came toward her, toward Sal and his corner. He worked his hood off. Despite herself, Logan gasped. The way his jaw tightened, plus the narrowed slant to his eyes, he looked downright mean. Very unlike the man who'd kissed her so gently last night.

Sweatshirt, T-shirt and pants were handed over to Sal in exchange for a bottle. Keane drank deeply and poured the remnants over his head. A fine line of water cascaded down his face, down his chest and along the swirl of his tattoo. Not enough to puddle the mat. But more than enough to make Logan's mouth go dry.

He shook his head like a puppy after a bath. Blinking away the moisture, his eyes fell on her. Briefly. He scowled and turned away. But at least Logan knew he'd spotted her. Knew she sat there, close to his corner. Just in case he needed her.

Fucking hell. He wished to God Logan had changed her mind. Keane had more than his share of problems right now. Not only did he have to worry about injuring this kid, but he knew, despite what she said, Logan had no clue how brutal a fight could be.

He could see her out of the corner of his eye. When he landed a well-placed kick and caused the kid to stumble, she covered her face. When he let Young Willie nail him in the mouth and bust open his lip—an effective tactic used to draw the kid closer for a takedown—she jumped to her feet. He needed to ignore her. Focusing on the kid took every ounce of his willpower. He couldn't afford a mistake. He might hurt him. Or worse.

He took his time, let Young Gun run out of ammo

from all the jogging about, defensive tucks and swivels he was so fond of using. The horn sounded. Five minutes had passed and Round One was over. Willie was winded and grinning like a madman. The silly kid thought he'd done well.

Keane followed Logan's movements with the Round Two ring card around the cage toward the stairs. There was no avoiding her. Willie stopped and said something to her. Something that made Logan blush. Every muscle in Keane's body flexed, ice-cold rage filling every pore. Right then, Keane decided he'd had enough with this kid. Time for a tap out.

"Your lip! Are you okay? Why did you let him hit you like that? Put your hands up next time."

Seemed like everyone was a mixed martial arts expert these days. Instead of voicing his thoughts, he grunted and pushed past her. Or tried to, before she blocked him with the damned sign. Outmaneuvered by a ring card.

"I've never had to announce a second bout. What is going on? Is it Willie's training in Chewbacca juju-juice or however you say it?"

"Jujutsu."

"Yes, that."

"Look. Announce this bout and then disappear."

"I'm an Octagon Girl, not a magician."

"Just do it," he said threateningly, dodging her sign to descend the steps.

Sal rushed over and handed him a water. They stood there next to the cage and waited for the blessed horn.

"Don't say a word." The old man closed his mouth, heeding the warning. Yet his eyes spoke volumes. Especially when they widened, and widened still further as

Logan strutted by in butt-hugging hot pants, skimpier and more fuckin' revealing than the last pair.

She finished, descended, and wouldn't you know it, brushed right past him, making sure to stay just out of his reach. "I can't. Chloe…" Luscious muttered. Dragging her up the ramp, locking her into a locker room, and ripping those shorts off her suddenly seemed more important than the fight.

Double fuck. Time to finish Young Willie off. Fast and with care.

The horn rang out.

Willie strutted back into the cage like a prized peacock. Certain of his abilities and underestimating his opponent. Stupid kid.

Keane waited for him and took a kick in the ribs. Willie thought he'd done some damage and lessened the distance between them. While a quick uppercut or kick to the kidneys would finish Young Gun off, Keane discounted it as too risky.

The next time Willie moved in, Keane struck. Ducking, he wove one arm beneath a leg and broke the kid's balance. He was on him in seconds and executed a quick, clean butterfly guard. Young Gun had nowhere to go but down on his back, with Keane on top of him.

He stretched Willie's arm across his own and with the other hand, bent it to the mat.

The kid deserved some credit; he tried bucking Keane off but without any luck.

"Tap out."

His face turned beet red and his teeth clenched together.

"It's done. Tap out." Damn it, either this guy was crazy or just plain stupid. He'd seen Afghani rebels who weren't this reckless. Probably quick with a grin or cracking a joke too. Just like fuckin'…

"Do it or I'll break your goddamn arm." Keane pressed harder and hyperextended the kid's elbow, enough to make him flinch.

Young Gun tapped out a second later. Blissfully unaware of the rush of emotions raging through Keane. Clueless, but safe.

Chapter 14

POSITION: How a fighter strategically places himself/herself during a bout

Logan was officially the last Octagon Girl standing. Soon after Keane's bout, drunken Miss Texas swayed once, then went down for the count in her seat. She thanked her lucky stars Chloe had held it together and passed out before the full effects of the liquor kicked in. The press would have gone nuts. One notorious ring girl was one too many in Logan's book. Logan became the go-to Octagon Girl for the night. Fortunately, no one paid attention to this slight change in plans.

Jerry was running around, frantically organizing the second wave of bouts for each weight class. Sal and Keane had disappeared back into the locker rooms. The media interviewed fighter after fighter, taking over any unoccupied space in the aisles, in front of the cage, and, eventually, inside the cage.

Logan took it all in from her place next to Chloe. Drawing attention to her condition would only garner negative press. Besides, Keane's locker room was likely overrun with fighters, making it impossible to speak to him.

The mention of welterweight contenders drew her attention to the reporters standing near Keane's corner inside the Octagon cage. As predicted, they'd pulled their mics up closer to their lips, preparing for what Logan thought of as the "pre-show," where they bantered about the fighters, revving up the crowd, and each other.

"Who's the guy you want to see go up against O'Shea next?"

"Several welterweights dominated tonight, showed crazy skill and easily won their bouts. Tenacious Beast is one. But my money is on O'Shea fighting either the Mad German or Caden Kelly. Mad meaning crazy because this German dude is totally insane. He's fearless, has a high tolerance for pain, and has a reach that is phenomenal—he can practically punch his opponent from across the cage."

"Ahem, I think that's a damn big exaggeration there, Felix. Let's not overlook the facts. The guy's six feet five, one of the tallest fighters in the sport."

Chloe groaned, but Logan shushed her. It was hard enough to hear the two reporters over the crowd. She didn't like the sound of the crazy German fighter, especially because if Keane had that much difficulty beating Willie, how would he stand a chance against this beast?

"Caden Kelly won big today," Felix continued, "but is he ready to go head to toe with O'Shea?"

"Rumor has it Caden's done with partying. Giving up on his playboy lifestyle. Feels he's not being taken seriously. He wants a comeback real bad."

"Caden Kelly might be the biggest surprise tonight. After all, with his modeling gigs and sports drink endorsements, he's not exactly hard up for money. So, this huge payout isn't his motivator. Why is he fighting again?"

"My guess is he's got something to prove. Maybe he's tired of being an Ultimate American Male underwear model. Remind everyone of the warrior beneath his pretty boy persona. Who knows? But we better be careful or he'll have our jobs next."

Logan knew who Caden Kelly was—what woman didn't? His more than ample package, wrapped up in virgin white briefs, was displayed on every billboard in Pittsburgh and probably across the country. She jumped to her feet and peered around for Jerry. Kelly was the perfect opponent for Keane.

The broadcasters thought so too. "You know, the MMA isn't professional wrestling or boxing. These guys have six-packs like nobody's business."

Eight-packs, but who's counting? Logan grinned, thinking about a certain somebody's oh-so-sexy business.

"O'Shea could easily land himself endorsements, too, with those good looks. I'm hoping these two pretty boys will battle it out next."

Logan's grin widened. Granted, Keane was drop-dead gorgeous but pretty boy? It just didn't stick.

"Hey, check out Luscious lusting after Boom-Yay."

Twist my tutu. Her gaze slowly lifted up toward them to find Felix pointing down at her. A second later, the widescreen television filled with her image. Logan froze, feeling like she'd walked in on someone butt naked at the very moment they'd realized they had company. Froze because of the sudden media spotlight. Froze because at this angle she blocked the camera from zooming in on Miss Comatose Texas sprawled out behind her.

Jerry saved her, waving wildly from inside the Octagon cage before snatching a microphone out of an announcer's hand.

"Quiet, everyone. We're about to announce the fighters moving on and their next match-ups."

Thankfully, the camera swung off her and toward Jerry. These bouts followed the standard three five-minute round format used by most organizations, except the UFC. If a fighter didn't submit to his opponent within this time frame, then a panel of judges decided upon the outcome. Jerry finished listing off the next match-ups in the featherweight class, and moved on to the next weight class.

What if Keane were up against the lunatic German? If that kid could make him bleed, what might the Mad German do to him? What if he got hurt? Or lost?

"Welterweight Boom-Yay O'Shea, weighing in at one hundred and sixty-eight pounds, will fight—"

"The Mad German!" a spectator screamed out, interrupting him.

Logan cringed. Her worst fears were coming true. From what the announcers said about this giant German, he was as tough as Pittsburgh steel. Not that Keane was anyone's pushover but she'd seen him fight that kid, how he'd let him get close enough to be hit, repeatedly. Would he use the same tactic on the German, and let himself be hurt in the process?

"Eh, not the Mad German." Jerry's face pinched in. *No, don't change your mind, Squirrel Face.*

"Why the hell not?"

Logan wasn't sure if it was the same irate fan or a different one, but whoever it was, he'd better put a lid on it. She jumped to her feet, and with her best Keane glare, swiveled around toward the obnoxious voice.

Jerry began again, with more assurance. "Boom-Yay O'Shea, weighing in at 168 pounds, will be fighting…"

She inhaled deeply. *Please let it be the David Beckham of the MMA world, Caden Kelly.* Surely Keane could beat an underwear model.

"Mr. Scorpion himself…Jaysin Bouvine."

The crowd went wild, but not in a pleased, happy way. Instead, mayhem broke out.

"You've got to be fucking kidding me!"

"What a scam. Bouvine is like a bulldog, man. All bark, no bite."

On and on the crowd screamed their displeasure. Jerry turned beet red. The announcers exchanged raised-brow looks. Chloe snapped out of her comatose state.

"What's going on?" Chloe shouted over the rest. "And what the blazes are ya doing, Logan?"

Logan raised her fist once more into the air and pumped it. *Yes. Oh, yes.*

Less than an hour later, Logan's fist was pressed tightly against her mouth, attempting to stifle her cries of dismay. "Boom-Yay" was a fitting nickname—and the horrifying reason why was being played out within the cage.

Keane lit into Bouvine over and over. Fists and kicks turned his opponent into a bloody mess. At one point, Keane lifted him straight up and sent him flat on his back on the mat. Bouvine barely got up in enough time.

With sick fascination, Logan watched it all.

"Whoo, did you see that, Felix? O'Shea snuck in a sharp uppercut. Absolutely stunned Bouvine." The excitement of the announcers was contagious, for all except Logan and Chloe.

Logan wasn't quite sure what she'd expected, maybe a bout like the earlier one, where Keane seemed to go through the motions, somewhat reluctantly too.

This fight left her breathless, because for the first time, she understood what MMA fans loved about Keane. His power was tremendous, but it was balanced by a grace within his movements and the intelligence within his attack. Every step, every turn was well-planned and controlled. He had fans on the edge of their seats, anticipating his next move, only to be dealt one surprise after another. He was an artist, a warrior, a man's man, and a woman's wet dream.

And, by the look of things, Bouvine's worst nightmare.

Bouvine dodged another fist by jogging away and heading straight back to Keane's corner. For some unknown reason, he began swiveling his head around in his manic the-scorpion-is-about-to-strike movement, as if he wasn't seeing stars from the elbow he'd just been nailed with.

Then he spotted Logan, and did something even more unexpected. He grabbed his crotch and gyrated his hips in a crude and stupid gesture. Was he still upset with her for abandoning Plan B, or was inciting Keane his sole purpose? Or—and she couldn't rule this out—maybe he was just plain nuts?

In mere seconds, all eyes were on Logan. The Jumbotrons filled with her scowling face. Several guys pointed down in her direction, displayed on screen behind her. One guy even stood up and mimicked Bouvine's gyration.

Logan prayed the arena floorboards would swallow her up. She'd worked so hard at coming to terms with her image. Like the flick of a switch, positive press was dimmed for negative news. Or in this case, utter humiliation. She slid down into her seat.

But not for long.

When Bouvine let go of his crotch, Keane was there. Step by step, Keane stalked the source of today's humiliation, backing him up until his back pressed against the cage.

Logan had a clear view of the savage expression on Keane's face and goose bumps formed on her arms. This was the reason Sal had warned her away. One mean, tough bastard had Bouvine trapped in the corner.

Cameras zoomed in on his face. His mouth was twisted into a sneer as he flexed his fingers. She'd never seen such unbridled fury. For a brief second, his eyes shot her way—or so she thought.

Then he struck. Keane was merciless. For two minutes, he pounded fists and slammed elbows, pummeling Bouvine left and right. His opponent looked stunned and shook his head, trying to awaken from his daze.

"He'd better watch out for Boom-Yay and his elbows," Felix's voice boomed over the sound system.

With Bouvine pinned in the corner, Keane pounded him with a series of blows to the head. Bouvine ducked the last, but his chin connected with a swift elbow. Then Keane pulled back his fist and punched. Blood splattered and rained down on the fighters and the spectators in the front row. Logan's row.

Down Bouvine went.

The referee began to count. An announcer screamed, "Boom-Yay wins with a knock out!" Chloe wiped her face, took one look at the speck of blood on the back of her hand, and promptly barfed off to the side of her chair.

Logan stood and wiped away splatters of blood on her cheek with the back of her hand. Appalled. Disturbed. Wondering why she'd never noticed that this man she cared so deeply for was so brutal. Violent. Someone to fear.

The crowd had witnessed his savagery, stood up and cheered for what she couldn't help but watch. Logan held her gaze steadfastly on Keane. His chest, sprinkled with blood, heaved. Fists hung at his sides. He'd placed a forehead against the weave of the cage and his eyes closed.

Bouvine clambered unsteadily onto his feet. Facing the audience, he shook his fist in the air as if saying, "I'm back up and ready for more." Keane ignored him.

Logan should have felt elated. He'd won again. Her paycheck from tonight would be enough to cover her remaining medical bills. The rest would be deposited into savings for her ballet school.

Bouvine left a trail of bloody footsteps as he pranced about while Keane stood immobile, his chin down and forehead still resting against the cage. Keane had won but from the way both men were acting, it seemed like Bouvine was the winner.

Keane straightened and his lips moved. "Fuck." With a jab to the net, he turned and stalked out of the cage, past snapping cameras and eager reporters wanting an interview. He moved past Jerry, who tried to gain his attention by wildly waving his arms. Sal appeared out of nowhere and ran off after him. At least someone was looking out for him.

Logan grabbed Chloe by the arm and led her through the crowd. Fortunately the press corps was madly re-capping the fight and paid them no mind.

Jerry caught up with them at the top of the ramp. "Hurry up! No one wants to see you two pretty Octagon Girls covered in blood. Looks like the Mad German's girlfriend—a freakin' model who happens to want some airtime—will take over for you. You can call it a night."

"I need to find Keane," Logan muttered, anxious to clean up and head home.

Jerry reached into his pocket and pulled out two thick green rolls of bills. "Remember, you get him here tomorrow and if he wins, you win. He's my ticket to a Tetnus championship."

He handed each of them their pay. So much for a fancy paycheck, but hard cash suited her just fine.

Logan grasped the wad of money. It felt heavy in her palm. A symbol of all she dreamed about her future. She was nearly back on her toes. So why did she feel like the ground had dropped out beneath her...again?

The downtown skyscrapers lit up the Pittsburgh night on the silent ride home. The hour was late, it had been almost eleven by the time a freshly showered

Logan had followed Keane out of the arena. She didn't know what to say…not that his somber, mean disposition invited conversation.

His hair was slightly darker, damp from showering. It had done nothing to improve his mood, though. His raw knuckles turned white around the Jeep's steering wheel and his narrowed eyes focused straight ahead as he drove.

Logan looked out the window. Fighting offered him a physical release—she understood that, dance had been her outlet—yet the man sitting next to her was wound up tighter than an old-school permanent wave.

A cold pea compress, a few Advil, and her special blend of chamomile tea should soften him up. A good night's sleep, too.

She stifled a yawn, worn out from the evening's events. A cab had been called for Chloe while Logan had waited near the locker rooms, unsure of Keane's mood. When he'd exited, he simply nodded for her to follow. A relief, albeit an annoying one.

Two lucrative fights were under her belt. Tomorrow, she'd deposit her roll of cash, head back to Mrs. Debinska's house, and give a kiss goodbye to that dusty pile of bills. The second wave of fights wasn't until evening. Not that she was looking forward to it, or to Keane being in the cage again.

Keane turned the Jeep onto his block. She knew he was a man of few words but he hadn't spoken the entire ride. Not once. Did he forget she was even sitting there?

She fiddled with her coat, casting a sideways glance toward him.

"I'm not gonna rip your head off."

Finally! She gave him her best as-if snort. "Well,

if you'd stop acting as if you've lost your best friend and—" The minute the careless words sprang out of her mouth, she realized her mistake.

Keane visibly stiffened.

"Keane, I know you don't want to talk about this, but bottling up your feelings isn't healthy. Can't we talk?"

He pulled up alongside the curb, put it into park, and jumped out. Before Logan could guess his intentions, he opened her door.

She clambered out and stepped toward him.

With his chin tucked in, he sidestepped her and made his way back around the Jeep. "Spare keys are in the planter." He pointed toward his porch.

"It's late. Where are you going?"

It took three shots of tequila and two Coronas for the knot in his neck to disappear. Keane contemplated the fourth shot being offered to him, though not from a shot glass. No, his two busty companions, tired of trading body shots with each other, had turned their attention to him. His next drinks were liberally drizzled between each set of tits. Rosie was an old pro at making a man hard, and tonight, she was in rare form.

"Come on, Keane. The drink's *on us*."

Except, he wasn't turned on. Shit, two obviously eager females within reach and drenched in tequila, and he wasn't biting. He was numb. Uninspired. Uninterested. Even in the amply displayed curves of Rosie's rack. They paled in comparison to another set of tits, more luscious and much more to his liking.

He rested his head back against the booth and closed his eyes. Envisioned nestling his face in her soft flesh and breathing in the clean sent of her skin. Feeling the warmth from her soft swells on his cheeks before his feast began. Hearing the sexy moans from deep within her throat as he suckled each taut nipple. Making her beg for more.

He thumbed his cell phone in his pocket. One brief phone call, asking Logan to catch a cab and pick him up. His cock stirred at the thought. He wanted her with such an astonishing intensity, his balls hurt.

The vinyl cushion shifted, making him open his eyes. Rosie's friend—what was her name?—knelt before him with both breasts thrust in his face. "I've heard a lot about you. Wanna know what you and I have in common?"

Keane grabbed his beer and took a long swig. He couldn't care less, but his lack of interest didn't stop her from talking.

"You're every girl's fantasy in the bedroom and I'm…"

"Leaving."

He choked on his beer. *Damn*. Logan had tracked his ass all the way to Finnegan's. His cock stirred in his pants as he caught sight of her, standing at the foot of the booth with her hands on her hips, glaring at them all. Too beautiful for words. Plus, she'd saved him a call.

"You too, Miss Kleptomaniac. Go prey on some other drunken fool."

Rosie scooted off the seat across from him. The woman on his cushion did so as well, though neither one made a move to leave. Instead, they folded their arms under their breasts and guarded him like two Rott-weilers watching over a bone. Logan was going to have her hands full with these two if he didn't say something.

With his mind dumb from drink, his responses were slow. Way too slow.

"The drink's on us," Rosie screeched. Amber liquid splashed Logan in the face and splattered onto her sweater. She sputtered in surprise.

"Leave us," he barked, giving full vent to his irritation. His bottle dropped onto the table, rattling from the force of impact. That did the trick. His two jealous companions stalked off in a huff.

The object of his earlier fantasy was here, sticky liquid dripping from her chin and glaring at him like he'd grown two heads.

He patted the cushion next to him, wanting her close.

Logan's lips tightened. She ran a hand across her face and then placed her coat on the knob on the side of the booth. Though her gestures were smooth and controlled, he knew her well enough by now to know she was pissed off.

She hesitated and then, grasping the hem of her sweater, worked it up and over her head. Fascinated and pleasantly surprised, he watched the tight, white camisole stretch across her breasts as she hooked her sweater on top of her coat.

Despite his best attempts to the contrary, he couldn't help himself—his lips raised into a broad smile. After all, it wasn't every day his fantasy came true, and someone so damned beautiful, someone he wanted so bad his cock hurt, ripped off her clothes for him.

She rolled her eyes, he caught that much as his gaze shifted to her face before she slid into the booth. He couldn't help but grin at her as he leaned closer.

"Baby, you're every man's fantasy."

"And you're hammered."

Damn, she smelled so good, like the vanilla cream wafers he'd stockpiled while in the Marines. He shifted and moved his arm around the bench behind her. Yep, sweet vanilla wafers. He'd give anything for a lick.

"Guess I scared away your entertainment."

He snorted, reaching with his free arm for a half-filled shot glass. Tequila swirled around the edge as he lifted it to his mouth. "Guess I'll have to make do."

She raised her eyebrows. God, he loved it when Logan got mad. Her green eyes brightened, her plump lips pressed into a tight line, tempting him to run a finger across the seam and pry them open. How her spine straightened, all stiff-back and proud.

"You know," she snapped, her eyes blazing, "when you say things like that, it makes me wonder why you rearranged our…business agreement. That was your fault entirely. Heck, I don't even know if you like me."

Leaning in, he nuzzled her neck. "Don't you, now?"

She went to move away from him but he wove his free hand behind her and firmly drew her in, closer. Still, her stiffening body said it all.

Lightly, he flicked his tongue over her earlobe. Then he exhaled. He felt her shiver against his arm. "I'm nothing but trouble."

She turned slightly and that green gaze bore into him. He knew her perception of him had changed after knocking Bouvine senseless. She'd witnessed the beast within that wouldn't quiet without a pounding. The rage inside him fighting its way out. In truth, that obnoxious ass deserved everything he got. Wait and see how fast he grabbed for his crotch next time. Keane just wished Logan hadn't seen it.

He'd scared the shit out of her tonight. *A sure sign of what was to come—of all that's in store for her, aside from a good time in bed.*

He downed the shot of tequila, shuddered and licked his lower lip. "You should have stayed home, baby. Fucked up." Even he knew his words were slurred. That fourth shot was a keeper. Sweet release numbed his mind.

She shifted away. Despite the message he was trying to make sink into that stubborn head of hers, he wanted her body closer…didn't want her to leave. He tugged her tighter against him.

"Why are you doing this to yourself? I'm trying to understand why you have such a strong aversion to fighting, yet you trained fighters for the Marines. Why is fighting only a release… When did it all change? Surely you must have enjoyed it as a trainer?"

"You're not gonna like the answer." He leaned forward and poured another shot. Shit, here we go again. Fuckin' Jimmy must be laughing his ass off from his perch high above, knowing how much Keane valued his privacy and also knowing that Keane was about to spill his guts. Unless… "I want you to do something for me."

"Um…okay."

"Pull your hair back off your shoulder."

"What? Why?"

He grunted. "Just do it, honey." His cock swelled in anticipation. He wanted a taste of her, a reminder of everything he had, even if it was temporary.

"I'm sticking to my guns this time, Keane. You're not going to dissuade me from getting some answers

here. Can't you see I want to help you? Want to understand you better?"

Shit. Trust me, you don't.

"Make you a deal. Do as I say and I'll answer a
question."

God bless her, Logan's eyes lit up, eager and full of
promise. He wouldn't mind waking up to those eyes
again…and again.

She swept her hair off of her neck and bared a shoulder blade. "What are you—"

Carefully, he drizzled tequila on her smooth skin.
"Body shot."

He ran his tongue from the bottom of her neck down
along her shoulder, then further down, following the tequila trail until it was no more.

Despite the liquor, he saw desire sparkle deep within
the green depths of her eyes.

He kissed her, ignoring his bruised lip. Deeper and
deeper until he lost track of place and time.

It was Logan who had to catch her breath first.

"Um…before we continue this *at home*, you owe
me an answer. What is it about fighting that upsets you
so much? What changed for you? I know it must have
something to do with—"

"Shhh." He pressed a finger to her lips. "I get to pick
which question."

She exhaled with exasperation, or so it seemed. "The
truth, okay. Let's have it."

"You asked me if I liked you."

"Huh? Oh, no. Keane, that wasn't what I meant by
wanting answers. You—"

He bent forward and pressed a light kiss on her lips.
That silenced her. Good thing, because the tequila was

really fucking with his mind. Better tell her now and show her later.

"Like you, all right? Baby, more than anyone. Anything."

Chapter 15

NO CONTEST: When a bout is too close to call, and there is no official winner

Her hot mess of a man weighed a ton. With Keane's arm slung around her shoulders and hers around his back, Logan finally managed to maneuver him into bed.

"Come here, Luscious. Need you."

"Sleep is what you need. What the bleeding leotards were you thinking, Keane? You'll hardly be in any shape tomorrow. Should I text Jerry and cancel?"

She caught his shake of the head on the pillow.

But her conscience battled out what to do. A few more wins and she'd be home free. All her future dreams would come true. She'd get her life back. With double the salary for working the next four bouts—*if*

Keane won—then there would be enough for a few months' rent on a dance school.

Keane's breathing changed. Now clearly passed out, he looked uncomfortable lying there on the bed, fully dressed. She studied his long dark lashes, a delicate contradiction to the brute strength of his muscular body. Fierce, raw gorgeousness. Sexy as sin. Yet battling some inner turmoil that made him gnash his teeth even as he slept. Her heart constricted.

His lower lip was swollen and a bluish bruise had formed on one cheek. And his poor knuckles were more raised and battered than the first time she'd placed her peas on them.

Frozen peas were a good idea. Two for his fists and one for his lip. She silently moved across the room.

"Fuckin' Jimmy. Told you to see a doctor." His voice was hoarse and filled with pain. The room grew silent but Logan's suspicions loudly resurfaced within her mind. Her instincts had been correct—something about Jimmy's death wreaked havoc on Keane's conscience. She froze in the doorway, hoping he'd reveal more. After a few minutes, it was clear Keane was out for the count.

With a sigh, she headed for the kitchen, retrieved the peas, and returned to treat this troubled, unconscious man's injuries. Peas gently propped in place on his lip, she restlessly roamed around his room. Should she text Jerry at this late hour and cancel Keane's fights?

She pulled her cell phone out of her coat, realizing that in her struggle to manage Keane, she'd completely forgotten to take it off. As she slid out of it, it occurred to her that Sal might know what to do. It was worth a try.

A quick text was sent: LOGAN: *Keane passed out drunk. Think he can fight without injury or do I cancel?* She took a deep breath, and waited. If Sal didn't respond soon, she had no choice but to call him and hope his ringing cell phone might awaken him.

Her cell phone vibrated.

SAL: *LOL. Typical Keane WOO. Always fights with a wik'd hangover. Company calls, gotta go.*

She shuddered. Clearly, Viagra had broadened the playing field along with Grandpa Romeo's WOO—*Way of Operating*, or at least that's what she thought the acronym meant. Poor woman.

Keane muttered incoherently. So, he'd done this sort of thing before…but why?

She crossed the room and stood before his dresser. Moonlight reflected off the dresser's mirror. Her eyelids looked puffy. Heavy. Tired. Her skin radiated tequila, the smell strong beneath her nostrils. A shower was sorely needed.

Leaning in for a closer inspection of her bloodshot eyes, something on the dresser caught her eye. A business card. Why was she surprised? Women from all walks of life, from bottom dwellers like Rosie to fancy Pittsburgh socialites—hell, why wouldn't they?—likely plied Keane with their telephone digits.

Against her better judgment, she grabbed the card and took a peek. A local phone number was listed, she could tell by the area code, along with a name—Dr. Susan Felter. But Logan almost dropped the card when she saw the message scribbled on the back: *Keane, You gotta call her. Best shrink around for PTSD. Love you, bro. Stevie.*

PTSD? As in Post-Traumatic Stress Disorder? Hell,

reports of guys coming home from Iraq and Afghanistan were getting more and more coverage in the news every day. Could this be why Keane had trouble sleeping? The reason he was so mixed up about fighting—training his ass off one second and bent out of shape about it the next?

She took out her cell and entered the number, just in case. It was late. She'd think this over tomorrow.

Right now, she had a bigger issue to tackle. Like the one sprawled out on the bed, breathing heavily.

Tossing her coat on a chair, she stripped down to her underwear and crawled in beside him. As if sensing her presence, he rolled toward her.

The icy pea pack shifted off his lip. She turned on her side and propped it back into place. With her leg wedged between his and her arm wrapped around his body, she snuggled in closer.

I'm going to find out what's bothering you and together, we'll fix it, she silently promised as she closed her eyes. After all, that's what you do when you love someone.

Logan wrestled with two bags stuffed to capacity as she unlocked the door. "Mrs. Debinska, I've brought you some groceries," she called to her landlady. She didn't hold a grudge against the woman. Who knew how the frail, elderly woman had ended up on videotape holding a bra? Logan didn't blame her for the negative press. The fault lay with a relentless, hungry media. And most certainly with her fame pimp of an ex.

Payback is a bitch. Soon, Pierre. Just you wait.

The thought perked her up. She'd woken tired and cranky. Keane had tossed and turned like nobody's business and when he was still, he muttered and swore incomprehensibly between clenched teeth. Delusional, him thinking falling asleep in a pissed-drunk stupor was helping him sleep better. She'd correct him on that fallacy later today.

Mrs. Debinska greeted her at the door. "Logan! *Witaj.* You are a dear. Thank you. *Daj mi to*, give them to me." Logan handed over one bag and waited for her to return from the kitchen.

"Hi, Mrs. Debinska. How are you? I hope the reporters have left you alone."

The old lady moved past her to look out the door. "I'm good…good. Eez here? Dat fighter?"

Crinkle my camisole. It seemed Keane's appeal extended to women of every generation and nationality. "Um, Keane isn't—"

Mrs. Debinska cut her off. Pulling her brown housecoat tighter, she brushed past Logan, stepped into the hallway, and eyed the front doorway. "Tak, Keeenee."

"No…no, he's not here."

The old woman looked crestfallen as she moved back inside her living room. "Okey-dokey. Bye." She took the second bag of groceries from Logan's hand and shut her door.

Inside, Logan's apartment was cold and empty. She quickly took inventory, making sure the few items of value were in place, which took less than a minute. Her painting had collected a coating of dust on its frame, as had the two Waterford lamps. *Soon, you'll have company, once a lawyer takes my case against Pierre*, she promised her few precious possessions. She shook her head. Clearly, exhaustion had rattled her brain and caused her to make promises to simple objects. After she'd written out the final checks and paid off her medical expenses once and for all, she'd take a nap.

The morning had been busy. Her savings account had breathed a sigh of relief from her substantial deposit—after paying off the balance of her bills, she was left with six thousand dollars which was enough to cover three months' rent on a place, plus start-up expenses if she started out humbly. It should have been enough to put a spring in her step. Except the grocery store was packed, the bus to Friendship was late, and thoughts of Keane preoccupied her mind. Thoughts about how to go about…helping him.

Just because she was falling for him didn't give her the right to butt into his business, right? Though that was exactly what she planned on doing. It all made sense now: Stevie's surprise visit to check up on Keane, the subsequent conversation she'd overheard, the brief note he'd left. His friend was trying to help.

Logan sat on her couch and indecisively thumbed Stevie's business card, the one he'd offered her back on the sidewalk in front of Keane's house. She'd kept it in her coat pocket, never thinking she'd need to contact him. Not until today.

Though before enlisting Stevie's help, she'd called Dr. Felter and had set up a tentative appointment.

That had been the easy part.

Long after she'd hung up, the doctor's words echoed in Logan's head. "Tread lightly but don't give up. He might not accept the fact that he has a medical disorder and needs counseling. A lot of guys don't—they see it as a weakness."

Keane was a walking billboard for PTSD. From what she knew about the disorder from the news reports, people who suffered from it tended to be easily aggravated. They frequently had trouble sleeping, flashbacks and headaches. Sometimes, their emotional switch faltered. Soldiers were trained to suppress emotional or traumatic events, and the transition to civilian life—and back into the warm bosom of their families—could be rough. Painful, even. Was this what was going on with Keane? He'd made it home safe but was now struggling with everyday life?

Hell, Logan had worked through the agony of dancing on blistered feet, growing so accustomed to it, it seemed normal. Keane had been conditioned to block out an entirely different kind of pain, the pain of war.

No way could she leave Keane to his own devices without support.

Logan removed her coat, took a blanket off her bed and settled down onto the couch. *You're not dealing with this alone, Keane.* She grimaced, remembering his hatred of surprises, and how poorly Stevie's first attempt at an intervention had gone. That's what Keane's friend had been trying to do—gently pressure him into getting professional help. She bit her lip. Why hadn't she realized this earlier, when all the clues had been staring her in the face?

She retrieved her cell and dialed Stevie's number.

Another intervention was in order.

This time, she was on board.

Logan awoke to the abrasive sound of a car horn. She blinked, adjusting her eyes to the darkness. Oh no, how long had she slept? Jumping off the couch, she grabbed for her cell phone on the coffee table. And blinked. It was 5:05 p.m. *Bleeding leotards.*

Her hair tumbled out of the loose ponytail and God only knew the condition of her makeup. But Logan didn't care. She had to talk to Keane about everything. Make sure he was physically and *mentally* fit to fight.

She grabbed her mail, tugged her door firmly shut and rushed down the narrow hallway. Breathless, her hand wrapped around the front doorknob and she yanked it open. Silently, she stepped out onto the porch. That's when the shouting began.

"Luscious, over here."

"Octagon Girl, who do you think will win tonight's fights?"

"Dat's her, Logan. Keeenee, dat fighter, eez no ere."

The entire front lawn was covered with cameramen and reporters. Her landlady, dressed in her brown housecoat, carried a pitcher of lemonade on a tray, as if she were hosting a summer picnic. Logan stopped as Mrs. Debinska appeared on the porch and waved at her. As if she hadn't just sold Logan out in the name of fame. Was Logan the only person who didn't want to be a celebrity? A celebrated ballerina, yes, but that was different. And impossible now.

Well, there was Keane. While other fighters talked the talk, pumping themselves up for the press, Keane took another approach—he scowled, effectively keeping everyone at arm's length. Or he disappeared. The man valued his privacy more than Logan did.

Fortunately, he wasn't here to witness this wild spectacle.

Squaring her shoulders, she made her way down the stairs. All that needed to happen now was for someone to roll out a red carpet along the sidewalk, which was bordered on both sides by the press.

"Is your boyfriend Boom-Yay O'Shea going to win tonight?"

"Speaking of Boom-Yay, what do you think of O'Shea's nickname? And I'm not talking about fighting, if you get my drift?" *Who uses that expression anymore?* Logan picked up her pace and stepped away from the smarmy paparazzo.

She prayed they wouldn't follow her down the block. The bus schedule was unpredictable and it would be beyond humiliating if the cameras followed her there just to catch her waiting for her ride. *Soon, I'll get my car fixed and not be at the mercy of public transportation.*

"Logan, would you like to comment on Pierre's latest statement?"

Well, that explained a heck of a lot. Her ex had stirred the pot once more. She was *really* getting tired of this. She tucked her chin in and kept walking.

"Rumor has it that Pierre's coming to Pittsburgh to attend tomorrow's final qualifiers. He's taking a break from filming *America Gets Its Groove On*. Says he's a big fan of the Mad German and is anxious to see him fight."

The faux smile slipped from her face. She stopped short. *Remember, pride cometh before the fall. Don't respond. Don't do it. Don't…* The self-control she prided herself on snapped. Stiffening her spine, she turned to face down the reporters. "Why, I didn't know Pierre was an MMA fan. I'll have to introduce him to Boom-Yay, personally."

"You sound confident that O'Shea will qualify for the final bouts?"

Logan turned and gave the cameras a jaunty smile. She waited until everyone had framed their close-up money shot for effect. "He's fit and has never been more eager, more prepared. O'Shea is ready to kick butt and smash some faces. Pierre won't want to miss it. See you tonight."

The press buzzed with excitement over her statement. Her lies. Given the condition she'd left him in, Keane might not last until tomorrow. Hell, she wasn't sure he'd even make it to the arena tonight. And if he did, she wasn't even sure if she wanted him to fight, knowing what she now knew. The only truth in the pack of lies she'd told was about Pierre. How he was going to get a close, bird's-eye view of just how violent an MMA fighter could be—when Keane planted his fist in his face.

And if Keane wasn't available, then the world was going to experience their first Octagon Girl tap out.

Chapter 16

CROSS PUNCH: A go-to power punch thrown with the back fist, and with a fighter's full weight behind it

Mayhem broke out in Mellon Arena a few hours later. Jerry looked as though he'd cashed in a winning lottery ticket. Sal gestured wildly with two thumbs up. The crowd chanted, "Boom-Yay, Boom-Yay, Boom-Yay." Day Two of the qualifiers was well underway, with Keane easily winning his first of two bouts.

Tenacious Beast had been a solid opponent. Hell, afterward, he'd even tapped Keane on the elbow in silent acknowledgment, as if saying you-just-kicked-my-ass-and-I-didn't-feel-a-thing. Rule number one in fighting was to know when you'd been dominated and to learn from your mistakes. If Keane's performance was as clean as this in the next three bouts, he'd have the championship in the bag.

For a moment, he'd felt like his former self. Let the rush ride over him, the kind a fighter gets when facing a challenging opponent. Guys like those he'd fought those first few years in the Marines, leading up to his qualifying for MCMAP and fourth-degree black belt. He'd handled them quickly and efficiently. Shit, he missed those days when fighting was such a sweet adrenaline boost instead of one massive psyche-fest.

His life had become way fuckin' complicated.

And, despite himself, Keane found himself searching for the woman who'd stirred up all his shit. He rubbed his jaw. Damned if he could figure out where she'd disappeared to.

His recollection of last night was vague at the very best. Rosie and her friend. Logan pissed and glaring. Jimmy laughing down at him because…why? Hell. His friend had always had a way of seeing past all Keane's bullshit to the heart of the matter. Jimmy'd told it like it was. But had he?

Did I say those three damning words? Not that it mattered, it felt like he did, which was just as bad. Not only did she stir up his shit, but did it with a big-ass spoon, causing waves so high he thought he was drowning.

She'd stayed with him through the night, the warmth from her head on his pillow still present when he'd awakened. Crazy how much he'd wanted her next to him. He'd inhaled her light vanilla scent, though it was faint compared to the strong tequila smell coming off of his own body. She was gone when he'd gotten up and hadn't come home by the time he'd left for the arena.

Logan had somehow managed to get so far inside his head that just the sight of her sent him spinning. Man alive, he couldn't deal with it. She was becoming a drug he craved, knowing it would only lead to pain. Hers. And his own.

Last night's drunken confession had made him feel vulnerable. Another mindfuck—he couldn't endure it, he already had enough emotional baggage to deal with. He was never going down that bloodbath of a road again. He didn't want to examine his *feelings*—or feel anything at all, for that matter. All he wanted was peace.

Fuck, he had to set the record straight in case she'd gotten the wrong idea about them.

An attractive, dark-haired Octagon Girl smiled shyly at him as she lifted her sign overhead and announced the next fight. He brushed off a few reporters and headed back toward the women's locker room. His second bout wasn't for another hour or two, since his had been one of the first fights of the evening.

Laughter greeted him, a throaty, sexy sound that made him lengthen his steps. At the end of the stadium corridor, he stopped short.

Logan stood with her back against the cement wall.

Keane looked his fill. Camouflage sneakers at the bottom of long, shapely legs. Mid-thigh-length shorts in a shade of green similar to his military jacket. Less revealing than her two previous outfits. From there up, all he saw was skin. Tight stomach, a rib cage that accentuated her midriff without making her appear anorexic, and…more skin. Two triangular camouflage patches held in place by tiny strings *almost* covered her luscious rack. Pulled high, the bottom swell of each breast played peek-a-boo every time she goddamned breathed.

From a few feet away, Keane noticed it all. And he wasn't the only one.

Some fighter leaned in toward her and had his hand on the wall by her head. Keane couldn't hear what he was whispering but there was no doubt what this player was up to.

She was smiling at this guy and laughing at the sweet nothings he was whispering in her ear.

Last night, he'd been in a similar position, had run his tongue across that expanse of her soft skin, from her neck and lower. He'd seen desire spark in her green eyes. She'd wanted him, perhaps even more than she wanted him to fight. Lord knew, the feeling *was* mutual but going nowhere. But seeing her eyes light up for this moron made Keane want to punch the cement wall.

Asshole. Damn, he must have said it aloud. They broke apart and two sets of eyes shot his way.

"Keane, come meet Caden Kelly. He's a welterweight, too. And still in the running for the title."

Figures. The freakin' underwear model. Keane glared at him.

Both smiles fell. Keane had to give the welterweight credit, his eyes didn't shift away like a meek mouse. The muscular model straightened and folded his arms across his chest.

"Breached the walls of the wrong hen house, I gather?"

"Looks that way."

"No harm done. This gorgeous hen wasn't pecking anyway. See ya around, Logan." The guy offered her a quick grin before striding off down the hallway.

"Did he just call me a chicken? What is it with this man lingo?"

Keane closed the distance between them. He smoothed his hands over her breasts and, because he couldn't help himself, tugged the two specks of cloth lower and tucked her lusciousness away.

She gasped and her pupils darkened. Until her eyes refocused on the fury within his gaze, and then a second gasp escaped her lovely lips.

Here he'd been worried about exactly how to wedge some big-ass wall between them without hurting anyone's freakin' feelings, and she'd been flirting with this asshole. *Good. That's what you fucking want, right? To let her go before things got too deep, too complicated, too dangerous?* He inhaled sharply, letting the frustration boil up inside of him and drawing on it. He had to hand it to her, she'd just made his job of distancing himself a hell of a lot easier.

"I've been looking all over for you." She reached into her pocket and pulled out two blue pills. Tylenol or some shit that wasn't gonna help in the least. Still, she held them out for him to take. "Take these. The water fountain is on the wall. I'd be a bear too with that hangover."

He took the two pills, squeezing them tightly between his fingers as he stalked over to the fountain.

"You're not going to like this. But I know how much you dislike surprises…"

One after the other he popped them into his mouth and swallowed hard. Water wouldn't help the rawness within his throat.

"What?" he grunted, turning toward her.

"I called Stevie and he's coming to Pittsburgh. He'll be here tomorrow."

What the fuck? "Call him back. Tell him—"

"Part of our business arrangement. The *new* one."

"We're sticking to the original plan. Got it? I fight, we fuck, and then we move on with our lives. *Separately.*"

He saw her flinch. Then she stiffened and put her hands on her hips. "A lot of guys returning from Afghanistan are struggling with PTSD. You're not alone, Keane. And Stevie and I want to see you through this."

"What else did that asshole tell you?"

She sighed, and lowered her voice. "That a professional is the best kind of help. You can talk to a physiatrist, Dr. Felter."

"Jesus, the shrink Stevie's been harping about?"

Logan grimaced at the fury in his tone, but plowed ahead. "She knows techniques for coping with this disorder. You said so yourself, the booze doesn't work. Hell, last night is proof enough."

"You wanna help me?" he demanded. "Worry about your own shit, and leave me to my own. I'm not talking to a goddamn shrink." Fuck. The last thing he needed was a professional stirring up memories he was trying to bury—right alongside Jimmy. "Call that troublemaker back and tell him to stay out of Pittsburgh."

"There's nothing to be ashamed of—"

He stepped back away from her. A preventive measure. No way would he ever strike her or physically harm her, no matter how upset he got. Not intentionally. Unintentionally, now that was the bigger problem. But right now, he felt like she'd kicked his ass, like he'd been kicked in the kidney in a move so evasive, it made him dizzy.

"Do you want me to fight or not? Because if the answer is yes, this topic is dead. Understood? Or I walk."

She stood, with her lips tight but her eyes thoughtful.

Jesus. Was she about to say no? He had to get away from her. *Why don't you cut the freakin' cord and quick.*

"There's one more thing I have to tell you."

He held up a palm, as if it would stop her. He didn't like the funny expression on her face. Not. One. Bit. "Look, I've got a fight to win."

His heart was pounding along with his head in one mindfuck of a performance. Man, he needed a drink. Or better yet, a brawl. Shooting her a fierce scowl, a clear warning for her not to follow him, he stalked away, his strides long and purposeful.

The alarm in her tone echoed off the cement walls, glaring like a bullhorn signaling a tap out. "I'm not going to let you just slip away from me. You hear me, Keane?"

Logan made her final turn of the day around the Octagon cage to Metallica's "Sandman." Appropriate introductory music for Keane's second bout on his second evening of qualifiers, especially the bit about hushing and not saying a word. Boy, those lyrics fit him to a T.

Boom-Yay's fans enthusiastically sang along. She nodded in silent solidarity.

Now what?

Keane wasn't ready to accept that he had PTSD and was set on fighting, as if he thought it was a cure or something. However, she'd come to suspect that Keane's bigger fight came after his wins. He didn't relish his victories like most athletes. No, instead he acted like he'd *lost*. If she pushed him away, not only would he stop fighting like he'd threatened earlier, he'd distance himself from her, no doubt about it. Sure, she needed the money from his wins. But placing herself in a position where she couldn't help him, that wouldn't bode well for the intervention plan.

A no-surprise kind of plan Stevie and she had discussed in length over the phone, with a third-party conference call to Dr. Felter. It was going to take a lot of patience, compassion and perseverance, helping this very private, strong-willed man. But no one said it would be easy.

Hell, it had to be such a struggle on Keane's end, as well. Fighting, booze, pills—those were Keane's crooked crutches. A temporary escape from the trauma. Not a permanent solution only a psychiatrist could provide.

But sex? Was that really also a coping mechanism?

Logan blushed, refusing to accept Dr. Felter's take on the matter, having first-hand experience of Keane in…action.

Her skin still tingled in memory of his tongue's trail across her body. Her mind raced over the snapshots in her head: Keane's sultry smile, the lust in his eyes, the way he looked at her as if she were the only woman in the place. His words made her heart dance: *Like you, all right. Baby, more than anyone. Anything.*

Crazy to think how her playful lover had morphed into such furious warrior mode. PTSD was the likely culprit for his swift changing moods. Perhaps after finishing the qualifying bouts and Tetnus, he'd retire from fighting? That would be the healthiest choice— the MMA world was brutal enough without him in it.

But how do you help someone who isn't looking for help?

By showing him you care, she thought.

By showing him how well a person managed after a fall, when they had to dig deep to deal with the bruises, the external and internal kind.

This morning, before she hit the grocery store, she'd found a potential dance school near her apartment. The rent was reasonable and the money she'd earned so far was enough to cover a few months and construction expenses to convert the space into a proper studio. The downside was that her class size would be limited due to the small room, which was why she was debating holding out for a more suitable space. Plus, three more wins, and she'd have peace of mind in knowing that not only was her bank account healthier, but there'd be money for advertising and promotion to build up her roster.

Everything hinged on Keane winning the next three bouts. *A win for her, but at what cost to him?*

She tugged the sign higher and headed for the stairs.

"Luscious, Luscious," the raucous crowd chanted, bringing her attention back to the present.

Funny how she didn't mind her nickname anymore. The deep, throaty ways Keane said it replayed in her head, a sexy cacophony.

The music recommenced, signaling that Keane was about to enter. But she wasn't going to let him stalk by on the ramp without seeing her. He'd sidelined her earlier. No way was she going to hang back in the shadows.

In fact, she was about to deliver a surprise cross punch of her own, and prayed he could take it. It was the easiest-yet-hardest way of making him realize how much she cared.

What Keane needed was tough love mixed with a healthy dose of attitude, accompanied by a swift Octagon Girl kick. A reminder that his stalking away from her wasn't acceptable. She inhaled sharply. A few seconds later, she'd channeled enough frustration to fill an arena, providing her with enough courage to propel a Nike-clad foot forward.

Keane and his entourage headed down the ramp, and Logan moved up it.

A beefy arm snaked around her waist, pulling her close. "Gotcha, Octagon…ahh!" the guy screamed and bent over to cup his privates.

"Did you see that, Luscious kneed that guy in the balls. Wouldn't want to piss her off," Felix said.

You hear that, Keane?

Cameras began snapping, probably hoping to catch them lip-locked on the ramp. That was *so* not going to happen. Boom-Yay needed a wakeup call without lustful distractions.

Sal caught sight of her first and motioned for Jerry's guys to make room on the ramp. When the entourage fanned out and moved past her, she spotted Keane. It felt like déjà vu. His dark sweatshirt was unzipped, revealing eight-pack abs and pecs so taut a quarter could bounce off them and keep on flying. The sight of him stole her breath away.

Handsome playboy Caden Kelly had nothing on Keane.

She squared her shoulders, knowing what she had to do, and getting all hot and bothered by him wasn't helping.

He raised his eyes to meet hers.

For a second, it was just the two of them, no entourage, no crowd, nobody but them. She wasn't sure what she saw in those deep, blue pools. Regret perhaps. Lust, most likely. Caring and adoration, she hoped with every fiber of her being.

Whatever it was, it was gone with the narrowing of his eyes. Just as well, his actions justified her own.

Keane shifted off to the side and made room for her to pass.

She sidestepped too, blocked his path, and forced him to stand still or plow smack into her. He stopped dead in his tracks.

The fine lines around his eyes deepened. That fierce look of his was likely to reach uncharted depths after she'd had her say. He needed to understand exactly why she'd overstepped the fine line between them. Why she'd butted into his business, which was likely what he'd thought she'd done.

His entourage had moved on down the ramp and out of hearing range. Perfect.

He stepped sideways to follow.

So did she.

"For fuck's sake, Logan." He yanked his hood off his head and rolled his neck. But all of his attention was on her.

"I wanted you to know I'm holding you to our business arrangement, minus the perks."

"Great. Later."

She took a deep breath and plowed on.

"I have one more thing to tell you, Boom-Yay, and I'm not moving until I do it."

"That's what you think." Quick as lightning, he wrapped an arm around her waist, tugged her close and scooped her up. His body shifted around.

No way was she going to let him manhandle her like a sack of Pittsburgh coal. Two could play at this game. She wove her arms around his thick, stubborn neck but did so just as he was relaxing his hold on her. Which resulted in her scrambling to hang on to him, with her chest pressed up against his own, before he tugged her in tighter.

Obstinate, seemingly mean, strong in mind and body, he was all that. But the bottom line was his actions spoke volumes; he *cared*. Which is why it was so important to tell him the truth. "Second order of business. Only then will I let you go."

Oh, she had no intentions of letting him go—for tonight, perhaps, but not in the future. He was as much a part of her future as her own dance school.

"Logan, the whole goddamned arena is watching us. What?"

Pride cometh before the fall, Logan. This was the biggest gamble of her life, her *heart*. Pride was not going to hold her back. She swallowed hard.

"I love you."

Jimmy's mindfuck dulled in comparison to the one Logan had just hit him with.

"Later," he managed to growl out as he placed her down gently. He couldn't freakin' breathe. The quicker he put some distance between them, the better.

"Man, what I wouldn't give to be you. The way Luscious was looking at you...what was she saying?"

"Zip it, Sal."

Keane shook his head. Hell, he didn't see that one coming. Love him? She hadn't seen all of his bullshit yet. Didn't know what a miserable, guilt-ridden bastard he was. A poor excuse of a friend. Too bad Jimmy wasn't around to explain it all to her. Maybe she had a thing for fuck-ups. Shit, look at that loose-lipped, tights-wearing ex of hers.

He ripped off his sweatshirt as he approached the cage. Whoever Smithy was, he'd better be ready. Keane meant to draw blood and work out his frustrations in the way that worked best for him, with quick kicks and solid, deadly fists.

This bout, he'd win for himself. Prove he could do this, that he was in control. The final two would be for her. First fulfill his fucked-up needs and then their business agreement—which ended tomorrow.

Rolling his neck, he headed into the cage and took to his corner.

"You've got this one in the bag, O'Shea. Mickey's a young one, fresh out of MMA boot camp. No match for your experience."

Sal's excitement wasn't mutual. Fuck, Keane had missed Jerry's announcement. That jerk-off was trying to make damned sure Keane qualified for Tetnus by pairing him up with these kids. Didn't he get it? Keane didn't want to fight opponents green behind the ears. Opponents who might get killed.

Jerry announced the fighters, the bell rang out, and after that, the bout was a blur. All Keane was conscious of was that his frustration was building and that no way in hell was he gonna beat down on this kid.

In fact, he did the opposite.

"Looks like Boom-Yay's new nickname should be 'No-yay.' His opponent is kicking the living shit out of him."

Not to be outdone, a second announcer added, "It's hard to believe this is the same guy who'd put such a brutal beating on Bouvine."

The referee jumped in between them. Keane stalked over to his corner and spit blood into a small bucket.

Sal shouted at him, snapping him out of his daze. "Keane, what are you doing? You're not even putting your hands up. What did Logan say to you on the way out? Did she cut your balls off or something?"

More like a kick in the balls. Logan and her *I love you.* Was she out there somewhere watching all this? Watching how weak he was, how goddamned *broken*? His fists clenched as all of the frustration holding him back peaked.

Spitting another wad of blood into the bucket, he turned. Smithy came at him with a high kick. Keane blocked it with his left arm and pushed the kid's leg off to the side, fucking up his equilibrium. This left his opponent well open for attack.

Keane balled up his right fist, brought it back, and punched.

It connected with the welterweight's chin. He was literally lifted off his feet from the impact. In the next hauntingly familiar second, the kid was out cold.

"Boom-Yay lands a solid jab and Michael Smith is down."

"O'Shea wins with a knock out!"

"Smithy's not moving."

Everyone was shouting but Keane zoned them out as he hovered over the prone kid. "Get a damned doctor, fast," he hollered, but the huskiness in his voice smothered his words.

He looked away from the kid. Spotting Jerry's smiling face as he talked to a reporter by the stairs, Keane stalked over to him. Grabbed him by the throat. Pushed him up against the cage. Ignored the cameras flashing.

"Ten seconds for a doctor or you're gonna eat your teeth."

Keane released the shaking man, who sprinted down the stairs like the IRS was about to hand him an unpaid tax bill. He strode back to see the damage he'd caused once more.

The kid groaned. Sal placed a wet rag on his head as Keane stood there, helplessly.

The air in his chest compressed like a balloon before it burst.

An emergency crew brushed past him, the hose from the oxygen tank they carried swinging.

He needed a hit of O2 as well, feeling dizzy. But first, the kid…Michael.

The oxygen did the trick and Smithy's eyes opened. Blissful semi-consciousness.

"Is he all right?"

"Yeah, we're going to lift him outta here and give him a full check-up," an EMT yelled up from his crouched position next to the kid. "Boom-Yay, think I can get an autograph later on?"

Keane flexed his sore knuckles. The cheering crowd, the media and everyone else shouting was too much to bear. Fans yelled and pointed, as if they'd just witnessed the best thing since Mike Tyson bit Evander Holyfield's ear off. In Keane's mind, this was as equally appalling.

He'd had enough. The kid was in good hands, with professionals equipped to help him. They'd give him a thorough examination and make sure no lingering effects remained, only to be triggered at some later date. Or so Keane hoped, from somewhere deep within the pit of his shattered soul.

Chapter 17

KNOCK OUT: When a fighter is unable to get up off the mat and back on his/her feet due to a lethal strike

"Logan, any comments about O'Shea's knock out?"

"What do you think about the beating he put on Smithy? One punch. Utterly ruthless."

"Do you think Pierre is looking forward to being introduced to Boom-Yay tomorrow night? *I'd* be worried after watching how O'Shea turned the bout around and utterly annihilated Mickey Smith."

Keane watched from his spot by the exit as Logan's blond head snapped up. The swarm of reporters moving along with her stopped almost as abruptly as she did.

That braggart announcer Felix chimed in—another

freakin' guy with a hard-on for her. "God knows how O'Shea managed it, after getting his ass kicked, bleeding all over the place with a busted lip and an ugly gash on the eyebrow…you okay, Luscious?"

"I didn't see the fight. Was he hurt?" Even from this distance, the worry in her voice rang out. He ran a finger along his swollen brow bone. She was about to hear, first-hand, what a violent son-of-a-bitch he was.

"The medics think he'll be okay. Concussion, so they'll keep him at Pittsburgh Medical Center overnight."

"Oh my God. Can one of you give me a lift?"

Keane took a step forward. And stopped. If she wanted to go rushing off and check on the kid, who was he to stop her? Hell, he had better things to do with his time right now—one of them involved Red Label Johnnie.

"Come on! You guys owe me big time for pestering me. Someone drive me to the hospital. How bad was Keane injured? God, this is all my fault. Here's news for you: I don't want him fighting anymore. Print that."

A couple of reporters had moved aside, giving him a clear view. With her hands on her hips and her eyes fired up, Logan was a force to be reckoned with, a tigress protecting her cub.

As it turned out, *he*—the meanest, surliest, most-standoffish bastard of them all—was the cub.

Damn. His temple throbbed and his lip hurt like shit. *Logan wasn't worried about Smithy. She was worried about me.*

The swarm buzzed with confusion but no one corrected her as they slowly moved out into the parking lot. One reporter dropped his camera bag, noticed Keane when he scooped it up, and sounded out the alarm. "Hey, there's O'Shea over by the exit."

Too late to duck. Keane had two choices: head back inside or join Logan in the parking lot. He looked in her direction and their eyes met through the parting crowd of reporters. She looked beautiful and surprised. What, was she expecting him to be laid up in some emergency room?

"What are your comments on tonight's knock out?"

Another reporter with a Napoleon complex shoved a mic in his face. "We'll ask you the same question we asked Logan. What are you going to say to Pierre tomorrow night, when he makes a semi-announced celebrity appearance at the arena?"

He ignored them, strode toward Logan and muscled his way between the few foolish reporters who'd blocked his way. Her eyes were wide. Her lips pressed tight. She seemed so small, so fragile standing there amidst the persistent reporters.

"I thought you were in the hospital?"

This wasn't good. It was better if she didn't care. Easier to drop her off and head off toward the downtown city lights to deal with his demons. Alone.

"Wrong guy." He tucked his arm around her waist and tucked her against his side. "Let's go."

"Lead the way."

Reporters followed but gave up their chase once they'd reached his Jeep. He yanked the passenger side door open and nodded his head toward the seat.

God, he was wired up. Climbing into the driver's seat, he cranked up the heat and noted the time on the dashboard clock. Ten forty-five. No way was sleep a possibility—not when the need to bash someone's head in or drink himself senseless persisted. He felt like howling at the moon from all the emotions raging through him. *She loved him.*

His knuckles tightened around the steering wheel. He didn't deserve her. But he didn't have the strength to push her away. He should have done it earlier. He should be doing it right now.

Logan sighed, a throaty, just-woke-up sound that did it for him. She was buttoned up tight in her fancy coat with her long skinny-jeaned legs stretched out before her. Her blond hair wildly framed her face, an unusual break from her neat, smooth ponytail. No, this was more like a sexy-as-hell bed-head look. For a second, he wondered if that underwear playboy had anything to do with her mussed-up hair; another reason to kick the guy's ass from Pittsburgh to New York. As soon as the thought finished, another replaced it: *sweet Jesus, he was jealous.*

He caught her reflection in the passenger side window as the Jeep left the reporters behind.

"You know, I can see you scowling at me in my window. Guess you're anxious to get rid of me, and get a head start on your evening?"

Her disapproval was clear yet something else lurked beneath her words. She sounded resigned and…hurt. Had she expected an outpouring of emotion from him? "I love you," she'd declared, guns blazing. And like the heartless prick that he was, he'd swiftly dodged her bullet. Any fool knew that that kind of shot—one to the heart—was the deadliest. Any fool could tell you love wasn't enough to keep someone around when the going got tough. And his tough goings-on were a constant event.

He couldn't look at her, didn't want to show the conflicting thoughts written all over his face.

When he caught sight of the underwear model swaggering across the parking lot, the blood vessel in his forehead throbbed. *Mine. She loves me, with all my fuck-ups.* He felt like staking his claim and making sure Marky Mark knew where things stood.

But Keane didn't. He didn't *know* where things stood. His head was like one of those rides at a carnival that spun topsy-turvy, just out of control, with screaming kids and all.

All he wanted was peace and quiet.

And…her. *Shit.*

Keane glanced over at the quiet figure next to him. She was studying her hands and not paying one iota of attention to the playboy out in the parking lot. She seemed sad. And he was the cause.

What was he going to do with her?

He'd faced car bombs and bullets. Seen men killed before his eyes. Fuck, he relived it on a nightly basis. But this was a different kind of fright. More for her sake than his own, and more having to do with what he might do to her than what some shithead terrorist might do to him.

The Pittsburgh skyline illuminated the night sky, the brilliant light seeming to reflect off the stars. A blinding light that clouded his judgment. No, he couldn't see dropping her off. Getting shitfaced at Finnegan's was his post-fight standard but that's not what he needed. Hell, the opposite, really—he needed her near him tonight. Someplace neutral and serene. A place to calm his pounding heart. Before he could change his mind, he tugged out his cell phone and shot off a text.

"Are we taking a road trip?"

"You'll see."

The Jeep climbed steadily up Mount Washington, away from the hubbub of the city below. Away from all of Pittsburgh's nighttime temptations and the vices Keane had grown dependent on.

His restlessness hadn't really subsided, but as he breathed the crisp, cool mountain air, the peacefulness of this place he remembered most settled over him. The tension wound up in a knot inside him began to unravel. A few minutes later, the Jeep ambled into an empty parking lot which, considering the late hour, was to be expected.

Logan leaned forward in her seat and peered at the sign flickering on the small building in front of them. "Duquesne Incline. Wow, you're full of surprises. A cable car?" Her lips twitched as she turned toward him.

"Come on."

A teenager sat behind a counter inside the small building at the base of the incline. His face lit up when he saw Keane. "Holy shit! It's you. I'm like, the hugest MMA fan. How you feeling, Boom-Yay? I watched the fight on Pay Per View. That was some knock out tonight. I—"

"What do you want me to sign?"

The kid's mouth broadened into a wide smile. "I know the deal is one autograph, but you know, my friends are huge MMA fans."

"No problem. Get whatever you've got."

Reaching underneath the counter separating them, the kid pulled out scraps of lined notebook paper, one rumpled "Rumble on the Rivers" T-shirt, and a baseball.

Keane rolled the ball in his palm and tossed it back at the teenager. "Save it for the Pirates. But I'll sign the other stuff." As he got busy scrawling his name, the teenager placed another stack of loose-leaf papers on the counter and stared at Logan expectantly.

"When Dad told me Boom-Yay texted him wanting a private ride tonight I hoped you'd come with him, Luscious."

"Just like your old man. Freakin' Mr. Opportunistic Jr. here," Keane muttered good-naturedly.

Logan giggled.

The girly sound made him smile. It felt as rusty as an old tire iron. It was rare to find something to smile about these days. But Logan was a good sport, signing her own pile of autographs. Tapping his foot, he waited until she had finished. "Ready?"

"Text me when you want to descend. I've got home-work to keep me occupied. A half hour cool?"

Keane nodded.

They climbed inside the bright yellow-and-red car, vibrant even on the inside, although softly lit. It hadn't changed much since the last time he'd ridden it, a life-time ago, with its polished wooden ceiling and walls. A rectangular bench framed the space below massive arched windows.

Logan crossed the car and settled onto the bench. He sat next to her, stretching out his legs and resting an arm on the seat back. So conscious of the woman next to him and so fucking careful to not make contact. Peace was what he was aiming for tonight. And, if the weather cooperated, a great view.

The car shifted into motion.

Fortunately, Logan seemed content to gaze out the window.

The round, flickering lights from the bridges below

looked like rows of full moons floating along the rivers. Everything seemed clearer from up here, and not simply the spectacular downtown views.

He'd set Jerry straight about pairing him up with these freakin' green-as-grass fighters. If he wanted Keane to win this thing, then he'd better find him a partner with a thick skull. One who could take a beating. No more repeat performances of his fights with Young Gun and Smitty. Not with Keane's sanity at stake.

The tension in his neck eased as the car ascended.

"All my years growing up in the Pittsburgh suburbs and I've never been on an incline." Her voice held a note of awe in it. Pittsburgh had a bum rap for being a gritty, tough steel city but it had an attractive side as well. He liked that he was the first to take her up here.

"Too busy dancing?"

Her lips turned upward but not into a full, knock-me-on-your-ass smile. More resigned. "I sacrificed a lot of things for ballet. Dancing was my whole life, my purpose. Though, in retrospect, dancing *isn't* my life but *is* something I love doing. Does that make sense?"

"Yep."

Her head cocked sideways and her eyes fell on him. "Was that how fighting used to be for you?"

He drummed his fingers on the bench's smooth wood and looked away. "Guess so."

"So, what changed?"

His fingers kept up their rhythm on the bench. He shifted, his gaze drawn once more to the bridge lights far below. Rows of parallel lights from the skyscrapers downtown reflected off the rivers. Well-balanced and orderly—like his life used to be.

Touching his forearm lightly, she murmured, "If you didn't want to talk, then why'd you bring me up here?"

"Dunno," he heard himself mutter. He relaxed, knowing how much he *liked* having her nearby, and also knowing that he'd be an idiot to admit it—no good would come from leading her on and making her think there was something more between them than…*holy shit*. He stiffened and pulled away, separating them by a fraction of an inch which felt more like a mile.

He felt her fingers squeeze his arm before letting go. "It's ironic. All that time spent hung up on becoming a prima ballerina, and it took becoming an Octagon Girl for me to realize how unfulfilled my life has been. Dancing gave me joy but it was everything else interfering with it that I regret. So caught up in the fame, glamour and money, I forgot about making decisions for myself."

He heard her sigh. A frustrated sound that caused him to look back at her.

"That silly reality TV show is a prime example of just how ridiculous my life had become. In a way, my broken ankle healed me." She paused and gazed at the skyline. Light reflected from the glass to her earnest eyes. She looked so freakin' beautiful. Something deep inside him stirred.

Mercifully, she continued, unaware of the change in him. "My life was dance. Period. I couldn't imagine anything else. Look at what I've been missing. Would you look at that skyline?"

She wasn't the only one who had missed out on life. His lapse in living was more recent, post-Jimmy's death until…shit, he was in the muck of it, all right.

As she shifted on the hard seat, her arm brushed against his.

He flexed in awareness. *Forget about it, no can do.* He struggled to bury the sudden rush of desire for her. Wait for later and take care of business alone, without her around.

She swiveled toward him on the seat and her face lit up. "I would never have pegged you as a romantic. This view is magnificent. Thank you for bringing me here. It's so beautiful."

Him, a romantic? Jesus, did she have it all wrong. Still, he heard himself say, "Gets better on top." *Damn.* On top was where he wanted to be, and it wasn't Mount Washington he was thinking about.

"I can't imagine anything better than this."

Keane tightened his lips in determination because he most *definitely* could imagine something that would trump the view, something along the lines of sinking into her warmth until all his demons disappeared.

The cable car swayed, sending Logan sliding up against him. She twisted and wiggled away, but his arm shifted protectively from the back of the seat and curved around her in silent, inexplicable protest.

She sighed and leaned back toward him so her head rested in the curve of his shoulder.

The heat in the cable car kicked in. His inner thermostat ran hot to begin with but now he was uncomfortably warm inside his army jacket. Yet he did nothing about it. Didn't want to move away, even though he knew he should.

"This mountain used to be called Coal Hill. I remember my father describing how they were restoring these cars to their original condition. I always wanted to take a ride on one. It's hard to believe people used foothills to walk from downtown to the top of Mount Washington."

Keane grunted, and studied the view of the Golden Triangle below. The downtown lights reflected in a perfect V where the three rivers angled out from a single point. The rivers tenderly surrounded downtown Pittsburgh, much like the way his arm and body nestled Logan's head.

Shit. He was so fucked.

Gently, he wrestled his arm out from behind her, and stood. Used the pretense of removing his jacket as explanation for his sudden movement. He was still too damned hot, burning up really. Tossing the jacket on the bench, he unzipped his sweatshirt, peeled it off, and dropped it on the pile.

"Good idea. I can't imagine what year heat was installed in these cars, but there's no doubt about it working." Logan stood up and unbuttoned her jacket. It joined his pile of clothing.

His gaze fell on her bared shoulder.

He froze. She had that damned sexy-as-hell sweatshirt on.

"Come here." Keane's voice was barely above a whisper, the gravel in his tone husky and warm.

Logan resisted the urge to roll her eyes in frustration. She'd been laying subtle let's-rock-the-incline hints all night but he hadn't taken the bait. The sexy, brooding man standing in front of her was a poster boy for exasperating. No, beyond exasperating, with his tight-lipped, no-nonsense attitude, which in truth, caused her pulse to quicken as it drew her in.

One minute he blew hot, the next he was as cold as winter steel. She realized his coldness was a defense mechanism, that whenever she'd overstepped the boundaries between them and hit a nerve—his PTSD being the mother lode of all nerves—his response was consistent: he pushed her away.

She stepped closer.

He reached out and cupped her chin in his big, burly hand, then caressed her cheek with his thumb. His face was tight, unreadable, but his fingers were gentle.

"So goddamned beautiful."

His words caused her heart to thump louder than wooden floorboards after landing a *grand jeté*. She inhaled sharply. His soapy, clean scent was laced with the fresh mint of the gum he had been chewing.

He closed his eyes and ran his fingers across his lids. As if in pain. As if he'd said too much—as if that was ever a possibility. His eyes snapped open, and her breath hitched. His gaze was so open, so intense, so filled with pent-up need, she really couldn't breathe.

She nearly missed his next knee-trembling words, his voice was that low and soft. "You make me feel things. Want things. Want *you*, more than anything, ever."

He undressed her with his eyes. If his comment hadn't induced a state of shock, she'd have stripped off every stitch of clothing right then and there.

The exchange was too intense. Too raw. Too nerve-racking.

"What are you waiting for?" She cocked her head as she issued her corny, light-hearted challenge.

Straightening, he cocked his head and simply stared at her. Hard. Then, faster than she could say "crinkle my camisole," he was on her.

He grasped her arms and pulled her in close.

She lifted her face and kissed his tense jaw. "I want you too. I love—"

His mouth came down and opened against hers in such a hot, intense kiss, her toes would have curled under if she hadn't been standing on the tips of them. He slid a hand under her sweatshirt and his palm flattened on top of her stomach. Her abdomen was on fire, burning from his touch. She didn't think she wanted anything in life as much as she wanted this. *Him*, a big brute of a fighter so different from anyone she'd known. A man so sexy her mouth dried up at the sight of him.

Not that her mouth was dry now, as his tongue twirled in a sensual dance with her own. She raised one hand behind his head and held his lips to hers, demanding more.

The car abruptly stopped, breaking them apart as they fought for balance.

"Take off your clothes."

Hell, who was she to disobey such a direct order? And from a retired Marine, too.

Bending, she unfastened and stepped out of her boots and socks, then kicked them aside. Next to go were the skinny jeans. She stripped down to a pair of tuxedo-themed panties, black with a white lace fringe and a cute bow affixed just below her navel. Her sweatshirt was tugged off next, revealing a matching tuxedoed bra. Silently, she thanked her newfound sexuality for prompting her to put on this ensemble rather than her dependable, conservative tighty whities.

Keane's eyes burned with desire beneath heavy lids. "Nice bow." His response made her brave.

She folded a bra strap over a shoulder and ever so

slowly, freed her arm. The second strap received the same treatment. Angling both arms behind her back, her fingers reached for the clasp.

"Leave the bra on." He sauntered forward, closing the distance in a few steps. His left hand slid down her stomach to the top lacing on her panties. A middle digit slid beneath the elastic, paused and rotated. A flush of moisture dampened the part of her that craved his touch.

Her legs spread apart as if they had a mind of their own.

His right hand cupped a breast and his thumb rubbed across the swell of her chest and then down into her bra and over her hardening nipple.

"Can't get enough of you, Luscious." Something flashed in his eyes. The rawness of his voice vanished, replaced by his normal, bossy self. "Go sit on the bench."

She silently moved over to the bench, tugged his coat over it and sat. Her bare legs rubbed against the coarse material, but she didn't care. All she cared about was him.

"Spread 'em." He moved and stood directly in front of her a few feet away.

Wanton, naughty and sexy as hell, that was how she felt sitting there with her legs spread, opening herself to him.

"Hard and rough, baby. That's what you're gonna get."

Her lips twitched, remembering how gentle he'd been the last time such a declaration was made. "Famous last words, Boom-Yay. I'll believe it when I see it."

His smile was so incredibly sexy, a rush of moisture

coated her panties. He untied the string on his track pants as his gaze roamed over her hungrily.

"Spread 'em a little wider."

Her chin notched up slightly at the challenge in his voice and she opened her legs broadly.

He knelt onto the floor between her thighs, grabbed her behind the legs, and tugged. She slid down until her head rolled against the seat back.

One hand cupped her left thigh. His other hand began to roam. Over the soft silk panties and the swell of her until his palm came to rest on her core. His finger looped into the side of her panties at the crease of her leg. And, without hesitation, pulled them aside.

"You're gonna scream for me, Luscious."

His head ducked. It took all of her willpower not to thrust her hips off the seat when he licked her like an ice cream cone, his tongue moving in one upward sweep. Another lick and her legs trembled. It was earth shattering, the combination of his hot, wet tongue and the gentle press of his fingers against her mound where he held her panties in place.

Then he got down to business and laved at her over and over, until not only did her body hum, every inch of her, from her head to the tips of her toes, sang, bellowed and danced. She moaned and shifted. His palm nudged her left leg away.

"Now you're gonna get it." He pulled back. Briefly straightening his body, he grabbed a foil packet from his wallet. Her mind was numb, blissfully oh-so-pleasurably numb. He grasped her hands and brought her to her feet. His fingers curled under the elastic of her panties and he stripped them off her in one fluid movement.

"Step." She lifted her legs out and the silk pooled on

the floor. Her entire attention was focused on Keane as he stripped down to his briefs and kicked them off as well. His cock sprang out, enormous and thick.

She reached out and wound her fingers around the long, hot shaft. A few strokes and he was rock hard. Retrieving the condom from his hand, she made quick work of rolling it over him.

With a growl, he reached for her and ran his hands across her bottom down to her thighs. He lifted and her legs clasped around his waist. The full tip of his erection rubbed against her center as he moved them across the room, to the floor-to-ceiling windowed doorway.

He pinned her back against the glass pane. For a second, she wondered if the entire population of Pittsburgh was gazing up at her naked ass pressed up against the window. All errant thoughts vanished as the thick head of his penis slid up into her and split her deliciously apart.

"Oh, my. Keane." His hips thrust and suddenly he was buried so deeply inside her, she saw stars. Bright white lights that outshone those far below.

He withdrew and plunged back, even deeper than before, if that was possible. In and out, over and over.

"Wanted this all fucking day. From the time I found you with that playboy, maybe earlier."

Just hearing him talk made her hot and wet. Man oh man, feeling her inner muscles tighten around his hot shaft was the best prize of all.

"What playboy?"

His next thrust was less gentle, more powerful. She loved every brutal inch of him.

"Freakin' lame-ass underwear model."

He'd promised her hard and rough, and his powerful plunges took her breath away. She arched her back against the windowpane, angling for something to push off of, wanting to meet him thrust for thrust. Her stomach rocked against his. His pace quickened.

"God, I need you. Want you. I…" Keane rumbled, his tone thick with need.

She gasped for breath at his passionate onslaught. His hip muscles flexed and thrust in wild abandon. Her skin was hot, but the juncture between her legs, so amply filled, was on fire. A molten, liquid heat so intense, so shattering, she lost awareness of everything except the feeling of him sliding in and out of her.

"Shit, Logan, you're so tight, baby."

"Maybe because you're hung like a rock star. You know…oh, yes. Mmm." A blaze of fire shot through her and she strained for release. The muscles of her legs flexed in his arms. He grunted in awareness and held on tighter.

He shifted so all of her weight bore down onto his thick staff. "Ahh…" she cried out but his mouth claimed hers and cut her off. His tongue plundered her mouth in rhythm with his thrusts. Her arms wrapped around his big neck and she held on for dear life. Her chest rubbed against his, the friction of her bra stimulating her nipples as they moved.

He broke his kiss, and grunted. "Come on, baby. Let's do this."

His biceps flexed and he lifted her high. He let go and she slid down hard on the full length of him. Once more, his biceps flexed. She shattered as he lifted her and the long, fast plunge caused her to cry out her release.

"Keane."

"I've gotcha. My turn."

Flex and lift, flex and lift, three more times and suddenly her back was back up against the window. His face nuzzled her neck. He moaned into it, his breath warm against her skin. "Logan…ahhh. So fucking good." His entire body shook from his release.

She felt his heart beating against her chest. Her arm was still wrapped around him, his hands cupped her buttocks, and her legs dangled aimlessly beside his body.

A wave of contentment washed over her. She loved this wildly passionate man, and she believed in him. But instead of giving voice to her emotions—having had a taste of how he'd likely respond—she decided that keeping the air light and easygoing was the better approach.

But she wasn't willing to cut the thin thread that bonded them together. The doors of communication had opened, albeit mostly physical, hands-on communication. But it was better than nothing. No way was she going to let it slam shut again.

He grunted against her neck. She was lifted then lowered onto her feet, his cock sliding out of her in a warm, wet farewell.

"Do you want to know what I'm thinking?"

His arm tensed as he stepped away from her.

Not so fast, my love. Reaching out, she grabbed his wrist and yanked it. He didn't move but his eyes shot to her face, surprised and cautious. It was like an iron mask snapped into place, impenetrable and unrelenting.

Or maybe not, she thought as she adjusted her bra strap under his unwavering gaze. He followed her every gesture as the second strap was smoothed into place. How would he react if she ran her hands down her body to the juncture of her legs? She was tempted, but instead she murmured, "One of the reporters has finally gotten it right."

The tight cheeks of his beautiful ass flexed as he retrieved his sweatpants and put them on. "How so?"

Good, she still had his attention.

"Your nickname."

He stood and ran his fingers through his hair. His tattoo rippled tight across his torso and down to his abs as his arm rose overhead—even in repose, his massive strength was visible.

She stepped closer and retrieved her own pants. Her silky underwear had eased the friction between the denim and her skin, but they remained where she'd stepped out of them on the floor. It took some doing but she finally wiggled herself in.

He made a noise and she glanced up, catching the slight upward curve on his lips. Good, he'd relaxed. That was a sign of how the rest of their evening was going to be, if she could manage the man's moods.

"Boom-Yay. I'd say the nickname fits…perfectly."

The curve of his lips remained in place as she put on her sweatshirt.

"Okay, you got me. How so?"

Her hands found her hips and she gave him her sauciest smile. "Well, you promised me hard and rough."

"You got it, babe. Bet you can't even walk straight."

She felt like fist pumping the air. He was biting, and it felt wonderful.

"Boom-Yay. Didn't you hear your nickname ringing out in your head?"

"Fuck, no. Why would I think about a bunch of

rowdy men heckling me while I was having amazing sex?"

God, she wanted to hug him. *Amazing*, was it? She was so pleased she felt like dancing.

"I'm not referring to your crazy fans. I'm talking about us. How every time you pushed up inside of me with a *boom*, I answered you with a *yay*. Bleeding leotards, I must have shouted *yay* at least a hundred times."

She wasn't sure if it was her rechristening of his nickname or her reference to one hundred times, but whatever it was, he grinned like a madman.

"Hmph…Boom-Yay. Yeah, I like it."

"So do I. It suits us—Boom-Yay and Luscious." She held her breath, waiting for him to object to her linking them together like a couple.

"What time is it?" he asked, in a neutral, unreadable voice.

She reached into her jacket, pulled out her cell, and showed him the screen. Eleven fifty-five.

"We better hurry." He placed his thumbs in his track pants and yanked them down.

"What are you…doing?" The question was ridiculous; his intentions became clear, *very* clear, when she caught sight of his emerging hard-on.

"Strip. Time to sink my Boom-Yay into your Lusciousness, and test out your theory, baby." His smile took her breath away. Five minutes later, his Boom-Yay had her humming faster than a hummingbird's wings.

Chapter 18

TURTLE: A protective maneuver where a fighter curls into a ball to block his/her opponent's punches

Naked as a jaybird, Logan lay on her back, studying how the early morning light deepened the golden hue of Keane's lovely tin ceiling. He was full of surprises, this sexy hunk sleeping soundly next to her. Life with him would be as rich and complex as he was.

Last night was as unexpected as a Pittsburgh Indian summer. Her body still hummed from their wild ride on the Duquesne Incline. What they'd *done* in that beautiful cable car registered way off the mind-boggling charts. Incredible. Stupendous. And a ride she'd repeat again and again.

He wasn't just hot as hell and able to put the spring in her step with a simple glance. He was caring, loyal and trustworthy. Dependable, too—he'd made her a promise and put aside his own issues to fulfill it, all for her. More proof that his conscience ran deep.

Whether he liked it or not, she was going to help him. Stevie'd be in Pittsburgh today—it wasn't like she'd had time to call him back and cancel their intervention. Not that she wanted to, despite knowing how pissed off Keane was going to be.

She glanced down at him. *Boom-Yay has hit the hay. Seems I've worn him out!* There was a bruise on his eyebrow and his lip was swollen on one side. Not that it had stopped him last night. Not that either injury took away from his rough, handsome features. Reaching out, she ran her fingers across his cheek in a gentle, loving caress.

Without warning, Keane shot up like he'd been burned, wrapped his big body around her, and rolled over and off the bed. Fortunately a pillow pinned between her head and his arm cushioned her fall. He landed on top of her, knocking the wind out of her. One hundred sixty-eight pounds of muscled welterweight had her trapped, with her arms tucked against her sides and legs spread wide open.

If she wasn't so astonished, she'd have laughed at finding herself in this situation once more, with a naked Keane sprawled out on top of her. But this was different. *He* was different. *What just happened?*

His face was mere inches above hers. His eyes were vacant and his mouth tight. A fine sheen of sweat covered his brow and his cheek ticked. If she didn't know better she'd think he was ready to go kick some ass. Or worse. He wasn't himself—this wasn't the man who'd made such passionate love to her last night.

"Keane!" Her voice was sharper than intended, and full of worry.

He blinked, and blinked again. His eyes refocused, filled with surprise, and then awareness.

"Fucking hell!" Quicker than he'd wrestled her to the ground, he was off her and onto his knees beside her.

She tried to sit up.

"Don't move. I need to check you out."

Silently, she obeyed. Aside from the tightness in her throat from his desperate expression and the tenderness between her legs, she was fine. Shocked, worried and trying to control the heart attempting to burst out of her chest, but otherwise fine.

"Jesus. Logan, are you okay? Where did I hurt you?"

"Keane, you just caught me by—"

"Shit, holy shit. I'll call an ambulance." His voice was hoarse, almost panicked. The sound of it forced her out of her dazed state.

"Listen, I'm fine. The pillow cushioned my head. You weigh a ton but I'm okay. No harm done."

"You're gonna see a doctor, anyway. To make sure."

She clambered up onto her knees and faced him. Cupping his jaw in her palms, she tried to soothe him as she struggled to come to terms with what had just transpired. "Shhh, I'm okay. You woke up out of a sound sleep because I touched you. You reacted. But you snapped out of it and realized I'm not the enemy, or whomever you were picturing in your head. At least, that's what I think happened."

"Fuck." He pulled back and covered his face with his hands, mumbling something inaudible.

Logan stood. She didn't move away, but instead hovered over him, desperately trying to figure out how to help him.

Moments passed yet the tension remained. Keane's fingers flexed as he pulled his hands away from his face and rose to his feet. His expression was horrible, like he'd lost a fight or worse. His hardened gaze scanned her from head to toe, pausing on her belly.

"Christ, what is that? Did I do that to you?"

Logan gasped at the pain in his voice. She lifted her arms away from her body and searched for whatever had him so alarmed. A bluish-red mark stood out on her otherwise pale skin, marring the area near her bellybutton. Come to think of it, a matching mark was probably on her neck, too.

"It's a love bite. Remember last night when you ran your tongue over my stomach and…well, you know. I think there's another one on my neck."

He exhaled in a rush.

"I'm here, Keane, for you. I—"

His lips tightened and caused her to hesitate. She had promised him not to pry but this was important. He needed to know she would help him. "Is fighting your way of dealing with all of this stuff? A physical release, even if you don't enjoy it?"

"What about it?" He stood in front of the antique dresser with his back to her. The metal handle rang out against the wood as he fiddled with it.

She sighed. He wasn't making this easy. Moving over to him, she placed her fingers on his bicep and squeezed reassuringly.

His arm tensed beneath her touch. Her heart raced with emotion—she wanted her touch to absorb all of his pain. Gently, she placed a feathery kiss on his neck, then whispered, "I'm here for you, Keane. This isn't something you have to deal with alone. I can go with you to see a professional, if you want. An expert who has counseled a lot of guys going through similar issues."

His body stiffened as he brought a balled-up fist crashing down onto the dresser. The wood vibrated from the impact. She jumped back, alarmed more by his anger than his physicality. She'd expected him to have softened from her touch, but instead, was now faced with a tense, brutish street fighter.

Turning around, he narrowed his eyes at her.

"Okay, so you're not ready to talk about it. Can't you see I want to help you? Sure, the timing stinks—you should be focusing on the next fight, right? Focusing on not getting hurt. Winning, even. But given what just happened, you can't ignore this."

"You don't know shit."

"What *shit* don't I know then, Keane?"

"Why are you sleeping in here?" His voice was brutal, accusing, but she noticed his hands were shaking. "Don't you see?"

Her back stiffened. "All I see is that you didn't give me much choice. I was trapped beneath you for most of the night." She pointed to the bed, hoping he'd be reminded of their wild night together. Hoping it might calm him down. Soothe him.

He pinned her with his gaze and clenched his jaw. "Logan, this isn't gonna work out for me. I need my space back, I need my freakin' life back."

"What are you saying, Keane?"

"Look, I warned you. No strings attached. No commitments."

"Rettino, where the fuck have you been?" Squirrel Face appeared at the end of the row of lockers.

Logan gasped at the sight of him. It looked as if he'd gotten into a fight with the locker door and had lost, with his cut-up face, swollen lip and bruised cheek. So disheveled and out of sorts, she wondered why he seemed so focused on her showing up and not on cleaning himself up. Hell, a man after a bar brawl was in better shape than him.

"I look like an asshole every time I send that nitwit out to announce the bouts when they're asking for you."

Asshole pretty much had him covered, bleeding lip and all. Chloe was not a nitwit, but Logan had to choose her battles carefully right now. "Why did you pair Keane up with the German? Isn't there anyone else he can fight, someone less violent?"

"Sweetheart, this isn't one of your fancy ballet shows. These guys out there want blood—to taste it, smell it, lick it, breathe it."

Lick it? Ew! Whoever had done the number on Jerry's face had scrambled his marbles as well. "So what are you saying? You're sending Keane to be butchered by that giant German so the crowd can turn into a bunch of testosterone-induced vampires?"

Jerry patted his mouth with his fingers, seemingly checking for verification that his lip was indeed the size of a golf ball. "Hmph, what have you been drinking? Your boyfriend is the butcher in this match-up. He's not exactly passing out roses tonight. Mean fuckin' bastard. Do you see what he did to my face? But I'm not holding a grudge, especially against my champion."

Logan frowned. *Did Jerry believe Keane would win this bout?* It certainly appeared that way.

"You fell asleep with your arms and legs wound around me. How's that for attachment?"

"It was just sex."

Leave it to a fighter to know how to deliver a knock out. He couldn't have picked a better way of tearing out her heart. Her fingers curled into her palm so tightly, her hand numbed.

She marched over to the other side of the bed and gathered together her clothing scattered on the floor. Scooping up her jacket from the chair, she headed for the door.

"Thanks for the *sex.*" She shot out, passing him by.

"Logan, wait," he murmured, his voice tight once more. "I don't want to hurt you."

"Too late."

If the darned city bus moved any slower it would be going in reverse.

Be right there, Jerry.

Getting fired seemed minor in comparison to her mixed bag of emotions about Keane, minor compared to her much-needed over-the-top salary even. His rejection smarted.

It sucked knowing her love was one-sided and unrequited. She'd worked her way through a lot of bullshit this year. Falling in love had been unexpected. Falling in love with a fighter had been startling.

Falling in love with a troubled man like Keane had been a mistake.

"This is for the best," Keane had said as he dropped her off at Mrs. Debinska's and drove off without so much as a goodbye. Logan wanted to bury her head underneath a feather pillow and stay there until her heartache subsided. Instead, she sucked it up and forced herself into taking a step toward fulfilling her *other* dream. She checked out another potential ballet studio.

The space was small and the rent more than she could afford, despite being in a less than desirable industrial area. Instead of cheering her up, it forced her to reassess her present situation. She had two choices: take the sales associate exam at Boscov's and nickel and dime her way into saving enough for six months' rent, minimum. Plus expenses. That was going to take some time.

Or she could high-tail it over to Mellon Arena and hope Jerry would cut her a break for being late.

Deep down, she knew a year at Boscov's was better than watching Keane getting a knuckle sandwich from his next opponent, the Mad German. They'd certainly pulled a one-hundred-and-eighty-degree shift—she didn't really want Keane to fight, and he now seemed hell-bent on doing so.

Talk about a yin-yang of conflicting emotions.

She needed him to fight but was worried. Everything she'd heard about the Mad German said he was bad news. Was Keane prepared for someone so huge and vicious? *Physically*, maybe. Lord knew Keane had as much fat on him as a celery stick—zip, null, zero. But was he mentally prepared for this kind of bout?

The way he'd withdrawn after such a wildly passionate evening was proof enough she'd gotten too close for comfort. This morning's events, him tackling her off the bed, had freaked him out bad. He'd overreacted, and worse still, he'd pushed her away.

The bus halted a block away from Mellon Arena. Logan briskly walked the short distance, passed secu-

rity at the side door, and made her way to the wo[r] locker room.

"Sugar, thank God you're here!" Chloe greeted he[r] a rush. "Ah tell ya what. Jerry's lookin' for ya and h[e] been throwing a hissy fit, barging in here like clock[] work every five minutes, wanting to know if ya arrive[d] yet. Madder than a rattler, with him grumbling about ya being one lucky broad. I reckon ya boyfriend struck a deal, by the look of things. Jerry kept mumbling on and on how Keane and free publicity is what's keepin' ya ass from gettin' fired."

Logan frowned. Her boyfriend, a man more complex than a spider's web, who'd flat out told her their relationship was just sex—casual, like he didn't give a rat's ass about her—had gone out of his way to save her job as an Octagon Girl. Was she that predictable that Keane expected her to show tonight? Or was it his guilty conscience making him act on her behalf? Whatever his motives, it bought her time.

Unlocking her locker, she eyed the two remaining Octagon Girl outfits. Even through the plastic wrap, she could tell by the colors that these were different than the bright yellow number Chloe wore. Logan caught sight of the wording printed on the back of a pair of purple shorts. She sucked in a breath. Jerry had lost his mind completely with this stunt.

"I'll wait outside and keep an eye out for ya."

"Thanks, Chloe," she said, her eyes glued to the [out]fit in her hand. *Great bleeding leotards. What [did] Jerry have me wearing this time?*

The sound of a crashing locker room door s[ignaled] her boss's arrival. So much for Chloe stoppin[g]

"You've kept them waiting long enough. Let's go."

She had no choice but to follow Jerry out of the locker room and down the long corridor. Tiny goose bumps spotted her skin by the time they arrived at the ramp into the arena. Something in Squirrel Face's suddenly cheerful disposition triggered her inner warning bells. "Jerry, when you said I kept *them* waiting long enough, you were referring to the crowd, right?"

He ignored her question. "That outfit is going to put this MMA event on every goddamn television network from here to Australia."

Her goose bumps multiplied in number. *Whatever Jerry is hedging at, it's going to be bad.*

His hand smacked her across the ass, forcing her forward into the arena. But not before she forcefully shoved an elbow back into his stomach. "Humph," Jerry grunted. She didn't wait around for the fallout.

The crowd spotted her a quarter of the way down the ramp. A familiar cheer greeted her. "Luscious, Luscious." This wasn't so bad. Predictable. Familiar. A day in the life of a popular Octagon Girl.

"We love you, Luscious!"

"It's Pete's birthday. Give us a smile." She plastered a grin on her face and waved at the birthday boy.

"Is Boom-Yay ready to take on the Mad German?"

I wish I knew, buddy. I wish I knew he was going to be okay. She gave a thumbs-up.

A crowd was gathered at the end of the ramp, without leaving much room for Logan to pass. As she approached, she immediately recognized the striking, dark red-haired woman overdressed in a deep navy business suit—*of all things*—blocking her way. Her arm hooked around Logan's own and tugged her close. "Logan, your manager said you'd give me a few minutes for an interview. Ready? Lights, camera, action."

Logan blinked at the cameras' blinding white lights, stunned and horrified to find a mic in her face.

"This is Sophie Morelle reporting live from the Mellon Arena. I'm here at day three of Mixed Martial Arts Monster Mayhem bringing you a live, uncensored, special report of the final fights for a chance to compete in the Tetnus championships in Las Vegas. I'm here with Luscious Logan Rettino. So, Logan, you were an accomplished ballerina, had a huge fan base as a contestant on *America Gets Its Groove On*. How hard was it for you to make the switch from classical ballet to *this?*"

Logan's mouth opened and closed like a beached fish fighting for its life. Nothing squeezed out but a long exhalation. *Great, just great.* She was about to make a fool of herself on national television for the second time this year.

Logan kept her fingers laced together across her backside, just as she'd done since entering the arena. Careful to hide the source of further humiliation from sight. How long would it be before they caught on?

Sophie didn't miss a beat and addressed the crowd. "What do you think, guys? Hasn't Logan rocked it as an Octagon Girl?" The camera swung away and zoomed in on a few hard-core fans. Logan flinched as the other woman's fingers squeezed her arm. She looked up and caught her conspiratorial wink—or so it seemed. The popular television host had saved her the embarrassment of answering. Yet, with Sophie on her side, who needed enemies. After all, the woman was notorious for her abrupt surprises.

"Gentlemen, before we let Luscious strut her stuff up

there in the cage, I want her honest reaction to what's been plaguing viewers the most since her unfortunate departure from *America Gets Its Groove On*."

Logan wished she could curl up into a tiny insignificant ball of nothingness and roll the hell out of there. Even in this more conservative outfit, there was no hiding them—her slightly above-average breasts were about to be remeasured, reassessed, and reevaluated once again. What was wrong with America when breast size captured more media attention than a Japanese tsunami and a Chilean earthquake combined?

Man, how she wanted to fold her arms across her breasts, but didn't dare move them from behind her. Because what was printed on her ass was beyond embarrassing.

Sophie waved her mic at a group of people and they shifted off to the sides, clearing space for her near the stairway. The reporter had considerately let her off the hook once again, or so it seemed.

Logan relaxed and stepped toward the opening in the crowd. *That wasn't so bad. This woman gets such an undeserving bad rap.*

"Reunited for the first time since Logan's abrupt departure from *America Gets Its Groove On*…" Logan didn't hear the rest. At the unexpected sight of *his* smirking face, that helpless, falling feeling returned, like the ground had shifted out beneath her and the person standing in front of her found it more delightful if he *didn't* catch her.

Logan braced herself for the second time that day. There was nothing else she could do.

Chapter 19

CLINCH: *Where two fighters face off, before one grabs the other and pulls him/her in tightly*

"If this is your doing, you're gonna eat some teeth."

Jerry visibly winced at Keane's threat before slinking off down the hallway. Clearly, the asshole hadn't learned his lesson from the beating he'd earned earlier. Keane turned back from his place at the top of the ramp, scowling at the Jumbotron and the so-called "surprise reunion" playing out on it. More like "vicious ambush."

The reporter seemed pleased with herself for surprising Logan like that. Her ex had a twisted grin on his face, clearly pleased with his stunt. Logan's face filled the screen, her glossy, widened eyes and half-parted lips making her look like someone who'd lost her best friend. An emotional punch Keane was all too familiar with.

"Jerry set her up. I heard him tell that reporter she could have an interview," Sal commented from his spot next to Keane. "I might be past my prime but I've got a few more jabs in me with Jerry's name on them. Jeez, Logan looks like she's gonna…hang on, what's her ex saying?"

"…and I'd like to personally invite you to watch me perform with Anya on the finale of *America Gets Its Groove On*." Pierre reached out and the cameras zoomed in on the envelope he was offering to Logan.

Sal swiftly headed back into the corridor with a parting, "I'll crank up your entrance music."

Keane snarled, his words indecipherable. If this crowd wanted a show, he'd give it to them, and he wasn't about to wait for some freakin' music. Stepping forward, he started down the ramp.

"Yo, Keane! Wait up, man. I had a hell of a time getting past security and had to pull out an old photo of you, me and Jimmy as proof we're buddies. I can't believe I almost missed this. Good thing your girl called me."

Stevie jogged up next to him.

Luscious hadn't left enough alone.

"Dude, you sure you're up for this? Fighting might not be the healthiest thing for you right now. Not until you work out some…issues."

"Zip it, man," Keane shouted and lengthened his stride. He'd left strict orders for no visitor's passes. Period. Just in case. Who the fuck had let him in?

Stevie shadowed him as he stalked down the ramp toward the group gathered cage side. "And this isn't a fight you want to take on. This German guy's the real deal. I know you're tough, but you've been out of action for a while. Even on your best day—and God knows you've had many of those—this guy would have given you a run for your money."

Keane felt his friend's hand on his arm and shrugged it off. All of his attention was zeroed in on Logan's beautiful-yet-stunned face spread out across every Jumbotron in the place. Her ex was in for a surprise—after Keane kicked his ass, he'd move on to kicking the German's, then Jerry's. Stevie would be next in line if he kept harping on things best left alone.

Stevie and Logan were two persistent thorns in his side, unsatisfied until he bled. Avoiding them both seemed paramount to his survival; hell, they didn't realize how close he was to losin' it with Jimmy's death eating away at him like ants on a slice of pie. Beating the shit out of this German was just the cure he needed. And should have been his absolute focus right now, if he hadn't caught the close-up of Logan's pained expression.

"I'm starting to think you've got a death wish or something. Come on, Keane, listen to what I'm saying. This fight isn't worth it. You're hurting yourself, man."

On the Jumbotron, Twinkletoes took a step forward and Logan shifted backward. Keane's fists clenched even tighter.

The feedback from a microphone trilled loudly, then music filled the arena—Aerosmith's "Dream On." The crowd jumped to their feet. All eyes swung his way. Their mouths moved. Keane thought they chanted, "Boom-Yay" but all he could hear was Steven Tyler singing about paying your dues in life. Just like fuckin' Pierre was about to pay his dues.

Keane stalked toward the group. He caught the shift in images on a huge screen, and now his tight expression replaced Logan's. *Good. Let 'em see what's headed their way.*

Stevie deserved some credit, for his buddy stuck to him like glue in spite of his menacing expression and the overwhelming attention it garnered. Thankfully, Keane couldn't hear a word of what his friend was yakking nonstop about.

Striding toward the cluster-fuck surrounding Logan, he muscled his way inside. Three sets of eyes widened in surprise. Two sets of eyes immediately filled with fear, and with good reason. Keane had been waiting for this asshole to show up so he could teach him a lesson.

A third set of surprised eyes, as clear and as lovely as grass in an otherwise bleak desert, met his own.

"Keane," her lips mouthed his name. His eyes raked over every inch of her, from the top of her forehead to the tip of her Nike-clad toes. Her arms were folded behind her, thrusting her lovely breasts outward and upward. A desert storm had nothing on the emotions blazing through him. Look but don't touch. Not again. Never again, or he'd be unable to stop. Running his hands over her body, that's not what this was about. No, sex was easier.

This was deeper, this was him struggling to hold the fuckin' floodgates of emotion at bay. *You can't have her. You're not the man for her, someone who'll protect her. Keep her safe.*

His gaze was drawn to the swell of exposed skin at the top of her breasts, then up to her face, to eyes brimming with hope. And love.

Something inside him snapped.

And he lost his mind, completely.

Logan wasn't sure what surprised her the most, being waylaid by Sophie Morelle, provoked by a smug-faced Pierre, or Keane's abrupt appearance.

But what she did know was this: Keane never looked so fierce, with his beautiful tight lips and piercing blue eyes, possessive and conflicted. Pierre never looked so nervous, as if he'd been cornered in a pen by a wild animal. She knew with certainty that what goes around, comes around, and things had finally swung full force in Pierre's direction. Keane was going to kick his lame ballerina ass if she didn't stop him.

Fear of consequences made her jump between the two men. Keane would suffer more for attacking a spectator than Pierre would from the well-deserved beating. As much as she'd love to see her ex laid out on the floor—just like he'd left her all those months ago—she couldn't let Keane be hauled off to jail on her account.

Keane's hands shifted to her waist in a familiar move. *Oh, no, Boom-Yay. You're not moving me out of the way so easily.* Ignoring everyone but him, she stepped in closer so their bodies touched. Keane tried to sidestep her, but she was ready and moved along with him.

"Logan…" he warned, his mouth close to her ear as he scooped her up. Mercifully, her sequined bottom was hidden by his embrace.

"Don't do it. I know you promised but he's not worth it. He's not worth your getting into trouble." Despite her plea, he spun her around and moved her out of his way. Her mind worked frantically for a solution, some way to prevent this inevitable debacle. She thought about wrapping her arms around his neck and holding tight. Hell, it had worked once before. But the tightness of Keane's jaw reflected his determination. Logan would have to resort to more drastic measures. Surely, God would forgive her for the white lie she was about to tell.

"Ah, Keane. I've a slight problem here," she began, yelling loudly in his ear. His scowl told her he was listening. *Good.* Better to play it up like it was a final performance at Lincoln Center. "The knot on my top is loose."

Keane kept moving, a runaway train of a man unwilling to stop.

Then she did wrap her arms around his neck, pulled him tight, and leaned in closer. "Do *not* put me down. Wardrobe malfunction, here. I'm about to lose my halter top."

His gaze narrowed on her face, assessing her words.

She opened her eyes, in what she hoped was an innocent look, and added for good measure, "If I reach back to retie it, *everyone* will see."

"Damn."

Logan smiled up at him. He cared enough about her to barge into this crowd and kick Pierre's butt. He cared enough to prevent her from hosting her own Octagon Girl peep show. He *cared.*

"Don't think this is over, Twinkletoes." Keane turned and with the side of his arm, gave Pierre a strong shove, sending her dumbfounded ex flying backward. Tugging her in tighter, he headed up the ramp.

The crowd loved it. Not one to miss an opportunity, Sophie Morelle's face filled the Jumbotron, as she added her take on what had just transpired. "Gentlemen, listen up. *That* is how you treat a lady. I'll say, it's the most romantic thing I've seen. He literally swooped in here and swept her off her feet. Nudged…well, maybe it was a bit more than a nudge…his rival for Logan's attention out of his way. To hell with all this fighting. Those two lovebirds are the real deal."

The real deal. More like a raw deal, once Keane realized her little white lie. Or maybe not. As soon as Keane cleared the entranceway, Logan unwound an arm from behind his neck and pretended to stretch.

Arching an elbow in the air, her fingers found the knotted string holding her top in place behind her neck. Deftly, she untwisted the bit of material and loosened it. No one was the wiser.

"Stop squirming," he breathed into her ear.

"Um, my hair's stuck. There we go."

And there it went, the unraveled string falling freely across her back. Her lips twitched upward.

Steven Tyler's crooning ended, replaced by the sound of approaching footsteps echoing on the cement floor. A Boy-Who-Cried-Wolf-like moment began playing out, as her top jiggled free and slipped from the sides of her breasts. Only her nipples, pressed tightly against Keane's chest, remained covered. *Pimp my plié*, she'd asked for this. To make matters worse, instead of a wolf drawing closer, it was a massive, six-foot-five German. Hastily, she wrapped her free arm back around Keane's neck.

The German and his entourage stopped. "Isn't zis sveet."

Keane shot out, "Yea, you'll see sweet in five." He brushed past the puzzled giant and his entourage, who were rapidly translating Keane-speak into German, and strode down the hallway.

His foot connected with the locker room door and it crashed open with a large boom.

"Don't come any closer, Jerry, or I swear my daddy will pull financing for Tetnus quicker than an angry bobcat," Chloe's startled voice cried out from behind the lockers.

Keane stopped short and abruptly set Logan down.

Logan called out to her friend in warning. "It's me, Chloe, and I'm not alone. Give me a sec, okay?" In one quick rush, Logan's tank top dropped to the floor.

"Jesus," the beautiful man standing before her muttered. Logan racked her brain for a way to make him stay. His gaze raked over her and a lusty look she was all too familiar with briefly replaced the fierceness within his eyes. But with Chloe just around the lockers, seduction was out of the question.

Yet she didn't cover herself. Let him look his fill and remind him of what he was missing. Postpone the fight a little longer. Buy her time to try to persuade him once more. *Make him love me.*

Her breath caught in her chest at the last ridiculous thought. There was no making Keane do anything. Besides, she wasn't about to force someone into loving her—no matter how her heart was breaking.

Pushing aside her own rampant emotions, she forced out, "He's a beast. I'm worried about you being prepared to fight him." *Mentally, not physically,* she wanted to add but refrained. Bringing up PTSD again was a bad idea right now.

He stepped closer, tension rolling off his muscles.

Reaching out, his fingers swept across her stomach. Warm and gentle. She leaned closer, wanting more.

"No faith, you and Stevie."

Logan had spotted the shocked expression on Stevie's face as Keane hauled her out of the arena. Help had arrived, but he was nowhere to be found at present.

With a whisper of a touch, his fingers ran back across her stomach. The air seemed thick with unspoken lust. A distraction she couldn't afford to give in to, not with Chloe close by. Not without having her say before he battled it out with the German.

"You can back out of this. I won't hold you to our agreement." Her voice raised as she spoke, distracted by his touch. "No question that Jerry's already canned my ass, so you won't be doing me any more favors."

His fingers had every nerve cell humming. Her body remembered the feel of him so well, his big hands on her, the way he filled her up and made her cry out her release.

"Wanna bet?"

"No he won't, Logan. I'll talk to Daddy on your behalf," the sly, curious and evidently wealthy eavesdropper declared from behind the lockers.

Crinkle my camisole, Chloe. Logan couldn't blame her. Given the situation, she'd have done the same thing if their roles were reversed. But the damage was done. Keane snatched his hand back and straightened to his full, unbendable height.

"Fix your top," he said over his shoulder as he stalked out of the room.

The German and his crew were already in their lion's den when Keane mounted the stairs and headed into the cage. Sal wildly gestured to him from his own corner, and he met up with the old-timer in six long strides.

"Boyo, that was some show you and Luscious put on. But we've got bigger fish to fry here, lover boy."

Keane scowled down until Sal shifted uncomfortably on his feet. Everyone doubted Keane's ability to win against the Mad German, everyone except himself. His opponent was aggressive, with a skull as thick as granite. A worthy opponent. This was the kind of bout where he could let loose, maybe even enjoy himself, without worrying about killing the guy. He'd finally be able to unleash the mounting anger raging just below the surface.

"I can't see how this guy made weight. Must be all flab, or someone's tomfoolery is at play here. Either way, you're gonna need to keep your distance because this guy's reach is incredible."

Keane jogged in place, loosening his muscles. His irritation grew as Sal voiced his doubts. Anger was good. This wasn't freakin' family fun night or a show you'd take Grandma to see. There was no place for *nice* here in the cage. Judging from the sly, intense looks the German was shooting him, *nice* was on a sabbatical.

Hell, there was a shit load of recent situations to fire up his rage. He visualized Logan's stunned expression at Twinkletoes' ambush. What had she called him, the fame whore? That ass had some balls showing up at an MMA bout and harassing her, just so his freakin' face stayed in the papers. Yet Logan had interfered again, and stopped him from smashing his face in. Well, Keane was gonna remedy that. When he was done with the German, Twinkletoes' swollen face would be the last thing home viewers expected.

He let a few punches fly. These days, thoughts of Logan set him off quicker than a car bomb.

She had a way of maneuvering him to her will, just as she'd done a few minutes ago. Man, every fuckin' guy in the place had a definite hard-on for her. Himself, included—but fuck knew it was a lot easier managing an untimely stiffy than the organ pounding away inside his chest.

He rolled his shoulders back, feeling the stretch in his muscles. Taking it to the mat was the only way to beat a brawler with a punching range like the German's. Fist to fist wasn't gonna do much. He threw a few more jabs and hooks, hoping his opponent misinterpreted his intent, and refocused on dredging up his hostility. It wasn't hard to do.

Darting a hostile glance at the German, Keane swiftly pummeled the air, imagining the rodent-faced promoter standing to his left, and Logan's asshole ex to his right.

Wouldn't you know it, Jerry entered the cage at precisely the moment Keane stopped for a swig of water. The man had nine lives for sure. He seemed oblivious to Keane's glare as he approached center cage.

With the bout seconds away from starting, Keane gave in to the biggest demon on his shoulder, the source feeding his anger like a twenty-four-hour virus: the asinine move he'd pulled this morning.

Sweet Jesus, when he'd snapped out of the nightmare and discovered Logan beneath him, he'd just about lost his mind. Unsure of what exactly had transpired but knowing oh-so-well what he was capable of doing. Combat had suited him well overseas but those days were over. Days he tried like hell to forget.

He'd come a hair's breadth away from breaking loose on her. His fists had been balled tight and ready to fly. When he'd spotted the bruise on her creamy, pale stomach, he thought he had socked her a shot.

That was why he slept alone. Why Rosie and company were a few hours' entertainment at best. The type of woman he should have stuck to.

God knew, Logan was different. Special. Someone he'd hugged close as he fell asleep. Someone he wanted to wake up to every day.

Someone he needed to shut out of his life as fast as possible—for her own good. And for the sake of his own freakin' sanity. Move on and forget her, already. Forget *everything*.

Tonight, he'd prove his worth. Show her, and Stevie, that he was one tough son of a bitch. Prove once and for all he didn't need help. Make them forget they'd ever bore witness to his fucked-up weaknesses. All he needed was time to figure it all out, and reconnect with the pleasure of pummeling a worthy opponent into pieces.

"Ladies and gentlemen, sorry for the delay in the main match-up of the evening. I'd like to draw your attention to our favorite Octagon Girl, Luscious Logan Rettino."

Keane's head snapped toward the stairs and spotted her. The Round One sign was firmly in place over her head. His features softened, though, as he glanced at her conservative deep purple halter top secured back in place. *Move on and forget her, already. Forget everything*, his mind repeated his newfound mantra.

He ignored her, Sal, Jerry and even Stevie, seated front row and center a few feet below. The German had his undivided attention, and was about to bear the brunt of all the unleashed emotions caged within him for so long.

Jerry returned to the mic and announced the bout. The horn blared, and with a few strategically misleading jabs, Keane stalked toward the center of the cage.

Chapter 20

HAYMAKER: A lethal, diving punch. If landed, it will likely change the outcome of a fight

"Nice shorts."

Logan blushed and ignored Stevie's comment, firmly planting her butt down in the seat next to him. Front row, behind Keane's corner. An earthquake wouldn't be enough to stir her from her chair. What was bedazzled in brightly colored sequins across the bottom of her fluorescent purple shorts was too humiliating for words. It took some work keeping them hidden, first by holding the card behind her, then, as she made her rounds, by keeping her bottom toward the cage. It had been a miracle Sophie Morelle, the crowd, and, most importantly,

Keane, hadn't spotted them. Still, who knew if the Jumbotron had zoomed in on the words displayed there.

Pierre was probably laughing his ass off somewhere in the audience. Funny how the thought didn't bother her much.

Stevie intently studied the cage. "If he doesn't keep a lid on his emotions, he'll lose this match for sure."

Logan snorted. If the lid containing Keane's emotions was screwed on any tighter, she'd never tug the damned thing off. It must be a Marine thing, restraining all feelings to the point of having none at all. She supposed that's what made a fighter an effective one during combat. What had Stevie noticed about Keane that she'd missed?

Nothing was out of the ordinary. With narrowed eyes, Keane glared at his opponent like a puma ready to pounce. He had the kind of quiet, contained ruthlessness that intimidated even the toughest of men—she'd witnessed this first-hand. In Logan's opinion, the German even seemed nervous, with the way he swayed back and forth, keeping his distance within the eight-sided cage.

She gave voice to her thoughts. "Keane is a study in self-control. Believe me, I've tried to break through and get in close but every time I see a flash of…*whatever*…he shuts me out. He literally dropped me off on my stoop this morning without so much as a goodbye."

Stevie ran his fingers across his chin thoughtfully. "Oh, he's been bitten by the love bug, all right. I've never seen him so possessive about a woman before, and believe me, he's had his share—no offense. Women have always loved Keane, that much hasn't changed.

For the most part, he's loved 'em and left them. You, Logan, are the exception."

Logan shook her head. "Stevie, have you been listening? Keane and I are no longer…" *What were they, even? Partners? Boyfriend/girlfriend? Lovers?* "He's done with me. Things are different between us."

"Listen, I know him better than anyone. Keane totally digs you. What *is* different is that he used to be more social, less distant. He's more closed off and harder to reach these days. Like Dr. Felter said, a lot of guys experience the same issues after coming home. Believe me, I know. I've been working on my own issues all year. Try not to take it too personally."

"He doesn't want to hurt me—that's what he keeps saying."

With a small smile, Stevie glanced at her. "It's a start, him admitting something is up, that he's worried about how he handles you. See, your intervention wasn't the failure you made it out to be. I've been trying to get him to speak with my therapist. Got to start somewhere."

"He's stubborn, that's for sure."

The fans erupted out of their seats, screaming and pointing at the fighters. Logan forgot everything she was saying, even the question on her lips about Keane's so-called hang-up, as her gaze swung toward the cage and fell on his bleeding cheek. Before her widening eyes, the Mad German's fist connected straight on with Keane's nose, and the impact forced him backward a few steps.

With clenched fists, she angled her body for a better view of him. He seemed unfazed by the punch in spite of the blood.

The announcers were having a field day, speculating how fast the German was going to finish him off, but Logan tuned them out. Surely the referee would call the fight with one man injured?

"He better stay out of that dude's reach or a broken nose isn't all he's gonna get," Stevie shouted.

"Oh my God! Is his nose broken? Why is he still in there?"

"Shhh, don't scream any louder, Logan. Keane will blow a gasket if he hears you. That's what happens in MMA fights, things get broken."

Logan shifted in her seat and looked around for the EMT crew. They'd know what to do, right? Except they were off to the side of the cage, nodding and laughing. No help there.

Keane wiped away the blood with his forearm, rolled his neck and jogged slowly around the cage, just out of the German's reach. Intense and focused. Even with a bloody, swollen nose, he was too beautiful for words.

The German was just the opposite. An enormous brute with at least three inches on Keane, and twenty pounds. How had he even made weight? No way had this man's underwear knocked off a pound or two on the scales. Logan's gaze came to rest on Jerry standing off to the side of the cage with a smirk so broad he resembled a circus clown. *Did Jerry screw with the damn scale so this heavy brute seemed to weigh less?* She swallowed deeply. She wouldn't put it past the jerk.

An explosion of activity rocked the cage. The German charged, his fists swinging. One connected with Keane's arm. A big, beefy leg followed, hitting Keane in the same place and making him stagger back.

The fickle crowd roared with appreciation.

"I don't think you should watch this, Logan. How

about sitting this one out in the locker room?" Stevie shouted over the brouhaha.

Logan tightened her fingers around the undersides of the chair. She wasn't going anywhere. She had to know he was okay.

Surprisingly, Keane was smiling. Her heart clenched. It was a rare occasion to get even a fleeting grin out of the man, yet there he was grinning like a cat who'd eaten a fat German canary. Had the punches to his face rattled his mind? Was he *enjoying* this?

Stevie spoke, his voice filled with trepidation. "I've seen that look before. Things are about to get ugly."

Logan jumped to her feet, but Stevie grabbed her arm and tugged her back down. "Don't distract him. I had it all wrong. Just watch."

"Another kick like that and Boom-Yay is going to become See-yay," the voice of an announcer predicted enthusiastically.

Once more, the German charged Keane. Closing in on him, his big, beefy bratwurst leg lifted and swung violently. Logan resisted the urge to squeeze her eyes shut, knowing she was about to witness a savage beating. "Keane," she screamed and, wrestling her arm out of Stevie's grasp, jumped to her feet.

What happened in the next few seconds was so fast that Logan barely had time to process it. The Mad German's kick was short but close enough for Keane to wrap his arm underneath the man's knee, lift it upward, and twist, knocking him belly down onto the mat. Without missing a beat, Keane was on top of him.

Logan fell back into her seat as Keane pushed the German's head into the cage a few feet away. Keane's arms flexed tight as they angled around his opponent's body, his face tight with intent.

"Lukas, get your knees in. Get your knees in," a corner man warned the other fighter.

Logan's eyes widened. Surely, forcing an opponent onto his stomach and hitting his head into the cage wasn't the way to win? Punches and kicks seemed more effective.

"Would you look at that? Man, I owe Coach an apology." Stevie laughed beside her. "Wonder what he's aiming for?"

Logan heard the admiration in his voice, as clear as day. The announcers went silent and, except for the German's trainer screaming out directions and the grunts of the two men wrestling around on the mat, an uncharacteristic hush fell over the arena.

Keane thrust his chest into the German's back and came up onto his knees. Shifting off to the side, he angled his arm over and underneath his opponent's neck.

Stevie sprang to his feet and fist pumped the air. "That's it, Keane. Get 'em in a headlock."

Logan gripped the seat tighter, not knowing what to expect. The German's eyes opened wide and, for a second, focused on her. It occurred to her that *he* knew what was coming a moment before it happened.

Keane pushed up to a crouch and then, in one fluid movement, sat back on the mat. His legs wound up and around the German. His arm flexed around the man's neck. Logan gasped and came to her feet as Keane rolled backward. With disbelief, she watched him flip the German over his body.

Stevie jumped up and down next to her. "Shit, shit, shit. He's going for it—a Peruvian necktie. You're witnessing the most lethal choke hold of all. Very few fighters have mastered it. Keane's making it look like a walk in the park, too."

This was a Peruvian necktie? The almighty MMA move that seemed to excite everyone from fighters to fans? Logan shook her head. She'd always thought it sounded like something a fighter passed around as a joke, a way to showcase how refined he was—like wearing a black silk bowtie at a wedding. What a misleading name for such a brutal maneuver.

Euphoric chaos broke out in the arena as the German tapped Keane three times on the forearm.

"Boom-Yay, Boom-Yay, Boom-Yay," chanted the fans.

The announcers sounded stunned. "The Mad German submits to a masterful Peruvian necktie."

An open-mouthed Stevie still hopped in place next to her, his eyes fixed on the cage.

The German lay on his back, coughing and gasping for breath, as he stared up in what could only be bewilderment at the man hovering over him.

Astonishment, fanatical pride, and respect echoed throughout the voices in the arena. The same sentiments filled their eyes. Logan had seen vaguely similar expressions spread across fan faces at a Pittsburgh Steelers Super Bowl party she'd attended while on tour.

"Boom-Yay, Boom-Yay, Boom-Yay!"

Her gaze fell on the source of their admiration. *Keane.* Her breath hitched. He didn't seem surprised, or euphoric, or proud. She had a clear view of his beautiful, battered face as he stood over the German. He looked…miserable.

She marched forward, grabbed hold of the cage, and

looked up at him. "Keane," she called out. He looked up and their eyes connected. The air rushed out of her lungs at the unspoken emotion within his blue depths. *This is not a normal reaction from a guy who'd just outmaneuvered an opponent twice his weight and size.*

"Keane," she shouted, uncaring who heard or about how terrible her timing was. "I love you, you hear me? I love you, no matter what."

Her declaration did the trick, all right. Something changed in his expression. A brief softening. And in the next second, it was gone and replaced by his oh-too-familiar tough-as-nails expression. Logan empathized with the German—Keane caused her throat to restrict enough that she felt like coughing and gasping for breath. His rejection stung.

Sal sprinted up and tried to dab Keane's nose with a towel. Keane brushed it away. He was so good at that, pushing people away. Sal was a stronger person than she was, she noted, watching him shuffle off, hot on Keane's heels. Logan watched Keane stalk away, out of the cage, and out of the arena. Every Jumbotron captured the image of the ferocious fighter's abrupt departure.

"There he goes, ladies and gentlemen. The welterweight who will now be going up against Caden Kelly for the championship later this evening. Don't go anywhere."

She needed to get a grip. If Keane truly wanted nothing to do with her, she had no choice but to let him go. Her heart raced inside her chest but she tried to ignore it. Moisture coated her eyes but she blinked the tears back. She had to get out of there before the media caught sight of the Octagon Girl who'd just received her own version of a Peruvian necktie from the man she loved.

Stevie interrupted her self-inflicted pity party. "Ah, Logan. Don't take it so hard. I don't think he heard you—"

"My father way out in San Diego heard me. I couldn't have shouted it any louder. I'm done here. I might love the guy but if this is the way he reacts to it…"

He took her by her arm and moved her over to the chair. "Sit. I'm going to explain something to you, whether Keane wants me to or not."

Logan cut him off. "I know more about PTSD than you think. A lot of veterans suffer from this, right? You don't see them fighting in MMA bouts with broken noses. Acting all nice and sweet one minute and surly and tight-lipped the next."

Stevie smiled, and Logan wanted to smack him on the side of the head. "Nice and sweet, huh? I'd have loved to be a fly on the wall for that. Keane's never been the type to be *gentle*." His face became more serious. "PTSD does fuck around with a veteran's emotions. Depression, anger, and even sadness might ambush a guy emotionally. You can't even fathom the shit we've seen—*done*—in the line of duty. It's nothing people stateside can begin to relate to."

"Well, it's your turn to convince him to get help. I tried, and he showed me the door so fast my head spun."

Stevie studied her, assessing her words.

Am I really just going to walk away from him? It wasn't like she'd been given a choice in the matter. Keane was calling all the shots.

"You know the expression 'the people you love hurt you the most'?"

"I sure do. Along with the expression, 'Love like you've never been hurt.' Well guess what? Here's a quote for the originators of these ridiculous expressions: 'Bite me.'" She looked around for Jerry. Retiring from her gig as an Octagon Girl was the first thing she was going to do. *Boscov's, here I come.*

"When you suffer from PTSD, sometimes the people you love the most hurt you with their kindness, and with their love. Weird, I know. But after some of the shit we've done, love isn't something we feel worthy of. See what I'm getting at here?"

"Now *you* can bite my ballerina behind, Stevie! Keane doesn't love me. He doesn't even like me."

"You didn't see his face when he hauled your ballerina butt outta here. If that wasn't love, then I don't know what it was. But there's more to Keane's issues than PTSD."

Logan folded her arms across her body as if they might keep her heart from falling out of her chest. She thought about the other conversations they'd had, and Keane's brutal withdrawal afterward. She knew the direction this conversation was headed. "Jimmy?"

"Yep, fuckin' Jimmy."

"Okay, you've got me. His name has come up so many times, I feel like I know him like a brother…" Logan's voice wavered. Something in Stevie's manner made the hair on her arms stand up.

"You got to understand…it's bad."

"Okay. But you've got to understand. I love him."

Stevie smiled, fleetingly. "Keane's gonna kick my ass for telling you this. But hell, I've been trying to help him since the funeral." He shook his head as if in disbelief and added, almost to himself, "And, here he goes, and falls in love, despite the load of shit he's bearing."

Logan wanted to believe him, hoping her feelings

weren't one-sided, and that Stevie was right—that Keane loved her.

"I know him well, know he's struggling. I don't want to see him push you away. Not when I think you're the only thing keeping him going…"

"Please, just tell me." So far, the media was busy recapping the fight. Most of the crowd was refreshing their hot dog and beer purchases. Jerry had run off to who knows where. All while Logan's world was crashing around her and she didn't even know why.

"Keane killed Jimmy. At least, that's what he thinks."

An invisible sucker punch knocked the air out of her. "What?"

"Keane and Jimmy fought in a championship bout sponsored by the Marines. You already know Keane was a trainer for MMA fighters. Jimmy had been his sparring partner for God knows how many years. The Marines wanted a morale-boosting event, something to take the guys' minds off of car bombs and Afghani rebels." Stevie ran a hand over his cheek, deep in thought, before continuing, "Keane won with a K.O.—"

"He knocked him out? That isn't so surprising."

"Yeah, guess not. It's what MMA fighters aim to do, right? Typical."

"And…" she pressed on anxiously.

"Jimmy was out, and I mean O-U-T, for a few minutes. But when he came to, he refused to see a medic or go to the unit. I remember Keane cursing out him for being so headstrong."

"How did Jimmy die? Did it have something to do with Keane knocking him out? Or was he killed in the line of duty? I don't get it."

"After Keane and I finished our last tour and headed

home for good, Jimmy was deployed to the Afghanistan/Pakistan border. During an attack, he had a freaking brain aneurysm. He was the main cover for his unit as they moved across an abandoned terrorist encampment. Turns out, it wasn't abandoned. He barely got a round out of the machine gun before the aneurysm happened."

Logan bit her lip hard, tasting blood. Oh my God. Poor Jimmy. And…Keane.

"Most of his unit was slaughtered," Stevie continued. "When an investigation into the matter revealed the cause of his death, it made the military papers. I knew Keane would see it, and that he'd totally lose it. Fuck, they were best friends. Then I got a hold of him. He could barely speak as he spilled his guts. Afterward, he closed up. Shut me out. End of discussion. The guilt was—*is*—eating him up inside."

Logan squeezed her arms tighter. Her heart thumped loudly in her chest. She thought about Keane's reluctance to fight. The expression on his face every time he did so. His anguish over knocking that kid, Smitty, out. The misery in his eyes when he hovered over the German. PTSD wasn't the only issue Keane needed help addressing. It was the lesser of the two evils. "Keane genuinely believes—"

"—he killed Jimmy *and* the men in his unit."

Chapter 21

GRAPPLING: When fighters take the action down to the mat

Logan was waiting for Keane when he came out of the locker room. She had more determination than one of his former drill sergeants, prodding, hassling and trying to wear him down during interrogation training. Big Sarge's goal had been to make Keane crack and spill the beans. Hell, if Logan dropped the L-bomb again, shouting *I love you* so loudly the arena shook, she might just succeed at accomplishing what Sarge had failed so miserably at doing.

"Bleeding leotards, your nose!"

Keane ignored her and tried brushing past. She blocked his path. No tame missus here, she had reason to fear him yet she planted her Nikes firmly on the concrete floor and stood her ground.

He loved the way her eyes flashed green when she was riled up. The way her hair unfurled from its ponytail and framed her lovely face. How her lithe, graceful movements reflected her self-discipline, the same type of control he'd trained for himself, first as a Marine, then as a fighter.

Her luscious curves jiggled underneath her conservative purple halter top. Her hands found her hips. She cocked her head and stared him down. Man, Logan was a force to be reckoned with. There wasn't a lot he didn't love about her. He just couldn't go there, for both their sakes.

"When are you going to stop punishing yourself?" she demanded.

"In case you missed it, the German ate the mat. I'd say I punished *him*."

A strand of blond hair fell into her face. She blew it away. "That's not what I'm talking about. Stevie told me *everything*, Keane. Even about Jimmy."

A brutal, mental ambush—that's what this was. Wait until he got his hands around Stevie's neck. She *knew*.

Yet the sudden rush of anger didn't come. Nor did the urge to beat up a locker or lay a kick down on someone. Instead, he felt empty. Dropping her back home on her stoop like that should have been her red flag. A clean break. *Nice knowing you. Don't need you around to witness how my life's fucked up way beyond hope*. He pressed his lips together, stepped around her and heard her sigh.

"Okay, you don't have to say anything. All I want you to know is you don't have to deal with this alone.

I'm here for you. So is Stevie. And professional help is available. But I can't lead a horse to water. This is something you're going to have to want."

"All I *want* is to get this fuckin' fight over with. Later." He feinted left, then dodged her on the right. Out of his peripheral vision, he caught her flinch. Softly, he added, "Got a dance school to fund."

"Please…I don't want you to fight. I'm good, really. A few weeks at Boscov's and I'll have my studio. This isn't healthy, Keane. I know it, Stevie knows it, you know it. Forget about Tetnus and Jerry."

Yeah, like that was gonna happen. What did she think all the booze, pills and women had been for? To *forget*. The word was like a slow poison gnawing away at him. He couldn't fuckin' forget, that was the point. Not Jimmy. Not…her.

Shit, he couldn't seem to shake thinking about her: the way she looked in the mornings, with her hair all rumpled and sexy as hell; how damned good she felt curled up next to him asleep; how every time he set eyes on her, something shifted inside of him. Logan and Jimmy—they'd both found a way to crawl beneath his thick skin and mess with his freakin' soul. But no way was Logan going to suffer the same fate as Jimmy.

"I know you're a private man. How you hate being harassed about anything, by Stevie or me. I'll say it once more, and that's it. You need expert advice, from a professional like Dr. Felter. There's no shame in it. Just contact her, okay? Talk to her and let her help you. Calling her is the first step toward figuring stuff out. I'll *wait* for you."

"Nothing to figure out. So don't waste your time."

He lengthened his stride, yet only made it a few

steps down the corridor before she shouted his name. Although he should have ignored her, he stopped and turned around.

"Don't you think Jimmy would want you to be happy? Have a life? To *care?*"

Her words pierced him like daggers. But it was the hurt in her tone that really dug deep.

Fuck, hurting people was the only thing he was good at.

He shoved back the feelings swelling up in him, and instead focused on the sexy sway of her hips as she narrowed the distance between them. Hips that said she was full of purpose. Damn if Logan wasn't looking for a way to make him tap out.

He rolled his neck and acted as if he didn't give a shit.

"Was it all a lie? What happened between us in the cable car? Did I get it all wrong?"

She had to go there, and bring up the cable car. His throat tightened and he fought for control. Man, it had to be written all over his face. He was gonna lose this battle, big time.

She stepped closer, unaware of how precarious a situation she was in. "You are not fighting again tonight, or any other night. Got it?" Poking him in the chest with a finger, she continued, "I'm going to go tell Jerry right now that you quit."

"No," he stated. *What the hell was she thinking? He'd fought a goddamn kid for her! He wasn't turning back now. This was their shit-ass plan, after all.*

"Yes. You owe me something, Keane," she rasped.

What the fuck—stop the fight? Was she trying to emotionally bribe him? "No can do. I'm finishing what's been started." Man, her words got to him, like she was asking him for something he didn't want to—*couldn't*—give her. He'd fight, all right. And she'd get that money for her school and go on with her life.

Without him.

Her expression changed, softened. A warning as clear as a bullhorn. A fighter should always be prepared for a jab, yet he saw it coming a second too late. "For the record, no matter what happens from this moment on, I still love you."

She pivoted on her Nikes, and stalked away. His attention was drawn to her freakin' boy shorts, and instantly, he felt like he'd been hit with a surprise cross punch, full force. One that knocked the wind out of him.

In bold sequined letters, the word *Boom* ran diagonally down her left cheek. A horizontal dash crossed at her waist. On her right cheek *Yay's* was diagonally written so the two words combined into a V shape right above the curve of her ass. Boom-Yay's. Running straight across the bottom of both buns was the word *Girl*. The print was small—hell, her ass was small. But when the cameramen caught sight of her glittering butt, the Jumbotrons would make the words pop out bolder than any billboard. *Boom-Yay's Girl*.

There it was. His feelings printed on her damned shorts for the world to see. Might as well add the word *love* to the sparkling mess. Plaster it smack on her ass in brilliant sequined emotions.

He rubbed his fingers over his temples. *Would the pain of loving, then losing, someone ever go away?*

He had no choice.

Sprinting down the corridor, he caught up with her and scooped her up into his arms.

"What? Keane…"

"This changes nothing, Logan," he barked, hoarsely. Stalking down the corridor, he stopped in front of the ladies' locker room and kicked the door open.

"Oh no, you don't. I have to find Jerry," she firmly stated, catching on to his intentions.

"Chloe!" he bellowed.

"This is not going to happen. Don't think my friend is going to go all Benedict Arnold on me. Octagon Girls stick together, right, Chloe?"

He'd heard the other woman gasp from behind the lockers. "Get over here, Chloe!"

Logan squirmed in his arms but he held on tight.

Chloe appeared from around the corner, breathless.

"Get Sal. Fast." Logan kicked him in the shins.

The tension inside him was unbearable, the kind only satisfied by getting physical—pounding some flesh, hard. Fast. For as long as it took to calm the fuck down. To forget.

"Chloe," Logan warned beneath clenched teeth. "Remember whose side you're on. Think about who took care of you when that bottle of Stoli grabbed hold of your senses. Who gave you tips for overcoming your nerves, without a liquid diet. A friend who—"

Keane bounced her in his arms.

Logan clawed at him.

As Chloe sprinted out of the locker room, he heard her say, "Be back in a flash."

Setting Logan down gently, he rooted her in place with his hands so she couldn't follow her ditsy cohort. Much like how her words rooted themselves in a place deep inside him. Logan, with her *I love you*. Shit.

"Promise me you won't fight."

"This was our agreement and I'm sticking with it."

"Fuck the agreement."

His hands almost fell off her hips at the rawness of her curse. "It's for the best."

"What? Locking me inside a locker room so I can't watch you get hurt. Physically and emotionally? I can't let you do this."

"That's not what I'm talking about." He grabbed a soft blond lock and rubbed it between his fingers before smoothing it back behind her ear. Everything about her felt nice. His chest tightened. "It's for your own good."

"What is?"

Shit. Didn't she realize he was doing this for him and *her*?

"I love you. No matter what."

Who was he kidding? He was a mixed bag of unresolved issues. But he'd deal with them on his own terms. He'd do this, for his sanity. And for her sake.

"Everything."

"I know you can hear me, Sal!" Logan pounded on the locker room door and paused for her unsolicited bodyguard's response. Grandpa Romeo was uncharacteristically quiet. "Come on, Sal. This is important. I've got to talk to Jerry."

She kicked the door, then pressed her forehead against it. In a low voice, she asked, "Sal, do you see the way Keane is after every bout, whether he dominates his opponent or not? He's not euphoric like Jaysin Bouvine or any of the other fighters. Fighting isn't healthy for him. I can't tell you all the specifics, but you have to let me out of here."

"Nope. Jerry will fire you for sure. Keane said as much."

So at least he was out there. "What do you mean 'nope'? Nope as in you don't notice how miserable Keane gets after a bout, or nope as in you're keeping me hostage here in the ladies' locker room?"

"Sorry, Logan. Wha'd you say? My lady friend's pissed the bouts aren't over yet. Just texting her back."

Twist my tights. At this rate, she'd never get out of here in time.

"Keane says you've lost your marbles. What are you thinking, stopping the fight? The way Keane handled the German, the model's gonna be a piece of cake." He sounded distracted, as if Keane's wins were an after-thought.

Something slammed against the door and Logan jumped back in alarm. "Sal?"

Sal muttered from the other side, "Flowers and chocolate weren't enough for her."

"Please let me out. Don't make me call the police," she lied, knowing her cell phone was dead.

The door shook once again, vibrating loudly on its hinges. She almost missed Sal's next comment. "She broke up with me for a pizza delivery boy. Says his hours of work suit her needs better."

Had Grandpa Romeo been listening to anything she'd been saying? Maybe her approach was all wrong. "Let me see the text, Sal. I'm sure you're misreading it."

"'Don't call or text me again. Antonio gives bet-ter…' humph." It sounded like something was caught in his throat.

Poor Grandpa Romeo. Looking for love in all the wrong places. Not that Logan was an expert on the subject, given the way Keane'd dropped her faster than an overcooked Polish kielbasa. *Wait a minute...* "Sal, I'll make a deal with you."

No response came from the other side of the door. She hoped he was listening. "If you unlock the door and let me out of here, I'll fix you up with a lovely woman. Someone more your speed. Someone who'll crave your *humph*."

"Your sister, maybe?" Sal sounded hopeful.

Logan felt hopeful, herself. "Ah, not *exactly*. But I can promise you, there's no way she'll ever dump you for an Italian dough boy. And I know for a fact that her bra size is much larger than mine."

The door opened so fast, if Logan weren't so nimble, she would have fallen through it.

"Deal." Grandpa Romeo grinned at her. "So what's her number?"

The excited chatter of the MMA fans calmed Logan's racing heart. She'd made it out of the locker room, down the corridor and to the arena in time. The fighters hadn't yet been announced.

Standing on her toes, she scanned the crowd until she spotted Chloe's dark hair by the cage. She seemed uncharacteristically calm and collected. Guess there was only room for one Octagon Girl freak-out per bout.

Logan saw Stevie standing over by Keane's corner. From this distance, he was a speck among the masses. Maybe Stevie could talk some sense into Keane?

Jerry was over by the broadcasters' table, animatedly chatting up the reporters and trying to drum up more financing for his fighters headed to Tetnus. *Damn. Damn. Damn.* Horrible timing. What she had to say to him was best done in private—for so many reasons. Who knew what Jerry would do if she confronted him now? A horrible, way-too-public cuss-fest was more than likely.

The same helpless feeling she'd had the moment her ankle snapped returned. Just like then, she struggled for some sense of control.

She desperately needed a Plan B.

Adjusting her top, she worked her way down the ramp. Closer to Stevie. Closer to where Keane would be.

"Hey, Luscious." She waved in the general direction of the fan who'd called her name. When her gaze swung back around, she noticed Sophie Morelle standing by the cage at the end of the ramp. The reporter hadn't seen her yet, she was too busy scribbling in her notebook. Alone. Intent on recording whatever it was inside the big black book. Presenting a prime opportunity for Logan to approach her and set the record straight about Pierre.

Strike fast and move on to more important matters, Logan. The righteously vindictive part of her spurred her on.

It was a perfect chance at revenge.

But she'd held out on airing the dirty laundry this long. Pierre counted on it, didn't he? Knowing how much she hated the notoriety. Banking on her to keep her mouth shut and growing more and more confident in her silence. Her problems were so insignificant compared to Keane's, yet the first step to solving them was admitting you had one. That was Dr. Felter's recommendation. That's what Logan had told Keane.

It was time for her to take the good doc's advice.

"Over here, Logan," another fan hollered. She shot him a grin over her shoulder but her attention remained on Sophie, who was still busy writing her notes. Perfect.

Swift and fast.

But before she took another step forward, she spotted him. The biggest, smuggest, most self-serving ass she'd ever regretted crossing paths with was now hovering in the aisle, smack in between her and Sophie Morelle. It wasn't a coincidence how close he lurked to the reporter.

Logan was about to give *him* an earful. This time, she was ready for him.

In her short career in the cage, her world, priorities and heart had shifted. Now he stood in *her* place, *her* Octagon arena, with hundreds of *her* adoring fans. And even if tonight was her last as Octagon Girl, Pierre wasn't the star. She was.

What goes around, comes around, Pierre. Revenge was going to taste oh-so-sweet. Fame…he could keep it. Logan planned on hitting him where he'd least expected it, in his pocket.

She squared her shoulders and strode forward until she was close enough to hear his wheezing exhale.

"Pierre."

The jerk didn't even greet her, just began speaking nervously, "About the finale. You know, Anya and I are slated to win. The hip-hop duo and belly dancers aren't *real* dancers. But any negative press could really hurt us, affect how America votes."

"You are so damn arrogant. What won't you do for fame, huh?"

"The show's executives think you should be there."

Logan gave a mental fist pump in the air. Surprise. Surprise. The wholesome family show was fed up with his bullshit, that's what he really was saying. This was perfect. Upon spying Pierre, she'd made a split decision—she was going to take him down, with money instead of fists. Though she wouldn't walk away from the opportunity to land a well-deserved kick. Make him sing instead of dance.

She decided to forfeit some of her savings for lawyer fees. Her salary from Keane winning the fifth bout was enough to cover a few months more in rent, plus initial lawyer fees. Money well spent. But knowing the networks needed her to make nice—that Pierre needed her—that was priceless. And she'd thought his showing up was a publicity stunt. Ha.

"It's reality TV, Logan. Everyone wants their favorites to win or there's no show."

Pierre ignored her Keane-worthy scowl, and continued on, "I'll apologize on television about the fall—"

"Drop it, Pierre. We both know the truth," she stated, her tone suspiciously calm, void of all the heartache he'd caused. Hell, she had bigger heartaches to contend with. *Make it fast, or it'll be too late.*

He swiveled his head around and nervously eyed the crowd, as if his lie had been announced over the loudspeakers. "Ah, about that—"

"One million cash, or I tell all. Tonight." She bit her lip, then added, "Plus payment of the full sale price on the co-op. All my antique furniture, china and porcelain collectibles."

Pierre's face flushed a beautiful scarlet shade. "That's nearly everything I'm making off the show…"

"…and I keep the painting."

That did the trick. The vein in Pierre's forehead popped out like a sugar beet root. "You told me it had been stolen. Why, you…liar!" All self-control gone, he stomped around the ramp, enraged.

Sophie Morelle's head snapped up from her notebook.

Logan had Pierre exactly where she wanted him. Now he was the one about to get dropped on his ass.

The arena reverberated with the opening chords of a Def Leppard song. Not that it stopped Sophie Morelle and her cameramen from heading up the ramp. Or Pierre, who was in full temper-tantrum mode, flailing about like a child who'd had his toy snatched away.

But the music signaled the beginning of the bout, forcing Logan's hand. She could finish off Pierre and expose him as a liar once and for all. It would be so easy to hand that bloodhound of a reporter an Emmy-worthy story of lies and deceit. Or Logan could high-tail it over to the cage and hastily figure out Plan B with Stevie.

Pierre was going through some kind of metamorphosis on the ramp, his face flaming red, his fingers clenching and unclenching, but grinning like they'd just had the most pleasant conversation. Clearly, he'd caught sight of Sophie and company.

"So my breasts caused you to drop me—*that* was your lame-ass excuse?" she began, raising her voice high enough to earn some attention. How far could she push Pierre? His fear of being thrown off his precious show was priceless. Bad press? It was his turn to grovel. "I wonder what Sophie's going to do when I clarify things; tell her how you need beginner lessons in ballet 101, where most dancers learn how to position their feet in preparation to catch their partner. Helps with a little thing called *balance*."

Sophie Morelle was sprinting toward them. Pierre saw her, too. The blood drained out of his face. Good, she had the jerk right where she wanted him.

Someone cranked up the music. "Bringin' on the Heartbreak," a Def Leppard classic.

Of course, the song had to be about heartbreak. *Damn. Damn. Damn.*

The bout was beginning momentarily. The source of her genuine heartbreak was headed toward the ring.

Payback was within her power.

Sophie bit her lip and paused. And then she let the perfect moment for revenge slip away. Nothing was more important than the man headed toward the cage. She had to stop the fight.

Logan stepped back. In a total Keane move, she feinted left, hustled by a surprised Sophie on the right, and headed down the ramp without a backward glance.

Chapter 22

GROUND AND POUND: A wrestling move, where a fighter secures his/her opponent to the mat and punches them, in an attempt to get them to submit

Keane jogged in place at the top of the ramp. Figures the underwear model would select such a lame-ass song for his entry music, some crap about heartbreak. He watched his opponent pause and lean in toward that abrasive redheaded reporter below. A similar gesture to the moves he'd been putting on Logan. This crowd-pleaser was a real ladies' man. But could this Marky Mark handle himself in the cage?

Not your problem. Not like he's a kid.

His temple throbbed. The days of fighting for pleasure were long gone. All he seemed to do lately was agonize over putting a beating on guys who'd willingly entered into the cage, most of them trained in mixed martial arts moves Keane hadn't used in ages. It was incredible he'd been able to even pull off a Peruvian necktie on the German. A move he planned on never using again, not after the way the German had been fighting for breath.

When are you going to stop punishing yourself?

He rolled his shoulders as if the gesture might shake off the question foremost in his head. And shake off the image of Logan, with her piercing green eyes and her throaty voice so full of...*love*. She should have known better than to get involved with such a mean bastard, should have listened to Rosie's warning the night of the snowstorm. She should count her blessings he'd be leaving her in one piece, unharmed and better off.

A Marine always finished what he'd started, it was part of a fighter's code of honor. Stuff the emotional shit. Hell with sentiment. *Love.* Keane felt a familiar fury wash over him, and he took comfort in it.

If he had a hood, he'd have yanked it over his head. A way to block everything and everyone out. Bare-chested was one thing, but bare-headed left him...exposed. Gritting his teeth, he headed down the ramp.

The fans jumped to their feet and fist pumped the air. "Boom-Yay, Boom-Yay, Boom-Yay." He ignored them and focused on the welterweight standing with the reporter and her crew. Judging by the way the redhead's attention kept angling Keane's way, she intended to interview both of them, like this was some demented freak show or something. Fuck that.

He lengthened his stride, planning on brushing by the group.

"Hey, Boom-Yay, wait up." *Freakin' great, the underwear model.* "Don't take this personally but I've got moves the German's never seen. Just thought I'd warn you now—this is gonna be some match-up."

Keane snorted. The mics picked up on it, and cameramen shifted their gear high on their shoulders, ready to capture the unscripted drama unfolding on live television.

The welterweight smoothed things over. "Never seen someone pull off a Peruvian necktie like that. Man, you've got mad technique." Assuming a fighter's stance, his opponent lifted his fists chest level for a knuckle tap. A perfect photo op.

At least he'd stopped yapping. Keane didn't want to hear anymore, didn't want to *like* the freakin' guy. Get the picture over with and get out of Dodge. He lifted his fists.

The redhead nudged her way between them. "Hold up, guys. One sec. Ready? Lights. Camera. Action. This is Sophie Morelle reporting from Mellon Arena and the match-up of all match-ups for the welterweight championship. The winner of this bout will move on to Tetnus in Las Vegas this July."

Keane shifted, but Sophie grabbed him by the arm.

"You can't begin to imagine how buff these guys are, how *strong*." A red fox had nothing on this sly redhead. Yet, it was equal rights for all, as she dropped Keane's arm and snagged the forearm of his opponent, who—to give the guy some credit—looked equally displeased.

Caden tried stepping back. Keane spotted how Sophie's leg wound around the back of his ankle, stopping him. How she easily manipulated a six-foot-three, one-hundred-and-seventy-pound brawler as if he were a toddler.

"This guy's got a body like a Greek god. C'mon, ladies, you know you've seen his package plastered on every billboard from Pittsburgh to Los Angeles."

At the mention of the billboards, Caden's brows narrowed so much, Keane spotted two thick creases form on his forehead. Man, he felt sorry for the guy.

His opponent's hand snaked around Sophie's waist and nudged her away.

Sophie held her ground, and with a surprising combination of lethal hip and carefully placed foot, she gyrated into him. Except he moved sideways. Everything was a freakin' blur after that.

His opponent angled away from the reporter. She went flying by him and straight into a cameraman. Like a slow-motion movie, the cameraman lost his balance, the huge camera on his shoulder tottered and came crashing forward, smack into the back of Caden's head.

Keane reached for him. But it was too late. His eyes rolled into the back of his head and then Marky Mark was out for the count.

"Get the medics, now!" Keane bellowed, kneeling over the guy.

"He's not…dead?" Sophie cried out, falling to her knees beside the unconscious man and grabbing his wrist. "Thank God, a pulse."

Cameras flashed around them. Pandemonium broke out in the arena. A few people standing around them looked stunned.

Keane took it all in until his chest contracted so

tightly, he had to gasp for breath. His skin felt damp and cold. This situation was way too familiar for comfort.

His opponent didn't so much as twitch. Damn, it wasn't a good sign. Keane should know; Jimmy hadn't twitched either.

Jimmy had been flat on his back, one leg bent, his head twisted sideways. His brown eyes blank and unresponsive. His teasing smile muted. An image Keane tried to forget, but couldn't. He'd killed his best friend with a knock out—except it had taken him months to die.

"Where are the goddamned medics?" he yelled again, tearing his eyes away from his opponent and searching the crowd for help.

"What have you done to my welterweight?" Jerry was the first to burst into the melee, jockeying for position between the arriving EMT crew and the hordes of converging reporters. "If he isn't able to fight in the next bout, I'm going to sue you, your parents, your boyfriend, your television station, the whole lot," he threatened Sophie. Jerry turned toward the medics. "You too. Either do your job and fix him or you're all gonna pay!"

Jerry's wild gaze fixed on Keane. "You! What do you think you're doing? Get up and get the hell in the cage. We've got a fight to win."

Keane stood and blinked. At least this asshole had snapped him back into the present. "He gonna be okay?" Keane asked one of the EMTs as he helped lift his unconscious opponent onto the stretcher.

"We'll need to check him out at the hospital. A knot on the head the size of a baseball might mean there's swelling inside. Nasty concussion. Ah, think I can get an autograph? I'll get his later."

Jerry tried to body block the stretcher. "No, no, no. Where are you taking him?"

"Enough!" Keane barked out and snatched the medic by the scruff of his neck. "If you interfere, you're gonna be laid out on a stretcher headed outta here too."

"But what about the bout?"

Keane couldn't bear looking at Jerry, let alone express the obvious answer. He had to get outta there before he lost it completely. Turning, he noticed Logan hovering just outside of the circle, studying him intently. Watching how freakin' weak and raw he was. *How the fuck did she get out of the locker room?*

"Ladies and gentlemen," Felix's voice boomed. "For the first time in MMA history, by way of K.O. the *loser* in tonight's much-anticipated welterweight bout is... Sophie Morelle."

Keane heard Sophie cry out, but ignored her. The stretcher cleared the top of the ramp.

"Are you okay?" He felt Logan's warm hand on his chest, over his heart. A quickening heart that'd give a racecar driver a run for their money. Thump. Thump. Thump. *No, I'm far from okay.*

"Sal," he snapped at the handler who'd come up next to her—another face gawking at him like he had two heads. He narrowed his eyes on the trainer. He couldn't look at Logan, unwilling to watch her expression fill with pain from what he was about to do. Time to call it quits.

"I'm done. Make sure she makes it home okay."

"Aw, Keane—"

"Do it."

Sal stood undecided, looking like a sad old dog. Keane didn't dare look Logan's way.

He'd held up his end of the bargain. She knew from the get-go where this was leading. It was for her own damn good. Still, he hesitated. The bout hundreds of times worse than the one that should have gone down in the cage played out in his head.

The pain of it all was too much to bear, and he made up his mind.

Keane didn't wait around. Barreling past the spectators abuzz with excited chatter, he pushed through the crowd, stalked up the ramp, headed down the long cold corridor, and out of the arena. Not once did he look back.

Chapter 23

TAP OUT: When a fighter taps the mat to signal his/her defeat

"Eez here! Dat fighter." Mrs. Debinska banged on the door. "Keeenee, eez ere!"

Logan groaned. This was the second Keane sighting in a week. Mrs. Debinska was on the lookout, but with those thick bifocal glasses, she wasn't likely to see much. Yet Logan's breath hitched in her throat just as it had done the last time. She rolled off the couch, yanked the door open, and hurried down the hallway into Mrs. Debinska's living room. Her landlady pulled back the curtain from the bay window, and they both peered out.

She pointed to the street. "Eez waz there."

All Logan saw was a newscaster firing up a barbecue

grill on the front sidewalk. Nothing out of the ordinary. A camera flashed, and she tugged the curtain closed.

"Valeska is right, Keane was out there." Logan flinched at the sound of Grandpa Romeo's voice. Adjusting to her new job as a Boscov's sales clerk had been much easier than adapting to the hot and heavy romance unfolding here on Morrison Avenue. Once more, she peered out from between the curtains. No Keane in sight.

Sal softly scolded her. "You should have taken his winnings. He wanted you to have it for your school."

"Zut, zut," Mrs. Debinska clucked at her. "Dat was a lot of monee."

Logan wrapped her arms around her landlady and gave her a tight hug. "I know, but I couldn't take his winnings. That's blood money. A reminder that he's going to Vegas."

Sal grunted. "Jerry didn't give them two much choice after declaring both welterweights as champions. If you ask me, Jerry was desperate to have one of his fighters qualify for Tetnus."

"I know. But fighting is the last thing I want for Keane…" Logan bit back the words. There was no fixing what had been done, not the way things stood between them.

Sal cleared his throat and patted a mustard-colored cushion on the couch. Logan sat down next to him. "Honey, let ol' Sal give you some advice on *love.*"

Twist my tutu! She resisted the urge to run for the slate hills.

"True love isn't some guy sweeping you across the threshold. Nope, if you genuinely love someone you've got to get your hands dirty and flounder about in the muck right along with them. Ride the highs, and battle out the lows—together."

A bittersweet smile spread across Logan's lips. Grandpa Romeo's long, passionate kisses with Mrs. Debinska, like the one Logan had witnessed this morning in the hallway, were both sweet and too gross for words. Yet, at this moment, Sal's loving and sentimental nature couldn't have touched her more deeply. It seemed Sal knew a thing or two about love, after all.

Keane found himself jogging through the streets of Friendship. Searching for one avenue, in particular. Morrison. His third trip this week. Each time, he hoped a run-by might ease his mind, and more. He had to know that she was okay.

Halfway down the block, he slowed, stopped and tugged his baseball cap lower on his forehead.

The small front lawn looked like a line for Springsteen tickets, with tents, lawn chairs and beverages. Vans with satellites attached to their hoods had double parked up and down the street. Reporters and cameramen alike stood around, chatting with their counterparts from different networks. Every few seconds, one would turn and look at the house as if anticipating Logan's exit.

Damn. He hadn't expected them to completely clear out, but was unprepared for this freakin' festival. And *he* was now the cause of the fucked-up publicity.

With a shake of his head, he realized there was nothing he could do, except leave. If they spotted him, it would only make matters worse.

He touched his track pants pocket. Inside were the pieces of the ripped-up check Sal had returned to him, along with a message: "Money isn't what I want from you."

But what she didn't realize was how he was one massive shell of a man. Nothing inside but trouble. She deserved better, someone with their shit pulled together. Loving her—and man, did he love her—it just wasn't good enough. But it was enough to let her go.

A week later, Sal's words resonated in her mind as Logan stepped off the Shadyside bus. March hadn't come in like a lion as the weathermen predicted. An uncharacteristic warm spell had hit the Burgh. Logan raised her cheek to the sun, loving the feel of the warming rays on her face. Today was the perfect day for a roll about in the muck. Especially with a six-foot-two hunk with an eight-pack for abs and a broken nose that didn't lessen the impact of his beautiful face.

Logan hesitated on Keane's curb. His Jeep was gone. With a sigh, she headed up the stairs onto his lovely wrap-around porch and knocked on the door. When no one answered, she hunkered down on the front steps and waited. After all, no one said finding the muck pile was going to be a simple task. Given the last few months, why would she expect anything different?

She'd visited a few prospective studios. She'd passed on the small one, and others were either also small, awkwardly laid out or way out of her price range. Once more, she questioned her sanity. *Why did I rip up his check?* It was going to take a lot of time to save that kind of money as a sales clerk.

Bleeding leotards, Logan. You did it because you love him.

Arching her head back, she let the sun fall on her

face and contemplated her other mind-boggling option. Pierre's desperately pleading phone call, and subsequent monetary offer.

Turns out, the show's ratings had plummeted. Network executives were anxious to quickly wrap things up so instead of an April finale, they'd backpedaled to March. LaFool—as Keane had so poignantly dubbed him—would do anything in the name of fame.

A million dollars. Plus the full sale price of the co-op. The painting was still being negotiated. All Logan had to do was show up at tonight's *America Gets Its Groove On* finale and cheer the fame whore and Anya on. He'd even reimburse her for the car rental. New York City was an eight-hour drive and there was time enough for her to make it there, if she wanted to.

Yet Logan stayed on Keane's stoop until the sun's rays vanished and the last late-night bus back to Friendship was about to depart. He hadn't come home.

Images of the alpaca-stealing thief weighed heavily on her mind as she made her way home. Something sounding like a cat yowling echoed along the hallway, and she quickly fumbled for the keys in her pocket and opened her door. Slipping off her coat and hanging it on the hook, Logan settled down on the sofa and flicked on the television, feeling numb and desolate. Searching for a distraction to take her mind away from Keane.

Crinkle my camisole, why the hell not? Like a driver passing a car wreck, she grabbed the remote and clicked it on to *America Gets Its Groove On*. Two smug faces filled the screen. Watching Pierre's victory dance was the kind of sick closure she probably needed. Besides, it was the least of her heartaches.

The host was finishing his recap of the prior two performances. "A round of applause for our rocking hip-hop performers and the exquisite belly dancer, Sukeshi. And now I'd like to say a few words to our ballet dancers, who many viewers predict will *win* the title along with a major dance contract with Rockefeller Studios, the one and only Pierre LaFeur and his beautifully talented partner, Anya Melankova."

The camera zoomed in on a smiling Pierre peering down on Anya like she was the love of his life. If this didn't pan out for Pierre, acting might. Logan had a similar picture she'd meant to rip up within her photograph album.

"Pierre, we understand you contacted Logan about cheering you both on tonight. Can we safely say her fingers will be dancing as she texts in her vote for you?"

Logan's middle finger itched to dance but she rolled her eyes instead. These past few months proved beyond a doubt that anything could happen in the name of show business.

"That's right. We talked." Pierre pouted, like a sulky child unable to hide his disappointment.

"Okay then…without further ado, we'll begin. Will the two of you take your places? I watched these guys rehearse and what you are about to witness, ladies and gentlemen, is a dance sure to go down in the record books." The host left the stage, the lights dimmed, and the music started.

It was such an over-the-top performance, Logan was sure Mikhail Baryshnikov was off somewhere banging his head. Still, it had enough flair to excite the untrained eye. Lifts and pirouettes galore. Logan had seen enough, and went to click off the television. But the way Pierre was standing as he positioned himself for Anya's final

jump caught her attention. His feet were too close together, something *they'd* worked on repeatedly.

Anya completed a series of *jetés*, then raced across
the stage. Her arms stretched overhead as she leaped
full force toward Pierre in a breathtakingly beautiful arch. She did as expected and landed hard against
Pierre's chest. But he did the unexpected—unexpected
that is, to everyone except Logan. He tottered backward, and then back onto his ass, with Anya sprawled
out on top of him.

The cameras didn't miss a thing. Not the host's fish-
mouthed expression, Anya's stunned reaction, nor
Pierre's crimson face as he stood and viciously chewed
Anya out, as if the fiasco playing out on national television was her fault.

Logan pressed the off button on the remote.

Payback was a bitch, after all.

In May, a second check, postmarked Cleveland,
Ohio, had arrived in the mail. No note or greeting—or
hey-how-are-you-doing-after-I-tore-out-your-heart?—
had been attached. But the money was message enough.
Keane was honoring their business agreement and
wrapping up loose ends.

The money was substantial, more than enough to
purchase a large dance space, when she'd been hoping
to simply afford rent on a place. She hadn't expected
Keane to offer up his own money. Whether or not Jerry
had paid him handsomely for winning five of the six
qualifiers—six technically—was irrelevant. Turns out
that Keane and Caden had both been declared the welterweight champions, by default. Not that it mattered to
Logan anymore. She'd lost the bigger battle, after all.

Just like the first check, she tore it up. Except she didn't know where to send the pieces, along with the chunks of her shattered heart.

Maybe Keane had found out how Jerry refused to pay her for the final two bouts? She couldn't even argue with Squirrel Face, it wasn't like she'd worked them. No, Jerry wasn't someone she'd miss. Surprisingly, what she did miss was being an Octagon Girl.

Performing for an audience was something she enjoyed, and though carrying an octagonal-shaped sign around overhead wasn't technically a performance, she'd somehow come to like the job. Well, Chloe would have to handle things now. Logan placed a cold Evian on her cheek. She'd perform again, this time as a dance instructor. In a studio she'd rent with her own money.

She padded into the living room and stared at the Renoir-like painting over the sofa. Logan hated the idea of selling it. It symbolized so much in her life; how she'd struggled to become a ballerina, how Pierre had duped her, and how the small girls pirouetting about were her future. Bittersweet, nevertheless.

Sally's lawyer friend suggested that Logan had a strong case against Pierre—criminal charges were even a consideration. But she hadn't entirely decided yet. She was prepared to hit Pierre where it counted, in his pocket. As long as the lawyer got back everything that was hers—especially the money from the co-op—she suspected that between that and Pierre's public humiliation, she'd be hard pressed to take it further.

In one massive wave, the paparazzi had disappeared from Mrs. Debinska's front lawn the night *America Gets Its Groove On* rebounded in the ratings, and in fact became the top-rated show in reality TV history.

The same night, Pierre became the most hated man in America. A few reporters inquired into Logan's opinion on the matter—had her fall also been Pierre's mistake? Though tempted, she'd remained silent. After that, the media left her alone and moved on, like sharks feeding on a bigger, more *newsworthy*, pool of fish.

The cold condensation from the Evian bottle felt nice against her neck. Between her shifts at Boscov's and a regimented ballet practice schedule, Logan kept herself busy.

Logan's cell phone vibrated next to the lamp. Sal. After all, he was the only person she knew who'd rather text than call her.

SAL: *Luscious, need ur help with Valeska's wedding ring!!! meet me at Joe's luncheonette on market st. at noon. come. important. hurry. Sal.*

Grandpa Romeo and Mrs. Debinska certainly hadn't wasted any time. *Bleeding leotards*. Hastily, she threw on a tank top, shorts and sandals and headed off to catch the downtown bus.

Barefaced, and with her hair wildly springing from the clip on her head, Logan tried to quiet her heart as she exited the bus a few doors down from Joe's Luncheonette. The same place Keane had brought her for breakfast precious months ago. Jimmy's uncle's luncheonette. Dare she inquire about Keane, or was it best to simply…let him go?

"Logan, my girl. I can't tell you how good it is to see you!" Joe greeted her as soon as she walked through the door. His surprising hug made her wonder if she'd better head back out into the June heat. Yet it was filled with affection and kindness, as was Joe's face. "Yes, indeed, it's good to see you."

"Hi, Joe. Um, I got a text from Keane's handler, Sal, to meet him here. Do you know where I can find him?"

"I sure do, dearie. I sure do. Follow me."

Logan froze and bit her lip as Joe headed out the front entrance. "I didn't know Market Street had a jewelry store—?"

"What are ye waiting for? Come on, honey. Before he gets away."

She frowned, puzzled, but followed him a few feet down the block. They stopped in front of Rachel's Antiques. "Go ahead, 'es in there."

"Sal's buying a wedding ring from Rachel's Antiques?" An odd place for a ring, but then again, nothing about his speed-dial romance with Mrs. Debinska was normal.

Joe chuckled. "Oh, it's not Rachel's Antiques anymore. Covers half the block too. Plenty of room. Two main entrances. Prime downtown location. Go on, get yourself in there." His hand touched her shoulder and gave her a nudge.

Logan held her breath as she entered. The welcome blast of air conditioning eased her nervousness somewhat. This year's twists and turns made even a ballerina feel dizzy, hesitant and gun shy from one too many surprises. *What on earth is Sal doing in Rachel's Antiques with—or without, she couldn't be sure—Mrs. Debinska's wedding ring?*

"Excuse me, miss," a workman said from behind her. She shifted to the side and watched two guys carry a massive mirror down the length of the enormous open-spaced room. But Sal was nowhere in sight.

"Sal?" she called out. Glancing over her shoulder, she caught Joe's wave from his spot outside the door.

Hovering, smiling, and...waiting for something? Maybe he was excited for Sal's upcoming proposal? Her attention swung back to the workmen and the open space. Except someone else stood in the middle of the room. Someone unexpected. Someone so strong and beautiful, her breath caught.

"Logan."

Despite the air conditioning, the temperature in the room spiked. A rush of emotions twirled around in her: happiness, sorrow, love, anger and confusion. She didn't know how to react, whether to throw herself at him and never let go. Or smack him on the side of his head for the disappearing act he'd pulled.

"I know, baby. Come here." His deep, throaty voice was so tempting.

She stood her ground. "Don't *baby* me."

He strode across the room and narrowed the distance between them. Logan stayed rooted in place. "Shit, I missed you."

No words came out; her breath hitched tightly in her throat.

His fingers reached up and caressed her cheek. She held her head firmly in place.

"You are so fuckin' beautiful with your green eyes flaring and your hair all messy."

She had a hundred questions for him but remained silent. Let him do the talking for a change.

"Why didn't you cash the checks?"

You know why, Keane. She gave him a look, the answer written on her face.

"Not making this easy on me, huh?" He flexed his fists and shifted on his feet, but his eyes devoured her, full of hunger. Need. Want. Brimming with unspoken emotions she could only guess at.

His hand snaked out, caught her waist, and pulled her closer. "I took your advice," he muttered, smoothing a stray strand of hair around her ear. He smelled good, clean and soapy and with a hint of mint. The past weeks, she'd dreamed of a moment like this, where he'd come back to her. But for how long?

"What advice?" she whispered, needing to know.

"All of it, baby. All of it."

She cocked her head and looked up at him, unsure what he was saying.

"You said you'd wait for me, remember?" he muttered. Keane sounded…unsure.

Instinctually, her hand covered the warm expanse of chest over his heart, and she stepped closer. Stunned. Excited. Breathless with the realization of what he must be telling her.

"I'm seeing a psychiatrist. Getting help with the PTSD. And Jimmy."

Logan wound her arm around his back and pressed up against him. "Oh, Keane."

"Quit fighting professionally. You were right, it wasn't helping." He angled his head and captured her mouth. His tongue danced with hers as her heart beat against his.

Seconds later, his head lifted. He lifted her by the waist and gently moved her away from him. "Like it?"

She grinned. *Oh, she liked it, all right.*

"The place. You like it?"

Her eyes fell on the guys far across the room, hanging an oversized mirror on the wall.

"Figure we'd split the space."

Her mouth opened and closed. And opened. "You bought Rachel's Antiques?"

He grinned so broadly her stomach did a pirouette. "Yep, your dance studio is over there."

"Oh, my God. You're not kidding."

"An MMA training club on this side, for returning veterans. Dr. Felter's satellite office in back."

"How am I going to afford this place?"

He crossed his arms and his eyes narrowed on her. "You're not. I am."

She couldn't let him walk in here, sweep her off her feet, and then fulfill everything she'd dreamed about since The Fall. Could she? "What about our business agreement? You've managed your part, and I'll manage mine."

Foolish, stubborn pride. That's what this was. But pride had carried her through the bad times like a trusty, dependable pair of ballet slippers.

He rolled his neck and grunted. Unfolded and refolded his arms. Then he stepped closer. She imagined the muscles beneath his black T-shirt flexing as he moved. His hand found her waist.

"One more thing—might tip the scale."

God, the memory of his naked ass at the weigh-in made her feel lightheaded. She leaned into him but his eyes captured hers.

A grin spread across his face. He seemed younger, more carefree. Happy. She laughed. "I'd say you tip my scale every time you look at me. What were you going to tell me?"

Wouldn't you know, his grin broadened? Six foot two of broad, mean hunk was smiling down on her like she'd given him the world.

His next words made her feel like he'd offered the world to her on a golden plate.

With blue eyes glimmering with emotion and his voice deep and rough, Keane whispered four words that meant more to her than ballet, more to her than anything.

"I love you, Luscious."

Chapter 24

DECISION: The outcome of a bout; when a winner is declared

Six months later

Chloe was a regular at Jimmy's Fight Club. Perhaps it was the constant influx of hot, retired Marines flexing their stuff as they worked out their issues, both in the cage and back inside Dr. Felter's satellite office. Or maybe her inner child connected with the young, fresh-faced ballerinas in the making. Or most likely, she needed an escape from ol' Squirrel Face and the ever-present media attention. After all, Chloe was the most popular Octagon Girl ever to strut her stuff around the cage. Her daddy had made sure of it.

Logan stood with Chloe off to the side of the sparring cage, watching Keane instruct a veteran on how to make an opponent tap out. That's what Logan thought was happening anyway.

She liked staying late, well after the kids headed home from their ballet lessons, to eyeball Mr. Eyegasm while he went about his business. Oh, Keane still had his surly moments, growling about some of her ballerina costumes or about the way the guys sometimes hung around and watched her dance. But he seemed happier. Content. And late at night—after he'd taken her breath away in ways she'd never imagined—he told her he loved her.

Chloe sighed next to her. "Boom-Yay's really something, huh?"

"Yep, *my* something."

"Well, if ya can tear ya eyes away from him for a dang second, I brought ya a copy of the *Pittsburgh Press*. Y'all made the front page, again." She unfolded the newspaper and handed it to Logan.

Chloe hadn't lied—there they were, front-page news. Three pictures and a few paragraphs of text. The headline read: Pittsburgh's Favorite Couple Making a Difference. Keane was going to hate the first picture, a reprint of their first kiss on the ramp at Mellon Arena. But a smaller picture showcased two veterans posing inside the cage. The text underneath outlined the goals and purpose of this first-of-its-kind club and summarized it neatly: "Jimmy's Fight Club aims to help veterans readjust to life back home." Good publicity always helped. How else were these guy going to know about it? *Keane's going to hate this one too*, Logan thought with a grin.

Logan's hand tightened around the newspaper as she studied the third picture. Why had she chosen that outfit the day the reporters trickled in?

"I think that's the most beautiful picture. It reminds me of the one on the wall over yonder, but better." Chloe pointed to the painting of the two young girls dancing. Logan nodded. The shot was priceless, despite her skimpy outfit.

In the photograph, Logan stood against the barre with her leg stretched high overhead. Two little girls flanked her sides, their tiny legs mimicking her posture. Logan had an arm around each in support, although a team of special needs aides were on hand to help. Jenna's wheelchair was pushed off to the side and barely in the picture. Joanna's crutch was underneath her armpit. All three of them grinned into the mirror like kittens after a bowl full of cream. Out of all the students attending her ballet classes, these girls were her favorite.

Tomorrow, Logan was sending this newspaper clip off to the art store to frame for her dance school. She had the perfect spot to hang it, too—right next to Pierre's painting.

"Come here," Keane demanded from his place on the stairs. "Why so teary-eyed?"

"No reason," Logan shot back, but Keane stalked up to her and took the newspaper from her hand.

His eyes scanned over it. She knew the exact moment he spotted the outfit because his mouth tightened and his features took on a gruff expression. She leaned up and kissed him hard, until his lips parted, his arms pulled her in tight, and *her* body felt like dancing.

In a year full of surprises, one thing was sure: life with Keane "Boom-Yay" O'Shea would never be dull.

* * * * *

TAP OUT

As a kid, heck, even as an adult,
I'd love to listen to my father's stories.
"True stories" about him and his eight siblings, his
father, his mother, my mother. About growing up
poor but with a love that was greater than what
money could buy. His stories were often repetitive,
except that the main characters would change or
there'd be a new plot twist previously unmentioned.
If I could count the hours spent listening to him,
I'm sure they'd add up to years. Time I deeply
treasure and am so grateful to have had.

This book is dedicated to my dad,
the greatest storyteller to have ever graced this
planet. Although I miss you every second of every
day, your stories, your amazing sense of humor,
your heart and love live on.

Acknowledgment

I'd like to thank my publisher, Carina Press,
and my amazing editor, Kerri Buckley,
for all the wisdom, support and hard work. A
huge thanks to the New Jersey Romance Writers,
a wonderful group of women with generous spirits
and a willingness to encourage all authors,
no matter the stage of their writing career.
Thank you to my extremely talented
critique partners, Joanna Shupe and Jenna Blue,
who help tame my crazy. A heartfelt thanks to
my extended critique group and friends at the
Violent Femmes. Finally, a huge thanks to you,
readers! For caring about my characters and the
world I've created, enough to discuss and share
your thoughts and feelings. Thanks for being
so enthusiastic about my books, and
for having been so supportive of a debut author.

Chapter 1

*MIXED MARTIAL ARTS FIGHTER: A fighter
with thick boxer arms, a massive wrestler chest,
formidable kickboxer legs, and an ego rivaling
any professional athlete's*
              —The World of Ultimate Fighting
                    According to Sophie Morelle

On the road, St. Louis, Missouri

Interstate I-70 traffic was at a dead standstill, and so
was Sophie Morelle. Her legs turning to lead smack dab
in the middle of the four-lane cluster jam, two buffalo
chicken hoagies clutched in her grip and the last man
she'd expected to lay eyes on, the scourge of her exis-
tence—MMA fighter Caden Kelly—up ahead.

In his underwear.

Like a moth to a brazen flame, her gaze was drawn to him, standing warrior-like, biceps flexed, arms folded across his chest, and legs spread wide. Naked, except for his virginal white, one-size-too-small briefs. The narrow elastic waistband rode tantalizingly low on the finely chiseled furrows beneath his hip bones.

A larger-than-life portrait of the welterweight, shamelessly displayed just a few yards away. Smirking down at her from the billboard hugging the far right lane, as if to say, "*Take a gander at this, sweetheart.*"

No mistaking him, with that impressive bulge so blatantly outlined in his designer tighty-whities. Matter of fact, everything about Caden was massive. Thighs, chest, biceps. Ego. Playboy lifestyle.

Rubberneckers who normally ogled fender-benders stopped for a long look at Ultimate American Man's infamous underwear model looming indecently overhead.

Forget road rage, this was interstate insanity.

The sandwich wrappers crackled beneath her fingers, and she pulled her eyes away. She couldn't get back into the sweet comforts of her new BMW fast enough.

"Hey, Sophie! Remember, sexy is as sexy does!" a guy sitting in a late-model Volvo wagon hollered, his friend beside him waving wildly.

Sophie flashed her signature grin as she dashed by, yet her stomach turned. Hearing her tag line so ardently parroted by fans always did that. Couldn't the network executives have kept it simple, like Idol's Ryan Seacrest, with his classic "over and out" sign-off? Branding— that's what they'd told her when they came up with the silly phrase. As if viewers would somehow otherwise miss the blatant sexual overtones of her show. Unlikely. That's what was expected of Sophie Morelle, the sharp-witted, smooth-talking queen of late-night smack. Ex-queen, anyway.

Both men stared back at her. As if they'd never expected a celebrity to acknowledge them.

A horn sounded, kicking off a cacophony of angry beeping as the drivers in the center lanes realized they were the only ones not rolling forward.

July tended to be hot in St. Louis, but today was a scorcher, the heat sizzling off the asphalt like a Sunday griddle. All the more reason to hurry back inside her lovely Beamer, even if it was held at the mercy of the unexpected midafternoon traffic.

Her car had progressed mere inches in the five minutes she'd been gone. Sophie sprinted for the passenger door her best friend and semi-reluctant travel partner, Lauren, had pushed open for her.

"Hang on to your hats, folks. What's a few more minutes in traffic going to cost you, eh?" she shouted over the blaring horns before slamming the door shut. "Jeez, you're never going to believe what's causing this mess." She passed her friend a freshly made sandwich, courtesy of the Boar's Head men in the truck behind them. "Your favorite. Buffalo chicken."

"You're crazy."

Sophie nodded in agreement, and for the first time in a long while, found herself genuinely grinning.

"It's a delivery truck, not some full-service corner deli. I was *joking*," Lauren gasped, then paused to consider her. "But I suppose if anyone could finagle two hoagies out of some random truck stuck in traffic, it would be you."

"You said that once you were fed, you'd take the wheel. Well?"

Lauren rolled her eyes. "Uh…still starving, and I'm *currently* driving."

"Finally driving, you mean?" Sophie added smoothly, straightening out her soft, silk blouse as she made herself more comfortable in the passenger seat. She should be treating her friend to lobster salad at the Ritz, not a hastily made sandwich. Her support and encouragement—as illustrated by her agreeing to this mad road trip—was rock solid.

Lauren chuckled. "You *always* win. Smart-ass." She shot Sophie a pointed look. "But man, you're so good at making men do what you want."

Sophie winked at her, and moved the hoagie to a more comfortable position on her lap. Boy, how she loved matching wits with Lauren. It helped keep the mood positive and light, in spite of the desperation tightly held at bay within the pit of her stomach. An amusing way to pass the time while logging 602 miles, which was exactly how far they'd traveled since leaving Pittsburgh two days ago.

"I almost feel sorry for those fighters," Lauren added, shaking her head. "They have no idea who they'll be dealing with."

Sophie bit her lip, very aware of who *she'd* soon be dealing with. *You need to ignore your dislike of the arrogant playboy. Remember, he's your golden ticket to success.*

The Chevy ahead accelerated. Lauren placed her hand on the stick shift and hit the gas. The Beamer's engine purred back to life.

"If you wait a few seconds, you can pull over so we don't have to eat in the car."

Her friend shot her an evil eye but didn't protest,

knowing how Sophie liked things neat and clean. Eating sloppy sandwiches in a moving Beamer was a recipe for disaster.

"After all these years, you still pull stuff that surprises me," Lauren further commented, adding emphatically, "totally bonkers."

Bonkers was right. Deciding to film a documentary on a day in the life of a mixed martial arts fighter was necessary, but weird, even considering Sophie's nearly manic research of a sport more foreign to her than a used tire sale. Chasing a tour bus full of mixed martial arts fighters cross-country was downright crazy. But the nuttiest of it all was she'd have to interview Caden Kelly, the one welterweight she'd never hoped to see again. By comparison, sequestering two Boar's Head guys in their truck for food was mildly insane on the crazy scale.

She turned her attention toward one of the men in the Volvo, who was still signaling for her to lower her window further, as if she hadn't heard him shouting.

They wanted a slice of her time, for sure. They all did.

Once more, her lips formed the smile she'd perfected over the years, and she pressed the power button on the door handle. The window smoothly lowered. "Sorry, did one of you say something?"

Lauren's giggle echoed around the interior.

"Hey, Sophie. So, what's your gripe with Caden Kelly? That was some bash—"

With a quick jab, Sophie's finger hit the button and the window switched direction, blocking out the nonsense spewing out of the man's mouth. Given present circumstances, what had she expected, really? A request for her autograph? A photograph?

Darn. She felt Lauren's eyes on her, but didn't need to see her expression to know what she was thinking. Instead, she ran a hand across her silk blouse and smoothed out any wrinkles that might have cropped up in the few minutes since she'd previously straightened things.

Lord knew, she liked order in her life. One overzealous fan wasn't going to upset her tidy apple cart. No siree. Still, her heart thumped erratically in her chest.

"You cut him off midsentence," Lauren commented, unaware of the sudden change of temperature within Sophie's soul. Cold. So darn cold an Alaskan blizzard seemed like a summer day at the beach. "Never knew windows reversed direction so smoothly—must be a new Beamer thing."

Sophie struggled to keep her demons at bay and ignored the two guys gesturing in the next car over. *Sorry, interview's over.* Instead, she murmured, "We'll stop and eat first, then check out tonight's venue—if we ever break free of this cluster jam."

Thankfully, Lauren let it go, teasing instead, "Don't you mean cluster fuck?"

Sophie flinched, and then grimaced at her silly reaction. On her show, she'd quipped numerous times how "shit regularly hit the f-bomb fan." She offered Lauren a half-hearted "yep," then fell silent.

As a successful late-night TV host, she'd played the quest-for-ratings game better than any of her all-male competition. That didn't mean she agreed with half the raunchy things that came out of her mouth. Conversations about ginormous tatas and teensy wee-wees, lewd exchanges with porn stars, naughty questions with alcoholic celebrities, and, most recently, showcasing a bitter ballerina and his smear campaign against his former partner—who just so happened to have turned herself into the most popular Octagon Girl ever…well, the ratings had been through the roof. Sophie's career had seemed indestructible.

She'd done it all—whatever whet the public's appetite.

At times, she wasn't proud of herself. But being able to afford luxuries like the gorgeous Beamer reminded her just how far she'd come from her childhood home in Hawley, an old run-down coal town that was one step up from trailer park. No one made it out of Hawley without developing a thick skin, and without being a bit ruthless. Or at least, appearing to be so—no matter how much it hurt on the inside. She shook her head, refusing to go there.

Lauren interrupted her thoughts. "You have this weird expression on your face. You okay?"

"Caden's responsible for this." She resisted the temptation to say more, not wanting to overexaggerate that troublemaker's hand in her recent downward spiral, and wondered when Lauren's eyes would roam upward and spot him. "You'll see. Mark my words."

Her friend looked at her and laughed. "For the traffic? Or for those two guys gawking at you? A tornado could rip through here right now, and you'd think it was Caden's divine doing."

"Hmph. The only thing he's divine at doing is looking good. Cornered the market in that department." Sophie couldn't argue that point.

The mixed martial arts fighter was the hottest ticket

around. His reputation was notorious, both in and out of the Octagon ring. He'd become every girl's oh-so-naughty fantasy date—or more. Every guy's way to live vicariously through the life of a mixed martial arts fighter.

Rumor had it Caden out-earned both David Beckham and Tom Brady as a model for Ultimate American Male underwear. And UAM had deep pockets, paying her network a ridiculous amount of money advertising their handsome athlete. He was a sure thing, after all. Viewers never seemed to get enough of the panty pimp's package. Which was why when UAM pulled their advertising from her network and went with their competitor, Sophie's career had come to a screeching halt.

Sophie knew it was an excuse not to renew her three-year contract, which, after rather tense salary negotiations, was an executive signature away from being a done deal—or so she'd been led to believe. Not only did the network cancel *Late Night with Sophie Morelle*, but to add insult to injury, they came up with the brilliant idea of offering her two alternative shows, at one-fourth the pay. A reality baking show—to the woman whose box-mix muffins were a dental nightmare—and worse still, a godforsaken housekeeping tips show. Yep. One heck of a minor incident had resulted in one major excuse executives had hatched up. All to save themselves money.

"I've lost everything because of Caden Kelly," she said, the thought as familiar to her as steel stacks in Pittsburgh. "They're hoping I'll disappear and not make a stink about how one of the good ole boys has filled my late-night spot. Guess you get what you pay for."

Lauren snorted. "I still can't believe they'd cancel

one of the most highly watched shows. Talk about bad business." She turned in her seat. "So, pitch another show to another network. You're famous. People love you, and that smart-ass, ballsy mouth on you."

"I have one month remaining on my no-compete clause. After that, I'm a free agent. And once this documentary is completed, they're going to regret driving me off and replacing me with some lackey at half the salary. The more I think about it, the higher the price of the rights to my documentary gets."

"Still, don't you think it best to leave your Channel 27 days behind, and look for a network who will appreciate the talent they've hired?" Sophie could hear the censure in her friend's voice, the same that had been there the last time a similar discussion had taken place. Heck, they'd been traveling for two days and this was a hot topic. "Why even dangle the option to purchase your documentary in front of those morons, given how they've treated you?"

"You don't understand. I'm not going to let them drive me off, shamefaced, be 'taken down a peg or two,' as one executive named Walt practically spat at me. I was in a similar situation…years ago. Where every damn person in town sold me out, and you know what for?" Sophie swallowed hard. "Money. Boy, did I learn a valuable lesson. Money talks, all right. No way. I'm not going to let them win. They can cancel my show, not re-sign my contract and hope I'll quietly go away. But brush me off as if I didn't matter? I don't think so. When all is said and done, they are going to respect me."

She felt her friend's eyes on her. Probably surprised the heck out of her, considering how Sophie never talked about her troubled—to say the least—teenage years.

"Jesus, and I'm partially responsible for this crazy plan," Lauren stated, wisely choosing not to continue down the dark, dismal path their discussion had taken. Keeping it light, just like they always did for each other.

"My sister in crime," Sophie added softly.

The old Chevy ahead rolled forward and gained speed. Even 5 mph seemed fast at this point.

The guys at the network loved mixed martial arts. Had turned into fanatics, really. And they weren't alone. MMA was hot right now, the fastest growing sport this year, with millions of viewers tuning in on pay-per-view for each bout. In a blink, the sport's popularity had spread from man caves to kitchens around the country. The buzz was that every major station was out to land the mother of mega waves and buy the rights for broadcasting Tetnus, the largest Ultimate Fighting championship to date.

Advertisers were prepping to spend beaucoup dollars. Obsessed fans were primed and ready for an in-depth look at their fighter heroes. Sophie'd have her pick of networks to sign over the rights to her documentary. But it'd be a cold day at a Vegas craps table before Channel 27 would get their penny-pinching hands on her hard-earned work.

She grinned. They wouldn't see her—or the carrot that she'd soon be dangling in front of them—coming.

All Sophie needed to do was figure out the ungodly reason why MMA fighters held such appeal, and present it in a way even her grandmother would appreciate. A woman's view on a sport that was so blatantly male, it reeked of sweat and blood.

Yep, she was going to have them begging her for the privilege of airing her documentary. Kissing her feet, and showering them with money, so much money, it would be piled up to her knees. Prove that someone wealthy *and* decent could make it out of Hawley. Even if her late-night persona led people to believe otherwise.

Once more, traffic slowed to a crawl.

"Look. Isn't that your fighter?"

Though she knew it was coming—he was hard to miss—Sophie's heart still accelerated faster than her V8 engine. Her gaze followed the upward angle of her best friend's finger.

"God, he's gorgeous," Lauren stated the obvious.

"His looks are irrelevant. He's the cause of this blasted traffic, I'm telling you." Still, the sign was more erotic than…anything. "Indecent. The billboard *and* the man," she muttered.

"Ha, this coming from the ex-queen of late-night drama," Lauren scoffed, shifting in the driver's seat and drawing Sophie's attention away from Caden's ginormous crotch. "If America only knew what a prude you really are."

"Soon to be reigning queen," Sophie murmured, her gaze instinctively shifting back to the billboard—and *him*, the catalyst of her disgraceful plummet from prime time.

Caden smirked back at her with a cocky grin.

The last time she'd seen him, he hadn't been smiling.

"I hope this delay won't make us miss the bus again," Lauren groaned, changing the subject. Her friend wasn't exactly patient—though neither was Sophie. Plus, traffic brought out the worst in both of them.

"Are you sure there's an appearance scheduled for St. Louis tonight? After all, the last two towns were duds, nothing but pissed-off farmers in Dresden and obnoxious college kids in Oxford, and in both cases, everyone mad as hell that the Ultimate Fighters On Tour was a no-show." Lauren paused to snort. "The whole idea of mixed martial arts fighters touring around on a bus like rock stars is ludicrous, if you ask me."

"One of the managers, Sal, promised me they'd be in St. Louis this afternoon, well in advance of tonight's appearance. As for the bus, *ludicrous* is too mild a word. I wouldn't be caught dead traversing cross-country on one. A sleek European roadster, now that's an entirely different beast." She glanced at Lauren, hoping the allure of riding in the Beamer still sounded appealing.

Perhaps not, given that Lauren raised an eyebrow at her.

"I'll interview them at each stop, film some footage of a bunch of gung-ho guys preparing for Tetnus, and in a few days, we'll have some fun in Vegas while they slug it out. We'll be driving back to Pittsburgh in under a month."

Sophie drummed her fingers on the soft leather doorframe, praying her words would ring true. "One shamefaced journalist, with one tiny camera, on a mission to interview a busload of bulked-up, testosterone-laden fighters."

"A bunny in a wolves' den."

"Exactly." Sophie paused, looked at Lauren, and winked. "And because of this traffic, I've had time to figure out their appeal. Or at least the new angle I'm taking, one that will have American women trading in their football jerseys for MMA T-shirts."

"I think the bunny's lost her carrots."

Lauren's gaze lifted, and so did her lips, into a very knowing female grin. Sophie's gaze followed.

From this vantage point, ultimate package appeal was hard to miss.

Sophie's eyes narrowed as she considered the billboard. "No telling what might happen after I get an exclusive on *him*..."

"Hate to say it, but you tried that once before, and look how that turned out."

She ignored the comment. After all, the one fighter who'd make even a Sunday afternoon knitting group sit up and take notice was staring her in the face. "Do you think he's a legitimate fighter? Hard to imagine someone so attractive, so dang sexy, getting his nose bashed in."

Lauren laughed, deep within her throat. "Hmm, his mad fighting skills might be the only truly legitimate thing we know about him. That and all his naughty extracurricular activities, like that scandal with the model. A nun would have found it impossible to ignore those weekly tabloid play-by-plays. Quite a lover and a fighter, our boy Caden is."

"Well, his *package* is legitimate. No question about that."

Legitimate was putting it mildly.

A horn sounded. Traffic began to ease up, and suddenly Sophie was anxious to get to their destination, some ungodly venue called Hair of the Dog.

Her inside contact, an old-school trainer named Sal, promised to help ease her way in with the fighters. "This handsome fella knows everything there is to know about fightin' boys," he'd informed her. Of course, he seemed "to know" a heck of a lot more after Sophie'd agreed to roll his name in the ending credits. Despite her natural skepticism, and her history with

Caden, Sal assured her the fighters would be more than eager to be filmed. She'd have begun taping already, if they'd only stuck to their scheduled appearances. But that, too, was water under the bridge now. "Time to let bygones be bygones. Stop thinking how every time I set eyes on Caden Kelly, my luck turns bad."

"You can con the pants off any man, Sophie. And hey, Caden's given you a head start," Lauren mercifully interrupted, jerking her thumb upward. "He's one beautiful fighter, all right."

And once more, Sophie's gaze unwillingly rose upward. Was it possible he'd grown even bigger? She was just about to comment on it, but caught sight of brake lights ahead of them.

"Lauren, watch out!"

The hoagie shot off her lap, rolled onto the floor, and wedged beneath her heel as she braced herself for impact. Something wet—Buffalo sauce?—leaked into her patent leather pump. Thankfully, Lauren hit the brakes in time to avoid rear-ending the old Chevy.

Sophie said a silent prayer, thinking they'd come out on top, if the worst of it was a slimy ankle. Until she glanced into the rearview mirror and spotted the polished chrome pig.

"Hold tight," she shrieked out in warning.

Part of the reason she'd bought the pricey BMW was its high crash-test ranking in *Consumer Reports*. The sense of safety had provided incentive, the kind of incentive that justified splurging on such a wallet-stretching purchase. Still, you never expected to put such rankings to the test.

Even crazier—they were about to be rear-ended by a Boar's Head truck.

Thwunk.

The force of the truck traveling one?—two?—miles per hour propelled Sophie's sedan forward as if it were a toy. Her foot squished through the sandwich, coming down hard onto the floor mat. She braced against the headrest. Her eyes rose to the heavens for help.

And saw Caden Kelly smirking down at her like the devil incarnate.

With one solid crunch, the BMW collided with the Chevy.

"Holy shit," Lauren gasped as the airbags ballooned out of the dashboard, sending a hail of white powder raining down and pinning both women into their seats.

For a moment, Sophie sat there, paralyzed more by fear than any injury. She wiped the chalky powder off her arms, then shook out her blouse, trying to make sense of what had happened. The Beamer's state-of-the-art airbag—that's what happened. It felt like a cement ball had ejected out of the dash and into her. Bet *Consumer Reports* missed that little safety feature by-product.

Her arm smarted, as if in agreement, a sure sign of a nasty, forthcoming bruise. She blinked, and looked around. The interior looked like it'd been the victim of some Disney ride gone wild.

"You okay, Lauren?" she whispered, struggling for breath.

"Yes…that damned airbag hit me in the forehead. But no serious injuries over here. You?"

Sophie tested her neck, arms, legs. Everything was in working order—everything except her car. Which meant…

"I'm…fine."

"Liar."

Zip it, she silently replied, choosing instead to inhale a deep, calming breath. It wouldn't help the situation by resorting to Mademoiselle Freak-Out mode, even if every fiber of her being screamed bloody murder. So what if her new car was totaled? So what if she'd never catch up with the fighters and film her documentary, her one chance at proving to the network that she wasn't going to be overlooked? Passed by. Or traded in for a cheaper model.

So what if Caden Kelly was to blame?

This was another test to see if she'd manage to stay calm, cool, and collected.

"Um, Sophie, I hate to be the bearer of more bad news—"

"Hmph, can it get any worse?" *Mind over matter*, she thought, sitting up straighter in her seat in spite of the wariness grasping hold of her, stealing her breath.

"—but is that the tour bus? The one with that shabby banner outside the window? There's a bunch of men hanging out of the windows gawking at us."

"What?" Sophie screeched, swatting away the airbag and following Lauren's finger, expecting to find a high-end, state-of-the-art vehicle large enough to transport several BMWs—the kind of wheels celebrities used while on tour. What she saw made her blink.

It couldn't be. The monstrosity four lanes over looked like a 1980s school bus, complete with chipped paint and exhaust billowing from its tailpipe.

"I thought you said they were stopping for the night in St. Louis?"

"They *are* stopping in St. Louis. Sal said they'd be

pulling into town sometime today." *And the last time you checked your text messages was when?*

"Well, its right blinker is on and it's about to take the exit toward Memphis."

As Sophie gazed at the Chevy ahead, her hand located her bag wedged between the door and her seat. Digging inside, she retrieved her cell. Her heart beat erratically against her chest.

"From what I can see from around this airbag, that old tank we rear-ended has barely a scratch on it," Lauren murmured.

Sophie had already drawn the same conclusion. No injuries. A measure of relief there.

"You're handling this incredibly well, which leads me to believe you're about to lose it," Lauren said. "We'll need a tow truck, but at least we're okay."

Sophie shifted the air bag to peer at Lauren more clearly. Her plans shifted as well. And Lauren was surely going to be the one to lose it. "Let's get one thing clear. I am *not* okay, okay?"

She squeezed her lips together, hating to snap at Lauren.

Her phone vibrated. Holding her breath, she read:

SAL: Bad news. Mutiny on bus. Now headed south to New Millennium Inn in Arnold. Hurry. Might be able to catch us cause bus is stuck in traffic.

Some dummy wrecked his BMW right underneath Caden's billboard.

She shook off the dummy comment and dropped her cell into her purse. "Lauren, that's it. My wrecked

Beamer is in better shape than that monstrosity."
*Breathe deep. You can do this. Just think how much
more time you'll have with them.* Her future depended
on this. Nothing—not even a Boar's Head-induced
fender-bender—was going to get in her way.

Sophie fought her way out of the clutches of the
airbag, grabbed her purse, and heaved her door open.
"Slight change of plans, Lauren," she hollered over the
pitched roof.

Lauren followed Sophie's lead, clambering out on her
side, and making her way toward the trunk. "What? Oh
no you don't. Don't even think about—"

"I'll pay you back for the Greyhound ticket, tow expenses, whatever it costs to make it back to Pittsburgh,"
she pressed on, Plan B—Get On That Bus—firmly ce-
mented in her head.

"No. No way are you leaving me here like this.
You've completely lost your mind."

"It's a mind-over-matter kind of situation. I've got
to get creative and…resourceful."

"And I thought that you conning two guys into making sandwiches in the back of a truck, smack in the
middle of I-70, would be the extent of your so-called
resourcefulness."

The truck was a few feet behind them and its passen-
gers a few feet further, engrossed in a heated argument
about eating while driving. *A little late to hammer this
issue out now, guys*, Sophie thought. She ignored them
and moved around to the trunk to assess the damage.

There had to be some way of opening it so she could
retrieve her suitcases.

Four lanes over, the lame excuse of a tour bus idled,
stopped dead in traffic.

Lauren must have caught her frown. "Oh my God. You won't last a day."

Sophie ignored the urge to agree with her. With the help of a piece of broken bumper, they were able to wedge the trunk halfway open.

"You were dropped on the head as a child," Lauren said pointedly.

"You thought your Cabbage Patch doll was your sister until your mother broke the news to you…at the age of twelve." Sophie attempted a smile as one suitcase cleared the trunk.

"You're the only person I know who packs her underwear and nighties in a separate suitcase. Definitely nutso."

They grabbed the smaller suitcase of delicates. Underwear always seemed to get lost within a suitcase filled with clothing, so why shouldn't it have its own case? "And you're the only person I know who doesn't even pack lingerie."

"I do too."

Gotcha. "Granny undies don't count."

"Hey, that's a low blow." But Lauren said it laughingly, knowing she'd lost once again. "Are you sure about this?"

"Nope. But what can happen when the worst has already happened? You'll stay with the car and handle the paperwork?" She paused, and considered Lauren. "You'll be okay?"

"Um…no."

"It's not like we're at fault. And, if the police give you a hard time, blame it on the real culprit. *Him.*" She gestured to the billboard. "Pileups are probably a daily occurrence around here since that thing went up," she added angrily beneath her breath.

Seconds passed, until finally Lauren rolled her eyes up, as if seeking advice from above. "How are you going to make it across four lanes of traffic with three suitcases, wearing three-inch heels?"

"Watch and learn. Journalist boot camp training. And plenty of practice getting in quick for the scoop with all my essentials. Clothing, video equipment and camera—"

"Suitcase full of underwear."

"Well, if there's an emergency, and I end up in the hospital…"

Lauren's gaze shifted toward the bus and then back on her. "Judging by the condition of that bus, it seems more than likely."

Sophie shot her friend a smile. "Got me."

She set her smaller suitcase on top of the larger one, looped the flexible handle over the plastic, retractable one, and expanded that handle with a solid jerk. The third suitcase containing her equipment had straps like a backpack, and with well-practiced movements, Sophie hoisted it onto her back. "I really appreciate your help."

"You're really going to do this?"

"Yep."

"Call me. I want a firsthand account of Caden's reaction when you show up on his bus—if he doesn't spot you dashing across I-70 and make a run for it, that is."

Sophie straightened. Common sense said *she* should make a run for it, far away from that hunk o' junk. Not toward it.

Weaving her way across the interstate, she focused on her objective and ignored the angry horns and shouts from cars backed up so far they'd fill a stadium parking lot. The racket blocked out the sound of her fist against the glass door window on the far side of the bus, but hey, she'd made it this far. Whipping out her cell, she texted Sal.

It took three tries for the door to open enough for her to squeeze her gear through. Mustering her last bit of strength, she hauled her bags up the four steps, situated them in the aisle between the first row of seats, and tugged the hem of her blouse back into place.

An errant bead of sweat trickled down her cheekbone, but she didn't care.

She was back on the road to success, via this ridiculous four-wheeled bucket of rust. She'd done it.

It took a minute to realize the bus was quiet, the silence so profound you could hear a pin drop on the worn aisle floor.

A moment for Sophie to look up and find all eyes fixed on her. One by one, the fighters' faces registered their recognition, then hardened. Quicker than a car air bag—and packing just as much punch—all hell broke loose.

Chapter 2

*ACHILLES LOCK: When a fighter grabs his op-
ponent by the ankles and holds on for dear life*

Brakes squealed, and so did Sophie, as the bus hit
another pothole, sending its riders airborne like skiers
taking a mogul wild. Her small suitcase full of undies
shifted halfway out of the overhead and bobbled precariously over the aisle. She prayed the fickle latch would
hold tight if it headed south, though it wouldn't matter if this rustcan hit one more pothole and fragmented
into chunks of metal.

Bad enough, the grumbles and glares coming from
the you're-not-welcome-to-our-ride committee had
only intensified with every teeth-shattering bump. The
Boys—as Sal had dubbed his assembly of oversized

fighters—had only just ceased directing a less-than-subtle tirade of curses her way.

Hopefully, they'd forget her. Go about their usual business of playing video games on their iPhones, pounding their chests and dragging women around by the hair. She was too wired to nap, which was what usually happened once she'd settled into her seat, much to Lauren's annoyance. She needed a moment, time to calm herself, gather her wits about her and reevaluate her plan of attack. She glanced over her shoulder, spotted a stiff middle finger gesturing her way, and quickly averted her gaze.

"You said no women on the bus. So what's she doing here?" someone cried out, parroting the general theme of their insults to date.

Oh, Boys. Here we go again.

"It's unlucky. She's unlucky."

"Downright destructive."

Sophie didn't have to turn around to know they were all staring at her. "You didn't tell them about the documentary," she stated, narrowing her eyes at the old-timer, her lifeline, her "way in," who seemed oblivious to the tension around him.

Sal's cheeks flushed red. "Um…Jerry already had 'em all riled up. Didn't think mentioning you up would settle the fellas down. Sorry, honey."

She smoothed a lock of hair behind her ear and tried not to let the news, Sal, or the glowering Boys rattle her. So what if getting them onboard for her documentary was going to be more difficult than expected? A bunny didn't enter a wolf's den without expecting some drama.

Perched on his knees, Sal looked over the seatback and addressed the busload of fighters from his spot on the worn spring-riddled seat next to her. "The receptionist at the New Millennium Inn told me over the phone that there's Wifey and a tech room. I know how you fellas love playing Pac-Man on that box. But listen up—no drinking. You're gonna end back at a Motel 6 if Jerry catches you imbibing."

Jerry was the less-than-amiable promoter/fight manager who'd helped organize Tetnus. He was also the East Coast chairman of the Xtreme MMA Federation, who'd sponsored the championship qualifiers back in Pittsburgh. She'd had a run-in with the horrible man just before the unfortunate incident with Caden and wasn't looking forward to their unavoidable confrontation on the road. For now, she had to deal with the problem at hand—figuring out exactly how she was going to win over this group of pissed-off pirates.

"Whose 'wifey' is going to be entertaining us, you old rascal?"

"Think he means WiFi."

"What the fuck is *imbibing*?" another fighter questioned.

"Still doesn't explain what *she's* doing here."

Sal cleared his throat, his focus on her rather than on the confusion he'd caused. "Don't look so panicked. The Boys need time to adjust. Get used to the idea of you riding along with us. Warm up to the notion of you filming them. See, they don't trust you, honey. Not after you—"

"They hate me," Sophie commented weakly. She waved off Sal's obligatory reassurance that somehow she'd misunderstood. That the last thirty-five minutes hadn't been filled with a tension so thick, you could slice it with a knife and serve it up like a piece of humble pie.

"Hate's a strong word. It's more like…despise."

"Gee, I feel much better," Sophie muttered. She tried to look on the bright side. Caden was mercifully absent. Though his presence was felt in every snort, angry glare, and unsubtle curse directed her way.

Sophie let out a long breath of air that she hadn't realized she'd been holding as the bus jerked to a halt within the hotel parking lot. Jeez, she'd barely lasted a half hour. Did she really think she'd survive the bus ride to Vegas? The hotel couldn't have been a more welcome site.

New Millennium Inns catered to business folk with two large convention rooms, a heated indoor pool with sauna and Jacuzzi, a fully equipped gym, spa treatments, and a restaurant with bar. Nicely decorated rooms with fully stocked mini-fridges, and, if one was lucky, a view of the pool.

This one, just outside of Arnold, Missouri, was large, with two wings off the main entry section. Quasi-expensive, too. She'd stayed at enough of them while on assignment to know the deal. Back when she earned enough money to afford the presidential suite.

Now she'd be lucky enough to afford a room overlooking the air conditioning unit.

A shiver ran up her spine, and she tried to shake it off. Fear of abject poverty ranked right up there with automobile accidents—and look how that had turned out.

A smashed BMW was just the beginning of her troubles. As if her day hadn't been filled with enough problems, her wallet wasn't inside her purse. ID, checkbook, credit cards, were all tucked securely within the expensive leather interior. She thought about asking Sal to help her locate a Pittsburgh Trust, but without a valid form of identification and with the additional identity theft protection she'd placed on her account, she'd have to jump hurdles to get everything replaced. For now, she was one piece of plastic away from failure.

A corporate credit card, which she kept separate and tucked within a billfold along with her now useless business cards, was her only hope. That is, *if* the network hadn't yet cancelled it.

"Listen up," Sal addressed the fighters. "No booze, no women, and no trouble."

The Boys groaned collectively, just like little boys.

"I understand. Before I married Valeska..." His voice wandered off. Sophie warmed to the older man, who clearly loved his wife. A sign of a good, kind man, a much-needed rose blooming through the frost. Even if his warmth wasn't directed at her, it helped calm her growing nerves.

With a shake of his head, Sal waved the grumpy lot of fighters off the rustmobile. He retrieved her large suitcase and rolled it outside. Another kind act, one that nevertheless smacked of pity. She grimaced. He felt sorry for her, and for the way the Boys had behaved, as if she'd stolen their favorite WrestleMania figure, or worse, ruined *their* chances at winning a million-dollar purse.

Nothing has gone according to plan, Sophie thought, peeling her silk blouse away from her sticky body. The traffic, rent-a-wreck, less-than-stellar reception and lost wallet, combined with the heat, had thrown her off her game. What she needed was a cool shower and a fresh change of clothes. Refresh. Regroup. Rethink her approach. Then sweet-talking Sophie Morelle would be out to play hardball. The Boys wouldn't know what hit them.

"Think you can handle the little one?" He pointed to her lingerie bag jutting out of the overhead, then shook his head. "Just like a woman to overpack."

Sophie didn't respond. Handling her luggage was the least of her worries. Her gaze wandered toward the larger one that he had placed in front of the bus, just in time to witness a passing fighter giving it a swift kick.

"That's it." She squeezed past Sal and hurried down the stairs. But the fighter was already a few long strides away and out of the range of her designer purse, despite its long leather strap. She watched him disappear behind the sliding glass entry doors.

Sal came up beside her. "Don't worry that pretty head. I'll smooth things out with the fellas. It's Jerry you've gotta worry about. He's booked at the hotel. If you think the Boys are in a snit about you being here, Jerry's gonna flip his lid, no matter how good of a negotiator you think you are." Sal rubbed his jaw, and looked at her, considering. "And Jerry's reaction will be mild compared to Caden's."

"Think about your name in the credits, Sal. Tied forever to an award-winning documentary." Moving her hands, she framed out an imaginary sign in the air. "Famous. All you have to do is get Caden to agree to talk."

The old-timer's eyes lit up, if only briefly. "Think it's a bad idea, you interviewing him, after what ya did in Pittsburgh—" With a shake of his head, Sal headed off toward the hotel.

"But you'll still help me, right?" she hollered after him. Terrific. Her only ally was having doubts, and that thin thread of allegiance binding them was snapping. Squaring her shoulders and grabbing her suitcase's handle, she followed him inside.

A welcome blast of cold air greeted her as she wheeled her suitcase into the lobby. She unclasped a few buttons on her blouse and tugged the cami beneath it away from her overheated body, allowing the air to circulate over her damp skin. Cotton would have been a better choice, but when it came to clothing, Sophie always dressed for success. You never knew when an opportunity would present itself, and the cameras would be rolling.

Sometimes the best stories were spur of the moment, and a journalist had a certain image to uphold—especially a female reporter. Weren't women in all walks of life always held to a higher standard? Besides, a late-night television host turned documentary filmmaker had a certain image to maintain. That thought had plagued her the entire sweltering bus ride, while she'd been tempted to slip off her silk blouse and simply wear the cami.

Oddly enough, the receptionist seemed to be quite warm herself, even in the air-conditioning. Sophie watched, fascinated, as the girl unbuttoned a few buttons on her green polyester New Millennium Inn uniform. Both women were so intently watching what seemed to be the security camera stashed away behind the reception desk that they were oblivious to Sophie and Sal.

"See, Jessica," the receptionist admonished her coworker, "I told you it was really him. I'd be able to spot that hunk of man meat anywhere."

"You owe me five dollars. I told you he's hung like a

stallion. That wasn't just extra paint on the billboard," her friend added, snapping her gum.

"Faux-cock. Stuffing. They slide it into his briefs before each shot," Sophie mumbled, biting back the rest of her lie.

Slowly, both receptionists came out of their Caden daze and glared at her. The one with a fiver in her hand asked, "How many nights?"

"Two," Sal responded, holding up two fingers.

Sophie did the same.

"Together?"

"I'm…um…a married man. Maybe a year ago—"

"Separate," Sophie interrupted, her voice filled with laughter. If the old man thought to shock her, he'd forgotten he was dealing with *Sophie Morelle*.

"I'd like a room near Caden's, preferably a connecting suite," Sal continued. His tone had changed, growing softer. The kind a man used on a woman to get her into bed, except coming from Sal, it was more like an older man trying to get a piece of cake he wasn't allowed to have. Everyone, including Sal—heck, even *herself*—seemed to be fixed on one tantalizingly well-hung slice.

Sophie nearly rolled her eyes.

"I overheard you talkin'. See, ladies, I'm Caden's handler. I need to be close to him, oversee things. He's gotta get into fighting shape for Tetnus so I gotta put a tether on him, reel him back in a bit. Tame his wild side. Of course, I've been known to be something of a ladies' man myself."

This time Sophie did roll her eyes. Once more, she was reminded that she wasn't the only one attempting a comeback.

Seems the playboy had missed getting his handsome

face bashed in inside the Octagon ring—having it *so* hard with all the modeling endorsements, partying, and naughty escapades. Epic, on all accounts. A sure bet, that's what he was, at a party, on television, in bed. A tabloid go-to, you could count on Caden to spike daily viewership with tales of his wild antics.

So when he mysteriously disappeared out of the fashion spotlight only to reappear as a welterweight in the qualifying fights for Tetnus, Sophie had found herself in the right place and the right time, and seized the opportunity for scooping an exclusive interview. She remembered the rush of excitement she'd felt, just before that silly incident ruined everything.

"I don't know how he managed dodging these appearances without Jerry busting a nut," Sal added, more for his own benefit than anyone else's. "Being his prized fella, and all."

Interesting tidbit, how Caden had missed his appearances. She'd have to pay attention to exactly how he planned on getting to Vegas. Clearly he'd been avoiding the bus—proof he was smarter than he looked.

Both girls sprang into action, searching the computer screen intently and muttering about shifting around a reservation, then smiling brightly at the old-school lady-killer next to her.

Sophie cleared her throat. "I'd like a room far away from Caden. Maybe in an entirely different wing, if available." She didn't want to chance bumping into him unexpectedly in the hotel corridor. The timing of their surprise reunion—with Caden being the *only* one caught off guard—was going to be well-planned out.

The receptionists' raised eyebrows said it all. *Crazy lady.*

"If you tell me where he is right now, I'll get signed autographs for you," Sal promised.

"The weight room!" they replied in unison, each waving a plastic key toward the main hallway. One key went flying, and when both girls bent to retrieve it, the second key dropped.

Dang-diggity. A relaxing soak in the Jacuzzi, that's what she needed. Relieve the tightness in her neck, possibly whiplash, definitely tension. A brief but necessary reprieve to mull over her next steps. Then she'd shower. Afterward, she'd tackle the Boys issue and strategize exactly how, where and when she would approach Caden with her proposal for an exclusive interview. One that would benefit his comeback plans. And hers.

But first things first. What were the chances that the Jacuzzi was near the pool and far, far away from the weight room? With the way her day was going…

"Where the fuck did *she* come from?"

Sophie's heart dropped. Turning, she found a tall, wiry man glaring daggers at her from across the lobby.

"You're on your own, kiddo. Off to call the wife. See ya, Jerry." Sal laid the camera bag next to her large suitcase and grabbed his key from the receptionist. "Don't forget your other bag on the…" Sal nodded toward the parking lot and bus.

"I'll handle Jerry. All I need from you is to fill the Boys in, get them onboard and do whatever it takes to make them agreeable to being filmed," she urged in a low voice.

With an apologetic glance delivered quicker than a blink, and as fast as his short legs could carry him, he left her to face the music alone. Jeez, she'd take a country ballad over having to listen to Jerry's hotheaded chorus any day.

Sophie adjusted the puffy sleeves on her blouse and mentally prepared for battle. She'd show this bundle of joyless that bunny had a set of teeth bigger than his cojones.

Judging by the red flush on his cheeks, the bundle was rapidly unraveling as he thundered up next to her.

"You career wrecker! If you—"

"Career wrecker?" She calmly picked up her plastic room key off the counter and shifted into full Sophie Morelle mode. "You destroy everything you touch with that foul mouth and even fouler temper. Heard talk about how your wife left you, Jerry. I'd say your temperament had something to do with it." She gave him her back as she pulled up the handle on her suitcase, picked up her camera bag, and stepped away.

There was no dealing with Jerry with kid gloves on or he'd plow right over her. She had an ace in her pocket, knew his weakness for money and fame would bring him around to her way of thinking. Except she was tired, grimy, and trying to avoid a nasty scene in the middle of the New Millennium Inn lobby. She'd prefer negotiating with him some other time.

She felt a firm grasp on her forearm a second before she was yanked none too gently back. Her heart pounded, but she ignored it. No one was allowed to mess with Sophie Morelle; she'd brought better men to the verge of tears for lesser offenses. Sophie let her temper rage, replacing the fear that had her heart aflutter. In seconds, she was sure the fire in her cheeks matched the manhandling creep's coloring.

"My fighters. My arena. You mess with them, you mess with me."

"If you don't release my arm this instant, the police are going to have a *mess* to sort out. Assault charges..."

"Bitch. It's a wonder your network didn't can you earlier." His hand dropped, though his fingers formed a fist on the way down. Sophie stepped back, waving her room key in his face like a sword fending off the enemy. Things were about to get ugly if she didn't defuse the situation.

She bit back her irritation and squashed the numb sensation in the pit of her stomach that appeared each time a man got overly aggressive with her, and calmly stated, "You're going to have more money than you know what to do with if you hear me out."

Though the pigheadedness in his piglike eyes remained, Jerry paused. Instinctively she knew the moment for violence had passed, though her stomach churned and her throat burned.

"Lady, I don't know how you got here, or what you're up to, but you're bad news and I don't like you. Fuck, don't you think you caused enough freakin' damage?"

"When you're feeling more chipper, we'll discuss how you are going to ride the Tetnus wave and *double* your winnings. And I'm going to make it happen, whether you like me or not."

Jerry frowned, considering her words. With a grunt, he turned and marched away, but not before issuing a parting shot. "Like you? Much as I'd like a bullet to the head."

Join the party...jerk.

She made her way down the long corridor toward the

elevator bank in the east wing. The wheels of her suit-case rolled across the carpet, churning along with her thoughts. As a teenager, she'd learned the hard way how to deal with powerful men. Just like so many people in her past, nothing motivated them like money. Jerry was no exception.

Truth be told, she was just as easy. Heck, the reason she'd taken the *Late Night with Sophie Morelle* gig was the stellar salary. She'd sold herself out. Intentionally. Crossed the fine line between morally correct and im-morally lurid. Cheap, too. Jerry'd be just another notch on her jaded belt.

Sophie wasn't proud of what she'd become. Often she didn't even *like* herself. But it was a world better than those early years, when a pigheaded man just like Jerry had snatched away her dreams. Temporarily, anyway.

The scars on her soul didn't count.

"Woot! Woot! That's twenty laps, Caden honey. That means—"

Caden dove and held his glide, effectively silenc-ing the chatterbox. God, that woman loved the sound of her own voice. More annoying was that the chatter consisted of a single topic—him. Not that he let the con-stant praise—even of the most minor stuff, like the way he flossed his damned teeth—feed his ego. Caden was tired of his fame, and the bullshit that accompanied it.

Mouth closed and legs spread wide. Fuck, that's what he wanted. Just like any average Joe. Her moaning and 'im coming hard. Not all this yacking about his pecs 'rwear collection.

'f he stuck it out for twenty more laps,

Chatty'd get the hint and disappear? He'd been more than direct after the Oral-B remark this morning. It'd been fun, but her number was up. Which was why her appearance at the end of the pool had him swimming more laps than necessary, considering the ten-pound weights strapped to his biceps and ankles.

Despite Cathy—or whatever her name was—being an enthusiastic bed partner, his boredom had returned full-force. Exactly what he'd come to expect from the countless relationships he moved through as swiftly as the tepid pool water. It didn't pay to bring anyone in too close; taking a shallow dip every now and again fulfilled his physical needs just fine.

Caden kicked harder, feeling the burn in his thighs. The gym attendant had more than enough money to update the entire exercise room with what Caden had paid him for the weights. Worth every penny too, judging by his fatigued muscles. A shame the slight-yet-never-ending headaches, which plagued him since his concussion a few months back, wouldn't tire out as well. His path down comeback road wasn't as easy as he'd thought. But it was bound to be a hell of a lot easier than when he'd first started out fighting, when he'd had to dig in deep and keep on going. Mind over matter.

Starting today, things were going to change. Hey, he'd already made some progress by finding a way off that yellow freak-show ride.

Breaking the surface, he forced his arms and legs into action and sliced through the water freestyle with precise, fluent strokes. The wall of the Olympic-sized pool came up quickly and he turned, pivoted, and pressed off the side without hesitation, though his muscles screamed in agony. No pain, no gain—he'd learned that lesson long ago, though was only reminded of it recently.

Several more laps followed—he lost count, and along with it, the chatterbox, who'd deserted her spot at the edge of the pool somewhere between laps twenty-five and twenty-eight. Probably headed off to greener pastures, likely joining the Boys and other MMA groupies for some late-afternoon fun in the oversized hot tub. Though Caden couldn't see them, the racket coming from behind the rattan fence was reminder enough that it was time to finish up. The party was a distraction he couldn't afford, on so many levels.

Hell, back in the day—days way too recent to count—he'd have been the main attraction. The life of the party. The guy everyone loved to be around. Back when his life had been one endless booze fest. Endorsements, liquor, women, money, fame—all one suffocating blur. Caden ignored the burn and kicked harder. Fighting the hollowness inside. Hell, for three wild years, he'd managed to lose himself in all the who's, what's, and where's, dull everything, except the memories.

Which was why, this time around, he had to get his shit together. Clean his act up and not give into temptation. Shake off his bad habits and make a crack at controlling his numerous appetites. Finally accomplish the one thing that had been within his reach until he blew it: the MMA welterweight title.

Four more blissfully peaceful, agonizingly brutal ~~he~~ decided, and he'd call it a day.

~~'d~~ begun training for real, he felt stronger

and more in control. It felt…good. Damned good. He picked up the pace into a full-on sprint, determined to do it right this time. This time, no one—not even himself—was going to get in his way.

Chapter 3

GUILLOTINE CHOKE: A move a fighter had best beware of, especially if his opponent is French

How many fighters does it take to fill a hot tub? Sophie wondered, trying to find humor in an otherwise exhausting day. *One. Two, max.*

From the sound of things, the entire entourage from the bus was putting it to the test. They'd congregated in and around the Jacuzzi, cordoned off from the pool area by a tall, rattan fence and some artificial palm trees. Drinking. Surrounded by giggling women. And partying so raucously that everyone else around the pool had headed over for a piece of the action.

Everyone except Sophie, and the lone swimmer making his way across the length of the pool.

Sophie filtered out their laughter. Being that the Boys were preoccupied and had forgotten her, she'd settled down on a clean patch of tile and had dangled her legs over the side. A cool drink would have been nice, but the Tiki bar had been wheeled over to the party.

Probably Caden's idea. The unwelcome image of him flitted through her mind—his big body filling the hot tub, drinks in both hands and two bikini-clad women vying for a spot on his lap. Leaning back on her elbows, she concentrated on the blissful lapping sound. Content to simply kick her legs and create tiny waves with her feet.

She was definitely out of place with her silk blouse unbuttoned and her pencil skirt hitched up on her long legs. A swimsuit would have been a better idea but she'd have to make do. The suitcase with her lingerie and swimwear was currently held hostage on the bus and Sal had informed her that Jerry had the keys. Being she'd had her fill of *him* for the moment, she didn't pursue it any further.

At least she'd had her flip-flops. Always kept a pair on hand—this pair being her favorite because of the bright, cheerful daisies. A habit, she supposed. Kids from Hawley spent a better part of the year in flip-flops. More affordable, and practical, than the Prada pumps she'd grown so fond of as an adult.

She kicked her legs, deciding never to think about Hawley again. Letting herself enjoy the smell of chlorine and the feel of the water washing over her skin. Letting the pool rinse away her troubles. Letting herself contemplate something, *someone*, much more appealing.

She took in the swimmer's broad shoulders, thick

arms, and tight butt in a long, gawking gape. His build rivaled any of the Boys'. Her trainers at the fitness club—when she'd had time to go—always encouraged her to take up swimming. Exercised all the muscles, or so they claimed.

Mildly curious, she eyed the eye candy slicing through the water and heading toward the other end. He wore some kind of black armbands on each bicep. Floaties? No, not the way he cut through the water with long, powerful strokes. Certifiably hot.

Sophie leaned back, let the sun warm her face, and sent up a silent prayer that the next time she looked, he'd be doing the backstroke, so she could ogle his chest.

Down, girl. She kicked her legs as if trying to tread the murky waters of her thoughts. It had been a while since she'd been intimately involved with a man.

Over the past few years, she could count on one hand the guys she'd dated. Most didn't get past the first date. A television executive, who after wining and dining her, thought he'd take her for a spin on the casting couch. She'd threatened to file sexual harassment charges— clearly that so-called date hadn't ended well. A few average guys who turned out to be fans, expecting a raunchy, *kinky*, Sophie Morelle, got instead…nothing, not even a kiss.

Two short-term boyfriends: one who lasted a few months until Sophie's schedule became so hectic she didn't have time for him. The second guy, Jeff, lasted a few more months, and was someone who genuinely cared about her—which freaked her out more than the television executive. On one dreary Mademoiselle Freak Out evening, she'd cut the cord and broken his heart.

Commitment phobia? Hung up on her past? Possibly both? Sophie didn't like to dwell on things she couldn't control. Or change. As far as relationships were concerned, better to let sleeping dogs lie and live in the present, or so she told herself. And judging by the splashing water, her present was making his way toward her.

The sound of wet feet slapping across the tiled pool deck caused Sophie to snap her eyes open, just in time to spot the two fighters headed her way.

Was it too much to ask luck to work for her, and not against her? She was so sure they'd be too preoccupied. How the heck had they spotted her?

Sophie hurried to stand, slid into her flip-flops, and turned to make a hasty retreat. But she was too late.

"Lookie who decided to join us," the fighter with the weird scorpion tattooed on his head slurred. Jaysin someone? It didn't matter. What mattered was getting away from this drunken crew.

Sophie tried to reason with them. "Listen, Boys. You have company…better company than me, over there in the hot tub. We'll talk tomorrow about how I am going to make you superstars." Both men paused, listening.

Suddenly hopeful, Sophie continued, "Men who'll be admired by every athlete out there, including Jeter and both Mannings. You'll see I'm not the 'washed-up clumsy bitch' Jaysin here accused me of being on the bus ride over. I'm the woman who's going to rock your worlds."

She eyed them both as they processed her words. She took a few measured steps backward, just in case.

Jaysin grunted. "Think you can make me a bigger star than him?" He angled his head toward the pool.

She frowned, her eyes following his gesture, but a loud shout made her jump and turn in alarm.

Two more Boys sprinted up to them, both grinning like devils. Jaysin tried to run interference, only to be jostled to the side.

"Where's your bathing suit, sweetheart?" An arm snaked around her waist and she was lifted off her feet. His grip wasn't too tight and if she arched her body just so...

"Hey, Anthony, I think she wants you to let go."

Sophie stopped squirming, realizing the brute holding her had stepped to the ledge of the pool.

"One."

"No. I—"

"Two."

"—can't—"

"Three!" they yelled in unison, drowning out Sophie's own scream.

"—swim!"

Sophie hit the water face-first, landing hard and flat into a body-jarring belly flop. A childhood spent in a coal town didn't exactly lend itself to swim lessons. Oh, she *owned* several bathing suits, for hanging out in hot tubs, sipping piña coladas and networking with celebrities, whomever her feature guest was going to be, back in the day. Not for swimming. Ever. She'd likely *drown*.

Fire spread across her midriff and her cheeks stung. The undignified belly flop hurt like dang-diggity. She literally had the wind knocked out of her, like she'd slammed up against a brick wall. Stunned, she felt the water wash over her.

As she sank, regret was what surfaced. The kind that came with the realization that her life had taken the wrong path, when in one huge gulp of chlorinated water, she regretted not sticking to her dreams, the goals she'd set for the future. Goals that didn't include talking trash on late-night television. Sure, she had something to prove to her former network. But more importantly, she had something to prove to herself. And now, she might not get the chance.

All I wanted was to be like Christiane Amanpour. A genuine journalist, one making a difference in the world. Really do it right this time.

A knee connected with the bottom—oddly malleable, but hard enough she thought she heard her teeth rattle. She pitched sideways.

I need this documentary! Is this really how I want to go out?

The pool floor *gyrated.*

Did she really want to go out wearing a silk blouse and skirt, and one yellow-flowered flip-flop, with her biggest story being not one she covered—but caused? Be remembered for all time as the woman who'd knocked out cold the most celebrated of celebrities and winningest of fighters, Caden Kelly? Nearly ruined his multiple careers. Completely ruined her own.

No siree.

Sophie flailed her arms overhead and kicked her feet hard. The sole of her foot connected with the pool's bottom, which felt more like a carnival moonwalk ride, but she didn't dwell on it. The lightbulb in her head had switched on to survival mode. With every ounce of strength left in her, she pushed off and shot upward toward the light.

Pumping her arms and legs wildly, she cleared the surface.

The welcoming rays of sunlight greeted her. With one long, jagged inhale, she realized her head was above water. She opened her mouth and let life's breath fill her lungs. Her future was hers for the taking. It wasn't all over.

The next instant, she was underwater.

Wildly, she kicked her legs, attempting to break free of both the water and the vise gripping her ankle. Something, or rather *someone*, had yanked her back under.

She reached out. Her hand connected with something soft and slippery, something to grab onto and use as leverage. Hastily, she worked her fingers up to the elastic waistband and wrapped them tightly around it. The material resisted, dragging the top of her hooked-on-for-dear-life fingers down along a warm, hard surface in a wet caress.

Still, it worked. Warm sunlight caressed her cheeks as she surfaced, gasping for breath as her head bobbed above water. She'd been given another chance. *This time, I'm not going to blow it.* The thought flickered through her mind like a passing sunbeam. Briefly. Before she went under once more.

An arm—the swimmer's!—wrapped around her waist, pulling her in tight against his side. And, blessedly, upward, until her head broke the surface.

She sputtered and blinked away the pool water from her eyelashes.

Her silk blouse spread out around her like a bright purple jellyfish but Sophie didn't care.

Laughter rang out loudly. She glanced at the Boys, pointing and fist pumping the air like their favorite wide receiver had just scored a touchdown, and ignored them and their less-than-sympathetic sense of humor.

Not even the Boys were going to buzzkill the feeling of euphoria sweeping over her. She'd been given another chance.

"Are you nuts, pinning me to the bottom of the pool like that? You nearly killed me."

Sophie tensed, horrified. The taut arm holding her pressed up against his side flexed. Caden.

Utter humiliation. Figured he'd be the cause. *Crapola.*

"I barely touched you," she snapped, trying to figure out how to work herself free of his hold without drowning before he recognized her.

"See this?" He flexed a bicep and her gaze fell to his enormous, well-defined muscle before shifting to the floatie. "Weights. Plus my muscles are shot from swimming extra laps."

Was there anything unattractive about the man aside from the floatie strapped to his arm? She pushed the wayward thought aside, turning her head to eyeball the rim of the pool. A hopeless cause—she'd never make it, even if she launched herself off his body. Better get their reintroduction over with. Bracing herself, she flipped her hair off her face and glared at him.

"Holy shit on a brick, you've got to be kidding me!"

She opened her mouth to give him a what-for but his hold on her slackened and she slid down his wet body. Her nipples pebbled up. Reminding her that not much separated her boobs from his rock-hard body, aside from a soaked silk blouse, sheer cami, and thin, lace bra.

Holy shit on a brick is right. This was Caden. Her savior? The cause of her intense, immediate arousal? CADEN. DANG IT! She flexed her fingers, frantically searching for the elastic, leverage so she could hoist herself up and off of him. Hoping somehow she'd manage to keep her head above water, then miraculously morph into an Olympic swimmer and sprint the heck away from him. She found the elastic, and then some. And then more some, a heck of a lot of more some.

"What the hell do you think you're doing?" He pulled his hips back, breaking himself free from the contact the tops of her fingers had made with...*sweet Mother Mary.*

The water rippled as the elastic snapped back into place against his taut stomach. She made a grab for his bicep. *Think documentary. You just landed—literally—on the hottest welterweight around. One within reach. Several long inches of him. Get a grip, Sophie!*

He tried to shake her off.

Kicking with both feet, she squeezed her hand, pulled herself up and then managed to weave her other arm around him.

"Are you fucking insane?" His emerald green eyes smoldered with anger. He tugged his arm back but she steadfastly held on even as her body slammed up against his chest.

Caden flexed beneath her. She didn't have to look to know that, unlike other fighters, his chest was free of tattoos, but her gaze lowered anyway. His body was a work of art in itself. Taut, tanned sculpted curves like sweet caramel on a vanilla cone. An immediate gastronomical-gasm in one long lick. Punch-drunk, that's what had happened to her, taking in the way his muscles rippled as he tried to break free. She made a sound deep within her throat, something between an exasperated grunt and a short low-toned moan.

He stopped moving, and as she glanced up, his gaze pierced her.

"Let go."

"No."

Caden's jaw clenched.

"Thought the restraining order said if you stepped anywhere near me, no matter the circumstances, you'd be locked up. Where the hell did you even come from?"

Oh, she'd give anything to dunk his arrogant, troublesome head underwater. A warning, that's all it had been. She'd been thrilled *not* to have the privilege of coming anywhere near the panty pimp. Though the network had reacted…badly. Loss of advertising *and* a temporary restraining order? Reluctantly, Sophie admitted that it had likely been the final blow, the additional ax in her contractual beheading.

A renewed sense of anger swelled up inside her. She fought for control.

Remember Christiane Amanpour. Make nice, or drown without your documentary. She cleared her throat. "It expired. You never officially filed, or went to court…"

"Attempted murder. Hell, a second attempt—"

"Both accidents."

"I thought being wacked in the head by a three-hundred-pound camera hurt like hell until—"

"Hardly three hundred pounds. How could my cameraman carry such a weight?"

"—being trampled on at the bottom of a pool by a hundred and fifty pounds of demented redhead with some sort of vendetta against me."

She sucked in a breath, exasperated yet struggling to find a way to make the best of the situation. No time like the present to clear the air, right? "Can we discuss this logically? Preferably somewhere safer? You've got to be getting tired of treading water. Especially while holding *one hundred and thirty-five pounds* of certifiable redhead, one who doesn't have a vendetta against you."

The look he shot her screamed *demented.* "I'm standing."

"What?" Sophie looked down. Sure enough, she could see his big feet through the water. She searched the tile wall until she found the sign painted on it that indicated the depth—or lack of it. Six feet deep. A few steps to the right and she'd be able to stand on her own.

He laughed unpleasantly, in amused disbelief or something closely resembling it. Once more she itched to dunk him.

"Idiot," he muttered, moving a few feet forward into shallower water, dragging her along. With a firm tug, he freed himself. Her arms fell to her sides as her toes connected with the pool bottom.

He turned, and she watched as the one fighter certain to make her documentary a success trudged his way through the water toward the cement stairs in the corner.

She really needed to work on not pushing the panic button every time things spiraled out of control. Heck, back in the day, Sophie Morelle would have swallowed pints of chlorinated water, drowned, and resuscitated herself in order to get the story. Her attention narrowed on the man climbing out of the pool. And from this angle, she had all the validation needed—with buns like that, undoubtedly every woman in America would want more of the troublesome fighter.

Except Sophie. That would be a disaster worse than a little tap on the head or a ruined career. What she needed from him was strictly professional. A means to an end. And then that would be the end of her interaction with *him*.

"See you around, Caden," she shouted. He'd better get used to the idea she wasn't going anywhere anytime soon.

"Not a fat chance in hell, sweetheart. No way are you gonna ruin my career...*again*," he warned from the side of the pool before stalking away in one wet, handsome mess. The Boys wandered off after him.

Sophie tiptoed her way toward shallow water, yet her steps were determined and certain. Like Caden, she wanted her career back, and more. Move over, Diane Sawyer. Sophie Morelle was about to reinvent herself.

No man, in any shape or form—muscular heartthrob or unpleasant memory—was going to stop her.

Chapter 4

HEEL HOOK: Typically employed by a female fighter, when she sticks a stiletto in her opponent's eye

Caden adjusted the weight on the bench press bar, just enough for a few final agonizing lifts. Fatigued, he was ready to catch some early evening Z's, and be asleep by ten. A far cry from his party animal past, of boozing it up all night and lounging around in bed all day. With company, of course.

Tomorrow, he'd head over to the St. Louis Mixed Martial Arts Club to pick up some hardcore sparring partners. Battle away the years of abusing his body, along with any lingering doubts about just how committed he was to winning the welterweight title. The bruise on his elbow barked as he completed a lift. He tried to ignore it, and thoughts of the woman who'd caused it.

No way was Sophie in Missouri on vacation. Seemed more like the Cabo San Lucas type. High end. High maintenance. Not that he knew her well, or hardly at all.

He had caught a few episodes of *Late Night with Sophie Morelle* back when he could stand the sight of her. Every bar, café, and goddamned sports pub on the planet tuned their televisions to watch the gorgeous television host talk smack. The guys Caden knew loved the bullshit spewing from her mouth, and respected her for having balls of steel when a belligerent star got freaky.

Sophie held her own, all right. Never seemed at a loss for words or had a hair out of place. The consummate, smart-ass, sexy-as-shit television host. So what was the fuck was her deal?

Clenching the bar, he pushed up, held the position, and slowly lowered it, feeling the shake in his tired biceps. Fighting for control of his movements. Fighting for focus on tonight's training.

Fighting against the direction his thoughts had taken, and the image of *her*, with her runny mascara and her hair looking like a shampoo commercial gone bad. For a second there, she'd looked human. Not the demon spawn he'd built her up to be in his mind since he last saw her in Pittsburgh—before his world went black.

Fuckability factor aside, that woman was trouble.

Tried and *proven* trouble. His chances at a comeback had crashed to a halt when that camera had smashed into his head. Knocked him out cold and almost ruined his shot at qualifying for Tetnus. Luckily, greedy Jerry declared him a winner anyway. Caden had heard it was an accident, that Sophie had been tripped, causing her to fall into the cameraman. But he still hated the sight of the mouthy reporter.

After eleven more repetitions, he released the bar. It clanged hard back into place on the bench press.

What he did know about her, he didn't like. She was dangerous. Relentless when it came to getting her story. Uncaring of who she hurt. Unfazed by the drama that always seemed to unfold around her. No one's wind was strong enough to knock her sailboat off course. And she sure as hell knew how to suck the very breath out of a man. *Literally.*

Caden didn't believe in coincidences. He needed to put a finger on some logical explanation for her sudden appearance in Missouri. He'd bet his rental car—a sweet ride in the form of an Aston Martin DB5 convertible—that it had something to do with him. Sophie Morelle was not the kind of trouble he needed in this stage of the game.

"How in the blazes did you get out of tonight's gig? Dang it, I needed you there," Sal's voice reverberated loudly as he approached the bench.

Caden winced. Was it too much to ask for a peaceful workout? Bad enough his thoughts had screwed with his focus.

"Ah, what does it matter?" Sal continued in a low voice, drawing up a small stool.

Caden sat up and wiped the sweat from his forehead. The old-timer seemed frazzled, with his white hair standing up in all directions. "Late-night wind kick up out there?"

Sal didn't seem to hear him as he searched in his pocket for a worn leather flask, which he withdrew and opened with shaky hands.

"How's it going, Sal?" Caden pressed. All joking aside, he was worried about the busybody of a man.

"Just a sec and I'll tell ya just how it's *not* going." Bringing the flask up to his lips, he took a long drink, then wiped his mouth with the back of his hand.

"Easy there, big guy. What have you got in there? Whiskey?" The smell of booze was hard to ignore.

Normally, Caden avoided getting involved with other people's business. But he'd grown fond of the old-timer, one of the few people who didn't bend over and kiss his ass every time he frowned. Sal had been around long enough to know not to get caught up in the celebrity shit.

"No offense, but do you think you can handle that?"

Sal nodded, and took another long swig. *Oh, fuck.*

"Never seen Jerry so pissed off."

Caden began his warm down, and rolled his shoulders. "Can't say that I'm surprised. What else did you expect to happen at a biker bar? Nothing but trouble. God knows why he's scheduling appearances at dives. Starting to cost me a pretty penny—and more—having to bribe my way out of making them."

"And more" was putting it mildly.

It had taken some serious finagling to get out of tonight's appearance. Since flying into St. Louis two days ago, Jerry had been nagging him about joining the Boys and trying to renege on their agreement. Caden'd greased the man's palm big time to only having to make two appearances and to not having to ride on that crap-for-wheels bus. It didn't stop Jerry from busting his balls and pressuring him into doing more.

Whether or not he liked Jerry was irrelevant. Caden was part of his fight team, sponsored by him, and most

importantly—and what he'd best keep reminding himself—was that notoriously tight-fisted man was also a
major sponsor of Tetnus.

Go figure.

Clearly Jerry had high hopes for his team—*him*—
winning.

At least they shared a common goal.

Caden was already regretting what else he'd offered
up in exchange. "You know, with the wad of greenbacks
lining his pocket, that asshat should be grinning all the
way to the bank. And…God help me, he's riding along
with me for the rest of the trip in my rental car."

"Not anymore. No wonder he's madder than a fighter
caught in a choke hold. Bad enough all hell broke loose
tonight. Jerry totally flipped his lid right dab in the middle of all the hoopla, cursing and screaming threats. He
promised the Boys that he'd be on tomorrow's bus." Sal
took another hard swig.

"Tastes better when you sip it," Caden lied. The news
about Jerry's change in transportation plans made him
smile. "Okay, I'll bite. You gonna fill me in on all the
hoopla?"

"The bus is leaving tomorrow at 6:00 a.m. sharp. He
told all the Boys to either be on it or forget about Vegas,
and that shot at the title."

"Bullshit. No way is he going to can his best fighters." It'd probably take Sal all night for him to spit out
the truth about tonight's fuck-up, given how he was
three sheets to the wind.

"Told everyone that he's driving the bus himself, so
he can monitor who gets on and off. Don't know how
I'm going to break it to her." Sal murmured the last bit

in a low voice, causing Caden's ears to strain to catch his words.

There could only be one *her*—the troublemaker in high heels. Man alive, she seemed to have occupied his thoughts for the better part of the day. But something else was up, and he intended to find out what it was. "What's got you all riled up tonight, old man?"

"My word is my honor. My reputation. This means a lot to her. You should have seen her handle the Boys on the bus. And tonight."

"You're talking about that reporter, right?" he asked, already guessing the answer. Caden gave himself a mental pat on the back. Keeping himself off that bus was money well spent.

"*Most* of the Boys seem to have taken a liking to her."

"Imbeciles. What was Sophie Morelle doing at our gig?"

"Jerry's face looked like a parsnip. The man must take blood pressure medication or else he'd have been wheeled outta that place on a stretcher. Bad enough only ten people showed up. Bad enough the Boys downed enough liquor to fill a stadium. The worst of it all happened after Sophie moseyed on in. That's when the night went from bad to life-threatening."

"Usually does when she's around. She was at the gig because…?"

Sal looked at him, and something crossed his face, something slightly devious. Or was it perturbed? Or most likely nothing, except mad-ass drunk.

"Trust me, Sal. Whatever happened, that woman will get over it. She's a survivor. What did she want from you, anyway?"

Sal looked like he was ready to tear his hair out.

Good thing he had so little to work with. "Dang, I hate to disappoint a pretty lady."

Caden snorted.

"Now I'll never see my name in the credits."

Caden tossed the towel onto the bench, braced his elbow on his legs, and leaned forward, angry. "What exactly do you mean, *credits*? Like television credits?"

Sal opened, then closed his mouth. But the truth was written all over his face.

"Fuck! You sold me out, didn't you? How much?"

"It's not what you think."

"Figures the one guy I trust in this whole operation pulls a classic Wall Street move by going all public and shit. Here, everyone thinks Jerry's the shark when the manatee swimming beside him is much more lethal." Caden shook his head in disgust, as Sal ran his hand over his belly, clearly missing the point.

"I know you said that you could give a fudge about being a celebrity. Hanging your hat up for good. No more interviews or…"

Caden glared, causing Sal to fidget on his stool.

"Exactly *who* drank enough liquor to fill a stadium? What were you thinking?"

"Can't an old man get his five minutes of fame, like that Andy Holwar fella? Like…you?"

Caden laughed, a shallow sound. It was that or give voice to the stream of cusses he was barely holding back. Fifteen minutes of fame for any other reason than fighting was time wasted. *Years* wasted. "I wouldn't sell someone out. Besides, how would you feel about having your crotch plastered on billboards nationwide?"

Sal scrunched up his face, considering the question.

Jesus. And Caden had been thinking Jaysin Bouvine

coveted his celebrity the most. Little did they know what a load of bull it all was.

Caden considered the money he'd been dishing out to Jerry. "You could have given me a heads-up. Not sell me out like that. What's she up to, anyway? Filming fighters? Busting balls?"

"She asked me to help her out. Wants to follow you fellas around, get some interviews for a documentary. The lady's dang persuasive. She had most of the Boys feeding from her hand, before Jaysin got fresh."

"I knew she was up to no good. Poking her nose in our business. I'll bet my ass that woman doesn't know jack about MMA."

"I'm gonna need more than my name in the cred-its now. Gotta pay for the damages caused by tonight's brawl. Jerry put a number on it, in the thousands," Sal muttered, his voice hoarse and pained. "Valeska is gonna kill me."

He shot Sal a look, then said softly, "Didn't I warn you that woman was trouble?"

The old-timer's fist shot out, a bitch move that would have hit a lesser fighter square in the face. He would have grazed Caden, had he not spotted it coming at the last second and dodged it. For an old feller, he packed a punch.

Both men jumped to their feet. No way did Caden want to take down Sal, but if he threw one more…

"You got a hard-on for Sophie Morelle, old man?" he taunted.

Sal swayed on his feet, looking disoriented. Sud-denly, all the air blew out of him in one long exhale, and he sat down. "Thought you were talking about Valeska."

"Easy," Caden said with a shake of his head, the rush

of adrenaline he always felt before a fight vanishing as abruptly as it came. Sal had really pissed him off, breaking his trust like that. Something to take note of for the future, then move on. Caden wasn't a hothead like some fighters. Preferred to keep his head on his shoulders and fight a well-planned, logical battle.

"Listen. It's late and I need to be up early to train. Spit it out, man. Sophie showed up. A fight broke out. Some chairs got smashed." He should have known better than to ask about her, but found himself doing so anyway. *Damned curiosity.*

Sal cleared his throat. "No panty lines."

"What?" The image of the wet redheaded reporter came to mind. With her blouse clinging to her like a second skin and her pert nipples at full attention beneath the soggy, body-hugging material. Man, that woman had curves in all the right places. Her ass was tight but curvy, just the way he liked it.

He shrugged, and hardened his voice. "Let me guess. Sophie Morelle crashed the gig in some expensive, red spandex number, and in full commando mode." His cock sprang to life within his worn sweats. "Must have been some sight. Shame I missed it."

"Back in the day, a woman wouldn't think to leave the house without painting her lips. Girls these days..." Sal paused, grinning like a cat who'd licked a shitload of cream.

Caden shook his head. "The brawl...?"

"Jaysin Bouvine seems to have taken a liking to Sophie. Or maybe he wants to be a superstar, like yourself. He was all over her, a goddamned octopus, with his hands everywhere."

"Let me guess. She liked it," Caden bit out, his voice

sounding harsher than expected. He flexed his fingers, unwinding them from the fist he'd made.

"Guess again. Who do you think started the brawl? Smacked Jaysin's hand hard with the back of one of those killer shoes. Broke the heel clean off, too. The other Boys—hell, the entire bar—had to jump in and pull him off of her."

Caden tensed. No matter how much he disliked Sophie, she didn't deserve to be taken down by the likes of Bouvine. Caden was going to have to have a fist talk with the asshole. "Was she hurt?" he murmured, his tone sounding threatening even to his own ears.

"Nope. A bit mussed up but as cool as a cucumber. Even when Jaysin announced to the entire bar how she didn't have any panties on. I was hoping she'd reach for that other killer heel. If I were a betting man, my money'd be on Sophie. Of course, Jerry had a fit. Blamed the entire event on me, 'cause I brought her aboard."

"I'd say you got off cheap, given her history." Caden stood up and stretched his legs. "Think I've heard enough about Sophie Morelle. Night, Sal."

Caden tried to conjure up an image, any one of the numerous women he'd had, suddenly feeling horny as hell. The thickening swell in his pants was begging for release, something he planned on remedying as soon as he hit the hay. But as he made his way to his room, thoughts of a pantyless, spandex-clad Sophie lingered.

Her hotel room door clicked shut, and Sophie found herself in the impossible situation of being locked out in the hallway with a bottle of tequila tucked under an arm, a tray with a container of orange juice and an egg-white omelet clutched tightly in her grip, and a patent leather heel on one foot and a mismatched daisy flip-flop on the other one.

And worse still, a cowboy in the next room crooning out melodies as if he were at the Grand Ole Opry.

How could anyone think straight with that racket going on?

Sophie grimaced. Bad enough earlier this evening she'd endured being tackled to the ground by a three-hundred-pound meathead with a hideous-looking scorpion tattooed on his scalp.

But come on already—*country* music?

Oblivious to the drama unfolding in the hallway, the cowboy sang on, this time about a prison dog. His rich baritone didn't miss a note. Clearly, her beating on the connecting en suite door hadn't fazed the crooner in the least. Heck, she'd even unlocked the darn thing and tried to rattle it, but it was locked on the other side.

Crapola.

Visions of tabloid headlines ran through her mind: *Sophie Morelle Caught in Hotel Hallway, Tipsy, Wearing Wrinkled Blouse and Odd Shoe Combo.* Not exactly a smooth transition to comeback queen.

She thought about the empty miniature vodka bottles lined up neatly on her nightstand. Going on a well-deserved bender had been a horrible idea. *All Willie Nelson's fault, too.* Relax and regroup? Yeah, right, it'd been impossible to recover and quietly lick her wounds with that ruckus. She glared at his door.

Now what?

She could have sworn the tequila bottle did a little I-can-help-you wiggle beneath her armpit, similar to what the vodka bottles had done earlier.

The elevator far down the hallway sounded.

Sophie had no choice.

It took three solid raps for the music to be lowered and precious seconds to tick by before the door was opened. But when the crooner's fingers found her elbow and tugged her inside the darkened entryway, she let out a small squeak of surprise.

"Damn persistent thing, aren't you? Thought I told you we're over?" a husky voice murmured, his warm breath on her ear. "One more night, sweetheart. That's all I'm promising," the sexy, *familiar*, voice added. Instantly, every mismatched emotion she'd ever felt for Caden Kelly surfaced—fear, discomfort, loathing, mortification…lust—which shot off the charts a second later as she took a gander at his broad naked chest.

Oh, my.

The expression "you could bounce a quarter off it" certainly applied to the broad, cut muscles on display before her.

"Quiet for a change, huh? Good. Nice way to end things. I'll take that. Get over on the bed before I change my mind."

She grabbed the tray tighter as he drew closer. Reaching over her head, he shoved the door closed.

"What'd you bring me, honey, breakfast in bed?"

She froze, breathlessly waiting for the other shoe to drop. For Caden to realize his mistake.

What was he doing in the room next to hers anyway—aside from singing? *And apparently sex, lots of sex.*

The receptionists. Ugh. They'd mixed up the keys. No wonder her room was more upscale than a standard. Would Sal even notice his less-than-stellar digs?

She tried to step back, away from the caress of Caden's fingers on her elbow. Her balance faltered. The pitcher capsized and a small tsunami of orange juice splattered the fighter's abdomen in a direct hit, sending a cascade of juice running down along his gorgeous six-pack and lower, coating his crotch and legs in a sticky, orange mess.

"Jesus. What the hell…" Caden reached behind her and flicked on the foyer light.

Sophie balanced her weight on her one pump, trying to steady herself. Watching teardrop-sized pebbles of orange juice slide down his chest. Waiting, breathless, for the angry outburst sure to come.

She bit back her own irritation. Typical—this was entirely the panty-dealing, wannabe cowboy's fault.

They both opened their mouths to speak, but an angry male voice from out in the hallway interrupted them. "Are you sure this is her room?"

"That's what the old-timer was grumbling about. Look, Jaysin, why don't you let bygones be bygones? The hole in your hand's healing up nicely. Don't tell me a little hurting like that still has you pissed off?"

Sophie shuddered. Jaysin Bouvine was the last person she expected at her door. What the blazes did he want, another round with her one working heel?

"Lady's got a potty mouth. Didn't you catch her show? Thinking I'll put those dirty lips to good use."

She raised her chin and stared at the door. Clearly, the fighter hadn't gotten her hands-off-meathead message. Annoying, and a tad disturbing, that he'd come knocking at this late hour.

Caden made a noise and, feeling his stare, her attention shifted to his face. He looked at her so hard her stomach did a cartwheel. For a moment, they stood like that. Eyes locked, him growing more furious by the second, so obviously so her breath hitched, mid-cartwheel. His jaw clenched, and for the first time, she caught a glimpse of the fighter within him. His hand found the knob, and he yanked it open.

Then he was gone.

"Hey, what the shit! Where did you come—?"

Sophie jumped as something smashed against the outside wall. The pounding of fists connecting with flesh—a sound she was well acquainted with after her earlier encounter with Jaysin—lasted for a good minute.

A voice broke the silence. "Man, you're done. Come on. I'll help you walk." The shuffle of footsteps on carpet followed.

Sophie moved over to the table by the window on the far side of the room, unsure of what had just transpired out in the hallway, and just as unsure about what was headed her way. Her stomach rolled and her hands shook, sloshing the remaining juice dangerously close to her blouse.

An Italian leather wallet had been casually tossed on the glass tabletop. Next to it was a set of keys with a *Luxury Car Rentals Inc.* tag on it. Dang it. Caden was smarter than she'd given him credit for. Clearly, he had no intentions of riding on the tour bus.

And clearly, she needed another drink.

Dropping the shaking tray onto the table, she grabbed the tequila, twisted off the cap, and filled a glass. Hey, opportunity knocked, right? And Sophie wasn't one to pass on one, however unexpected it was. Tonight, she'd have to work her magic on Caden, just like she'd done with hundreds of other celebrities.

With her mind made up, she poured a second glass—a peace offering in the face of adversity.

She felt the warm burn of tequila on her throat as she swallowed deeply, listening to the soft tread of his bare feet on the carpet as the door closed and he approached.

His reddened fingers wrapped around the glass she offered, but he set it on the table without taking a sip. She noted the rise and fall of his breath, how normal it seemed. No physical signs that he'd just clobbered old bughead outside in the hallway.

No man had the right to be this beautiful, with light green eyes framed by long, dark eyelashes. High, chiseled cheekbones drew the eye downward to a set of full, sensuous lips. Heck, his billboard didn't do him justice. Though the part of him most prominently featured on it was mercifully tucked away. And Sophie didn't dare sneak a peek in that direction.

Caden licked his bottom lip and turned to stare at her. She wondered if he noticed the sudden flush in her cheeks. His eyes lingered on her face, then raked over her messy clothing.

Her cheeks were now ablaze with humiliation, and… no…*holy crapola*. Her belly felt warm. And a raging inferno had sparked in her happy place.

I'm never drinking tequila again.

He let out a low whistle. "Sweetheart, you're just full of surprises, aren't you? Here, I'd been imagining you in a little red number."

His gaze lowered, and lowered further, coming to rest on her mismatched shoes.

Sophie wasn't exactly sure what he meant, but she'd take sarcasm over anger any day. "You know what they say," she murmured, hoping she sounded nonchalant, as if this situation wasn't awkward in the least. "Variety is the spice of life."

Dang-diggity. Talk about poor word choice. She was forgetting who was dealing with—his sex life was probably spicier than a slice of jalapeño pie. Sophie shifted, the thought throwing her off her game before she slammed it back into the recesses of her mind.

"You don't say," Caden murmured, sounding like he just woke up from a deep sleep after partaking in a sexual marathon. "Must explain why I'm considering adding a bit of paprika to my diet. Not every day a man is propositioned in his hotel room by a natural redhead."

Her spine bristled but her traitorous heart executed another quick cartwheel. Was Caden hitting on her? No way. More likely, he was trying to intimidate her.

"So what do you want?" His voice was smooth and buttery. Sexy. Loaded and full of meaning.

Sex. Wild, spicy sex. "A one-on-one, full-access interview."

"You looking to use me good and hard, huh, sweetheart?"

"I wouldn't say *use*..."

"What would you call it, then?"

"A mutually beneficial arrangement. We're after the same thing, Caden. You want a comeback as much as I do. I'm in the position to make you the most celebrated MMA fighter around."

"Tell you what. I'll give you ten minutes of my time if you do something for me first." Caden ignored his drink, sauntering off into the bathroom only to return with a damp washcloth. Settling down on the edge of the bed, he leaned back on an arm, stretched out his long legs, and nonchalantly began working the cloth first over his chest and then down along his abs, following the trail of sticky orange juice.

Sophie stepped closer. Ten minutes was hardly enough time. With the way he was rubbing that dang cloth across his magnificent body—inch by inch by mouthwatering inch—she'd never get the question out. Because, just like every cell in her body had decided to turn traitor by doing a sizzling rendition of a naughty Irish jig, her throat had dried up as well.

She swallowed hard. If she could just pull herself together long enough to get back in the game, an awful lot could be revealed in ten minutes.

She decided to play along. "Shoot."

He looked up, pinning her with an amused stare. Like he knew she was breathing in his every wicked movement. "I'll start. Flats or heels?"

She cocked her head. "What is this, your version of truth or dare?" *This will be easy.*

Caden smiled in response, and her body bounced back into high alert.

"Uh, hum. Time's a ticking."

"Heels. The higher the better. My turn. Why give up a modeling—"

"Color?"

"What? Bla…" she began, but stopped, suddenly inspired. "Red," she stated, squarely, keeping a neutral tone. "Bright, shiny red. Preferably Italian leather. Let's discuss your disappearance from the MMA circuit and you resurfacing at the Tetnus qualifiers."

"No."

"Okay, fast forward to Tetnus. Do you think someone with your good looks, your notoriety, can—"

"Forget it."

Sophie stepped closer to the stubborn man and stood before him with her hands on her hips. If Caden Kelly thought he was going to bulldoze her, he had a surprise coming his way. Two could play at this game. "Boots or Nike flops?"

That brought a lady-killer smile to his lips. "Boots. Preferably American leather. Cowhide."

She flipped her hair. A brazen tequila fog had settled over her, pushing any lingering caution aside and spurring her on. "Color?"

"Hmm." He seemed to contemplate the entire rainbow, all the while running that darned cloth down across his drum-tight abdomen. "Man, you really pulled a number on me," he grunted absently, his—and her—attention drawn downward over the sticky mess she'd caused. His thumb hooked into the waistline of his sweatpants, tugging them down so he could reach lower. Revealing that sweet spot on a man, that indentation slightly lower than his hipbone, that stirred up her libido like nobody's business. Up close and personal like this, Caden had one mouthwatering sweet spot. Without warning, he looked back up.

It took all of her willpower not to look away.

He tossed the washcloth onto the floor.

"Red," he stated, "like the color of a woman's lips after kissing. Bet yours turn bright and shiny..."

"Care to elaborate?" she heard her sassy self say. The player was trying to play her. *Game on.*

He propped himself up onto both elbows and his lips lifted into a naughty smile, one full of promises. "Depends."

"Why don't we get down to business?"

His eyebrows lifted at that.

"I'll need my recorder for our conversation. You can even sign off on everything discussed when we're done, so they'll be no surprises. Be right back." She stepped toward the en suite door.

"Close the door behind you…chicken."

That stopped her short. As if she—the queen of smack—would be frightened away by his overtly sexual banter? Exactly who did he think he was trying to one-up? Well, it wouldn't be the first time she'd transcribed an interview based on memory alone.

Turning, Sophie got to the point. "Why return to such a brutal world? Surely it's not for the money— even if you win Tetnus and the million-dollar purse, your Ultimate American Male contract is worth more." She tried to block out the image of Caden in his underwear, a difficult feat considering the way his pants had shifted even lower. Tricky given her body's shift into another untimely jig. "Less bloodshed and pain, too," she continued, absentmindedly.

"That right?" Caden slowly got up from the bed and sauntered toward her. Sophie stood ramrod straight, unwilling to back down. Reaching out, he placed a finger high on her chest. Both the location and lightness of his touch surprising her. What was he up to?

She glanced down, and instantly regretted it. In one smooth movement, he ran the tip of his finger along the soft skin of her throat, skimmed it up and over her chin and then flicked her on the nose.

Her eyes shot to his face and, noticing his smirk, narrowed. Wrong woman to pull such a little boy move on.

He straightened. "Enough. Five minutes remaining…"

"You've been as cooperative as ice on a sunburn."

"Tsk. Tsk. You haven't even begun to burn yet, honey. Or melt."

"Sounds unpleasant. I'm a redhead, remember, with a strong aversion to the sun. As far as melting…"

"I'm amending our deal," Caden said, changing the topic.

"We didn't agree on one to amend."

"I'll give you what you want, answer any questions you have within our remaining four minutes. But I want something in return. Something legit. Something material."

"So if I give you what you're asking for—something material, like the cold omelet over on the table—you won't hold back in answering my questions? I'll have to postpone our interview if you want money."

"Thatta girl, back to thinking like a reporter. Out to get her story no matter the cost. What I want is better than money. That's why there's a condition." Caden's gaze raked over her from head to toe before continuing, "If you can't produce the goods, I get a consolation prize, without having to answer a single question. So, we on?"

"Depends." She mimicked his earlier tone exactly and issued her own naughty smile. A lame attempt at disguising her excitement about getting a shot at interviewing him. "Is it something expensive?"

"I'm sure you can afford it."

"Is it something I'll miss if it's gone?" She had to admit, the prospect of uncovering what exactly he *wanted* from her was downright titillating. Her gaze fell on the rumpled bedspread, then catching herself, slid back his way. That bed held a whole assortment of sordid prospects, all of which were downright titillating.

"Kind of the point of the whole matter..." he murmured, vaguely. "A case of curiosity. Genuine curiosity."

Sophie frowned, and weighed her options, quickly making her decision. "Agreed. Believe it or not, I hate surprises."

"Take off your panties."

What?

"I want your panties. A token of our new—albeit brief, at three minutes and counting—business arrangement."

Oh, how she wanted to give this man a wake-up call with a quick knee between the legs. Did training for the Octagon ring include honing some kind of woman-gone-commando radar? Likely, given what some of these fighters wore in a bout and what those ring girls paraded around in. How was she going to hand over her panties when the only pair not locked in a suitcase on the bus was hanging out to dry in her bathroom?

"Be right back." She stepped toward the en suite door next to the bed. It opened without a problem.

"Nope." He slapped his palm against the door and slammed it shut. She turned and shot him a deadly look.

The smug lift of his lips was still sexy as hell. "Now." He held out his palm and leaned over her. It took all her willpower to maintain a cool, collected, professional expression. Caden was clever, she'd give him that.

"What's the forfeit?" Sophie asked casually, as if she hadn't picked up on his game. Dang, the sly devil must have heard about her fiasco at the Hair of the Dump. Clearly Caden planned on winning—knew what wasn't underneath her skirt—and had no intention of giving her an exclusive. In a way, she couldn't blame him.

Heck, if this was how he planned on getting his frustration with her out…

"It'll take you a second to wiggle outta them. If you need help…"

"I need to know my options. The forfeit?"

The devil leaned in closer. Sophie was acutely aware of the size of him. So big in all the right places.

"Our conversation has me thinking…" he rasped softly, his voice a rich throaty baritone. "About something moist, and red."

Lay one on me, baby, every hormone in her body sang out. Sophie ignored it, fighting for control. "You know what they say about a man who thinks too hard?"

Caden paused, and gave her a lopsided grin. "What do they say, sweetheart?"

"Within the time he needs to act, the moment's gone by."

"Guess time's up for thinking then," he shot back, lowering his head. So close she could smell the sweet bubble gum on his breath mixed with the heady scent of his cologne, all spice and tangerine. Two choices: back down or step it up.

Sophie Morelle was no coward.

She placed her palm onto his stomach and gave him a lame shove. Caden grinned down at her, triumphant, and shifted slightly backward.

Hooking her fingers around the hem of her skirt, she began to lift it. Slowly. Her eyes locked in battle with his. His smug grin disappeared, and his lips tightened into a thin line. She could have sworn his nostrils flared.

Gotcha. "Seems you're thinking too hard, *sweetheart.* Thinking, does she or doesn't she?" Despite her brave words and even braver actions, no way was she

going to go Hollywood starlet on him and flash Caden
her coochie.

Her mouth was just below his. Close enough to feel
the warmth of his breath as he exhaled sharply. Close
enough for her to straighten on her tippy toes and narrow the distance to mere inches. She moistened her lips
with her tongue.

A raw, intense heat flashed between them. She felt
him bend down, a fraction of a second before his mouth
covered hers, warm and oh-so-blatantly male. Bold and
demanding, as his tongue moved inside to tangle with
her own, sending every tiny nerve into a flurry of sensation. She thought about pushing away but logic fell
victim to desire. Later, she'd blame it on the liquor.
Now, in this moment and against her better judgment,
she wanted *all* of him.

She grabbed his shoulders and tugged up against
his big, bare chest. He felt so darn good. His mouth
opened further, devouring her, leaving her breathless
and wanting more. No question this wicked man could
kiss. Could probably do a lot of things well. And, didn't
you know it, she wanted to find out just how naughty
he could be.

He pressed her back up against the en suite door,
pinning her in place with his massive chest. He shifted
his hips forward, pushing his big erection up against
her belly, hard and powerful.

Holy dang-diggity.

Someone moaned. Him. Her. It didn't matter; nothing mattered but the swell of desire flowing out of her
in one sensual wave after another.

His big hands moved beneath her skirt and cupped

her bare bottom, his palms warm and assertive as they raised her up and tugged her lower half closer.

"Jesus," she heard him breathe against her ear, before his mouth reclaimed hers. He rubbed his erection over the warm spot between her legs in tempo with his tongue. Once. Twice. She spread her legs further, losing count, and counting on the lovely tension building within. Whoa. Had she ever climaxed during foreplay? His hands, his fingers, weren't even involved, except for being fixed on her bottom to anchor her in place as he moved against her.

All she needed to do was tug her skirt up around her waist. Take the full length of him out of his sweatpants and into her. Climb up his big body, wrap her legs around his back, and enjoy the sweet ride.

She broke free of his mouth. Moved her hands off his shoulders and to the sides of her skirt. Relying on pure, feminine instinct.

Caden stepped back, forcing her to follow. His hands dropped and their bodies separated.

Before Sophie could even miss his warmth, miss the lovely feel of him against her, catch a chill from the polar vortex that had blasted its way between them, she was nudged to the side.

He reached over her head. "Nice locking lips and all," he rumbled, his voice deep and aroused, as he yanked the door open and pushed her through it. "But time's up."

Chapter 5

OMAPLATA: What a fighter says when his plate's empty

One tap on the gas pedal and the convertible's engine hummed like nobody's business. Man, Caden loved this car. With a top speed of 210 mph, the sleek black Aston Martin DBS shot from 0-62 in 4.3 seconds flat. He itched to hit the pedal harder, test its worth out on the nearly deserted highway. The sweetest ride around, when it wasn't stuck behind a piece-of-shit school bus.

More proof that asshat Jerry was cheaper than air.

Fortunately, Caden had caught on to the promoter's tight-wadded ways in enough time to have his manager arrange for this sweet ride. A miracle worker, considering Harold had done it all from their home base in

Nashville. Best business manager around. Not exactly the busiest one, though.

Not since Caden had bid *adios* to his endless schedule of endorsements, appearances, and other trivial bullshit. Next up for Harold was terminating his contract with Ultimate American Male. That'd keep him busy for a spell.

Caden ran the pads of his fingers over the leather steering wheel. Renting the Aston was a splurge, reminding him just how much money he'd be giving up by not re-signing with the underwear line. One reason he hadn't yet parted ways. Hell, he'd learned at a young age what it was like to have your stomach churn in hunger, and though his savings account was nothing to complain about—thanks to Harold's keen investment sense—memories of those dark nights in the alleyways of Nashville were hard to shake off.

Winning Tetnus and the million-dollar purse would lessen the blow to his wallet. Lessen the anxiousness in his gut, the fear of losing it all. His money. Pride. Even his fucking sanity. Again.

Go big or go home. And Vegas was just the place to do it. Once Ultimate American Male executives laid eyes on him after Tetnus was over, they'd probably be more than happy to rip up his contract. He'd traded in a life of sin for getting his face smashed up in Sin City.

"There isn't even a bathroom on it? Gotta be nuts to travel cross-country on an old school bus," Harold's voice came back over the Bluetooth. Given the early morning hour, Caden was sure his call had woken his manager up. Nothing bothered the guy, and he'd stuck by Caden through the worst of it. Caden trusted him as much as he trusted anyone, which wasn't saying much.

"That sums it up," Caden replied, rolling his neck and wondering if he'd warmed down enough after this morning's training. He'd been up before daylight and hit the pavement for a run, sprinting hard and mentally pushing himself even harder. A lame attempt to sweat out the restlessness that had him wired and needing either a good fight or a good fuck. His cock had been hard all night. Not much he could do about it, except whack off. His other option had been to jerk open the en suite door and give that cheeky redheaded tease part two of what'd turned into a very hands-on interview. Thank God he'd settled for his own hand.

Man, he'd enjoyed battling it out with Sophie. The memory of her standing with her hands on her swaying hips, a rosy flush on her cheeks, played out in his head. The way she'd grabbed her skirt and gave him her best Dirty Harry impersonation—hell, she was full of surprises. Rarely did anyone go tit for tat with him, or give him back what he dished out. Especially a woman. His last few flings did exactly what he wanted, and left his bed with smiles on their faces.

Damn if Sophie Morelle didn't spike his interest, and in such an unexpectedly provocative way. Sure, the feel of her tight curves in his palms, even the way her eyes flashed when he'd touched her chest in that silly taunt, had snagged his attention. But even more than her hair-trigger response time, he liked her fearless attitude, how she didn't give a half shit about him being a celebrity who needed to be treated with kid gloves. That smart, sassy mouth on her, the challenge of her, was such a fucking turn-on.

But locking lips with her, getting it on with that reporter—a celebrity in her own right—was a bad idea.

The bottom line was he didn't need any distractions. Good thing Sophie Morelle was just an image in his rearview mirror. Now he could concentrate on what was ahead.

He tapped on the gas to punctuate the thoughts.

"So the promoter stopped you out in the hotel parking lot and threatened you?" Harold asked, his voice sounding higher than normal. Caden rolled his neck again, trying to wake up. Certain he'd missed part of the conversation. "Don't tell me you paid him off again?" Harold continued.

Caden scowled, remembering his early morning confrontation with the greedy man. "Yep. At the rate I'm paying him off, I'll be broke before Tetnus begins. Anyway, I dodged him when I headed out for my run. Avoided the bus entirely when I went back inside to shower. But wouldn't you know it, he was leaning against the trunk of my rental when I came back outside. Demanded I take him for a quick ride while Sal watched over the bus."

Harold laughed, then added, "Did you ask him why the venues he's scheduled for appearances are complete dives? Every single one of them. Cheap and shady. The kind of places amateur fighters might go for an unofficial cash-in-hand bout."

"Told me it was money issues, then bust into a long-winded tale of hardships and woe. Realized it was nothing worthwhile. That's when I hit the gas pedal. Figured at a hundred miles an hour, it'd be hard for him to yip-yap without swallowing a whole lotta bugs."

"Well listen to this. On the schedule you faxed me, he scratched out Wichita Athletics. I can barely read what was swapped in, but I ran a search for what I can make out—Wichita Fight Club? There's no legitimate venue listed under that name."

Caden grunted.

Harold's comments only confirmed Caden's suspicions. Something about Jerry's choice of venues didn't add up. Sure he was tight-fisted. But beyond that, the man was a bona fide media whore. Loved the attention, the spectacle of a larger venue. The more Jerry's ugly mug appeared on the screen, the better payouts his fighters received—or that's how it seemed. So, why the biker bars and obscure VFW halls?

"I'll let you know when I know more." Caden made a mental note to keep his eye on the man, get a take on whatever stupid scheme the promoter had concocted. "Figured I'd make the two appearances I'd agreed to—or one, if Wichita is a no-go—and see what's up." The upcoming venues couldn't be any worse than the holes he'd started fighting in. "On the upside of things, if no one but a couple bikers show up, I'm game with that. I'm not looking for any publicity. Been there, done that." Caden paused, and frowned. "Speaking of unwanted publicity, did you find out what that reporter's up to? She showed up at my door last night looking for an interview."

"Oh my God. Does that woman have balls, or what? Thought the temporary restraining order would have done the trick?"

Caden squinted at the odometer. If the bus moved any slower… "You thought wrong. I wasn't going to pursue it, anyway. What happened was an accident." *Though the devil in high heels was completely at fault.* He contemplated telling Harold about the near drowning in the pool, but it was too early in the freakin' morning to get all worked up about nothing.

"That woman is something. Said so yourself. Hot as hell, and just as bloodthirsty—your exact words."

He thought about the look of bliss on Sophie's face after locking lips with her...*Jesus*. "And mad as hell, when she wakes up and discovers our entourage headed out without her."

"Serves her right."

"Yeah. So? What'd you get on her?"

"Nada. Her former network has distanced themselves from her. Said she was on some kind of sabbatical. Whatever that means. Not sure when, or if, she'll be back on air. I get the feeling they're done with her."

Caden leaned back into his leather bucket seat, wondering just how much backlash she'd received when Ultimate American Male cancelled his ads. Served the little spitfire right. That woman was as confident as she was curvaceous—and God help him, he'd spent enough time thinking about those curves.

"Keep searching. I wanna know exactly what that fireball is angling toward."

Harold inhaled faintly. But it was enough for Caden to pick up on it before the sound blended in with purr of the engine. *Here we go again.* "Um...I know this isn't a good time to rehash this issue, but Ultimate American Male is waiting for your decision."

"Right. Bad timing. Let you know soon. Talk to you later." He pressed the disconnect button on the dashboard, feeling guilty for stringing Harold along.

Miles flew by, giving Caden ample time to contemplate what lay ahead of him.

He loved the hardcore sport of mixed martial arts.

Nothing better than a well-planned and executed fight, where his heart rate accelerated and his mind was in perfect sync with his body. In the Octagon cage, he'd be expecting the punches and kicks. He'd be in control.

Signing another modeling agreement would be the kiss of death to his MMA career. The Boys were getting younger, stronger, and more technically skilled in abstract fighting strategies like Brazilian Jujitsu and Muay Thai. He'd missed his opportunity three years ago. Ended up modeling instead—easier to maintain a wicked stupor and numb his demons when all he had to do was flex some muscle and smile. He dealt with his less-than-stellar childhood the best way he could.

In retrospect, his hardcore lifestyle had been a form of escape.

Escape. Just like when he was a teen, taking to the streets with his brother Bracken, deep into the underbelly of Nashville. Always on the move. Always on the go. Always struggling to get by. They'd had each other. They'd survived.

Bracken seemed to have come to terms with his demons. When he'd been promoted to second grade NVPD detective, Caden had to scratch his head. Such a one-eighty from his hell-raising youth. He was rumored to be damn good cop, too. Their eldest brother, Michael, who'd escaped their father's fists by heading into the Marines, would have been proud of Bracken.

Except Mikey was dead. Killed in an Afghani roadside bombing three years ago. His posthumous Purple Heart had come by mail, and was now tucked safely away in Caden's wallet.

The Kelly men were fighting men. It must run in their DNA.

There'd come a point where all the hard living had come back to bite him. It was now or never to get his head on straight and his body in top form. The thought caused Caden to readjust his long legs, suddenly growing antsy. Man, he was actually looking forward to picking up the pace of his training.

He tugged his iPhone from the overnight bag wedged between the front seats and plugged it into the auxiliary jack, anxious for some music to break the dismal silence. Thumbing through his playlist, he found the perfect Blake Shelton song to blast away the memories. A silly song about a bee, of all things, always cheered him up. Caden cranked it and sang along in harmony.

The sun began to rise, and so did Caden's spirits. He needed a strong cup of coffee. But first, he had to ditch the bus. To hell with Jerry and his temper; he'd meet up with him and the others in Wichita.

Caden maneuvered the Aston into the passing lane and gave it some gas. The car picked up smoothly. The Boys' faces filled the windows, their shit-eating grins full of envy, and Anthony gave him an approving thumbs-up. Caden hit the accelerator hard, ready to blow past the bus, hoping to catch sight of Jerry's furious mug in his rearview mirror and not a moment sooner. The man had to be livid, after passing up such a sweet ride to drive that can of rust on wheels.

He was two-thirds of the way past the bus when suddenly something sailed out of a window. Small like a finch. But bright, fuchsia pink.

It landed on the shiny black hood and slid across the polished chrome all the way up to the windshield. Caden stopped singing and his eyes narrowed. A thong?

"Panty fight!" one of the Boys screamed, rolling the

material in his hand into a tight ball and hurling it toward Caden.

Lingerie in every shade imaginable soared out of the bus. One after another, in a wild array of rainbow silk. Blue briefs whizzed overhead, accompanied by a matching bra made out of fishing twine, or some other transparent material. Caden ducked, avoiding a yellow nightgown. An interesting assortment of naughty nighties, panties, and bustiers followed. Inexplicably, his hand shot up and snagged a bit of black lace.

"Whoo hee. Sophie Morelle's got some sexy underwear," another of the Boys hollered. "Guess now she's really going to be the Commando Queen."

Caden glanced down. Purple, not black. Lace-trimmed, silky and fuck-all transparent. He tossed the negligee into the back of the car, as if it had sparked up and burned him. What the hell? Knowing she slept in a sheer bit of material was an image he *so* did not need after last night. Thinking about her off somewhere, panty-free, made his cock stiffen.

"Damn, that's a hell of a lot of lingerie," he muttered, as the hail of undergarments began to dwindle. "Serves her right."

Caden had a pair of boxers for each day of the week—a simple, no-nonsense plan, despite the fact that Ultimate American Man's signature garments were form-fitted briefs. Sex sells, and Caden had been the biggest attraction they had, which equated to a hell of a lot of brief sales. Which was why they were still hounding him to resign a multimillion-dollar contract.

He was crazy turning down that kind of money.

Jerry gestured violently from the driver's-side window. Caden shot past him, cranked the music up another notch, and with an overhead wave, headed off on the long expanse of highway.

He approached the I-70 on-ramp in record time. Spotting a Cuppa Joe sign at the last exit, he slowed and turned smoothly off the road. Grabbing his overnight bag from the middle console, Caden stretched his long legs as he ambled out. No need to put the top up as the car was fully equipped with an anti-theft system. All he needed to do was secure his bags in the trunk.

Shifting the driver's seat forward, he lifted his suitcase out of the bucket seat. Took two steps toward the trunk, and stopped. Frowned. And turned to take a closer look at the back seat.

The sheer purple nightie was gone.

Caden's attention sharpened on the object. *What the fuck?* Tucked away behind the passenger's seat was a large, bulky blanket that he hadn't noticed before—man alive, it hadn't crossed his mind to check the back seat in the early morning darkness. Besides, Jerry had had his head spinning.

The balled-up material looked suspiciously like the bedspread from the New Millennium Inn.

He stalked around to the passenger's side, pulled the door open, and flipped the seat forward. The bedspread moved.

A stowaway. One he knew, undoubtedly.

In one swift movement, he yanked the bedspread up and off.

She was curled up in a ball on the floor, neatly wedged between the back bucket seat and front passenger seat, clutching the missing nightie like it was her last possession.

"Out," he demanded. *Hell, if she doesn't have balls the size of Vegas.*

Sophie angled her head and gave him a bold smile. "Nice ride."

"I should have followed through on that restraining order," Caden murmured. His body was straight and tense, but his lips twisted wryly. "Damn, you are persistent."

Sophie climbed out of the back of the Aston Martin, feeling the pins and needles in her legs from being crunched up for so long. She saw Caden's gaze shift to the nightgown in her hands and quickly stuffed it inside her pants pocket. She sucked in a breath. "So," she began nervously, yet her voice sounded smooth and unaffected.

"So?" he responded, in a low, sexy tone. Her toes curled upward at the sound. His gaze raked over her in a bold caress, from her head to her curling toes. *Humph.* Was Caden trying to intimidate her? Or make her feel bad about hitching an uninvited ride?

Sophie decided to soften her approach. "James Bond's car, right? An Aston Martin."

His lips lifted for a fraction of a second before he nodded agreeably. *Dang-diggity.* "DB5."

It seemed he wasn't going to make this easy on her.

He tossed his luggage back onto the back seat, reminding Sophie about the fate of her own bags.

She hoped Sal had managed to secure her camera bag and large suitcase in the luggage bin underneath the bus. He'd promised to take care of things earlier this morning when they'd discussed her plans—though plan

A, hiding on the bus, had been shot to pieces once she'd spotted Jerry prowling around.

Shifting toward the car's hood, she scooped up her thong and tucked it safely away in her pocket, to keep company with her nightie.

Out of your cotton-pickin' mind with crazy plan B, she scolded herself for the hundredth time.

Clearly, she'd been too hungover when making this rash, by-the-seat-of-her-pants decision. Without considering the massive consequences, most notably six foot three of lean, muscled welterweight. A man with eight-pack abs, who now stood before her looking bemused, pissed off and indecisive, all at the same time. Eyeballing her like a schoolmarm he'd caught being naughty. It made her want to show him just how naughty she could be.

Jeez. What she needed was a cold blast of water on her face.

She straightened her blouse. What did Caden expect, after all? It wasn't like she had a choice. Staying behind was out. Her three attempts at boarding the bus without Jerry knowing had failed. She'd had a fleeting window of opportunity to climb into the Aston Martin and become invisible—between the time Caden silently dropped Jerry off and headed into the hotel, and seconds later, when he'd returned. She'd hoped to high heaven he wouldn't spot her. For once, luck had been in her favor.

Raising her chin, she looked back at Caden. Her luck had run out. *Or possibly not*, she thought, as he ran a thumb along his jaw, deeply contemplating his options, or so it seemed. She worked her fingers through her hair, as much to loosen the messy knots as to loosen him up further with a classic feminine move. Perhaps he wouldn't be all that opposed to some company.

Sophie pressed on, wanting to make light of the situation. Take advantage of the sudden change in him. "Loved how James Bond and the Queen jumped out of that plane during the Olympics. Talk about a great PR campaign."

"Listen, I'm gonna get a cup of coffee. This isn't the safest of neighborhoods, so this is what I'm going to do. I'll take you as far as the Park-'n'-Ride at the top of the I-70 on-ramp, then you're on your own. Catch a bus back to wherever the hell you came from. Man, I'd love to see the look on Jerry's face when he sees you standing there."

Sophie snorted and ignored his last comment. "That's the safer option? Heck, there are more missing persons reports along interstates—"

"Like hiding in the back of a stranger's car is safe?"

"You're hardly a stranger." Sophie grimaced, thinking how false that statement really was. Drooling over someone's billboard, following their career in the tabloids, and having a minor altercation with a person— well, a few minor altercations, if the pool and the kiss qualified—hardly fell under the category of "Getting To Know You." "I know you can hold a tune, but your choice of music stinks. And that you wear briefs like nobody's business."

A deep V formed on Caden's forehead, and Sophie gave herself a mental kick. Mocking the man's music wasn't earning her any points here. "You are attempting a comeback and are rumored to be the best welterweight out there. What else do I need to know?"

"I don't do interviews anymore. No exceptions."

Ouch. "Well, you know what they say…"

"She who expects nothing, won't be disappointed. No exceptions."

Double ouch. Darn, Caden was quick. "More like it's better to expect the unexpected. So maybe over a cup of coffee, you'll listen to what I have to offer."

He straightened and the tension in his big body seemed to disappear. He pinned her with his gaze. This hunk positively gleamed with sex appeal. Sophie considered adding an addendum to her offer: *Be mine for a night.*

"Jesus," he muttered, and she wondered if he felt the sizzling energy too. Heck, she'd been about to sexually combust before him. "Watch my luggage. I'll get the coffee, and then you're history."

Sophie stood with her hip on the trunk and watched Caden stalk away, telling herself she needed to keep things in perspective. Though the perspective of his tight body so beautifully wrapped in worn jeans was downright distracting.

What could she possibly offer Caden that would entice him enough to let her ride along, and more importantly, give her a genuine, God's honest interview? Naughty visions of the nightgown in her pocket came to mind, her in it and Caden on his knees, a smirk on his lips, willing to do whatever she demanded. Except they were back at the New Millennium Inn, not in a Cuppa Joe parking lot. And, let's face it, Caden wasn't exactly the submissive type.

Furthermore, although TV host and journalist extraordinaire Sophie Morelle was known for her brazen, no-holds-barred style, the real Sophie would never sell herself short by offering her body for a story. Locking lips, as Caden had so eloquently put it, didn't count.

Someone made a loud clucking noise, and Sophie turned. A large man in a Cardinals baseball cap and another stout guy with long, brown hair walked up to her. "This your car?"

They stepped a bit too close for her liking, invading her space. But Sophie held her ground. Years ago, she'd learned that fear was something a predator could smell miles away. Fear was hard to shake once it grasped hold of the senses. And Sophie had to inhale deeply as it welled up inside her. "My boyf—fiancé's car. He's standing inside by the window. Hi, honey!" She waved at the small, dirty store window.

The bulkier guy snorted. A low, disconcerting sound. Hard to tell if he was buying her story or not.

"When he's not beating the pulp out of someone, my fiancé likes cruising around in his car."

"Hear that, Pete? We've got a tough guy on our hands."

Pete cracked his knuckles.

"Pete here packs quite a punch. Would hate to see him finally lose a fight."

Oh, crapola. "He'll just be a second…and has the car keys."

The two men looked at each other, sending an unspoken message that Sophie read clearly. *Trouble.*

She stepped back until her bottom pressed up against the trunk. "You're not mugging me in a Cuppa Joe parking lot. Heck, there are cameras *everywhere*."

The tall mugger pulled his cap lower on his forehead while the stout one looked anxiously around the dirt parking lot—one better suited to a truck stop than any sort of retail space.

"Empty your pockets."

She thought about reaching into her pocket and texting for help, like they did in the movies. Except her Smartphone was buried inside her purse, which was tucked away safely under the passenger seat.

"Look, I don't have any money."

Both men looked from the Aston, to her, to her bulging pant pocket, incredulous. "Sugar, you've got something stashed away. I can see it." Pete offered her his palm.

"No."

"What did she say?"

Sophie straightened, putting her hands on her hips. No way in crapola was she giving up the contents of her pocket. "N.O."

Pete stepped forward, so close she could smell his breath. The man certainly could use some lessons in oral hygiene. He grabbed her arm and held her still while he jammed his hand inside her pocket. The pink thong fell to the ground as he held up the nightie. His expression was one of utter stupefaction, until it changed. Then he looked like he'd won a prize at the local fair. "What have we here?" he exclaimed.

"What *have* we here?" Caden repeated, his voice deep, calm and surprisingly unaffected as he strode up to them. He bent, scooped up her thong and tucked it into his pocket nonchalantly, like he was gathering rocks for his collection. Sophie frowned, then noticed how he wasn't carrying any coffee.

"Quite the little fiancée you've got, buddy. Hot and

ready for some action, huh," Pete mocked, his mouth twisting into an ugly grin. "Sure you can handle her?"

The man was still way too close, close enough for her to give him a quick knee to the crotch. She contemplated whether to escalate the situation or let Caden handle matters. Judging by Caden's laid-back manner, as if the redneck had asked him if he liked cold beer or big-busted women, she'd better act. Sophie flexed her leg, warming it up for action.

"Uh, Pete. We gotta head out. Nice meeting you, Mrs. Kelly." The tall man began to walk away. Pete, however, wasn't biting.

"Nah, man. I'm taking a ride."

Pete wasn't looking at the car. Sophie felt an icy chill shoot up her spine, even though the only ride she planned on giving the man was a long trip in an ambulance. How hard did a woman have to knee someone in the groin to warrant major surgery?

"Come on, Pete. That's Caden freakin' Kelly." The mugger with a newfound conscience—or was it perspective?—turned toward Caden. "Honestly, he didn't mean any harm to your fiancée."

Stepping several feet back from Sophie, Pete's full attention swung toward Caden. He stood impassive, with his arms folded across his body like he was waiting on the tide, like the jerk had offered her flowers instead of trouble. His focus wasn't even on Pete. Instead his attention fixed on her, as if he was assessing her worthiness as his better half, or something.

Sophie contemplated giving Caden a swift kick to wake him up. Was he just going to stand there, without doing or saying anything?

He shook his head. *God, was he enjoying this?*

"Don't do it," he warned. Something more than amusement was in his tone, but before Sophie could put her finger on it, Pete made a serious attitude adjustment, changing from aggressive ass to obsessive ass.

"Hey, man. I'm a huge fan. Didn't mean to cause any trouble here. I'll just be going…" He turned quickly on his mud-crusted boots. Sophie moved even quicker, and snatched her expensive nightgown out of his filthy grasp before he trotted off. This garment was not going to join the trail of undies senselessly thrown onto the highway.

Caden's eyebrows lifted, bemused. "Jesus, one surprise after another with you. Pure trouble," he remarked, before finally deciding to form a complete sentence. "Good thing I caught your wave, sweetheart," he murmured sarcastically.

Without waiting for her to respond, he retrieved his luggage from the back seat and popped the trunk. His biceps flexed as he hefted his suitcase and carried it to the back of the car.

Muscles that big and on a body that tight should come with a warning sign. *Holy stud alert.* "Didn't even get my coffee," he grumbled, unaware of her perusal.

Her mouth went dry.

"Hmph, cat caught your tongue for a change?" He stopped and peered at her more closely. The sun seemed hotter, like it was midday instead of 7:00 a.m. "You might be a nuisance, but nothing was going to happen to you."

"Damn straight." Gosh, he had her cursing now. It was well worth it though, when a generous, panty-wetting smile crossed his face.

"That's what I like about you, Morelle. You've got gumption." Caden turned away.

Sophie couldn't stop herself from basking in the warmth of his compliment, a feeling akin to her certain reaction if he'd signed on for an exclusive interview. Softening her in a way only a woman can be softened when garnered with hot male attention. And in the afterglow, she soaked up every little bit about him. The way he filled a T-shirt like nobody's business. The tightness of his buns in those faded jeans. There was so much more to Caden than a pretty face, but boy-oh-boy did his body just do it for her. Like that drool-worthy biceps…

Caden froze, suitcase hoisted midair. His whole attitude changed from laid-back beach bum to scowling fighter. Exactly the reaction she'd been expecting a moment earlier—which was why the change in him caused her breath to catch.

"What the fuck is this doing—?"

Sophie's eyebrows shot up. She tried to peer around him to see what was in the trunk, figure out what caused the sudden shift in him, but his big body blocked her view.

Stepping back, he slammed the trunk shut with his elbow. The sound of metal on metal echoed off the broken asphalt. Shooting her a deadly look, as if daring her to comment, he pitched his suitcase into the back seat. Without further explanation for his mood swing, he climbed into the car.

The Aston Martin roared to life.

Sophie stood there, stunned and immobile, trying to reconcile what just transpired. It felt like someone had jerked a rug out from under her while she'd been dancing. And singing. And just realizing the possibilities of the hunk before her.

Her gaze fell on the closed trunk and her investigative instincts kicked in. What exactly had he seen inside that had caused such a harsh reaction?

"You've got two seconds until goodbye," she heard him growl, his voice hard as steel.

Sophie squared her shoulders and walked calmly over to the passenger door.

Goodbye was not going to happen, not by a long shot.

Just like James Bond always got his woman, Sophie Morelle was going to get her man, and his story. And, she was beginning to think, maybe even something else.

Chapter 6

SLICK SUBMISSION: When a fighter gives up and uses hair gel

Sophie kept her lips pressed tight and held back a smile as her visual on the Park-'n'-Ride disappeared from the rearview mirror. She pretended to stretch her neck, angling her head for a better view of the man next to her so she could scan his features from beneath her lashes. Trying to decide if whatever preoccupied Caden's thoughts had made him forgetful or, better still, want her along for the ride.

Hard to say, with his nondescript poker face and the mirrored sunglasses hiding his expression. No telltale signs for the reasons behind his sudden change of heart. His laid-back, laissez-faire attitude had changed as well, replaced by a palpable tension in the air between them. What was in the trunk that had him so riled up? Her curiosity had been piqued but with him scowling and taking the on-ramp at this asinine speed, she thought better of questioning him about it. She'd bide her time and wait for him to initiate the conversation. Instead, she'd relax and enjoy the ride. She glanced at the odometer and grimaced. Eighty-eight miles per hour.

Sophie slipped off her heels and reclined into the safety of the comfortable leather bucket seat. Forced herself to relax by studying the massive expanse of Missouri sky. Like one endless blue blanket with an occasional worn white patch—it never ceased to amaze her. Nothing like the gray Pittsburgh skyline, littered with mountains and row after row of skyscrapers. Out here, the world was never-ending.

Such a long time had passed since she'd watched the scenery drift by. Deadlines had to be met, celebrities lined up for interviews, ratings maintained. Who had time for a mental nature walk?

The Aston Martin flew by mile after mile of farmland, interrupted by the occasional small town. Quiet. Uneventful. Almost peaceful, the silence broken only by the rushing wind and the sound of Caden's fingers tapping the leather steering wheel. They skirted around Kansas City, Missouri, and crossed into Kansas.

"Fuck."

Sophie jumped in her seat, surprised. Glancing toward Caden, she waited for him to continue. But it seemed that one word was it. *Great.*

The scenery had changed and become more commercial, with multiple gas stations and self-storage units. The latter made her smile, finding humor in the thought that even with such an abundance of space, people didn't have enough storage room. Sophie thought about the damage she could do renting one of them, for shoes alone. Her mood lightened, and lightened further when she spotted the large billboard up ahead. This time, traffic wasn't backed up for miles.

Instinctively, her eyes rose.

Take a gander at this, Dorothy.

Her heartbeat thumped into overdrive, having forgotten just how large… She snapped her attention back onto a faded, orange Rent-a-Unit sign and prayed to God Caden hadn't noticed her gawking at his billboard.

Caden grunted, and Sophie fell back into her seat as he gunned the gas pedal.

"Your luggage is at the hotel?"

"What?" His abrupt question caught her off-guard. *Luggage? Really?*

"Your stuff, is it at the hotel?"

She frowned. "Why would I leave my suitcases behind? Sal took them both and secured them under the bus…I hope," she muttered the last part, worried the Boys had decided to scatter her clothing across the Midwest. Having one pair of underwear—two if you counted the pair Caden had stuffed inside his pocket—plus one skimpy nightie was a problem. But having no clothing whatsoever would really suck eggs.

Who knew how long she'd have before the network spotted the charges on her corporate card? She'd had her excuse already formulated in case they challenged her, that a month left on that no-compete clause meant an additional month of credit, right? So far she'd been able to charge food and the hotel room fees without issue. But a quick shopping spree would draw too much attention to the fact she still had an active card, one they'd be cancelling quicker than you could say "dang-diggity." Then what would she do? Besides, Sophie'd rather die or do something really unpleasant than have people see her in a cheesy tourist T-shirt and Chucks, should she decide on a shopping spree at some cheap Midwestern truck stop.

"And that's everything?" His tone of his voice was anything but playful, which was fine with Sophie because the reminder of her undergarment status really set her off. Patting her pocket, she stated, irritably, "You know darn well what happened to my lingerie suitcase. In fact, you have something of mine. Hand it over."

The tightness around his beautiful jawline disappeared. *Dang.* If mentioning her thong was all it took to snuff out the tension in him, she'd have brought it up a lot sooner. Her cheeks warmed. Uncharacteristically so—Sophie Morelle had had more conversations about underwear than she could count. But the man next to her had gotten under her skin in a way she hadn't expected.

"What do you want from me?" he demanded mildly, turning her way. He'd shifted his sunglasses up onto his head and he pinned her with his gaze.

What do I want from him? Her libido pulled an Aston Martin, hustling forward from zero to 120 mph in one second flat.

"Uh…an interview." Her voice sounded hoarse. A sure sign of the blatant lie she was feeding him. Oh, she wanted the interview. And her thong back. But at that moment, her entire body warmed from wanting *him*, from the tips of her toes, between her legs, up her chest, and into her cheeks. So hot for him she contemplated adding the word *naked* to her interview request.

Great, just great. A naked interview? The thought only made her warmer.

"Man alive." He shook his head. "Okay."

"Okay to what?" she blurted out, disturbed her thoughts had been that transparent.

"I'll give it to you…an exclusive. Shoot."

Dang-diggity. Sex was Caden's weapon, one he wielded subtly yet expertly. For the second time within twenty-four hours, she caught herself being lured in by his sexcapades. Jeez, he must think her gullible.

"Bull crap."

He laughed. "Bull crap? That's hardly a word. Bullshit, now that's better."

"Don't change the subject. Do I have the word *sucker* tattooed on my forehead?"

"Sucker, huh?" He cocked his head and shot her a naughty smile.

Holy crapola. Why did it have to be him—the playboy panty peddler with a grin that'd melt the iciest of hearts—she was counting on to be her featured fighter?

"I swear to God, if you are playing me the way you did last night…" Her voice trailed off as she bent forward, grabbed her purse, and retrieved her notepad, still doubtful he meant what he'd said and that her exclusive would soon be underway. Still, the familiar motions jarred her back into reporter mode. She wondered at his abrupt shift back into the easygoing player she'd expected. Something had been bothering him. But whatever it had been was gone.

He didn't answer her. Instead, he reached into his pocket, pulled out a pack of gum, and offered her a piece. When she declined, he popped the stick into his mouth.

A giddiness washed over her, making her breathless. For whatever reason, Caden was giving her an interview. Scoring an exclusive with the very man who'd ruined her career, by making amends with their past, by showing the world that all had been forgiven, she'd find redemption in the public eye. Sure, reporters would put a scandalous spin on it. In her experience, negative press drew as much attention, if not more, than a positive, upbeat review. Fans—not to mention her former employers—were going to get a gander at the new Sophie Morelle, the investigative journalist who'd outmaneuvered every major network by getting the inside scoop on Caden Kelly.

Better begin before Caden changed his mind. She started out strong. "What made you want to come back to the mixed martial arts world when you were in the middle of such a huge…um…amazing modeling career?"

"Next question."

"What's wrong with the first one?"

"Tell you what. I'll give you the lowdown on what this is gonna be about," he replied, his voice going deep and gravelly, like he'd just woken up.

Whose interview was this? She'd best establish exactly who was the interviewer and who was the interviewee. "My documentary is going to provide a series of insightful glimpses into the day-to-day life of an MMA fighter. You're rumored to be ruthless in the cage, right? A top contender for the title. Out to prove you're the toughest fighter in the country. I plan on shooting an in-depth look at the makings of an ultimate fighter, with you as the featured star. Show viewers why someone would put a lucrative career in jeopardy by getting his face bashed in. Why MMA? What makes a guy like you, with a huge modeling contract, risk his handsome assets for a chance to fight in Tetnus? You'll be the main feature, the comeback kid. That's the angle I'm going for."

"What about drugs?"

Talk about coming out of left field. What was he saying that she thought the Boys were a bunch of coked-up warriors? Doubtful. No one would be that fit without having some self-discipline, and sitting around dropping acid didn't exactly fit the bill.

Caden shot her an assessing look, reminiscent of his earlier dark mood before the tight line of his lips relaxed. "Forget it. Let's talk about sex. How much I like it. Often. What a woman's face looks like after working my tongue over her sweetness."

Curse the man! Sophie wiggled uncomfortably in her seat.

"Honey, I assume you've read the tabloids. True, most of it."

She flipped through the blank pages of her notebook, the lines swimming before her as she tried to quiet the furious pounding of her heart. "Hmph, three women in one bed. They don't make mattresses that big," she challenged, grabbing her pen a bit too tightly.

"Bent over the bed, not *in* it."

"Sounds like a lot of work," she shot back, but not before he grinned at the reddening of her cheeks.

"The most pleasurable kind."

"Care to elaborate?" Sophie drew spiraling lines on her notepad. Even they seemed indecent, forming the bit of male anatomy she was so desperately trying forget about. She could feel his stare, assessing her response.

She knew his intention was to get a rise out of her by the way he'd said *pleasurable*, the word rolling off his tongue as if he was about to pull the Aston Martin over and demonstrate the definition.

"I like to get down and dirty. Kinky too."

Sophie snorted, trying to sound unaffected. "The American public is well versed in your kinky liaisons— that Victoria's Secret model was quite candid in her interview. Leather restraints and tethers."

"Caroline loved to play the submissive to my—"

"No, the other model, the one with the breast implants gone wild."

"So you *have* been following my career."

"Listen, sweetheart, you're a hard man to miss. Between the crotch shots on billboards in every major city and the tabloid headlines, it's safe to say everyone from New York to San Francisco knows the intimate details of your sexual escapades." Perfect. She was starting to sound like her good ole self.

"Not everything, *sweetheart*. Maybe it's time for a slight detour." He stepped off the accelerator and shifted into the slowpoke lane.

Sophie tried to not let him frazzle her. "I've got your number, you know."

"Yeah, what number is that?"

"You're deflecting."

Caden struggled to keep his smug grin. The instincts that had carried her so far in her career seemed to have struck a home run.

"Care to elaborate, Sophie? You wanna fill me in on something I don't know?"

What could she possibly tell this walking sex bomb about sex that he didn't already know? It was like comparing a Hollywood starlet's love life to that of a Girl Scout troop mother.

"Wild stuff, kinky acts, quickies, these aren't the most satisfying kinds of sex." She gave a mental chuckle. The very voice of inexperience was speaking to Mr. Sexpert about the downsides of wild sex.

What Caden didn't know was that the real Sophie Morelle had spent the better part of her adult years shying away from anything but predictable, comfortable sex—without complicated issues like intimacy.

"Putting ideas in my head, darling?" He gestured toward the dashboard clock. "We've got time, you know."

"Deflecto-mundo. What are you hiding from?"

Caden glanced at himself in the rearview mirror, then turned his focus back to the roadway.

"I'm sitting right here next to you, aren't I?"

He took the exit ramp slowly. Purposefully. Trying to throw her game. A Best Western sign caught her attention.

To her relief and utter disappointment, Caden pulled into a gas station. He didn't wait for her to comment. "Fill 'er up," he told her, tossing a few twenties onto her lap and striding off into the station convenience store.

Curse the man. His shock-jock approach had gotten him out of her interviewing him once again, and there'd been nothing she could have done about it, aside from stripping down naked and calling him out on his calculated innuendos. She watched him disappear into the building, so sure and confident. Yet, her instincts told her she was correct—something was up with him. All this talk about sex had been a smokescreen.

All Sophie needed to do was get to the bottom of it and uncover the real Caden Kelly.

* * *

Caden almost left her behind at the rest stop. Sophie was too smart for her own good. Pure trouble, and just the nosy, inquisitive, and damn-too-perceptive person he didn't want as travel companion.

Not with a duffel full of drugs and syringes stashed in his trunk.

He looked over at her, his thoughts well concealed beneath his Oakleys. She didn't look like a steroid-toting queen or that she knew the stash even existed. Sure, her stowing away in his car the same time the drugs appeared was suspicious.

She uncrossed and recrossed her bare ankles, having slipped off those killer heels, as she studied the passing scenery. Sexy ankles, the flash of skin drawing his interest. Not his usual mode of operation, granted, but from the way she'd turned in the seat, he couldn't check out her chest. Not that he'd find the swell of her tits inside that conservative blouse.

He'd have thought the ballsy late-night host would be flashier. Using her sexy body along with her smart-ass tongue. Still, the blouse was...*nice.* Feminine. Neat and tidy. Suited her softer side—like now, when she was quiet, sleepy, and so contrary to the woman he'd thought he knew, and spent so much time loathing. It was prim, not the kind of blouse someone taking illegal risks would wear, or so he thought.

Last night, the car had been clean. Caden had checked it out, including the trunk, excited to see what his new sweet ride had to offer. Someone had to have stuffed the duffel bag—which was bursting at the zipper with hundreds of prepackaged baggies of green and white pills, not to mention a fair number of stray syringes—inside the car earlier this morning. Performance-enhancing drugs, one of several designer steroids becoming more and more popular. The colorful coating was a dead giveaway. And the needles—supplies for blood injections—spoke volumes. Whoever was dealing was doing so hardcore, and on a larger scale.

In his modeling days, steroids had been just another item on the endless smorgasbord of drugs available. Caden had seen…done…all kinds of shit over the past few years. Cocaine and hard liquor being his go-to poisons. He'd done his share, all right, before leaving it all behind. Fortunately, the high from recreational drugs wasn't something he'd needed over the long term. Booze, though, had been harder to quit. Cleaning up his body. Life. Freakin' career choices.

Never steroids.

So what the fuck was a gym bag filled to capacity with the stuff doing in his trunk?

Better to keep the nosy, inquisitive reporter close. Find out if she'd seen anything—after all, she'd have had her eye on his car the entire morning while waiting for her chance to hide inside it.

Fucking great. One more distraction he didn't need. One that could land him in jail, or just as bad, cause a tabloid feeding frenzy. If Sophie Morelle spotted the pills, if she didn't have enough common sense to know they weren't Caden's, he could kiss his comeback goodbye.

Despite the risk, he was going to hang on to the stash and keep the duffel hidden in the trunk. Until Nevada, where he'd turn it over to his brother Bracken, without any unnecessary fanfare. Let him investigate the source and figure out exactly which fighter was doping and, worse, dealing.

Once more, he studied his companion, now fast asleep, sprawled out in her bucket seat, her long legs stretched out and her head rolled to one side so her cheek pressed against the leather. Her auburn hair was neatly combed into a ponytail, with one long stray strand blowing in the wind. The rich color contrasted nicely against her pale skin. No apparent freckles or birthmarks on this redhead. Long, dark eyelashes, high cheekbones, and full, pink lips, the lower one slightly plumper. Attractive in a natural way. Wholesome.

Far from his usual type of woman.

Caden shook his head and looked away. It was all an illusion—after all, this was the queen of smack, Sophie Morelle, sitting here. The antithesis of wholesomeness.

The sexy reporter must have been up damned early to have stashed herself in the Aston. Or maybe she hadn't slept at all. He couldn't blame her for conking out. The flat farm country, stretching on for miles, was starting to look the same in every direction.

Caden didn't mind the open roadway. And, truth was, he was growing more accustomed to the idea of company.

All that talk about sex had affected him more than he wanted to admit. Hell, he wondered if she knew how close he'd been to following through on his subtle promise. Gotten a room at the Best Western and turned the glimmer of arousal in her eyes to one heavy with lust.

That'd be a fine sight to see.

Fuck. He should have left her behind at the gas station.

A Rascal Flatts song came on the radio and he turned

the volume up slightly. Driving music. Singing music. Lovemaking music.

It was gonna be a long ride to Wichita.

Caden contemplated texting his brother to get his take on this shitty situation. But Bracken would tell him to ditch the drugs. Shield himself from the consequences. Keep his nose clean, and out of someone else's illegal business.

But the fact that another fighter headed for the championship bout had been doping pissed Caden off. MMA was considered a clean sport. Untarnished by reports of steroids and performance-enhancing drugs. Unlike other sports, like cycling and baseball. Dopers cheapened the efforts of someone who'd legitimately trained, who'd put in the physical hours and mental discipline.

MMA fighters were well-known for steering clear of chemicals, for following a natural diet of lean protein, carbs, and greens to round out their extensive physical training. Prided themselves on their mental preparation too—Zen shit, and all. Polluting their bodies wasn't part of their sports culture. Caden wasn't about to let some asshole tarnish the sport he loved or sabotage his comeback.

He considered asking Harold how to deal with this, but he thought better of it. His manager wasn't in a position to help. Hell, the only person he could trust this fucked-up problem with was Bracken.

Tetnus was more than a championship fight. It was a chance to prove to his brother—fuck, who was he kidding, to prove to *himself*—that Caden Kelly was no joke. His shit was together. Those restless years were behind him. He was capable of committing to something worthwhile, and finishing it. He was in control.

Focused. In the present. Not so deep inside his head that his thoughts were defeating him quicker than any opponent.

Fighting was his choice. Within his power. Not something he'd been forced to do.

Not like when he was a kid.

"Let me get this straight," Caden summarized, his tone sarcastic and light. "You're saying Sal was inside the hotel lobby, waiting for the prick patrolling the bus to turn the other way so he could stick your luggage underneath the bus. That that prick Jerry was like a fly in a fly trap, stuck to the bus and nothing but the bus. Unbeknownst to Jerry, you, being a shrewd operator, slipped by him and stowed away in my car. And that no one else was in the parking lot?" He placed his well-defined forearms on the red tablecloth and cocked his head.

"Um…don't you think one of the Boys would have sounded off a Sophie-alert? It's not like they've come around to my way of thinking. Yet."

"Heaven help them."

Roughly half an hour ago, he'd pulled off the highway into a run-of-the-mill diner for lunch. She'd conked out during the ride, which of course only added to the awkwardness between them now. Her darn narcoleptic tendencies were a nuisance. Back in the early days— before selling out—she'd spent a good portion of her time on the road. A good reporter needed to keep alert. Who knew when a story might be around the next bend? Airplanes, cars, the Pittsburgh T—she'd nodded off in the worst of places. It was downright embarrassing.

Like today, when she'd woken, found the car idling

in front of a diner, and Caden's face parked inches from her own. So close, she could smell the cinnamon gum on his breath. Close enough to kiss, if her foggy mind had connected the dots a bit quicker. Falling asleep wasn't exactly a savvy reporting strategy but perhaps his willingness to talk would make up for the missed opportunity.

His silence before she'd fallen asleep had been like a third travel companion, and the subtle undercurrent of tension emanating from his beautiful body, a fourth. Given the size of the Aston, something had to give. What was up with him, anyway?

Gone was the light banter and sex talk. His shift in manner dumbfounded her as much as the complexity of him unnerved her. Who would have expected it of an underwear model and a man who fought for a living?

Caden leaned in, closing the distance between them, and she sensed that he was waiting for her to do the talking.

With a flat-out faked calmness, she sipped her coffee. "I didn't call Jerry a prick, or myself a shrewd… an opportunist, but yes, in effect, that's what I said."

He nodded and jabbed his fork into the last slice of steak on his plate, looking away as he did so.

Sophie relaxed and shifted the few remaining leaves of lettuce in her Cobb salad around with her fork.

"Did you see anyone else but Jerry near the Aston before you pulled your stowaway act?"

"A smooth act, you have to admit. I might have made it to Wichita if not for the parade of panties. To answer your question, no. I waited for Jerry to disappear around the back of the bus and then climbed inside the Aston.

Why the inquisition? Did someone put a ding in the bumper or something?"

He shot her a bemused smile, and relaxed back into his seat. "Sweetheart, it's not the car that's got me thinking." Caden pinned her with his gaze, making sure she was watching him as he licked a drop of salad dressing oil from his bottom lip. Purposefully. Knowingly. And dang it, if Sophie didn't just about slide off the bench.

His come-on—lame as it was—was still a turn-on. Caden was smooth, she'd give him that. Tossing her napkin at him in an attempt to recover, she opened her mouth to comment, but was cut off by the return of their waitress.

Or rather Caden's waitress, Miss Attentive.

"How was your steak and salad?" Her words were slow and deliberate, like she was asking him how he'd liked a rub-down with a happy ending.

"Never tasted better. Thanks." Amusement roughened his voice but his answer wasn't directed at Miss Attentive.

Sophie's heel shot forward, a natural reflex, and connected with his leg.

Caden gave her a lopsided grin.

Sexy devil.

She scowled, hoping Miss Attentive would catch her drift, but the waitress was fixated on Caden. Heck, who could blame her?

The desire for some major heel thumping rose up inside Sophie. Her reaction surprised and angered her, to the point that she contemplated smacking her own head with her heel. Knock those ugly images of Miss Attentive bent over a bed and asking Caden how he liked his steak and salad clear out of her brain.

"Can I get you dessert?"

Enough already. "He ate enough salad to feed the state's entire rabbit population. I'll take the check."

The waitress flounced off with a huff.

"How'd you know I'm saving dessert for later?"

"Do I have *amateur* written on my forehead? You're deflecting again, Caden. You promised me an exclusive. All these questions, your lame attempts to rile me up with enticing words…gestures…"

Caden leaned forward again, his forearms on the table. She wondered what was playing out in his mind, for his eyes changed with his mood, deep emerald one moment and an almost transparent green in another.

Big-O-factor material, those eyes.

A rush of adrenaline made her heart quicken. He winked. A confident gesture, full of intent. Pure trouble. "Who would have thought a bit of verbal foreplay would make you, of all people, blush. Such a pretty red, too. Matches the color of your hair." His grin broadened. "Maybe it's too hot in here. Maybe it's time to go."

The devil was full of innuendos. Sophie didn't know how to respond, so instead she pushed her plastic glass of water toward him. "Here. It's on me. Cool yourself off." It didn't matter that the waitress had refilled his glass of water at least six times already.

Whereas before she'd been perched ramrod straight on her bench—her late-morning siesta in the car had wrinkled her blouse and she was trying to give them time to fall out—offering him her water brought Sophie closer to him, within arm's reach. And dang it all if Caden didn't take advantage.

Reaching out, he clasped a lock of her hair between his fingers, winding it around his pointer and rubbing it with his thumb. "A natural, earthy redhead. Like chili powder. Suits you." He stopped rubbing and leaned in closer, like he wanted to whisper naughty words to her.

She'd interviewed a lot of hot guys, but none of them brought out the crazy in her like Caden did. Spoke to her baser instincts. Had her consider the possibilities of him, her, and them performing a horizontal tango. Yep, Caden was charming, charismatic, with a sexual energy about him that made promise of a good time. Promise of an almighty O-factor.

Correction. Multiple-O-factors.

No wonder he drove her crazy. Promises. Promises.

"You're prettier in person than on television, chili cakes," he remarked. His head cocked to the side as he studied her, a hint of his infamously naughty grin on his lips. Her cheeks flushed warmer, heart raced quicker, and her imagination ignited with the possibility that maybe, just maybe, Caden saw right past her carefully constructed persona, and *liked* what he found hidden there.

She angled in, his tender touch as surprising as his gentle words. Yet it was her response, the wonder at what it'd feel like to let go, let him inside, bask in an intimacy that had always been on the horizon but never within her grasp—heck, she never wanted it to be attainable, until now—that was the greatest surprise of all.

A second later, his fingers released her hair and he leaned back, breaking contact. Breaking the connection that had been sizzling between them. A fork replaced her lock of hair in his hand and as he shifted restlessly in his seat, his attention wandered about the diner, everywhere but on her.

She ignored the sudden feeling of loss sweeping over her. A familiar feeling that wrenched at her soul and robbed her of air. She was a teenager all over again, discovering her reputation had been twisted and crushed through no fault of her own and she was left to pick up the pieces of her shattered life. Uncomfortable feelings she'd fought to silence. Forget.

A kick in the stomach would have been less of a wakeup call. So Sophie did what she always did. She focused on her objective.

Three years ago, the fighter across from her was the guy to beat. He'd had it all, and was on the verge of winning Warrior's Wager, the first-ever MMA title. Had battled some fierce opponents to get there. The news channels buzzed with excitement over the handsome warrior's rise to glory. Even Sophie, who didn't know a thing about MMA at the time, knew about Caden. She'd gone as far as placing him on her guest list.

Then he'd up and quit.

Some speculated he'd been afraid. Others suspected he knew he wasn't tough enough, not with that pretty face. His reappearance in the spotlight as a model validated their suspicions. But only one person knew the truth and he was sitting right across from her. Fiddling with his fork and with tight lips and narrow eyes, granted. But right there.

And she was going to get him to talk. Better hit him while he was being all warm and cozy. "You traded in your gym shorts for designer underwear and a million-dollar endorsement. Why throw it all away by returning to fighting?" she asked, hoping her change in tactic would illicit some nugget of useful information.

He twirled the fork in his fingers.

Sophie had the impression the question had pissed him off. It was hard to tell by the blank expression on his face, but his playfulness disappeared. *Too late now.* She stiffened on her cushion, anticipating his response.

A few more twirls, then he tossed the fork on the table. It clanged loudly on the Formica. "Sex."

The word was said casually, like he'd said the word *pencil* or *paper.* Emotionless. Monotone. And Sophie realized he could have said any word, in any manner, and her woman's place would moisten in response. Dang. She'd never get her story if her hormones over-ruled her instincts.

"Come on, Caden. You're not exactly hard on the eyes, so don't tell me you did it to lay babes. Heck, Miss Attentive over there was serving up more than steak and salad."

Double darn.

"Miss Attentive, huh?" He glanced at the waitress's station. A second later, his gaze was back on Sophie, raking over her like she was his next ice-cream sundae and he knew exactly where to place his cherry.

He blinked and shook his head. "I seem to keep forgetting exactly who is keeping me company," he muttered, almost to himself but loud enough that she caught the bite in his words. Abruptly, his entire demeanor hardened.

The sweet fantasy of the sundae clung stubbornly in her head. She realized, too late, it had soured beyond saving.

"Kind of thought that sex was the whole premise of your show, sweetheart. Celebrity confessions, and all

that bullshit. It's what you're all about. And you want
me to trust you? Confide my secrets and hope you don't
twist me into being something I'm not? For fuck's sake,
I'm out to prove something here—and it's not how fast
or how quick I can get you off, honey."

Darn it. Sophie bit her lip. Sure, she'd used sex to
boost ratings. All journalists did it on some level, *except* maybe Christiane Amanpour. It didn't mean she
liked doing it. Truth be told, it rubbed her nerves raw
every single time some celebrity got out of control. Like
she'd led them down a slippery slope leading into the
darkness, where all their skeletons lurked.

She thought she'd come to terms with herself, and
what she'd done for fame. But something about the
way Caden was looking at her—like she was a bottom dweller of the worst kind, searching for her next
victim to exploit and over-sensationalize—felt like a
dagger piercing her skin. She saw herself through his
eyes, a foul-mouthed, former talk-show star who he'd
toyed with and tolerated, and was now tempted to bid
farewell to.

It…hurt.

Her cheeks felt moist. She blinked then stiffened.
Egad, tears? With the realization came her instinctual
response of drawing upon that iron core of pride she'd
built brick by bloody brick, pride that she'd developed
as a teenager, when life couldn't get any darker. She'd
survived, and had seen to it that awful man had been
locked up for good.

*Don't forget the slap in the face the good citizens of
Hawley gave you when they chose to support that child
predator. Chose greed over respect for an innocent kid.*

Since then, her skin was thicker. More prepared for the curveballs hurled her way. And, in the years that followed as her career took off, there'd been more than at a World Series. Seemed the world was bent on pulling another Hawley, in one form or another.

Like the hunk sitting across from her in the booth.

Sophie Morelle did not cry. Not for anyone. Not anymore.

Respect. How was one little word so massively hard to attain?

This was unfathomable. He was another good-looking jock who'd had the world handed to him on a silver platter. Who'd given up an MMA title for a money-shot of his crotch plastered on billboards across the country. Just another man who thought that because of his position of wealth and power, he could get away with anything.

"I've got the check," she said, her voice sounding raw and several octaves deeper. Pressing her lips tightly together, she did her best to mask her emotions as she slid her card into the cheap plastic bill folder, stood, and without looking at him, hurried off toward the rest room.

She blinked back her tears, forcing them away. *Sophie Morelle does not cry. Ever.* She should go back out there and thank Caden for giving her a much-needed reality check. She didn't need anyone digging up memories best left dead and buried.

Keeping people at arm's length was a skill she'd mastered long ago. She should have known better than to relax her guard, and let Caden's pretty face—and her own dang lust—lull her into a false sense of security.

Better get her exclusive, edit her documentary, and get on with her life.

When she returned to the table, every hair was smoothed back into place.

She reached for the bill folder to sign her receipt.

"Your card has been *declined*," Miss Attentive said snidely from behind her.

Declined. Stuck in the middle of Kansas with a panty-peddling jock and zip, nada, nil to her name. She bit down on her lip, hard, noticing how her hands shook while she grasped the table like it held her last meal. In a way, it did.

Someone—her?—made a pained noise.

Caden stood and pried the plastic folder from her death grip. "Got it," he said, his tone nonchalant, as if he didn't notice the absolute mortifying flush on her cheeks. "Look, I'm—"

She held out her hand. Shook her head and stopped him. It was too much. The loss of the card was horrible enough. But he'd hit a nerve. He'd seen past her walls all right, caught a glimpse of the real woman behind the polished exterior. What a shocker for him, too, having expected Ms. Cool-and-Confident and finding Ms. Far-Too-Damaged lurking there instead. Fragile, insecure, and with a soul beyond repair.

It was too much to bear. From now on, she'd be better prepared.

Her voice was steady as steel and just as cold. "You promised me an exclusive and I'm holding you to it. Say goodbye to Miss Attentive. I'll meet you in the car."

Tossing her hair as if she hadn't a care in the world, Sophie headed out ahead of him.

"Don't hold your breath," she heard him murmur. It was the final bit of icing on the cake she needed to put things back into perspective. Going forward, Sophie meant business.

Chapter 7

PERUVIAN NECKTIED: When a hot fighter shows up in nothing but the fancy silk tie he picked up in South America

Caden slowed the Aston, the GPS instructions telling them they'd arrived at their destination. He scowled, taking in first the worn neon welcome sign a few feet off the road, cocked at an odd angle and missing an *e*, then the motel behind it. The place sure gave the bus a run for its money in the "shitty abode" category, looking like a cross between a shady beachfront motel and a 1990s strip mall. Its brown awning and matching aluminum siding were chipped and dirty. The rooms were going to be a nightmare.

"Sleepy Time Motel? Oh, no. This is not where we're

staying tonight. Is it?" The horror in her tone matched his own dark thoughts. And God knew he'd lived in a few hellholes, some that actually made this motel look like a palace.

Yet the accommodations worked to his advantage. No way was he planning on keeping her around. She'd served her purpose—he'd realized she knew jack shit about the drugs or who might have stashed them in the trunk. And he needed to keep it that way.

Damn, if she wasn't looking at him right now, expectantly. Or was it hopefully?

He shrugged, the gesture relaxing the tension coiled inside. "Hate to tell you, chili bean, but the sign likely sums up the place. Sle-*e*-ping isn't gonna be part of your overnight experience."

His words caused her cheeks to flush a pretty shade of pink.

Man, he liked how easy it was to rile her up. A welcome distraction, one long overdue.

Since the diner, their ride through Kansas had been all business, with Sophie prodding him about his life and with him tactfully questioning her about the duffel bag. Neither had gotten anywhere, except frustrated. And man-oh-man, add in the raging hard-on...damn, if his cock didn't want to show her an overnight experience, an evening she'd remember for a long time.

All the more reason to get rid of her. Fast.

"Not with the volume of traffic passing by," he added as an afterthought. Less playful. Less full of vinegar and more salty. Not wanting to be the type of guy who'd tease a woman without following through.

"Guess it'll have to do," she said, her tone taking on a harshness that caught him off guard.

The kind of reaction you'd expect from Sophie Morelle, he reminded himself. The woman was determined.

He'd learned a lot about her during the ride. How she deftly angled her approach to questioning, baited her hook and waited for a bite. She was good. Clever and smart. Almost had him too, with her surprising knowledge of MMA. He'd caught himself a few times, falling into a deep discussion about Peruvian Neckties, the lethal tap-out maneuver, as she'd accurately dubbed it.

Time to part ways. Who knew what she'd have him blabbing about next? He couldn't afford to mess up.

Caden parked and turned off the ignition. He ignored the impulse to cruise on away from here. Instead, he climbed out of the Aston. Two appearances—that's what he'd committed to, with Wichita being the first and Phoenix the second. Being that there was no Wichita Fight Club, God only knew what surprise venue that sleazeball Jerry'd pull out of his sleeve.

Except for an enormous awning that had obviously been recently erected in the graveled parking lot that ran along the side of the motel, everything was as expected. A once-white plastic railing separated the concrete walkway from the long expanse of parking lot out front. Doors to each of the front rooms faced the roadway, their paint chipped and worn from neglect.

He spotted the office tucked away in the corner of the L-shaped motel. The dirty window facing the front had a "No Vacancy" sign blinking with a slow pulse. *Perfect.*

"Mind waiting with the car? I'll check us in." He caught her nod as he grabbed his bags from the back seat.

Five minutes later, his bags were piled on a chair in

his room. He was feeling more relaxed. The hotel manager had offered up his personal parking space in a garage around back, so the Aston would be secure and out of sight. His room was out front but if he cranked up the A/C unit, it would drown out the traffic noise. Now, if only making arrangements for his unwanted travel companion would go as smoothly. Judging by the soft click of her heels on the worn linoleum floor announcing her arrival, he doubted it.

"Looks like the Sleepy Time Motel is booked solid," he informed her over his shoulder. He grabbed the phone on the table by the bed. "I'll call around and see what else is available." He'd memorized the Hilton's 800 number. Chances were, they had rooms. If not, he'd call Harold and give his business manager something to do other than pester him about that damn contract.

"Last time I was in this neck of the woods, I had a massage at the Hilton. Great spa there."

Her silence surprised him. No way in hell was she buying that load of crap. He turned, ready to add a line about happy endings just to provoke her, and dropped the receiver back into place. Sophie was no longer in the doorway.

Hell.

Striding down the walkway, he entered the manager's office and scowled. A set of keys dangled from her fingers.

He heard her laugh just as she caught sight of him. "I'm recommending this motel to all my friends. Terrific service. Ralph has been so accommodating."

"Guess the sign was wrong then?" He glared at Ralph, who was leering at Sophie like he'd won a date with a porn star.

Sophie answered for him. "I explained how Jaysin developed a summer flu bug and wouldn't be needing a room. Shame to let his room go empty, with all that hard-earned money Jerry had spent on a non-refundable reservation. Better retrieve my luggage before our interview. See you later."

Double hell.

She sashayed on by him, her lips lifted knowingly.

It served him right, underestimating her. A clear reminder he'd better not let his guard down with her, or his mug might end up plastered on the front pages underneath the headline 'Roid *King*.

Still, he was amused. Her luggage consisted of the contents of her enormous purse and the bulge in her pocket. That was it, besides the little number he had stashed away. He shook his head, wondering why he didn't just hand over the thong. It wasn't like he was ever going to see her in it.

His stomach rumbled but food would have to wait. He needed to be ready for whatever Jerry had planned for tonight's exhibition. Plus, a workout was long overdue. No pain, no gain. No winning Tetnus. Meanwhile, he'd give Harold the task of ordering Chinese takeout to be delivered to his room, the kind with whole grain rice and non-MSG-laced chicken. Hey, if his manager found the Aston in the middle of nowhere, finding an organic Chinese takeout restaurant should be simple.

"What room did you put her in?" he asked, surprised to hear himself inquiring. *Damn.* His head wasn't on straight, and tonight someone was gonna knock it off his shoulders if he wasn't careful.

Bad enough the scorpion on Jaysin's head was gonna come unglued when he found out that Sophie was in his room and he was sleeping on the bus. She probably thought the hurting she'd put on his hand with her heel last night had done the trick, and had put the asshat in his place. But Caden knew differently. *Which is why I need her sleeping close by*, he rationalized. *That's why I'm asking, no other reason.*

"Room 33," the clerk interrupted his thoughts, surprise evident in his tone.

"I'll take 34. Or 32. Move whoever you need to into my room." He tossed the keys back onto the countertop.

The man looked at the keys like Caden had tossed a rattler onto the counter. "Uh…room seven is nicer. Much nicer. And it'll be quieter than the rooms down the other end by the cage."

The cage. The awning had been a red flag waving in the wind. Shame he'd been too focused on Sophie to see the set-up in the parking lot for what it was, or Caden would have kept on driving. *Damn Jerry.*

A cage, as in of the low-class, cheaply constructed, pseudo-Octagon kind. Leave it to that asshole promoter to bring spectators out to the freakin' hotel parking lot for a backstreet fight. Wichita Fight Club, a true no-frills venue, except for the shoddy awning—in case it fucking rained on Jerry's parade. Not that the hardcore crew who frequented these types of fights cared about a little drizzle.

Gamblers, amateur fighters, street punks, you name it, this was their preferred entertainment. Better than video games. Spectators who appreciated blood spill over skill set.

As for the bouts, they were the bare-knuckle type, organized for the purpose of lining promoters' pockets with illegal betting. Cockfights, but of the human kind.

With fixed winners and with losers so beaten they often needed medical attention. Or worse. Anything could happen. Dangerous fights. Even deadly.

Brutal, hardcore fights that sucked the breath outta a man and turned him into an animal. Fuck, Caden should know.

He'd been weaned on them.

Sophie expertly maneuvered a slice of gingered chicken between her chopsticks and discreetly studied the man sitting in front of her. His legs were flexible despite thick muscles, given the way he was sitting, Indian style, with his plate perched on one thigh. She'd mimicked his position, realizing too late how difficult it was to use chopsticks while holding a paper plate. So far, she'd managed to not splatter Sichuan sauce all over her bed.

He'd told her he was going to feed her then take her to a better hotel.

She'd told him she wasn't going anywhere without getting her exclusive.

So here they were, with him fresh from showering, and her licking her lips, mentally devouring every inch of him like he was the naughty fortune inside her cookie. She hadn't gotten a straight answer out of him yet.

His crotch, she noticed, was framed snugly by gray Adidas sweatpants that outlined the long length of him against his thigh. *Billboards do not lie.*

"Do you want more?"

Sophie's eyes shot to his face. His hair was a shade darker, still wet from his shower, and the clean, soapy scent of him filled her senses. What did he say? *Well, duh...yes, more.* "No, I'm full. Your plate is empty again, go for it. While you're eating, can I ask another question?" She switched up her strategy, aiming to get some answers out of him while his guard was down.

He grunted. But a grin formed on his lips for the first time since he'd come knocking on her door, bearing large bags of Chinese takeout and an even larger scowl. "You asking permission now? After bombarding me with hundreds of questions and working all your angles?"

"What can I say, I'm inquisitive."

"Good trait for your line of work. How about this, I ask you a question and you get to ask one in return?"

She shot him her best scowl. "Haven't we been down that road a few times already? And look where it has taken us. Nowhere."

He paused, his full chopsticks frozen in midair above the now empty container. Since he'd entered her room and situated his big body on her bed, he'd been so serious. Now, amusement with a hint of mischievousness roughened his voice. "I'd say our lockin' lips had gotten us somewhere. Hell, I'm in your bed right now. Bet I could be inside your panties in a heartbeat. Now, that would really be somewhere."

"Not going to happen. Know why?" she asked calmly. Well, on the surface, anyway. So much for setting perimeters. "I'm not wearing any."

A naughty smile curled his lips. Thankfully, she'd worn a light pair of linen slacks instead of a skirt.

She did her best to ignore him. "Why is it that every time I try to get a straight answer out of you, you change the subject? You're good at it. I'll give you that, Caden. A deflecto-mundo king. But here's the thing. I need this interview. So, no matter what you throw my way, it's not going to affect me."

"Me neither."

She released a long rush of breath. Back to business as usual. "You don't understand how important this is—"

"—I meant underneath these sweats. Nothing. Nada."

Focus on his face. Do not look down.

Caden winked.

Now why did he have to throw dry twigs on an already raging fire? She shifted and her empty plate slid off her pants and onto the floor.

"Guess you figured that one out on your own, huh?" he added.

To her utter humiliation, her cheeks heated. *Dang-diggity.* For the first time in a very long time, she felt like she was in over her head.

"For someone so unaffected, your cheeks sure do flush a lot, chili bean."

She wished the mattress would open up and swallow her whole. No one got over on her, not even as an amateur reporter. She'd learned early on how to manage people, from powerful politicians to over-the-top celebrities to beautiful, model-type guests. All this hunk had to do was mention panties and she was fanning herself. Get. A. Grip. Looking up, she caught his knowing smirk.

A few choice responses came to mind. She kept quiet, though, fascinated by the transformation in him. A somber Caden was easy on the eyes. A laughing Caden had her mind racing and her libido on high hot-stud alert. That easygoing grin tugged at her heartstrings, reached right into her and yanked out all the fragile, long-denied desires.

To her mortification, he seemed to look right into her, know her thoughts. As if he'd seen right past the walls she'd so carefully constructed. Right to the genuine core of the real Sophie Morelle. Again.

"What happened? The network give you the boot?" His tone was mild, curious.

"You happened."

His eyebrows furrowed.

"I'm sorry, you know. For ruining your comeback. Someone tripped me. That's why I fell into the cameraman." She paused, regretting the direction of their conversation as the sparkle left his eyes. "The network is a tough place for anyone to survive for any length of time. Especially a woman. Our incident, the loss of UAM advertising—the restraining order, too—was their excuse to replace me, and save themselves more money. They'll soon see how wrong they were."

"So that's why you're chasing these assholes across the country."

"Your turn to answer a question." She stiffened, hoping he'd take the hint that this line of discussion was over. Her reasons were complicated, and not up for his analysis.

"Deflecto-mundo," Caden commented, the bright sunshine of his smirk returning. "Okay. A few questions. Keep them current and relevant. Then, we'll… drop you off at the Hilton. Deal?"

She paused for a split second. "Do you think you can win Tetnus?"

"Yep." He closed his mouth. Some unidentifiable emotion flickered across his face, then was gone. He shook his head before adding, "It's all I've wanted for a long time." His tone was so low, she strained to hear him.

He seemed *vulnerable*.

She fought herself to keep from reaching out and touching him. Whenever a door opened, Sophie'd kick it wider, getting to the heart of the matter, finding her story. What made Caden Kelly tick? That was the million-dollar question and the answer would sell her documentary.

But, truth be told, it wasn't the documentary that motivated her now. It was something more. Something personal. And, despite her reporter's instinct, she couldn't do it. Couldn't kick down the walls of Caden Kelly and get inside of him. Not now, anyway.

"You're not cut from the same animalistic cloth as the other fighters—like Jaysin Bouvine, for example. Do you really think you can outfight them?" she said, giving voice to her fresh impression of him.

He moved forward and placed the empty Chinese container and paper plate on the nightstand. The old bedsprings rang out as he settled back. She realized how close their bodies were, his legs a hair's breadth away from her own. So close, but still, she wondered if he'd heard her.

She continued, emphasizing her point. "You're refined, not like the Boys with their tattooed bodies, out-of-proportion muscles, and bad manners. You're like a golf pro, with your calm attitude." He made a noise that sounded suspiciously like a snort, which made her glance at him.

His lazy smirk was gone, though it didn't detract from his perfect features. Why would anyone who looked like that want his face smashed in? "You're a model. Soft while these fighters are hard. Mild while they're wild, dangerous. Jeez, the only thing dangerous about you is your naughty reputation. Hardly something that will strike fear in your opponents."

His expression changed, reflecting a myriad of emotions that caught her off guard. Before she could put her finger on one, wonder at what he was thinking, the moment passed. His gaze lowered to her throat, watching her swallow back the lump wedged inside. He offered her a naughty smile. That was her only warning.

He rose up onto his knees, placed his hands on either side of her legs, and leaned in. The mattress shifted beneath him and she rolled forward. His head tilted, mere inches from her own. She inhaled sharply, the scent of ginger and soy sauce and clean soap filling her senses.

"You've got me pegged all wrong, chili cheeks," he murmured, "except for my naughty reputation. You're gonna get a firsthand account of that."

In the second it took him to pause and lick the smudge of Sichuan sauce off his bottom lip, Sophie knew exactly how bad he was going to be.

She blinked.

He swooped in and kissed her.

Hard. Aggressive. Oh so wild. And with such force, she found herself falling backward, with him on top.

His tongue tangled with hers, rolling and licking. An assault on her senses. Hot and sweet and relentless.

She answered by mimicking his actions, and he groaned into her mouth. He pulled back to lick and bite her lower lip. Taking it between his lips, he sucked briefly before slipping his tongue back into her mouth.

His lower half pressed into her, his erection hot against her thigh.

She shuddered. Nervous. Beyond excited. She'd never felt anything like this. Like him.

He deepened the kiss, so wild, so intense, then pulled back. "Sweet, so sweet. Why is that?" His mouth reclaimed hers before she could reply.

The room began to shake. At first, Sophie thought it was desire messing with her head—Caden rocking her world and all. Until the alarm clock vibrated off the nightstand, ringing out as it hit the bed frame and crashed to the floor. An obnoxious beeping noise, like that of a truck backing up, echoed loudly around the room.

Sophie yanked her head away, peered around the room, then back at Caden. "What the heck is going on out there? Do you feel, *hear*, that?"

"Hell."

Caden slid off the bed and yanked open the faded brown curtains. Where before there had been an awning and some police tape, now there was a tall, metal fence being secured in place. From Sophie's spot beside the bed, she could see more steel and metal pieces being hammered together.

"Fuckin' great," Caden ground out. He didn't look too happy about the commotion outside. "Too late to take the Aston out now," he added, more softly.

"What's all this?" She marched over to the window.

"Do yourself a favor. Stay in your room tonight until I come back, okay? There's going to be a lot of seedy characters roaming around with hard-ons for violence. Stay put. I'll let you know when I'm in my room and you can knock on the wall if you need me."

She snorted. "Surprise. Surprise. You didn't answer my question."

"Damn. What a fucking headache," he softly stated, tugging his sneakers back on. "Should have headed over to the Hilton. What was I thinking?"

His tone made her bristle. Jeez, she'd left herself wide-open. Vulnerable. His words tugged at her heart. "That's not what you were thinking a few minutes ago," she snapped.

He finished tying his shoelace, stood, then looked at her. "You don't want know what I was thinking. Don't have time right now. Later…maybe."

Stalking over to the nightstand, he grabbed the trash, scooped her empty plate off the floor, and tossed them into the waste bin by the bathroom door. Further proof he wasn't a Neanderthal like the other fighters. Still, his comment was the reality check she needed. If he thought for a second that they were going to continue what they'd started, she'd show him a side of her that he wasn't expecting. This was business. Nothing more.

"Stay inside. Bang on the wall if you need me. I'll knock when I leave and return. Got it?"

"Got it. And just so I'm clear, you are now my go-between with the other fighters. It's the least you can do, given how you keep derailing our interview with your charming personality and clever remarks. So we locked lips. No big deal. But I intend to make you stick to your promise. You're going to personally reintroduce me to the Boys. You're taking me to tonight's venue."

He shot her a look, like she'd grown two heads.

His attitude really pissed her off. "You're my in with the Boys, and I fully intend to get the job done, no matter what happens."

Caden arched an eyebrow. Then he was gone.

* * *

Sal arrived on her doorstep, sporting her camera bag and a bloody nose.

"Are you okay? What's going on out there?"

Stepping into the room, the old-timer slammed the door shut. "Animals coming out of the cornfields for a chance of fighting the Boys. Might have gotten mistaken for one when some big guy made a grab for your stuff. Luckily, I know how to handle myself."

Sophie frowned in confusion. Plucking a few tissues from her purse, she handed them to him. Luck likely had a lot to do with Sal surviving the altercation, but she didn't give voice to her thoughts. Chilling that someone would even think to target the older man.

"My apologies, honey. Maybe when things quiet down out there, I'll get your bigger bag from the undercarriage. As for your ugly gym bag, stuffed to the gills with golly-knows-what bursting from the seams— something pricked me, darn-gone-it…mascary maybe? Hurt like the dickens. Hope you found it in—"

A loud banging noise outside caused them both to jump.

"Don't worry about my suitcase right now, Sal. What exactly is going on out there? Caden's been gone for a few hours. I've been banging on his wall for the past hour. Did you see him outside anywhere?"

"Jerry's gonna be pissed if he broke their agreement."

"When isn't Jerry pissed? Wherever Caden ran off to, I'm tired of being cooped up in my room. And the clanging of metal and shouting has my nerves on edge. I'm starting to believe that the circus act being constructed outside *is* the next venue. I wouldn't put it past that tightwad Jerry to set up shop in a motel parking lot. Praying I'm wrong."

"Nope. You're right on target."

"But why the makeshift cage if the Boys are just signing autographs and taking pictures? Or…not." *Darn it all.* "Jerry?"

"Yep, he pulled a fast one. He's trying to reach out to the wannabes. The parking lot is full of them, mostly street gangers and hoodlums, along with a few boxer types, looking to be the next new flavor on the MMA scene and beat one of the Boys. Old-school, bare-knuckle, underground fighting. The dark roots of MMA. No good can come from tonight's shenanigans."

"The Boys are fighting random locals?"

"For their lives. See, the rules in these types of fights are discombobulated. Not like the official MMA regulations. Weight, skill level, experience, forget about it. A last-man-standing kind of fight. A betting man's fight."

Sophie shuffled through her purse for her notepad. "I read that MMA began in the streets as unsanctioned street fights. No-holds-barred kinds of fights, where there were no rules."

"You could say that."

"Height, weight, skill—or lack of it—doesn't matter, right? I am hoping to quote you as a source, Sal."

That perked the old rascal up. "But believe me, most guys don't wake up one day and say, 'Hey, I'm going to kick some booty.' No, they've trained for it. See the difference is that it's a no-holds-barred fight, like you mentioned. No rules except destroy your opponent as fast as possible. Not what our highly trained, technically skilled Boys are used to."

She'd scribbled Sal's comments verbatim in her notebook, replacing the word *booty* with *ass*. "Fists and kicks, right?" She tried to picture the Boys fighting, punching heads, kicking bodies, and wrestling around on the mat.

"Fists and kicks. Plus nails, elbows, teeth, you name it."

Sophie paused. "Biting? The sounds rather immature, like little kids fighting."

Sal shrugged. "It's what happens when there aren't any rules."

A horn blared and they both jumped. Paused. And looked at each other, knowing full well what was going down mere feet away from her motel room.

Sophie reached for her camera equipment bag, still strapped on Sal's back.

The old-timer stepped out of reach. "Are you nuts?"

"I'm a journalist, remember? This is what I do. Jerry has unknowingly handed me the opening to a documentary everyone is going to be talking about. No-holds-barred fighting at its finest. I'll show America what this sport is all about, from its old-school roots to its rise in popularity into mainstream culture, beloved by sports fans and non-sports fans alike, to its prestigious world-renowned championship fight, Tetnus. Listen, I've been in bad situations before and I've survived. I *need* this story. Hand over the bag, Sal."

"You don't understand—"

"Yes I do." She gritted her teeth and stuck out her hand. "Give it up."

"Valeska is gonna be pissed if she finds out I let a little lady like you go out there."

"I'll send her some flowers. Come on, the fights have already started."

"Stick to the back. And here, put this on." He tugged a worn Pittsburgh Pirates baseball cap out of his thin jacket. Sophie took it, with no other intention but to calm him down enough to get her camera equipment. No way was she wearing someone else's cap.

It worked. "Wish me luck," she told him, her tone excited and determined. Caden hadn't exactly come through with an exclusive but in a way, this was far, far better. Because, let's face it, her chances of seeing— *videotaping*—a real, down-and-out street fight were limited. She'd be a fool not to take advantage of filming the one that showed up on her doorstep. Literally.

"Text me if you get into trouble. Remember, keep your head down and hover around back where I can see you from your room window. In case I need to have another go at one of those hoodlums."

"Got it. Thanks for everything, Sal."

Sal grimaced. "You won't be thanking me, honey, once you step outside that door."

Chapter 8

REAR NAKED CHOKE: What happens when you wrap your legs around a fighter's neck while facing the wrong way

"I want my room back, you bitch!"

Jaysin's murderous bellow was the first sign of trouble. Sophie fixed her attention on holding the camcorder steady and kept filming. What was Jaysin going to do, anyway? Roll off the stretcher that carried him away from the Octagon ring and make a grab for her? He was bleeding like a stuck pig from his arms, chest, even his chin. A horrible sight.

Her viewers were going to eat this up.

Jaysin's fifteen minutes of fame had lasted no more than sixty seconds, too quick for her to make it to the cage in time to film the bout. No way was she going to miss capturing the agonizing aftermath, or his bughead being hauled out on a stretcher. Aside from disliking the brute, this was great footage—or would be once she'd edited out a few choice words. The bitch persona of hers had to go.

A bullhorn blared loudly, signaling another bout. The sound of pounding fists played tenor to the alto of curses that followed. The latter came from pumped-up bodies with attitudes to match. Bloodthirsty and scary as hell. Yikes, her viewfinder did not lie—the parking lot looked like a Wichita State Prison field trip.

Sophie quieted her panic and focused single-mindedly on her objective.

The rawness of the event was palpable. A seething anger rumbling toward the surface, ready to explode. Oh, Sophie understood that kind of rawness. Squared off against coal mining folk whose loyalties lay with the almighty dollar rather than an innocent girl, she'd felt the kind of rage that made you want to strike out, hard. She wasn't sure if her viewers were ready for that kind of raw pain. Heck, was anyone? By filming the Boys in action, fighting in some underground parking lot fight, her documentary would take on an unplanned edginess. A tension—a brutality—that'd be difficult to re-create, not without this flock of jailbirds. Doubtful they'd make it past midnight without being arrested.

Besides, she could always cut the footage if it didn't pan out, right?

She elbowed her way closer to the cage, raised her Canon XA10 HD camcorder high, and adjusted the zoom lens. A clear shot was impossible with the metal winding its way around all eight sides like an oddly shaped prison cell. She'd have to make do. Plus, the metal framing her footage would be a subtle reminder to viewers how hardcore MMA's origins were.

Sweat and body odor, thick and dank, mixed with the acrid smell of blood. She held her breath to keep from gagging, only to let it out in one rushed exhale when she recognized one of the Boys. One who'd tossed her in the pool, and who was now getting the living heck beat out of him.

A man that outweighed him by nearly two hundred pounds—those rolls around his middle didn't lie—held the Boy in place by the throat with one hand while pounding on his stomach with the other. The gleam of something wrapped around the brute's knuckles reflected off the metal cage.

Sophie frowned. Brass knuckles?

Doubtful she'd missed it in her research. Organized MMA bouts did not include brass knuckles. Official bouts were won based on skill and technique, not on the type of weapon wielded. Was this what Sal had meant by bare-knuckle fighting? The Boy didn't stand a chance.

Not that the crowd minded. Nor did the referee, standing off to the side, screaming and jumping around along with the rest of the spectators.

She couldn't watch. Instead, she scanned the crowd, looking for someone to film next. The baseball cap Sal had given her hung from her slacks' belt loop. Bringing it along now seemed like a good idea. Suddenly, she wanted something to hide beneath, protection from these thugs. She tugged the cap free and was just about to secure it on her head when her gaze fell on Jerry.

He'd set up shop at the far side of the cage. He wasn't

even paying attention to his fighter being butchered a few feet away. Instead, he was focused on the long line of men winding their way toward him. Interesting. What was the tight-fisted terrier up to? She turned the camcorder on him and zoomed in.

One by one, the men handed Jerry a wad of greenbacks. In turn, Jerry recorded something on a pack of papers. Each time, he'd pause, count, and either nod or shake his head and beckon with his fingers to pay up. She was on to something, she just knew it. *Dang-diggity.* Her documentary was becoming more interesting by the second; something more than entertainment was going on here.

What she needed was a close-up of his face.

Shuffling along the front row while keeping her camera fixed on the fighters proved to be difficult and tedious. Progress through the mass of bodies was slow. Spectators who weren't flashing her a stiff middle finger for blocking their view were patting and pinching her backside. She ground her teeth, trying to maintain her camera angle while warding off the offensive hands.

The further alongside the cage she moved, the more she realized her mistake. Talk about being in the thick of things—huge, towering, and a few even toothless things, out for blood or whatever sport they could get.

With Sal's cap, she swatted first at the unwelcome touches, then at the massive bodies blocking her pathway, trying to draw enough attention that they'd step back so she could squeeze through. Which in effect, did nothing. So, she resorted to the one thing that always seemed to work with thickheaded guests.

She lied. Hell, wasn't her whole persona the greatest lie of all?

"KAN News," she hollered, hoping these barbarians had basic television service and watched the news. Shouting out "Late Night with Sophie Morelle" at this point would just be asking for trouble. "Let me pass."

At first, no one heard her over the raucous shouts. She raised her voice, and hollered even louder.

A few guys in muscle shirts caught on. "KAN. KAN. KAN" echoed softly. One by one, the spectators seemed to stand up straighter, preening at the chance of being filmed for a newscast.

Now that was progress.

Until one big-bodied brute who was attempting to flip his hair moved too aggressively and slammed into her. She struggled to hold onto her camera.

"Hey."

"Sorry," the enormous guy, six feet five or more, apologized. Surprising from someone sporting a worn leather jacket and a matching leather bracelet with metal spikes protruding from it.

Turning, she cocked her head and pretended to consider his camera-worthiness. "Ever been on television?" she demanded, knowing full well the answer. No one wanted to flip on the television and be scared silly by this guy.

The man looked surprised. "No. What gives?"

"An interview. A die-hard fan's take on tonight's bouts. With you, after this is all over, when I'm not screaming to be heard. In return, a favor?"

He grinned.

Bingo. Lauren would be so proud of her resourcefulness. By bribing this beast with a fake interview in exchange for his protection, those Amanpour genes were kicking in all right.

"Will I·be on the nightly news? Gotta call my girl and let her know to TiVo my shit."

"I really need to get this footage and am having a heck of a time recording the fight with this crowd. If you'll be my bodyguard for the next few hours, I'll guarantee an interview later on."

His elbow shot out and hit the man next to her. The one guy in the entire parking lot who'd been minding his own business and focused on guzzling his beer had been laid out flat.

Her bodyguard grinned manically at her, looking for approval.

Crapola. She'd better think of a smooth way out of this. No predicting what this brute might do if he figured out she was full of it.

Yet his actions were confirmation enough of his helpfulness. She offered him a weak smile, and feeling slightly more at ease with the situation, shifted her attention back to the ring.

Piles of crimson-colored towels littered the mat, soaking up the blood from the latest battle. Brutal evidence of what had gone down seconds ago, all that she'd mercifully missed. She grimaced. Better develop a thicker skin or she'd never make it through the night. As if to prove her point, she focused in on the bloody mess.

This wasn't normal, right? Jeez, no way had Caden's handsome face seen this kind of brutality, men carried off by stretchers, broken and in serious pain. His type of fighting was probably just like him. Edgy yet slightly sweet, like lemon ice. Wholesome.

Don't forget naughty. Her cheeks warmed at the memory of their kiss. Yep, he'd probably smirk his opponent into submission. Well, his female opponents, anyway. Was he out here and watching this bloodbath unfold? She scanned the crowd with her camcorder, trying to get a visual on him.

"What the fucking hell do *you* think you're doing?" Jerry's ugly mug filled the lens from inside the cage. Great. The last thing she wanted was for him to suspect she'd caught him counting his blood money red-handed.

Keeping her camera rolling so it picked up their conversation, she shot off a question to him. "Don't you care that your Boys' chances at Tetnus might be ruined because of all this? Why would you organize such a bloodbath?" *Because you're charging locals money for a chance to fight an MMA superstar?* She pressed her lips together, and waited for him to sink his own ship.

His face flushed deep red. *Bingo.*

"Jaysin Bouvine is a fan favorite. Will he recover in time to fight in Tetnus? Or have you ruined his chances?" She prayed the smugness in her voice didn't translate in the video's audio. Jaysin was a jerk who well deserved the beating he'd gotten.

"You don't know what you're talking about. So, a few guys had an off fight. Not my fault. I'm warning you, better get outta here or you're gonna get hurt." Jerry raised the bullhorn and pressed the red button.

The giant next to her spoke. "You wanna see a wicked fighter? The dirtiest street thug around? Thrives on putting a hurting on his enemies. Paralyzed one kid. Knifed another to death. He just got out of the penitentiary." He paused dramatically, pointing at a huge thug who'd appeared by the side of the cage. Sophie couldn't tell if her bodyguard was stating the truth or exaggerating, until he added, "You got that on tape?"

"Sure did."

Still, a shiver ran up her spine.

The thug now prowling around the outside of the cage was bigger than the giant next to her, in all senses of the word: his belly massively round, his arms like tree stumps, his neck equally thick. *Badass* was written all over him.

Jerry sounded the horn once more.

Instinct told her to head back to her room. Watching this giant kick butt was going to give her nightmares, and it wasn't like she needed any more of them. The ramshackle cage screeched in protest as the brute climbed the stairs, entered the cage, and stalked around the interior, kicking away the bloody towels that obstructed his path. He didn't seem to mind that the mat was a breeding ground for blood-borne pathogens or that the worst of Wichita had drawn in closer, blocking his exit.

Sophie could feel rivulets of sweat running down her neck and the humid air reeked with body odor. Her bodyguard was the only thing in between her and the masses of men whose every breath was spiked with violence.

Once more, she shook off the instinct to flee. Instead, she raised her camera and angled it toward the inside of the cage. This introduction into the evolution of MMA from the streets to a professionally organized championship was the real deal. She'd missed two bouts and despite her fears, she was determined to film this one from start to finish. She just hoped no one got too hurt. Or died.

Sure, the networks would love the drama of it all, but she needed to reposition herself over by the steps, where there was a gap in the chain link. Fans at home had short attention spans, and would predictably grow tired of watching a fight obscured by a metal cage. Easy viewing pleasure—that was the name of the game.

She waved the giant on. "Need to get over there."

"Better lights for the interview?"

What part about *later* did this guy miss? Even if Sophie's later was nonexistent. "Yep. Bigger spotlight."

The giant plowed through the crowd. Sophie tucked herself safely in behind him and followed. The crowd parted angrily. Ready to fight for their position by the cage, until they realized the magnitude of the man pushing his way through.

"Things are about to get ugly," her bodyguard remarked. As if the entire spectacle unfolding out here in the motel parking lot wasn't ugly enough.

Sophie moved up onto the steps and angled her camera toward the massive bald fighter stalking around the Octagon cage.

He prowled toward the stairs, his mug filling the frame.

Sophie held position, swallowing hard. Breathless. Waiting for him to tell her he was going to kill someone and eat their liver with fava beans and red wine. Meanness personified.

Jerry paced around the outside of the cage, looking like he wanted to kill someone as well. His earlier greedy gaze was gone. Every bit of his tall, lanky body was stiff and furious.

Jerking the horn over his head, he kept his finger on the red button. The blasted horn blared endlessly, further upsetting the crowd. Not that Jerry cared. To him, the hyped-up spectators were like rowdy students, and he, the unpopular professor from hell, was demanding their attention.

Great footage. Her camera captured it all.

"Freakin' shit on a brick."

Sophie jumped at the snarl, so close she felt the heat of his breath on her ear. A memory. Nothing more. He wasn't close enough for that. Caden…*Caden? What was he doing here?*

"What the fuck are you doing? Do you have some sort of death wish?" She felt his warm hand on her elbow. Briefly.

Then it was gone.

The sound of flesh connecting with flesh, followed by a long groan, made her jump and turn.

Her bodyguard was on the ground, cupping his side.

She focused on Caden, standing at the foot of the steps, now eye level with her. His body language was relaxed, like he'd just crawled out of bed and was limbering up. Except his fist was clenched. Did he just knock her bodyguard on his back with one punch?

His eyes told a different story. Hard. Piercing. Full of some unidentifiable emotion. Disappointment? Anger? It couldn't be good. Whatever it was, it affected him deeply. But the second she realized it, it was gone.

He was wearing a tight, black Ultimate American Male T-shirt, gray shorts, and ratty sneakers. Even dressed down, the sight of him caused a surge of pleasure deep within her. The sight of him… *Oh crapola. No.*

Common sense seemed to reach out, grab her by the throat and shake her until logic sank in. "What are *you* doing?" The answer hit her like a three-hundred-pound weight, stealing her breath and making her head spin. No, this was not happening.

"For fuck's sake, go back to your room."

"I've been pounding on my wall for hours. Where the heck have you been? And more importantly, what do you think you're doing?" she repeated, this time with more force.

Caden grunted, looking past her to the fighter prowling around the cage.

"You're not stupid enough to fight that man? Jeez, he just got out of jail."

Ignoring her, he grabbed hold of the bottom of his black T-shirt and stripped it up and over his head. Every muscle in his abdomen and chest flexed.

He climbed the steps until he was beside her. Somehow, he seemed bigger. Bigger in every sense of the word—his entire being, not just the packaging.

His fingers touched her arm and gave a gentle squeeze. Sure, there was lust but it was quickly overwhelmed by the tight knot that had formed in her stomach, leaving her breathless. Talk about conflicting emotions. Which, in truth, was how she always felt around Caden. Confused. Turned on. *Worried.*

"You're a well-respected champion in the making. Not someone who fights in some ramshackle ring, in some thug fest. I didn't peg you for being the kind of athlete who'd participate in this kind of brutal bloodbath."

"Sweetheart, you don't know the first thing about me. If you don't head back to the room, forget about me helping you. Fuck, forget that you know me at all," he literally growled into her ear.

Releasing her, he moved up the stairs and into the ring.

Sophie descended, hoping to give the appearance

that she was actually listening to him and following orders. But the last thing she wanted to do was abandon Caden to that beast, without knowing the extent of the beating he'd received. How many broken bones needed resetting, or the depth of medical attention he would require. If he survived the fight.

She paused, and looked around for the EMTs, all the while muttering to herself. "Foolish. What is he thinking? He's going to get throttled, ruin his beautiful face, end his modeling career for good. Disappoint women across the country. Get himself killed. Damn. Damn. Damn."

Her bodyguard snorted as he got to his feet to stand beside her. "About our interview, can it wait? Gotta go place a bet. No one's gonna expect this. I'll make a killing. Meet up with you by the bus out front—the yellow one, can't miss that hunk of junk. Okay?"

Sophie ignored the comment. Something had to be done about this fight, and fast. Her bodyguard was turning out to be more useful than expected.

"Organized betting? Sounds shady to me. Who's collecting the money?" She already knew the answer. This was for the camera alone.

He pointed in Jerry's direction. Darn. She needed him to say it. Quickly.

"Joseph somebody?"

"No, the tall guy inside the cage. The one with the horn in his hand."

Terrific.

"Jerry Batelli? The promoter," she emphasized, making sure the censure in her voice translated well. She glanced toward the cage and met Caden's glare.

The knot in her stomach tightened in a death grip.

Knowing he was going to lose was heartbreaking, an unexpected elephant on her chest, pinning the breath within her lungs. Aside from lusting after the hunk, she was surprised to discover she *liked* him. Liked the protectiveness he'd displayed earlier, with his insistence she knock on the wall if she needed him. Liked how he was sensitive enough to know when he'd hit a nerve and backed off without going for blood. Heck, he'd probably agreed to help her simply because he felt sorry for her.

There was much more to Caden Kelly than jaw-dropping good looks. Charisma. Humor. A keen sense of intelligence. The elephant bore down to the point where pain welled up in her chest. He was better than this ramshackle ring, this brutal bloodbath. He should have his comeback without having to lower himself to Jerry's unorthodox level of chaos in order to do it. Caden was going to ruin his good looks *and* his chance to compete in Tetnus, big time.

She shook her head at him. *No. Don't do it*.

He scowled, then nodded toward the motel. A short, sharp gesture.

Abruptly, he turned and sauntered toward the far corner, effectively dismissing her.

"Yep, that's right," her bodyguard continued, oblivious to the wave of emotion playing havoc with her heart. He moved toward the ring and shouted, "Hey, Jerry. Hold up!" Without waiting for the shady promoter's reply, he hustled off, leaving Sophie feeling anything but victorious, despite having recorded confirmation of Jerry's wrongdoings.

She knew moving away from the ring wasn't an option. Escaping the mass of testosterone-infused bodies, safeguarding her exclusive interview, shielding herself from the drama about to unfold, none of it was important. What mattered was the fighter in the cage.

The bullhorn sounded. Sophie pushed until she managed to squeeze right up next to the metal fence.

Caden sauntered forward, offering his fists in greeting to the bald prison escapee. The classy gesture was lost on the man. Instead, he took a pot shot at Caden, who ducked and narrowly missed being slammed in the side of his head.

Then he smirked.

Sophie cringed. *Madman.*

Glancing around, she waved to the EMT guys, clearly identifiable within this crowd, their white uniforms like cream in an Oreo cookie, surrounded by black and brown. They responded by waving back. She noted their proximity to the cage, close enough to reach Caden when the time came. Judging by Caden's reckless, nonchalant behavior, it would be sooner rather than later. Couldn't he tell the guy wanted to kill him, and would resort to any means necessary to do so?

Baldy charged across the ring, fists raised and shouting like a wild man.

Caden didn't budge. His arms hung loosely by his sides, his stance relaxed and unthreatening. Quiet movements, so unlike the man himself.

The oversized beast threw his entire body weight at Caden, and ended up face-first against the cage. She zoomed in on Baldy's very pissed-off response. The indentations from the cage's wiring looked like deep-set frown marks on his face.

She would have laughed, if it hadn't been for Caden turning and slowly heading across the cage. Toward her. His back was to Baldy. Any fool knew what a huge mistake that was.

He didn't seem to notice her. Three choices: duck out of sight, brazen it out and watch Baldy pummel him, or…warn him?

Once more, Baldy charged.

Sophie opened her mouth. "Caden," she shouted, "watch—" Her words were interrupted by a gasp, as Caden turned at the last second and swung his leg around full throttle.

They connected with Baldy's side, smack in the kidney. Baldy bellowed in rage.

Caden leaned in toward his opponent, saying something. Sophie didn't need to hear his words to figure it out, having been on the receiving end of Caden's wry humor. Something provocative, for sure.

Judging by Baldy's snarling curses in English, Spanish, and surprisingly, Chinese, the word *provocative* was putting it mildly.

Baldy whipped a shiny object out of his pants.

A mixture of admonition and admiration rumbled through the crowd like a dark, treacherous wave. Light flickered off the object, and Sophie gasped.

A knife.

Not a butter knife, either. She refocused the camera lens for a closer look. A curved blade the length of a large banana. Baldy must have had it sheathed within his sweatpants. Holding the camcorder steady, she looked around the parking lot. Someone had to stop this. Brass knuckles were bad enough. Now knives?

Didn't Sal warn you there are no rules tonight? her nervous mind scolded.

Her windpipe constricted, making her lightheaded.

No one had stepped forward to help. And she felt…
helpless, a feeling so long buried that it took her a second to recognize it.

Where was her bodyguard? He was big enough to end it.

Caden gestured with his hands, drawing her attention back to him.

Oh. Crapola. He was taunting Baldy. "Bring it on," his hands motioned.

Helplessly, she looked around once more. Someone had to stop this fight before Caden goaded his opponent into committing murder.

The crowd's attention was fixed on the fighters. Sophie's hands shook so hard she was forced to lower her camera. Tucking it beneath her armpit, she angled it up toward the cage and left it running.

Baldy charged, forcing Caden's back against the cage. Sophie swallowed hard; the rage on Baldy's face was purely animalistic. In one swift motion, the knife swung through the air and sliced Caden's arm. Blood sprayed from the cut like from a lawn sprinkler, showering the cage and the spectators below. A fist came sailing from the other direction, connecting hard with Caden's cheekbone with a resounding crack.

"Damn it, Caden. Move!" she heard her own hoarse cry, wiping his blood from her arm with the hem of her cotton blouse. Darn, the stain was never going to come out. She didn't care. All she cared about was Caden fighting for his life in that cage.

He moved, shifting sideways so she could see his profile. See the vicious cut on his arm. See the look of utter rage he shot her in a single glance.

"Get the fuck outta here," he shouted. "Now."

Baldy laughed sadistically. "What? The handsome pussy wants me to leave his pretty boy face alone? Got news for you. I'm not going nowhere. And the only way you're leaving is by the ambulancia. Dŏng mā?"

Caden rolled his shoulders, then his neck. Warming up. Jeez, now? Or was he too hurt to know that the time for preparation had long since passed?

He glared at her. With so much fury, it was like someone sucker punched her, stealing her breath.

Then his face became completely void of expression. He shifted on his feet. Relaxed and composed, or so it seemed. Contrary in every way to Baldy, who was all huff and puff, with steam blowing out of his flaring nostrils.

Seconds passed. Despite all the noises coming from Baldy, Sophie's gaze rested on Caden. He looked ready for a nap. Or the beach. Or…bed. He didn't look her way again, and hopefully he'd forgotten her. What did he expect anyway? She had a job to do. She…*needed him in one piece.*

The warm summer night had turned sweaty with crowds of men packed in shoulder to shoulder. Still, the camera humming against her side felt cold. She felt chilled to the bone.

Baldy raised his knife again. Then everything became one crazy blur.

Caden kicked his wrist, sending the knife flying across the cage. Pivoting and raising his uninjured arm, he elbowed Baldy squarely in the nose, surely breaking it. His fist followed, swinging up and hitting Baldy underneath the chin. The brute was literally lifted off his feet by the impact.

Baldy landed on his feet, and stepped backward.

His eyes popped out of his head, surprised as hell. His crooked nose spewed blood down his chin.

Sophie could relate. Awestruck, she was speechless as she focused on the stranger in front of her. A fine sheen of sweat coated his taut chest. His jaw clenched tightly but his hands hung loosely at his sides. So different than what she'd thought. So incredibly virile. Deep inside her, something stirred. A primal feminine reaction to his pure, unadulterated masculinity.

The crowd was eerily quiet. Waiting with bated breath for Caden to go in for the kill.

Caden smirked briefly, a reassuring glimpse of his sarcastic self hidden within the vicious fighter standing nonchalantly before her.

Nonchalant. No way, she thought, just before Caden sprang forward. His fists pounded both of Baldy's sides, then his face. Rapidly. Repeatedly. Viciously.

It wasn't the brutal punches that made her cry out, though. It was the look that fell across Caden's features. A look so fierce it caused her to want to hug herself protectively.

Never in a million years would she have guessed that behind that lazy smile, breathtaking good looks, and sharp, sarcastic wit, lurked such a brutal man. A warrior. The kind of guy you wouldn't want to get involved with if you valued your life. Gone was the man who'd made her knees tremble from his kisses, her heart do a jig at his touch.

And to make matters worse, he *liked* this, wanted it, gave up a safe, comfortable career for this…the beatings and bloodshed.

Sophie shuddered. Clearly, she wasn't the good judge of character she'd credited herself with being.

The EMT crew sprinted past her for the stairs.

Caden swung his leg high, connecting with Baldy's thigh, and the man crumbled to the ground. Caden was on him a second later, pinning him to the mat.

Blood poured out of his cut. His bruised cheek had swelled up. Yet his relentless fists pounded his opponent's side again and again.

Baldy raised his hand and tapped the mat.

"Tap out! He fucking tapped out," chorused the stunned spectators.

The camera nestled against her side was still rolling, right in unison with her heartbeat. Her documentary had taken a surprising turn, and had the makings of being something spectacular. She'd heard he had mad skills but this model/playboy had a down-and-dirty side. A brutality you'd expect to find in a back alley brawler, not America's favorite loverboy. One thing was clear, though. Caden was a champion no matter the cage he fought in. Viewers were in for a wake-up call.

"Killer Kelly, Killer," the crowd chanted. *Holy crapola*.

Sophie looked on in horror as it took three EMTs to pull Caden off his opponent.

That sexy smile, the light-hearted playboy appeal depicted on his billboard, had been a lie. The man she knew—or thought she'd known—was an illusion.

Chapter 9

LAY AND PRAY: When a fighter plays dead, and prays his opponent will fall for it and stop beating the hell out of him. Seems like the best way to get out of the cage alive

The fists pounding on his motel room door echoed loudly around the bathroom. Or was that his pounding headache beating in time with whoever the fuck was out there? Whoever it was clearly hadn't seen the fight. A rational person, or even someone with a smidgeon of common sense, would know enough to leave him alone. Give him time to recover and work through the second battle playing out in his head.

Rage. No other word described what had happened back there in the cage. A killing rage. The crowd picked up on it, all right, chanting Killer Kelly like they'd been cheering for their favorite baseball player up at bat.

He'd lost control. Allowed the demons to resurface, and along with them, anger and hurt. His daddy's fists. Bracken beaten to near death, with cracked ribs and a broken nose. Child Protective Services, who did more harm than good by separating the brothers. Foster homes suitable for tough, hardcore, mean-looking kids, not an attractive boy looking for someone to love him. Life afterward, in the backstreets of Nashville, fighting for food. Fighting to survive.

Since he sobered up, he'd gotten good at redirecting his pain, using it as motivation to rise above it all. Win Tetnus. Prove once and for all that he mattered.

Tonight, that pain had eaten him whole.

A quick, hot shower hadn't been enough comfort. He needed a hiatus from the promise he'd made to himself. A bottle of booze was just what he had in mind.

His mind flashed full of Sophie. Her hair fanning out on the mattress, her lips swollen from his kisses, her eyes shimmering with pleasure. The image was all wrong. She was officially off limits. Tonight, she'd pissed him off like nobody's business.

"Knock if you need me," he muttered. She'd promised to stay put, then had blatantly ignored it, putting herself in unnecessary danger. Man, he should have expected it from her. Typical woman—couldn't be trusted. Caden wore two belts, figurative ones. The first notched with all the women he'd fucked, and another with the women who'd outright lied to him. The latter was beginning to catch up to the first.

Promises were something he didn't take lightly because, in spite of the endless letdowns he'd experienced over the years, Caden had never made an idle one. His word was his word.

That is, except for the promises made to himself. Breaking them were the biggest letdowns of all.

He hurled the damp towel clenched in his fist onto the bathroom countertop. Tugging on a clean pair of sweats, he scowled at the sharp pain from the wound on his arm. The EMTs had looked at it and given him some antiseptic and bandages to bind it with after he'd showered the stench from his body.

The pounding continued. Relentless and unmerciful. One more ballbuster to be dealt with. "Just a fucking second," he shouted at the door.

The combination of somebody's blaring television and whoever was beating the hell out of his motel room door only worsened his headache. Just like the woman in the adjacent room—the one that had better be in there, and not banging away outside.

Fuck. One more reason not to answer it.

Shit. And double shit. Was she in trouble? His head throbbed at the thought, knowing he'd promised her his protection and hadn't exactly hurried to the door.

Without further thought, Caden stalked over and yanked it open.

"Boy-oh-boy, that was something," Sal murmured, stepping past him into the room. The man was as annoying as hell, and just as oblivious. "Jerry's mad as the dickens, too. Thought you were a no-show—he didn't see your car out front, you didn't check in to the room he'd reserved. So he put his mouth and money on Jaysin. Lost big time."

The news wasn't surprising. Caden had dealt with his share of Jerrys in his lifetime, sure. Guys who were

slaves to the dollar, who'd use fighters any way necessary to fill up their bank accounts. Fuck, for the better
part of the evening he'd been watching the man, waiting to catch him red-handed. But a guy who traded in
human flesh *and* sold dope? That took the cake...

Sal stood with his hands on his hips, his gaze searching the room. "I bet you didn't expect Caden to put a
licking on that felon?" he loudly asked. Dried blood had
formed beneath a nostril, signs that the old-timer had
seen some trouble. Knocked loose some marbles within
that head of his, with the way was talking—like there
was another guy named Caden in the room.

"Holy tarnation," Sal continued, eyes searching, then
widening. "She's not here. Thought she followed you
back. I've been waiting for her to...eh...finish up in
here."

Fucking tarnation.

"That was you in Sophie's room, with the television
amped up to 100 decibels?" he demanded, knowing full
well the answer. He stalked over to the chair, grabbed
his black T-shirt off the back, and slid it over his head.
The cut on his arm smarted but he ignored it as he slid
on his sneakers.

The room fell silent, drawing attention to the fact
that the commotion outside had died down. No news
to be had out there. Bad news for Sophie, any way you
looked at it. He had to find her, and fast.

Sal was already at the door. "I'm going to get her,"
he announced, drawing the same conclusion.

Caden scowled. *Shit on a brick*. Lord knew what Sophie had gotten herself into out there. He moved past
Sal, jerked the door open, and strode out into the parking lot.

Light from a full moon illuminated the area enough for him to spot the huddle of thugs lurking over by the deconstructed cage. No one else was around. The thought that Sophie might be held against her will by those shitheads, or worse…

He headed toward the group, lengthening his strides. Sal's loafers sounded on the pavement behind him, hustling to keep up.

Caden heard her voice, coming from deep within the circle, but he had to see her. Had to see for himself that she was okay. The fact that her voice sounded polished and professional, calm even—that it was the voice she used while interviewing celebrities—was lost on him.

"What else do you want to say to the MMA fans out there?"

"Uh…"

Caden elbowed his way into the thick of them, guided by the sound of her. He paused once to glance over his shoulder and make sure the old-timer was close by.

"Come on. Don't be camera shy. Let me remind you: *Live* on KAN. Anyone else care to comment?"

He pushed through the front line of bodies and stopped short. His gaze landed first on her, then on the camcorder.

Sal drew up next to him and sucked in a breath. "Holy Toledo."

Sophie stood on the second step of what remained of the stairs. Her blouse was wrinkled and her pants creased, but despite the worse for wear, she seemed unharmed. Dead serious, with her camera held high. Holding court to all of the thugs, riffraff, and street punks who lingered about after a fight, looking for trouble.

Guess they found it. All five foot seven of her.

Except they hadn't figured it out yet. That she was pure trouble. That the Pittsburgh Pirates cap on her head was a dead giveaway that she wasn't from these parts. That she wasn't a reporter for a local news channel.

That the fucking camcorder wasn't even on.

"Please, somebody speak up. Remember, we're on *air.*"

He wanted to punch the three assholes closest to her, all of them smiling manically. Gullible as shit, but built like tanks.

She hadn't noticed him.

Her gaze darted toward the three thugs, nervously. A sign that common sense hadn't entirely vanished.

"Okay, guys, a little change in topic, here. Any comment on the illegal betting taking place tonight?"

A rumble of angry curses came out of his lips, overshadowed by the louder rumble of voices rolling through the crowd. Like a dark, ominous cloud over an already torrential downpour of bad losers. Caden was willing to bet they'd bet against *him.*

"How many of you gave Jerry money?" Sophie continued, unaware that it was about to rain on her parade. Damn. Given her profession, you'd think she'd know when danger surrounded her. The tension had grown so thick, a chainsaw wouldn't slice through it.

Sophie shifted her weight and tucked a hand into her pants pocket, with the dark lens of the camcorder held steadfast on the crowd.

"That weasel got me for a hundred bucks. Told me that fucking fighter of his, the one with the scorpion on his head, was un-fuckin'-beatable. If he hadn't been hauled out on a stretcher, I'd beat the shit outta him myself." The fan's face grew redder as he ground the words out from between clenched teeth.

The guy next to him chimed in. "Got me for a hundred, too. I want my money back. The fights were fixed."

Silence fell, and then the men's eyes swung Caden's way, finally noticing him.

Caden ground his teeth together, readying himself to have at it.

"Don't do it," Sal said, surprising him.

He grunted, his gaze shifting off the trio and onto Sal.

The old-timer was shaking his head at Sophie.

Hell. His gaze quickly fell back onto her. Man, this woman drew trouble to her like honey drew butterflies.

He let out a healthy stream of curses as she stepped down off the makeshift stairs, drew out a small notepad from somewhere beneath her camera, and stepped closer to the trio.

It was too late to stop her.

"Tell me, how much does Jerry charge amateurs to fight professionals? And how does he get the word out and find the hardest guys? Does he cull from local prisons? Detention centers?"

"Cull? Like seacull? Honey, do I look like some damned bird?" The red-faced fan growled. "You're the reporter. You get stuff done. So, go get my money."

"You know, KAN sucks. How about—"

"Woo, bitch, is that thing even on?"

It wasn't their words, or the fact that she'd been made that sprung Caden into action. It was the look on the faces of the three thugs, staring at Sophie as if they'd been interviewed by the devil in high heels.

Great, he was going to have to fight his way back out of here, with a headache that felt like an iron vice squeezing his temples.

In three long strides, he stalked up to her and grabbed her beneath the elbow.

Sophie jumped, yanking her arm from beneath his grasp, but he held on firm. Turning, her eyes widened on his face a second before her arm relaxed beneath his fingers.

"Show's over," he stated, loud enough for the crew around them to know he meant business. "Let's go," he added in a softer voice, tugging her arm and leading her back through the crowd.

"Hey, what time can we watch our interview?" the guy who'd been crowding Sophie as he approached the ring. Clueless as crap.

"Eleven o'clock news," Sophie calmly lied through her teeth. "Run home and turn your televisions on."

It was well past midnight. Good thing this crew wasn't the watch-wearing sort.

"Sophie, sweetheart, I hate to rustle your feathers but do you know that your camera isn't even—"

"Zip it, Sal," he growled, shooting him a clear look of warning.

Man alive, no way was he making it outta here without a battle.

His temples throbbed along with his splitting headache. The sharp pain in his arm matched his sore cheek. He ignored it all. Fuck, he'd fought through worse situations, before he'd even learned how to defend himself.

The biggest guy decided to play hardball by blocking his path. Showing off for the crowd more than anything else. Large-oaf syndrome.

Caden shot him a warning look. For a second, the guy looked nervous enough to step aside. He shuffled around on his feet, his movements hesitant before stupidity had him holding ground. He felt sorry for the man. Now it was about saving face.

Before any chants of encouragement could begin, Caden balled up his fist and sucker punched the guy in the stomach. A shame, but he had to make his point clear.

Sophie's arm jerked beneath his grasp. He heard her gasp.

What the fuck did she expect? His fingers tightened around her arm as they made their way without further incident back to his room.

He released her arm, and she rubbed the spot with her hand, as if to wipe away his repulsive touch.

"Inside."

She didn't hesitate, stepping around his body in the doorway. Careful not to brush up against him as she passed.

He studied her face.

She tucked her chin and avoided eye contact.

"Hell," he murmured, exasperated.

She shied away from him and hurried into the room.

Letting out another stream of curses, he followed her inside. Her reaction pissed him off.

She'd been cool as a cucumber surrounded by street punks and ex-cons. Resourceful and hell-bent on getting the goods on Jerry. Nervous yes, but fearless nevertheless. And unbelievably stupid—any number of things could have happened to her tonight, if he hadn't interfered.

Had he hurt her? He rubbed his temples, hard. It didn't help the drumming in his head.

Fuck. What she'd witnessed in the cage earlier more than justified her fear.

Sal stood shifting on his loafers, just outside the doorway.

Freakin' great—the old-timer too?

Sal moved about nervously on the cement walkway. "Wow, that was a close call. Thought I was going to have to take that guy down. Unfortunately, you beat me to it. The least I can do for you, Caden, is go and get something for the swelling. Motel manager has got to have ice or something."

Caden frowned, and then winced in pain. People fussing over him left a foul taste in his mouth, as if he couldn't take care of himself. But he nodded in agreement anyway. Less noise with Sal gone.

"You got it. And, Caden…um…she's not all that bad. You might wanna cut her some slack. Even though it looked like she was handling herself okay—"

He slammed the door before Sal finished. Stalking into the bathroom, he unwound his bandage, grabbed a towel, wet it, and pressed it against the oozing cut on his arm.

The soft tread on the carpet as she paced around in the room told him she hadn't fled. Horrible instincts for a reporter. She was uncharacteristically quiet. Knew enough to leave him alone to regroup. Or was she afraid of him now?

He grunted. If that was the case, her instincts were spot-on. Guess that wholesome illusion of him had been shot to pieces. Tonight, she'd discovered the truth. How his looks, humor, sharp tongue were a ruse. He was damaged. No good. A rough kid, inside and out.

He'd thought this side of him had been smothered and contained. A single amateur fight with a bald street punk had forced years of disciplined training down the drain. He knew it and Sophie had seen it, which was why she was so skittish. It pissed him off to no end.

It doesn't matter. Nothing matters.

He was sick to death of living a lie. The bottle, women, money and fame…none of it had helped. Fighting brought him closer to the truth. Made his blood pump and mind clear. The training and commitment were nearly satisfying enough. Winning would give him the satisfaction of knowing he could overcome all kinds of odds—physically demanding challenges and the mental demons nipping at his heels. Fighting professionally was the catharsis he prized the most. Hell, it offered the level of physical action he needed *and* could control.

When he didn't fucking lose it, like tonight. How reminiscent of his dad. A real chip off the ole block.

Stalking back into the room, he grabbed a water bottle off the nightstand, opened the bottle of aspirin next to it, and tossed down a few with one long chug. He caught a glimpse of the bruise on his cheek reflected in the mirror. A reflection of his mood, as well. Black and darkening still.

"Okay, then. I'm headed back to my room," Sophie murmured, interrupting his thoughts. "Too much excitement for one night."

He'd been thinking the same thing. Bid *adios* to Miss Meddlesome. Say hello to a bottle of Jack. To hell with training. But now that she said it, so quietly and without a trace of the gumption he'd grown accustomed to, he realized being alone was the last thing he wanted.

Getting lost in drink probably wasn't going to be enough to satisfy him tonight. Why the hell not? He'd send her packing just like all the others, afterward.

She stepped toward the door.

He didn't stop her. The bottle of Jack would be better company. No personal questions or unreasonable demands. Simple relief from the tension in his head.

Granted, the tension in his body usually called for something more physical. And lately his thoughts were full of one woman in particular—one who was ready to hightail it out of his room if he didn't do something foolish and stop her.

No can do, his voice of reason returned. He ran his fingers through his hair. Lifting the bottle of water, he took another long drink. Rolling around in the sheets with the reporter was a horrible idea. Irrational. Illogical. Downright idiotic. The punch to his head had fucked up his thinking, for sure.

Nah, tonight he'd settle for getting loaded instead of laid.

A knock sounded on the door. Sophie jumped, and hastened back a few paces.

Moving past her, he yanked it open.

Sal pushed a frozen sirloin steak into his chest. "This is the best I could drum up before Jerry found me. Man, he's livid. Someone slashed all the tires on the bus."

Caden snorted. Poor judgment, leaving that hunk of junk parked out front. What did the sleazeball expect after inviting every lowlife in Wichita over for some bloodletting? Lining the motel manager's pockets for his garage space was proving to be a smart move.

His gaze shifted to Sophie. Those full red lips of hers lifted, stirring something deep within the pit of his stomach. And lower. *Damn.* What was it about her that had him thinking about tossing her onto the bed and burying himself deep inside, despite his assembly of aches and pains?

"Wanna hear the best part of it, what's got him madder than a python?"

"I'm game, Sal. Though I can't picture what a pissed-off python looks like," Sophie laughed, clearly relishing Jerry's dilemma.

Who could blame her? The man was a pure, unadulterated a-hole. At least she seemed more relaxed. More like herself. The thought calmed him as well, his humor returning despite the pain in his cheek.

"Not python. A rattler—they're venomous, like Jerry." He heard Sophie snort in acknowledgment, and realized that his headache was gone. "Sal, you coming in, buddy?"

"Can't. Never hear the end of it if I don't go help Jerry get these tires fixed, and fast. He's been screaming about being late for our next appearance. Said it was really important that we stop there," Sal said, looking worried. He turned, and took a step away.

Caden felt Sophie's stare. Silent communication that she was searching for answers. Information he wasn't about to share, not until he figured out the extent of Jerry's racket, and how deeply involved he was in pimping performance-enhancing drugs. Not to mention the illegal betting and death matches set up in shady venues from Wichita to Vegas. At the same time, there'd been plenty of opportunities tonight to distribute to a target market—wannabe fighters. And Caden hadn't seen Jerry hand off a single pill. Pushing aside his suspicions, he shrugged his shoulders and caught her scowl.

He gave her a smug grin. Any remnants of tension vanished as he took in the sight of her, so cute in that baseball cap, with her blouse unbuttoned and wrinkled beyond belief. Naturally pretty, with her pink cheeks and lips a shade darker.

"Come on, Sal," he prompted him, his mind at ease, and back on their discussion. "Don't leave us hanging."

Sal stopped, and chuckled. "Eh...forgot. Right. Someone got to the sign, too. Jerry said it cost him 'a shitload' of money."

"What sign?" Sophie demanded. "That dirty banner from the side of the bus?"

"Wichita's got a sense of humor. They crossed out a few letters. Now it reads 'Tits on tour.'" Sal emphasized every word, relishing every syllable, oblivious to the grimace on Sophie's face.

Ironic how the queen of late night was so easily offended.

There was an awkward pause, before Sal caught on. "Sorry, Sophie. The Boys are gonna be ornery when they see what those hoodlum have done." He rolled his eyes at her, meant to be an apologetic gesture, or so Caden thought.

Once more, Caden found himself unexpectedly drawn to her. Curious why she, of all people, was bothered by the harsh language.

"Hmph," she grunted, breaking the silence. "That took some imagination. Who would have thought it with the boneheads roaming around outside? Don't tell Jerry, but if you blacken out the first t and a few other letters, the sign will read: It Tour. Hey, it's better than nothing, right?"

Caden smiled. Man, that brain of hers was always in fifth gear, never at a full stop. Yet he bet Jerry'd prefer *tit* over *it*, any day.

Sal nodded emphatically. A sure sign he was going to tell Jerry, just to calm the drama king down.

He looked past Sal and out into the empty parking lot. Hundreds of beer cans littered the space, flickering in the moonlight like warped Morse code. Maybe an EMT worker would think someone needed help, and come check out his addled brain. Hell, was he—a champion welterweight, a street-bred fighter—really playing Scrabble with douchebag Jerry's sign?

The empty lot was a welcome sight. No one would be bothering Sophie. "Thanks for the steak." He waved the useless frozen sirloin at the old-timer and shot a pointed look at Sophie. "Knock on the wall if you need me."

Sal headed off around the corner of the building.

Sophie didn't budge.

"Time to call it a night. Go ahead, no one's gonna mess with you."

Instead of leaving, she moved further into his room and out of reach. "Where did you learn to fight like that?" Her voice was soft and raspy. Like her words came from the back of her throat, all innocent and naïve. Gone was the confident, demanding tone, the rapid-fire questioning. Her tone held a raw quality to it, like she was saying a final goodbye. As if his answer mattered. As if he mattered.

Her awareness of the brutal, no-holds-barred side of him made him clench, then unclench his free fist. An attempt to keep the calmness that he'd found only moments before intact.

"Listen, it's late. Save your questions for tomorrow." He narrowed his eyes at her, trying for uninviting.

Her shoulders relaxed. *Fucking terrific.* Miss Meddlesome had gotten her second wind.

He might as well flush gentlemanly behavior down the drain. Tonight, being a bastard seemed like a better approach.

"Fine. We'll pick up where we left off tomorrow." She moved slowly toward him, her camera bag and notepad in one hand and a tissue she'd pulled from her pocket in another. "Here," she offered, "your arm is bleeding."

When he didn't move to take it, she reached out. Patted his arm with the rolled-up tissue, gently. Her features softened. Gone was the hellbent reporter. In her place was someone softer, someone who seemed to… care. *Fuck.*

Caden tugged his arm away. The bruise on his cheek throbbed. His temper he held precariously in check. He didn't want someone mothering him. Hell, that feeling was alien—as *upsetting*—as the emotional aftermath of the beating he'd dished out.

"Go," he growled.

"No," she calmly replied. "I can't. You don't look well."

Well? If how he looked matched the fresh wave of pain churning around inside his head, that was the understatement of the century. Especially with the damned steak clutched against his chest and with her patting his arm like an obedient dog.

On top of it all was a wave of lust that stirred his cock to half-mast.

"What the fuck more do you expect from me?" The warning in his tone should have sent her running.

Her eyebrows drew together stubbornly. "Expect? You're standing inches away from me with a deep gaping wound, a cheek the color of a bruised peach, and a puffy eye, growling like a wounded animal in need of attention. You don't remotely resemble the laid-back guy I hitched a ride here with."

"Exactly. Sorry to disappoint you." He folded his arms across his chest, unsure whether the action was intended to protect himself or intimidate her. He chose the latter. "I'm warning you, what you see is what you'll get."

Her brows drew together. "What I'll get is peace of mind knowing you're okay. Let me help you. Return the favor for saving me from those criminals."

Jesus. Couldn't she tell that he was ten times more dangerous at this very moment than any of the amateurs stalking around the parking lot? All he had to do was maneuver her near the bed… If she didn't catch on to his change of heart—didn't get that he was gonna bury himself so deeply inside her she'd forget what he was, forget what she'd seen, forget everything but the feel of him pounding into her—she didn't stand a chance in hell of walking out of here.

She stepped closer, so close he could smell the delicate floral scent of her auburn hair. Without hesitation, she ran the back of her fingers whisper-soft across his stiffening jaw. So warm and tender.

He shifted, pulling away.

She followed, her back to the bed.

That was it. "You wanna help me, huh?"

"Of course. It's the least I could—"

He stepped forward into her space, his heavy, burning erection straining against his sweatpants.

She retreated two small steps. The back of her knees connected with the bed. With one well-placed nudge on the shoulder, she gasped and tumbled onto the mattress.

Too late to stop now.

Reaching out, he plucked the baseball cap off her head and tossed it aside.

Her auburn locks tumbled loose, framing her face. Man alive, she was gorgeous.

"Couldn't leave me alone like I wanted." He ran his finger across his jaw following the same path her fingers had taken seconds earlier, conscious of the way his body reacted to her. Conscious of how this was such a bad idea, and not giving a flying fuck.

"You're going to get more than peace of mind, chili buns. That's all I'm promising."

Chapter 10

NO-HOLDS-BARRED FIGHT: A type of bar fight instigated by someone whose hands are as loose as his lips

This wasn't the kind of help she'd had in mind. But at the moment, she didn't care.

Caden's moods shifted like shadows in the moonlight. Swift, dark, and fleeting. There'd been hurt in his eyes, something he'd tried to hide. She'd bet her bottom dollar the cause wasn't his battered body. Not with the way he mercilessly pressed the tissue to the nasty gash on his arm. He didn't wince once. When she'd gently touched his jaw, something in the way he pulled back made her think it was more of an emotional than physical reaction. A sign that he was suffering.

Heck, she was an expert on burying pain, like a squirrel preparing for the long haul of winter, digging deep to stow its nuts. Except squirrels were absent-minded, they forgot where they hid things. No matter how many years passed, she couldn't seem to forget what the good citizens of Hawley had done. No matter how hard she tried to shake it off. And, with every fiber of her being, she knew that Caden had his own Hawley to contend with.

What hidden wound caused him pain? And if her trash-talking persona was her coat of armor, what was his? Was it possible all his sexcapades, his entire in-her-face-and-then-in-her-panties approach was just a masterful front? Because let's face it, once you headed down that tantalizing pathway, no way in heck were you looking back.

She inhaled sharply, catching the clean, soapy smell of him. His hair was wild, like he hadn't combed it after his shower. Reaching up, she smoothed an errant curl off his forehead, wanting…needing…to comfort him.

He smirked, naughtily. Knowingly. *Masterfully.*

Then he was on her, pressing the full length of his big body over her like an oh-so-hot blanket. And presto, wouldn't you know it, she wasn't just headed down that pathway, she was sprinting down it, with no further thought than the feel of him. On her.

He rubbed up against her.

Her breath hitched, her body in tune with his own.

His grin widened, and presto, his beautiful features transformed back into the man she'd thought she'd known. *Dang-diggity.* His sex appeal could melt steel. Melt all rational thought. Melt even her jaded heart, if she wasn't careful.

"Couldn't leave well enough alone, huh? I knew you'd be trouble," he breathed into her ear. Pulling back to watch her expression, he shifted and ground his thick erection over her moistened core.

She parted her legs wider.

"Jesus," he groaned, low and deep and appreciatively. Leaning in, he captured her lips with his. Hard, aggressive, and oh-so-sweet. His tongue twirled wantonly. She answered in kind, allowing all the pent-up passion out in a kiss to end all kisses.

"Let's get one thing straight." His lips moved against her own, before he pulled off her, taking his weight onto his forearms. His eyes seemed lighter, pale green framed by jet-black lashes.

She tugged his head down and kissed him hard. After a few seconds, she ended it, and instead ran gentle kisses along his jawline, starting near his mouth and working her way to his ear.

"I'm going to make that sweet body of yours sing." As if to prove his point, he took her hand and placed it on his rock-hard erection. "You're gonna get an exclusive, all right. And if you keep looking at me that way, it'll be *multiples*. My specialty."

Oh holy hell. A shiver of excitement coursed through her.

"Bring them on, killer," she heard herself whisper, not knowing what else to say as her mind had already fast-forwarded to the idea of his so-called biggest asset expertly moving inside of her.

Which was why she swallowed back a groan when he stiffened and abruptly broke contact, as if she'd said the L word or something equally outrageous.

"*Killer* is right. I'm not sure how many celebrities

you've interviewed—or freakin' slept with. Who's sprinkled rose petals on your pillow and whispered sweet nothings in your ear. If you want flowers and chocolate, I'm not that guy. Not tonight. Not ever." He paused to readjust himself. Then he leaned closer, so close she could feel the warmth of his breath on her skin. "I'll make it worth your while, darling. Take it or leave it. But make your mind up fast."

"How's this for fast?" Sophie balled up her fist and smashed it against his uninjured cheek. "Get off of me, you jerk."

Immediately, he rolled off her and onto his back. "Hell," he muttered, massaging his cheek. Sophie sat up and straightened her blouse, trying to calm her temper.

She came up onto her knees on the mattress and glared down at him, lying on his back with his arms behind his head, seemingly oblivious to the sucker punch he'd issued to her heart. "Flowers. Fucking candy. How many fucking celebrities do you think I've *entertained*?" She winced as her ugly cuss words filled the space between them.

"Hate to break it to you, Sophie, but no chance in hell of a red-blooded American male ever confusing you with a virgin. Not with that mouth of yours and all. You put on quite a performance five nights a week. America's got your number, you made certain of that. After all, 'sexy is as sexy does.' And I'm game for finding out exactly what that means."

Damn. Her own words had come back to stab her in the throat. Moisture coated her eyelashes. Double damn. Would she ever be able to shed her *Late Night* persona?

"Don't think I give two shits, sweetheart. It's not like they're rolling around on the mattress with us."

"You think I slept my way to the top." She blinked her tears away and sat up straighter. This was her fault for allowing this playboy jock to manipulate her. Letting his sullen brooding act suck her in. Letting him get closer to her than any other man. She'd been played by the king of players. And, boy, did it smart.

"Hey, I'm not judging you." His head was back on a pillow and he was staring at the ceiling. She felt like grabbing the other one and smacking him in the head.

"Just wanted to let you know how it was gonna be," he muttered petulantly. "Thought I was being considerate."

"Bullshit."

He shifted his weight. She momentarily lost her balance, and had to place her hands on his thigh to stop from toppling over and on to him. The big jerk.

She wanted to scramble off the mattress but the beast was blocking her way. Hell, if he wanted Sophie Morelle and her smart mouth, he was going to get it.

"You know what? I've been overly considerate of you and your mood swings. You're one coldhearted bastard." She snorted and poked him in the thigh. "You're good, all right. Playing me like that. Making me feel sorry for—"

He rolled, twisted and rose onto his knees. A second later, she was back underneath him.

"I don't want your pity. Got it?"

She blinked, and blinked again. His eyes were full of pain.

For a brief moment, their gazes locked. Then he shut her out.

He hadn't been playing me.

He rolled onto his back and studied the ceiling.

She moved onto her side, propped her head up on her hand, and swiped the hair out of her face in order to get a better look at him.

With his hands beneath his head, he looked as if he'd smoked a fine cigarette in bed and was enjoying the effects. This time, she wasn't fooled by his seemingly heartless act. Maybe, just maybe, she'd gotten through to him.

"You're not a *killer*, okay?" She pronounced *killer* slowly, deliberately. "Jeez, one little word…" Taking a deep breath, she waited to see how he'd respond.

"The door is over there. Use it."

Deflecto-mundo. "Message received, loud and clear."

He grunted. As if to say, *end of discussion.*

She searched for some neutral ground, words to lighten the tension that rolled through the room like midnight waves. That, or she could leave. But his reaction proved her right, there was a fragility within him. A side of Caden she needed to figure out. Just like she sensed *he* needed *her* right now.

"So, do you think Sal could have taken the guy who blocked our way?"

He stiffened, sighing. For another awkward moment, he didn't budge or say anything. Then, he turned her way. "If the old-timer can produce a sirloin out of the blue, I'm not counting him out. But that man is proving to be a real nuisance." Reaching beneath him, he pulled out the still-frozen steak.

She grinned.

"I'm sorry, you know. About my bad attitude. About hurting you. I'm not fit for company, especially after a fight like that."

She felt her smile drop, both from shock and from

something more. Something deeper. "Do you want to talk about it?"

"Nope."

She sighed. "You were way off the mark, you know. Being one of the few women on late night was hard. But I earned it, and not by rolling around on the network couches. Heck, I graduated from the Walter Cronkite School of Journalism. Magna cum laude. Bet you didn't expect to hear that."

"Nope. But I'm not surprised, either. That's what I like about you the most, your gumption." Reaching out, he cupped her cheek and ran his thumb over her skin. Her face warmed, along with the rest of her. "I'm listening," he prompted. The arrogance, the hurt, was gone from his tone. He sounded gentle, almost humble.

"You realize *I'm* the reporter and *you* are the guy I should be interviewing."

"Deflecto-mundo. Go on."

She wanted to roll her eyes. His thumb continued across her cheek and softly ran along her jawline, all the way to her mouth.

"I landed a freelance spot at the *Arizona Times*. My seventh assignment earned a *Courage in Journalism* award from the International Women's Media Foundation. I was part of a team that exposed an underground drug cartel working the border. They were busted and arrested on my twenty-fourth birthday." She shook her head. "I don't know why I'm rambling on and telling you this." *Maybe, just maybe, you'll confide in me.*

"Yes, you do."

She stiffened. Had she been that transparent?

He grinned.

Perceptive man.

"Why late night?"

"Big mistake." She drew in a deep breath, then blurted out the truth. "I sold out for the money and fame. And some sort of warped respect, like being someone people knew and quoted on the streets was important. Prove to the people back home in Hawley, especially that Hank Cawfield…" *Oh, no. Damn. Damn. Damn.*

She tugged herself away from his touch and rolled onto her back.

To his credit, he repositioned his head on the pillow next to her.

It seemed like hours before he broke the silence. "This documentary means a lot to you, huh? An exclusive with me," he snorted, "won't be as spectacular as taking down a drug cartel, but it should draw some attention—for what it's worth."

"Yeah." She didn't trust the tremble in her voice enough to say anything further. Maybe now was a good time to grab her camcorder and head back to her room.

"Who would have thought we'd have such a shitload in common?"

"You're tired, too? Better head back to my room then."

He responded by sliding off the bed, crossing the room, and returning with two bottles of water. "I have something stronger stashed away in the nightstand."

Sophie shook her head. After the catastrophic night they'd had, hard liquor was asking for trouble. Heading back to her room was the best idea. A safe environment where she could regroup. Alone. She didn't know which was worse, feeling Caden's pain or her own.

Caden reclined back onto the bed and took a long drink of water. When he finished, he carefully placed the half-emptied bottle on the nightstand, and turned her way. "I would have offered you something to eat along with the drink, but it's frozen solid over there on the carpet."

She offered a weak smile and took a sip from her water. The tepid liquid soothed the dryness in her throat. She almost choked when she looked up and saw the concern in his expression. Noticing *her*, Sophie, not the trash-talking woman he'd commented on earlier. Looking long and deep, like the way he'd polished off his water.

Like he understood, and wasn't running for the hills.

She took another sip, longer this time.

When she'd finished, he reached over, plucked the bottle from her grasp, and set it beside his own. "Relax."

Really? Relax? They'd been riding an emotional rollercoaster for half an hour and he wanted her to relax?

"Take off your pants."

"What?"

"Change of plans. Take 'em off. Quick, before I nod off."

Caden was as alert as ever, nowhere near sleep. Maybe he had bouts of narcolepsy too. She doubted it.

"Ten. Nine. Eight."

"Um…I'm not wearing—"

"Seven."

What the heck, it wasn't like she hadn't taken the plunge in this direction moments earlier. Wasn't like the anticipation wasn't killing her. Wasn't like she didn't want him.

"You asked for it, buddy." Without further comment, she raised her hips off the bed and shimmied out of her slacks. Shook them out and folded them, then rolled toward the edge of the bed and placed them on the nightstand.

Caden made a strange sound, like the wind had been sucked out of him.

She rolled back his way and gasped when she caught the look in his eyes. *Oh. My. God.*

A lifetime passed as his gaze roamed over her body. Inch by inch of her warmed under his regard. Second by second his eyes grew hotter. Then he flashed her a smile, one that gripped her heart and squeezed, making her breathless.

With a finger, he touched her bare midriff. Oh-so-slowly, his finger drifted down around her belly button and lower still, until his digit found her soft curls. Tracing slow circles, he stroked her mound. The pad of his finger swirled first one way, then the other, shooting sparks of pleasure through her entire body. She lifted her hips, but not enough to cause his digit to shift lower, where her nub was doing a flag salute. Not enough to find her wetness.

"Beautiful. The color of chili powder." His voice deep and full of gravel. "Let's find out how many times we can make you explode."

He moved so darn fast his comment was lost on her. Her long, bare leg rested on top of his thigh. With one hand, he deftly unbuttoned her blouse. His other hand lingered, stubbornly refusing to shift lower, to the delicate nub swollen with need. Just a little attention, that's all she required. Caden promised an explosion, not realizing that the powder keg of lust begging for his touch was about ready to blast the roof off this motel.

Sooner, rather than later.

Her blouse fell open and he worked an arm free and

slid it off her. He worked his palms over her breasts and grinned at her moan. Grabbing the hem of her cami, he worked it up and over her head.

Then his fingers returned to her curls while his other hand cupped her breast, testing out the weight of it.

He pinched a nipple, gentle but with enough force that a jolt of electricity shot through her.

Light as a whisper, he thumbed her nub. Just enough to make her buck toward his hand.

Caden laughed.

She reached over and cupped the rigid length of him through his sweats.

His laughter stopped. But, boy-oh-boy, his fingers certainly didn't. His thumbs played her body like a song, alternating between a firm rub of her nipple and a slick slide over her folds.

She grinned at the feel of his cock jerking beneath her palm.

In the next cycle of thumbs, his at last sank into her warm wetness. Then he rubbed his digit over her nub, moistening it. "Tsk. Tsk. Why so serious?" he murmured playfully.

Curse him. This devil knew just how to play her and get her revved up and raring to go, both in and out of bed.

He traced the trail of moisture left by his thumb with a finger, over and across her curls and, with a gentle nudge, worked it inside of her. She opened to him like a spring rose as he added another finger and established a mind-altering rhythm. His fingers plunged deeper, more forcefully, and he shifted her leg higher on his hip.

Her body began cresting in a slow-rising hum.

Suddenly, he was gone.

She bit back a cry of protest.

Then cried out in surprise as he rolled their bodies so her back was to the mattress and her legs spread open with him between them.

He laughed. "I'm about to wipe that frown straight off your face, chili bean. Know what I want?"

Oh, multiple responses to that question sprang to mind. Dang, if she didn't want the same things, all of them. *Now.*

"Now?" he chuckled.

Oh, crap. I said it aloud.

"Now, now, patience comes to those that wait." He bent over and licked a nipple.

Yes.

He pulled back. "Are you getting the drift of where things are going?"

Jeez. "Can we get there already? Please, take off your sweats."

He sat back, still straddling her with his legs bearing his weight. "No can do."

She growled low in her throat.

He laughed. "That's the spirit. You see, I need to know the answer to a question that's been on my mind."

"Listen, Chatty Cathy…"

He snorted, then burst out laughing, deep and genuine, like he'd been holding it back and waiting for the right time to grace her with the sound of it. When it ended, he tilted his head and bit down lightly on her other nipple. His other hand found her core and his fingers drew a line between her wet folds.

Instantly, her body picked up where it had left off seconds ago. She spread her legs wider.

"Point taken. But one more thing," he whispered in

her ear. She didn't care, as his hands were talking as well. "I wanna know how sweet chili pepper tastes."

Holy crapola. His words stirred up a lust so swift she nearly climaxed on the spot.

The bed shifted. His breath warmed her stomach. His tongue caressed her skin. Lightly at first, then more firmly as he licked his way along the same path his fingers had taken earlier, around her belly button and down a straight line to her curls. He paused and with both hands, spread her legs wider. Then his tongue was everywhere. Roaming over her nub, licking between her folds, and plunging so deep inside of her, she groaned.

He didn't say another word. That gorgeous tongue of his—what else did she expect?—did all the talking.

She'd swear she saw a smile on his face as he sucked, licked and plundered her.

Nothing in his actions were rough or hard. The complete opposite, in fact, with the expert way he played her body. For the first time in her life, she felt cherished.

So close.

Her fingers wove into his hair, tugging him in. Feeling the heat from his tongue's long strokes as she peaked and spiraled out of control.

Chapter 11

HAYMAKER: A good ole fashioned punch, most often witnessed in barnyards

Caden cursed under his breath as he plucked the last pink petal off the single rose he'd purchased back in the manager's office. What made him dream up this dumb move, he didn't know. He sprinkled the final handful onto Sophie's pillow.

She murmured incomprehensibly. The smile that *he'd* put on her lips remained.

Another considerate gesture from an inconsiderate guy.

Thoughtfulness wasn't his usual mode of operation. A long, hard fuck or women pleasuring him, not the other way around, that was the deal. Hell, he was a self-

ish guy. Usually he held his women physically close—
hell, buried balls deep inside them—but kept himself
emotionally distant. No romantic bullshit. No regrets.
No weird desire to climb back in bed and freakin' spoon
up against her.

Sophie sneezed and her eyelashes fluttered, but she
didn't wake.

He grinned down at her, pleased she was exhausted.
He'd brought her to climax twice, first with his mouth,
then with his fingers. Enjoyed it, too. Thinking about
the way her skin flushed pink and the little moan she
gave as she peaked made him hard.

Once more he contemplated crawling back into bed
and wrapping himself around her, just the position he'd
found himself in when he'd woken up.

His cold, calculated manner—one of several steel-
thick layers protecting his own vulnerability—hadn't
discouraged her in the slightest. Though for a second,
when he'd mentioned how she'd slept her way to the
top, he'd thought he'd actually hurt her. As for throwing
her off track with sex talk, that had them both wanting
to get down-and-dirty quicker than a country swing
dance. Shaking his head, he moved away from the bed
and finished stuffing his clothing into his bag, leaving
a fresh set out to change into.

Sophie'd seen past his bullshit.

Neat, tidy, unemotional and mutually satisfying.
That's how he liked to keep things. Sentimental sui-
cide, that's what this was.

All the more reason to hightail it out of Dodge.

Which was what he'd been trying to do for the past
half hour, having woken the motel manager up to get
the garage keys. And the goddamn rose.

As he stripped, the nagging sensation that he'd made some kind of unspoken promise persisted.

He looked around the room, spotted the camera bag she'd placed on the chair by the wall, then turned back to the woman sleeping soundly in bed. He'd seen a side of her he hadn't expected. Someone had hurt her, likely an ex—Hank Cawfield? That the pain still lingered was clear. It left her softer than expected, more vulnerable.

Surprising. Yet nothing about last night was typical.

Suddenly, he had the desire to leave her with something, something more than the petals he'd tossed on her pillow and the smile he'd put on her lips.

Striding over to the chair, he removed her camcorder from the bag, then returned to bed and settled back down on the mattress beside her. Adjusting the sheet around his nakedness, he flipped open the viewfinder, held up the camcorder, and hit record.

"Hey, there. This is Caden Kelly. I decided to throw a bone out to Sophie Morelle, who's been relentlessly bugging me to reveal all." He paused. Yeah, he'd like to do nothing better right now than throw the covers off, reveal *all*—namely his thick, heavy member—then throw *her* the bone and fuck her right out of his system. *Shit for bricks*. Absentmindedly, he moved his free hand to her pillow and lifted a lock of auburn hair before he continued on with a safer topic. Wrapping it around his fingers tempered the resurgence of lust that had gripped him by the balls. "First, let's start with two of my favorite fighting styles, Sanshou and Greco-Roman wrestling, and how I trained with masters in each specifically for Tetnus."

He went on to describe how learning to kick properly was the foundation for a fighter's being effective in the Octagon, and how a well-balanced fighter needed to be trained in multiple disciplines, and have a wide variety of maneuvers perfected if they wanted to fight professionally. Lost himself for a good five minutes as he shared his passion for mixed martial arts, until Sophie let out a thunderous sneeze and brought his attention back to her.

Guess I'm not being an attentive enough bed partner, he thought wickedly. Lifting his hand, he studied the smooth strands of hair curled around his fingers. He smirked into the camera before lowering it to reveal his chest, then…her.

Man, she was gorgeous, her cheeks still flushed pink with pleasure and her hair spread out across the pillow like dark, rich sunbeams.

The thought caused him to frown. What time was it? The morning sun had begun to break through the dingy curtains. A signal—time to bolt, and with a clearer conscience.

He'd finish their exclusive in Vegas, after he'd time to get his head back on straight.

For now, he'd settle for putting some mileage on the Aston.

Though the company he'd be keeping wasn't as sweet. Call it goodwill or whatnot, he'd granted her another favor by agreeing to take Jerry along for the ride. She could have free rein over the Boys on the newly repaired bus without the sleazeball's interference.

Besides, time with Jerry meant time to figure out what he knew about the steroids. While filming, it had dawned on him that he could record the loudmouth using an iPhone app and get solid proof that the man was dealing drugs. Then turn both the duffel bag and the audio over to Bracken when they hit Vegas.

Better the media focus on the hardcore bouts and martial arts skills that set MMA fighters apart from other athletes, than substance abuse. A scandal would ruin Tetnus, threaten his comeback, put him back to work as a cock jockey quicker than you could say "chili bean." Caden hadn't come this far to have some asshole ruin it all.

Running his hand through his hair, he raked his gaze over her. Liking how her creamy pale skin seemed even more flushed than it had earlier. Naughty minx. Was she dreaming about him? Man, how he liked the idea that he'd rocked her world. His lips twitched as his eyes fell on the pale pink rose petal plastered to her cheek.

She sneezed once more, his signal it was time to split. On his way out, he turned the A/C unit off.

Hell, he didn't want to like her.

"Gosh darn it," Sophie exclaimed, struggling to find her equilibrium on the hard, vinyl bus seat. Grabbing hold of the seatback in front of her, she braced herself for another pothole. The day had gone from bad to worse, and was headed toward horrific. It was all playboy extraordinaire Caden Kiss-'n'-Dash Kelly's fault.

She hoped someone put a ding in the Aston Martin and his insurance premium skyrocketed.

"Bobby Tom, ya think you can take those pits in the roadway a bit slower? My teeth are about to fall outta my gums," Sal hollered at the bus driver from his seat next to her. "Hate to say it, but Jerry did a helluva better job in the driver's seat. Of course, the gas pedal could've nipped him in the ole ankle and he'd still refuse to press down on it." Sal attempted to murmur under his breath, but his kind of quiet was loud enough the entire population of Vegas probably heard him.

The bus driver pumped the pedal and slammed into another pothole. It seemed like Sophie wasn't the only one looking for retaliation of some sort.

"One more pothole, and I'm taking over the wheel," the old-timer grumbled, settling back into their seat and closing his eyes.

She grimaced.

The action caused an immediate burn on her face, but she tucked her hands beneath her legs and refused to give into the itch. Scowling was a surefire way of aggravating the rash covering her left cheek and a large expanse of her upper chest.

No one deserved to wake up as she had, feeling as if an invisible pillow was smothering her, suffocating her. What she initially thought were pink candy wrappers sprinkled over the pillows and sheets had turned out to be rose petals. Harmless pink candy wrappers? *Wrong-o-mundo.*

Lethal, allergen-laden pink roses?

Exact-o-mundo.

Sophie frowned, and ignored the resulting itch. What had Caden been thinking? Leaving flowers for a woman after sex was tacky as hell. But when the woman was highly allergic to flowers, it was plain ole hellish, like he'd littered the bed with African snapping beetles, or worse.

Bad enough it felt as if massive cotton balls had been shoved inside her nostrils. But her cheek and chest swelled up too, irritated beyond belief and itching like holy bejeezus.

Was he trying to kill her?

Not that Caden would have stuck around for her funeral, or anything. Heck, he could have at least have woken her up after...

She frowned. What had she expected from the king of players, anyway?

Not toxic roses, that's for sure.

Bet Mr. Houdini himself couldn't have pulled off such a well-executed vanishing act. His missing bag had been all the proof she needed that he hadn't simply stepped outside. Nope. Caden had made a run for it, disappeared, and was probably long gone. She hadn't seen it coming—not after what had transpired last night.

No words. Nada. Except for the stinking rose petals.

Fortunately, he'd taken Jerry with him. Left her with semi-helpful Sal, albeit on this lame excuse of a bus that stank of bad aftershave and that was warmer than a sauna in the Sonoran Desert.

She rubbed her cheek and instantly regretted it. The Benadryl hadn't yet kicked in. Mercifully, Sal had made the bus take a pit stop at Target, where she'd purchased some supplies. It took some stealth avoiding the Boys, by being the first person off the bus and the last one back on it, though most had had their butts kicked in last night's street fights and were sleeping away their defeats or hanging their heads.

Anger rose up inside of her, thinking about the money she'd used to make the purchase.

A single bill from the substantial roll of Franklins had covered everything. Caden had left a thick wad of hundreds on the nightstand on her side of the bed. Payment for her services, which was ironic in itself, considering last night had been all about her pleasure.

She'd reimburse him, hundred by bleeding hundred, when her documentary took off. Or—and boy, did this strike a nerve—was this some form of compensation for a broken promise? Payment for dodging his exclusive once again?

Houdini Jr. had better believe that she meant to hold him to his promises.

She stood and grabbed her camera case from the overhead bin, reminded how there were much more important things to think about than him.

Sal snored gently in the seat next to her. So much for him smoothing things over with the Boys. Yep, the old-timer had been as helpful as a rock. Sophie was reminded once more that she had no one to depend upon but her own resourceful self.

Carefully, she headed toward the back of the bus. Heck, maybe her rash would make the Boys take pity on her, empathize with her, considering their own battered faces and coagulated cuts.

Misery loved company, right?

"How the hell did she get back on the bus?" someone snorted. Sophie tottered forward in search of a friendly face.

"She's got that camera out again."

"Bad luck, a woman traveling on our bus. Look what happened to us last night."

A superstitious crew? Or just ignorant of the fact that Jerry was the person actually responsible for their battered bodies?

Midway down the aisle, the bus rolled. Sophie caught herself before she tumbled face-first into the laps of two of the Boys to her left. Before she could fully collect her footing, a flash of green landed at her feet.

She caught Anthony—sitting solo in the seat to her right—honing in on the thick wad. His eyes lit up with interest.

Sophie seized the moment.

Scooping up the bills, she waved them in front of his face. "Look, I know I got off to a rocky start with you guys—"

He grunted loudly, cutting her off. "Jaysin better not wake up and find you on this bus or things are gonna get ugly."

It was Sophie's turn to freeze. Jaysin? "He was released from the hospital?" she whispered. No way would she have gotten on the bus if she'd known he was on it.

"Jumped outta the ambulance before they could haul him away. Ripped the IV right out of his arm. Took out two of the medics when they tried to stop him."

Nervously, she glanced back down the aisle and contemplated returning to her seat up front. Play it safe and hide out until they stopped. As much as she wanted this documentary, Jaysin was too unpredictable. Too unstable. Too dangerous. She'd sneak off the bus with Jaysin none the wiser.

If she made it to the next pit stop alive.

Or she'd befriend another bodyguard. Her gaze fell back on Anthony, who was still eyeballing the money. Before he could guess her intent, she climbed over his lap, squirming her way between his body and the seat back. Nudging him over and away from the window, she smoothed out her slacks and put her camera bag on her lap.

His massive bulk would be a buffer between her and Jaysin, if he spotted her. Anthony opened his mouth but closed it at the sight of the bills she waved in his face. She hit him with her best Sophie Morelle smile.

He stiffened beside her. *Okay, wrong approach.*

One slick-talking exclusive had snuck out on her this morning and she was about to miss another opportunity with Anthony. Somehow, she had to connect with him. She searched her mind for the right words to butter him up. In a low voice, she began. "You could be the next big thing in MMA."

"Like Caden?"

She clenched her teeth before answering, "Bigger than Caden."

His head tilted slightly to the side, seemingly interested. *Good boy.*

"I'd like to show America what a day in the life of an average fighter is like. You'd be one of only a few fighters featured in my film."

"I'm not an average fighter," he growled. "Find someone else." He squirmed away from her, like a child upset by his mother's reprimand.

Dang it.

She let a few minutes slide by and focused her attention on removing the camcorder from its case. Oh, she was getting this interview, all right. "Don't you want the recognition you deserve after all the physical training you've done for Tetnus?"

Anthony ignored her.

"This documentary is going to be the first of its kind. Think fame. Think endorsements."

He moved a fraction of an inch closer.

Good, she had his attention.

"I'm willing to pay you for your time." *With Caden's*

pimp money. Oh, she'd fork over a piece of her profits to Houdini Jr., along with a piece of her mind.

That caught his attention. "How much?"

Bingo. "How does a couple hundred sound? But first, you need to sign a waiver giving me permission to use the footage." She shuffled through her camera bag and retrieved the authorization packet and a pen. "Here. Read through this, and initial on the lines by each clause. Then sign on the bottom line on page three. By the time you're done, my camera will be ready to roll."

"How do I know I can trust you?"

"Ask me anything you want and I'll give you a direct answer."

"What happened to your face?" He looked horrified. Was it really that bad? A sudden flash of vulnerability bubbled up inside of her, as if the rash on her cheek left her open and weak. Sophie did not like the feeling. *Not. One. Bit.*

"Some asswipe pumped me and dumped me. He thought roses would make me feel better. Moron—I'm allergic." *Alrighty.* She sounded like good ole Sophie Morelle at her finest.

Anthony jerked back as if she'd tossed a scorpion onto the seatback in front of them. She'd shocked him for sure.

"Go on. Fill out the paperwork. I'll be ready in a second." Unfolding the viewfinder, she went through her meticulous routine of checking the battery life and monitoring the GB usage on her SD card. The percentage shown caused her to shake her head. She hadn't filmed much of anything yet, except last night's fiasco. Maybe her camera had been on during her KAN interviews after all?

She hit Rewind and waited a few seconds. Her eyes shifted to Anthony, who was initialing the agreement like a good boy. Remembering the footage shot of shady Jerry, she positioned the camcorder comfortably on her thigh, angled it so Anthony couldn't see the screen, and pressed the mute button. Then she hit Play.

Caden's smug face filled the viewfinder.

She fell back in her seat as if he'd reached out and sucker punched her.

"Careful or you'll make me smudge my initials," Anthony warned.

When had Caden gotten a hold of her camera? Her eyes narrowed as the answer became obvious. There he was, bare from the chest up, with a sheet tugged over his lap and the yellowed headboard from the motel behind him. Smug as could be, lying beside her. He must have filmed this after they'd…

The camera tottered precariously on her leg as her heart jumped in surprise. He was talking, his expression first thoughtful, then animated. She thought about moving back to the front seat and listening to exactly what Caden Kiss-'n'-Dash Kelly had to say for himself. It couldn't be good.

With her attention fixed on the screen, she watched as Caden rambled on and on, wondering what he was up to and wishing she could raise the volume—but she didn't dare. If he was giving a recount of last night…?

Anthony asked her a question. She answered yes, not really hearing him. How long was this footage?

Her breath hitched when Caden stopped speaking and shot the camera one of his infamous grins. His eyes danced. She realized deep down inside, she hoped he'd been reliving their evening, hoped that smile might be for her.

He panned the camera lower.

Her mouth went dry, and drier still, as it shifted across his torso, followed the thin line of hair leading downward over his abdomen. The sheet barely covered him. Most viewers would think he was as naked as sin.

The camera jostled, up at the ceiling and then down onto... *Oh. Holy. Crapola.*

There she was, grinning in her sleep. Looking like she'd gone to heaven. His finger was in the shot, a lock of her red hair twined around it.

"Here you go. So, what do you want to know about me?" Anthony was shoving his release forms toward her.

She fumbled with the camera and hit fast-forward. "One second, okay?" Relief filled her senses at being found out. But it was mingled with disappointment. What the heck was that video all about—with him curling her hair? Some weird form of sex tape, taken *after* the fact?

Caden had snuck out on his exclusive...and on *her*, she reminded herself. This giddy nonsense had to stop. *Must. Focus. On. Documentary.*

She sat up straighter on the hard seat. "Ready. The first few questions will be background stuff, okay?"

Anthony grabbed a small black comb from his pocket and ran it through his hair. Once satisfied with the results, he tucked it away, and faced her. Lifting the camera, she pressed play. "Rolling. Tell us a bit about yourself, Anthony. Where you're from and what you liked to do as a child," she directed.

"My name is Anthony Mastrantonio. I'm an Italian-American." He looked at her for approval.

Sophie nodded. "Such a grand name, Mastrantonio. I'm guessing you're from a family of fighters, all built like brick houses, right? Muscular and in prime shape. Brothers whose butts you kicked all over Chicago—or wherever you were raised? Practicing and honing your immense talent?"

Anthony shook his head. "I'm an only child, from New Haven, Connecticut. Mom and Dad are both doctors. They wanted me to go to medical school but I couldn't pull the grades. Guess I didn't inherit the smart gene. Plus, I didn't care for school much. Rather be outside, running around. I have focus issues which didn't help. Do you know what ADHD is?"

"Attention Deficit Hyperactivity Disorder. A common disorder that a lot of successful people just like yourself have. Come to think of it, I bet you'd make a terrific spokesperson for an ADHD organization, being someone who's overcome challenges and achieved their goals, like fighting in the Tetnus championship."

"My parents might disagree with you on that one. I wanted to be a quarterback or first baseman. Took a long time to convince them that I wasn't doctor material. They caved, and let me go to a public school to play." He grunted. "They didn't know about the underground fight clubs. I found out awfully quick I was good at something. I fucking love this sport."

Sophie frowned, thoughtfully. "You went to a private school before that?"

"Yep, Shady Brook Prep."

"You know, I'm glad you agreed to do this interview," she commented, honestly. "The general impres-

sion of MMA fighters—the Boys, which is what one of
the old-time trainers has coined this group of athletes,"
she clarified for the camera, "is that you're kind of like
the WrestleMania guys. You know, with every move
pre-choreographed."

Anthony's eyes hardened.

His reaction was clear enough for viewers to pick up
on. "Or," Sophie hastened to redirect their discussion,
thinking back on Caden, and how the mere memory of
wrestling around on the mattress with him caused a curl
of lust to fire up inside of her, "another misperception
is that MMA fighters are a bunch of rough-around-the-
edges, beefed-up brawlers, with no rhyme or reason behind their fighting. Street punks and no-holds-barred
fighters. Not private-school kids."

She peered over the camera at him to assess his reaction, hoping her comment didn't hit another nerve.
He seemed puzzled so she added, "Like hardcore back
alley city boys."

"Like Caden, you mean."

"What?"

"Street-bred. With skills you can't learn in a gym or
from a teacher. If you're talking hardcore, he's the real
deal. One time, he took on this total animal, a fighter
with at least fifteen pounds on him. Won the bout in
three seconds, giving the guy a hammer fist to the nose.
See, it's not just skill, but mad instincts. Guess when
you grow up on the streets, where you survive by defending yourself…hell. Hey, are you okay?"

Okay? She couldn't find her breath.

"If you could only see the expression on your face.
Never judge a book by its cover, ain't that right?"

"Could you please clarify what you mean when

you say *street-bred*?" She hoped the lift in her voice wouldn't be easily detectible to viewers. A curveball had been tossed her way, and Sophie's journalist's glove instinctively reached high to claim it. Oh, she'd known there was more to Caden Kelly than met the eye. Something the general public would be more than thrilled to discover. Last night, she'd succumbed to his charm instead of pressing him for information. Given the state of their relationship, she couldn't afford to make the same mistake with Caden. No matter how much hearing the truth bothered her.

"Ah, I don't know that much about him. Just repeating what I've heard."

"Which is?"

"That Caden's one tough motherfucker, much tougher than he lets on. A lot of guys underestimated him—still do. He's the man to beat at Tetnus, though. I'd bet my last dollar on him." Anthony crunched the hundreds in his palm, a thoughtful look on his face. "The way he handled himself last night…"

Good thing she kept the camera fixed on Anthony because her cheeks were scorching, the rash only adding to her misery. *If he only knew.* Man, at the next stop, she was *so* going to delete Caden's sex tape.

"Explain for the viewers what you mean by how he… um…handled himself. I saw him land a few solid kicks, and some solid throws." She frowned, remembering the way Caden sat on top of the bald thug, raining punches down on the guy.

"Well, Caden can read his opponent like nobody's business. When a fighter comes at him with a haymaker, Caden's elbow is already up and he's feeding the guy a mouthful of teeth. Or else Caden's wrapping him up and taking him to the ground. That's where street smarts gets you, into the head of your opponent. Mix that up with mad martial arts skills, and you've got yourself one helluva fighter."

"Haymaker," she began to clarify, "is a lethal punch. Don't let these names fool you. It's not two fighters wrestling around in a barnyard." *Or two consenting adults making hay of each other on a motel mattress.*

Anthony looked at her like she'd just taken a roll around the grimy bus floor.

She continued, thinking hard about what she'd learned about MMA striking skills. "It's a standard tough-guy move, like when someone winds up, swings, and puts their entire body weight behind the punch. If you know it's coming, all you need to do is block it with the outside of your elbow. Leaves the guy completely open for retaliation from either a punch or a take down."

"Correct," Anthony said. She could tell she'd surprised him with her explanation. "A take down," he added, "is when a fighter is wrestled to the mat."

"But Caden didn't wrestle his opponent to the mat last night."

"Nope. That's why he's got mad street smarts. Instead, Caden used a spinning hook kick. Now, that's usually used on an opponent's head, but Caden nailed him in the leg. Knew he had the guy off balance. Knew he'd put a hurting on him big time."

She remembered the way the EMT crew had rushed into the cage. The way it took three men to yank Caden off the guy. A street fighter with the good looks of someone who'd been weaned at a country club. A street fighter with a gentle side.

If she hadn't been so wrapped up in him last night,

she'd have realized he'd shown her both sides of himself. The mean snarling brute had demanded she leave, and the more wholesome guy had been nothing less than spectacular. She might be pissed at his Houdini act but she had nothing negative to say about his skills between the sheets.

Anthony turned away from the camera. All this talk about Caden was probably making him weary. The guy wasn't even here and he'd still managed to steal someone's thunder.

"What would you get out of winning Tetnus, Anthony?" she questioned. "Besides the million-dollar purse."

Anthony grunted and turned back her way. "What any fighter wants. To be recognized as the toughest man in America. Fame. A better name for himself. Better future fights. Better life. The money doesn't hurt though." Her eyes fell to the crumpled bills in his hand, and she wondered at what the real cost had been for him to leave the comfy confines of Connecticut for this hell ride to Vegas.

As if guessing her thoughts, he held out his palm. "Here. I don't want your money. I was only messing with you."

Dang-diggity. A fighter with a conscience. She smiled weakly, and accepted the bills.

A time long ago, when she'd been desperate to get out of Hawley, she'd have done about anything for money.

"You know, Sophie, you're not the bitch I thought you were."

"I kind of like you too, Anthony. Maybe you'll become a star because of Tetnus. I hope so." Her comment was genuine, and not for the cameras.

The bus hit a pothole, sending Sophie airborne. The new driver Jerry'd hired wasn't any better than the rest of the lot.

A chorus of dirty curses sounded from the back of the bus.

Time to seek shelter far up front.

She clicked off her camera.

Disappointment was written all over Anthony's face. "It'll do you justice. You'll be amazing, I promise you," she whispered. "But this rolling sardine can isn't the best place for this. I'll compile a list of questions and we'll resume our discussion in Vegas."

Anthony looked puzzled, which gave her pause. According to her schedule, Vegas was the next and final stop. Something Sal had said earlier, back in the shack motel, about the next appearance, not *final*…but *next*. Dang-diggity, this joyride wasn't taking another unplanned pothole, right?

After carefully packing her equipment away, she climbed over Anthony and made her way back to her seat, far away from Mr. Scorpion King.

Sal slept on, oblivious to the raucous noise taking over the bus.

Sophie sank down in the seat next to him, wondering how much longer until they reached the next pit stop.

Chapter 12

ANACONDA CHOKE: A camping trip gone horribly wrong

Somewhere in the middle of the desert between Albuquerque and Phoenix, the Aston Martin blew a head gasket.

Caden could deal with engine problems. He could put up with the oddball route Jerry'd mapped out for the trip, having them head south, then west, then north, instead of in a more direct northern route to Phoenix. He could tolerate the one-hundred-twenty-five-degree temperature—the baseball cap he'd dug out of his bag helped. But he was about to quiet Jerry with a fist if he didn't change his tune. Fast.

As the heat spiked, so did Jerry's frustration. And,

judging by the manic way the douchebag was pacing up and down the barren asphalt highway, kicking at the desert dirt and muttering curses, his temper was about to skyrocket. If heatstroke didn't do him in first.

Caden was close to his breaking point, as well.

Three hours ago, Harold had arranged for a tow truck. They'd bummed a lift a half mile down the highway to a dilapidated 1950's-style gas station.

Two hours and fifty-nine minutes ago, Jerry had pounded the digits on his cell phone and demanded the bus pick them up. Seemed the mechanics needed a specialized part which had to be driven in from God knows where.

Caden expected to wait five hours, minimum, for the bus to rescue him. He hoped it'd happen sometime before he took Jerry by the neck and shook him, a sure way of ruining his chances at Tetnus. He needed the asshole, he kept reminding himself. Which was why, after three long hours, Caden was surprised to spot the vehicle way off in the horizon. Hard to miss it.

Not a moment too soon.

"If I have to cancel tomorrow night's appearance in Phoenix, it's coming out of your pocket." Jerry's voice rose, drawing Caden's attention back to him. Boy, the cheap-as-shit promoter had some mad sense of entitlement. Last night, they'd had time to kill, the bus was that far behind. Per Jerry, it had driven nonstop through the night so as to make it to Phoenix on time. Which meant Caden had ended up paying for Jerry's hotel room, meals, and extensive beer tab, without receiving so much as a thank you. He'd gone on this freakin' road trip because Jerry had demanded it of his fighters.

Yep, Jerry had served his purpose—as useful as an electric heater on a day like today.

Based on Caden's subtle questioning and Jerry's big mouth, it was doubtful the promoter had anything to do with the steroids. Surprising, but true. Oh, he'd bragged about being the mastermind behind the illegal bets run at events he'd scheduled. The way he double-dipped, taking money from the top, fifty percent of admission, and the bottom, the lucrative betting system he had going on off on the side.

But when Caden brought up the topic of drugs, Jerry didn't even flinch. In fact, he'd described in detail why he'd never deal. It had nothing to do with morals, which hadn't surprised Caden, and everything to do with money. The man was invested heavily in the MMA scene and, like Caden, hated the idea that performance-enhancing drugs might hurt this sport—like all those baseball Hall of Fame records now under scrutiny.

Beyond the money, Jerry had an aversion to blood. Ironic, given that the Boys spewed enough of it during bouts. But blood transfusions were all the rage in steroids. An athlete could purify his own blood, making it rich in red blood cells for added energy, then inject it back into his body. A nasty practice, yet much harder to detect during mandatory drug tests. Caden passed the time last night telling horror stories about having seen dudes doing this. Jerry'd turned green, revulsion written within the deep lines of his face. It had become pretty clear Jerry probably wasn't dealing. As for being a manipulative, money-hounding, flesh-betting bookie, Jerry was numero uno on the asshole list.

So, which fighter was the dealer?

Caden covered his eyes and squinted at the bus. It

would do Jerry some good to take a long humbling ride on that piece of crap.

"Phoenix was gonna be the biggest turnout yet. Sold out the place. Fifty bucks for every seat. That's five thousand dollars in my pocket, less the venue fee of nine hundred plus change. Your piece of crap vehicle is gonna cost you big time."

Caden flexed his fingers, but tuned him out. He willed his thoughts toward something more pleasant, and they turned to Sophie, as they tended to do of late.

Guilty conscious? Perhaps. He imagined the pleasure in her eyes when she'd woken up to find herself sprinkled with rose petals and significantly richer than she'd been when she went to bed. If she'd had extra cash around, he doubted she'd subject herself to the bus. *Had she watched the video?* He grinned at the thought.

What had begun as a serious one-sided discussion about fighting styles had ended on a naughty note— for her ears alone. Hopefully, her editing skills were as strong as her reporting skills, or America was going to get an eyeful of a well-satisfied woman. His on-screen antics had been amusing. But in the bright light of day, he wished he'd stuck to his original intent of giving her an exclusive, and then washing his hands of the matter.

Still, he wondered at her reaction.

"Damn it all. There's the motherfuckin' bus. Time to get out of this hellhole."

Jerry's excitement was palpable. Caden couldn't have summed it up any better.

The two mechanics came outside to witness the bus's arrival, as if an unnatural phenomenon was barreling down the empty roadway instead of a banged-up junk heap.

"Need to take a piss. Be right back." Caden took advantage of the moment. He retrieved the duffel bag full of drugs and syringes from the trunk and pulled the zipper tight before heading off to the men's room. He propped the bag on the bathroom sink while he took care of business. Returning to the roadside, he nonchalantly set the duffel next to his other gear.

A dark cloud of exhaust billowed up in the desert sky. Whoever had the back seats were either asphyxiated or wearing gas masks. No way was he getting on that thing. But he had to play his hand with Jerry, just to make sure. He needed to be one hundred percent certain sure his instincts were correct and Jerry wasn't the dealer.

If Jerry noticed, and commented on the duffel bag, then bingo. Caden would have the proof he needed. He'd confront the jerk and get it all on audio as planned.

"Phew-ee, I ain't seen a vehicle that beat up since Leonard's four-by-four bed rusted right off. Out here in the desert, we don't get much cause for rusting," one of the mechanics commented.

The second man chimed in. "If this don't beat all. *That's* what you're traveling to Phoenix in, instead of the James Bond mobile we've got in the garage? I'll be damned."

So will I, Caden thought.

Dust kicked up as the bus bore down on them. Whoever was driving it must have been mad as hell because the vehicle swerved back and forth across the invisible center line. When it reached about the one-hundred-yard mark, Caden reached for his gear and headed over to the gas pumps. The bus didn't look as if it were going to stop.

The two mechanics seemed to think so too, and beat a fast retreat inside the garage, near the Aston.

Not so much Jerry. He marched into the roadway and held up his palm. It was like that scene in *The Terminator*, except Jerry was no Arnold Schwarzenegger.

Yet he stubbornly held his ground as the bus bore down on him.

As much as Caden detested the slimeball, he didn't fancy seeing him end up as New Mexican roadkill.

At the last second, it dawned on the foolish man that he wasn't God, and that whoever was driving the speeding sardine can wasn't stopping for anyone. As fast as his wiry legs could carry him, Jerry bolted out of the way.

The bus shot on by.

A cloud of dust billowed up in its wake, making Caden cough. Blinking away the grime, he caught sight of something that made him want to gag. Agitated gestures just inside the bus's back door window. Bodies moving around inside.

A fight. Rather a full-blown, flat-out brawl. He made out a rapid whirl of auburn hair as it brushed against the emergency door windowpane.

Caden hit the asphalt at a dead run, his heart racing. Knowing who he'd find mixed up in the middle of it.

The wheels of the vehicle gave off a high-pitched screech a quarter mile down the roadway. A sudden jerk followed, and the bus finally halted. If the fists flying inside hadn't killed anyone, the jarring stop might have done the job.

The rear door swung open, violently smashing against the worn yellow steel with a loud clang.

Caden picked up his pace. Sweat beaded up on his forehead and he swiped it away. God, if she was hurt…

A suitcase spiraled through the air. It landed on the asphalt ahead, bounced and rolled, but stayed closed. Just inside the frame stood a tall man with someone slung across his shoulders. *Jesus.* Someone whose fists were flailing and whose legs were kicking wildly, like an Olympian swimming the 100-meter freestyle—airborne.

Jesus. What the hell was Jaysin Bouvine doing on the bus? He'd thought the man was recovering in a Wichita hospital. Turning, Jaysin filled the doorway, a manic expression on his face and a struggling Sophie in his arms.

The last few remaining treads on Caden's personal head gasket burst. Jaysin was going to wish he'd never set eyes on Sophie Morelle. And if he hurt her, if he tossed her from that bus—which was what appeared to be his intent—she was going to be the last thing the asshat ever saw.

Caden's long legs took him over the suitcase and a few lengths from the door.

Jaysin was cursing like a madman.

Sophie swung her camera bag over Jaysin's head, nailing him in the face. She repeated the action, over and over again, causing him to grow more and more furious with every whack.

He lifted her higher into the air. Manhandling her. A defensive gesture or in preparation to hurl her out of the bus, it didn't matter. Jaysin had just signed his own death warrant.

Caden stopped short, panting and so freakin' pissed off, he struggled over his words. Rule number one as a fighter was to never let them see you sweat, but that's just what Caden did, his tone sharp and his temper bordering on uncontrolled.

"Hand her down to me. Gently. Or you are going to wish you were never born."

"Well, looky here. If it isn't our tough guy model, shouting like a little bitch. What happened, is your underwear on too tight? Making threats you can't possibly keep? I'm gonna dish out a beating you won't forget for jumping me in the hallway back in Missouri. Long-term memory—that's what I've got, and you're gonna pay for it."

That was it.

Caden grabbed hold of the door and hoisted himself inside.

The shock on Jaysin's face was priceless—almost as priceless as the look of horror that replaced it when, in one fluid motion, Caden head-butted him.

A similar expression must have spread across Caden's own features, after Sophie's camera bag nailed him in the back of his head. Hard enough, he was guaranteed an egg-sized knot.

With one hand, he yanked the bag from her grasp. With his other one, he shot a fully loaded punch into Jaysin's already-bloodied nose.

Sophie's legs swung around as Jaysin jerked sideways beneath the impact. His arm loosened its vice-like hold and, with a gasp, she tumbled backward onto a vacant seat.

Caden swung an arm around the asshat's neck and pinned him against the side of a seat in a choke hold. Immediately, Jaysin's hand tapped the worn vinyl, like this was some kind of organized bout. With organized rules of conduct. Boy, was he in for a rude awakening.

"Come on. Let's hear it." He sounded calm, yet he was struggling to control himself. This guy needed a lesson in manners, and in why it was never wise to underestimate your opponent. "Sing for us." Man, he wanted to put a hurting on him. It didn't help that Sophie had composed herself enough to sit up, and was watching the events unfolding before her. Her expression was a complex mixture of surprise, admiration and horror. Definitely horror, Caden was sure of it.

A horror that mirrored his own when he noticed her red, swollen face.

Bouvine was a dead man.

"That bitch is bad luck. You know it…"

One quick uppercut silenced the fool. This was followed by a vicelike squeeze as Caden pulled his elbow in tighter around Jaysin's throat. Squeezing harder. And harder still.

Caden inhaled deeply, desperate to calm his rage and not cross the fine line between leaving him temporarily breathless and murdering him. Sophie was watching it all go down—watching him turn into the street thug, the boy with a deep, uncontrollable rage. The boy nobody wanted. A wild kid with a violent streak who lacked self-discipline and control. But he'd learned his lesson, he'd changed, right? He was no longer that guy, an apple that had fallen from an abusive father's tree. All that crap about "like father, like son." Bunch of bullshit he was still coming to terms with.

Moments like this…the thought of Jaysin manhandling Sophie… He was one firm squeeze of the asshat's throat away from proving this theory wrong.

Sophie sang out, off-key and out-of-tune, her face flushed a bright shade of pink, clearly furious. "'You know, I'm bad, I'm bad, you know it.' Sing it, bughead. Let's hear your best Michael Jackson impersonation."

Caden felt his temper mellow.

He almost burst out laughing when the throat pressed up against his arm began to vibrate with song. "Bad, bad, really, really bad."

"What have we got going on here? A goddang symphony?" Sal asked, his tone filled with concern.

"Show's over," Caden told him, and the rest of the Boys dispersed. It was a wonder the bus hadn't been lifted onto its back two wheels under the combined weight of them. "Get your bag. You're coming with me." He nodded at Sophie. He turned and spotted the duffel over in the distance by the pumps, exactly where he'd left it. *Good.*

She wiggled out of the seat, scooted around Jaysin, and was out the door before Jaysin could finish his next verse.

Caden relaxed his grip. Here he was, trapped in the desert in one-hundred-twenty-five-degree weather, on a bus with no air-conditioning, with a bunch of overheated fighters ready for a brawl. He'd been close, so close, to finishing Jaysin off. Somehow, he'd managed to rein in his volatile emotions. Somehow he'd managed to avoid killing the fucker. "We'll finish this in Vegas," he promised.

Jaysin coughed, greedily sucking air into his lungs.

It was over. No one was seriously hurt. Sophie was okay. Caden peered around, thinking how he was more upset than the lot of them. Mimicking Jaysin's actions, he sucked in a long breath.

A high, ear-shattering scream rang up from the asphalt.

"What the hell is *she* doing on *my* bus?"

* * *

Gone was the easygoing, playful Lothario Sophie had grown to know. Gone too was the viciously brutal fighter. Both sides of this beautiful man seated beside her had been lost somewhere between Kansas and New Mexico.

Sophie was crossing into Arizona with a total stranger.

Once more, she found herself speeding along a long stretch of roadway with a driver so quiet the hum of the Aston's engine, accompanied by the occasional thump of a thumb on the leather steering wheel, were the only breaks in the silence.

He'd lied to Jerry, telling him the Aston wouldn't be ready for hours and basically giving the fool no choice but ride on the bus, leaving them alone in the middle of nowhere. A half hour later, they were on the road, but not after a few tense moments when she thought he was going to leave her behind.

Sophie adjusted the A/C vent on the dashboard and was rewarded with a cool blast of air on her face. The lack of air-conditioning on the bus was no surprise. Though, combined with a pack of sweaty, overheated men—who probably didn't know that you needed *antiperspirant*-deodorant, not just straight-up deodorant, when dealing with unbearable heat—the hell-ride had been toxic.

Her skin itched more than ever. Her shirt was crumpled. Her pants dirty from Jaysin dragging her down the aisle. Especially her bottom. And she was exhausted. It must be nerves. And the heat. What she wouldn't give for a cool bath and a sweet iced tea.

The journey into Arizona had been as uneventful as

the land around them. It seemed urban sprawl hadn't reached this part of the Southwest. Sophie remembered reading an advertisement in the *Arizona Times* for free land. Pay the taxes, put in a claim, and the land was yours. Quite alluring, for modern-day pioneers. She peered around the vast landscape, thinking how easy it'd be to lose yourself within the great expanse of barren desert, just like the lost pioneers from days gone by.

It wasn't until they passed a *Welcome to San Carlos Apache Nation* billboard and, right next to it, a colorful advertisement for a casino, did Sophie realize just how wrong she'd been. Absolute confirmation came a few miles further, when another billboard loomed indecently overhead—even the desert had been touched by Caden's charm. Or charms, rather.

"Fuckin' A," Caden growled, accelerating past the sign at an ungodly speed.

Sophie wanted to laugh. The Ultimate American Man actually grimaced, visibly appalled by his own billboard. Leaving Sophie wondering at his reaction, wondering why the multimillion-dollar endorsement seemed to rub him the wrong way. It wasn't like Caden had body perception issues, of that she was certain. Though the crotch shot was pretty provocative, he had to have known that ginormous fact during the shoot.

Still, he refrained from commenting further as the desert swallowed them up.

The Aston sped along the endless highway in silent solitude. Sophie knew she should take this opportunity to lure Caden back into conversation, get something useful recorded. She just couldn't muster up the energy.

Besides, she had no clue what Caden had left for her on that sex tape. In Vegas, she'd soak her weary bones and wash away the day's troubles. Then she'd play the tape.

Did he explain his Houdini act? Doubtful, given his reputation.

Sophie sat up straighter and smoothed out her pants. Not that it mattered one iota. She could handle a wild night of sex. It wasn't like she wanted something from him other than an interview and his help in buttering up the Boys. *Or fighting them off me.*

They flew by the next sign, announcing the exit to Las Vegas, and continued west."Um…I hate to interrupt our stimulating conversation," she offered. "Or is it companionable silence? But you need to turn around. Vegas is north. You missed the turn."

Caden rolled his neck, his gaze fixed on the roadway. "Stimulating, huh? I could go for some companionable stimulation about now. Just say the word."

Sophie sighed, both pleased and exasperated by his response. Memories of Caden between her legs came to mind, his athletic body maneuvering her into positions she'd only read about in *Cosmo*. "Word," she said weakly.

He rewarded her with a panty-wetting grin.

"Seriously. Not to be a backseat driver, but you missed the exit to Vegas."

"No, I didn't."

What was it with men and their addled belief that some internal GPS system was genetically encoded within every member of their gender?

"Yes, you did," she shot back, letting Caden know by her tone exactly how she felt on the subject.

"Nope. We're—"

"Listen, double-oh-seven." Turning in her seat, she

leaned over the console and closed the distance between them. It was more like double-O, as in *orgasm*. "The sign back there—*miles* ago considering we're driving like we're being chased by a crazy desert assassin— said Vegas is 256 miles *that* way."

She pointed at his driver-side window, hoping he'd turn around. Hoping the warning bells ringing around in her head were wrong. "You are headed west," she added weakly.

"We're making a pit stop in Phoenix."

She stopped glaring at the rearview mirror as if it were responsible for the renewed tension in the car. Her tension, not his.

"Crapola, I knew it. Phoenix wasn't on the schedule." Unbelievable. Just great, she'd be dealing with the Double Mint Jerks—Jerry and Jaysin—sooner than expected. God knew what was in store for her.

For Caden.

She ran her hands over the hem of her blouse, but her efforts did nothing to smooth out the wrinkles, or her worries. What if Jerry had another twisted fight planned for tonight? What if, this time, it was Caden carried away in an ambulance? "I can't believe after what happened in Wichita, you'd agree…"

"Do you want to drive?" He didn't wait for her to reply, slowing the Aston to a stop and unwinding his big frame from the bucket seat.

Sophie felt a surge of excitement. Sliding back into her heels, she climbed out of the car.

"My only condition is that you keep it over a hundred, chili cheeks."

"No problem, butter buns."

Caden burst out laughing. "That the best you got?

Makes my glutes sound like a flab fest." He turned and inspected his backside.

Her hand instinctively—*yeah, right! She knew exactly what she was doing!*—shot out and gave his butt a pat. Oh boy, she *wanted* to cop a feel. Wanted to run her hands all over that gorgeous body of his, starting with his taut cheeks. Maybe even work her way around the front of him, where his butter buns met his Ultimate Male Package.

The midafternoon sun must have scrambled her head. This was Houdini Jr. she was flirting with. She shook her head, just to be safe.

"I've got a long night of training ahead of me. So, try not to be a sissy behind the wheel, okay?"

The last she'd seen of his player ass *was* his ass, on the way *out*. Now he had the gall to insult her driving skills? "Hop on in, cowboy," she said, in the sexiest voice she could muster.

He raised an eyebrow, unconvinced, but did as he was told.

Sophie took her sweet time adjusting the driver's seat. She could feel his gaze on her, watching her careful movements. It took her minutes to rearrange the rearview mirror. A futile task, as she preferred looking over her shoulder for signs of trouble. Always waiting to be blindsided once more. Though today, trouble wasn't behind her but sitting right next to her.

"First thing I'm doing in Phoenix is showing Jaysin Bouvine an up-close-and-personal view of my haymaker. That's some job he did on your cheek," she heard him say, dead serious.

"I'm highly allergic to roses, you jerk."

His eyebrows rose.

She gunned the gas, and was immediately rewarded by the way he tumbled backward in his seat.

"Oops. How sissy of me."

Caden burst out laughing, the sound as attractive as the man sitting next to her. For the moment, her worries of what might or might not happen were erased, like a fading cloud. Replaced by a horizon rich with promises of what just might happen again.

Chapter 13

TRIP: What happens when a fighter sports a pair of stilettos—though highly unlikely they'd be caught doing so and even less likely their big feet would fit. But it would be amusing as heck to watch

"Can I ask you a personal question? Off the record?" Sophie asked. The clear sky was slowly giving way to a grayish cloud of smog, a sign that Phoenix, the fastest growing city in America, was close.

Somewhere in between the San Carlos Apache Indian Reservation and Mesa, Sophie'd unplugged Caden's iPhone, abruptly putting an end to his soulful country crooning in the hopes that he'd talk to her. But when she'd pressed him about dodging his interview, he'd given her an odd look, smirked, and then had fallen silent. Miles later, she missed the rich gravelly voice that had plagued her memory since Wichita. Heck, she could *so* get used to country music.

Yet she'd gotten him to open up about his preparations for Tetnus, and he'd given her a glimpse into his world as a fighter.

His passion for the sport was undeniable. The way he described the detestable diet of chicken and broccoli, and all kinds of "barely edible crap" mixed with an occasional carb boost. Caden had gone a hundred steps beyond all those lame salads she'd consumed to keep herself fit for TV. And his workouts? They made hers seem like a kindergartener warming up for recess. The hours he put into training. The discipline required, and how his rigorous schedule kept him in line from taking a damn drink, from polluting his body. The frustration he felt from his routine being interrupted by the few days of driving, leaving him only two weeks for him to get into top form.

A vulture cruised overhead, its wings wide and foreboding, momentarily catching her off guard. How could such a magnificent bird be so cruel? A chill ran up her spin, but she ignored it and tried to focus on more pleasant thoughts. Instead, she turned her attention to the hot mess of a man next to her, a myriad of unidentifiable emotions playing across his face. So cruel in his own sexy way. He seemed deep in thought, staring up at the sky.

He sighed. "Go ahead. I'm not promising you'll like the answers."

She snorted. "Let me be the judge of that, sweet buns."

The slight twitch of his lips caused her heart to race. "How old were you when you had your first fight?"

"Four."

Her foot lifted off the gas and the car decelerated. "What?"

He grinned, yet it didn't reach his eyes.

"Are you ever serious?" She quieted and settled back into her seat, well aware of how his carefree demeanor easily misled a person into believing he was a good ole boy. Except this good ole boy's six-pack was an eight-pack, and better suited to licking than chugging. Still, it deflected attention from the serious man within. She'd had a taste of that side in Wichita, and her instincts told her that his street-smart ways had something to do with it. "You get into a lot of brawls, like back there with Jaysin…?"

"I'm a trained fighter, not some amateur punk, if that's what you're getting at." His tone seemed harder, but not angry. Not playful either.

Interesting, how Caden seemed to despise the thought, yet Anthony had nothing but respect for Caden's natural, street-honed instincts. Exactly how street smart was Caden?

She'd bet her last dollar, which wasn't saying much, that there was some truth to his words. Something had flashed in his eyes when he'd said it. But what four-year-old was a brawler? Especially one who was cute as a button—which Caden surely had been. It was difficult to fathom that the man beside her was an infant brawler turned street-smart thug.

She decided on a blunt approach. "You're the farthest thing from being a punk. But you also hate it when people discuss your playboy good looks."

He scowled.

Point proven, she noted, deciding to change her line of questioning. "Hey. Before you go and get all pissy on me for mentioning it, tell my why the sight of your own billboard makes you grimace, like someone stuffed a lemon in your mouth."

"Is this how you conduct all your interviews?" He rolled his neck, then relaxed his shoulders. In an entirely different tone, deeper and with more of a Southern drawl to it, he added, "I like lemons. But I'll tell you, I love blood oranges more. Reminds me of something else I like to stuff my mouth full of."

The car accelerated, jerking Caden backward in his seat. *Naughty man.*

He laughed.

"Are you going to answer my question?"

"Does it matter?"

Jeez, he was infuriating.

"My interview with Anthony took less time and was full of interesting information. Plus, I filmed it, so less work is required of me. You, however, have provided me with nothing but shallow promises."

Lazily, Caden leaned his head against the headrest and angled his head her way. "That right?" The gravel was fully back in his voice.

She flushed, the memory of him between her legs proving her wrong. It took all of her willpower to recover. "*That* is right. He gave me juicy stuff. Ripe and sweet. And he promised me more when we meet up in Vegas."

"Guess he's got nothing better to do than interviews."

She shrugged, yet noted how he scoffed at all those interviews when he'd given so many of them. Almost like he was mocking his own livelihood. But why? What had changed for him?

"I'd say Hank Cawfield's got some competition."

Sophie hit the brake hard. They both flew forward. Only their seat belts prevented them from hitting the windshield.

"Holy fuck." Caden braced his palms against the dashboard, cursing a blue streak.

Sophie clambered out of the car, breathing hard. *Damn, oh damn.*

That man's name coming from Caden's beautiful lips—it felt like his mighty fist clasped hold of her heart and squeezed it into pulp.

Hank. Hell. *Hawley.* They all began with *h*'s. All three ugly stand-ins for her loss of innocence, how the world wasn't the perfect place she'd thought it to be.

She was back in Hawley all over again. Alone in her hole of a house, her father out with some buddies. A knock on the door had interrupted her homework. She remembered being shocked that Hank Cawfield had come calling. He was the wealthiest guy in Hawley, had financed the construction of a new town library, soccer field, playground and soon-to-be-built municipal building. He was running for mayor, going house to house to shake hands with potential voters. Sophie hadn't even yet turned sixteen, too young to vote. As it turned out, a handshake wasn't what he wanted from her.

She glanced up at the sky and spotted the bird spiraling overhead, still searching for prey. A natural predator, looking for his next innocent victim. Which was exactly what Hank had done years ago.

Grabbing the largest rock she could find, she hurled it up at the vulture. "Bastard," she screamed.

Physically, he hadn't hurt her, aside from the bruises around her neck and chest. No, it was the emotional anguish from the aftermath—what the good citizens of Hawley had done—that hurt the most.

How long had she been standing in the hot, barren roadway, desperately trying to catch her breath? Long enough for sweat to coat the inside of her blouse. Long enough to feel a relentless stream of moisture trickle down her cheeks.

Damn. Oh damn. It still hurt.

She heard the crunch of stone at Caden's approach. She sucked in a breath, waiting for the sick chill of nausea to finish its onslaught within her belly.

He came up behind her, grasped her hand, and pressed something warm into her palm. With the back of her free hand, she swiped at the moisture on her cheek, blinked the stray tears from her lashes, then glanced at the object in her palm.

A rock.

Surprised, she turned his way.

His gaze was skyward, fixed on the circling bird, but…far away, deep in thought. He didn't say anything—didn't need to. She'd been bleeding on the inside, and he seemed to know it. The silence gave her time to put a mega-sized Band-Aid on it, but not before one last throw.

Winding her arm behind her head, she chucked the stone high.

This time, it worked. The vulture cried out in displeasure, then flew off into the horizon. Immediately, she felt better. That's exactly what she'd done to Hank years ago.

Sent. Him. Away.

Bastard.

"Thanks," she muttered, her throat dry.

"Ready?"

She nodded. More than ready to put Hawley behind her for good.

Once in the car, he handed her a bottle of water and silently took over the wheel.

It wasn't until he offered her a napkin did she realize they'd reached the outside of the city limits. Pulling a compact out of her bag, she shuddered at the sight of herself. Tiny mascara marks framed her eyes, smudges of grime coated her skin in random places, and her clothing was a soiled, wrinkled jumble. Well, if she were to look on the bright side of things, her rash had faded.

"Guess I'm the new definition of one hot mess, huh?" Her lame joke felt forced, even to her own ears.

"You're talking to a fighter, chili bean. I like my woman sweaty and hot." But he added softly, "A little bit of dirt's got nothing on you, gorgeous."

She wondered briefly what he was really thinking but she was too drained to hold on to a coherent thought.

They fell back into a more comfortable silence, heading into Phoenix where the city skyscrapers swallowed them up.

Her spirits lifted when Caden pulled the Aston into the valet of the Arizona Saguaro Resort and Spa. Without a word, he climbed out and pulled her dirty battered suitcase, along with his own, out of the back seat.

"Listen, I'll check us into a suite…"

She managed a stupid grin, suddenly feeling much better.

"…but, I'm not going to be around much. I've got to hit the gym hard. You're on your own for dinner, too."

"Perfect." A long, cool bath. A nap. Clean clothes, now that she had her suitcase back. Contact Pittsburgh Trust and figure out the fastest way to get a replacement card—maybe Lauren could fax a copy of her birth certificate, which Sophie kept in her nightstand back in Pittsburgh, along with some other form of identification? Heck, and just maybe she'd treat herself to a manicure and pedicure at the spa. After today—after this week—she deserved it.

"How about we meet later, in the hot tub?"

Her heart pulled a cartwheel. She nodded weakly, afraid to look at him. Her inner Marvin Gaye crooned softly: *Hot tub, baby. Bed, baby. Wherever, honey, let's get it on.* Why not?

"Bring that recorder of yours and whatever questions you want to ask me. We can finish with a videotape. Maybe that sweet smile will be even bigger by the time we're done."

She laughed, the genuine, carefree kind, one that sounded foreign to her ears, having been stifled inside her for far too long. Figured Caden would be the one to bring it out of her. With good ole Marvin urging her on, she replied, "I won't be the only one grinning, baby."

His eyebrows lifted, then he reached over and ran his thumb across her bottom lip. "That's what I like about you, Sophie—always a challenge. One I aim to win."

If the valet attendant wasn't headed over, she'd have wrapped herself around the naughty hunk, climbed up his body, and made him forget all about the Jacuzzi.

Instead, she gave him something to think about.

"The contents of my lingerie case are all over a Kansas highway."

He raised an eyebrow.

"Bathing suits included. Nothing except a few freckles and a lot of bare skin."

His eyes glimmered with promise. "Perfect."

Caden lounged in the doorway of Sophie's bedroom, studying the gorgeous woman spread out on the king-size bed. Sound asleep—she'd been that way for ten hours straight. So much for tracing an imaginary *C* on the pale skin of her abdomen, like he'd planned on doing, first with his fingers then with his mouth.

He'd come in from his early morning run well before the desert sun rose and had stopped to check in on her. She'd kicked off the covers, offering him a cock-jerking view of the slip of material she had on. Thank the Lord he'd snagged it from midair or it'd be another bit of wasted underwear. It looked much prettier on Sophie than littering an interstate highway. Rich purple silk with black lace along the edges rose up on her thighs and contrasted with her cream-colored skin. The lace *V* between the swell of her breasts rising and falling with her breath. Her position on the bed hadn't changed. He might do something about that, all right.

Rubbing the stubble on his chin, he wondered what it was about Sophie that had his head so twisted. She'd worked her way into his thoughts, and with her typical gumption, wouldn't budge. She'd preoccupied his mind during last night's grueling workout. Images of her in the hot tub…*Jesus*. Man, he needed to scratch this itch, and fast, before it turned into something deeper and without a doubt, more painful.

She shifted on the mattress, then quieted.

He'd gotten seven restful hours of sleep, but was still envious. What he wouldn't give for a few more hours, next to her…inside her.

The next two weeks leading up to Tetnus promised to be grueling. Training was as much mental as physical. He needed to get into the zone, where nothing else mattered but his physical and mental preparedness. Which meant he had to resolve this steroid issue fast. Then he'd figure out what to do about getting Sophie out of his head. Give her what she wanted. A fuck. An interview. A rocking documentary. A drama-free ticket for a nonstop flight back to Pittsburgh.

He paused, frowning. One more thing—after Tetnus was over, he'd find Hank Cawfield and beat the living fuck out of him. It had to be bad, whatever that asshole had done to her.

First things first. He wandered back into the living area, plucked his iPhone off the table and hit Bracken's number. Ruling out Jerry as the drug dealer was progress, but Bracken did this bullshit for a living. Kind of ironic, because to the outside word, he was the last guy anyone would trust. Hell, what did you expect from a street thug turned undercover narcotics detective?

Bracken looked like the leader of a motorcycle gang and his manner was abrasive and coarse. The muscled size of him scared the shit out of most men. *He* should be fighting in Tetnus—there wasn't a fighter alive, including Caden, who could beat him. Chances were high that Bracken was going to knock some heads in when he found out about the duffel bag. Still, time was ticking and he needed to get his big brother involved.

Except Caden got his voice mail. *Damn.*

He left a brief message about tomorrow's arrival in Vegas and hit end. Feeling like he had to do something to tidy up these loose ends, he found himself back in Sophie's bedroom.

She hadn't budged. He wanted to give her a wake-up present but thought better of it.

If her kind of distraction kept up, no way in hell would he win Tetnus.

He grabbed her camera bag from where she'd left it by her bed. Heading into the privacy of the living room, he positioned the camcorder on the table, and unfolded the viewfinder. He clicked it on and set a chair up in front of it. Without giving himself time to back out, he hit record.

"Hey, this is Caden Kelly speaking once again with reporter Sophie Morelle. You probably know who I am but there's a hell of a lot you don't know about me. And, being as Sophie Morelle is one of the best investigative reporters out there, she's conned me into spilling all the juicy details. So, here you go…"

"The bus ride to Phoenix wasn't the same without you, Sophie," Sal said by way of a greeting. Sophie noted the tall, half-emptied glass of vodka in his hand. Before she could predict how many refills the old-timer had guzzled, he added, "Just joking."

Someone had found his sense of humor on that rust-mobile.

Good humor seemed to be the prevailing theme at tonight's venue. The refurbished nightclub was decent. Clean and spacious, with a sunken dance floor filling the center of the room, three bars lining the walls, and several well-endowed waitresses carting around trays of appetizers. The place was packed, sold-out, with fans buzzing with excitement. The kind of effervescent delight some people felt after getting up close and personal with a celebrity. Sophie had had a similar sense of giddiness when she'd started on *Late Night*—a few days on the job and she'd gotten over it.

Jerry appeared amiable, working the sold-out crowd and pretty much ignoring Sophie's presence. She couldn't have asked for a better arrangement. Except for the hats, boots, and mechanical bull off to one side of the dance floor.

"Where's your hat, darling?" Anthony came up beside her, his faux Southern drawl thick and heavy with Texas flavor. She wanted to roll her eyes at the prep school fighter from Connecticut, but he'd been more than cooperative tonight. She'd spent a good hour interviewing him off in the corner. He was handsome and photogenic, pleasant and well-mannered. Someone the audience was going to love. After she filmed him greeting his fans, she'd begin part three of their interview. She'd scoped out a small room down the hallway past the restrooms, which offered the most promise for a quiet, interrupted exchange.

"I can't see my viewfinder clearly with a ten-gallon hat in my eyes," she replied. God knows where someone had procured the pink cowboy hat adorned with blue sequined trim and a brightly blinking tiara. The dang thing had flickered out in protest as she'd jammed it into her empty camera bag. No room for bling—Sophie meant business. She gave a thumbs-up to the group of fighters she'd assembled. "Okay. Ready. The camera's rolling. Three. Two. One. Action."

The first image that appeared was Sal with a shit-eating grin. Clearly, he loved the attention, and Sophie found herself smiling. "Okay, we talked about your aspirations to win Tetnus," she addressed the group. "We discussed what the million-dollar purse would mean to you guys and your careers. Now, I have a few more personal questions."

Within the small entourage of Boys—six to be exact—five of them exchanged glances. Rightly so. Perhaps they sensed she was about to grill them on Jerry's shady dealings. She plunged ahead.

"Tonight, there are no scheduled exhibitions or fights. Why is that? Isn't your promoter, Jerry, interested in showcasing your fighting skills? You've been kind enough to explain—"

A few voices responded at the same time, all with various versions of the same. "No more exhibitions, not after the bullshit Jerry pulled in Wichita." *Bingo.*

"So no illegal betting tonight, either?"

The group *laughed.*

She glanced around the room and spotted Jerry. The sleazeball was decked out in a brown polyester suit and thin, red tie. He seemed in good humor tonight—a result of the appearance being sold-out—and was talking animatedly with a group of men. No greenbacks being exchanged.

"Am I missing something?"

Anthony gestured for her to follow him. Holding her camera tightly, she panned the crowd socializing and chatting with their heroes as they headed out of the main room and down the hallway to the bathrooms. The Boys and Sal stopped outside the men's room door.

"I don't think this is such a hot idea, Anthony. If Jerry finds out we let her film this…" Sal trailed off.

Anthony looked at her. "Put your cowboy hat on so you don't draw attention."

Hmph. Well, it was better than nothing. Tugging the abomination from her bag, she plopped it on her head. "Don't tell me there's illegal betting going on in the men's room?"

Anthony tapped out a sequence of knocks on the door opposite the men's room, the one she'd tried earlier and found locked. Interesting.

The door opened. A small man in a fancy black suit and black cowboy hat ushered them inside. Sophie stopped short and looked around in amazement.

Six tables were lined up in three wide rows. Men in 1970s suits similar in color and material to Jerry's outdated duds sat behind each of them, talking to small groups of MMA fans clustered around. Sophie kept her camcorder running steady as she wandered down an aisle, taking in the computers, credit card machines, stacks of money, and what looked to be piles of paper with brackets on them—the kind basketball fans fill out for March Madness to select their favorite teams. She scooped one up and held it in front of the camera. The brackets on the outside section of the sheet contained each of the fighters headed for Tetnus, grouped by their weight class. Sure enough, she noted Caden's handsome mug—the first she'd seen of him all day—grinning up at her from the welterweight page. The faces of the other welterweight Boys were there, as well. Jeez, quite a bit of preparation had gone into this.

The Boys wandered off, probably hoping to find out where they'd place in the bets. Sal remained by her side, silent for once.

A man in a mud-colored suit glanced at her then

back at his computer screen. All business—well, so was she. "That thing on?" he asked, not really seeming to care if it was.

She shook her head no and shot him a bright smile, just in case.

It worked. "Pretty lady, you looking to place a bet? We take cash, credit cards, and Paypal. Of course, the charge will show up on your statement as *Lots of Luck*. Tax purposes, mind you. Minimum bet is a grand."

"A grand as in one thousand dollars?"

"You got it." The man's gaze fell from her hat to her camcorder. "Do you have permission to bring that thing in here? And why is the light on if it's not running?"

"She's good, pal. I heard Jerry tell her so," Sal chimed in.

She hastily added, "Jerry's outside, eagerly issuing personal invitations to fellas about coming in and placing bets. He's too busy to witness how well managed things are in here. May be—" though she intentionally said it as *maybe* "—Jerry's planning on keeping this agency open on a more permanent basis?" She let the idea of that dangle in the air like a Southern drawl. "May be that's why he asked me to record how efficiently things are running back here."

Sal tugged at her elbow. "Time to skedaddle."

"Hang on. Jerry wanted me to find out one more thing." Ah, she'd just have to edit her little lies out of the footage. "How much have we raked in so far?"

The man scowled. *Darn it.* He'd caught on to her game. "Tell Jerry," he ground out through his teeth, "that we'll count the cash later, as agreed." He pulled something up on his computer. "Credit card receipts total seven hundred."

"I thought you said the minimum bet was one thousand?"

He glowered. Luckily, his annoyance with Jerry—who must be up their butts asking for minute-by-minute totals—overshadowed any suspicion. "Seven. Hundred. Thousand." He emphasized each word. "So far. Cash count will probably double that."

Score one for Sophie. It didn't get any juicier than this.

"I'm going to make sure Jerry knows he's not paying you enough. See ya."

With Sal in tow, she headed for the door. Anthony and two other Boys followed. The remaining three were likely pushing to increase their odds by betting on themselves.

Sal wisely waited until they were in the hallway to say, "Sophie, I didn't know how much of a setup Jerry had going. Thought it was a simple operation, like betting on the horses."

"Do all the Boys know?" *Does Caden know?*

Anthony nodded. "You kind of expect it with Jerry running the show."

"Aw, don't pull such a sour look, honey. I know you're disappointed in us," Sal stammered. "It's the way things are around here. Other sports do it, too." The old-timer was a bit twisted but his conscience was like pure spun silk.

"Did you get it on film? I'd love to see his face when you bring him down, Sophie. What he deserves after that stunt he pulled in Wichita." *Hmph. So that's why Anthony ratted Jerry out—payback time.* She couldn't blame Anthony or Sal.

"Between Wichita and tonight, I'm off to a good start

as far as footage is concerned." But she wanted to get a closer look, without them around. In a more serious voice she said, "I expected more from you, Anthony." She turned to give Sal a similar comment. He blanched like she'd already ripped him to pieces. Relief washed across his face when all she did was gesture over her shoulder with her thumb. "Ladies' room."

Safely inside, she exhaled, grateful for a moment to quiet her nerves, and let the weight of what had gone down fully sink in. With her back to the mirror, she leaned against the sink counter and tapped her foot. Jerry's offside betting scam was the brightest light to shine her way in the past twenty-four hours.

The video she'd taken of the betting room was something out of a mob movie. Thousands of presumably tax-free dollars lined Jerry's deep pockets. The IRS might find that tidbit helpful, for sure. *Thank you, Anthony.* Sophie was beside herself with excitement. Her earlier manicure and pedicure didn't even come close.

Granted, it didn't relieve the disappointment she'd felt when she'd woken up and realized her exclusive with Caden had been botched once more.

Two cocktail waitresses came into the restroom and eyed her hat before continuing their conversation. Sophie felt like plucking the pink abomination off her head and giving it her best Frisbee throw, when it became apparent who they were talking about.

"He's more ripped in person."

"I'm on a mission to find out if they padded his junk in the billboard ad or not."

"Doubtful. Did you see the size of his arms?"

Dang-diggity. "Tons of padding," she heard herself say. For good measure, she added, "A reliable source told me he's an inch bigger than an average thumb." Ignoring their shocked expressions, she grabbed her camera and left them to consider the possibility. It served that playboy Houdini right. Who knew where he'd been all day. She stepped into the hallway and missed bumping into Jaysin by a heartbeat.

Fortunately, he was preoccupied repositioning the handles of three large duffel bags in his hand while deep in conversation with another guy.

"Everything set for Vegas?" he asked his partner, his words lingering in the hallway as they headed into her interview room. Common sense told her to head in the other direction. Her instincts told her something was up. She wouldn't put it past Jaysin to have a second side-betting operation in place.

Quickly, she took out her camcorder and followed them. Instead of entering the room, she stood off to the side of the door, in position to angle her camera and tape whatever was transpiring inside while keeping her eyes on the hallway in case someone spotted her. Which, with this cowboy getup on, was likely.

Luck was on her side. She was able to get a few solid minutes of footage before they shook hands, signaling whatever was going down was done. Hopefully, the mic was strong enough to pick up their mumbled words. Neatly folding her viewfinder back into place, she pulled her hat low, strode down the hallway well ahead of them, and partially reentered the ladies' room, propping the door open enough to squeeze her lens through but not be seen. She needed to get a closer look at Jaysin's partner.

The guy was enormous. His muscles seemed unnatural, his neck thicker than both her thighs combined.

Another fighter, a heavyweight, maybe? A foreigner, probably Russian? The heavy duffel bags were so heavy Jaysin had struggled to carry them. Yet this guy had slung all three over his shoulders like sacks of feathers. Whatever was inside, was important to them. Money? Heck, that seemed to be the common theme tonight.

"I'll call you when the missing bag shows up," Jaysin told him, his voice low.

Sophie barely heard him over the excited fluttering of her heart, which continued long after the two men disappeared back into the main room.

All kinds of juicy side-events were going down, ripe for the plucking.

The night couldn't get any more interesting than this.

Chapter 14

SUBMISSION HOLD: The act of giving a fighter the cold shoulder until he's acknowledged the pile of laundry, dirty dishes, and housework waiting on him

Normally, two long-legged blonde cocktail waitresses were precisely what Caden needed after a grueling day. But these two women rubbed his nerves raw. He sipped his drink, wondering why his ordering a water with a slice of lemon was so goddamn funny. He was shot, his body needing some recovery time after the full-blown workout he'd had, yet he'd committed to making this lame appearance.

Bracken was M.I.A., probably working undercover and unable to return his calls. *Fuck.* The last time his brother had been deep within an investigation, it'd taken nearly a month for him to call Caden back. Still, he punched in his brother's number, hoping he'd pick up, but got the same monotonous recording, "The person you are trying to reach is unavailable at this time. Please try back later."

Caden's mood was sour, to put it mildly. And as his restless gaze came to settle on the woman he'd been searching for, it blackened further.

It was hard to miss her.

Holding court with several fighters and a few fans, Sophie's face was animated as she spoke. The fact that she was gorgeous, despite that ridiculous hat, wasn't lost on the men surrounding her. Especially that fighter she seemed so fond of—Anthony. Caden felt like smashing his fist into the man's face as he threw his head back, laughing. Lamely trying to butter her up so he could worm his way into her bed.

A hand touched Caden's arm. He glared at the blonde waitress and was rewarded with her nervous giggle. She'd better check in with that player Anthony and brush up on her come-on skills.

"Do you know that woman over there in the pink cowboy hat?"

He nodded, his eyes wandering back over to the woman in question.

Both the waitresses fell into a fit of giggles.

Caden's evening shifted from shitty to shittier. His eyes narrowed as Anthony put his hand on Sophie's shoulder. He finished his drink, gestured the waitress back over, and set his glass on her tray. She lingered by his side until he looked at her.

Pretty enough. Just not his type…*shit.*

"We didn't recognize her at first, with that hat and all. But you wanna hear what Sophie Morelle told us?" The waitress lowered her voice, earning his full attention. "She said that your crotch was padded for the billboard shots."

His eyebrows shot up, then knit together. "She did, did she?"

"Yep," her friend chimed in. "But we didn't believe her. Look at the size of your feet, for jiminy's sake. No way you're as small as she says."

Nothing like a stereotype to end the night. He rose and, before they could finish, strode across the room and shoved his way into the pack.

"You know what the little fuckheads at the network told me? That my blue-balling days were over. As if I've ever left one of my boy toys unsatisfied. God forbid."

A few of the Boys blanched at Sophie's words. The minx knew exactly the effect she had on them by telling them that story—laughter brightened her eyes to a clear, iridescent blue.

Until she spotted him. That wiped the smile off her face.

"Let's dance," he ground out. He grabbed her elbow and led her toward the dance floor.

To her credit, she didn't protest. Looking over her shoulder, she shouted, "Watch my stuff, Sal."

An old Garth Brooks song was playing. He pulled her in tight against his chest and followed the rhythm of the music. In those heels, the top of her head reached his chin. She melted into him and tucked her face in the crook of his neck. His arms relaxed around her and the tension inside him vanished.

She felt good in his arms, swaying against him. Her hair smelled nice, all flowers and cinnamon spice.

Gently, he tugged her in closer.

He heard her sigh. Maybe, just maybe, she was finally feeling how sexy country music could be.

The thought made him grin.

"Where have you been all night?"

He pulled back and looked at her. "Miss me?"

She rolled her eyes. "Like a cat misses a dog."

"Better watch out. I might be tempted to nip you."

"Yeah, right," she shot back. "I saw you talking to the cocktail waitresses. Any ole bone will do."

That's right, Caden. Better to remember that.

The song ended too soon and changed to one with real Southern grit. Tired as he was, the music lifted his spirits. Grabbing her waist, he twirled her around, moving with the other couples on the dance floor.

Her laughter rang out, genuine and pretty-sounding.

The music picked up in tempo and a couple's dance turned into a full-scale honky-tonk stomp. Doubtful Sophie knew what that was but it didn't hold her back a bit. Sashaying away from him, her hands found her hips and her high heels tapped the floor.

Her hair tumbled free of her ponytail, framing her face with auburn wisps. Her blouse had come undone at the throat, exposing the sensual valley of her neck. He wanted to run his tongue along the sweet curve of that sensitive spot. She wiggled her hips, drawing his gaze to the tight skirt accentuating her ass with each gyration.

Man alive, she was something to see.

He moved closer, aching to place his hands on her backside and tug her in against himself. Let her feel the full length of him. Show her the stuff his cock was made of—one hundred percent hardcore male. No padding needed.

For the first time in a long while, Caden felt the lightness of life. Sophie brought that out in him. She was spectacular, the way she managed to adapt to any environment. Like now, the way she was rolling her hips in rhythm to the music, innocently rubbing up against his hardening cock, seemingly unaware of the effect she had on him. He tugged her in closer and relaxed, liking the feel of her against him as the beat slowed, guiding his movements. Yep, his mood had certainly lifted. Who would have thought he'd be enjoying himself at one of Jerry's appearances?

"Mind if I dance with her?" Anthony stepped between them, grinning like a kid at a carnival cotton candy booth.

Caden's light faded to black and he was two seconds away from smashing his fist into Anthony's smug face.

To his credit, Anthony hesitated. "Guess not."

Fuck. *What am I doing, anyway?* With a shake of his head, Caden headed off the dance floor and repositioned himself at a small, two-seat table.

He sat there and watched them dance. Watched her sashay and laugh and simply let herself go. Thinking about all the reasons he shouldn't—shouldn't want to bury himself deep inside her, shouldn't want to hear her scream his name, shouldn't care that another man might get there first, shouldn't care if he did. But he did care. Too much, in fact.

The song ended. Through slitted eyes, he watched her shake her head no. She left Anthony on the dance floor and retrieved her bag from Sal. Then she headed his way, her hips swinging and her eyes alight with excitement.

He stood up. Knowing he shouldn't.

Clasping her elbow, he nudged her in the direction of the door.

Knowing exactly what he was going to do.

Sophie squirmed in the backseat of the cab the entire ride back to their hotel. Caden's silence made her nervous. As did the funny look in his eyes, a mix between wanting to drop her off and wanting to get her off—or so it seemed.

"Blue balls, huh? Wanna tell me about it?" he asked, his tone laced with humor and something less identifiable. He'd stretched out his long legs and reclined back into the seat with his head on the headrest and his eyes closed. So contrary to the determined way he'd led her out of the club. He was a man on a mission no more. Or maybe she'd gotten her signals crossed and what she thought had been a lustful attraction was…what? The sexual inferno that had flared up between them on the dance floor had been real, right? She sighed.

With a slight shrug—as if her raging libido didn't matter—she said, "I'm reputed to be a girl's best friend but a man's worst nightmare, which meant I had no one in my *Late Night* corner when things got a bit testy about salaries." She paused, realizing the sting of being let go had faded. Still, she had something to prove to them. "Ha, wait until they get a load of my documentary. Little do they know my blue ball days are just beginning."

"Morons."

"Dickwads," she chimed in, surprising herself.

Silence followed. Was he considering her story or sleeping? It was hard to tell in the dark confines of the cab. The answer became clear as they rolled to a stop in front of the hotel. Caden paid, snatched her hand, and led her toward the elevator.

His lips twitched as he caught her scowl. The elevator chimed.

A few seconds later, they entered their suite. It was the first time they'd been there together *and* awake.

"Hmph, so that's what happened to you. Those wimps couldn't handle a hot little chili bean of a woman, huh?" He moved her camera bag off his shoulder and set it down on the table. With his hand on her back, he led her into his bedroom. Letting her go, he grabbed a bottle of water off the nightstand and took a long sip.

A bead of moisture formed on his bottom lip. Her tongue darted out of her mouth and she licked her own lip, so ready for it to be his but not sure how to re-spark the flame smoldering between them.

Turned out, she didn't have to worry about it. Not. At. All.

"Know what I think?" he added softly. Deceptively so, as his gaze was full of intent.

Her heart did a quick cartwheel. Boy, was that a loaded question.

She grinned, certain his balls had never been left hanging blue.

"With your gumption, smarts, and good looks? Hell, you can do or be anything you want to be."

This was so not the way she imagined their conversation going. She heard herself say, "Way before I was on *Late Night*, I was on the path to being a darn good investigative reporter."

He chuckled. "I'm not surprised. Look, tonight you had an entire crew of badass fighters eating out of your hand. They'd share their darkest secrets with you, if you asked." He frowned thoughtfully.

Dang it. She did deserve better. Playing some foul-mouthed sexpot in order to boost ratings. Tits and cocks over content. Vulgarity over genuine talent.

"You're missing a button." He reached out and placed his finger between her breasts.

Crapola. Panties. Heel. Now a blouse? At the rate she was going, there'd be nothing left for her to wear by the time they arrived in Vegas.

She glanced down.

He ran his finger up her chest, over her throat and chin, then flicked her nose.

The devil.

A long exhale escaped her—like she'd been holding her breath far too long, and unexpectedly, the weight disappeared.

She was going to get her career back on track. And, without further distractions, get Caden back on track. She tossed her hair and licked her lips.

Game on.

Caden grinned, a lady-killer of a smile.

And, just like that, the room combusted and the inferno between them reignited.

"I've got my own theory on your blue-balling abilities," he murmured. "It takes a real man to know how to handle you."

The invitation in his voice was clear.

She couldn't wait any longer. "Humph, I could have sworn a real man had been standing—"

Caden was quick.

With a low growl, he strode toward her. Gently, he cupped her cheeks with the palms of his hands, leaned in, and kissed her.

He stole away any lingering thoughts, replacing them with his lips. His mouth moving over hers. His tongue sliding along her own. The warmth of his body as he tugged her in closer, and deepened the kiss. She felt his hands draw downward across her arms until they rested on her elbows, pulling her in tight and holding her steady. Good thing; the way he worked her over, her knees had begun to buckle.

She groaned into his mouth.

He withdrew, licked his tongue along her plump lower lip, and shot her such a lustful look, it hit her deep between her legs and deeper still inside her heart.

Briefly, they stood like that, with his hands on her elbows and hers finding his hips, staring lustfully at each other and wondering when he'd make the next move. *Naughty man.*

Withdrawing a few steps, she tugged her blouse free of her skirt. Slowly, she unfastened the button between her breasts. Then, making certain he understood who he was dealing with, she winked.

The fingers weaving small circles on the inside of her elbows stopped dead in their tracks.

Bingo. Her hands moved to the bottom buttons and she slowly worked her way up. She felt like ripping her blouse off, when deep within his throat, he made a low noise. A shiver of excitement ran down her spine. More. She wanted more. Wanted to better understand the dangerous undercurrent that she'd sensed within him, and find her way into the heart of Caden Kelly, discover what exactly made him tick.

She paused her fingers at the last button, her arms preventing him from stealing a peek. "Bet you're thinking, will she? Or won't she?"

"Chili bean, I'm thinking how many *will she's* will she have. Multiple, guaranteed."

Dang-diggity. She couldn't strip down fast enough. With shaky hands, she unfastened it, wiggled, and let her blouse fall to the floor.

His arms fell to his sides. He raked his gaze over her leisurely, as if he was making a mental checklist of her body and what she offered up. His lips lifted, wickedly, as he zeroed in on her underwear. The sheer demi-cup bra lifted her breasts nicely. Cherry red—his favorite color. She'd purchased it, along with several other much-needed undergarments, earlier. All with him in mind.

She swept one strap then the other off her shoulders and onto her arms. Her hand shifted to the clasp between her breast and she unfastened it, pinching the material together between trembling fingers. Wanting him so much it hurt. Wanting to make him want her so much it hurt. Jeez, her whole body shook with emotion.

He drew in a long breath. Desire flickered in his eyes, like a summer storm passing over fresh cut grass.

"Do it."

The material slid from beneath her fingers. Her breasts bounced free, brazenly bared for him.

"I wanna see all of you," Caden growled. He stepped forward and reached around her waist. Her breasts brushed up against his chest and her nipples turned to pebbles. A groan caught in her throat.

He unzipped the back of her skirt and smoothed the material from her hips. It fell to the floor, leaving her in nothing but her sleek black heels and red thong.

The warmth of his breath caressed her cheek, and her heart accelerated.

She wanted him. Now. What had happened in their past, whatever the future held, it didn't matter.

"Beautiful," he said, his voice deep and husky. His big hands touched her waist. Lifting her up, he turned her around and gently set her back onto her heels. "You're so fuckin' beautiful." His hands roamed over the curves of her buttocks and gave them a squeeze. The spread of his fingers left a hot trail as they shifted to her hips, then beneath the side string of her thong.

Biting her lip, she anticipated his next move, and wasn't disappointed when he moved the strings down, over her hips. Wiggling, her thong slid down to her ankles.

"Step," he demanded.

She lifted one foot, then the other. For good measure, she kicked the material away. "My heels—"

"Leave them on."

She heard his soft tread on the carpet as he moved away. The zing of a zipper undone. The rustle of his clothing being removed. Her anticipation mounting with each slight sound.

With his palms, he caressed her bare cheeks. A sensual, intimate gesture. But brief. Her skin went cool when he removed one hand and reached around to cup her breast. Gently, he massaged her, catching her nipple between two fingers. His lips kissed the sensitive tendon on her neck, just below the ear.

She shifted up on her toes, wanting more.

"Hungry yet, chili cheeks?" His tone wasn't playful. Before she could reply—*yes, sweet*—he moved.

His bare chest pressed against her back, forcing her

closer to the wall. He pinched her nipple and she shuddered as hot, slick moisture coated her folds.

Lips parting, she arched her head back, savoring the feel of his lips on her skin, the gentle caress of his fingers trailing across her hip and into her trim nest.

His lips lifted and she felt his breath on her ear. "Spread your legs."

She did so, leaning forward and pressing her elbows against the wall.

He rewarded her by spiraling a finger over her nub. Tiny starbursts flickered across her bare skin. Shifting, she widened her stance.

His laughter rang out, so sexy, so guttural and raw with need, it caused a second burst of pleasure within her. This time, however, it ignited deep within her heart and grew stronger with his every touch, leaving her breathless.

He repositioned the hand on her breast between her legs, distracting her from the sudden swell of emotion before she had time to consider it further. He played with her slick folds, making sure she was thoroughly drenched before sliding two fingers inside. His thumb rotated in slow circles over her highly sensitive pearl.

She groaned.

He pulled away and she arched her hips back. The sound of ripping foil made her want to thank the heavens. She wanted him inside her. Fast.

She heard his grunt.

"What...?"

He didn't answer, but he lifted her and cradled her in his arms as he strode toward the bed. She bounced on the mattress where he dropped her, arms and legs

wide. Shifting onto her elbows, she opened her mouth
to speak, but swallowed her words.

He stood at the side of the bed, shaking his head.

She didn't have time to process the emotions playing
out on his face because her attention was drawn lower,
and lower still. She swallowed hard. Sure, she'd seen
him shirtless. Devoured him, inch by delicious inch.
His taut, muscled chest. Eight-pack abs, with its rolling curves and valleys. That sweet spot just below the
hipbone. But his full-blown erection made her want to
lick her lips. And then him.

He was enormous. Swollen and ready with need.

Clearly, this was not the reason he hesitated.

Reluctantly, her gaze shifted back to his face. Her
breath hitched, as she caught the look on his face. His
eyes slid closed, briefly, then reopened. As if he'd come
to some sort of decision.

"I can't fuck you against the wall like I'd planned."
He moved forward and dropped onto the bed, pulling
himself over her and wedging himself between her legs.

She reached up and cupped his cheeks, dragging
him down to her lips. She couldn't grab a taste of him
quick enough. Plunging her tongue into his mouth, she
devoured him. Hungry with want, and need.

His manhood pressed against her core, using his
hardness to coat her with her own juices as if readying
her for him. *Like she needed it.*

He groaned, or maybe it was her, the sound swallowed whole by his mouth.

She ran her tongue over his teeth.

He did the same, before breaking their kiss.

She spread her legs wider, and her pussy quivered
as the broad head of him slid a fraction of an inch in-

side of her. Her folds clenched and unclenched around his massive girth.

"I want to watch you as I make you come." In a smooth thrust forward, his entire length filled her tight, slick channel.

She gasped in pleasure, surprised at how completely he filled her.

True to his word, he was watching her. His pupils darkened as he withdrew and thrust. Again and again.

She wound her legs around his waist, lifting her hips for him.

He thickened deep inside her, and bells chimed sweetly in her head. He was too beautiful for words. Her body hummed with pleasure as the root of him filled her completely.

He quickened his thrusts and she lost her mind.

"So fuckin' tight, my sweet chili bean. Look at me." His thrust deepened and he cursed beneath his breath.

Her eyelashes fluttered open as the tension inside her swelled and crested.

"Let. Go."

Wave after wave of pleasure spread through her. Her ears rang with sweet bliss.

The tempo of his hips increased, his thrusts deep and long. She ground against him, her release a sweet, agonizing peak.

Caden let out a shout, shaking slightly as he climaxed hard.

His big body blanketed her and pressed her into the mattress. She didn't mind. For the first time in her life, she felt complete.

Moments passed by. The sound of his breath whispered in her ear.

She sighed, contently.

"You okay?" he demanded, coming onto his elbows and gazing at her intently.

She raised her head and kissed his lips. "Perfect."

His lips twisted up into a smug smile. He rolled off her, climbed out of the bed, and strode into the bathroom, glancing at the bedroom door.

She lay back in his bed and snuggled beneath the sheets, her mind relaxing along with her body. Sex with Caden had been everything she'd expected. And more. So much more her heart danced.

Sometime later, she heard the water running in the bathroom. "Are you okay?" she murmured, her voice heavy, her words jumbled.

He didn't respond, likely didn't even hear her. She wondered about it, then at her own dang satisfaction, and her corny reaction to it. A good-loving kind of daze washed over her as she relaxed back into bed. Heck, if she were a smoker, two cigarettes would be dangling from between her lips. Maybe she'd offer one to Caden or better still, she'd make him work for it. *What is he doing, anyway?* Her eyelids drifted shut. Instead of sheep, she counted the passing time of Caden's growing absence. A minute. Two. Three, until she frowned, a second before all her thoughts quieted.

Chapter 15

STREETFIGHTING: A kind of fighting learned on the streets—like battling it out for a cab or parking spot

Sophie gave him a wink, then put the Aston's top down as the car began its winding incline into the cooler climate of the Sedona mountains. Sexy, *satisfied* minx. Caden kept his sunglasses up on his head, not wanting to spoil the view. And it wasn't the scenery that held his attention.

Today, Sophie looked younger, more relaxed and playful. Less formal than usual, yet still tidy and neat. She was wearing a crisp white blouse with tiny pearl buttons and a stiff, starched collar. The white set off the brightly colored flowers on her short, flowing skirt. Still the reserved professional, with no outward signs—except for the soft glow about her—that he'd fucked her six ways to Sunday.

At first glance, you thought you had her all pegged. But if you looked closely—and man, Caden couldn't seem to take his eyes off her—her spiciness shined through. Like her flame-colored fingernails. Fuck-me nails that stood out against the creamy skin of the thigh where she'd rested her hand. Like the fact she wore no hosiery on her long legs. Like the tiny thongs and sheer teases of bras she was fond of wearing.

His cock stirred in his shorts and hardened further at the sight of her bright red toenails, playing peek-a-boo with him out of her open-toe heels. *Damn.* He was losing his mind, getting all worked up over her toes. He pulled his gaze away, knowing it wasn't just her toes. Sophie was the whole package. She was the real deal. *Shit.*

He forced his focus to the subtle beauty of the Northern Arizona landscape. The crimson buttes and majestic rocks were something, nature's subtle way of claiming a man's soul. Guess Mother Nature had a fight on her hands, because the woman beside him had already…

Freakin' love-drunk idiot.

His heart balled up tighter than a boulder. This was not what he needed. Or wanted. *Don't forget don't deserve*, he reminded himself, as if he'd ever forget.

He avoided looking her way. Instead, he studied the sun reflecting off the mountains until the emotional twattle inside his head settled.

"You be my sweet pea. I'll be your bumblebee," Sophie sang out sweetly, extremely off-key, with the lyrics all wrong. His jaw relaxed its tight hold. Man, this woman had a way of calming him and making him smile. Even if she was responsible for stirring up all of his better-left-dormant emotional shit.

Though she couldn't carry a tune to save her life.

But, man-oh-man, how she could make his body hum. The third time—in the wee hours of the morning—he'd been so deep inside her, it felt like he'd already won Tetnus. The satisfaction in her eyes as she peaked caused him to come so hard the bed shook. Something he'd never forget.

He felt a weak smile on his lips. "Honey bee, not bumblebee. What kind of guy would be harping on and on about a bumblebee?"

"What kind of fighter loves country music so much?" she replied, leveling him with a look.

"I spent time in Nashville."

"Finally! Something personal. Are you volunteering a tell-all?"

Caden arched an eyebrow, then murmured, "Guess you haven't watched the videos." He heard her sigh.

"The sex tape? I briefly skimmed over it. Unfair move, you taking a video of me sleeping."

"Isn't that what happens to celebrities?" He saw her stiffen, clearly uncomfortable. Such a different reaction than what one expected of her. He changed the topic. "I wanted you to see the smile I put on your face, chili cakes."

He wanted to groan as she grinned. It was a mixture of shyness and sweetness, with a hint of embarrassment. *Interesting.* Man, he liked getting her all riled up, though.

"Come on, Caden," she prodded, "you promised.

Tell me something no one knows. So, you spent some time in Nashville…"

Nashville. *Fuck*. "You really wanna hear all my shit?" he ground out.

"Your shit is what's going to sell my documentary."

"Tell you what, if I spill my guts to you right now, you let me do what I got to do in Vegas."

She nodded.

Instantly, he regretted his promise. Man, maybe he'd come so hard it rattled his brain, his common sense. What was it about her that made him want to roll over and bare his soft side?

"Don't you dare back out now," she threatened, sensing his hesitation.

What the hell—it's not like it mattered. Not anymore. "I lied. I wasn't four. I was eight. Not much of a stretch, huh?"

"What? Are you talking about your first fight? Now it's eight?"

He ground his teeth. Perfect. This was what he wanted, right? Mercilessly, he forged ahead. "I'm telling the truth. My first fight was at eight. Behind Wilson Elementary School after dismissal. My foster mother was dating a Brazilian Jiu-jitsu instructor."

"She arranged for a slug fest behind the school?" Sophie's tone was disbelieving.

Caden laughed, but it came out hoarse. "Nah. She arranged for a few freebie lessons at her boyfriend's mixed martial arts school. Thought it might help get a scrawny kid into shape, build muscles and stamina. Plus, it was a good way to blow off some anger."

"Oh my God. You're serious. You were in foster care at eight years old? And fighting? I never imagined…"

She paused, probably realizing her questions were more like declarations—outraged declarations on his behalf. Inhaling sharply, she continued in a softer voice, "I'm having trouble understanding it all."

"Hmph, I'm still trying to get a grip myself," he muttered, flashing back to the fight and to the memory of Mickey, the biggest bully and strongest puncher at Wilson, spitting out mouthfuls of playground sand. Caden was instantly the kid no one fucked with. Too bad it was short-lived.

"Did you win?"

"Yep. Guess you could say I won. The class bully seemed to think so, anyway."

"What was your foster mom like?"

"The kindest of the bunch. Desperate, but nice. The tree-hugging type, anti-violence. Honest to a fault." *Kept her hands to herself.* His mouth tightened. "Guess her hiring a trainer to teach an eight-year-old to kick ass so she could get laid wasn't her wisest move, with all the trouble I caused afterward."

"You're a fighter. Clearly, she got over her dislike for the sport."

"Nope." He tried to keep the bitterness from his tone, not wanting Sophie's pity. Give her the facts—that's all.

"Did her boyfriend teach you these mad skills I keep hearing about?"

He grunted. "Mad skills, huh? But yeah. He was a decent guy. Taught me the basics, and laid a foundation, though I didn't know it at the time. I thought I was tough."

He'd learned the hard way how weak he'd really been.

Taking the water bottle out of the cup holder, he took

a chug, then moved on to a safer topic. "Do you know what Jiu-jitsu is?"

"Sounds like a kind of juice you drink at Girl Scout camp." She winked at him.

His lips curled briefly.

"Do you think you're dealing with an amateur here?" she tossed his own words back at him. "I did my homework." In a more serious voice, she said, "I want to make MMA accessible to everyone, from the hardcore fans to the average viewer who won't understand the nuances of this sport. Cover both perspectives, mine and yours. So tell me in your own words, where does Jiu-jitsu fit in among the other skills an MMA fighter must learn?"

Her hair was pulled off her face, neatly piled in a stylish bun. He resisted the temptation to reach over and mess it up. Keep things light before he shed more rain on their already washed-out parade. Thank the fuck for the change in topic. Little did she know how close the drizzle was to being a full-fledged downpour.

His eyes fell to her heels, shifting his thoughts from the past back to the present. Who in their right mind but Sophie would take to the road to cover these animals wearing three-inch heels? You'd think someone invested in teaming up with a group of fighters would be in comfortable sweatpants or shorts, T-shirts, Nikes.

"Do I have something on my skirt?" she interrupted his thoughts.

He wiggled his pointer finger at her, and she blushed. He gestured to her heels.

"America should see the shoes you're marching around in. Those are sexy as hell."

"We're discussing Jiu-jitsu, not my choice of footwear."

He decided to cut her a break and help her out. Hell, help himself out—a safer topic, one he could handle without giving too much away. "Jiu-jitsu uses the manipulation of joint locks and choke holds to make the opponent submit. The theory is that a less-muscular fighter can force a more traditionally trained one like a boxer, wrestler, or karate master to tap out."

"And joint-manipulation works?"

"Hurts like hell, unexpectedly so. You think a punch to the muscle causes damage, but throwing a joint out of whack can be agonizing."

"And your stepmother's boyfriend taught you how to do that?"

"Yep."

"He must have taught you a lot of useful skills?"

He shook his head.

Sophie frowned. "Why not?"

"They broke up. She bailed, said she couldn't handle me. I got shuffled to another home. Wilson seemed like a country club in comparison."

"How many foster homes were you in?" Sophie demanded, unable to censor the alarm in her voice. "I thought you'd grown up with your brother."

Damn.

"Caden?"

"Six."

"Six? Then what? You got your freedom at eighteen?"

He snorted. "I got my freedom way before then."

"What do you mean?"

"I took off."

"To?"

"Nowhere. The streets. Until my brother Bracken tracked me down." He felt her eyes on him so he plucked his sunglasses off his head and put them on. Safer that way. "Look, that stuff's not important."

"Of course it's important. Your past is what molds you into the person you are today." Her voice cracked, teeming with emotion.

Her pity was like a solid strike to the abdomen, then a tight squeeze. It hooked into him, took hold and yanked everything out, leaving one freaking hellhole of a mess. He should've known she'd zoomed right in on his weaknesses. Fuckin' scary how she'd seen right past his bullshit. At least she hadn't gotten it on video.

"That's what Anthony meant by you being streetwise. You lived on the streets with your brother."

Anthony. Hearing the fighter's name coming from her lips was like tossing dry wood onto the emotional bonfire already raging in his head. He struggled to find another topic before he lost it completely. And failed miserably.

"We're survivors, you and I," she added softly.

He glanced at her. She was gazing up at the sky. That asshole Hank had done a number on her. Caden planned on returning the favor.

Man alive, what had he been thinking? Two people with this much baggage would never be able to haul it around for the long term.

Sophie must have come to the same conclusion because she was mercifully silent.

Her leg flexed as she pressed the gas pedal.

He sat back in his seat and closed his eyes.

End of discussion.

Sophie held the Aston at a solid eighty miles per. Guess he wasn't the only one eager to hit Vegas.

When it came to talking sex, Caden was in the driver's seat. It was the kind of verbal foreplay he excelled at. The perfect wall to throw up between them—keeping the conversation light, the tension that had been like a third passenger at bay, and as they crossed the Nevada state line, leaving any lingering thoughts about his misspent youth back in Arizona. Relief washed over him when she took the bait, and started sassing him back.

Her clever responses made him grin, but the flush on her cheeks his sexy promises had put there was what was really turning him on.

Ironic how she was going tit for tat with him, yet seemed so innocent. Matter of fact, he was pretty sure her *Late Night* persona was a lie.

"Let's talk about the kinky things I'm gonna do to that hot body of yours."

He could tell she liked that by the way she fidgeted with the hem of her skirt.

"Let's talk about how you better put your money where your mouth is, sugar."

"My mouth, huh?"

He heard her inhale sharply as she caught his look of unadulterated lust. "I meant the rest of the interview."

"Oh yeah?"

"Ohhh, yeah." She extended the *oh*, making it sound sexy and passionate.

"Wish I'd caught on tape how you looked with my mouth between your thighs and my tongue working over your clit."

She wiggled in her seat and grasped the steering

wheel tighter. Her widened eyes were focused on the roadway. A shame. He wanted to see the fire burning there. Yep, he was the one doing the driving, and he was loving every minute of it.

He paused, giving her time to gather her thoughts. He loved her mind, the way she always had a quick comeback. G-rated compared to his R-rated, he noted, further proof that she wasn't the person people expected her to be. Her reaction to him turned him on, big time. Not that he needed any help in that department.

"As soon as we get situated in Vegas, I'm deleting your sex tape."

"Better watch it first, chili bean."

She blushed a pretty shade of pink. Still, he knew what it was like to be in the celebrity spotlight, and made it a point to reassure her.

"It's not a sex tape. Or sex tapes—I recorded myself three times."

"Three? When? What did you say?"

"Not much substance in your first recording, that one was more a narrative on fighting in general. In the second, there's a bunch of bullshit the public will want to hear. My sponsorships and what it was like being the body for Ultimate American Man."

"Oh my God. Really?"

"Yep. Even gave you a real exclusive, how I'm ending my contract with them, and how I'll be focusing all my energy on fighting."

"You are?" She turned to peer at him.

"Yep.

"Why?"

He knew that was going to be her response. Silently, he thanked the heavens she didn't ask about the third recording. The footage he'd shot earlier this morning like some besotted moron. What the fuck had he been thinking? Somehow, he had to get his hands on her camcorder and delete it. One major sentimental blood-letting. It would lead to nothing but broken hearts and tears.

He shrugged, and focused on answering her question honestly. "My billboard days are done. I texted my manager. He's terminating my modeling contract. No one knows this yet. You've got the exclusive you wanted so badly. See, I've a bone to pick with myself. Learned a lesson—all the time training, getting into peak physical shape and ready to fight, it isn't enough without mental discipline. Without drive and commitment, a fighter will never advance. Those mental battles are the bloodiest, get my drift?"

She sat up straighter in her seat, stiff and proper. Yeah, she knew exactly what he was talking about.

It took her a second to recover.

He could tell she realized that he hadn't answered her question by the silence that followed. After a long exhale, he muttered, "Just watch the tape."

"So, you were that guy—physically ready but otherwise unprepared?" she promptly asked.

"Yep, a poster child for it."

She turned her eyes from the road, cocked her head, and studied him. "What happened?"

"My older brother died in Afghanistan. Mikey."

She peered at him closely. "I'm so sorry. I didn't know you had another brother."

"When Family Services broke us up, he headed into the army. I didn't get to see him before he died."

She frowned, quietly considering his words.

"Ultimate American Male isn't who I am and was

never what I wanted. My life kind of derailed after Mikey died. Winning Tetnus is something I need to do for my brothers, and for myself. Like you said before, it'll be proof that I'm a survivor. I've got big plans to get my shit back on track."

He heard her sigh. "You and me both."

He balled his fist in his hand, and added, "Tetnus is all I've wanted for a long time. I'll do whatever it takes to win."

Hell, he needed to get a grip, and rid his head of all the soft, lovey-dovey nonsense rattling around inside. A man like him didn't deserve a woman like her for the long term. She brought out things in him—a hope in him, *feelings* within him—that were best left dead. Better he shake it off now, before things got out of hand, as if his pile of bullshit wasn't high enough with the issue of the duffel bag.

No, he needed to clear the air, then clear his head. Make sure she knew to keep things light. Give himself a solid haymaker of a reminder, as well. He was going to finish this thing, for himself and his brother. Without her.

"I don't—can't—do relationships. No long-term commitments. Best you know that now. What this is, is casual. Temporary."

A small huffing sound was the only indication she'd heard him.

Sophie averted her gaze, studying the horizon for a while and taking measure of what he was telling her. Smart woman. Silence accompanied them down a long stretch of desert roadway, though his brain kept chanting *bastard, lying bastard*, until Sophie asked in a low voice, "Winning Tetnus is that important to you?"

Shit, he had to delete that freakin' third truth fest of a video. Better for both of them if she remained oblivious to his bleeding heart. "Yep. Nothing else matters."

"Deflecto-mundo," she murmured.

Terrific. She wasn't falling for his crap—it seemed she knew him better than he knew himself. Jesus, all the confirmation she needed was on her camcorder.

"So, you're saying that if I pull the car over, get out, strip naked, and bend over the hood, it wouldn't matter to you in the slightest?" she quipped, though the tightness around her eyes suggested her taunt held more than she was letting on.

How easy it would be to let someone like Sophie in. It was his turn to squirm in his seat. Except he couldn't because his cock pinned him in place, swelling up like a long iron weight and growing heavier by the second. The tension that had been building since their repartee reignited. Thank God she was steering him back into a more comfortable ride, one with him in the driver's seat.

"You're saying that if I got down on my knees between your—"

"Pull over."

Out of the corner of his eyes, he saw her shake her head.

"Pull. The. Car. Over."

"Tell me it doesn't matter."

Shit.

"Tell me that when we get to Vegas and Anthony becomes the new focus of my documentary, that won't matter to you."

He heard a low-pitched sound. From her? Or him?

"I care about you. Tell me that doesn't matter that I'm

falling…" Her voice sounded hoarse, deep and filled with emotion.

He thought about her back in the desert, hurtling rocks into the sky. Her strength of character. Her stubbornness. She was a survivor, just like him.

"Oh, darn," she added. "Damn. Damn. Damn."

That was it.

"Pull the car over, chili cheeks."

"No."

"Do it."

"Fuck you."

Her words surprised him. He grinned. Hell, maybe winning Tetnus wasn't the only thing he needed in his life.

He reached over and placed his palm on her thigh.

She jerked away as if his touch burned her. His heart felt like someone had set it afire and it had started to blaze uncontrollably. Knowing what he'd been—a neglected, troubled brawler. Knowing where he was headed—to become the toughest fighter around. Knowing this, she still cared.

The thing about professional fighters that set them apart from the amateurs was that they recognized the exact moment when their opponent whipped out skills they'd never even imagined. Mad skills. The kind that forced a fighter to his knees and to accept defeat. And Sophie'd thrown him one motherfucker of a punch. Falling for *him*. This was the tap out of all tap outs.

"Sophie," he said softly, "pull over, sweetheart." He gently squeezed her thigh so she'd look at him.

She shot him a glare that would melt ice.

"I lied." He shook his head, closed his eyes, and reopened them. What he saw was her staring at him like he was someone worth loving.

Maybe, just maybe…he could live up to her expectations. It was well worth a try if he could keep his shit together. He relaxed, his decision made.

Just like Tetnus, nothing was going to stop him from winning *her*.

"Vegas can wait. I'll show you…"

The car bounced, cutting Caden off, as they catapulted backward against their seats. The rear of the Aston fishtailed and Sophie focused all of her energy on safely steering the car off the roadway. Crapola, she must have hit something.

"Holy shit," Caden exclaimed, throwing his hands on the dashboard as they jerked to a stop. Then he laughed. "You trying to tell me you're tired of driving or that you want me up inside you fast?"

Maybe I'm trying to tell you I see beneath your sexpot exterior—that every time you throw sex into the mix, you're deflecting from the truth. Caden climbed out of the car before she could put her thoughts to words.

She followed, scanning the long expanse of barren roadway for some signs of life. The air was cooler than Phoenix but hotter than Sedona.

He nodded toward the hood. "Bend over."

"Right here on the side of the highway?" Man, she was shocked the idea was such a turn-on. Naughty, like something Sophie Morelle might do. Maybe she was a bit more like her alter ego than she'd realized. And Caden sure knew how to bring this side of her out to play, all right.

"This was your idea, chili cakes."

It certainly was her idea. "Is this your idea of make-up sex?"

Caden took a long look up the road one way and then the other. Finally, his eyes fell on her. "More than that, okay? Much more. But that's all I'm saying."

Sophie blinked, and her heart mimicked the movement.

She eyed the hood. When had she ever done anything remotely wild? Or exciting? With someone she cared about? Stepping closer, his hands touched her sides and he turned her so her back was to the hood.

"What if a car passes us?"

"We'll see them way before they can see us. Keep your eyes on the horizon, honey." His hands found the buttons on his Bermuda shorts. He opened them and was working his cock out of his boxers before she could even say the word *horizon*.

"Drop your panties and get on up on the hood."

"I thought you wanted me bent over the hood?" she stated, saucily, the idea that they were about to get it on along a deserted stretch of Nevada highway downright titillating. Still, she added, "That hood's got to be hotter than heck."

"Come on. Vegas is waiting. I'm waiting."

Oh, boy, was he ever.

"You won't be seated there for long, and I wanna take good care of you first."

Oh. My. God.

Before she could process what that meant, he lifted her up and placed her on the hood. His warm palms caressed her thighs on their journey upward, slowly, until a finger slid beneath the elastic of her thong, and in one long stroke, caressed her nub. Her hips lifted off the hood and her throat went dry as a desert.

"Keep your eyes on the roadway."

Yeah, right. At that moment, a parade could have been marching by and she wouldn't have cared.

Deftly, his hands found her hips and shifted her slightly upward as he yanked her panties free.

She heard the rustle of her skirt being lifted. Her eyes nearly rolled right off the horizon when she felt his tongue touch the sensitive skin on the inside of her knee. With his head beneath her skirt, he traced a path between her thighs.

He laved her, running his tongue deep between her folds.

She didn't know what was hotter, the heat of the hood, the flush of moisture at the juncture of her legs, or the wild devil between her thighs.

His finger worked her folds open as his tongue delved in her depths.

She leaned back onto her elbows on the hood and looked at the sky, watching it fill with stars as her climax came fast and hard.

Her skirt fell back into place but not for long. She heard the sound of foil unwrapping, and a renewed wave of moisture pooled between her legs. He slid her forward, tugged her upright, and lifted her clear off the hood.

"I've been dying to get inside you all day. Hold it up."

Grabbing both sides of the waistband, she yanked her skirt up and wrapped her legs around his waist. Immediately, his cock found her center and pushed into her.

"Never seems like I can get enough of you, Sophie,"

he murmured, thrusting deeper and faster. "Every time I'm near you, all I want is more."

Her heart sang out in chorus with her body. So beautifully, she wanted to cry.

He paused and searched the highway. "Let's move things inside." She felt empty at his withdrawal, and ached for more. He led her to the passenger seat and climbed in, his magnificent cock at full attention. "You keep your eyes south and I'll watch the northern horizon. Hop on."

It took a few awkward seconds to straddle him in the bucket seat but the reward was so worth it, as her moist core found his delicious hardness and she sank down onto him. He lifted her up by the hips, then let her drop. Over and over, until her body moved in perfect rhythm with his own.

He groaned.

Stars appeared once more overhead, shining brighter and brighter with every thrust.

His cock thickened inside her. So sweet, and so very sinful.

He touched her cheek in a gentle caress. A whisper of a smile curled his lips before his mouth claimed hers, his tongue delving inside her mouth in time with their movements.

Time was irrelevant. Nothing mattered but Caden, and the feeling building deep within her.

She broke free of his lips, arched her back and cried out.

With three long thrusts, he groaned, a raw, heady, lustful sound, and climaxed along with her.

"Holy dang-diggity, that was hot," she murmured

into his ear, nuzzling her cheek up against the warmth of his neck.

Her entire body seemed to quiver around him as his cock twitched in agreement.

Yep. Vegas could wait.

Chapter 16

TWISTER: The kind of fight you just didn't see coming

Someone cleared their throat. Loudly. Then repeated the action before commanding, "Please disengage and remove yourselves from the vehicle."

Caden froze beneath her. Sophie opened her eyes and peered over her shoulder. Sure enough, a man dressed in blue shorts and a blue shirt stood at the hood of the Aston, his gaze toward the sky. His sedan's flashing blue light in the background. Busted by a Nevada Highway Patrolman.

Caught like two horny teens. Not good. Not at all. Jeez, she probably looked a wreck. Or worse, like someone who'd just done the dirty in the bucket seat of a

James Bond mobile. Her thighs shook, from mortification and from the cramp in her right leg from straddling him. Luckily, her skirt covered them enough for Caden to disengage and readjust himself. He smoothed her skirt over her legs. Then he pivoted and climbed out of the car with her in his arms.

The officer was still looking at the sky. No question he knew exactly what had transpired. Sophie had never done anything so rash. So downright dirty. So against her moral code of what was proper, and what wasn't. This clearly fell into the latter. So mind-blowing she might have considered another round a few miles up the road.

She glanced up at Caden, expecting a broad smirk. But his lips, still moist from being locked with hers, were pulled into a tight, thin line. So serious. His gaze met hers. So pained, like he'd led her toward a life of crime, or something worse.

He tensed, then set her on her feet next to him.

It felt as if dark, ominous clouds rolled overhead, sending chills up her spine. Caden nodded his head, a slight gesture. What was he telling her?

The officer peered into the car, then gave a low whistle. "This is some set of wheels. Lordy, isn't this the car from the James Bond flick?"

"Yep. An Aston Martin DB5," Caden confirmed, his tone completely devoid of emotion.

"Yours?" the officer asked, more curious than with any sense of duty. Sophie could tell by the gleam of admiration in his eyes. At least it took his attention off of what had gone down in the Aston—literally.

"Rental."

"Didn't know you could rent a car like this. Next

time, I'll tell the wife a plain ole Mustang won't do. Can I see the rental paperwork?"

"Sure." Caden retrieved the rental agreement from the glove box and handed it off to the officer. She should have felt reassured by his presence next to her. The officer was being kind, too. But a sense of dread billowed up within her. She couldn't breathe. Her throat had dried up quicker than a raindrop on a cactus bloom.

"Who was driving the car?" the officer questioned, as he scanned the documents. "Hard to tell, under the circumstances."

Caden spoke up. "I was driving. I'm completely responsible."

The officer shook his head. "Out here, it might be a long spell before you see folk. Still, it's a risky move performing lewd acts in a vehicle on a public road."

Lewd? Sophie gave a mental groan. *What the hell had she been thinking? If this cop recognized her...* She tucked her chin down, hoping for the best but anticipating the worst.

Caden frowned and shook his head slightly. For a fighter, he seemed to have run out of steam.

"I can always issue a ticket and court appearance. You don't seem like bad folk—horny perhaps, getting it on in a bucket seat. Need your driver's licenses."

Before she could explain how she lacked identification, money…morals…Caden tugged his license out of his expensive leather wallet, and handed it to the officer.

She shot him a questioning look.

He ignored her.

The officer whistled and then grinned. "Caden Kelly? You the mixed martial arts fighter? Headed to Tetnus, huh?"

Caden nodded. Sure the situation was awkward. But he was acting funny—not at all like his sarcastic self. And if any situation ever deserved to be mocked, this was it. Still, Caden seemed to have withdrawn into himself. It gave her the chills.

"The fellas at the station are big MMA fans. See this?" He showed Caden his knuckles. "This is from messing around in one of the guys' basement. Mimicking your moves—trying to perform a perfect guillotine. Man, why'd you quit like that?"

"It's a long story," Caden responded. "If you want to know the details, you'll have to check out Sophie Morelle's documentary. She's gotten an exclusive interview with me, and has all the shit."

The officer glanced from Caden to her and back to Caden. "Sophie Morelle? Isn't she that foul-mouthed woman who was thrown off national television because she knocked you out with her camera? That woman looked like she was trouble."

Ah, trouble is standing right in front of you. Yep, she could tell he was a big fan.

Caden grunted.

"Okay, Caden. I'm going to let you and your female friend off with a verbal warning. Your loose cannon of a brother would have my head if I issued you a ticket."

Sophie wanted to laugh. That was it, a warning? Caden's fame—and his *brother*, a cop out here in Nevada? Go figure!—had come to the rescue. She was glad the officer hadn't connected the dots and recognized her. The infamous Sophie Morelle would have warranted a naughty reporter caught-with-her-skirt-up ticket and a subsequent court appearance.

She shifted in her heels. Close call. If the boys at her

former network—or God forbid, the public—heard what she'd been doing…

Maybe that's what the dark, invisible cloud of doom was all about?

As the officer scribbled out the warning, he added, "I'm not writing down the details because I'm a big fan of yours, and want to see you win Tetnus."

The silent man next to her nodded.

The officer continued, "Next time you decide to get it on in the sweetest ride to hit this neck of the desert, make sure you don't get caught. Heck, man, didn't you see my lights a mile away? Not like there's anything else to look at out here."

"*Next* time, we'll be more careful, officer."

Sophie glared at Caden. Great, his humor had been restored.

The officer shot Caden a grin. Subtle male, non-verbal communication—which was to say it was anything but subtle. A silent high-five, acknowledging how he didn't see anything wrong with a bit of kinky fun out in the Nevada sunshine.

"Think I can get an autograph?"

Caden shook his head and held out his hand as the officer handed him a scrap of paper he'd dug out of his pocket.

A welcome breeze kicked up. Even in the higher elevations, the sun was relentless.

The bit of paper caught the breeze, sailed through the air, and landed a few feet away. The good-natured officer chased after it.

He bent, stooped over, and paused. "Um, Caden. You've got a flat over here."

"Shit," Caden muttered. Something in the tone of his voice caused a tiny shiver to roll up her spine.

"Pop the trunk and I'll give you a hand," the officer continued.

Caden didn't budge. "You know my brother Bracken's deal, right?"

The officer frowned, his gaze running from Caden to the trunk. "The best undercover narcotics agent we've got. Shame how I.A.'s been giving him such flack for not following protocol. What's going on, Caden?"

Surely the Aston Martin had a functioning spare tire? Yet the man next to her was as tense as he'd been earlier, when he'd revealed more than he'd intended about his heartbreaking past.

When she'd realized just how much she'd fallen for him.

Sophie Morelle involved with a mixed martial arts fighter and former Ultimate American Male model. A man who took her breath away with one bat of his eyelashes.

Dang-diggity, she *was* in love with him.

"Let her call a cab, okay? You know how it is, with ladies looking for a quick celebrity ride. I picked her up in Phoenix, her bags are in the back seat. I rented the car, I was driving, I'm responsible for everything," Caden told the officer, his voice low but clear.

She gasped, but no sound escaped from her tightening throat. Like someone had kicked her in the stomach, then squeezed her esophagus so she couldn't cry out.

The last time she'd felt like this, the good citizens of Hawley were pressuring her not to testify.

That's what Caden had just done, pulled a Hawley

on her. The…traitor! *A groupie? An insignificant fuck out here in the desert?*

"I know you're doing your job. But in a few seconds, I want your promise that you'll call my brother. He'll confirm everything," she heard him say, his tone hoarse and deadly serious.

At the officer's nod, Caden headed around to driver's side, opened the door, and reached in and popped the trunk, the angry noise of the metal lock filling the air.

"Don't stand there. Call a cab. Have them take you to Vegas," he told her in an unemotional voice.

"A cab?" she whispered. She felt lightheaded, a sudden case of heatstroke but worse. Her heart was breaking. She hadn't seen it coming—any of it.

The officer shuffled forward and ducked his head into the trunk. Through the dead silence, she heard the sound of a zipper being unfastened.

Caden quietly moved closer to him, stretched his arms out in front of him, and crossed one wrist over the other.

"Darn gone it!" the officer exclaimed. "Bracken's bent the rules before, but this beats all. First thing we're gonna do on the way to the precinct is call him in. If I find out you're a doper or dealer…"

"She's good to go, right?"

The officer nodded. "But I'm warning you, you're gonna be fighting a whole different battle in jail."

Sophie felt her legs carrying her forward. She looked into the trunk, and gasped. Clear bags of unfamiliar green pills overflowed from an oversized duffel. Her gaze faltered as she spotted several plastic syringes sticking out of the bag as well.

"I take full responsibility. She had no knowledge of this. She's just a groupie, that's all."

No knowledge. No knowledge. The words echoed off the hot asphalt and burned into her head. No knowledge of what? Drugs? In the trunk of the Aston? *Oh. My. God.*

The two men moved toward the police car. Sophie was frozen in place. The duffel bag looked familiar, like the bags Jaysin Bouvine…

"For fuck's sake, Sophie. Call. A. Cab," she heard Caden shout, his voice sounding so far away, already.

The patrolman pulled out his cell phone, and handed it to her. She looked down at it dumbly. Listening to the officer address Caden. Listening to him address the playboy who'd just made love to her, who then chalked it up to a meaningless *fuck*. A man who had drugs stashed in the back of his Aston rental. A man she thought she'd fallen fall, and ended up flat on her face.

The patrolman's words sounded like a raging wave just at the point when it crests. "Caden Kelly, you better not be lying. Or I promise you'll be placed under arrest for possession of illegal, performance-enhancing drugs quicker than this sweet car can burn rubber."

Chapter 17

CUT MAN: The person in a fight most likely to break your heart

Three different drug tests, two nights in a jail on the outskirts of Las Vegas, and one wild story fabricated with his brother's help, and Caden was released without facing a single charge.

Caden had woven the first part of his story exactly as it had happened. How he found the bag of pills in the trunk. How he thought about dumping them or turning them in to local police, but had instead called the only cop he trusted—his brother.

Bracken had assumed complete responsibility by giving the excuse that his baby brother was doing him a favor by transporting evidence in the form of the duffel bag stuffed with steroids to him. He'd covered for him just like he'd always done.

Though Caden didn't doubt for a second that Bracken would have to answer for his lie. Fuck, if he'd only picked up the goddamn phone, returned his calls, Caden would have made sure he hadn't been kept in the dark.

Or "fucking blindsided," as Bracken had quietly, but emphatically, put it.

The fact that his brother was a credible Nevada DPS narcotics detective helped. And, in typical Bracken style, he'd turned the whole situation around to one that was mutually beneficial. Caden's brother saw this as a way into the underbelly of ultimate fighting, where rumor had it that illicit drugs—stuff worse than steroids, even—were being sold like hard candy. Headquarters had been pestering him to make a bust, and fast. Had him deep undercover for a good part of the year. For the most part, they ignored his wild-card ways because he produced results.

Until Internal Affairs pulled rank, threatening to pull him from his assignment and tie him to a desk job while they reviewed his too-numerous-to-count Code of Conduct violations. "Fuck-all politics. A slap on the hand for breaking the rules," he'd informed Caden. Bracken at a desk job was like putting a bull in a flower shop.

Man, if Internal Affairs caught wind of how far Bracken had just bent the rules on his behalf…

"Shit, wish I'd taken your calls. Couldn't." A stream of muttered curses followed, as his brother finished signing some paperwork.

Caden rolled his eyes. Bracken's curses were his hugs. He didn't know how to be soft. *Soft* wasn't a word in the Kelly brothers' vocabulary. Soft was the equivalent of death. And, if there had ever been any softness, it had vanished when the news came that Mikey had been killed in action. Caden would take Bracken's kind of mothering any day.

"Goddamn paperwork."

He grinned. Every officer in the precinct was probably thankful his brother was still on the streets and not one cubicle over. His brother's hard ballbusting ways were notorious. No wonder his sergeant had been so easily convinced of this plan.

Opportunity had come knocking with the appearance of the duffel bag. Bracken was headed to Tetnus with him, posing as a biker interested in becoming a fighter. Ironic, because if anyone could knock him around, it was Bracken. Caden would save him some time by providing him easy access to the behind-the-scenes shit—the locker room, the sparring facilities set up for practices, and anywhere else he'd need to infiltrate. With any luck, he'd make the biggest drug bust to hit Vegas in years.

The assholes involved with ruining his sport were going to have to deal with Bracken's kind of justice.

Bottom line—Caden had inadvertently provided the narcotics division with a lead in toward a bigger bust. Bracken was raring to go. And Caden was still in line to fight.

He studied his brother while he finished the last of the paperwork.

Although the same height, Bracken had at least forty pounds on him. All muscle, even his neck was thick, the size of a small man's leg. He was darker, with jet-black hair that hung ragged about his face. A matching beard gave him a wild, sinister look. And his demeanor was more somber than the T-shirt and jeans he wore in spite of the sweltering heat.

"We're gonna have a long fucking talk on the way into Vegas, bro," Bracken ground out, interrupting his thoughts. "Shit, good thing Serge has a hard-on for having his crew be the ones to beat the Feds in making a major drug bust. That, or he's so fed up with my shit, he'd do practically anything to get me off his back, and miles away from here."

Caden snorted, knowing the truth was probably a bit of both. "So? Let's bolt. How many forms do you have to fill out when nothing has really happened yet, besides me showing up with the duffel bag?"

Bracken stood and grabbed the stack from his desk. "One too many. Follow me."

After a quick stop at the front desk, where Bracken tossed the pile of papers onto the chair, they headed out into the blistering midafternoon heat.

A new day. A new start. With no one the wiser, not even the press.

Except for the people who really mattered. Except the one person who mattered the most.

Sophie.

Caden grimaced. She hadn't said a word to the media. No on-air appearances recounting what went down. No public statement to the press. No private calls. Nothing. He hadn't heard a peep from her.

Calling her a groupie after what had gone down… shit. He'd humiliated her in front of a state trooper. He was lucky his mug wasn't plastered on every news channel from Vegas to New York.

What did he expect?

He wasn't sure anymore. There was something about

her that just did it for him. Big time. Unlike any other woman, she was the whole package.

So much time had been wasted. Tetnus wasn't about the money. It was about him, and his fucking neurosis. Winning the championship bout was his way of moving on. Proving to himself, once and for all, that the fucked-up kid who'd been abused and passed on from family to family was in the best shape of his life. Mentally and physically.

He shook his head, trying to rid himself of the image of Sophie's shining eyes, bright with laughter from their wordplay. He got such a kick out of her—*being* with her, leaving her those videos…was she watching them now, wondering if it was all a lie?

Wants and needs, sometimes they're not the same beast, he reminded himself. A future with Sophie just wasn't gonna happen.

His future was fighting. Fortunately for him, Tetnus was still on.

"First it's baseball. Then basketball. And now MMA. What are athletes saying, that hard work doesn't count? Pop a pill so an unnatural Superman-like strength will win you the titles and glory? Everyone's looking for a shortcut. I'm going to end up watching golf, or something, if this keeps up," Bracken grumbled, as they headed back to the precinct parking lot.

Though a huge fan of golf himself, Caden didn't disagree. It pissed him off that the playing ground wasn't level, and that guys put all sorts of shit into their bodies. The exact opposite of sportsmanlike conduct. But less obvious, more devious. It all boiled down to winning, no matter what the consequences. Great message for today's youth.

His brother whistled low, breaking the silence. "Man, Caden, you've got style. That is some sweet ride, bro."

"Glad I'm leaving it in good hands. Sweetened the pot with your sergeant by agreeing he'd keep the Aston for a week—though he did seem thrilled to get you out on a case and out of his hair. To have been a fly on the precinct wall while you were confined to that cubicle…" He took out his cell phone to make the necessary arrangements through Harold.

A jingling noise made him look to his right. The keys to the Aston swung from his brother's pointed finger. "Need a bit of sweetness in my own damn pot." Without missing a beat, he unlocked the car and settled down into the driver's seat.

Caden arched an eyebrow, but kept his mouth shut. Moving around the car, he climbed in.

Seconds later, they were en route to Vegas.

"As much as I'm going to enjoy bringing these fuck-head drug pushers down, there's something else I need you to do," Bracken commented softly, breaking the silence. "You've come this far. Something for yourself, more than for me."

"Yeah. I'm all ears." Caden played it off, yet mentally prepared for a well-deserved reprimand. Things could have flipped and gone bad, for both of them, and all because of him.

Bracken turned his way and his lips rose into something that closely resembled a smile. "Win that motherfucking championship."

The biggest sinner alive had at long last arrived in Sin City. He'd checked into the MGM Grand last night, two nights behind schedule. Or so Sal had informed Sophie earlier this morning. Terrific. Just the kind of lying cheat she didn't want to see around the hotel. Another reason to revisit her plan and stay at a more affordable place, somewhere off the strip and as far away from Caden Kelly as possible.

Sophie had been battling with her conscience ever since Caden had been hauled off in the police car. Her journalistic-minded side screamed *inside scoop*. To go rogue, report the story and get herself on every network station, every news channel around the globe.

Performance-enhancing drugs seemed to be the scandalous flavor of the year, from cyclists to baseball players alike. It would stand to reason that a few mixed martial arts fighters had also been benefiting from a quick fix.

Jaysin Bouvine had been holding three identical duffel bags, her reporter instincts reminded her, *and I have it on tape*.

Caden wasn't acting alone in this.

She bit her lip, wondering at her surprise. Bit down harder, thinking about what a silly fool she'd been, falling in love with a handsome-faced liar.

For some unknown reason, the police had released him. Plus, he was still on the list of fighters vying for Tetnus. Sal had squeezed the list through, his curiosity apparent even within the inch of space created before she'd shut the door on his busybody ways.

Deep down, she was thankful knowing Caden wasn't stewing away in jail. On the surface, she felt like taking a bullhorn to the Vegas Boulevard and revealing to the world what a dishonest, heart-trashing liar he was.

But she'd kept *her* lips shut.

Sal had been pretty darn persistent in prodding her with questions, like a dog on the scent of some hopelessly wounded animal. The series of knocks on her hotel room door confirmed it. Sal wasn't going to leave her be. Two visits this morning had been two too many.

"Brought someone with me to cheer you up," the old-timer announced, entering the room and taking a long look around. "Jeez, did your surly personality cause the maids to bail on you this morning?"

Sophie tugged her complimentary MGM robe tighter, and with surly eyes, noted how Anthony had followed Sal into her room. The look on his face said that he'd watched *The Hangover* one too many times—it was like he expected a tiger to jump out at him. Heck, she wished one might, and put an end to her worrying about paying for this room, with little choice but to use the dirty drug money Caden had given her. She'd contacted Pittsburgh Trust, but they wanted her there in person and with two forms of ID. She felt like kicking herself for making a stink about their weak identity theft protection policies. Clearly, progress had been made.

Both men turned and stared at her, appalled. It was evident in the way they eyed her from her messy, knot-haired head to her bare toes.

"What the hell happened to her?" Anthony demanded, as if she weren't in the room and the subject of his concerned amusement.

"Dunno. Won't tell me a thing, but I think Caden's to blame. Pulled his typical M.O.O."

Anthony stepped forward, kindly intending to offer her a consolatory hug. She dodged him, ducking under his arm and moving over to the window. Tugging the curtains open, the room filled with light so quickly, she blinked. *Darn, that hurt.*

"Wanna know how many women he's slept with? Too many to—"

"Not particularly. Don't say another word, Sal."

Anthony chimed in. "What kind of question is that? No woman wants to hear about her, uh, boyfriend's sexcapades. And Caden, man, he's a force to be reckoned with."

It took the sound of a heavy wrought iron lamp rolling across the tiled portion of the floor for both men to shut the hell up. She stared, making sure her message was clear—end of discussion. Almost.

"For the record, he isn't, and will never be, my boyfriend."

Seconds passed. Then Sal softly stated, "Looks like you need one." His head turned and his gaze shifted around the room once more.

"What? I've made it this far on my own…"

"A friend, I'm talking about. Like good ole Sal here." He patted his stomach.

Sophie snorted, indelicately. "Yeah, well you know the expression. With friends like you…"

Sal bent and scooped up a pillow from the floor. "Told you she was full of sass." Moving to the sofa, he replaced the pillow and sat down. He patted the cushion next to him. "Sit. Anthony wants to fill you in on what's happening downstairs with the Tetnus preparations."

"If you still care," Anthony added.

Care? She frowned. A weaker woman would have rolled over and booked a flight back to Pittsburgh. Not Sophie. Not now. Not when she'd been a teen, questioning her decision to tattle on the creep who'd tried to take away her innocence. Tattle—yeah, right. That's what the local media and the good town folk of Hawley had called it.

They'd turned on her. How dare she accuse their wealthiest—and only—philanthropist of attempted rape. As if the fingerprints on her neck and breasts didn't matter. Money...now, that was what counted. The pain of their betrayal still hurt. Something Sophie knew how to deal with. Or so she'd thought, until Caden came along and put a different kind of hurting on her. The broken-hearted kind.

She'd found the strength to survive Hawley, and that same strength would pull her through this.

Sophie Morelle wasn't a quitter—she'd just taken a hiatus to regroup. Besides, it'd given her time to think about other things, namely that jerk Jaysin and what his duffel bags full of drugs meant. Just like any good investigative reporter, she was going to get to the bottom of it all. Including or excluding Caden's involvement.

Combing her fingers through her hair in a delayed attempt at fixing her appearance, she straightened and squared her shoulders. She had work to do.

"I'll get the video camera." Anthony marched over to the bedside table and retrieved the camera bag lying next to it.

"There is coffee on the table, and some clean cups... somewhere. Give me ten minutes to freshen up. In the meantime, I want you to come up with some interesting facts about Tetnus. The last-minute preparations fighters perform in order to become top dog, information like that."

Two weeks and counting, she thought to herself as she grabbed a blouse and her last remaining unwrinkled pair of shorts from the pile of clothing dumped on the bed.

Time enough to get this film rolling.

Time enough to reinvent herself.

Time enough for her Sophie Morelle persona to eat dust—a good old mouthful of it.

Caden, too. She hoped the Las Vegas dust coming his way tasted saltier than the tears she'd shed over him. A little farewell present from the real Sophie Morelle.

Chapter 18

DOUBLE-LEG TAKE DOWN: What happens when you wrap one long leg around a fighter's calf, weave your other leg around his shin, and follow with a strategically placed push to his chest

Vegas must have been a great deal in July. Booking Tetnus this time of year reeked of slimeball Jerry's tight-fisted touch. Five days and the temperature hadn't fallen below one hundred ten. A dry heat. Yeah, whatever—tell that to her darn armpits. Aside from the heat, by successfully avoiding the Double Jerks and having had to suffer through only one Caden sighting, Sophie considered her luck on the upswing.

"Thatta girl, roll those dice," one of the Boys standing at the side of the craps table hollered.

She downed the shot of tequila, and performed the same exact routine that had helped build her nest of chips. Cupping her hands and shaking the dice over one shoulder then the other and then finally over her head, she sent them sailing down the table.

"Six. Come on, Sophie. It's almost midnight," the same fighter encouraged.

Jerry had a strict curfew in place for his fighters. Not that they needed it because, much to her surprise, aside from an occasional night down in the casino, she'd never witnessed a more committed group of guys. They worked out constantly, running in the mind-boggling heat and weight lifting and sparring in three different gyms assigned specifically to Tetnus participants. She'd gotten it all, and more, on videotape.

The dealer moved the hockey puck onto the number six, whatever that meant. Sophie knew luck had a lot to do with her pile. It certainly wasn't her keen sense of craps.

She giggled at the word, or was it the tequila? The dealer handed back the dice.

Anthony took a handful of chips and moved them onto the board. "Come on, Sophie. One more great roll and we'll party like rock stars after Tetnus is over."

"No can do. I'll be somewhere doing correspondence work when this has all ended," she murmured. The room spun slightly, causing her to regret that last shot. But she deserved it. Had earned it, so to speak.

In three days, she'd accomplished more than antici-pated. The Boys had warmed to her and with Sal's en-couragement and Anthony's support, they'd filled her in on the ins and outs of mixed martial arts. She had more footage than she knew what to do with. More cuts and edits that needed to be pieced together.

The entire time, the question about Jaysin's involvement with those pills had nagged at her conscience. The manhandling jerk was up to no good. Before she did another thing, she was going to review the footage she'd shot in Phoenix. There probably wasn't enough incriminating evidence, just him with the duffel bags. It'd be an entirely different matter to catch him on tape with those green pills. That's what he was about, right? Dealing drugs to mixed martial arts fighters and wannabe fighters. She straightened at the thought.

Tomorrow, she was going to catch Jaysin red-handed.

But what was Caden's involvement?

Her throat burned, the lingering tequila adding to her pain.

She hadn't been able to bring herself to watch the three videos he'd left. Exclusive or not, it was nothing but lies. Lies from a lying cheat, from a less-than-credible source. A definite fast-forward, then cut.

Her palms cupped the dice tighter than necessary, and she focused on maintaining tonight's winning streak. She deserved it.

She repeated her die-rolling routine but this time, the dice hit the table with a bounce. One flipped three times and came to rest showing a one. The second kept rolling. Slowly. Briefly, it tottered toward a five. Five, that's the number she wanted, right?

All eyes were on the dice. The Boys looked worried. She noticed chips had been placed in front of almost everyone around. Were they piggybacking onto her good luck, luck that seemed about to end?

Sure enough, the die flopped over. Not a five. But a

six. *Oh, crap*, she thought, thinking how the game was appropriately named, and not wanting to shred the thin fibers of trust she'd woven between her and the Boys. Hopefully, one bad roll wouldn't overshadow her rather fortunate night.

On the next roll, the casino came alive with whoops and hollers so loud, the table shook. Sophie was hoisted into the air. "Five! She rolled five!"

"Just before curfew too," someone added.

Anthony put her down long enough for her to scoop up her chips and stuff them in her bag. A second later, she was back in this arms and being carried across the casino floor. The Pied Piper to a trail of boisterously happy fighters.

Sophie giggled. It looked like she wouldn't have to relocate off of Las Vegas Boulevard after all.

"Man, when I saw you the first time on the bus, I thought you were bad luck. Was I ever wrong," a younger fighter named Billy commented as he came up alongside them. His fist tightened around a bunch of chips and his smile grew even fuller.

Another guy chimed in. "Yeah, after the blow to Caden, and after watching your show, I thought you ate guys like us for dinner. You know, you're not at all what I expected."

"If Anthony doesn't put me down, I'm going make him my appetizer."

"Sounds good to me," Anthony shot back, his tone changing.

Great, just great. The last thing she needed was his interest. The sweet, bulky mass of a man had been a much-needed friend. And had turned into one of the focal points of her documentary. But that was it. He didn't even register on her would-consider-dating radar. She'd learned her lesson about mixing business with pleasure. She had donned her investigative reporter hat and no way was it falling off again.

They'd exited the casino, and had made it down a long carpeted corridor leading to the bank of elevators that would take them up to the hotel level. Anthony pressed the elevator button, his grip on her steadfast. At least they were surrounded by a small gathering of Boys, and not alone. Better do something about the situation, though, before it escalated any further.

"I think the tequila made me nauseous. One more step, and I'm not going to be able to keep it in," she lied through her teeth. Lightheadedness, perhaps. Giddiness, unfortunately. But Sophie wouldn't be caught dead barfing in public, *not* that she was remotely close to doing so.

Mercifully, her exaggeration did the trick, and she found herself out of Anthony's arms and back on her feet without further argument.

The door chimed and slid open. Hundreds of pounds of muscled fighters, plus a not-so-willing one-hundred-thirty-five-pound journalist, got on. Now, how to shed some weight and ditch them before Anthony and company decided to escort their lucky charm to her room?

She made a theatrical production of looking at her watch, then at her cell. "Golly, my battery must be acting up again. My watch says twelve but according to my cell phone, it's 12:05." Her words sounded way too obvious, like a pink neon sign flashing a false advertisement, one that read: "She's full of shit."

"Holy crap. Jerry said he'd disqualify anyone found lurking about Las Vegas after curfew."

"Damn, his room just had to be on the same floor as ours. We'll have to be super quiet."

Good luck with that, she thought. Lord help them, with their girth and height, they were going to sound like a stampede of elephants headed down the hallway.

She took out her cell and texted a message to Sal:

Call Jerry's room. The Boys made curfew. Won lots of money.

She shared her text with them. "If we time this right, Jerry will be checking his phone while you sneak back into your rooms. As soon as the door opens, I'll send the text. Wait a minute for Sal to call him."

"Damn, she's not just lucky but smart."

"Did she have to tell Jerry we won?"

Sophie grinned.

The door chimed. Sophie hit Send. And Anthony looked like a dog that just had his bone whisked away.

Brother. She needed another tequila and a moment to celebrate her small victory. Alone.

Change of plans. There was a bar one floor above casino level. One drink in celebration of beating the Vegas odds, and bamboozling the Boys into working with her. Tomorrow, she'd secured permission to film sparring matches at the temporary cage set up at the casino next door. Up-close-and-personal footage depicting exactly how an MMA fighter differed from other fighters. Show viewers the self-control and discipline professional fighters had, and balance the brutal footage she'd shot at the motel in Wichita.

The following day, she had some video to preview. Within the comforts of her room, she planned on viewing the material, deciding what to cut and what more she needed. Time to review, reflect and reconstruct her final plan of attack.

Yep, maybe an alcohol-infused mind might shed some light on what to do about Caden, as her rational mind turned to muck every time she thought about him. Should she finish the interview or delete him entirely from the documentary and keep him back in the dirt, in her past, eating her dust? The question continued to plague her as the elevator descended, then stopped.

The door opened.

She stepped forward, nearly tripping over her feet at the sight that greeted her.

Dressed in gray cotton shorts, a ripped white Rolling Stones T-shirt, worn running shoes, and dripping sweat like it was nobody's business, Caden should have been a sight for sore eyes—except he wasn't.

With his damp hair and wet T-shirt, he was a cautionary tale about the powers of raw and oh-so-male sex appeal. Heck, the lesson she'd learned was to avoid him like the plague. But despite herself, every nerve in her body shifted into high alert as her eyes unwillingly devoured him.

She froze in indecision. This time, there was no potted plant to hide behind, which was what she'd done a day earlier when she'd spotted him in the hotel lobby. Nowhere to hide, especially as his gaze pinned her in place, then slowly raked over her, starting with her hair, which dangled freely about her shoulders, and traveling all the way down to her open-toe pumps.

She felt an irrational tug deep within herself, urging her to step forward, wrap her arms around his neck and pull him in tight.

Her lips felt dry. She moistened them with her tongue.

His lips tightened into a fine line.

The elevator chimed and the door closed. If the elevator had legs, it'd be giving her a swift kick in the butt, knocking her both away from this man and some sense into her, the foolish, idiotic, irrational woman on her third ride within minutes.

Except it didn't move. Glancing down, Sophie spotted the reason why. Caden had stuck his foot in the door.

The doors slid open, allowing him entry, his big, sweaty body blocking the exit. He reached over and pressed Close.

She stepped to the right in an attempt to squeeze by him but he was too fast, blocking her just as the doors closed.

He shifted sideways and after a quick swipe of his room card, pressed the penthouse button.

Caden was staying in one of the luxury suites reserved for the very rich, or the very lucky. Or the very corrupt.

Her gaze shifted away from the illuminated button and met his bold stare.

He smirked.

Smooth operating bastard.

A bead of sweat followed a path along his cheekbone. He tugged the bottom of his T-shirt up and wiped it away, not before giving her an eyeful of exquisitely toned eight-pack abs and massively bulging pecs.

God, he was more chiseled, more defined than a few days ago. She'd run her hands along his chest and down to his abdomen as she straddled him in the Aston. Touching him was like sunshine on a winter day, you never got enough of it and never wanted it to stop. The feel of his sculpted physique was such a turn-on. And, wow, if Caden had been in fighting shape before, his opponents didn't stand a chance now. She couldn't imagine another man cut so beautifully in all the right places.

She swallowed hard, remembering what a masterful liar he was.

His eyes narrowed, piercing her. "What a difference a few days makes, huh? Where's your entourage? Ditch them after some fun at the craps table?"

She frowned. Keeping tabs, was he? His tone was mild, yet still felt like daggers. And, for some bizarre reason, she wanted to rattle his smug, self-serving attitude. "The Boys have been extremely supportive, helping me with my documentary. Except for Jaysin, I underestimated them. They're…sweethearts."

"Sweethearts? Every MMA fan in America is going have your head if you use that freakin' word to describe the Boys. Is that the kind of guy you want, a sweetheart? A sweetheart who's got you spread eagled on the hood of a car with his tongue in your honeypot."

She flushed at the memory but forced it away. Bastard. How dare he argue the merits of a word with a goddamned journalist. Way too confident in his abilities, too. Too self-assured. Too smug. And way too capable of pissing her off.

If he could toss down lies like shots of tequila, without wincing or fearing the inevitable hangover, well so could she.

"You're assuming one of my sweethearts isn't lying spread eagled, as you so eloquently put it, on my mattress right now."

He moved and punched a button with his fist. Number 25—her floor. The entire elevator rattled under the impact.

She jumped. "Are you crazy?"

"I'd say so." He stood glaring at her, like he'd been the one left stranded in the desert with an inoperable luxury rental car and a wad of large, unbreakable bills. The cab driver had been overjoyed to be handed a week's worth of fees. A two-week stint at the MGM Grand was pricey so she'd been thankful the officer had let him toss her the wad of money, even if it was dirty drug money. She intended to make a donation to the Nevada State Police after all was said and done. Sooner than planned, if her luck at the craps table continued.

"Fuck, you're bluffing," he muttered, his fingers unwinding from his tightened fists. Her breath caught, knowing her lie had struck a nerve. Knowing he cared.

And knowing, too, that she shouldn't give a damn.

"Ready to listen yet? Or are you going to keep avoiding me?" He folded his arms across his chest and cocked his head, his clear, green gaze holding her captive. "I deserve a chance to explain, considering our history."

Sophie snorted, trying to harden her heart and gain back some self-control. Respect, that's what this was about—or rather, his disrespect. *Groupie.* She'd gone and let him in, closer than other male, trusted him, and he'd gone and pulled a Hawley on her.

She struck her best Sophie Morelle pose—shoulders squared, hands on her hips, with one hip thrust out to the side. "History is learning from your mistakes. And you're my biggest one."

Instantly, she regretted her words—way too revealing. Rule number one when dealing with a lying male cheat was don't let him sense your weaknesses. And she'd laid it right on out there for him, on the Sophie-reveals-all table.

"Darling, there's no arguing size with you." He paused, his lips twitching, probably because he'd caught the flush spreading across her cheeks and down to her chest. But his demeanor suddenly changed, from aggressive male to a softer version of himself, more like the Caden she'd grown to love. "It wasn't mine, you know. The duffel bag. I was just trying to figure out what the fuck was going on. Who's taking or distributing the drugs."

Damn, the elevator was small. Nowhere to hide tonight.

"Performance-enhancing drugs, Caden. And needles, for what?" She frowned, thinking about the duffel bags Jaysin had exchange with his large friend. Her instinct reassured her that no way was Caden involved. Yet the evidence…

Caden snorted, interrupting her thoughts. "Shows you don't know jack about the sly ways some athletes get their fix."

That did it. "You're the voice of experience, huh? Bet there's not a drug out there you haven't indulged in."

"Not performance-boosting stuff. Never. I'm a lot of things, but a cheater—no way. I'll win based on my own merits, not because my muscles are souped-up on steroids or fresh blood infusions. Never done any of that shit, and don't do the other shit anymore, either."

She bit her lip and studied him.

He looked right at her, his eyes hooked on hers. Either he was a damned good liar—and of course he was, the man excelled at everything else, why not lies?—or he was telling the truth.

Her heart quickened, wanting to give in and believe him. Wanting him. "So how did that duffel bag get in the trunk of your rental?" she blurted out.

"Think about it, Sophie. Haven't I been trying to get the answer to that question from you the entire ride?" He straightened and turned away, as if he was disgusted with her. "Fuck, you know what? Believe what you want. I'm used to figuring things out on my own—why would now be any different?"

The elevator stopped, and a split second later, Sophie was maneuvered onto the exterior carpet.

"See you around," he growled, his tone teeming with frustration.

He was gone. Done with her. She'd been feeling the same toward him for days. So why did she feel so alone? Abandoned. And unjustly accused. So reminiscent of how she felt when the entire town of Hawley had turned on her. Maybe, just maybe, that's what she'd been doing to Caden.

The police had released him. Here he was in Vegas, training hard for Tetnus. Antisocial, keeping to himself rather than working out with the Boys. No time to solicit buyers or sell drugs, from what she could tell.

She'd been so ready to believe the worst of him. Heck, that's how she felt toward everyone—it was better to assume the worst than expect the best, right?

These nagging doubts played around in her mind all the way down the hallway and far into the long, sleepless night. Searching for a truth that seemed just out of reach.

"Another water with lemon," Caden ordered, nodding at the empty glass on the bar in front of him.

Bracken tossed back the rest of his tequila and wiped the back of his hand across his mouth.

"The shit I've had to do…" his brother mumbled, his way of explaining why he was drinking on the job, before he changed the subject. "That twat Jerry's not our dealer. You were right. Interesting guy, though, with his fingers in quite a few pockets, maybe even links to organized crime. I'm gonna keep my eyes on that fuckhead."

"So it's one of the Boys."

"Probably. Did you do as we discussed, plant the rumor that some hard-prick biker wants to meet a couple fighters, share the shit? That I was looking for some low-key fights, off-premise, an easy way to get in shape without the bullshit training?"

No-bullshit training was more like it. From daybreak to well past nightfall, Caden had been following a workout regimen that left no room for woes or aches of any kind.

Training for Tetnus was no joke. He had to put on muscle and then drop weight a day before the bouts to make fighting weight. And then put it all back on again. He followed a highly restricted, lean-protein diet, extreme carb-infused workout, and balanced it with weight lifting and stretches to elongate his muscles. Despite the vigorous training and dietary restrictions, it would all be worth it if he won Tetnus.

And some pill-popping peddler was looking to make things easier, ruin a fighter's credibility.

"Yep. Pissed a few fighters off, too. You're going to be an unpopular man with most of them."

Guys from around the country would give their left nuts to qualify for a chance at becoming the greatest fighter around. Sure, the argument remained that boxers were the toughest. Not so. What mixed martial arts fighters had over boxers was serious, mad-ass skills in a host of disciplines. Boxers…box. But an MMA bout was more than exchanging punches and whoever lands the best throws or whoever falls down first wins or loses, respectively.

MMA fighters trained in several styles of fighting. Hell, one of the MMA Gods, named Royce Gracie, proved that size doesn't matter. Six foot one and at 180 pounds he took on a taller wrestler who outweighed him at a whopping 486 pounds and won. He took down more fighters using Jiu-jitsu than any other guy around. Fuck, a mind-blowing headache wouldn't bother a guy like that.

The bartender placed another water in front of him, and leaned over the bar as she did so, flashing some skin. He could almost see her belly button, the way her low-cut shirt gaped open—a few more buttons had been unbuttoned since she'd served him the first glass of water. But when her gaze drifted to the man sitting next to him, she beat a hasty retreat back to the other end of the bar.

"Guess that's my signal to head out. I'll be out in the neighborhood following a tip. We'll keep in touch. Text me if you hear anything more. You're looking fit, bro. Rooting for you." Bracken faux-punched Caden in the arm, and left.

There was more than meets the eye happening behind the scenes out here, that much was for sure. The fact that the duffel had been hidden in Caden's rental car and no one had come to claim it was downright bizarre. Sure, Jerry was the king of shitty business practices but Caden, and subsequently Bracken, had ruled his involvement out.

Someone was missing something. But what?

Caden took a sip of water and felt the bartender's eyes on him. He ignored her. Another time, another place, another freakin' woman ago…

He hadn't seen much of Sophie since arriving in Vegas, except for a quick elevator ride the night before. She'd done something with her hair, was wearing it loose around her face so it curled against her cheeks. Not the prim, proper Sophie he'd grown used to. Her long, wavy hair offered her the perfect way to hide—which was exactly what she'd done, pretending she hadn't seen him. Yeah, like the surprised flash of desire that had filled her eyes when he'd entered the elevator wasn't enough of a hiya.

Sal got a kick outta keeping him informed of her whereabouts. Tonight, she'd kept to her room, located a few floors above the rest of the crew. Not far enough away from that bonehead, Anthony, though.

Last night, Caden had come in from his run and had been drawn to the casino by the Boys' shouts. The big bonehead had had his hands all over her. At the sight of him lifting Sophie into his arms, Caden charged forward, ready to act on an unexpected surge of violence. He wanted to protect her from that player's hands. Drive his point home to the fighter using some non-verbal communication, likely fists. Hands off. So reminiscent of the kind of anger he'd had as a kid—which was the only reason he stopped, turned, and walked away. Control was key in a situation like this. And Caden had been anything but in control of his emotions.

What did she see in the guy?

"Can I get you anything else?" the brunette asked. She'd come out from behind the bar and approached his barstool. Maneuvering herself between the bar and his legs, she thrust her breasts at him. "Anything you want."

He forced a smile onto his lips. "Tempting. But I'll stick to water, sweetheart." Damn, what he wanted was a stiff shot of Jack. And a woman, someone to bury deep inside and work off some tension. Hard, fast, and unrelenting—just like his daily routine. But somehow during his cross-country journey, he'd changed. A quick roll on the mattress wasn't enough, unless it was with Sophie.

Pushing his barstool back, he put some distance between himself and the buxom bartender. Glancing at his watch, he figured he'd bump up tomorrow morning's run, work off some of the bullshit clouding his thinking. The streets of Vegas were cooler after midnight. Jerry could go fuck himself and his curfew. Then, he'd head over to the adjacent casino where a sparring cage had been set up. Just as he'd done the past few nights, Caden hoped to pick up a bout or two. Perfect his skills on new blood, before the big finale with Tetnus. Work off his frustrations. His anger.

Spread a rumor here and there.

"Another time. I'm here all week."

Caden reached into his sweatpants pocket, pulled out some bills, and placed them next to the empty glass.

"Thanks for the drink. It was just what I needed," he commented.

She shrugged, and tucked a napkin into his pocket. No points off for effort.

For a second, he paused. Why the hell not follow through on what was so blatantly offered? A week ago, she'd have already been on her back with her legs spread wide.

Someone else came to mind, her legs spread and all. *Fuck.* She plagued him worse than any drug habit. With a shake of his head, he set off for the Strip. Man, how he wished he'd forget ever getting involved with—ever *caring* about—Sophie Morelle.

Chapter 19

CLINCH: The face a fighter makes when he gets the credit card bill

*O*ne for *Team Caden*, he thought, smirking. His cheek smarted, but he ignored it. The punch to his face left him invigorated. Alive. Knowing this peacock prancing about the cage underestimated him. He let him land a punch, a strategy used to draw the man in closer. Close enough where he could land a lethal kick and take things to the mat.

A few minutes ago, Jaysin Bouvine had put a hurting on a guy. Knocked the man out cold with a single jab. Concussion, or worse. Ruined his chances at Tetnus. But it gave Caden hope, because if a douchebag fighter like Bouvine could manage to win a sparring match, Caden's chances at winning Tetnus were in the bag.

Douchebag and his crew seemed to be having a premature victory celebration on the other side of the cage. Caden moved away from them, not giving a shit how much Jaysin thought he was going to somehow miraculously rise to the top of the MMA food chain and win. Dumb luck.

Not the kind of luck that had ever graced Caden's life.

Not the kind of luck he wanted, either.

His opponent stepped in and attempted a kick.

Caden stepped back, blocked it, and visualized exactly how he was going to take the man down.

A light flashed, momentarily blinding him. Enough time for the peacock to punch him in the kidney. Blinking away small, illuminated stars, Caden instinctively shot his elbow up, blocking another swing. Pivoting on his toe, he swung around and nailed the guy in the back of his legs. He buckled, unsteady on his feet. Throwing his weight on the man, Caden knocked him onto his back and fell forward with him.

They grappled and rolled.

Someone shouted—a woman—but his mind was locked on his opponent. He flipped him onto his stomach.

Caden had the amateur's head in a can-opener when another light flashed brightly, causing his pupils to dilate. His opponent wiggled free.

"Fuck me," Caden ground out, and searched the side of the cage for the obnoxious light.

His gaze halted on two familiar faces, one with a brightly lit handheld light meter, and the other one pointing a goddamned video camera at him. He shook his head, and gestured a time-out at his opponent. Stopping the sparring match wasn't part of the MMA rulebook, but the breathless guy was all too eager to take a coffee break.

"If you pull this shit during Tetnus, I'm going to give you a beating," he growled, leaning into the cage and glaring down at Sal.

A muffled noise caused Caden's gaze to shift to the woman standing next to the old-timer.

Her hair was tucked beneath a baseball cap, which was pulled low over her forehead. She was wearing a tight, pale blue T-shirt with the words *Tap Out* stretched tightly across her chest. Crisp white slacks covered her long legs. And she had on flats, pale blue, to match her T-shirt. A casual look for her, probably so she wouldn't draw attention to herself. Funny how that hadn't exactly worked out.

Sophie in a simple T-shirt was downright breathtaking.

Man, she was gorgeous, in a wholesome, natural way. He wanted to make the words on her shirt ring true. Make her tap out in submission as he pinned her to the floor. Hear her moan his name. Over and over. Until he found himself completely tapped out as well.

Stick to the plan, he reminded himself. *One that doesn't include her.*

Sophie shifted on her feet. Nervous?

Good. "Get that freakin' light outta my eyes," he hollered down to Sal, who was still holding the huge light fixture on Caden. Turning, Caden pinned his gaze back onto Sophie. "You filming me?" he demanded.

Her chin rose up a notch. "Yes."

"Gonna smack me over the head with your camera, sweet thing? Ruin another chance at me winning the title?"

"I thought we'd worked that out, darn it. It was an accident. Besides, you promised you'd help me. You promised me an exclu—"

"Exclusive? Shit on a brick. What more do you want from me?" He paused, and scowled.

"Aw, come on, Caden," Sal interrupted, "don't know what happened between you two out there in the desert. Bit by a rattler or something, with all the melodrama."

Caden snorted.

"Melodrama?" Sophie said, her voice high and sounding offended. "I haven't seen him in two nights."

"Oh, she's seen enough of me, all right. Seems like she's looking for another eyeful."

She cocked her head to the side. "Jeez, every woman in America is hoping for an eyeful of you and your baby jewels. Looks can be deceiving, isn't that right, sweetheart?"

"All you need to do, sweetheart, is open your eyes. The truth is staring right back at you."

She flipped her hair off her face. "Are you telling me I got it all wrong?"

Her voice was hoarse but it was the doubtfulness of her tone that felt like a kick to the kidneys. Caden leaned into the cage. "I never lied to you," he ground out, his own voice raw and vibrating with frustration.

She gasped. For a moment, they studied each other. Her eyes thoughtful. His, for sure, brimming with anger.

"Baby jewels? Is that what all this melodrama is about?" Sal demanded. "Sophie, honey, there's nothing baby about him. I've seen him in the showers, ya know. Caden, you do much better with the women when there's sugar in your tone. Want some advice?"

"No," Sophie quickly shot out, and stomped her foot.

"Sal," he warned.

The desire to pound a fist into the cage changed to a feeling of disbelief. The old-timer was either clueless, or had a death wish. Judging by the way Sophie stood glaring at him, Caden wouldn't have to get his hands dirty.

In his typical, oblivious fashion, Sal continued, "A nice bottle of wine, some candles, and soft music. Did the maid clean up your room, Sophie? Clothes tossed all over the place could ruin the mood I'm aiming for. And, come to think of it, Caden is in training…"

Man, she was gorgeous, with her hands on her hips and her eyes throwing daggers at the old-timer. Damned drugs. Whoever was responsible was going to pay dearly.

Yet Caden wasn't about to roll over and beg for her forgiveness. She was a reporter, let her fucking figure it out.

It all boiled down to trust. Something he didn't give lightly…or ever, really. Though he demanded it from others. Cleary, she had trust issues—hell, with everything she'd told him, he didn't blame her. But it rubbed him raw. He slammed a lid down hard on whatever silly emotion that had him wondering about a future. With her. A future that was decidedly better off without her. Like all the other women that'd come into his life, he'd give her what she wanted, then send her packing.

"Interview's over. Keep on filming, what the fuck do I care? But keep those lights out of my eyes."

He shot one parting glance at her, standing with her

hands at her sides and looking all hurt, like someone had given her a solid teeth-rattling takedown.

Sophie wiped her mouth, set the napkin on the room service tray, and poured a second cup of coffee, hoping the caffeine would help refocus her attention on the images flashing by in her viewfinder. According to her notes, she'd need to film a few additional sparring bouts, and then just the grand finale—Tetnus. She'd covered everything from the street roots of MMA to training to intimate snapshots of fighters—give or take Caden's incomplete exclusive.

"I never lied to you." *Damn. Damn. Damn.*

The Caden-coaster she'd been rolling around on since hitting Vegas was interfering with her objectivity. MMA fans would eat him up. It's not like she couldn't edit out the sexy bits he'd filmed for her eyes only. And, unless he'd lied to her in Sedona, he'd left her more exclusive information, too. Add the drama of his arrest to the mix... She swallowed hard.

That's what any credible investigative reporter would do, right? Caden had handed her a prime opportunity, heck, he'd tossed it into her lap. The title of her piece said it all: *Bets, Drugs, and MMA—Sophie Morelle Investigates.*

After all, wasn't that what the Double Jerks were all about? Taking bets and selling drugs?

But was Caden part of it?

She peered at the viewfinder. Her heart rolled about painfully along with the man projected there. She snapped her eyes shut, trying to block him out. Except her memories played out as well, frame by delicious frame.

With his hair tousled and wild from her fingers after sex. His smug look of satisfaction after she'd moaned his name as she climaxed. His piercing regard, and the hurt in his eyes when he'd asked her to give him a chance to explain. The rawness of his tone, as he'd glared down at her from the cage. "I never lied to you."

She hadn't expected him to be at the training ring— yeah, right, who was she kidding? Her conscience had nagged her all the way to the Octagon cage. She'd wanted a glimpse of him. Some small means of understanding him better, and what motivated him to do the things he did.

Or didn't do.

She wanted to believe him. Trust. The word of the century. She wanted to go out onto a limb, and trust him enough to hear him out. But the company Caden kept made it difficult.

Last night, she'd been discreetly filming Jaysin Bouvine for about an hour before Sal and Caden both arrived. What she hoped to record was something juicy and illegal. Catch him in the act of dealing drugs. Instead, she recorded Jaysin the jerk and genuine underdog, who, by all accounts—though mostly his own—was rising out of the fighter food chain and into the limelight.

His confidence level had pulled a 180-degree shift. His movements around the room, his brutal victory over a smaller sparring opponent and his subsequent boast fest smacked of self-importance. Cool and conceited beyond belief. Like Caden, Jaysin had bulked up. His biceps were enormous, along with his torso and legs. She caught him preening and flexing his way around the facility, posing for photographs and a few other reporters' interviews. A genuine showboat.

Heck, Sal had even gotten him to sign her release form to use whatever footage she'd captured of him for her documentary. Clearly, the man wasn't in the right frame of mind.

He'd changed. Drastically. Now he was bigger, meaner, and eager to be a moneymaking star. It was startling, to say the least.

Just what the world needed—another arrogant male meathead.

Boy, she disliked him. But fans loved an underdog story. They'd respond to how the lamest dog around transformed himself into a vital contender.

She prayed he wouldn't win. The manhandling jerk deserved what was coming his way. She intended to portray him in the right light, so to speak. Make fans love him so they'd hate him even more when they witnessed firsthand what a dickhead he really was.

She hit the pause button, deciding to review last night's footage while it was fresh in her head. Every minute counted, so she needed to decide if another night of filming was necessary.

Score five for Sophie. Five in-depth interviews, about Tetnus and with the Boys' opponents. It helped balance out her documentary by filming from a different angle, different points of view. Except no matter who she talked to, they all marked one welterweight as the fighter to beat.

Caden.

With fresh eyes, she examined the footage of him in the cage. He was beauty in motion, graceful and subtle in his movements. He didn't jump around like other fighters, bobbing on their feet around the mat. Caden either stalked his opponent, or stood his ground like he was waiting for a wave instead of a fight. Letting his opponents come in close and allowing them to hit and kick him. Sophie hit Pause and studied Caden's smug grin—the same one he used on her numerous times. When she'd gotten him all wrong and had read him the wrong way. Which was exactly what his opponent was doing, judging by the man's overtly confident gestures.

Caden wants his opponents to underestimate him.

She forwarded the footage several frames until she found their exchange last night. She hit Play, and watched closely as Caden said, "All you need to do, sweetheart, is open your eyes. The truth is staring right back at you."

She rewound it and hit Play again. And again.

Damn. Damn. Damn. This snapshot directly contrasted to the warrior in the cage who'd only seconds ago been frozen on her camcorder. Whose every action was purposefully trained on provoking his opponent. She frowned. What if he had been telling her the truth? That this bit of video was a glimpse into the real Caden. Raw. Open. Honest. That the truth was just like he'd said it would be, there in his face, his tone, and his gestures.

And in his eyes. The hurt she'd seen there that had stuck with her well into the night, because her instincts told her it had been genuine. *Damn. Damn. Damn.* He'd trusted her. And she'd gotten it all wrong. She'd done what his foster parent had done, doubted him and then bailed on him.

Her hand shook and coffee splashed out of the mug. *Shit.* She jumped up, grabbed a few tissues from the nightstand and wiped the dark drops off the tile. A few more drops landed on her fingers. She blinked.

Tears.

This wouldn't do. She stood and dabbed her eyes. She had a documentary to edit, damn it. And her indecision was messing with her emotions big time. She wanted to believe him. But one nagging question plagued her. If she'd gotten it wrong, then how did the duffel bag get into his trunk? And he knew about it—wasn't that evidence enough?

Jaysin? From what she could tell, he was the real criminal here. But how to prove it? And what to do about Caden?

All she wanted now was to take a ride up to the penthouse. Apologize, and offer to listen to his explanation. Give him the benefit of the doubt. Not pull a Hawley on him.

Damn. Damn. Damn. When the truth had gotten too blurred, too distorted, and too tough to handle, she'd shut the door in his face.

Slowly, she moved back to the table and carefully placed the mug next to her equipment. She dabbed the moisture from her cheeks, then reached to turn off her camcorder. No time like the present—she had to find Caden.

She frowned, noticing Jaysin's ugly mug filling the screen. Somehow she must have hit Rewind.

Sophie reached forward to hit Play, then quickly paused. She shifted the camera closer and tilted it up so the natural light in the room fully revealed the image paused there.

Jaysin. With his back to the group and a water bottle in his hand.

His other hand was raised, with something pinched between his fingers and almost to his mouth.

Something green.

Chapter 20

BRAZILIAN JIU-JITSU: A kind of juice served at Girl Scout camp

Shit on a brick, Caden thought, grimacing at the scene playing out inside the posh MGM locker room. For a fighter groomed in the streets, he was used to the sight, feel, *taste* of blood. Yet what that asshat Jaysin was doing made Caden's stomach roll.

Two syringes sat emptied on the bench. Jaysin hadn't winced once as the long needles pierced a vein in his arm. A heroin addict would have been proud of how easily he'd completed the act.

First the performance-enhancing pills, then illegal blood transfusions. Last night, Bracken confirmed that methamphetamines had hit the streets, and that there was some kind of connection to Tetnus. That he'd be nearby out following his lead. To call him if anything came up.

What was up was Jaysin and company. His blood was fully loaded with fresh, rich red blood cells. No wonder the guy was suddenly ripped. No wonder his arrogance knew no boundaries.

Caden had been watching the asshole for days, trying to catch him red-handed dealing pills. He'd bulked up fast and, from what Caden had observed, with very little work involved. What he'd witnessed Jaysin doing was just the lead he'd been looking for. Caught him literally red-handed, with his finger pressing against the hole left behind by the needle. It was both too disgusting for words and confirmation of exactly what was going down.

The problem was worse than he'd suspected. Caden clenched a fist. It made him sick, and sicker still knowing that after Jaysin's bullshit hit the fan, the sport of MMA and all the honest fighters training their asses off for a clean shot at Tetnus, would be considered guilty as well.

That Caden might not have a shot at the title.

That there might not even be a Tetnus if the police closed the place down.

The press was going to have a field day.

Jaysin straightened, dropped the tainted syringes into a duffel bag, and left. The locker room door slammed on his way out.

"You're gonna pay, you fuckin' deceitful asshole," Caden muttered, stepping out of the shower. He plucked the baseball cap off his head and pitched it onto a cleaner, untainted bench. The sight he'd witnessed made his stomach curl.

Tugging his sweaty T-shirt over his head and kicking off his sneakers, Caden considered his next move. He'd contact Bracken and fill him in on the sick twist of events. Hope his brother found some hard evidence, because as things stood now, it'd be Caden's word against Jaysin's. Sure, there were tests for this kind of steroid abuse, if you knew to test for it. Red cell counts within the blood had to be under forty-nine percent. No way had Jaysin been monitoring his intake, not with the way he'd packed the syringes loose like that, in those cheap duffel bags. Never suspected he'd be caught. Was it enough to lock him up, though?

A shame he hadn't caught Jaysin in action on his iPhone, having come into the locker room sweating like a dog from today's grueling workout, his cell left behind in his hotel room. The timing sucked, any which way he looked at it.

Man, he was tired. Physically, emotionally, and fuckin' psychologically, a whole goddamned plague of problems. That asshole's long-overdue drug bust. The memories of his father's fists and the insecurities that accompanied them, feelings of weakness and neglect. The overwhelming need to prove himself, once and for all.

Then there was Sophie. Her falling-for-you bomb, and then now, worse, her distrust. For a moment, he'd thought fate was going to shift in his favor—someone to love and who loved him unconditionally. Hell, the reporter was the last person he'd imagined falling for. Hard.

He should count his lucky stars it ended before it had even begun.

He yanked off his sweatpants and his own brand of moisture-wicking briefs. By the time his shower ended, he hoped to have his shit together, and a clearer idea what to do.

Stalking over to the shower, he grabbed the curtain. Something caused him to pause...a noise? His gaze shifted to the next stall, lowered to the bottom of the curtain, and to the gap separating the curtain from the tile floor. To the red polished toenails peeking out between open-toed pumps.

Jesus.

He shifted the curtain aside.

Sophie's eyes widened in alarm, until recognition dawned. She lifted her chin slightly, letting him know she meant business, despite placing herself in such a freakin' dangerous position.

If she'd been discovered... "Man alive. Do you have some kind of death wish? If Jaysin saw you—"

"He didn't. Besides, you were hiding in the shower next to me. I know things are strained between us, but you wouldn't have let him hurt me."

Caden opened, then closed his mouth. His head pounded, but it was the way his heart had wedged into his throat that caused him to choke on any coherent words. Didn't she realize how dangerous Jaysin was? If he'd spotted her hiding in the shower, watching him shooting up blood, he'd think nothing about hurting her. *Fuck.*

"I caught it all on tape."

His gaze fell on the camcorder she held clenched in her hand.

"The most disgusting, repulsive, creepy thing I've witnessed. Was that his own blood he was injecting? And you know what? I've been filming him all week, selling pills, counting money, all kinds of deviant activities. The blood…that was unexpected, I have to admit."

"Give me the SD card." He held out his hand, palm up.

It was Sophie's turn to open her mouth, then snap it shut. Unfortunately, it opened again. "No. All of my footage is on this card. I'm editing…"

"Sophie, listen. You don't know how deep this shit is. I need to get that SD card to my brother, so he can use it as evidence."

"My documentary—"

"Don't you have another SD card?"

"Of course I do. A blank one. This one is loaded; I'm at the end of filming. There's a lot of editing and review required before and after Tetnus. The documentary needs to hit the air while things are fresh and current. Two, three months from now max, with a lot of work in the interim. Plus, I need to show the networks a rough cut to sell it. How about I make you a copy?"

"Not negotiable. Hand it over. This is way more important than your documentary."

She pulled herself up straighter in her heels. Her head reached his chin. "You know how important this documentary is to me, just as I know how much you want to get to the bottom of things. Find out the extent of *Jaysin* dealing drugs…"

He narrowed his eyes. "How much do you know about that?"

"For the record, I believe you. I wanted to tell you, but…"

He dropped his hand as if she'd smacked it down. "There's a hell of a lot more riding on this than me cleaning up my shit."

"You dodged my question in the elevator, but you're not going anywhere without answering it. How did Jaysin's duffel bag get into the trunk of your rental? I *do* believe you, really. But this one fact has me puzzled."

"Hell. Why do you think I'd been grilling you for information since leaving Wichita? I thought you could explain it to me."

"So, you have no idea how the bag got there?"

"Do you?"

She shook her head.

He ran a hand through his hair, his abdominals barking from the stretch. After completing an insane amount of sit-ups, weight training, and cardio-blasts, his muscles were tight. Yet the muscle between his legs jolted to life as her gaze fell on his body. Her cheeks flushed a familiar pink. He thought he heard her sigh.

Terrific. Seemed his timing today sucked dirt.

Sophie's, it seemed, was spot-on.

Surprise. Surprise. Sophie had caught it all on film. Everything Bracken needed for a bust seemed to be on that SD card. Everything Caden needed to put behind him, so he could go on and win Tetnus. Earn Sophie's… Man, oh man. What the hell was he going to do now?

The clang of the locker room door smashing against the wall forced Caden into action. Gently, he pulled her away from the curtain and deeper into the shower. She gasped, and he placed a finger to his mouth, signaling her to be quiet.

"How much for a dozen?" someone asked. The soft tread of footsteps sounded on the industrial carpeting.

"What do you think, I'm selling eggs? One thousand for a bag of ten. If you want something that'll pass the drug test tomorrow…goddamn it, someone's in here."

Caden flicked the showerhead on and a cascade of cold water hailed down on them. Sophie shifted, tucking her camera under her shirt as she faced the back wall, trying to protect her equipment from water damage. Good girl.

"Who's in the shower?" Sophie jumped, clearly recognizing Jaysin's voice.

Damn.

Counting to three, then careful not to move the curtain too far and give Jaysin an eyeful of the reporter who had had her nose way too far into his business, Caden stepped out. He intentionally widened his eyes on the three men. Two fighters from another organization, and Jaysin. They must have pocketed the pills, though. Only the duffel bag was in sight, there on the bench. He could easily handle one of them. Three, especially given his fatigued body, would be brutal.

He shrugged his shoulders and stalked over to his clothing. "Forgot the damn shampoo."

His words had their desired effect, and all three relaxed.

Jaysin went so far as to puff out his chest. "Gonna be nice and clean for tomorrow so I can roll you around on the dirty mat, huh?"

He felt the challenge in Jaysin's glare but ignored him. *Tomorrow, asshat,* he silently promised the man. And frowned. Maybe there was a way to get Jaysin out of the locker room and ensure Sophie made a clean exit.

Hell.

"You'll be rolling around with me, all right, fuckhead. Just before you tap out." He slid into his briefs and sweatpants without drying off. As he bent to put his sneakers on, he watched Jaysin out of the corner of his eye.

"That right? Maybe you won't make it to Tetnus? Maybe you'll be too beaten to fight?"

Caden stood and nodded at the door. "Let's do it then. Or are you afraid to go at it with me in the cage without your babysitters?" He grunted. "Just what I figured—those muscles of yours are for show, right?"

Jaysin's entire body shook with rage. He snatched the duffel bag off the bench and with a silent glare toward his cronies, headed for the door. The two fighters paused for a second, grinning like kids invited to an ice-cream party. Then they followed Jaysin out to the cage.

Caden waited, long enough to know they'd gone.

"Go back to your room and stay there. Got it?" He hesitated, then added, "And, Sophie, for God's sake, keep out of trouble on the way."

He heard her muffled voice through the water. "You're soaking wet. Where are *you* going?"

"To do something I've been wanting to do for a long time. Feed Jaysin the mat."

The asshat should have seen it coming. Caden went in for a double leg takedown, sweeping Jaysin off his legs and taking him down hard. A hail of punches followed, brutal and fight-ending. But his opponent was either too stupid or so pumped up on steroids his brain was rot because he refused to tap out.

Just as well. The cheating drug pimp had it coming to him.

Trapping him in a butterfly guard, Caden flipped

him over his head and pinned him face-down to the mat. He grabbed Jaysin's arm and angled it into a V behind his back.

"Tap out, you piece of steroid-dealing shithead, or I'll break it. Good luck defending yourself in jail."

Jaysin must have been high on something else, as well. "That lying bitch. I'm gonna kill her for nosing into my business. She can't prove anything—I'll deny it all. I'll…"

Caden didn't hear what followed. He didn't say a word. He let his skill as an MMA fighter do the talking.

Using his full weight, he pressed Jaysin's arm into his back, and was rewarded with a snapping sound.

Jaysin howled, and tapped the mat.

Tonight, his kind of justice had been served—with fist and kicks, and a firm hold on his self-control, all inside the Octagon cage. He'd stopped and called his brother en route to the cage, and was thankful to spot his leather-clad figure just before the fight began. Now it was time for Bracken to take matters into hand.

Caden stood. The street moves had paid off, and for the first time in a long time, Caden felt solid. A worthy fighter. Someone to be admired, accepted. Not a thug, or an angry kid nobody wanted.

This wasn't just about nailing the steroid pimp in a drug bust. It was more. This was Caden's own private tap out—on his past.

In the time it took Caden to get an icepack for his cheek, Jaysin was taken out on a stretcher, to the hospital, then with the hard evidence from Sophie's SD card, off to jail.

"That was quick."

"I could say the same about you, bro," Bracken replied. "Nice work. You broke the bastard's arm."

They chuckled in unison.

"Let's finish this."

"Tell me once more before we illegally enter her room. She's got it all on film? The pills? The blood injections? All of it?" Bracken's tone was cynical, full of doubt. But he didn't know Sophie like Caden did. Her gumption. Her determination to get her story. Her desire to succeed with the freakin' documentary in spite of the danger involved. And then some.

Caden grinned. Damn, he was proud of her. Seemed that documentary of hers wasn't the sole focus of her filming—or so she'd told him. The truth was on that SD card. And, man alive, he didn't want to be around when she'd realized it had disappeared.

He was about to pull one shithead of a move.

They stopped at her door, and with Caden's silent approval, Bracken rapped on the door. His lips pressed tightly together, as they listened for no answer.

They'd waited for her to give up her search for Caden, had gotten lucky when she'd headed down to the casino. They'd told Sal to stick to her like glue, to keep her occupied and out of trouble. Five minutes, that's all they needed. He hoped the information that Sal had provided them when he'd returned was correct—that Sophie was at the craps table with "her chips piled so high, she'd probably outearn Jerry here in Vegas."

Bracken had no hesitations. He swiped a room key, and they silently entered the vacant room.

Caden was both exhilarated and annoyed. Excited that this whole ordeal with the drugs was coming to an end. And pissed off, thinking who Sophie was keeping company with—that blockhead Anthony.

"You better talk to your girl about leaving her valuables out where any fool could take them, Caden." Bracken unzipped the camcorder and plucked it out. Opening the viewfinder, he hit Play.

Caden sucked in a breath when the image of Jaysin shooting blood filled the screen.

"Sick bastard. Bet he'll be needing another shot of blood after the beating you gave him. Too bad he's going straight from the hospital to jail." His brother turned the camera off and removed the SD card. "Let's roll."

"How long is it going to take to make a copy? She's worked so hard…and it means a lot to her. She's going to go nuts when she finds out her documentary has disappeared."

Bracken folded his arms across his chest and scowled. "It's this, or I get kicked back to a fucking desk job—courtesy of my asshole brother. You owe me, dude."

"A day?"

"Jesus, man. A few days, with all the freaking paperwork to do. She'll get her documentary back after I copy what I need off her card."

Caden nodded. Bracken's word was golden. "Hang on." He felt around inside the case's side pocket until his fingers caught what he'd been looking for. He retrieved the spare SD card and smoothly placed it into her camcorder. "Better she not find out about her footage. She's going to know it was me, but I can't deal with upsetting her right now. I can't afford any more distractions if I want to win. One more day to prepare, and that's it. *Angry* isn't the word for how she'll react…"

"I'll do what I can, bro, to have it back to you ASAP."

His brother raised an eyebrow. Message read loud and clear. Caden's actions said it all—he cared about her.

Which, he told himself much later, after Bracken had left, was why he found himself outside the casino entrance, watching her as the pile of chips on the craps table grew higher and higher. He hoped to high hell she didn't realize her luck had changed for the worst.

And that Caden was responsible.

He turned and headed back to his room.

"Whoo, quite the pile of chips you've got going on there, Sophie. I came to warn you—be on the lookout for Jerry. He's blaming you for 'snitching.' Something about money, and a couple of fighters being disqualified. They were pulled and drug tested tonight, instead of tomorrow. Failed it. Jerry thinks you, with all your snooping around, are responsible."

Sophie grabbed Sal's hand and placed a stack of chips in it. "Don't mention the slimeball promoter's name, please. It might jinx me. Look—" she waved her hand at her pile "—I'm on another winning streak, Sal. The money I have in front of me is enough to put toward an advertising campaign for my documentary. Or better yet, the investigative piece I'm working on. Jeez, if I'd known how lucky…"

"I'd say the Boys at this table are lucky."

The Boys ignored him, their attention fixed on the dice in Sophie's hand.

"Uh-huh. Your luck has changed. Are you guys listening? Jaysin hurt himself tonight while training. He can't fight in Tetnus with a broken arm. He's done."

Sophie's fist paused midshake as the table almost shook from the Boys' excitement.

Was it a coincidence that Caden had left to spar with Jaysin hours earlier and the jerk ended up with a broken bone in the same time frame? By the time she'd dropped off her camera, changed into dry clothing and headed to the practice cages, they'd been nowhere to be found. She'd been to Caden's penthouse with no answer. Briefly, she'd waited in her room for him to call or let her know he was okay. Nothing.

At least he wasn't hounding her about her SD card. Sure, she wanted to help him but that would have to wait until tomorrow, after she'd had time to duplicate the card, then delete all the footage she shot for her documentary, leaving only the investigative pieces for the Nevada police.

Call her jaded, but it was too much of a risk handing over all her hard work, just like that. Who knew where her documentary might end up once it became evidence, and who'd get the credit for it?

But the police having a copy of her investigative piece added to her credibility as a reporter. She'd still make something work for prime-time television: *Behind the Bust with Sophie Morelle.*

Her lips lifted into a grin. She wouldn't have to focus on anyone's chest this time.

No way was she able to keep to her room in the state she'd worked herself into. She found the Boys—her form of protection against Jaysin—and set about calming her nerves.

Lucky you, Sophie. The news about Jaysin was the cherry on her banana split of an evening.

She raised her hand, ready to roll. "Caden was asking about you."

Her breath hitched. *You're telling me this now?* She scowled at the addled old-timer. "Where is he?"

Sal glanced at his watch, counted the minutes aloud, then nodded. "Twenty-five," he murmured, before proceeding to answer her question. "Last I saw him he was getting into the elevator with the scariest-looking dud around."

"Dude, Sal. Not dud. A dud is not scary." She sighed. "So you don't know where he is?"

The Boys began chanting her name, interrupting her. Not one to disappoint them—not anymore, anyway—she let the dice fly.

Six.

Cheers erupted. Except for Sophie. Had the ugly dud taken Caden somewhere and hurt him? She shook her head. Doubtful. Caden had proved over and over that he could handle himself.

So, where the heck was he tonight?

Carefully, she gathered up her chips and tucked them inside her purse.

Sal straightened next to her. "I'll walk you to your room. Remember you've got to avoid—"

"Jerry. Don't worry, Sal. He's probably off running illegal last minute bets for Tetnus, now that Jaysin is out of the picture. Tonight's been a big win, no matter which way you look at it."

The old-timer nodded, yet his eyebrows rose skeptically.

Tomorrow she'd improve her winning streak. Cash in her chips. Film the final day of training and the excitement leading up to Tetnus.

But first, there was something she needed to watch. And, being that Caden was off somewhere, and given the late hour, tonight seemed like the perfect time to play his sex tape, and whatever else he'd secretly recorded. Before she hit Delete.

Sophie finished her text to Lauren and, grinning like she'd won the lottery—which, in a way, she had—hit Send. A phone call would have been more detailed, but hey, Sophie had something else requiring her attention. If she could only track him down.

Dang-diggity. It felt great coming out on top for a change.

She placed her cell next to the camcorder bag, and gave herself a mental scolding for not zipping it closed. *Crapola.* It didn't matter, she had some long-overdue footage to watch. Tonight, she was in the right frame of mind, back on her feet, thinking clearly, and certain that as far as Caden Kelly was concerned, she'd made a mistake in judgment.

She was on a winning streak. No better time to face the sweet country music.

Let's find out exactly what I'm dealing with, what Caden had to say on those three videos.

A fist pounded on her door, causing her to jump.

Immediately, she relaxed. No way was it Jaysin unless he escaped the ambulance en route to the hospital, broken arm and all. Something to consider, but unlikely. Jeez, more likely it was either her watchdog Sal, who'd lost something, his marbles perhaps? Or Caden had come for the card. Either way, that knock meant business, judging by the force behind it.

"Coming," she hollered and turned the knob.

The door flew open, violently. The force of it smashed into her and sent her flying. With a gasp and a painful thud, she landed on her back. Shocked, she looked up and found a pair of small beady eyes glaring down at her.

"You ruined everything, you fucking bitch. I told you I didn't want you around or you'd get hurt. But no. Miss Busybody was too busy snooping into my business, messing with my fighters, and turning my event into a media circus."

Sal stepped inside, took one look at Sophie sprawled on the carpet, and jumped in between her and Jerry. "Calm down," the old-timer ordered, putting his palms out toward Jerry, as if he was ready to push him away.

Jerry's face flushed beet red. "Calm down? Calm down? My best fighter is out, injured with a broken arm. Fighter after fighter has failed the goddamn drug test. Steroids. The idiots have been taking frigging steroids. Thousands of guys are looking for a refund. And if the media finds out about this, I'm ruined."

Yoo hoo, you jerk. I'm the woman who's gonna get the job done, Sophie thought, struggling to stand. At that moment, she wanted nothing more than to show America the shady, *illegal* dealings the promoter had going on. Her hands found her hips, and she gave him her best "fuck you" smile.

His fist shot out, right over Sal's shoulder, and connected with her cheek. Sophie fell back down for the count.

Before Sal could retaliate—judging by the way the old-timer had his fists balled, he was about to—Jerry shoved him. Sal toppled over onto the floor next to her.

Thankfully, Jerry stalked away from them, his gaze roaming the room.

"Are you okay, Sal?" Sophie murmured, sitting up and leaning toward the old man.

"Just got the wind knocked out of me," he replied, breathless and nervous.

Sophie scrambled onto all fours, wondering if they should make a run for it and call security.

Her fingers touched her swollen cheek. The jerk had hit her.

But Sophie would have preferred another punch in the face to what Jerry intended to do next. "No," she shouted, as the promoter shook her camcorder free of its bag and whirled it over his head.

"Nobody's gonna know about this. Nobody. Got it? Or you're gonna end up like your busybody camera here. Broken. Into. Pieces." Jerry swung hard and let the camcorder fly. It hit the wall full throttle and shattered into chunky bits.

From her spot on the carpet, Sophie spotted the SD card lying next to the metal chunks of shattered viewfinder. Jerry headed over toward the wall for round two.

A distraction, that's what was called for. He had to leave that card alone, no matter the cost.

"You don't scare me, Jerry," she heard herself shout. He pivoted on his heels and glared at her. *Good.*

"Shut your trap or I'll shut it for you."

"Oh no you won't," Sal hollered from his spot next to her.

"You too, old man. Don't think I haven't figured out that it's your fault she was on the bus in the first place."

Sophie rose up onto her knees and squared her shoulders. Despite her efforts, her hands shook. "That's right,

Jerry. I was on the bus, in the parking lot in Wichita, and back by the men's room in Phoenix. And you know what I discovered?" She sucked in a deep breath, willing herself to continue and knowing full well the consequences. But that SD card had to be saved, no matter what. "You're going to end up in the cell next to Jaysin when I'm finished with your sorry, thieving ways."

"Aw, Sophie. No. Don't say anything else."

Jerry practically ran over to them, his body shaking with fury. Then he spit. A huge, wet gob landed on the carpet by her hand.

"When I'm done with you, the public won't wanna see what happened to that pretty face of yours anymore." She braced herself for another punch but he slammed his foot into her side. Hard enough that she crumbled to the floor.

"For God's sake, Jerry. Caden is going to kill you when he figures out you hurt his girl."

Jerry froze, midkick. Considering Sal's words, and the consequences of his actions.

Sophie glanced at the SD card lying unprotected on the carpet. Maybe Jerry was too stupid to know that it contained *everything*.

"Wimp," she shot out. "Beating up on a woman and old man. You throw a punch like a sissy, too."

The ding of the elevator sounded through the open door. With a parting glare, Jerry stepped toward the door.

Thank God.

"One more thing," Jerry said, almost to himself. He stopped, moved over to the wall and scooped up the SD card. Stalking back in front of them, he wedged it into the doorframe. Then, he slammed the door closed, and reopened it. With a growl, he repeated the action until the SD card became a small, twisted replica of her totaled BMW.

"If I hear a word outta you, if you trash me in the media or tell anyone about my shit, and the reason my Boys disqualified for Tetnus, and you're gonna look like this." He held up the SD card, then tossed it on the carpet next to her before he stalked out of her room.

Gently, she scooped up the card and touched it to her swollen cheek.

Her documentary. Her investigative report. Caden's evidence. All gone.

She inhaled sharply. The pain in her side forced out a gasp.

"Sophie, honey. You've got balls of steel."

She groaned. Her blue balls hadn't been any help.

"I'm sorry, so very sorry. Whatever I can do to help you out." She heard Sal way off in the distance. "You look like you're gonna pass out. Hang in there, okay. Be right back."

Her eyes rolled in the back in her head. The last thing she saw was the ceiling.

Chapter 21

FULL MOUNT: No comment

One fighter—that's what it took to pull Sal off Jerry.

Minor, compared to the four men struggling to separate Caden from the broken, bleeding man. Three rounds hadn't been enough to quiet the uncontrollable rage within him. The asshole deserved everything coming his way.

"I warned you Caden was gonna kill you," Sal said, his tone smug. And rightly so.

When Caden had found her crumpled on the floor and out for the count, he'd swallowed hard, as if it would hold back the black rage boiling up inside. He'd kept his control as he woke her up, fearful she had a concussion from that bastard's punch. Sal informed him that the asshole had kicked her, too. Gently, he'd touched her side and made her tell him about the pain, assessing if anything was broken—hell, Bracken used to do the same assessment of his injuries when they'd been kids.

He'd kept his cool after she'd refused to go to the hospital. Who could blame her with Jaysin sure to be a few doors down? Instead, he helped her into bed and asked Sal to arrange for one of the medics on hand to take a look at her, and make sure she was gonna be okay.

Sophie'd murmured quietly as she rested her head on her pillow—something about her car. Then she'd whispered his name.

Caden.

That's the moment he'd lost it.

Twenty minutes later, Jerry's nose was broken, his ribs probably fractured, and Caden was just warming up.

Jerry spat out a tooth. His eyes bugged out wide at the sight of it, which made him angrier, then stupid beyond belief. "You're disqualified," he threatened. "I'll file the paperwork and make a statement from the hospital. You're finished. You'll never fight a professional MMA bout again."

"Fuck you. Fuck your threats. I. Don't. Give. A. Shit."

Caden broke free and tackled Jerry back down to the ground. Over and over he pummeled the man's face. Then, he went to work on his body. With every punch, he realized his dream was done—Tetnus was over for him. He wasn't going to get away beating the promoter into pulp without consequences.

The image of Sophie curled up on the floor flashed before him.

Caden resumed his punches. If the guys hadn't pulled him back off, he'd have killed him.

"That's enough, Caden," Sal admonished. Sal nodded at Jerry, like a Godfather who'd overseen justice being dished out. "That last beating was for destroying her camera and her career."

When the EMTs arrived and silently loaded him onto the stretcher, the asshole still hadn't learned his lesson. "Thought she was gonna rat me out. Had it on tape, that bitch. Guess I took care of that."

"What is he mumbling about?" Caden glared at Sal.

"Sophie has been secretly filming him. Caught him running his shady bets, numerous times. He destroyed her camera and that tiny piece of plastic. The EZ thing-amajiggy."

"The SD card?"

"That's it. Turns out that wee little thing had her entire documentary. Gone. I think that upset her more than the beating."

No doubt it did.

"You're gonna wish you never laid a hand on me," Jerry continued, ignorant of the fact of how close Caden had come to finishing him off. "You're gonna regret this."

His hand flexed, sore from the two beatings he'd doled out tonight. *So Sophie had been taping Jerry as well?* Man, she had more nerve than any of his opponents, which was one more thing to love about her.

The thought calmed his racing heart. He stepped toward the stretcher, and immediately the four fighters tightened their hold on him. "I'm done, but there seems to be something Jerry doesn't know. I mean to enlighten him."

Jerry turned his head away as Caden approached the stretcher.

"It's you who's done, Jerry."

He stiffened on the stretcher, and grunted in denial.

"Tell you what. You disqualify me from Tetnus, and you're the guy who's gonna regret it. Wanna know why?" He grabbed Jerry by the jaw and turned his head toward him. The man's eyes flashed in alarm.

"I've got Sophie's real SD card. The one you ruined was empty. It's me, asswipe, who's got all your bullshit on tape."

Caden kicked off his sneakers and yanked off his sweaty gray running shorts. A cool blast of air greeted him. Housekeeping must have cranked up the air-conditioning after he'd headed out into the sweltering morning heat. The room smelled like sweet cinnamon and vanilla. Fresh, clean, and invigorating—so contrary to how he felt.

He loved her. But love wasn't enough to keep someone safe—especially from a guy like him.

Self-control was key. The test he'd been putting himself through—that he could keep a level head and still be the toughest man out there.

So much for that emotional drivel of a dream.

A chip off the old bruiser block, that's what he was. Last night proved he couldn't keep his anger in check. Fuck, if Jerry miraculously reappeared at tomorrow's event, Caden would do it all again. Despite his regrets. Despite knowing his brutal actions were likely driving the one thing he wanted more than Tetnus away.

He found little comfort knowing she was recovering

and that the events of the past few weeks were neatly falling into place.

Word came late last night that Sophie was fine, aside from a swollen cheek and bruised ribs. Jaysin was on his way to jail—the hard evidence on her SD card was proof enough. Jerry had taken his place at the hospital, and according to Bracken, would soon join Jaysin in jail. Two more Boys had been eliminated from Tetnus for testing positive for steroids—they seemed to be the last of the dopers, though. The police had Sophie's card. Everything was just freakin' terrific.

Everything except the bigger matter—what to do about Sophie?

He'd bought her a new camcorder, along with two SD cards. But hadn't heard a peep out of her. The medics told him she'd been sleeping the two times he'd knocked on her hotel room door. The third time, no one had answered.

Probably you're not what she had expected out of an underwear model, he reminded himself. Man, if she heard about the beatings he put on Jaysin, and then Jerry…hell, she'd better make a run for it before it was too late. And he did something stupid, like tell her that he loved her.

Too late for that, you fool.

Bracken promised he'd make a complete copy of the SD card. A complete copy, with everything included. *Everything…hell.*

Maybe Bracken wouldn't see it.

He rubbed a hand over his sore jaw. Sophie was going to be pissed off when she found out how he'd appropriated her card. Despite the fact that he'd unintentionally saved her documentary, and then some.

She'd paid the price for that card at the hands of that weasel…*fuck*. One more reason why he'd bought her the best camcorder on the market. She needed to finish what she started, after all. Little did Sophie know that she still had the inside scoop. That her blue-balling days had just begun.

News crews swarmed the casino—he'd dodged them earlier after his run. Man, they loved the negative bullshit. And athletes taking steroids was hotter than Vegas right now. So much for putting a positive spin on mixed martial arts. A shame—he'd been trying so hard to keep the drug abuse on the low and out of the press.

He rolled his neck, then headed into the enormous bathroom, bypassing the sunk-in Jacuzzi tub for the glass-enclosed shower. Turning the water on, he let it run until the bathroom fogged up. The water felt good on his weary muscles, his head.

It was done.

And, with all said and done, so were they.

He didn't want to cause her—*himself*—any more pain. Better let go now, because life with him would be no cakewalk.

He finished up in the shower, turned the faucet off, and ran a towel over his taut, muscled body. Top physical shape. The best shape of his life. An emotional train wreck.

Wrapping the towel around his waist, he headed into the bedroom. What happened in Vegas, stayed in Vegas, which meant he had to delete the fucking videos, and then get out of there fast.

He stalked over to the window and opened the blinds, letting the early morning light into the room. Time to get dressed, and take care of business.

Over by the bed, he stopped and paused.

What the fuck?

Frowning, he scooped up the small bouquet of flowers—red tulips. A small envelope fell to the floor. His pulse began to race as he retrieved, opened it and read: *Watch the video, sweet cheeks.*

He scanned the room. Sure enough, the camcorder he'd bought her was on top of the bureau against the wall.

With three long strides, he was there, hunkering down in the chair next to the bureau with the camcorder perched on his knee, and pressing Play.

Sophie sat on the edge of her bed, her face angled to the side, likely trying to hide the bruise on her cheek. Caden stiffened, but relaxed when she spoke.

"Ha. Seems you aren't the only one sneaking videos." She grinned, clearly pleased with herself, before continuing on a more serious note. "Thank you for the camera, Caden. You know what a setback it is to have all my hard work destroyed. I wanted to tell you this in person, when you came to my room, but I had to come to terms with it myself. I've come to realize that the documentary doesn't matter." She paused, inhaled, then looked directly at the camera. "You are what is most important to me. I know you kicked the Double Jerks' butts—thank you." She fist pumped the air and added, "Woot, woot!"

Okay, maybe she wasn't appalled by his brutal actions.

"My documentary would have exposed them both, but the ass-whooping you gave them was the next best thing. I'm leaving you this video to let you know I'm okay, to give you time to train without the drama that is my life, and to let you know that I'll be there. I'll be at Tetnus, cheering you on."

He inhaled sharply. *Fuck, now what am I gonna do?*

She continued, her voice trembling as she spoke. "And, afterward, I will be there for you, in your life, if you want me. You see, sweet cheeks, I love you."

A tulip petal floated to the floor. Caden released his death grip on the bouquet, ready to hit Rewind.

But it seemed Sophie wasn't done yet. Her eyes glimmered mischievously—a look he was all too aware of—as she stared into the camera. "And if you want to give a girl flowers, sweet buns, try a low-allergen variety, like tulips. I'll be on the lookout for them." She leaned forward, a close-up. He cringed at the sight of her blackened cheek.

Then she gave him the haymaker of all haymakers.

"Win Tetnus, and win big, Caden. But know I'll love you no matter what happens."

Within minutes of Sophie pressing Record, Caden won his first in a series of bouts leading toward the welterweight championship. Three kicks, a punch to the nose, and tackling one's opponent to the mat until he tapped out was all it took for Caden to win this match. His tough-as-sin brother was sitting up front and next to her, and was calmly assisting with her narrative, with Bracken informing her viewers that Caden had "taken down" his opponent, and Sophie translating that into layman terms—"a tackle with some wrestling about."

Caden made it seem easy. Sophie knew the truth, though. How hard he'd trained. The focus required to anticipate an opponent and outmaneuver him. The discipline it took to become the best fighter out there.

Her documentary might have been destroyed but she had a whole future to look forward to documenting Caden Kelly, the warrior, the lover, her love.

Or so she hoped.

This morning, she'd been surprised when the camcorder was returned to her without a response to her video. Zero. Nada. Zip. Of course, he'd seen it. She'd gone all out trying to draw his attention to it.

Did he know she was there in the audience, watching him fight? It was hard to tell because he hadn't looked in her direction once.

Strangely enough, she did draw some comfort from the fact that his big brute of a brother had sought her out and, with a few select words as way of a greeting, had taken the seat beside her. Talk about getting off to a rocky start.

"Nice camera, chili bean," he'd said. Her gaze had flown off the outdated camcorder he'd wedged into a beat-up canvas bag—so different from the top-of-the-line, state-of-the-art one Caden had bought her—and studied his dark, bearded face. Hearing someone else use Caden's nickname for her had made her warm inside, like he cared enough about her to share something special between them. Even with this street thug.

"It's Sophie. Nice to meet you, *Bracken*," she'd replied. His eyes had lit up briefly, confirmation enough that she'd guessed correctly. How else would he have known her nickname? Clearly this was someone Caden confided in. This brute was Caden's brother.

The cop. A contradiction to what she'd figured a detective would look like, who sported a worn suit jacket, belted slacks, and a pencil tucked behind an ear. When

Caden had talked about street-smart thugs, this hardened, leather-clad man was the image she'd pictured.

His appearance had been as shocking as his greeting, if that's what you'd call it. He was Caden's complete opposite in both appearance and attitude. Dark, unkempt, and formidable, with his crooked nose, long black shaggy hair and coarse beard. And for every hundred smart-ass words Caden had to say, his brother had only a few, because after he'd introduced himself in such a dismal manner—as if he was intentionally trying to get a rise out of her—he had had little to say, except to correct her MMA vocabulary.

Jeez. What had she been expecting, anyway? A hug and a "Welcome to the family?"

"Be back in a few," he stated, interrupting her silent assessment of him. Abruptly, he stood up, then paused and cocked his head at her, as if he were ascertaining her worth.

She sat up straighter in her chair and squarely met his gaze. That seemed to please him, because his lips slightly twitched. He nodded his head, and she watched him jog off to catch up with Caden on the walkway leading out of the arena.

Sophie sighed.

"I was waiting for him to leave so I could talk to you," Sal muttered. The first sane decision Sophie'd seen him make. The old-timer took the vacant seat beside her. "It does my heart good to see you back in action with that camera. Shame about your documentary."

She shrugged and patted the old-timer's arm. "It doesn't matter. How are you, Sal? Did the medics check you over too?"

The old-timer scowled. "A little shove by that minion like Jerry was child's play for a guy like me."

"I'm talking about what you did afterward, jumping on Jerry's back like that."

He gave her a sheepish smile. "Ah, you heard about that, huh? Hell, Caden did worse…"

"I know. If the roles had been reversed, and Jerry put a beating on Caden, I'd have been tempted to do the same."

Sal grunted. "The way you put a licking on Jaysin with your heel is something the Boys will never forget."

Sophie grinned, having forgotten about her first confrontation with the drug peddler. Heck, Wichita seemed like years ago. *Decades* ago.

A shell of a woman named Sophie Morelle had set out on this journey, but for every mile traveled, had come to realize she was so much more than a blue-balling television host. So much more than a victim of Hank, and the misguided people of Hawley. When she'd left Pittsburgh to film her documentary, little did she know her perspective on MMA fighters would change, and that she'd fall in love with the Ultimate American Man and top welterweight fighter himself.

But were her feelings reciprocated?

Suddenly, she knew what she had to do.

"Be back in a sec," she repeated Bracken's words to Sal. The arena had calmed down somewhat, the audience socializing with their neighbors as they waited for the next qualifying bout to begin. Providing an unobstructed exit out of the main event area and into the hallway leading to the locker room. She stood, repositioned her camera bag strap on her shoulder, and followed the same pathway Bracken had taken a moment ago.

Halfway to the locker room, a team of men filled the hallway and slowly headed her way. She stopped to record their progress, spotting the next fighter en route to the cage. Anthony.

Before she could wish him good luck, she was swooped up into his big arms for a bear hug.

"My lucky charm. God, it's good to see you're okay and back on your feet, Sophie. Jerry deserved everything Caden dished out to him. If I'd known what was going down, he'd have had a taste of my fist and kicks as well."

Once more, Sophie was reminded how wrong she'd been about the Boys. Sure a few bad steroid-induced apples had to be sorted out, but the majority of fighters—like Anthony—were decent, hard-working, disciplined men. She gave him a fond peck on the cheek, then asked, "Have you seen Caden?"

Anthony's arms stiffened around her before he set her back on her feet. "He's in the locker room with his brother."

"Is anyone else in there?"

"Not at the moment."

Sophie squeezed his arm. "Thanks. And, Anthony?"

"Yeah?"

"How do you like sassy brunettes? Because, boy-oh-boy, my friend Lauren is going to love you." Sophie made a mental note to get a hold of her best friend, and perhaps do a little matchmaking. That is, after she took care of her own affairs of the heart. She heard him chuckle, though her attention shifted toward the men's locker room. "Good luck in the cage today, okay," she murmured, then headed over to the door.

To knock or not to knock? Well, it wasn't like she

hadn't enjoyed seeing Caden's beautifully naked body. Multiple times, beginning with his all-too-revealing billboards.

She entered, but didn't see anyone. Her ears perked up, however, at the sound of his voice. He was describing a fighting technique, something about a Peruvian necktie. She strode forward, needing to see him in person, before his next qualifying bout, about the little ole issue of how she'd fallen hard for him. She wanted to see his expression, and know his response.

Caden let out a long stream of cusses.

Sophie stopped in her tracks.

"Here is where things start to get as sappy as shit, bro," Bracken said. He sounded louder, his voice carrying from the other side of the row of lockers.

"Hell," Caden said, sounding exasperated. "Turn it off, man. Just give me the copy you made, and forget what you saw."

"No can do, brother. Fuck, this is the first time I've seen you like this."

Sophie jumped as something banged against a locker door. A stream of curses followed, less muted, and sounding a heck of a lot closer. What was going on?

"I should have deleted it when I had the chance."

Someone drew in a long breath.

Bracken spoke. "It's fucking beautiful. I want you to hear yourself, hear what it sounds like when you love someone. You know why?"

"Why?" Caden growled, his frustration obvious. "So you can be reminded how fucking weak I am?"

Sophie winced, surprised at his words and distressed by the pain in his tone. Weak wasn't even on her Caden Kelly descriptive radar, yet that's what this discussion was about, right? Caden's misguided self-conception. And what was all this talk about…*love*?

Bracken snorted loudly. "Weak? Is that what you think?"

Silence followed. Sophie quietly tiptoed her way to the end of the row of lockers. She wished she could see their expressions and discover what was reflected on Caden's handsome face.

"Listen, man. This video isn't about weakness. It's about strength. Honesty. Courage."

Caden snorted.

Bracken continued, his voice so deep Sophie had to freeze so as not to miss his words. "You deserve to feel this way for once in your life, Caden. To dig deep, and acknowledge you love someone like that, takes balls. Especially given what we've been through. You made it, man. Got out of your head and into your heart." She heard him grunt. "I'm envious. Sit and listen."

Caden let out another stream of cusses. Sophie's heart raced at the sound of his low, gravel-filled voice.

Was this her video?

"This is way too early in our relationship to tell you this, chili bean. Fuck, I can hardly believe it myself. Mind-boggling, really," Caden addressed *her*.

Holy. Sweet. Crapola.

His video messages hadn't been destroyed—unless there was a fourth one floating around out there, which was highly doubtful. Had her documentary and investigative footage survived as well? Jeez, she should have watched all three of his videos a long time ago. So many questions and doubts could have been avoided. So much heartache, and distrust.

"Never thought I had it in me. But there is something about that smart-ass mouth of yours, the way you deal with stuff, with me, the way you blush after I tease you…" He paused.

Sophie cupped her palms over her mouth to keep from crying out, fearing she'd miss his next words.

"Fuck. Okay. I love you. Got that, chili bean?"

She blinked away her tears. Then sniffled. Dang. He'd made her cry.

"I don't deserve you but I do love you."

Bracken spoke. "That took real courage, bro. I'm proud of you."

Caden groaned, then murmured, "I'm deleting it. She'll never know if you keep your trap shut. Better that way."

"Your mistake. Yours to make."

"At least she'll have her documentary."

She heard a low whistle. "You're all she's got, for now. I'll need to collect this copy when you're done. I can't turn it over to you or her, not until the investigation is concluded."

Caden is all I've got. He's all I got for now. For always.

Sophie didn't know whether to laugh or keep crying. She almost did both, simultaneously, when Bracken came barreling around the corner and practically knocked her off her heels. He stopped short, his gaze running over the full length of her.

He reached out, placed a finger under her chin, and gently raised her head back up from where she'd bowed it. A dismal attempt at hiding her tears, anyway. His gesture spoke volumes.

Chin up, Sophie.

He whistled, a jaunty, upbeat tune, filling the silent locker room on his way out.

Sophie straightened, smoothed out her blouse, and wiped her eyes with the back of her hand. Inhaling deeply, she stepped around the end of the lockers and over to the other side.

Caden sat on a bench, hunched over onto the forearms on his thighs. Deep in thought as he studied the floor. An outdated camcorder—a loaner from the police station?—rested on the bench next to him. Thankfully, the footage of Caden talking was still running. Muted, but not deleted.

Silently, she stepped forward and approached him.

At first, he seemed not to notice her, completely absorbed by his own dark thoughts.

She tapped her open-toed heel, hoping the movement might catch his attention.

It did.

His eyebrows narrowed, briefly. Then slowly, his gaze traveled over her heels, up her bare legs, over her slim pencil skirt, along the neat row of buttons on her blouse, then at last, onto her face.

"You heard?"

"You are not deleting that video. Or you'll have a real fight on your hands. One you have no chance of winning."

"Hell."

"Hell is right." She paused, laughter bubbling up inside her at the shocked expression on his face from her cussing. The devil deserved to be surprised, as well, after the L-bomb he'd dealt her. Served him right she'd made a video for him, too. A bit of video payback—

if Caden hadn't erased it. Which made her softly add, "That's mine. And you're not deleting it. Ever."

Caden sat up and leaned his head back, his gaze fixed on her face.

She shifted forward, and lightly cupped his cheeks between her hands. "You said it first, back in Phoenix."

He snorted. She refrained from grinning like a madwoman, sensing just how unsettled he was about baring his soul on film like that. Jeez, was that why he'd kept demanding to know if she'd watched the videos? Unsettled or not, she wasn't letting him off the hook that easily. She'd come this far. Now she wanted to shake his world, her world, flip it upside down until they both didn't know which end was up. Until everything was clear, and beautiful.

"I told you in Sedona that I was falling for you. You said we were done—*knowing* you'd already left me that video."

He closed his eyes, then opened them. "Cowardly bastard," he murmured.

She sank to her knees and brought his head down to hers. "The bravest man I know."

His eyes flashed. He leaned in to kiss her.

"Say it," she demanded against his lips. "I want to see your face this time." She hesitated a second before pulling back. Then she gasped.

The transformation in him stole her breath away. Gone was the hard cynic. The doubtful lover. The warrior. Before her was the real Caden, a man filled with so much love that his eyes watered as his smile lit up her heart.

"You asked for it, chili cheeks. I love you. I want you. I need you. And I'm never letting you go. Got it?"

She laughed. "Got it."

"Heck, I'm tired of fighting."

"Me too. And you know what that means."

Caden's eyes sparkled, his green depths drawing her in like a sweet summer meadow. "Goodbye, Vegas. Hello…Pittsburgh?"

She shook her head. "What I mean is after you win Tetnus—you have to finish what you started, Caden—then, we'll see about doing exactly the opposite of fighting."

"Loving?"

"Exactly."

He tilted his head and slowly leaned in, closing the distance between them. "I'm not waiting anymore," he murmured, and swooped in for a kiss.

His tongue wrapped around hers, frantic and full of need. Sophie lifted herself up on her toes and leaned in closer. The kiss wiped away years of heartache, and promised years of passionate bliss.

In between the past and the future, was the near present. A documentary, investigative footage, and the story of two people falling in love. And it had all been captured on film.

She pulled away slightly and murmured against his lips, "So you're not deleting the video."

"Nope. Guess the cat's out of the bag."

Sophie stepped forward boldly. Time to seal the deal. "Now let's see if this cat can make you purr."

Chapter 22

TAP OUT: When a fighter taps his opponent's shoulder and says, "Let's take it from here, chili cheeks"

For the first time since her crazy quest to document the day in the life of an MMA fighter had begun, Sophie really understood what all the MMA hype was about. Bare-chested, barefoot, and barely breaking a sweat, Caden was hotter than his billboard as he dominated the Octagon cage.

With one quick movement, he'd flipped his opponent over his shoulder and took him down to the mat.

She conveyed her thoughts aloud, for the audio to pick up. "Caden has his opponent on the mat and is twisting the guy's arm into what has got to be a painful position."

"An Americana" she heard Bracken comment.

"It looks like Caden is trying to dislocate his shoulder while keeping him pinned in place."

Bracken shook his head in disagreement, and motioned for her to turn off the mic. She did so, and he quickly commented, "I'll narrate but keep my name out of the credits. Deal?"

"Deal."

Just as quickly, she flicked back on the mic, and Bracken began speaking in a low voice.

"Caden is a professional. What you are seeing is a rare and extremely painful maneuver called the Americana. See how Caden's got the guy's arm angled on the mat?"

He paused while she adjusted the lens to fully capture the movement.

"When you pin someone's arm to the mat like that, it pulls on the tendon in his elbow and shoulder. It's all about precision, and Caden has done it beautifully. If the guy doesn't tap out, his tendons will shred."

She glanced at Bracken. The pride in his tone spoke volumes. His gruff demeanor couldn't overshadow his love for his brother.

"Ready? He's gonna tap out in a few seconds. And Caden…he's just won Tetnus."

Bracken knew it. The crowd knew it, and began to cheer wildly. And just as Bracken predicted, Caden's opponent knew it. Four seconds later, he tapped out.

"Ladies and gentlemen," a broadcaster announced enthusiastically, pausing to make his way over to Caden, and move his arm into the air. "The winner of Tetnus, by submission with a surprise Americana, Caden Kelly!"

She caught it all on videotape, the crowd's fist-pumps, the broadcaster's pat to Caden's back, and the sheer look of pleasure on Caden's face. Heartbreaking.

Heart-stopping.

He turned in her direction and looked directly into the camera.

Or…at her.

Her pulse quickened.

Slowly, he sauntered across the mat until he stood directly above her. Her jaw went slack as she peeled her eyes off the image of him in the viewfinder and looked directly up at him.

He smirked down at her, then blew her a kiss.

The crowd went wild.

So did Sophie's heartstrings.

Everyone's attention was on her but she didn't care. The world was about to find out what a lovestruck softie Sophie Morelle really was.

Cupping her hands together, she pretended to catch his kiss and tugged her hands over heart.

"Locker room in ten," he shouted down at her.

"Or sooner," she hollered back.

He grinned in response.

Sophie made her way to the concession stand situated outside in the hallway. Caden had to be hungry, and she hurried to place an order for two chicken sandwiches, minus the buns and condiments, unsure how long his diet regimen would last.

Coincidentally, one of the guys from Channel 27 bumped into her—which meant he'd spotted her from his seat way up in the nosebleed section and had followed her into the hallway. Evidently, sometime between the locker room and turning her copy of the SD card back over to Bracken, Caden had had his manager contact her former network and told them to send out a field reporter, that Caden had something to show him. Caden had played her tape, pitched her documentary as the definitive piece on MMA fighters and the hottest sport around, *and* let it drop that she had the inside story on the doping scandal.

Seemed Caden was making amends for sequestering her SD card.

Money was not an issue for them, the network lackey told her. She'd sign an exclusive *four*-year contract, with annual bonuses, a car, and a new *Late Night* show.

In return, they'd be the sole network to broadcast both her documentary and an exclusive investigative report on doping in sports.

Poor guy. This lackey was going to get an earful when they heard her response. Calmly, she informed him, "I'm holding out for a national network. Rumor has it they're looking for a reporter to host a new investigative show. Something tells me I've got a pretty darn good shot at being hired."

"The network said if you come back you could name your salary."

"Right. What are they paying you, anyway?"

His flush said it all. Peanuts.

"Make sure you tell dear old Walt that Sophie's feeling confident that this other network will decide to quote take Sophie *up* a peg or two endquote. Got that?"

She grinned as the lackey jotted down her words on a small pad, verbatim.

"How does this sound for the name of my new show: *Inside Investigation with Sophie Morelle?*"

As predicted, the guy looked crestfallen. His own job was probably on the line if he didn't bring her back.

He's better off working somewhere else, she thought. She patted the guy's shoulder, a goodbye to him, her former network, and her crass, smart-ass persona.

Her image was about to pull a one-eighty. America was going to find out that the real Sophie Morelle was a smart, ambitious, caring person, and a dang good reporter.

She'd found her first interview, too.

Earlier, during Caden's weigh-in, she'd done a bit of show-and-tell herself—well, without the actual footage, it'd been more like tell-and-tell. Still, she'd caught the attention of a few reporters, who promised to share her news with their networks. Bracken had stood off to the side, his lips twisted slightly as he eavesdropped on her sales pitch. Afterward, he'd promised her the return of her SD card within the week and an interview with his sergeant about the investigation. Turned out, he didn't want to piss off his soon-to-be sister-in-law.

She'd smiled at the thought, thinking back to the incident in the Cuppa Joe parking lot, where she'd once claimed to be Caden's fiancée.

A self-fulfilling prophecy? Or had she known all along that Caden was her soul mate?

Her country-crooning, smart-mouthed, smooth-talking man.

She wouldn't change a thing about him.

Anxious to see Caden, she headed to the locker room. Raising a free elbow to knock on the door, she stumbled forward as it abruptly opened. Sal came barreling out, swinging a duffel bag over his shoulder and almost taking her out in the process.

The bag with the water and chicken breasts sailed through the air.

"Jeez," she muttered.

"There you are," he said, oblivious to the mini-drama he'd created.

She bent over to scoop the items up.

"There you are," a second voice commented, his tone rich with humor and laced with promise. His arms wove around her waist and tugged her in for a kiss.

"Uh-huh," Sal cleared his throat, interrupting them. "I brought you your duffel bag, Sophie. Found it in the luggage bin beneath the bus. Nothing pricked me this time. Nearly pulled my back out, same as back in Wichita. Just leave it to a woman to overpack."

Caden stepped away a second before she did.

"Hell."

"Holy crapola," Sophie echoed Caden's sentiment. "You put the duffel bag in the Aston, Sal?"

Sal looked at her, then Caden. Frowning his gaze turned back on her. "Good thing, or whatever is inside might have ended up like those pretty panties of yours."

Caden set her on the ground, then burst out laughing.

Sophie followed.

"Aw, guess what the Boys did with your panties was kind of funny."

"Do me a favor, Sal," Caden asked. "Go get Bracken."

"Does my ole heart good to see you two lockin' lips." Sal hovered, waiting.

Dang-diggity.

"Jesus, Sal. Can we get a little privacy?"

That did the trick, and the old-timer hustled off.

"Come here, chili cheeks. For once, the trainer's got the right idea."

Sophie stepped closer, and teased, "What makes you think I'd want anything to do with a hot, sweaty fighter?"

Caden just smiled, and looked at her, his eyes bright and full of love.

"Besides, you have something on your T-shirt."

"That right?"

"Yep." She placed her finger on his chest, and waited.

He glanced down. She traced her finger up his chest, ever so slowly over his throat and chin, and ever so lightly flicked his nose.

Laughing, he grabbed her by the waist and tugged her in close. "How about it, chili bean?" he whispered. His lips found hers and, in typical Caden style, he stole her breath away.

* * * * *

We hope you enjoyed reading this
special collection from Harlequin® books.

If you liked reading these stories,
then you will love
Harlequin® Blaze® books!

You like it hot!
Harlequin Blaze stories sizzle with strong
heroines and irresistible heroes playing the
game of modern love and lust. They're fun,
sexy and always steamy.

Enjoy four *new* stories from
Harlequin Blaze every month!

Available wherever books and
ebooks are sold.

⊕ HARLEQUIN®

Blaze®
Red-Hot Reads

SPECIAL EXCERPT FROM

 HARLEQUIN®

Blaze

*Military veteran Mia Brandt agrees to a fake
engagement to help sexy rescue swimmer Tag Johnson
out of a jam. But could their fun, temporary liaison lead
to something more?*

Read on for a sneak preview at
WICKED SECRETS *by* **Anne Marsh**,
part of our **UNIFORMLY HOT!** *miniseries.*

Sailor boy didn't look up. Not because he didn't notice
the other woman's departure—something about the way
he held himself warned her he was aware of everyone
and everything around him—but because polite clearly
wasn't part of his daily repertoire.

Fine. She wasn't all that civilized herself.

The blonde made a face, her ponytail bobbing as she
started hoofing it along the beach. "Good luck with that
one," she muttered as she passed Mia.

Oookay. Maybe this *was* mission impossible. Still,
she'd never failed when she'd been out in the field, and
all her gals wanted was intel. She padded into the water,
grateful for the cool soaking into her burning soles. The
little things mattered so much more now.

"I'm not interested." Sailor boy didn't look up from
the motor when she approached, a look of fierce concen-
tration creasing his forehead. Having worked on more
than one Apache helicopter during her two tours of duty,
she knew the repair work wasn't rocket science.

She also knew the mechanic and…holy hotness.

Mentally, she ran through every curse word she'd learned. Tag Johnson hadn't changed much in five years. He'd acquired a few more fine lines around the corners of his eyes, possibly from laughing. Or from squinting into the sun since rescue swimmers spent plenty of time out at sea. The white scar on his forearm was as new as the lines, but otherwise he was just as gorgeous and every bit as annoying as he'd been the night she'd picked him up at the Star Bar in San Diego. He was also still out of her league, a military bad boy who was strong, silent, deadly…and always headed out the door.

For a brief second, she considered retreating. Unfortunately, the bridal party was watching her intently, clearly hoping she was about to score on their behalf. Disappointing them would be a shame.

"Funny," she drawled. "You could have fooled me."

Tag's head turned slowly toward her. Mia had hoped for drama. Possibly even his butt planting in the ocean from the surprise of her reappearance. No such luck.

"Sergeant Dominatrix," he drawled back.

Don't miss
WICKED SECRETS
by New York Times *bestselling author Anne Marsh,*
available April 2015 wherever
Harlequin® Blaze® books and ebooks are sold.

www.Harlequin.com

Love the Harlequin book you just read?

Your opinion matters.

Review this book on your favorite book site, review site, blog or your own social media properties and share your opinion with other readers!

Be sure to connect with us at:
Harlequin.com/Newsletters
Facebook.com/HarlequinBooks
Twitter.com/HarlequinBooks

JUST CAN'T GET ENOUGH?

Join our social communities
and talk to us online.

You will have access to the latest
news on upcoming titles and special
promotions, but most importantly,
you can talk to other fans about your
favorite Harlequin reads.

Harlequin.com/Community

f Facebook.com/HarlequinBooks

y Twitter.com/HarlequinBooks

p Pinterest.com/HarlequinBooks

HARLEQUIN®

A *Romance* FOR EVERY MOOD™

Stay up-to-date on all your
romance-reading news with the
Harlequin Shopping Guide,
featuring bestselling authors, exciting new
miniseries, books to watch and more!

The newest issue will be delivered right to you
with our compliments! There are 4 each year.

Signing up is easy.

EMAIL

ShoppingGuide@Harlequin.ca

WRITE TO US

HARLEQUIN BOOKS
Attention: Customer Service Department
P.O. Box 9057, Buffalo, NY 14269-9057

OR PHONE

1-800-873-8635 in the United States
1-888-343-9777 in Canada

Please allow 4-6 weeks for delivery of the first issue by mail.